W9-ABL-433

FIRE
IN THE
BLOOD

ERIN M. EVANS

FIRE
IN THE
BLOOD

FIRE IN THE BLOOD
©2014 Wizards of the Coast LLC.

Published by Wizards of the Coast LLC. Manufactured by: Hasbro SA, Rue Emile-Boéchat 31, 2800 Delémont, CH. Represented by Hasbro Europe, 2 Roundwood Ave, Stockley Park, Uxbridge, Middlesex, UB11 1AZ, UK.

Printed in the U.S.A.

Lineage Diagram by: Mike Schley
Cover art by: Min Yum
First Printing: October 2014

9 8 7 6 5 4 3 2 1

ISBN: 978-0-7869-6529-8
ISBN: 978-0-7869-6552-6 (ebook)
620A6880000001 EN

Cataloging-in-Publication data is on file with the Library of Congress

Contact Us at Wizards.com/CustomerService
Wizards of the Coast LLC, PO Box 707, Renton, WA 98057-0707, USA
USA & Canada: (800) 324-6496 or (425) 204-8069
Europe: +32(0) 70 233 277

Visit our web site at **www.dungeonsanddragons.com**

For those who love the Realms above all else—especially Brian Cortijo and Ed Greenwood, without whom I could never have finished this book on time.

And for Kevin and Idris, always.

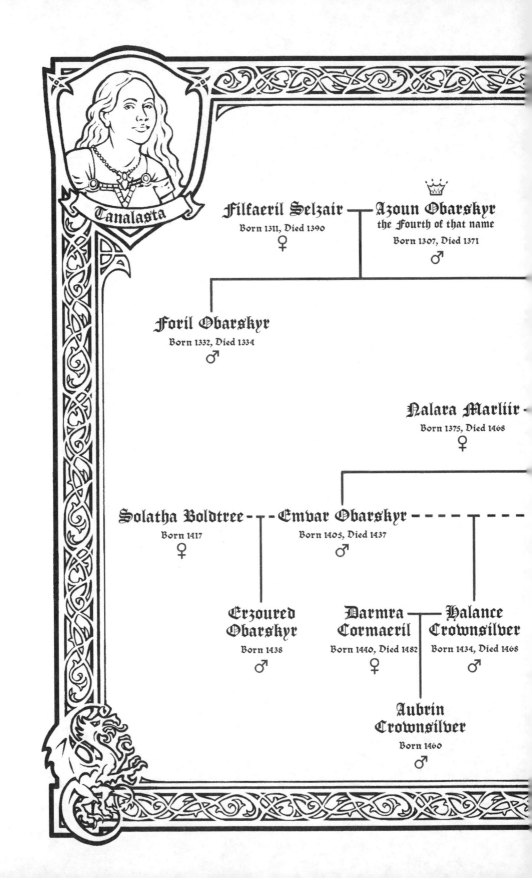

Tanalasta

Filfaeril Selzair
Born 1311, Died 1390
♀

Azoun Obarskyr
the Fourth of that name
Born 1307, Died 1371
♂

Foril Obarskyr
Born 1332, Died 1334
♂

Nalara Marliir
Born 1375, Died 1468
♀

Solatha Boldtree
Born 1417
♀

Emvar Obarskyr
Born 1405, Died 1437
♂

**Erzoured
Obarskyr**
Born 1438
♂

**Darmra
Cormaeril**
Born 1440, Died 1482
♀

**Halance
Crownsilver**
Born 1434, Died 1468
♂

**Aubrin
Crownsilver**
Born 1460
♂

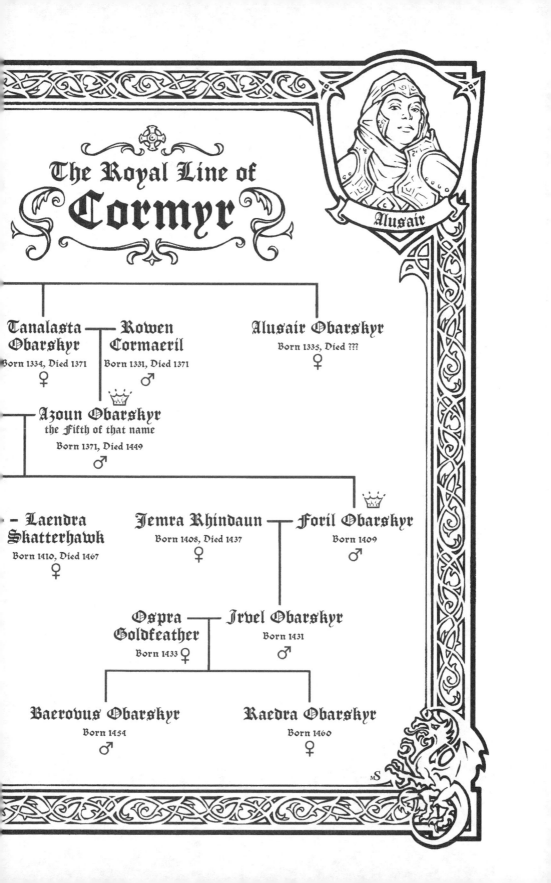

The Royal Line of Cormyr

Alusair

Tanalasta Obarskyr
Born 1334, Died 1371
♀

Rowen Cormaeril
Born 1331, Died 1371
♂

Alusair Obarskyr
Born 1335, Died ???
♀

Azoun Obarskyr
the Fifth of that name
Born 1371, Died 1449
♂

Laendra Skatterhawk
Born 1410, Died 1467
♀

Jemra Rhindaun
Born 1408, Died 1437
♀

Foril Obarskyr
Born 1409
♂

Ospra Goldfeather
Born 1433 ♀

Irvel Obarskyr
Born 1431
♂

Baerovus Obarskyr
Born 1454
♂

Raedra Obarskyr
Born 1460
♀

PROLOGUE

8 Mirtul, the Year of the Nether Mountain Scrolls (1486 DR)
Two days' march from Saerloon, Sembia

THE DAMNABLE RAIN DIDN'T HAVE THE DECENCY TO STOP WHEN SPRING came. If it would just stop raining, Irvel thought wearily, everything else would be simpler to deal with. The war, his children, the godsbe-damned succession . . .

And Lancelord Beliard Greatgaunt, stomping toward Crown Prince Irvel Obarskyr's tent through the muddy field, wearing a scowl that Irvel dearly wanted to order right off the good lord's face.

"He's coming from an audience with Prince Baerovus."

Irvel jumped at the sudden voice. He scowled back at the Lord Warder, a man as broad and burly as a bear, but wearing fine silk robes of dark purple. Unlike everything else in the camp, the war wizard wasn't even damp.

"For the last time, Vainrence," Irvel said, "don't creep up on me."

Vainrence raised his brows. "My apologies, Your Highness, but no one crept," he said, unapologetic as the Lord Warder always was. "I walked in through the other entrance, and announced myself, as asked."

"Damnable rain," Irvel said. He rubbed his forehead. "You have my apologies, Lord Warder. I find I'm a bit on edge."

"Perfectly understandable," Vainrence allowed. "I shall speak more loudly next time." He looked past Irvel at the lancelord, now standing at attention in the tent's main entry, his features schooled.

"Your Royal Highness," he said with a little bow—and that did not bode well either. "We have . . . That is, His Highness, Prince Baerovus, has made further requests of the cavalry."

Irvel considered the lancelord, giving himself a moment to curse inwardly. He should have found a way to stock the officers of his army with fellows whose company he enjoyed. Fellows who knew how to deal with his son's strange ways. He'd had the time at the start of the campaign.

"Oh?" he said. "What is it he wants?"

"His Highness feels that the horses would be better at ease if their pickets were spread farther apart," Beliard said in clipped tones that told Irvel all he needed to know about Baerovus's rambling lecture on the well-being of horses. "And that we should move them to the south side of the encampment. Because the cookfires

1

upset them. Never mind that to keep them under the shelter of the trees would mean the entire camp has to move fifty yards south."

Irvel suppressed a sigh. "And have you done so?"

"My lord," Beliard said, "we are nearly set. The men are tired. Reordering the camp on the prince's whim—"

"It is hardly a whim," Irvel corrected. "Baerovus is quite well-informed. If he says the horses will do better with such adjustments, I believe him."

Beliard frowned again. "Irvel, he's your boy, but—"

"And he's a prince of Cormyr," Irvel reminded Beliard. "Therefore due your respect and deference."

"So you're asking me to—"

"Present Prince Baerovus with a full assessment of what that exchange would take and with whom he must consult to achieve it." Knowing Baerovus, realizing he would have to argue with a dozen proud, baffled noblemen would make him back down—the lad could only handle so much conflict. He would be agitated after, but only Irvel would have to hear about the horses' needs for the next tenday.

Beliard hesitated, and Irvel waited, wondering if the lancelord would say what he was thinking: That Baerovus was odd. That he should have been left behind in Suzail. That Irvel really ought to figure out what to do about Baerovus before it came down to having a moon-eyed fool on the Dragon Throne.

And even though Irvel had thought the same at times, it wouldn't do to have the lancelord speaking ill of a prince of the blood that way. Nor would he stand there and let someone belittle his poor strange son. He stared Lord Greatgaunt down.

"Is there anything else?"

Beliard cleared his throat. "I will . . . make the necessary assessments. Thank you, my prince." Irvel nodded and waved him on his way. He waited until the lancelord was out of sight and out of earshot before allowing the smallest of sighs.

"Would you kindly have someone bring Baerovus to me?" he said to Vainrence.

Baerovus arrived soon after, tense and slump-shouldered and peering through the muss of his dark hair, marshaled by another war wizard in flowing, muddy robes. A man of thirty, and still Baerovus moved like a guilty boy. Irvel quashed another sigh. "Well met, Son," he said. "And good evening."

"Good evening," Baerovus said. "What did I do?"

"How are you settled?" Irvel asked. "Ready for a good night's sleep and an early march?"

"I suppose," Baerovus said after a moment. "I mean, we must."

Irvel's jaw tightened. "'Yes,'" he reminded the prince. "Say 'yes, saer.' A prince of the blood answers always with assurance and vigor," he said. "Remember, Baerovus: your answers are Cormyr's answers."

"Not precisely," Baerovus said. "Grandfather's answers are Cormyr's. One could say yours are Cormyr's—you're the crown prince. But, to be precise—"

"Son."

Baerovus fell silent. But a heartbeat later, he finished, "It's just I'm only a prince."

Irvel bit his tongue. He had ridden out of Suzail with so many bright hopes for this war: Sembia's armies would fall before them, Netheril would reconsider their reach, Baerovus would finally outgrow his oddness and become the sort of man who could inherit the Dragon Throne.

But then the rains had come, Sembia had retreated beyond Irvel's army's reach, messages came through the war wizards that Netheril had opened a northern front, and Baerovus was fussing with horses. And still the Great Rain poured down.

In two months, Irvel's only daughter, Raedra, was meant to wed the son of his dear late friend. It would take a miracle to get back to Suzail in time for the nuptials—they'd moved the wedding three times already, assuming Irvel would surely be back in time. Vainrence told him the minister of protocol was strongly advocating they not move it again, and so unless Irvel managed a miracle, he would miss his daughter's wedding.

He wondered privately if Halance Crownsilver's spirit would watch over the ceremony. He wondered if he watched his son, Aubrin, with the same puzzlement as Irvel watched Baerovus.

When the Crownsilver matriarch had produced Aubrin in court, Irvel had scoffed. Halance's son had died in a featherlung epidemic shortly after Hal was killed—Lady Helindra Crownsilver had sworn to it herself.

"For his safety, Your Majesty," Helindra had explained. "His father's claim to the throne shortened too many lives. I would not have laid a child in those same villains' hands."

The Hells you wouldn't, Irvel had thought, considering Aubrin.

Where Halance had been a fierce huntsman, a boisterous goblet-hoister, and a stout-hearted second in a scuffle, Aubrin was slight and quiet, with his great-aunt's penetrating gaze and a careful way of speaking that made Irvel always think he wasn't being forthright.

But Irvel's father, Foril—King of the Dragon Throne—had no such reservations.

"Watching Gods," the aged king had breathed. "He is my brother come to flesh."

No one could argue: the young man's boyish features held an unmistakable resemblance to his grandfather's, the former Crown Prince Emvar Obarskyr, the accidental architect of so many of the tangled threads that threatened to strangle the court these days.

"Though," Foril had added a moment later, "a bit *less* flesh. Quite short."

"Cormaeril blood," Helindra Crownsilver had supplied.

The war wizards made their tests, brought forth their results, and confirmed the Crownsilvers' assertions. And Irvel missed poor dead Hal all the more, for if neither of them could have made their sons into men of strength and legend, then at least they would each have had someone in whom they could confide their disappointments.

Baerovus is clever, Irvel thought to himself, as he watched his son staring off at the cavalry lines through the muss of his hair. He is a master with the bow, which is still a weapon, even if it's not a sword. He has a keen eye for detail—some detail—and a way with numbers. A king who is a strategist, not a warrior, is no great shame.

And as for Aubrin . . .

Raedra will straighten him out, Hal, Irvel promised his old friend's spirit. Or possibly drive him to drink.

What a pity Beshaba seemed to ignore all bribes, all entreaties at the prince and princess's births: his son as uncomfortable with the notion of a throne as Irvel would be of a dancing gown; his daughter, the spirited heir Irvel had hoped for, but born second and a girl. The nobles would never countenance Raedra when Baerovus was an option. They might not bear her when Emvar's bastard lines still breathed either. One tidy solution the marriage affords, Irvel thought.

"Are you going to tell me what it is I've done?" Baerovus asked. "I know you'd rather I knew for myself, but I never seem to be right about these things, and the war wizards only come for me when I've done something."

Irvel sighed. "Leave Lancelord Greatgaunt's horses alone, if you please."

"But he's wrong. Shouldn't I correct him?"

"He's a noble, they are frequently wrong," Irvel said. "Leave them to it whenever possible and you will have a long, happy reign one day." Watching Gods, he thought, give him a long, happy reign. And he wished Halance were there again, which brought another measure of grief. If Irvel hadn't seen in Halance a safer steward for his own young children, a regent who might hold the throne for them if—Watching Gods forfend!—anything should happen to Irvel; if he hadn't pressed the king to legitimize yet another bastard of the old prince . . . well, then, Hal wouldn't have been killed and Aubrin would not have become this curious puzzle.

At the very least, Irvel thought, watching his son, Raedra will make certain Aubrin stands beside Baerovus, and keep the baron off the throne. "Do make certain you're ready to leave in the morning, properly armored and all. Don't chase your squire off again, please."

Baerovus fidgeted. "I did not chase anyone off. I simply said I don't want to carry a shield. I can't shoot with a shield. No one can shoot with a shield. And it rubs my arm badly, saer."

"You are not hunting," Irvel said patiently. "You are leading a company into battle. You will carry a shield with your insignia and a sword. You will use them as you need, as befits a prince of the blood. And you will be ready to do so when we march again."

Baerovus stared down at the muddied rug. "Yes, Father. Saer."

"Go rest," Irvel said, dismissing Baerovus. After the young man had bowed and hurried off, he turned to see Vainrence, still watching.

"I'm sure my prince is aware he could assign Prince Baerovus a shield bearer," Vainrence said. "The second Azoun was renowned for his archery skills. Prince Baerovus would not be the first."

Irvel sighed. "Prince Baerovus has too many obstacles as it is. Let him learn to look like a king while he can. And Azoun the Second may have been an archer, but he never marched into battle without a sword in hand—don't tell me otherwise."

"I can still return him to Suzail," Vainrence said. "It would be safer."

"Suzail is as full of ill-settled assassins as Sembia." Irvel snorted, even though that wasn't so. He'd be damned if all the army saw him treat Baerovus as a weakling. "He is hale, he is here, and he will lead a company."

"As you like," Vainrence said. He bowed and slipped out the rear of the tent, quieter than the constant patter of rain on the oilcloth. Irvel allowed himself another small sigh, and said a little prayer to Tempus, Tymora, and Beshaba that they'd meet the Sembians in battle soon and nothing else would go awry.

PART I

SYMYLAZARR
THE FONT OF HONOR

. . .

The painting hangs beside the first window in the Hall of Gazes, charmed against fading or dust. The queen bathed in a flood of sunlight is Gantharla First-Queen, and the sword is Symylazarr, the sword all have sworn their oaths of allegiance and fealty upon since Varanth, its first bearer, fell against the goblins of Hlundadim. The young knight at her feet is Oric Redspear, who will die in his duty, defending the queen's son at Marsember. Archons linger in the corners of the painting, and the red-haired queen is stern as Kelemvor. The sword lies heavily on the kneeling knight, so thickly painted one could trace its edges with blind touch. All is solemn. These promises are unbreakable.

. . .

1

THE UNWELCOME POWERS OF THE NINE HELLS' PACT FELT LIKE THREADS of steel sliding up Farideh's veins. The tiefling woman focused instead on the fringe of scales just over her adoptive father's left eye and waited for the response she'd been dreading for tendays now.

Clanless Mehen stared back, silent. The rain hammering on the roof of the half-empty warehouse was the only sound.

"Think of it like . . ." her twin said, trying a different tack. Havilar frowned and met Farideh's odd eyes with her golden ones.

A curse, Farideh thought. A misfortune. A *blight*.

". . . having a sword that's weighted all wrong," Havilar declared. "It's really just an inconvenience more than anything. Almost not worth mentioning." Her tail lashed the packed earth, betraying her anxiety. "So really, we should just spar—"

"*Thrik!*" Mehen snapped, one word as sharp as a pike. Farideh looked down at the blunted short sword in her hands, at her bronze fingers—save the bone white third finger—clutched around it, at the line of the sparring circle Mehen had drawn just before she and Havilar had told him everything. The feeling of the long-neglected powers tugging at her, sliding along her nerves, demanded Farideh's attention. But they could not compete with waiting for what her father would say next.

"You tell me you're Chosen of Asmodeus," Mehen said, disbelieving. "The Chosen of the *karshoji* god of sin. You tell me Farideh sees souls and that the bursting into flames was all a part of this . . . this . . ." He blew out a breath that popped with tatters of electricity. "And now Havi."

"*Nothing's* happened to me," Havilar protested. "Maybe nothing will?" She twirled her glaive in one hand.

Mehen looked up at Farideh, his nostrils flaring, his tongue fluttering behind his teeth as he tasted the air for trouble. "I don't know," she said. "It might and it might not."

"What did you do?" he asked. "How did this happen?"

Farideh shook her head—nothing so simple. "We were born to the wrong people?" That was what Lorcan, the cambion she drew her pact from—the cambion who'd opened the door to this world of devils and danger and the chance to save people all the same—had guessed. That all the descendants of Bryseis Kakistos, the

Brimstone Angel, had been imbued with power by Asmodeus, to serve his needs in the changing world that threatened his divinity, and promised new avenues to power.

"Did Lorcan tell you it's just an inconvenience too?" Mehen demanded.

"Not exactly," Farideh said. "He says it's just a little benefit. A way for . . ." She swallowed—she still couldn't utter Asmodeus's name. "A way to show off, I suppose."

Meheh shook his head. "What do you have to do in return?"

Farideh shut her eyes, her thoughts full of the vision that had haunted her dreams ever since they had fled the Shadovar internment camp where she'd learned where the strange powers came from. Asmodeus, his ruby rod pointed at her, a strange blue glyph pulsing in his chest. *You have one task,* he'd said. *Stay alive, tiefling. Give no ground. You may find we have more than one goal in common.*

Since then, Farideh had heard nothing. Nothing but the echoing dreams.

"I don't know," she said, unwilling to believe Asmodeus had told her the fullness of his intent. "Nothing for now. Lorcan says . . ." She wet her mouth—she wasn't sure how much Lorcan's assurances should count. He might be the only one of them who knew anything, but she didn't trust him the way she once had. "He says they don't force things. That that's what *demons* do. That they'd rather just work with what I want, so everyone's happy." Mehen's yellow eyes flicked over her, and she sighed. "If nothing else, I should get a little warning."

Mehen paced the edge of the circle, so full of furious energy, Farideh could picture him knocking one of the towering piles of crates over with his fist. Havilar shot her another worried look, and Farideh could imagine exactly what she was thinking—they shouldn't have said anything. Havilar hadn't *wanted* to say anything, had stalled and faltered and it was only when Farideh had decided to tell Mehen about her own state—in the heat of sparring, what if she slipped and changed and frightened Mehen?—that Havilar had relented.

Havilar twisted the pointed end of her glaive against the packed floor and bit her lip—this was exactly why she'd wanted to wait longer. Farideh shook her head once—there was no keeping something like this a secret, not from Mehen. They'd waited long enough already.

Havilar sighed, all full of anxious energy—all of this trouble and now they'd be talking instead of sparring. Farideh reached over and squeezed her hand.

"There must be a priest," Mehen started.

"I don't think it works that way," Farideh said gently. "I think we can just hope he takes it back when he sees I'm not . . ." She shook her head again—not what? Not corruptible, when she'd already taken the infernal pact of a warlock? Not wicked, when she'd followed through on a terrible deal with a devil and aided a Netherese wizard in capturing Chosen? Not an agent of corruption herself, when she'd managed to trap herself and Havilar in the Hells for nearly eight years while the world passed by without them?

"Not the best he can do," she settled on.

That didn't calm her father. Havilar frowned at Farideh again—when Mehen got upset, when he couldn't do anything, he'd try to do too much. They'd be lucky if he didn't drag a parade of priests through here, shouting them down when they told him what he didn't want to hear and cursing the uselessness of gods.

"Does Brin know?" Mehen finally asked.

"No," Havilar said firmly. "Brin does *not* know and he doesn't need to know until something actually happens." Her tail flicked uneasily. "No one tells Brin a word until then. For all anyone knows, this is just Farideh's problem."

Farideh bit her tongue and wished she could unmake her decisions. She wished she could find the right thing to say to guide Havilar through the morass that suddenly surged around her once-fledgling relationship with Brin. She wished a little that he would end it, and at the same time that Havilar would get everything she wanted.

Farideh wondered what became of her when that happened.

"*Karshoj arsuzailominak*," Mehen sighed. "As if we needed anything else to make this blasted city more of a disadavantage."

"It's not *that* bad here," Havilar insisted. She swept her glaive to one side, back and forth like a deadly pendulum. "I mean the worst thing is that there's nowhere to practice, and Brin's solved that by making us this space."

Farideh did not agree—Havilar was leaving out several of Suzail's difficulties. Once more, they couldn't travel safely and easily without donning cloaks and hoods. Even then, getting out of the tallhouse Brin owned unseen was a challenge—"Lord Crownsilver's tiefling mistress" had become rather notorious.

And that all aside, there was the rain—every day, every single day, it rained. Whether it drizzled or dumped oceans from thunderheads, the sun was scarce and the storms never stopped for long enough to let things dry out. The garden behind the tallhouse—the only place Havilar might have practiced—was little better than a marsh, its stepping-stones steadily sinking in the mud, day by day. It was enough to make anyone cottage-crazed.

But having to worry about what people might think, what they might do, was not Cormyr's issue alone.

"It would be the same if we were anywhere else," Farideh told Mehen. "I'd still have to worry—"

"*We*," Mehen corrected. "This is *all* of our problems, together. Don't forget that."

Problems have solutions, Farideh thought, but did not say. This is nothing but a curse.

"Not to be *flippant*," Havilar said, testing the new word. "But do you think we might still spar?" She shifted on the balls of her feet. "It would give you a chance to think about things, Mehen. And I have been waiting for so long—"

"Has she checked you?" Mehen asked. He turned to Farideh. "Have you checked her? For signs . . . Can you do that? It has to show, doesn't it?"

"She's fine."

"Do it now."

Farideh hesitated. But Mehen's worried expression wore a hole in her resolve better than any god's will could. Farideh closed her eyes and tapped into the dark powers. The sudden presence of them gripped the back of her head like a hand made of knives and she winced against it before she opened her eyes.

In any other person, Farideh's unwanted blessings would change the intangible mark of their soul into a mass of light and shade and color—a mark to signal how corrupted the person was, how easily their soul might be claimed, or what god had already claimed it.

But in Havilar—much as it was when Farideh looked at her own reflection with the soul sight—there was nothing, only a blurriness as if someone had smeared unguent on Farideh's eyes, but only where Havilar stood.

Because the protection spell remains? Farideh wondered. Or because there is no soul in us to see?

"It's fine," she said. "Nothing's changed."

"See?" Havilar said. "Nothing's changed and nothing might even happen, and Farideh's fine. Now who's going to try and hit me?"

"Oh, I could start," a voice called from the dark end of the warehouse. A man strolled out from between the crates and bales, a scarf tied over his face, over his hair, hiding everything but a pair of hazel eyes.

Mehen cursed under his breath. "Turn around. This is a private warehouse, and you're trespassing."

"Indeed we are," the hazel-eyed man said. Farideh spun to see another man ease out of the shadows behind her, and a third and fourth come in through the main doors. Weapons drawn, ropes ready. Farideh hadn't even heard the doors open. Had they slipped past the carriage driver?

"Where, oh, where are your guards, pretty ladies?" the man behind Farideh said. He was spindly as a shadow, his blade pointed and sleek.

Mehen's falchion came out so swiftly it might have melted from its scabbard. "Some silks and rugs really worth dying over?"

"We're not here for goods," the hazel-eyed man said. "We've come for Lord Crownsilver's tiefling."

"I *hate* when people call me that," Havilar said, shifting her glaive around, ready to strike. Farideh felt the edges of shadows ruffling the borders of her skin, trying to hide her from this sudden threat.

"Whoever you are," Mehen snarled, "whoever sent you, this is your last chance to walk away." Farideh doubted the men knew to watch the sparks leaping between her father's sharp teeth. They didn't turn.

"We'll take our chances," the hazel-eyed man said. Four more bodies melted out of the shadows, four more assassins.

Mehen cursed again. Eight to three was no good at all—and Havilar was already dancing on the balls of her feet. The powers of the pact surged up Farideh's veins. She gripped the hilt of her sword hard.

"Carriage," Mehen hissed to his daughters. "Don't get cocky. Do whatever you have to, to get back in the carriage. Clear?"

"Clear," Farideh said.

"Havi," Mehen warned.

"Send the lucky girl forward," the spindly man said. "And we'll leave you to carry the message to his lordship."

Havilar laughed. "Oh, try it, *tiamash*. Let's see what you've brought."

"I said don't get cocky!" Mehen shouted at her as the attackers closed. "Fari, use the—"

"Sword. I know."

Mehen slashed at the man with the rope, forcing him back out of the blade's reach. "That's a *karshoji* practice sword. Toss it and set them on fire. Get your sister some cover."

The powers of the Hells flooded into Farideh, scaling her bones and pouring eagerly into her veins at the unexpected permission. She spread her hands and spoke a word of harsh Infernal. Missiles of brimstone burned out of the ether, sizzling the moisture from the air as they rained down on the hazel-eyed man and his companions.

Havilar slipped out of reach of the slim one's sword and swung the heavy glaive down into him as she did, striking him across the back and knocking the air from him. With the batting still wrapping the blade for safety, there was no cutting them.

Still seething with the powers of the Nine Hells, Farideh pointed two fingers at the glaive. "*Assulam.*"

A bolt of dark energy shot from her, crackling through the leather and batting, which burst into tatters and fibers of smoking wool. Havilar didn't so much as spare a glance for Farideh, but caught the advancing blackguard on the blade.

"Carriage!" Mehen bellowed.

"Havi!" Farideh cried. A strong hand clamped down on her shoulder, then another on her wrist. A man's foul, wet breath assaulted her. Unholy rage chased her fury and fear—the powers of Asmodeus's blessing threatening to overtake her.

Calm, she told herself, pulling against her captor.

"Which is she?" he shouted back at the hazel-eyed man.

"Grab 'em both," another answered.

That one reached for Havilar, but froze as a fork of lightning leaped through him, skipping to his nearer fellows, chased by a dampened *boom*. Two bodies lay at Clanless Mehen's feet, and the lightning danced in the gape of his teeth.

Farideh pulled hard on the powers from the Hells, thinning the skin of the plane enough to split it like an overripe peach's. She threw her weight forward, into a fog of shadow and brimstone, dragging the man with her and stepping free near to Mehen . . . and his deadly falchion. The man's grip tightened briefly as the blade struck, but then his wound was far more pressing than holding tight to Farideh.

"Havilar!" Mehen bellowed. "Stop showing off!"

Two of the attackers lay slumped on the ground at Havi's feet, a third retreating with his hand pressed to a belly wound. Two more circled her, no doubt reconsidering the wisdom of coming for "Lord Crownsilver's tiefling" so lightly armed.

The hazel-eyed man pulled a pouch from his belt and hurled it at Havilar's feet. It burst open, spraying a thin amber liquid over her.

"*Adaestuo,*" Farideh spat. Another ball of energy shrieked past the man's ear as the fluid thickened and hardened, trapping Havilar where she stood. She strained against the stuff, trying to move her feet. A fresh flood of terror washed over Farideh. The hazel-eyed man edged around her, a damp-looking rag in hand.

Behind her, Mehen roared as the last pair came after him. Farideh could feel the fire building in her blood, her bones, as she stormed toward Havilar. *Let it go,* that voice like a cultured thunderhead seemed to say. *They don't deserve any less.*

"Havi, duck!" Farideh barked, followed by the sibilant trigger word that peeled a bolt of flames off her fingertips. Havilar dropped under its path, the edges of its flames not nearly strong enough to singe a tiefling. The bolt streaked past and hit the hazel-eyed man in the face, setting his kerchief ablaze.

Havilar straightened, still trapped. Farideh's heart lodged in her throat as the big man came at her sister. Before he reached her, Havilar hefted the polearm up, grabbing it down low and swinging. The side of the blade caught him in the cheekbone with a meaty thud.

Farideh summoned another bolt of the ruinous energy, shattering the amber lump into a burst of shards. Havilar shifted her weight and pulled—once, twice, and then the substance shattered. She stumbled backward.

Do it. Make them sorry.

Make for the carriage, Farideh thought, as if shouting over the other voice. She grabbed hold of Havilar and once more leaped through the fabric of the planes, yanking her sister away from the kidnappers, across the warehouse, and within sprinting distance of the door. The driver, Arlo, a youngish man who'd always been nervous around the twins, sat slumped in the seat, his throat neatly cut. The horses pranced, agitated and uneasy.

"Get inside!" Mehen shouted behind them. Another tanglefoot bag *splatted* on the ground beside him.

Farideh and Havilar had hardly shut the door behind them when Mehen hauled himself up into the seat, his suddenness and smell startling the horses into motion before he could even touch the whip. The carriage jerked and jolted over the cobbled roads, and Farideh could feel the axles fighting to stay straight beneath them.

"What in the *Hells*," Havilar panted, "was *that* all about?"

Farideh peeked out the window. Suzail's trading coster yards rushed by, the streets widening as they closed on the city's center. The flood of rage and fire was receding, but her hands were still shaking. "I think," she said, "you'll have to ask Lord Crownsilver."

• • •

THE COLDEST THING in all of the Forest Kingdom—or so said many nobles—was the heart of Princess Raedra Obarskyr. She might have a lovely face and a pleasant figure, flashing eyes and flaxen hair. She might be as graceful with a sword as she was with a dance partner. She *was* the daughter of the Blood Royal and eligible even without such virtues.

But Lord Aubrin Crownsilver, the princess's betrothed, was regarded with a mixture of envy and pity nevertheless. After all, everyone had seen what had happened to the last fellow.

"Tell me"—Raedra said as she swept into her private audience chamber where Brin waited—"that I've heard wrong."

Brin stood, driven to his feet more by the presence of the two armored Purple Dragon knights that accompanied Raedra—glaring down at him—than by the princess alone. She and he weren't that formal—usually, he thought, taking in Raedra's stony expression.

"Much as I'd love to," he said, "I suspect I can't. Although if you told me what you'd heard, perhaps? Also, well met and nice to see you too."

"Don't you dare," Raedra said. "You vanish off to Waterdeep, without so much as a *word* to me. You're gone for tendays and when you finally turn up—"

"You won't see me," Brin finished, sitting back down. "If you were so deeply concerned about me, you could have seen me."

Raedra's eyes tightened. "When you finally turn up," she said again, harder, "you've got *her* in tow. What makes you think I want to hear anything you have to say to me?"

"You're going to have to hear it," Brin said gently. "We have to talk about what we're going to do."

"'We?'" Raedra laughed. "They say she's staying in the tallhouse. It sounds like 'we've' already decided."

"She's staying there," Brin said. "But I'm not."

"As if that matters to anyone watching. As if you don't slip in and out at your leisure. As if you've not made yourself a little blind-spot love nest in that blasted festhall." Brin looked away—Raedra's watchers were very keen. "We had an agreement," she said.

"And I've held to that," Brin retorted. "We explicitly agreed the other could have lovers."

Raedra shot a dark look at the Purple Dragon on her left—she waved both guards back, toward the door. Her jaw tightened, and she sat down on the opposite settee. "We agreed," she said quietly, "that whatever lovers you took, I would have the right to deny you if they weren't . . . acceptable. And short of my own mother, I doubt there is a woman walking Toril whose presence in your bed is more humiliating to me." She leaned forward. "You agreed to tell me before you did anything. You agreed we *both* had the right to refuse. I shouldn't have war wizards telling me there's a devil-child in your bed."

Raedra was right on that score. But Havilar had come back from being trapped in the Nine Hells and everything had changed so quickly. Forgetting Havi wasn't an option. Not going to her wasn't an option. And when Havilar had looked into his eyes and told him she was still in love with him, there was no part of him that would have left her behind.

"You knew this day might come," he said. "I won't tell you I'm sorry it has."

Now Raedra looked away. "I thought she was dead."

"So did a lot of people," Brin said. "But I never told you that." He hesitated. "We need to talk about postponing the wedding."

Raedra narrowed her eyes at him. "Absolutely not. Three postponements are bad enough. Making it four would say something."

"Really? So you're going to marry 'Lord Saddlesores, the failure of Calantar's Way'?" Brin demanded. "Who—on top of everything else—has a tiefling for a mistress?"

Raedra sighed heavily. "Tell your dear darling she chose an *excellent* time to return," she said dryly. "There is not a thing you could have done to stop Shade's armies opening a portal through that *blasted* ruin. Whatever everyone's saying."

"All the more reason," Brin said.

She looked up at Brin as if he'd just done something unspeakable on the rug. "Watching Gods, are you suggesting what I think you're suggesting?"

"I don't know what you mean."

"Oh, like the broken plane you don't! Say it." When Brin hesitated, she all but spat, "You want me to call it off."

"It would be simplest. Give me time. I can—"

"You can what? Find some willing nobleman to relieve you of the burden I am?"

"You're being dramatic."

"*I'm* being dramatic? How long did you know her?" Raedra demanded. "Before she disappeared, Aubrin, how long did you know her?"

"Two months," Brin said. "Seventeen days." And four hours, and if he could have counted the heartbeats, too, he would have. Those days were the happiest in his life, even if he didn't completely appreciate it at the time.

"And how long," Raedra said coldly, "have you and I known each other? No, wait, let's make it easy: how long have we been engaged?"

Brin shrugged. "Two years."

"Two," Raedra repeated, "*years*. She must be something *special*."

"This was never a love match!"

"No," she said. "It was a 'sensible arrangement' you offered me. And being so sensible, I should think you know better than to get all rosy-eyed over the first girl you bedded. Or is this some perversion no one without horns and a tail could satisfy?"

"That's enough!" Brin snapped. "You want to be cruel, be a little cleverer."

"*I beg your pardon?*" the princess of the blood intoned. On the other side of the room, the Purple Dragons tensed, ready hands on their blades. Brin cursed to himself. This was going all wrong, but had there ever been a way it turned out right?

"I'm sorry," he said. "You're right. You shouldn't be hearing these things from war wizards. That's why I've been trying to see you, though. Because I *did* want to tell you, and figure out a better arrangement."

"You'll forgive me if I have no interest in helping you find the smoothest way to ruin me."

"This won't ruin you," Brin said. "If anyone, it will ruin me. I promise, this has nothing to do with you, Raedra. I will do everything—"

"You're throwing me to the wolves and it has nothing to do with me?" Raedra stood, and Brin stood with her. "You want to ruin yourself, that's not my concern. You want to drag the Crownsilver name down in the dungbarrows by carrying on with some feral tiefling girl you met while running around like a vagabond, by all means please yourself."

Brin startled. "That's good of you."

Raedra smiled. "Oh, you misunderstand, *Lord* Crownsilver. I'm not calling off the wedding, and I'm not giving you two my blessings. You want to go through with this? You want to humiliate me again? Then grow some stones, do it yourself, and accept the *many* consequences."

Before Brin could utter another word, Raedra turned on her heel and stormed out, the Purple Dragons pulling the door wide before she could even consider reaching for the handle, and following her out.

Brin fell back onto the settee and ran a hand over his beard. The drum of rain on the windows, the constant accompaniment of the last many months, picked up as the storm sent slashes of water across the glass. Brin sat a moment, cursing his foul luck, Raedra's temper, devils, and Crownsilvers and anything else he could possibly blame. He cursed himself, his inability to have seen this coming, and the doubt that made him propose to Raedra in the first place.

"You aren't going to marry your lost demon-love then?" Raedra had said, a little archly.

"Listen, I won't pretend I love you. I won't pretend I will—I might. But . . ." He paused, so much he could say and none of it would make a difference. "It's not looking likely."

"You are such a romantic, Lord Crownsilver."

"I don't want the throne," Brin said. "I don't want a wife who will push me toward the throne. And I certainly don't want His Majesty dropping me in front of it, just because I look like his dead brother. He thinks he owes me this, owes Emvar this. I'm wondering if making certain I'm officially family would stop him from doing it."

"You want me to marry you so His Majesty doesn't legitimize you?"

"Yes," Brin said. "And so that you get a little respite from all that noble nonsense. You didn't betray anyone. You did the right thing."

Raedra had smiled then, a real, rare smile. "You don't think they'll talk just the same about me if I agree to wed not only a Crownsilver, but the lost scion of Emvar who everyone knows dabbles in dark magic and loves a demoness?"

"A tiefling," he had said. "And don't talk about her like that." He'd shrugged. "By my estimation, that would be people talking about *me*. Not you."

Brin cursed himself again, remembering it. But if nothing else, it had managed to satisfy King Foril's worries that his brother's grandson would be left out in the cold. Brin wondered if there were any hoping that it wouldn't come up again.

But that was a separate matter. At the moment all that he could hope for was some way to get out of the marriage without falling on his sword socially. If Raedra were angry enough, it would mean none of the nobles he relied on for intelligence would talk to him, and the ones he relied on for gossip would only talk about him. The Harpers would be stymied when they couldn't afford to be. He cursed again.

When there was nothing and no one left to curse, he left the parlor, turning new options over in his thoughts. There had to be some way to make Raedra see reason, to let him out quietly and marry someone else. Brin wouldn't give up, not yet. In the hallway beyond, his cousin, Constancia waited, her symbol of Torm bright on her armor, and her severe, dark bob sleek and unruffled.

"I take it that wasn't the smooth transition you were hoping for," the paladin of the god of duty said, falling into step beside him. "Perhaps you see it's not a simple matter."

"When was this *ever* a simple matter?" Brin demanded. Even before Havilar returned to the picture, things were complex: rival nobles, Raedra's status, Raedra's reputation, the balance of being a Harper and a lord of Cormyr, and the impending civil war nestled in the possibility that King Foril would return to the matter of Brin's father's legitimization. "I can hardly move but I step on a new trap."

"Only because you're complicating things."

"Maybe for Helindra."

"She'll want to know what came of all of this," Constancia said. "What should I tell her?"

"Tell her my love life is still not her damned business."

"Everything in your life is this family's business," Constancia said, stating it as if it were an immutable fact, nothing for Brin to be upset by.

"Then I assume you already know what to tell her. What is it you think I'm going to do? Hmm? I waited for Havi to come back, and here she is. You think my whole life is the work of Torm, so what is that? What's he saying to me?"

Constancia scoffed. "The gods are not the arbiters of every minor incident."

"Convenient," Brin said as they reached the carriage.

As much as Brin wanted to retreat to the tallhouse, his afternoon was filled with more appointments than he'd thought it could hold—conferences with other nobles, meetings with contacts, a stop in the market, and another dressing down from the Lord Magister of Suzail, Edwin Morahan, about Brin leaving his military post. The good lord's household was already preparing for evenfeast by the time Brin arrived.

"At least you chose a lucky time to run off," Lord Morahan said. "If you'd hit the Swordflow at the wrong time, you'd have been the first thing eaten by all those monsters that lady shade's stirred up from their nests. We'd be having a funeral instead of a wedding."

"When should I expect to head out again?" Brin asked.

"You're not riding up Calantar's Way *now*, my lord," Lord Morahan said incredulously. "Chances are too high you'll be shot full of arrows before you ever get to Arabel, end up some goblin's dinner, and then I'll be the one telling Princess Raedra." He shook his head at Brin, as if appalled Brin could suggest leaving him to such a fate. "Let the army handle it."

That wouldn't work, Brin thought. Cormyrean politics aside, he had Harper business relying on the fact that he made the ride north out of Suzail on a regular basis. "I'll manage. Others manage."

"If you'll pardon me saying, my lord, others aren't on the hook for an Obarskyr heir. We'll find a duty for you in Suzail."

Duty, Brin thought. Torm help him, he had grown to loathe that word.

"You think I failed by leaving," Brin said to Constancia, as they left Lord Morahan's house. "And yet, he has a point: If I'd been riding the Way, I'd likely as not have been killed. Was that my duty?"

Constancia didn't look at him. "*That's* a petulant question. To begin with, nothing says you would have been killed. Perhaps you would have carried the message quicker. Perhaps you would have killed a few more goblins."

Brin climbed into the carriage. "Perhaps I would have been torn from my horse and eaten."

Constancia had started to reply when one of his doorguards ran up to the carriage. "Lord Crownsilver, there's been an incident," he said. "You have to come back to the tallhouse."

Brin was about to leap from the carriage, to run the few blocks to the tallhouse, but Constancia blocked him and climbed in herself. "You will regret racing down the Promenade in the rain like an errand boy, *Lord* Crownsilver," she said, as the carriage lurched forward. "Whatever has happened, we will know soon enough."

"Stlarn and sod the bloody carriage," Brin said, but it didn't make him feel better.

• • •

THE BRACING SMELL of the poultice on her ankle made Havilar's eyes water even after it started to cool, but the ache was finally fading. Mehen sat on the opposite sofa—the softer one—while Farideh rebandaged the cut on his arm.

"Tighter," Mehen said.

"It was too tight before," Farideh returned. "I know what I'm doing."

Havilar considered her feet propped up on the padded stool—the twisted one by now hardly hurt more than the one that had been simply bruised. So long as she sat. "Is it wrong," she asked, "to think that was a *little* better than sparring?"

"Yes," Mehen growled.

Havilar sighed. "Then I'm wrong."

"The move where you swung the glaive by the end went well," Farideh offered. "I haven't seen that before." She smiled. "And I'd rather you did it to him than to me."

Havilar laughed. At the same moment, the door slammed against the wall. "Havi!" Brin shouted from the entryway.

"Here!" she called.

"Sit," Mehen warned when she moved to stand.

Brin came into the front room, his stormcloak dripping on the carpet, his expression fearful. He looked Havilar over, up and down, up and down. "What happened?"

"Got caught by a tanglefoot bag." She wriggled her toes—a twinge of pain went through her twisted ankle.

"Someone tried to kidnap her," Mehen said, as though it were Brin's doing.

Brin stiffened. "Did you catch them?"

"Eight assassins playing at kidnappers? No, I didn't catch them. They killed Arlo, by the way. I sent the new doorguard to get the Dragons."

Brin said nothing. Havilar fidgeted against the upholstery and caught Farideh's eye. Being in love with Brin had been complicated enough, but while the twins had been trapped in the Nine Hells, Brin had become Mehen's employer as well.

"Who did it?" Brin asked. "Did they say?"

"Someone rich," Mehen said. "Someone who doesn't think twice about spilling the kind of coin it takes to hire eight assassins to kidnap someone."

"What makes you think they were assassins?"

"The blade that took Arlo was very sharp and very quick. Not some sharpjaw's pocketknife," Mehen said. "Short weapons, quick weapons. Even the big fellow had daggers instead of a bludgeon."

"They slipped in while we were talking," Farideh added. "All eight of them. They never made a sound."

"Then why aren't you dead?" Brin demanded.

"Brin," Havilar said. He was mad, but that was too much.

"I mean," he said, trying again, "eight assassins should have made short work of you."

"They got confused," Havilar said. "They weren't expecting me to fight. They weren't expecting Farideh to cast spells. They couldn't even tell which of us was which, for pity's sake." She shook her head. "*They* got cocky," she said to Mehen.

"You cast spells?" Brin turned on Farideh. "What were you thinking?"

Farideh folded her hands in her lap. "That I didn't want them to kill us." Her voice was calm and measured, but Havilar knew her too well—her *and* Brin. Another fight brewing.

"Hey," Havilar interrupted. "Let's save it for the *henish* who sent kidnappers, right?" Brin turned to her and all the anger went out of him. He came to sit beside her on the hard sofa. "They were very little spells. Even Mehen said it was reasonable."

"The war wizards might not agree," he said. To Farideh he added, "I'm only concerned with your safety. All of your safety."

"Of course," Farideh said. "If they have concerns, I'll—"

"Don't talk to them," Brin said. "I'll deal with it."

Farideh looked away, and Havilar blew out a breath. She had been just as angry as Brin at Farideh, but . . . after so long it became almost a chore to stay angry. Much as she wanted those years of her life back, the more Havilar found out, the harder it was to point the finger at Farideh alone. And after what had happened in the internment camp . . . Havilar's eyes trailed to her sister's interlaced hands, the third finger that stood out, white as a skeleton's, where Adolican Rhand, the camp's keeper, had chopped it off as punishment, and a shoddy healing potion had grown it back. Farideh's mistake might have made Havilar's life harder, but she'd earned herself more than enough punishments.

Brin told her he understood. But he didn't act as if he did.

"Constancia, will you find out what the Purple Dragons know?" Brin asked. Constancia considered her cousin and Havilar beside him with a stern look. Havilar returned it—*karshoj* to her if she thought she could glower Havi away.

"I'll come along," Mehen said. "See what they missed."

They left, and Farideh and Havilar exchanged glances. "I'll . . . go see about evenfeast," Farideh said, all but leaping to her feet. Whether to give Havilar and Brin a little space or for her own reasons, Havilar didn't care.

"Well met," she said to Brin.

"Tell me you're all right."

"I've been hurt *far* worse than this, never you mind," she said. "I got a little practice and I only turned my ankle." A pang of guilt hit her. "Can you pay to raise Arlo?"

Brin rubbed his forehead. "I can try. I *will* try." He reached for her ankle, took the poultice off, and set his fingertips on the swollen joint ever so gently. "Loyal Torm, aid this servant of your justice."

The blessings of Torm weren't nearly as gentle as Brin, but the sharp pain passed quickly. "Much better." She turned, setting her feet on the other side of his lap. He slipped an arm around her waist. "Did you talk to her?" Havilar asked.

"Yes," he said with a sigh. "She's pretty angry. She doesn't want another postponement, and she doesn't want to call it off."

"Figures," she said. "What now?"

"Now, I try and find a way to force her to want to call it off."

"Like what?"

"Find something she doesn't want people to know," he said. "Find something she wants worse than a husband. Find her a better husband."

Havilar snorted. "This isn't about a *husband*. If it were, she would have seen you ages ago. This is about being right."

"How do you know?"

"Because I have a sister, and I *like* being right. Also, I've read chapbooks—if she's a princess, getting a husband isn't hard, even if you're pretty wonderful." She shifted away so she could look at him. "What are you going to do if there's nothing to hold against her?"

Brin hesitated for a terrible moment, then leaned in and kissed her temple. "Think of a new plan. Do you still want to go to Teneth's tonight?"

"I just nearly got kidnapped," Havilar pointed out. "Maybe you could stay?"

"I can't," Brin said. "Not all night."

"Then for evenfeast? And maybe a bit after? It's not as if anyone who cares hasn't seen you come and go."

"Fair point," Brin conceded. "And I would very much like to stay." He reached for the package Constancia had dropped beside him and handed it to her. "I brought you something."

Havilar picked apart the twine knot. "Jewels?" she teased. "Scents? Silks?" Brin laughed. "It's what you're meant to give your mistress, isn't it?"

She'd been trying to be light about it, trying to laugh. The whole thing was an absolute mess, and she believed Brin when he said it would end, he could fix it—but under that cheer, even Havilar had to admit not all of it sat right.

Brin regarded her seriously. "I don't have a mistress. And you don't buy the love of your life meaningless things like jewels and scents."

Havilar smiled, unfolding the paper. "What if I like jewels?" But what lay inside was far, far better. The nagging feeling that this might not turn out right dissipated as she lifted a stack of chapbooks from the wrappings and fanned them out. *The Prince of Al-Qadim. The Secrets of the Obarskyrs. The Giantess's Curse. Red Bess and the Kelpie's Regret.*

"I don't recognize any of these," she said with a chuckle. "I suppose all the stories we were reading finished ages ago."

"I'll track them down," he promised. "But these are all just starting. I don't know if they're any good—the seller said they were all the best she'd seen, but they always say that. We don't have to—"

Havilar leaned across the bench, pulled him to her and kissed him firmly on the mouth. "You're sweet, and I love you," she said, letting her hand linger on his cheek. "Although, I still hate this beard."

He took her hand and kissed the palm of it. "I love you too. And I'll shave as soon as I don't have to go to court anymore. Promise."

Havilar smiled, pulled a chapbook from the middle of her fan and thrust it at him, grinning. "Here. You start."

• • •

THE SPIRIT HAD never been to Cormyr in life—at least, not so far as she could remember. She studied her great-great-granddaughter, giggling over some frivolous printing, and wondered if the Forest Kingdom of old turned in the secret memories of the soul fragment nestled in the tiefling's own essence. All manner of answers, of stories, of ends might be trapped behind that vapid façade.

The broken ghost of Bryseis Kakistos had traveled so very far to find out what they were.

To the untrained eye, Cormyr had weathered the Spellplague and its attendant chaos and emerged nearly the peer of its historical self—albeit short a great many wizards. But the magic of the torn Weave still bucked and buckled and threatened to unravel the threads of magic Bryseis Kakistos had used to stitch her shattered soul back together. The holes that the lost fragments left behind felt so sharp and physical, she thought surely the little nobleman would have felt their absence as he passed through her insubstantial form—as if those bits of Toril were simply *missing*.

But he had not so much as shivered. Her powers were, after all, finite.

One fragment in each twin. Two pieces left tethered when the vessel that was meant to hold Bryseis Kakistos's spirit split in the womb. She would need both back, eventually. And then she would need a body to hold her soul in order to return to the world and seize what was theirs.

She caught herself. Not theirs. *Hers*.

Do it, a part of her urged, and had been urging since the first time she'd laid eyes on the lost heirs. Tear the souls out. Claim your due.

Not yet, Bryseis Kakistos reminded herself. She could not, after all, tear the fragment that was hers from the rest of the twins' souls—that would take the power of an archdevil, if not a god. Fighting against a pair of willful ghosts sealed to her spirit was not a state to stumble into.

A memory slipped through her, as if along the edge of one of the missing fragments—the feeling of being tethered to a ghost, the way it had of tugging at your own soul and a loneliness alongside it.

And then it was gone, just as so many memories were gone. She watched Havilar, needled by frustrations the young woman couldn't imagine, trying to remember exactly what her plan was. Why she had tethered herself to a ghost.

Everything in its time. She would make certain Asmodeus suffered for his trickery. That much she would never, ever forget.

In the little parlor, Havilar burst into a fresh cascade of giggles amid reciting some particularly ribald rhymes. The young man leaned over and stopped her with a kiss. The ghost hoped, quietly, Havilar was the disposable one. The one without the secret she needed.

2

26 Kythorn, the Year of the Nether Mountain Scrolls (1486 DR)
Suzail, Cormyr

B*ODIES STREAM PAST FARIDEH, AS IF SHE'S FIGHTING HER WAY UPSTREAM THROUGH*
a deep and brimful river, the current too strong to make any headway. She
presses herself against the island of a hut and watches the people passing,
hurrying for the buried rooms on the other side of the camp. Some she
recognizes—Oota, Khochen, Brother Vartan, Maspero and Pernika—most are
strangers. She can't find Lorcan, and if she doesn't soon . . .

She fights her way back into the torrent of people, squeezed so tightly by their
passing that she has to twist and stretch between them merely to keep her place.
She has to find Lorcan, and something terrible will happen if she can't. To the
left, one of the huts suddenly bursts into flames, but Farideh can't reach it—the
river of bodies forces her in the opposite direction. She has to find Havilar, or
something terrible will happen.

Another hut bursts into flames, and another and another—a chain of them,
whoosh, whoosh, whoosh. As if something is coming for her, leaping from building
to building. She shifts around more hurrying bodies. If she doesn't find Dahl,
something terrible will happen.

That stops her—Lorcan, Havilar, Dahl . . . This is a dream. She stands still,
buffeted by the fleeing prisoners, and tries to remember what comes next. When
she looks up, the ghost of a tiefling woman is blocking her path. She points a
skeletal arm toward the nearest hut as it bursts into flames, just moments before
a terrible maw breaks out of the ground, dragging the malformed body of a
wormlike dragon behind. The beast wavers for a moment against the gray sky,
before splitting down to the middle. The flesh falls, pooling around a stone heart,
where the god stands, terrible and beautiful, branded with a fragile sigil of blue.

Asmodeus points his ruby rod at Farideh, and speaks: "Stay alive tief-
ling. You may find we have more than one goal in common." Every
nerve in her body catches fire . . .

Farideh woke a heartbeat before Lorcan's summons came, sharp and unsettling as
a blade pricking up from under her skin. She scrunched her eyes shut, as if it could
scrub the nightmare from her thoughts with the motion. Outside the night was
complete—only the wavering light of streetlamps outlined the edges of the shutters.

She rubbed a hand over the raised edges of her brand, toying with the idea of ignoring the invitation. She might have slept through it, after all, and it would be better if she didn't encourage Lorcan.

The summons came again, softer this time and unsettling in a very different way.

Better than lying here trying to forget that blasted dream, Farideh thought, though she was already up and wrapping herself in a dressing gown. One eye on her sister's still and sleeping form, she slipped from the borrowed bedroom and into the hallway. Past Mehen's room and the stairs up to the servants' quarters, down to the entry on featherlight feet so as not to alert the doorguard outside. Through the hallway that divided the tallhouse in half and past the kitchen, so carefully the scullery on the other side might as well have been a dragon. Farideh's pulse raced—no matter how many times she met Lorcan in the sodden garden, it felt dangerous.

It *was* dangerous. If any one of Brin's servants spotted Lorcan, she'd have a great deal to explain. She slipped out the back door and stopped, sheltered by the eaves. The rain had let up to only a drizzle, and Lorcan stood in the middle of it, wearing his human disguise. If a servant did wake, all they'd find in the garden would be a strikingly handsome man in black leathers—no sign of horns or wings or burning red skin.

At least he'd listened about that much, Farideh thought. Reflexively, she pulled her robe close. "Come out of the rain."

"I thought I wasn't supposed to come in the house," he drawled. The trees scattered cold drops as a breeze blew through their crowns. Lorcan's dark hair curled as the rain soaked through it. "Are you afraid you'll get wet?"

Farideh felt her cheeks burn. "If you don't get out of the rain, I'm going back inside."

Lorcan's black, black eyes pierced her as he moved toward her. She nearly took a step back, just to get some more space, but she made her feet stay where she'd planted them. Things with Lorcan were different these days.

"Where are your boots?" he asked. "Your feet will get cold."

"Inside," she said. "I was asleep after all."

"So somewhere warm?" Lorcan smiled at Farideh and a shiver ran up her back—*that* might give him away.

"And dry," she said. "And quiet."

Lorcan took her hand in his, and Farideh shut her eyes as he opened the portal. Lorcan might have been gifted with a portal that could take him anywhere on Toril, but they had to step through the Nine Hells to do so. Another reason you should stop, Farideh reminded herself, as the crushing sensation of heat and rot and death pressed on her in that moment between the portal opening to Suzail and the reopening to their next location. But Lorcan held her hand tightly. And whether it was wise or not, she trusted him not to let go.

"Here we are."

Farideh opened her eyes again to a wide and treeless plain, the dancing grasses lit silver by the full disk of the moon. It was nearly bright as morning, not a cloud in the sky, and the stars that whirled overhead were so numerous, they looked nearly like seafoam upon a dark and distant ocean. Beneath her feet, the ground was sandy and loose. The remnants of her nightmare imagined a twisted dragon bursting out of it with ease.

She looked up at the moon. Don't ruin it, she told herself. "Where is 'here'?"

"The Shaar," Lorcan told her. "There is not a soul for miles. Nor," he added, "a raincloud."

Farideh rubbed a little warmth into her hands. "Chilly though."

"Two out of three isn't so terrible." Lorcan wrapped his arms around her. "And you can surely think of ways to gain the third." He kissed her neck, just behind her jaw, and there didn't seem to be a thing in the world that would be easier.

"Well, you don't make it very hard to guess," Farideh said dryly, eyes on the grasses, rolling into dunes of silvery sand. A desert, and before that, a lonely island, a dense forest, a cliffside overlooking a shining castle. "How far are we from Suzail?"

"Far enough." He turned her, pulled her against him by the hips. His mouth found hers—how many times had he kissed her now? Enough that it shouldn't have made her weak when he did, shouldn't have scattered all her thoughts like a slung stone scattered birds. But it did every time.

Her hands snaked up to his chest and for a terrifying, glorious moment, they went to unbuckle his leather armor. He wouldn't stop her.

She uncurled her hands and pushed him back, breaking off the kiss. "Stop," she made herself say. "It's . . . it's not a good time."

He clucked his tongue. "That happens an awful lot."

Farideh scowled at him. "You woke me from another nightmare, you know. I don't want to think . . ." She trailed off, not wanting to put it into words—Asmodeus pulled Lorcan's strings just as much as he pulled hers.

"Your problem," Lorcan said, sitting in the grass, "is that you think too much." Farideh rolled her eyes, but sat beside him, then after a moment, lay back staring up at the stars.

He stretched out beside her. "You could have a little cottage here. No one to bother you—much better than being so close to Almraiven would have been."

"In a desert?" Farideh asked. "What would I eat? What would I even do? There's nothing here." His knuckles lay against hers in the sand, and she thought about taking his hand. "We're probably a thousand miles from Suzail."

Lorcan chuckled again. "Close to two thousand miles."

Farideh shut her eyes. "I've never been so far from Havi." She laughed once, the distance so enormous and yet with Lorcan's magic, so inconsequential. "I can't stay here. I can't stay in any of these places."

"Hmm." Lorcan leaned over her. "You can't leave her, but she's allowed to leave you? How is that fair?"

"She hasn't left me."

"But she will—isn't that why you're stuck in dreary Suzail? Because she'd rather hitch her fortunes to the little lordling than stand by your side?"

"Brin and her have nothing to do with me."

"Exactly. You come with me, we'll find somewhere that suits you better. They'll stay behind and mope in Cormyr."

"If," Farideh noted, "things work out."

Lorcan's grin spread, slowly as a knife traced up her spine. "What an interesting idea. Is that why you've been playing swordswoman all these afternoons? Reminding her blood is thickest?"

"That's not what I meant."

"Of course," Lorcan said, clearly still amused. "You just like the sword. Well done."

"I like my sister. And I'll like her just as much if she decides to stay in Suzail. I just meant—"

"And then what? You'll find rooms there? You think the landlords who rent to tieflings are kind and generous sorts?"

Farideh watched the stars, burning through the fabric of the sky, her temper simmering. She didn't know. "They're probably kinder to a friend of Lord Crownsilver's."

"*Are* you friends?" Lorcan said. "Last I recall his only use for you was keeping Havilar happy."

"It's complicated."

"Only if you're an idiot. Darling, don't pretend you'll happily hang around Suzail if the little lordling decides to keep your sister on."

"She's not a servant," Farideh snapped.

"Do you think she's going to be his *wife?*" Lorcan said. "Darling, even if he chooses her and chucks the princess to the cleric—which is both incredibly foolish and exactly the sort of nearsightedness the little Tormite is capable of—do you think he can stay a lord of Cormyr and wed a tiefling who descends from one of the most vile sorceresses in the history of the Western Heartlands?"

A tiefling who is one of the Chosen of Asmodeus, Farideh thought. Her nightmare echoed through her thoughts.

"You forget it's Brin," Farideh pointed out. "He doesn't care—"

"He doesn't *want* to care," Lorcan returned. "But he does. Otherwise, why would you still be waiting? He's paralyzed, because he wants too many things and they don't fit together."

Farideh sat up and glared at Lorcan. "It's complicated," she said, more because she was sick of Lorcan interrupting her and sicker of him being right, than because of the situation itself. "I don't want things not to work out. And anyway, who says they'll stay in Suzail? They may come along with us."

"As if that's better," Lorcan said. "He'll be as much a sneering bastard in any other port." He leaned close again. "If Havilar's choice is truly a fellow who hates you for doing what you had to, are you really in danger of losing anything so dear?"

Farideh stood, the powers of Asmodeus rising with her temper. "Take me home."

"Oh, come on, darling—"

"Take me home, right now."

"Or what?" He stood and slipped an arm around her. "You'll start walking? I'm not saying anything you're not already thinking. Your sister isn't the best example of constancy after all."

Fire threatened to burst out of her pores. Calm, Farideh told herself. Calm. "Are you seriously criticizing Brin for being angry when you did *exactly* the same thing to me under worse circumstances? Are you truly claiming Havilar's the inconstant one?"

Lorcan's dark eyes narrowed. "I *apologized* for that. Are you going to keep throwing it at me?"

"I'm not throwing anything at you!" She could—oh, she could. He might be almost sweet now, but that didn't change everything. "You're the one who's bringing all of it up!"

The rage and fury of the Hells soaked her faster than the rain could have, her veins turning black in her arms. Stop, she told herself. Stop, stop, stop—

"We don't have to fight, darling," Lorcan crooned, even though he had been the one to start it, to pick at her. "Just calm down."

"Stop it!" she snapped, too far gone now. Farideh felt the powers slip from her tight hold, felt the flames leap from her skin—felt the dark horror of Asmodeus suddenly race out of her like a pack of wild dogs. She had only a moment to leap away from Lorcan, before wings of fire unfolded from her back. She shut her eyes and cursed and cursed.

But not before seeing the fear in Lorcan's face, the horror at the dark, terrible thing she'd become.

The wave of terror crashed and vanished. The flames guttered and went out—first the wings, then the rest. The breeze picked up, rattling the grasses. Farideh kept watching the dunes.

"Take me home, please," she said softly. She shut her eyes as Lorcan took her hand in his. There was nothing else either of them could do.

• • •

LORCAN STEPPED FROM his portal onto the bone-tiled floor of a little room at the tip of the farthest fingerbone tower, gritting his teeth. That hadn't gone well—it never seemed to go well anymore. There would be a next time, he reminded himself. She's not casting you off. And whatever Suzail's faults, it was safe, it was contained, it was predictable. Nothing about Suzail particularly countermanded his orders from Asmodeus.

Except that it left her in the middle of people she was terrified of failing. Pushed and pulled by guilt and grief. Any day now, she might do something drastic, thinking she could absolve herself.

Lorcan shook off the human disguise—red skin burning through, horns sprouting from his brow, batlike wings stretching from his back. He flexed his hands—the transformation was getting simpler. At least something was.

"*What*," his sister Sairché demanded, "was that?"

"Oh, good," Lorcan said, dryly. "You're awake again." Sairché seethed at him from her corner, hemmed in by a wall of force. Oozing scabs parted the silvery fuzz of her unshaven scalp and one wing still drooped as if it were wilting. Her gold eyes were hollow, her favored silver lashes tangled in her true ones, like dead branches caught in a canopy.

"How are we feeling today?" he said with exaggerated care.

"I want to kill you *just* a little more than I did the last time you asked," Sairché said. "You forgot to dismiss your scrying mirror, *darling*."

The mirror reflected the tallhouse's best bedroom, the enormous wooden bed, and Farideh, sitting on one side of it, staring at the opposite wall with a troubled expression.

Lorcan stormed over and waved a ring over the surface, making his own reflection replace Farideh and the tallhouse and the tangle of feelings he was most certainly not going to deal with. He glared at Sairché. "It's all your tampering. It's grown temperamental."

"Aww," Sairché said. "Are you angry I saw your little tryst fall apart? Honestly, that was without a doubt the worst seduction I've ever witnessed. And I once watched a polymorphed kyton try to go about it."

"First of all," Lorcan said, "you don't have the slightest idea how you seduce someone, so keep your criticisms. You also don't have the slightest idea how to manage a warlock pact—seducing her would be an idiot's move. After that, what do I have to tempt her with?"

Sairché smirked. "She's not going to be interested a second time, I gather?"

Lorcan ignored the lazy insult. Treading the line between too much and too little with Farideh was the worst of it. He shouldn't have ever kissed her like that—a line crossed, and then where could her attentions turn but to the next line? He would run short of promises all too soon.

But it had been necessary, he reminded himself. She was furious, ready to cast off the pact, certain to never forgive him, and running off into the snowy night with *Dahl*, of all people. And Lorcan, all seething with the dark powers of a Chosen of Shar, could only think he might lose her in that moment, he might never have the chance—

It was strategic, he thought firmly. Even if it was a poor move in the long term.

"I may not know how to manage a warlock," Sairché went on. "But I know the look of someone who—shall we say—wants to be an idiot."

"Well, the Lords of the Nine know you might well think I look like a planetar or a bear or a rotting turnip. Poor mad little Sairché." He clucked his tongue.

Sairché glared at him. "You know I haven't gone mad."

"What is it they say? 'The sanity of the sane defends itself'?"

"What is it they say?" Sairché shot back. "Don't send a shirking cambion to do a succubus's job? Just *hire* someone—surely you have a favor in your pocket."

"That sounds even madder than the last time I was here," Lorcan said, all false concern. "You must need more time to recover."

Sairché slammed the side of her fist against the invisible barrier. "I am *well*, and you *know* it!"

"Don't worry. Her Highness is aware that you put yourself in harm's way to battle the Chosen of Shar herself." The memory of those powers that drove the will to survive from a person's mind bit by bit made him grow cold, even now. Lorcan had felt the briefest touch of those abilities, and still he'd found himself distressingly maudlin, clinging to Farideh like she was a lover in a tale and not his warlock. Sairché had been locked in with the Chosen of Shar for well over a day, and he had no idea how she'd survived to even walk out shivering and scared.

But he smiled nonetheless. "I didn't mention it was a thirteen-year-old girl who reduced you into a weeping, jabbering mess."

"What do you think you're going to do with me?" Sairché demanded. "You're still bound to our agreement. Do you plan on 'protecting' me in this prison until time runs out and then hope I stand still while you drop the shield and run me through?"

"Of course not," Lorcan said. "Only a madwoman would think of that." He left the little room with its marrow-seeping walls, chased by Sairché's curses.

A pair of enormous erinyes—his and Sairché's half sisters—stood watching as he coaxed the locks of sinew and bone over the door. No one could enter the room but Lorcan, even if they watched exactly how he did it, and that was safest. Still, the erinyes—Leuctra and Noreia—studied his every move. Members of the elite *pradixikai*, both were larger and stronger than their younger sisters, their horns twisted and sharp, their hooves like cut glass.

"There's ways to take care of her," Leuctra said. "If you've the stomach."

"Don't underestimate how many schemes are intertwining here," Lorcan said. "If there were a way to kill Sairché and keep all the other pieces in place, I would have done it long ago."

Leuctra tilted her head, a thick streak of white hair, stemming from a patch of scarred skin, falling over one horn. "Would you have?"

There were a thousand things Lorcan wanted to do to Sairché after all the pain and trouble she'd caused him. Torture her, as she had him. Hand her to the erinyes.

Hand her to Invadiah, their furious mother to whom he owed a favor. Hand her to Stygia and the devil whose plans Sairché had helped Lorcan ruin.

Hells, even turning her over to Farideh—how swiftly would Farideh stop being his virtuous warlock when confronted with the architect of all her sorrows? The line between good and evil blurred awfully quickly when a helpless enemy landed in your lap.

But Lorcan had made a deal—and letting Sairché come to harm would mean he hadn't held up his end.

He didn't like to think about what happened to devils who didn't hold to their own deals.

Lorcan glared at her. "Glasya doesn't want her dead. Are you going to countermand Her Highness?" The erinyes's smirk faltered.

"An imp came while you were in there," Leuctra said. "Her Highness wants you to come as soon as you're available."

Lorcan's blood ran cold. "How long ago?"

Leuctra grinned around her fangs, but the fear in her eyes was clear. "It's been a while. Maybe you'd better run."

Lorcan spread his wings. "*You* can run," he sneered, and he leaped from the near window. The palace of Osseia rose out of the center of the layer, a massive skull transformed into the seat of Glasya's power.

The Lord of the Sixth, princess of the Nine Hells, had not been happy about how things had turned out on Toril. Lorcan had kneeled long hours in her presence, accounting for each step, from supplanting Sairché to helping the Chosen of Asmodeus escape the destruction of the Netherese prison camp.

"I suppose you did your best," Glasya had said. "My father, His Majesty, is not pleased, of course, though the blame is laid upon His Highness, Prince Levistus. But then, at least Shar has not benefited from Levistus's error." She had leaned close to Lorcan's ear and spoken in a voice terrible and wonderful. "I am *not* pleased, on the other hand, that Prince Levistus has benefited."

"None of us is, Your Highness," Lorcan murmured, eyes on the floor. He swallowed the bile that rose in his throat. "We stand ready for your orders."

"Why would I give orders against Prince Levistus?" Glasya said. But no devil hearing those words would mistake them for innocent. "What did you think I would do? Order the pradixikai to raid the Fifth Layer?"

"It's not my place to presume what you would order, Highness."

The bubble of Glasya's laughter put Lorcan in mind of boiling lead. "A pretty answer," she had said. "You'll do well."

Lorcan landed before the jaws of Osseia and hurried in, ignoring the pit fiends that loomed over the entry. Once, they would have given him no end of trouble; a mere cambion—a mewling half-devil—was hardly a step above an imp to a towering pit fiend. But since Asmodeus had laid his edict upon Invadiah's only son, every devil in the Hells seemed a little more circumspect.

It was not worth it, in Lorcan's mind. Lorcan was not meant for the audience of an archdevil or the leadership of the *pradixikai*. The spoiled son of Fallen Invadiah, Lorcan was meant for nothing more than collecting warlocks and staying out of anyone important's attention. Instead he had both Glasya's and Asmodeus's eyes fixed on him.

A hundred devils fixed the cambion with curious gazes as he passed through the court, led by a bobbing imp to a small antechamber. Unlike the greater part of Malbolge, the room would have delighted any fine lady on the mortal planes, apart from the lingering odors of blood and brimstone.

Glasya perched upon a gilded chair, ignoring Lorcan for an array of tidbits laid upon the crystal table beside her. She plucked a tiny, jewel-bright heart from a bowl and popped it in her mouth, like darkness enveloping a miniature moon.

"Where have you been?" she asked.

"My apologies." Lorcan fell on his knees. "The message was not conveyed quickly. I will deal with that."

Glasya chuckled. "You do grow bold, little Lorcan. But that isn't what I meant. Your portal. What is there of interest in the Shaar Desolation?" Lorcan kept his eyes on the pattern of the carpet, the lacy lines of vines and blossoms, the fearsome mouths hidden in their gaps. "The Moonshae Isles? The Calim? Hmm?" Glasya's hand slid through his hair, her nails like daggers, and a violent shiver went through Lorcan. "You've been very busy."

"Looking for a place to secure His Majesty's Chosen," Lorcan said. "It's only a matter of time before Cormyr becomes unsafe."

"Tumultuous," Glasya corrected. "When the world is ending, some take solace in privation, some will throw themselves headlong into sin. Suzail is more useful to His Majesty than the Shaar." She paused, the silence yawning like a hungry mouth. "Though it's come to my attention that this may not be your first error."

Lorcan didn't move, but it was only years of the Nine Hells hammering home what would happen if he did that kept him from fleeing like a hunted beast. "My apologies, Highness. What is that?"

"I can't help but notice, your Brimstone Angel isn't ours. Not really. Why has she not corrupted?"

"Circumstances haven't allowed it, Highness," Lorcan said. "She's a . . . delicate case."

"You may have been in the habit of collecting warlocks for your own amusement," Glasya said, sliding her sharp nails through his hair once more. "But you are no longer your own agent—you must bring the Hells their due. And I have no use for a virtuous Brimstone Angel. And unless you *know* something, I doubt my lord father has use for a virtuous Chosen?"

Asmodeus did not care about Farideh's virtues, Lorcan knew that much. He wanted her silence, her peace. Whatever she was to Asmodeus, first and foremost she was a secret—something the other archdevils shouldn't be concerning themselves with. Lorcan shut his eyes and said a string of curses to himself. "Yes, Highness."

"Do you *know* something Lorcan?"

"I know she won't go easily," he said, dodging the question.

"Start soon," Glasya said. "Farewell, little Lorcan."

The erinyes were waiting for him as he left the court of Osseia. They fell into step beside him, as Lorcan wound his way to his own apartments in the Skull Palace.

"Zela wants orders," Noreia said as they passed through the leaking, weeping hallways.

"I order her to put you all through your training then," Lorcan said, "until Her Highness has other ideas. And tell Zela she's perfectly capable of asking me instead of bleating like a lost lamb to you all."

Noreia tossed her long, wooly dreadlocks. "I think she's waiting for Sairché to come after you."

"She'll be waiting a long time," Lorcan said.

"Some of them are waiting for Invadiah to come back first," Leuctra said.

Lorcan rolled his eyes. "Since His Majesty and Her Highness seem to find me useful, I'd hope Invadiah has sense enough to wait until one or both of them change their minds before coming after me."

"Probably ought to make sure they know that," Leuctra said offhandedly. "Sulci for one."

"So she can kill me in a fit of pique?" Lorcan asked, as they reached his quarters. "Shit and ashes, I thought *Sairché* thought I was stupid."

The *pradixikai* swept the room once to check for intruders, then left. Lorcan went to stand before the wide windows looking out on Malbolge beyond—he was not supposed to be here. This was what came of getting too involved in mortal nonsense. This was what came of embroiling oneself in the sort of conflicts that shifted and twisted and changed all too fast, forcing one to shift and twist with them. Making decisions too quickly, without all the proper considerations, and what else would happen but he'd rise up the damnable hierarchy?

This is what came of letting warlocks get under your skin.

Behind him, someone cleared her throat. Noreia stood in the doorway, and Lorcan found himself mentally cataloging the magic rings he could reach that would stop her if she decided to attack him. Enough of the erinyes had, since Invadiah and Sairché had lost their positions.

But Noreia only regarded him curiously. She peered back out into the corridor, as if waiting to be sure Leuctra was nowhere near.

"If you want to know what happens if you try and take care of matters," Lorcan said acidly, "ask Sulci. I believe a broken arm and eighty lashes for the impudence is the answer."

Noreia gave him a withering look. "I'm not going to fight you. I have information. You might be interested."

"No," Lorcan said firmly. "I am not interested in any godsdamned erinyes gossip."

"This isn't erinyes gossip," Noreia said. "It's about the succubi—"

"I don't care," Lorcan interrupted. "I don't want to hear any gossip. I don't want to hear any information. I don't want to be dragged any further into Her Highness's sphere and I don't want any more of His Majesty's attention. Go away."

Noreia sneered at him. "You think you can avoid the hierarchy?"

"I think I can avoid diving into it as though it's a summer pond," he said. "Get out." As much as Noreia looked as if she thought she could beat him into listening, the erinyes followed her sister out of the room and back to their posts.

Lorcan stood before the window a moment longer, watching the layer beyond and listening to the faint, ghostly wailing of the skull palace, the remains of Malbolge's last ruler. He shut his eyes. "Shit and *ashes*. I shouldn't be here."

A second, smaller scrying mirror hung in the antechamber—this one unprotected and without the other's many charms and workaround magics. Lorcan watched his reflection in the faintly swirling surface a moment, before taking hold of the scourge pendant he wore and waving the trigger ring over the mirror.

Farideh lay in bed again, curled over on one side around a knot of blankets. Lorcan watched for long moments as her eyes flickered under their lids, her expression tightening as she watched some nightmare unfold. Some unwelcome part of him felt sorry for her. After all, had Lorcan never found this Brimstone Angel heir, Asmodeus wouldn't have either.

She pursed her mouth in her sleep, and Lorcan briefly thought of kissing her, and how far he was from meeting Glasya's demands—or even looking as if he were. Sairché was right—there were easier ways to corrupt her, but none of them ended with things going back to the way they were before.

Behind him, an enormous hourglass poured sand grain by grain to mark the days since he'd visited Farideh. If she was under the impression she held the reins, making certain that his attention did not come too often or too regularly would undo it. Ease her back to the way things ought to be.

There was an art to this, he thought, turning the glass once more. A way to make it work, and he just had to keep looking far enough ahead, make sure he didn't slip into easy acts with bad results . . .

• • •

Raedra eyed the edge of storm clouds just visible over the farther wall of the Royal Gardens. They didn't have long before it started raining again. Perfect, she thought. Everyone would have shot at that point, her cousins would be through showing off, and Raedra would have spent a fair few bells with her retinue—long enough to make certain no one felt slighted and no one thought she was sulking. Four young, hopeful nobles surrounded her, as well as four Purple Dragons and a war wizard—not counting the guards she couldn't see. And every one of them, to a soul, was waiting for her to crack under the strain of Aubrin's sudden madness.

"Put your elbow down," her cousin, Lord Maranth Goldfeather, called to his sister. "Honestly, you look like a chicken trying to shoot like that."

Lovely Lady Varauna Goldfeather turned and glowered at her brother. "Which of us has thirteen bull's eyes to her credit."

Maranth smirked. "It will stay thirteen if you keep your elbow so high."

The dark-haired noblewoman very deliberately did not lower her elbow. She let the arrow fly, striking just at the edge of the target's crimson center.

"A miss," Maranth declared.

"That is within the bounds and you know it, Lord Prissypants."

"Calm," Raedra said with a smile. "Varauna, count the shot and sit down." Maranth gave Raedra a look that clearly said she oughtn't to encourage proud Varauna, but Raedra waved him off. "The turn is yours, Sulue." Meanwhile the storm clouds eased nearer, slow as ladies in heavy ball gowns.

"Thank you, Highness." Lady Sulue Thundersword gave Raedra a shy smile and took the longbow from Varauna—who rolled her eyes at Raedra. Lady Thundersword, Varauna was fond of saying—often in front of poor Sulue—was so sweet she'd make your teeth fall out. And so Raedra made a point of keeping her close, to make up for Varauna's barbs.

"Perhaps it's not your form," Maranth drawled. "Perhaps your arms just resemble a chicken's by their nature."

"That's not what your fancyman says," Varauna retorted, taking up a glass of cordial.

"Children," Raedra said in mock warning. Maranth snorted and Varauna made a sarcastic little curtsy. Raedra smiled and sipped her own cordial. "Tell us then about your latest fancyman, Maranth."

"If you've found one," Varauna said, "you're more skilled a hunter than I. This war has created an absolute drought of eligible fellows."

"Not if you don't mind commoners," Lady Florelle Ambershield said. "Isn't that right, Varauna?"

Raedra pursed her lips to stop the smile that crept unbidden to her mouth. Florelle was no match for Varauna, and had yet to learn it. Varauna turned very deliberately and offered Florelle a winning smile. "My dear, that is hardly the same sport. You'd know if you'd ever managed to take a trophy of your own." Sulue's bow twanged as she shot her arrow wide and into a bush of snowspikes.

"All I get lately are desperate fellows who want to make a little trade to clear up the Goldfeather coin they'd rather keep," Maranth announced. "It seems half of them are *far* too old, half are far too young. And anyway, I detest desperation. There is nothing so unarousing as desperation."

"It's *something*," Varauna said. "I'm half ready to insist they let me take up arms, if only for the chance to ride behind some good-looking fellows with decent breeding and better backsides."

Raedra sipped her cordial. Better to enlist Varauna for her skills with the bow. And keep all the fellows from playing into her "how do I draw this?" act. She wondered what a commander in charge of Varauna could do to keep the noblewoman focused, and decided it was probably a task beyond most of them. Even if Varauna could shoot nearly as well as Baerovus. She watched the clouds creep nearer.

"It seems Raedra is the only one with decent prospects," Florelle said. "Not that anyone expected windfall from the Northern front, but having your betrothed home is . . ." She trailed off.

Raedra's heart skipped. She saw the shocked look Maranth and Varauna traded, the way the Purple Dragons stiffened slightly. Only Sulue seemed unaffected, releasing her arrow with a painful *twang*.

"I would rather Shade weren't ravaging the countryside," Raedra said coolly, "than have Lord Crownsilver home." Florelle paled and gave her a timid smile.

"Of course, Your Highness," she said. "I didn't mean—"

"It's a wonderful blessing," Maranth said. "That doesn't mean Shade's encroachment isn't terrible."

"Or that—" Florelle broke off as soon as she'd started.

"Or what?" Raedra said. Florelle shrugged and shook her head, her ash-blonde curls bouncing.

"It's gone from my mind."

Raedra stared at the stubborn clouds. "Could we not playact as if I never hear any gossip?" she said. "That is, I suspect, far worse than discussing it outright."

For a long moment, no one spoke. Even Sulue's third arrow waited, nocked in the bow.

"We could have her killed," Maranth said, in conspiratorial tones that might have meant he was joking, and might not.

"Killing her would mean she was a threat," Raedra said calmly. And I will not admit she's a threat, she thought to herself.

"Not at all," Varauna protested. "Just a nuisance."

"Send her off to the Tunlands," Maranth suggested. "Or your betrothed's wretched little citadel in the hinterlands. That's what you do with a nuisance."

"You could do better than him, Highness," Sulue offered. The others glared at the petite noblewoman and she blushed. "You *all* think it," she protested.

"Of course we do," Maranth said. "She could always do better. This time, last time. There is not a man walking Faerûn's face who deserves you," he said to Raedra. "Including Lord Saddlesores. But we all know marriage is about more than whether your friends would bed your husband. Aubrin brings many benefits to the marriage."

Such as the end of all that gossip, Raedra thought bitterly. At least that had been how it was supposed to work. But now the whispered attacks were worse—fiercer and just as numerous as they'd been in the shadow of her first marriage.

"Aubrin's decent," Varauna said. "And he doesn't care what you do on your own—that's something. Most men would have a fit at the idea of possible rivals."

Maranth shot her a dark look at the word *rivals*.

Raedra glanced up at the clouds just cresting the palace roof's edge, and drew a deep breath. If she fled now, every one of them would talk, dear as they were. They couldn't help it.

"Your Highness?" The war wizard, a tall young man named Ilstan Nyaril caught her eye as she turned. "I don't wish to interrupt, but you have an appointment with the minister of protocol and Princess Ospra very soon. Would you like me to send someone to tell them you'll be late?"

"No, thank you," Raedra said, standing. "Mother would be furious. I suppose I lost track of the time. I should go and change." She turned to her friends. "You all finish up before the rain starts again. I'll return shortly." She made her good-byes swiftly and headed toward the palace once more, trailed by Ilstan and the Purple Dragons.

"Thank you," she said, as soon as they were out of earshot.

"Of course," Ilstan said. "I can imagine you're growing weary of that conversation."

"Quite."

Raedra had become accustomed to having Ilstan watch over her and her retinue—enough that his superiors had grilled him as to their relationship. But there was nothing to find—she liked Ilstan well enough. He was trustworthy where Raedra was sure other war wizards turned around and spilled all her private exchanges to the Royal Magician, Ganrahast—and young enough to be a little fun too.

"I'm sure it will all sort out," Ilstan said. "Varauna is right; Lord Crownsilver seems a decent fellow. With many superior attributes."

"And a tiefling for a mistress," Raedra said lightly. "I know what I'm getting into. I'm well aware of its pitfalls and promises. And I know I am lucky to find such an arrangement after everything else. Unless something changes, I do intend to marry him."

Ilstan sighed. "Well, I hope you remember I'm on your side. And so are the others."

"Varauna's the one who's suggesting Aubrin and I are sharing . . . *her*, isn't she?"

"No, no," Ilstan said. Then, "I mean, she repeated it, but she didn't start it. That came from a Huntcrown."

"Of course it did," Raedra said with a sigh of her own. They reached her chambers. "Keep them away for a bell or two? And if Nell comes up before then, tell her to wait."

"Of course, Highness."

Raedra thanked the war wizard and the Purple Dragons again, and locked the door behind her. Thankfully, there were no servants within, the sitting room utterly silent but for the birdsong floating in the cracked window. Raedra pulled shut the drapes and fell into a chair—a chair unfortunately opposite the one Aubrin had proposed to her from.

She had returned late the night after her first revel as a widow—her first revel wearing the purple scarf that marked an Obarskyr's eligibility—to find the odd Lord Crownsilver waiting in her rooms. The Purple Dragons had drawn steel, Ilstan had nearly immolated him, but Aubrin hadn't so much as batted an eye.

"I have a proposition for you, Your Highness," he said.

"You want to marry me?" Raedra said. After a long night of nobles sniggering behind her back at Proud Raedra's fall, then turning around to praise her poise and grace, she'd heard enough offers to last her a lifetime. But, she thought, Aubrin wasn't one of the ones who'd mocked her openly—before or after Lindon's death.

"Haven't you heard?" she said. "I'm proud and I'm demanding—nothing and no one is good enough. Bitter, sharp, unpleasant. Frigid as the Great Glacier. You're doomed to disappoint me and end up with your head under Orbyn's blade. And I won't even make you king."

"All gossip. I'm sure you've heard *plenty* about me as well."

She had—Lord Aubrin Crownsilver, who was supposed to be dead at the tender age of eight, whose father had been named Emvar's bastard, whose legitimization as an heir to the Dragon Throne hung like a blade over the line of succession, despite the fact that it was simply not done to lift up bastards that way. Lord Aubrin Crownsilver, who spent uncounted coin on tomes of infernal magic, on charlatans who claimed to be able to access the Nine Hells. Whose heart had been stolen by a devil or a demon or a sorceress, and maybe he was just as cold as Raedra in that case.

Whether it had been his argument, his forthrightness, or the fact that she thought her grandfather reckless for even considering legitimizing this son of a bastard, a few tendays later Raedra had hung up her purple scarf, and announced her engagement. And Brin had been right—the whispers had stopped, all turning to mysterious Lord Crownsilver and how he'd been so lucky.

"It's advantageous. The Crownsilvers have a good deal of coin," her mother had said. "Though I wish you'd *considered* Cousin Maranth."

"His father was a good man," her father had settled on. "One of the best I've ever known."

"You don't love him," Baerovus had observed. "I thought you said that was important."

It had been, Raedra told him. But then, she'd been in love with Lindon, and look where that had gotten her. Perhaps advantageous and practical would be better.

"It makes sense," Baerovus had allowed. "Which means that other people will hate the idea, if my experience proves anything."

Raedra had laughed. "Rover, you're too wise."

And now poor Baerovus was out in the muddy fields of battle, while their father tried to turn him into a copy of himself. Raedra stood and pulled aside a tapestry, revealing a little door set into the stone wall. She unlatched it and slipped into the secret passage. Winding her way through the dark hall, guided only by memory and the occasional light leaking through peekholes drilled through the stone, Raedra reached a second door—this one smoothed into the stone so carefully that if one didn't know it was there, didn't know the chip that created a little handle to pull it open, one would never be able to reach the prince's chambers.

Even if some other had breached Baerovus's door, they would have to know which tiles to skip over—which ones made an alarm sound through the room, which ones were spread with sticky substances, and which steps would take one too close to the precarious stacks of armor meant to tumble and trip an intruder. Raedra slipped around all of these traps easily, through the maze of screens and mirrors and trunks that Baerovus left before every door.

"I like my privacy," her brother always said, as if this should be everyone's response.

Raedra stood in the silent, dusty room—untouched by maids since Baerovus had left—and imagined her dear brother, forced to bed down in a tent, cheek by jowl with all manner of strangers. Adapting was not Baerovus's strongest suit.

But then neither was standing up to Irvel.

"I'll survive," Baerovus had told her the night before the army marched.

"He'll survive," her father had said sternly.

"Are you so sure, my lord?" Raedra had said a little tartly. "Since I hear it's too dangerous for me."

"Raedra," her father had warned. "This will be good for Baerovus. And good for the men to see he can handle himself like a prince should. We'll rout these bumptious Sembians and be back before your wedding. I know you'd rather come along, but if anything happened to you, I'd have to deal with that terrible woman. So enjoy your wedding preparations and try," he'd added with a kiss on her forehead, "not to slit any Crownsilver throats."

But her planned wedding day had come and gone months ago, as the Army of the Purple Dragon hadn't returned. They'd pressed farther and farther into Sembia, farther and farther from Suzail. The Great Rain had begun falling on the Sea of Fallen Stars, and the roads had turned to mud. The army had wintered in Saerloon, and Raedra and Brin's wedding had been pushed off into summer, when—surely—the crown prince would have returned.

It was looking less and less likely. On multiple fronts.

What would Baerovus say about this new, wretched twist? Would it be more helpful than suggesting Raedra have the tiefling murdered—something *everyone* expected the "Ice Princess" to do—or just another bit of Baerovus's oddness? She could imagine him telling Raedra to ignore the other woman, to make friends with her, or suggesting they all move to Marsember—him and her and maybe

Aubrin too. She could imagine him not knowing what to say, because, though her brother loved her and cared about what upset her, he had no experience with anything like this—much as it vexed their parents.

"My dear," her mother had said quite seriously some months ago, "don't feel as if you need to wait for the wedding. Your brother . . . I don't expect much to come of introducing him to proper ladies. Or improper ones for that matter." She'd clasped Raedra's hands. "The throne needs heirs."

Raedra lay back on Baerovus's bed, staring up at the star-patterned ceiling. If the army returned, she'd have to make a decision about the wedding. If they stayed away, at war—or if they returned only to turn north to meet the growing threat of Netheril that the western army was ill-equipped to rout—then all the fear and worry about her brother, her father, her kingdom, would eat her away.

"Havilar," she said to the empty room, and she hated the sound.

The door opened with a faint squeal. "Highness?" Ilstan called.

"Here," Raedra replied. "Don't come in—I'm fairly sure there's a trip-wire over there."

"Your maid has come," Ilstan explained.

Raedra sighed and sat up. "I'll make my way back."

"Of course, Your Highness." Silence. "If there's anything I can do . . ."

"I'll let you know," Raedra assured him, smoothing her skirts and preparing to return to the here and now in the Court of Suzail, of reappearing tieflings, and the unyielding gossip of her peers.

Do not slit any throats, she told herself wryly. Particularly not your own.

3

16 Flamerule, the Year of the Nether Mountain Scrolls (1486 DR)
Suzail, Cormyr

HAVILAR TURNED TO THE SIDE, CONSIDERING HER REFLECTION IN THE long mirror. She pressed the deep blue fabric of the gown closer to her chest. "I think they're bigger."

"They're not bigger," Farideh said once more.

"Maybe yours aren't, but these stupid things have been throwing off my slice for tendays. They're bigger." She looked over at the seamstress who was staring at her as though she were a bear in a gown. Havilar made herself smile. "Though that's nothing to do with the dress," she said kindly. "I like it quite a lot."

The seamstress bobbed her head, eyes darting to Farideh and then Constancia, standing cross-armed beside the door like a sentinel. "Thank you . . . goodwoman."

"What are you going to do with a gown?" Farideh asked. "You hardly go out."

"I go out."

"Where?"

"None of your business, bossyboots."

"Do you go places where anyone cares how you dress?"

Farideh sounded curious more than chastising, but it irritated Havilar nevertheless.

"Eventually," Havilar said with a little acid, "all this will be settled and then . . . then I'm sure we'll go plenty of places." Somewhere, she thought. Maybe not Suzail.

Constancia snorted quietly. In the mirror, Havilar saw Farideh glare at the knight. "Fair point," she said. "But maybe you should save the coin until then."

"It's not my coin," Havilar said. "Brin's already paid for it. For yours too."

Farideh folded her arms around herself. "Well, I definitely don't need a gown."

"You might. Later." Havilar kicked the fabric of the skirt out, once, twice. "Can you make a sort of slit in it?" she asked the seamstress. "Something so I can move if I have to." Her foot made another billow of sapphire silk. "I can't imagine fighting someone in this."

"That . . ." The seamstress stopped herself. "Let me bring you some sketches." She shot another glance at Constancia, and hurried into the back room.

"Do you think you're going to be a fine lady *and* a bounty hunter?" Constancia said dryly. "One doesn't brawl in skirts."

Havilar turned to the knight of Torm. "*One* doesn't always get the luxury of choosing when she fights," she said airily. "It's my gown, I'll have it how I like."

43

"It's Lord Crownsilver's gown, come to that," Constancia said.

"She should take the hem up then," Farideh quipped. Havilar shot her a dark look—that wasn't helping.

"Brin can do what he likes," Havilar said to Constancia. "He wants to buy me a dress; I want to have a dress. I don't see where you come into it." She turned back to the mirror. "Not that a thing like that would stop you."

Constancia glowered at her. "We both want what's best for him, you know. There's no need for hostility."

"We do," Havilar agreed. She fixed her gaze on Constancia's in the mirror. "But *you* called me a silly slut. *You* told him to leave me. *You* pretend I'm not there, don't even look at me when we're in the same room. When I talk, when I say anything to Brin, you disagree—but not with me. You just say it to him, like I don't exist. Like I'm too stupid to notice." She fidgeted with the cuff of the left sleeve—that needed loosening too. "I don't know why you came along anyway."

"To protect you."

Now it was Havilar's turn to snort. "Please. You and your aunt probably sent the kidnappers in the first place." The fact that Brin hadn't figured out where they'd come from, why someone had wanted to drag her off, still worried at Havilar's resolve. Helindra wasn't at the top of her list of suspects, but she was close.

"You might not think much of me, but I handle my own enemies. With honor and openness. Sending assassins and kidnappers is a coward's act."

A persistent coward. Twice now, Dorn and Arven had chased off fellows lingering too long in the Promenade before the tallhouse. That very morning, the gardener had found a man's bootprints in the mud. Though, judging by Farideh's sudden blush, that had little to do with kidnappers.

"You had better tell me everything," Havilar had hissed as they climbed into the carriage. But then of course, Constancia had loomed over them and left no space for Farideh to confess.

"And Lady Crownsilver?" Farideh asked. "Is she so open and honorable?"

Constancia eyed the door to the back room. "You could find out yourself," she said, sounding almost nervous. Almost embarrassed. "Helindra wishes you to call on her. Today, if there's time."

Havilar spun on Constancia. "What? What does she want?"

"If you forced me to guess?" Constancia said. "She wants to figure out how to best make you go away."

Havilar's blood rushed to her cheeks, a half-dozen retorts coming to her lips, but Constancia held up a hand. "I'm not saying I agree with her."

"But you aren't saying you don't either," Havilar managed. "'Protect me'—what does Torm think of your lying?"

"Do you enjoy this?" Constancia asked. "Aubrin has put himself in an unenviable situation, and the simplest way to solve that is you walking away."

"He'd come after me," Havilar said. "Whatever your aunt does."

Constancia scoffed and shook her head, as if Havilar had made a bluff worthy of a child who didn't understand what she was dealing with. Havilar gritted her teeth—it wasn't a bluff, it was just true. Even if she decided the best, safest thing for Brin was for her to leave Suzail, he would come after her. She was sure of that, down to her bones. And if Helindra Crownsilver needed to be convinced it wasn't a bluff—

"You can get a dress another time," Havilar said to Farideh. "We'll go."

The seamstress returned, made more measurements, more cuts, more promises. Havilar hardly cared what she did. She was busy arming herself.

"Are you sure this is what you want to do?" Farideh asked when Constancia went to get the carriage. "I mean, I'll go with you, but—"

Havilar pulled her blouse on and laced her bodice. "Yes," she spat. She wished she had her glaive with her. "And no." She dropped her voice so the eavesdropping seamstress couldn't hear. "I hate trying to talk to them. It's like crossing blades with bloodthirsty bandits. Only with words. You think you're talking about the weather and all of a sudden they're acting all clever and saying things about your breeding. I'd rather they came at me with a knife. I can knock a knife out of their hands. But I'm not supposed to knock the words out of their mouths. Especially not Helindra, who's probably the *worst* of all of them."

Farideh reached up and pinned the end of Havilar's braid back into its knot. "So think of it like sparring. Give her enough space to show you what she's really saying, where her weaknesses are."

Havilar snorted. "Now *you* sound like a Cormyrean."

• • •

"I CANNOT BELIEVE you told them I was your equerry," Dahl Peredur muttered as the coster caravan crossed into the city of Suzail.

"What was I supposed to say?" Lord Vescaras Ammakyl replied. He nodded politely at the Purple Dragons who stood at the gates, already satisfied by the caravan master's writs and permissions. "Your cover story was ridiculous."

"I could be your business associate," Dahl said irritably.

"Are you an expert on wine?"

"I know things about wine."

The dark-skinned half-elf looked over at his colleague, one eyebrow raised. "What's the going price for a cask of aged Arrhenish? Why are the prices on last year's Murlkan so high this year? Can we bring the cost of the Laumark down by ten tradebars? What's the rain doing to grape yields for next year? When will we see more bottles of Zanzel? Shall I stop, or can you answer a one of those?"

Dahl scowled at the other Harper. "I could have learned all that on the road."

"But you didn't," Vescaras pointed out. "So you're an equerry."

Dahl shut his eyes and told himself it wasn't worth arguing with Vescaras over this. It would inevitably make this mission to Cormyr a nightmare—and it was already going to be rough. And then there was the side issue of Brin—none of the High Harpers of the Waterdhavian network had been pleased to find their Cormyrean handler was in the middle of a very high-profile political maelstrom that threatened to destroy everything he had built. Especially over something as selfish as which lovers he kept.

"No one wants to force him," Tam Zawad, the High Harper of Waterdeep, had said. "But, Watching Gods, at least find out what he intends to do and get him to do it a little faster. If we're going to lose all our high-level Cormyrean contacts in the middle of a war, alongside the low-levels, I want to know soon enough to tell their network they're on their own."

Dahl rubbed his smooth-shaven chin—servants needed to look presentable, according to Lord Ammakyl—and sighed. He knew Brin well enough to be sure he didn't have an answer. Too many pieces, too many people to let down, too many decisions he couldn't unmake—and Havilar.

"How are you trading so well in the midst of a war?" Dahl asked. "Half of Cormyr is being pillaged as we speak, and you're raking in coin."

"People like to drink when the world's on fire," Vescaras said. "What else can they do?" A question for which Dahl didn't have an answer.

"Lot of gossip last night," Dahl said. "They say that Shade's mad general has taken Arabel."

"I heard it's not fallen. Still just harried, maybe sieged. Lady Marsheena's stirred up the Stonelands, make no mistake, and the surrounding villages are done for. If you still have it in your head to make for Harrowdale when we're done here, I hope you're ready to disguise yourself as a bugbear."

Dahl blew out a nervous breath. His mother lived on a farm outside New Velar in Harrowdale, some six hundred miles north of Suzail. All of the intelligence he could set hands on said that Harrowdale was safe, an island in a storm of violence, protected by the elves of Myth Drannor. But Dahl wanted to be sure. Had to be sure.

"I'll find a way," Dahl said. There was enough to do in Suzail—things had time to change and he had time to worry about how he'd manage.

"A fair part of the gossip I heard had nothing to do with the war," Vescaras said, as the carriage pulled away from the caravan and through the streets of Cormyr, heading toward Brin's tallhouse. "If Brin's managed nothing else, he's given folks something to talk about."

"How bad is it?"

Vescaras shrugged. "What you'd expect. Details about his bedroom activities no one would know. Speculation that he doesn't have a mistress so much as he and the princess have a mistress. Lots of bizarre notions about bedding tieflings."

"What?"

"Apparently, several gentlemen had it on good authority that it's not only turned sideways, but it also has teeth."

Dahl looked pointedly out the window. "Ah." He fidgeted with the collar of the shirt Vescaras had loaned him. "When will you get more bottles of . . . Zanzel, was it?"

"The way the rains are coming, all the grapes will mold, and we'll be drowning in it next year," Vescaras said as the carriage rolled to a stop. "Pity it tastes like bad cheese."

• • •

THE PARLOR THE twins had been escorted to was far more opulent than anything in Brin's tallhouse. Furniture so fine Farideh wondered how anyone stood sitting on it day to day, for fear they'd dirty it. Havilar ran her hands over the silk upholstery.

"How many spiders do you think this took to spin?" she asked.

Farideh frowned at her. "That's not the same kind of silk."

"What do you think they get it from? Trees?" Havilar scoffed. "You're doing it, by the way."

Farideh brushed her sleeves, but the seeping smoke was still there. "Aren't you nervous?"

"No," Havilar said grimly. "I am done being nervous."

Farideh drummed her fingers on the wooden frame of the sofa. They'd been waiting, alone, for well on half an hour. She considered the portraits hanging over the fireplace, five steely-looking Crownsilvers in a row. The nameplates beneath identified them as Narvus, Draskos, Helindra, Neanae, and Pheonard.

Helindra in paint was a dark-haired young woman with Constancia's cool eyes and thin mouth. There was a cruelness to her gaze that the portraitist hadn't bothered to soften, and Farideh found herself wondering if the intervening years could have done anything about it either. Beside her was Narvus Crownsilver, a lean man with a lantern jaw and the same cool eyes—was there anything of Brin in these faces? That was Brin's father's father, wasn't it?

No, Farideh thought. Narvus was the one whose wife had dallied with the crown prince. Brin was a Crownsilver like she and Havilar were dragonborn.

"*That* is making me nervous too," Havilar said, nodding at Farideh's drumming hand. Her gaze lingered—no doubt on the bleached finger. Farideh tucked her hand back into her sleeve.

Havilar looked up at her face. "*Whose* bootprints are in the garden?"

Farideh felt her chest tighten, too many promises and worries pressing their points against her. "She'll be in any moment. Can't we talk about that later?"

"Oh gods," Havilar said. "It's Lorcan isn't it? Does Mehen know?"

"Of course he doesn't know," Farideh said. "*Please* don't tell him. I just . . . Lorcan's the only one who knows what's going on, even a little, and besides . . ."

"You haven't told Mehen about me and Brin going off," Havilar said, as if finishing Farideh's thought—even though that hadn't been remotely what she was going to say. "Although he *must* know." She hesitated. "Do you think he's being a little strange? I figured Brin and I would have gotten away with it once, and the next time I'd find Mehen sitting in front of the door. Ready to talk. And then the . . . other thing."

The other thing—the powers of Asmodeus—had indeed fallen into the uncomfortable space between secret and solution. Mehen brought it up, here and there, testing and prodding the edges of the curse. Could she control the powers? Was she using them? Should she be using them—honing them—so that they couldn't be a weapon against her? Did she want to go visit this temple or that? Was there any change in Havilar? And Farideh wished so hard she had anything of use to tell Mehen, but nothing changed.

"I don't know if he'd care about Lorcan so much," Havilar went on. "Like you said, he's the only one who knows what's going on with *that* even if it hardly comes to much." She eyed her sister and lowered her voice. "You're not sleeping with Lorcan in the garden are you?"

"I'm not sleeping with him at all!"

"That's probably sensible," Havilar said, sounding just a little disappointed. "Although," she added, "you're missing out—it's tremendous fun."

Mercifully, the door opened, and a woman with her steel-gray hair arranged in a crown of braids stepped in. She eyed first Havilar, then Farideh with Crownsilver eyes—icy and blue—her mouth pursed, as if she couldn't tell which of them to deal with. As if it didn't matter.

Havilar stood. "Well met," she said, holding out a hand.

Helindra's gaze traveled over both of them once more, before the Crownsilver matriarch crossed to the chair beside the fireplace, her walking stick tapping a muffled *thud, thud, thud* against the carpet. She seated herself, arranging her slate woolen skirts with a flick of her hand. "So," she said, and Farideh found herself reminded of the village midwife and long winters and mischief she'd been trying to stop in the first place.

"*Martifyr*," Farideh cautioned, slipping into Draconic.

Havilar sat once more, settling her hands in her lap. "Well met, Lady Crownsilver," she said. A moment passed, and Havilar could not help but be Havilar. "Do you want to tell me what you want? I don't think you want to be here anymore than me."

"A sharp tongue," Helindra said. "No wonder Aubrin favors you—he was always an impudent child."

"I'm not sharp with him," Havilar said. Helindra raised her eyebrows, her thin mouth pursed, but said nothing. Whether there was no weakness to reveal in her or Helindra Crownsilver was simply a better opponent, Farideh couldn't guess. She squeezed Havilar's hand a little harder.

Havilar leaned over. "*What do you do,*" she whispered in Draconic, "*if someone has a fit?*"

"It's not a fit," Farideh hissed back.

"*That is exactly the look Garago used to get—*"

"You will speak a proper language in my presence," Helindra said. "Do me a little courtesy, and I'll stay a gracious host." A maid came in with a tray of small glasses and a decanter of cordial with slices of lemon floating in it. She poured three glasses.

"Were you being gracious when you said my tongue was sharp?" Havilar asked, and Farideh wished they could just walk out. Havilar wasn't suited to these games, and Helindra hadn't even begun to play.

"I've asked you here to discuss Aubrin's future," Helindra said, "and yours. No doubt you're finding yourself very comfortable in his tallhouse? All your needs taken care of? All your wants satisfied? Havilar?"

Havilar shrugged. "It's nice enough. It's a house."

"Much better than your prior circumstances, if I understand correctly. Do you prefer linen sheets to a bed of leaves? Plush furniture to a fallen log? A solid roof and the depths of Aubrin's coin to uncertainty and want? Havilar?"

Farideh bristled at the way Helindra said Havilar's name—like it didn't belong next to her "proper language"—and she made sure the powers of the Hells stayed pressed firmly down.

Havilar wrinkled her nose. "Should I not like it?"

Helindra gave her a sly smile. "I'm pleased we agree."

Havilar gave Farideh a puzzled look, as if checking once more that Helindra wasn't having a fit. "She means," Farideh said, wishing it were a fight, wishing Havilar did have her glaive, "that you like Brin's things better than you like him."

Havilar made an indignant little cry. "I am not agreeing with that."

Helindra gave Havilar the sort of look reserved for children telling tales. "Here is what I propose," she said. "I will give you a great deal of coin—at least as much as Aubrin has been spending on you, plus enough for a house of your own, some-where quiet and comfortable and not here. In exchange, you will go away and never darken my portal again. What do you say?"

"You think we're together because you're wealthy?" Havilar said incredulously. "When I met him, I thought he was a runaway apprentice— I don't love him for coin."

"No one wishes to know how you're compensated, my dear," Helindra said, and Farideh clutched her sister's arm hard to keep her from leaping off the settee.

"I don't want your *pothac* coin," Havilar spat, her cheeks blazing. "I don't want anything to do with your crazy family, and I certainly am not for sale." She hesitated. "I mean, mercenary work aside, but that's not . . . You know what I'm talking about."

"I would suggest you reconsider," Helindra said. "Think about your family, your own resources. I can be very generous . . . Or I can be a very poor person to make an enemy of." She smiled slyly again, putting Farideh in mind of a weasel out of a fable, all cunning words and ready to raid the henhouse as soon as the guard went to sleep.

"You're the one who sent those kidnappers," Farideh said.

Helindra glared at Farideh. "Watching Gods forfend. Whoever did that has no sense of proportion or decorum."

"Anyone you send," Havilar said, "I can take them. I thrashed those bastards, I'll thrash the next round. It will give me something to do."

Helindra sipped her cordial. "You will find—Havilar—that there are a great many people who want for you to disappear from our lives. Only I am willing to compensate you for your time. And such a lot of time it's been already. I wouldn't be surprised if all this waiting on Aubrin has soured you on fair Suzail. Or Aubrin, for that matter."

Farideh squeezed her sister's hand tight. "*Martifyr,*" she whispered, as much for herself as for Havilar. Nothing would be helped by attacking Helindra—with words or fists or blades.

"Give it some thought," Helindra advised. "For I'm also the only one who doesn't mind if you take your time."

"Aren't you worried I'll drive your precious princess off?" Havilar said.

Helindra laughed in a stiff, practiced way. "My dear, you have no idea what sort of rival you have in Raedra Obarskyr."

Farideh felt her powers start to burn again, before Helindra added, "Besides, even if you win that war, all it means is that His Majesty returns to the issue of legitimization. If Aubrin shan't be an Obarskyr by marriage, then he shall truly be one by birth after all. Either way, the Crownsilvers have an heir to the Dragon Throne." She took another small sip of the cordial, then reached behind her for a tasseled rope that hung there. "Either way," she said as the doorjack came into the room, "you are nothing but an impediment and a tool I don't need."

The twins were ushered from the parlor and out into the streets with hardly enough time to get their cloaks on straight. Fortunately the rain was only thick and drizzly, nearly a fog against the ground. The rumble of thunder in the distance hinted at harder weather coming.

Constancia stood beside the carriage, her face a mask. "To the tallhouse then?"

Havilar stormed straight up to her. "Whatever you think of me," she said, "shoving him up on that throne isn't what's best for him. And you know *that.*"

"What he wants and what's best aren't necessarily the same thing," she said. Then, "You haven't considered the alternatives."

Havilar didn't answer, but climbed into the carriage, slamming the door once Farideh was inside, and leaving Constancia to ride on the back with the footman.

The carriage started forward, and Havilar stared out the window, seething. She kicked the cushion fall, and made a little screech.

"I," she proclaimed, "am trying *so hard* not to hate this *karshoji* city! But then there's kidnappers and princesses and Crownsilvers, and I am so *sick* of this stupid rain!"

Farideh thought of the Shaar, of brisk Narfell and muggy Port Nyaranzaru where Lorcan had taken her last tenday. "There's a lot of world," she said. "We don't have to stay here."

Havilar sighed. "Sometimes, it feels like I can't even move. Like none of us can move, or a thousand things are going to fall apart." She turned to the carriage window. "I'm getting really tired of waiting for things to change."

Kidnappers and princesses and Crownsilvers, Farideh thought. And Asmodeus and devils. And Brin. And the never-ending rain. "We're not trapped," she said, even though she wasn't sure she believed it. "Neither is Brin."

Havilar gave her a sour look. "If *she* doesn't change her mind, I don't know that he's not."

So then let's leave, Farideh almost said, but didn't. Even if it were the best possible option, even if Havilar's growing frustrations gave her a guilty glimmer of hope, saying so too quickly would just make Havilar angry at her again. And it had taken so long to get back to a place where they were friends.

"I'm with you," Farideh said instead. "It will sort out."

The carriage lurched, throwing Havilar across the benches and snapping Farideh's neck back. "Gods sod it!" the driver shouted. "Reckless bastards! Someone call the Dragons in!"

"My deepest apologies!" another voice called. "Here, here—let your groom—oh! Sorry, lady knight! Might you help us separate?"

Havilar climbed back into her seat and pulled back the curtain: another carriage sat right beside theirs, the wheels locked together.

"We should have walked," she said.

• • •

LORD CROWNSILVER'S TALLHOUSE sat on the Promenade, south and west of the Royal Court and palace. The house was freestanding, unlike many of its neighbors, with a stone wall around it and a wrought-iron gate guarded by a burly-looking fellow in a tabard marked with a black Crownsilver sigil—a dragon with a crown around its muzzle. The doorguard eyed Vescaras with more than a little puzzlement—half-elves weren't common in Cormyr, and a Turami half-elf with his dark skin and his hair in neat, gold-threaded braids was all the odder. In fact the doorjack looked a little fearful. Vescaras eyed the doorjack right back and cleared his throat. A moment later he glared at Dahl.

Right. Equerry.

"Lord Vescaras Ammakyl, here to see his . . ." Dahl fumbled—how much of Brin's title would the equerry of a foreign lord be expected to know? He couldn't remember. "Lord Aubrin Crownsilver," he settled on. "Do be quick."

"Ah. Yes, of course." The doorjack hesitated the briefest of moments before unlocking the gate and then the front door, and the two men were ushered through marble-floored hallways, up a sweeping staircase, and through several doors, to a sitting room whose window opened onto the road below.

"It's Lord Aubrin Crownsilver, Earl of Tethgard, Oversword of Calantar's Way, Horsemaster of the Realm, and Bearer of the Blood Royal," Vescaras said, jerking Dahl's attention back to the room. "I can't believe you don't know that."

"Of course I know it," Dahl said. "And you forgot 'Unproven of Torm.' But that doesn't matter: Would your equerry know it? And would an equerry spit all that out? Do I say 'Lord Crownsilver' or 'His Grace' or the whole thing? Do I act in a huff because some jack doesn't know who my lord is?"

Vescaras made a face. "No, to that one. That's terribly brightcoin. I'm not a damned Hedare, stamping my feet and demanding to be ennobled by every passerby."

"That was a bit more than just thinking you weren't noble."

Vescaras poured himself a small glass of ruby-colored wine from the sideboard. "Chances are he thought I was half-drow. Perhaps wholly drow—I wouldn't be too surprised."

"Are you joking?"

Vescaras sipped his drink. "Cormyr is not . . . let us say, 'diverse' in its inhabitants."

"'Not many non-humans' is a piss-poor reason to mistake a fellow for a drow."

"Hmm. Have you never been to Cormyr before? To Suzail?"

"Only briefly. A stop on the way to and from Waterdeep. Never had time to dawdle."

"Funny place," Vescaras said. "They feel themselves to be the pinnacle of civilization."

"They've lasted fourteen hundred years," Dahl pointed out. "They can afford to pat themselves on the back a bit."

"Fair," Vescaras said. "But the thing is, in all those years . . . not much has changed. And they like it that way. So things that don't fit"—he nodded at the open window—"stand out all the worse."

"Everyone knows that," Dahl said.

"Then you shouldn't be surprised when some haynose doorguard can't tell the difference at once between a drow and someone with elven and Turami blood together. Pointed ears, dark skin—he literally doesn't know the difference." He took another long sip of his wine. "At least he had the good manners to wait and see what we said we were about before doing anything rash. That's one thing much of Cormyr has going for it."

Dahl nodded at the decanter. "Pour me a glass would you?"

"Pour it yourself, human," Vescaras said with a smirk. "A lord doesn't serve servants."

Brin slipped in the door, looking as harried and frazzled as Dahl had ever seen him. "Before you start," Brin said, "be forewarned I have absolutely no control over what the war wizards overhear. They're none of them idiots—they know plenty more than most—and they probably have better things to do than listen in just now, but guard your tongues if it's sensitive." He frowned at Vescaras. "What are you doing here?"

"We're talking about your personal order of Arrhenish," Vescaras said. "It would be rude to send my equerry alone, wouldn't it?"

"I can't believe you made me your equerry," Dahl said.

"And I loathe Arrhenish," Brin said.

"For your guests," Vescaras said. He held up the wineglass. "Better than this stuff. Who do you buy from?"

Brin shook his head. "I got what you asked for." He crossed to a tall bookcase, shifted some of the titles around, and pulled down a case. "It wasn't easy. And I'm guessing you're not going to tell me who she was."

"One of us," Dahl said.

Brin raised an eyebrow. Dahl gestured to the air around them, the listening war wizards beyond. "Many thanks," he said, taking the case. "If we'd waited, gods only know who might have gotten to it first."

"Of course," Brin said. He blew out a breath. "I assume you were also told to chastise me?"

"Not exactly," Dahl said. "But he does want to know what you intend to do."

Brin rested his head in his hands. "I'm working on it."

"That's not good enough," Dahl said. "Cormyr is in the middle of the worst war they've seen in a century—"

"Oh, are we?" Brin shot back. "I hadn't noticed. Why in the Hells do you think I haven't just broken it off and been done with it? If I chuck Raedra to the cleric, there is not a noble in Cormyr who will risk speaking with me, let alone slip me information. My network collapses. Whatever good the Harpers or Cormyr could make of that information is lost. I know what I'm standing to lose here—what *we* stand to lose. I am working on it!"

"Raedra doesn't know you're with us?" Vescaras asked.

"I don't know. I haven't told her, and I don't intend to, if I can help it. But war wizards . . ." Brin gestured at the empty air.

Dahl hesitated. "Have you considered just marrying her?"

"I have considered everything at this point," Brin said, "and that isn't an option."

"It is if Havilar's the one you break it off with."

Brin glared at Dahl. "I said, that isn't an option."

Dahl bit back a response. Stlarning nobles and their stlarning pride. "Well, what is an option?"

Brin shook his head. "I've delayed the wedding again. Bought every scrap of silk available in the Heartlands so no one can make the damned dress, and my future mother-in-law won't have that—especially when she's secretly heartbroken the crown prince hasn't returned yet. Here's an excuse to give him more time to get home, and the minister of protocol can hardly argue."

"Which buys you time," Vescaras said. "But not answers."

"I met with a contact this morning, looking for ways out that won't destroy me."

"And?"

"And nothing."

"Nothing at all?"

"Nothing I'm willing to do," Brin said. "While spreading detailed word of Raedra's infidelities might get me some leeway, we've always agreed she could have her lovers. I'm not that sort of fellow."

"Well, you're going to have to pick which sort of fellow you are," Dahl said, "and soon. You've found nothing else?"

"I can throw in with the nobles that want to capitulate to Sembia—or worse, Shade," Brin said. "Or the sort of noble that wants to put Boldtree on the throne—that *henish* has attempted my life enough times that I'll back him when Myrkul returns and holds my soulless corpse's hand up in assent."

"*Henish?*" Dahl said. "Drop a few more of those and you're not going to have to worry much how to wriggle out of this." Brin shot him a dark look.

"Ignore him," Vescaras said. "He's taking poorly to his new position. What are you going to do?"

"I'm working on it," Brin snapped. "Gods, listen: Everything's still running. I've lost no one so far. If anything, more people are talking to me since . . ." He trailed off.

"Since?"

"Since . . . apparently," Brin said delicately, "Havi and I have . . . set a fashion." Vescaras snorted.

"Fantastic," Dahl said dryly. "So you have all the best intelligence on how many tiefling coinlasses and lads are operating in Suzail. Well done."

"It's not state secrets, but it's a step. You tell someone what's happening in your bedroom, you're opening up in a way that means you'll talk a lot more about other topics later on. Which, thank the gods, because otherwise I've lost hours of my life answering questions about tails that should be nobody else's business."

"At least you're talking about it," Vescaras said. "Silence just stokes the fires of rumor."

"Ye gods," Brin groaned. "How far has it spread?"

"Halfway to Proskur," Dahl said.

"Only the wildest ones," Vescaras assured him.

"Gods," Brin said again. "If this doesn't blow over soon—"

"You'll have an excellent use for a few crates of Arrhenish," Vescaras said smoothly. "Fifteen? Would you say?"

Dahl let his thoughts drift away from the other men's arguments of wine and gold. Brin's problems wouldn't be easily unsnarled, but at least they were clear and not likely to come to a head before Dahl could think of a second solution. "High Cormyr" could be replaced as an agent with only the average headache.

"Low Cormyr" was another story.

His second agent in Cormyr, a lutist called Marjana who played in several taprooms, had sent a message six tendays ago: *Signs of Shar in Suzail. Suspect plan to attack within year, though no more details. Following possible agent from the Brigand's Bottle. Return soon with information.*

But she hadn't. Four tendays later, a letter had arrived for her "stepbrother," regretfully informing Dahl that Marjana's body had been found floating in the harbor. Dahl had been ready to trek north and search for the remaining Shadovar internment camps, but that letter had changed everything. They had to find out what had happened to Marjana. They had to find out how much had been compromised. Dahl tapped his fingers on the case that held Marjana's last notes.

He could have passed this off. He could have left it to Vescaras and Brin to sort out—he could still see Tam's expression, the High Harper ready for Dahl to demur. He'd been through so much lately, hadn't he? No one would blame him for not leaping into the field on a case that had so many of the same earmarks as the one that had forced him from the field originally.

But even if Low Cormyr had not been his agent, Dahl would have come anyway. Cormyr was as close as he could get to the Dalelands to the north, to his mother's farm just on the edge of the wars with Sembia and Netheril. And while he sorted through Marjana's effects and hunted for a path to Harrowdale, Farideh was in Cormyr.

Vur ghent vethsunathear renthisj . . .

"I don't think Oghma is done with you yet," Farideh had said, when she'd told him the scrap of Draconic runes written upon his soul.

And after, my priest speaks . . .

He'd all but run from her after—he hadn't wanted to hear the rest, hadn't wanted to know. Whatever the god had left upon Dahl, it couldn't be good, not after Oghma had snatched back the gifts of a paladin from Dahl and led him on a merry chase for answers. Dahl had made Farideh swear not to look again, not to tell him.

And two days after she had left for Cormyr, he realized how deeply he wanted to hear the rest of it. How badly he wanted to understand.

How much he feared that she'd seen enough to know exactly how badly he'd failed.

A shout in the street broke Brin and Vescaras's argument over how many cases was cover enough. Both of them stood, reaching for weapons. Dahl went to the window.

"Couple of carriages locked together." The drivers were shouting at one another, grooms climbing down from their perches. He frowned, peering through the warp of the glass. "One of them has your crest on it."

The light from a sudden explosion briefly lit the gloomy street. "Son of a barghest!" Dahl cried. "Get your guards!"

4

HAVILAR HAD HARDLY FINISHED HER COMPLAINT WHEN THE DOOR against the carriage swung open into the other vehicle. Something small and heavy hit Farideh in the breastbone, followed by the splash of a thin liquid that thickened over her arms and lap, sealing her to the carriage seat.

In the same moment, a hooded man with a scarf around his face reached into the carriage, nicking Havilar's bare arm with a sharp, thin dagger. Havilar turned and slammed her elbow down onto the man's forearm, shifting to get her legs free.

Her hand slipped off the bench. She crashed to the floor, eyes glazed and lids drooping. The smell of citrus and burnt sugar and blood hit Farideh, as the reaching arms hauled Havilar into the other carriage.

"Havi!" Farideh cried.

The man from the warehouse with the hazel eyes nodded at Farideh, just as the carriage suddenly pulled off, unencumbered after all, taking Havilar with it.

Farideh threw the weight of her body against the tanglefoot bag's hardening ichor. It shattered on the third try, still sticking in great shards to her blouse and breeches. She lunged for the open door, tearing her sticky sleeve—the carriage was just picking up speed, heading east along the Promenade.

Farideh sprinted after the carriage, pulling her rod free of her torn sleeve. Quick as it was, the engines of Malbolge could spin much more quickly. "*Laesurach,*" Farideh hissed.

A rift opened in the cobblestones, throwing orange light against the gray buildings as the heart of the world exposed itself. Lava sprayed from the wound, and the horses reared and wheeled. The yoke trapped them, and in their twisting, both fell to the ground. Wood splintered, and the carriage overbalanced, tipping forward on one broken axle. People in the street screamed and ran in all directions.

All directions that led away from Farideh, at least. She glanced back and saw Constancia pick herself up off the ground, sword drawn, and Arlo watching fearfully from the driver's box.

Twenty feet from the disabled carriage, Farideh pointed the rod at the bit of wood still trapping the thrashing horses. "*Assulam!*" A burst of splinters and the faint scent of brimstone—the horses whinnied and pulled apart, lunging to their feet, no thought in their minds but fleeing the carriage and the strange magic. The driver pulled a wand as he clung to the carriage, eyeing her as the horses galloped past his reach, parting the growing crowd.

The first rock hit Farideh between the shoulder blades. She whirled, expecting another attacker, another tanglefoot bag. The second struck her shoulder. She threw her arms up to ward off a steady rain of pebbles, thrown by a pack of children.

"Ya! Ya! Devil-child!" an urchin shouted at her, racing closer. "Go back to the Abyss!"

She heard Constancia curse and swords clash. Farideh pulled on her magic, skipped backward through the plane, out of the stones' reach for a moment. Constancia fought off a pair of seeming-adventurers out of the crowd, their battle blocking Arven and Dorn's assistance. Another volley of rocks clattered on the cobblestones at her feet. The kidnappers were better prepared this time.

"Godsdamn it!" she heard the man in the carriage shout. "Quit dawdling and get us out of here!"

The driver with the wand eyed Farideh uneasily, but started casting.

She cast a string of blasts at the driver and the carriage as she ran across the gap. Stones struck her—hip, shoulder, cheek, chest. The last slammed into the side of her head, right against the curve of her horn, and she stumbled, vision swirling.

Footfalls, the shouts of children. "You throw one more stone," Dahl Peredur shouted from her left, "and . . . I'll feed you to my drow, you little miscreants! Get!"

Farideh straightened, surprised at the rescue. The man with the wand was attempting once more to finish his spell. But the hazel-eyed man had a wand of his own, pointed straight at her and Dahl.

Farideh grabbed hold of Dahl and pulled him through a tear in the plane, as close to the carriage as she could. A splash of green magic hit the cobblestones behind them, scattering a rain of rock shards.

The hazel-eyed man yelped in surprise. The driver chanted more quickly. The powers of Asmodeus filled Farideh's veins, stealing her attention. She could hold fast to them, or she could stop the kidnappers. She stopped breathing, focused all she had on the wizard's wand.

"*Assulam!*" she managed. The spell missed the wand, but hit the man's leather vest. It burst into a rain of scraps, startling him. The wand slipped from his hand.

Dahl darted toward the carriage, as if to grab hold of the hazel-eyed man and haul him out. But the man scrambled back, one hand reaching inside his vest. He pulled out an amulet, and with a wry smile and the momentary sense of someone snatching away a column of air, he vanished. The doorguards rushed the driver, and he placed his hands on top of his head before they even reached him.

Panting, Farideh took a step forward, and her leg buckled. Too much magic, too much blood pouring down the side of her face. The sheer number of people watching her—before she'd been aware of them as a mass, a single thing. Now a score of faces watched, judged.

Dahl caught her arm. "Did you get hit in the head?"

"The horn," Farideh said. "Is she all right? He poisoned her."

"And the face," Dahl said. "You're going to get a scar."

"Is she all right?" Farideh said again. Brin was suddenly there, Dorn and Arven beside him as he climbed into the carriage, cursing and calling Havilar's name.

"She's not waking," he shouted, all nerves and fury. He stuck his head back out. "Constancia!" The paladin stood over her fallen opponent, waiting—no doubt—for the watch.

"He stabbed her," Farideh said. "In the arm. There was something on it, and she fell straight to sleep."

"And you let him get away?" Brin demanded.

Before she could answer, the air reverberated with three sharp *twangs*, as if three fiddles had just snapped strings. Three wizards, garbed in severe black cloaks, suddenly stood arrayed around the remains of the carriage, wands pointed at Farideh.

One—a man so tall even Farideh had to crane her neck to look at him—smiled pleasantly at Brin. "Good afternoon, Lord Crownsilver. Are these people your guests?"

Brin's face closed. "Wizard of War Nyaril," he said. "Very good. I trust you're here to take this fellow into custody?" He gestured at the trembling driver.

The war wizard's pleasant smile didn't waver, nor did the war wizards' wands leave Farideh. "I think the Dragons can handle him. Please introduce us to your friend." When Brin didn't move, the man lowered his wand and walked toward Farideh, hand outstretched.

"Well met," he said, taking her hand. He was young, in his middle twenties, brown-haired and kind-eyed. A shiver of magic ran up Farideh's arm, skittering over her skin like a swarm of freshly hatched spiders. She shuddered and yanked her hand back. The man smiled. "My name is Ilstan. This is Drannon and Devora. We need to speak to you."

"My household—and my guests—have just been attacked," Brin said. "This is hardly the time—"

"The proper time," Ilstan said, more firmly, "was when she first entered the city. As you'll recall, Lord Crownsilver." He smiled at Brin. "You may, of course, make the necessary arrangements. Tend to the young lady's injuries. We'll just wait in your parlor."

Dorn and Arven carried the still insensate Havilar into the tallhouse. Constancia and Vescaras stood watch over the swordsman she'd disarmed and the driver who'd had the wand, waiting for the Purple Dragons to show up. Dahl helped Farideh into the kitchen, where the cook shrieked at the blood soaking her blouse and threatened to faint.

"It's not that bad," Farideh protested. Dahl wet a handkerchief and passed it to her. She pressed it to the wound on her cheek. "It only grazed me. I need to go see Havilar."

"Did you smell lemons when he stabbed her?"

Farideh stopped. "Yes."

"Then it'd be swiftsleep," Dahl said, sitting on the bench. "She'll be fine, if a bit out of sorts, within the next half hour. Until then, she's not waking up. Come here and look at me." She sat down, and he frowned at her.

"What is it?"

"I was going to see if you're skullscorned . . . I forgot you haven't got proper pupils."

She scowled back. "I got hit in the horn, not the head. All I have's a headache and a lot of bruises."

He turned her head gently so the side that had been hit faced him. "Did you black out? Maybe just for a breath?"

"No—it doesn't work like that. It just yanked my head over. My neck hurts, my forehead aches. I'm not skullscorned."

"Right," he said dryly, "because if you were, you could absolutely tell before those war wizards start putting you through your paces."

She turned back to him. "Your concern is noted, and if I start stumbling around and vomiting, you get to say you warned me."

Dahl looked away, but he smiled. "Well met, by the way."

"Well met," she said. "Where'd you come from?"

"Tam."

Farideh winced—carefully. "Is Brin in trouble?" She pulled the handkerchief away, Dahl pushed it back.

"Still bleeding. Not . . . *trouble*," Dahl said. "Though there's enough on the edge that it wouldn't take much. Did he *really* never bring you to the war wizards? Even I know you have to do that."

Farideh hesitated. Ilstan had seemed friendly enough—but she'd been warned about the war wizards, in jest and in earnest, more than a few times. "Do you know what they're going to do?"

"Suss out what you're capable of," Dahl said. "Somehow."

A chill ran down Farideh's spine, and she wondered how deep their magic would penetrate, if they'd see the connection to the Hells, or worse, Asmodeus. She wondered if she could run.

"How do you like Suzail?" Dahl asked.

"How do you think?" Farideh checked the handkerchief again, the wound on her face stinging as the air hit it. "I leave the house once every tenday and a half, and when I do, things like *that* happen." She touched the cut on her cheek. "I'm not ungrateful," she started. "But if Brin doesn't figure himself out soon, I may just . . . run off to the Shaar Desolation."

She thought of Lorcan, the stars burning through the cloudless sky, and the endless rolling dunes. He might rescue her from the war wizards, if it came to that. And then the quiet and the peace and the utter lack of villains who would use her as a pawn.

A little part of her laughed at that—no kidnappers sent by nobles, but there was nowhere on Toril she'd be free from Asmodeus.

Dahl gave her a funny look. "Why in the Hells would you go to the Shaar? It's a godsblighted desert full of mad elves."

Farideh felt herself blush. "Better than Suzail."

"Suzail has *water*."

"And war wizards." Farideh glanced back at the door.

"They're not going to throw you in a dungeon for destroying a carriage and wounding some sellswords. Hey." She turned to look back at him. "Would you mind if I came around again? There's something I want to talk to you about."

"If you have to come down into the dungeon, you'd better bring a key."

The trio of war wizards was waiting in the front room, with a furious-looking Brin. Ilstan smiled at her as she entered, as if she were joining them for a drink. "You are well, I trust."

"Bruised," she said.

"Better than your victims," the bearded man, Drannon, said.

"Assailants," the red-haired woman, Devora, corrected. "Be fair."

"I wouldn't have done anything," Farideh insisted. "Only I didn't see another way to stop them—"

"Do you think that's an excuse?" Drannon demanded. "That your Lord Crownsilver's standing is enough to protect you from the established consequences?"

Farideh glanced over at Brin again, who was giving her a grim look of his own. "I don't think Lord Crownsilver's about to protect me from anything. I didn't catch them, after all."

"What Drannon means," Ilstan said, "is that the sort of spells you apparently cast mean you were required to register with the Crown and the war wizards when you arrived in Suzail. Why didn't you?"

"You don't have requirements about warlocks," Brin said before she could reply.

"With all due respect, Lord Crownsilver, that's a technicality and you know it," Ilstan said. He turned back to Farideh. "Your friend should have made you acquainted with our laws. We're well aware they're not the clearest to all." He smiled and shrugged. "But they make our kingdom what it is, and they must be followed. All mages of a certain skill must be registered."

Farideh watched his face as he spoke, stiff with fear. But there was no malice in Ilstan's expression, no threat. "What are you going to do?" she asked.

"We ought to clap you in irons," Drannon said. "The both of you, Lord Crownsilver."

"Don't be overwrought, Drannon," Ilstan said. "She helped stop a crime." His eyes shifted to Brin, and grew just a bit cooler. "Prevented her sister's capture and perhaps the death of one of the Loyal Fury's finest.

"And," Ilstan said, "I made sure right away that—warlock or not—she isn't seething evil." He smiled at Farideh. "My apologies for the unannounced spell. I find it works best when people aren't expecting it."

Farideh nodded, more relieved than she dared show, but she was still thinking about the way he'd looked at Brin.

"All that remains is for us to see you properly registered. Just sit there, and we'll do the rest."

• • •

BRIN WATCHED THE war wizards from beside the entrance to the front room, arms folded, never taking his eyes off of Ilstan. Was it coincidence that Raedra's pet war wizard had come when Farideh had finally failed to hold back her spells? The war wizard was as merry as he ever was, unconcerned with the fact that their circling spells studied a tiefling, a warlock, and the twin of Lord Crownsilver's mistress.

How badly would this throw Brin off course?

How much further could he even be thrown? Brin wondered. Since he'd finally met with Raedra after returning to Suzail, one by one a handful of highly placed nobles had snubbed him—subtly now. A forgotten invitation. An insistence that they hadn't seen him standing there. The delicate game of playing off their pride and their sense of intrigue and adventure could be thrown into entire disarray by the chance to insert themselves into the drama of the Royal Court. A handful of nobles and already one of his routes was in jeopardy.

He watched Farideh, gray-faced in one of the needlepoint chairs, and felt a twinge of worry. She'll be fine, he told himself. Cormyr might not be.

Constancia came down the stairs. "She's awake. And cursing up a storm cloud."

Brin hurried up to the bedroom. "Any word from the Dragons?" Constancia asked.

"You know they'll take their time with this."

"Mehen?"

"I presume he's on his way."

Havilar was propped up on one side of the enormous bed, her eyes still glassy, her cheeks flushed. Brin sat down beside her. "How are you feeling?"

"I *slept* through an entire fight. I got dragged off like a sack of apples—how do you think I feel?" She pushed the covers back. "I thought you said you were going to fix this."

"I am," Brin said. "It's not as easy as it seems."

"Who sent them?" she demanded, each word as forceful as a thrown rock.

Brin shook his head. "We're still searching. The carriage was hired. The urchins were paid by someone they'd never seen—"

"*Guess*," Havilar said.

"I *can't*," Brin said. "I don't know. I have enemies. *We* have enemies."

"Your aunt?"

"A possibility."

"*Her?*"

"I don't know. I mean it—there are too many options. Helindra, Raedra, Baron Boldtree, some charged-up, would-be Huntsilver heir? Or someone new? I don't know."

"When are you going to know?" she demanded. "If I'm not allowed to fix this, then you need to. Now. Not later. Not when you can. I am not a *karshoji* treasure they steal from you, understand? I am not a piece in this big, stupid, *Cormyrean* game."

You are, he thought. We all are. "I'm working on it. We caught one of them this time. We'll have answers. We're working on it."

Havilar gripped his arms hard, her eyes wild. "Brin. Work faster. I love you. I trust you. I said I would wait for you. But you never mentioned *karshoji* assassins who you can't even *guess* the patrons of! You *never* mentioned your aunt trying to buy me off. You *never* mentioned being trapped in this tallhouse, and . . . and none of that goes away because you buy me some godsbedamned dresses!"

"Wait," Brin slipped his arms around her. She was stiff as iron. "Helindra tried to buy you off?"

"She said as much coin as you spend on me, plus enough for a little cottage." Havilar scowled down at her lap. "She all but called me a whore."

"You can't let Helindra get to you. Not a word."

"She's *threatening* me," Havilar said, "threatening my family—and if there are *karshoji* war wizards—"

"Havi . . ." Brin sighed. He could explain it a thousand times, and it felt as if it would never make a difference. "She's looking for a weak spot. An opening. Pretend she's a swordswoman trying to break your guard."

"I tried that," Havilar said through her teeth. "It does *not* make it easier." She tugged nervously on the end of her braid. "Is Farideh all right? Constancia said the war wizards came."

"They're just making sure of her."

The door opened, and Mehen came in. "What in all the broken planes happened?" he demanded.

"Kidnappers," Havilar said.

"And war wizards, I see." He turned to Brin. "You said she'd be clear."

"I said she'd be clear so long as she didn't cast anything flashy. Pushing a volcano through the street is the definition of flashy. We're lucky," he said. "They're just registering her."

"And if they find something they don't like?"

"What are they going to find?"

"What are they going to *think* they've found?" Mehen corrected. "What's there doesn't matter."

Havilar yawned so wide her jaw *popped*. "You have to rest," Brin said, knowing there wasn't a thing Havilar would want to do less. "Give the swiftsleep a little time to burn off."

"*Swiftsleep?*" Mehen cried.

"I'm *fine*," Havilar said.

"She's fine," Brin said. He patted her knee. "But, truly, you'll be happier if you nap a bit." Havilar frowned at him, and he shrugged. "I've gotten a dose before. Although I slept a good deal longer than you. I'll be right back." He kissed her cheek, and steered Mehen out of the room.

"Any luck?" he asked, his voice low.

"Don't change the subject," Mehen said. "The kidnappers were supposed to be dealt with. Your way."

"If my very recognizable bodyguard goes thundering through every low tavern in this city, whoever sent the kidnappers will hear and we will never find them," Brin pointed out. Mehen should know this—after eight years of this life, how could he not? "I'm narrowing it down."

Mehen folded his arms. "To how many?"

"Assuming it's someone I already know? Eleven," Brin said. "But it's not Princess Ospra and I'm fairly sure it's not Raedra—which means it's not out of reach to stop. The Dragons have the driver, the children they paid off. I'm waiting for answers, and we'll see then if the number comes down. Although, if I had to lay coin, I'd say it's that *henish* Erzoured and so we're never going to find the proof that it's him, and you might as well take her off to Tymanther—or whatever it is you're planning on doing—tonight."

Mehen looked down his snout at Brin. "Am I the wicked father out of one of your chapbooks now?"

Brin scowled at him. "Don't act as if you're not thinking about it."

"Don't act as if we're all set against you. Since they've come back," Mehen said, "you've been acting as though you're seventeen once more. Not a lord of Cormyr. Not a Harper. Not a grown man who's made something of himself, and certainly not a man who's worthy of the amount of turmoil my daughter's putting herself through. You're acting as though you're trapped, and there is absolutely no reason for it."

Brin heard the truth in Mehen's words, but it slipped through his soul as if it were nothing but a ribbon in a current. "How am I not trapped?" he demanded. "*Eleven*. Eleven well-connected people are willing to hurt the woman I love just to get a little advantage, jump a little higher in the line for the throne—which hardly *bloody* matters when Foril's already got a crown prince named, mind—and

I can't nail down which one, which means I can't be sure it won't happen again. Meanwhile, Raedra's turned the Illances squarely against me, which means I have no way of securing the eastern path and that's at least seventy-five folks dawdling in the wilderness, waiting for goblins. I've wasted a kraken's load of coin on locking up silk, just to delay the wedding long enough to figure out a way to either wrap up all these loose ends so that Garce doesn't run the godsdamned thing straight into the Dragons' hands and get everyone talking about how we ought to decide who can live in the city. And all the while blackguards keep turning up trying to take her away again, and yes—I'm well aware I'm doing a *shit* job of stopping it. I'm trying. Though all the good that will do when your shadow from Djerad Thymar turns up and you all run off for Tymanther."

"Are you through?" Mehen asked calmly.

Brin rubbed his forehead. The tirade had poured out of him, an avalanche of words. But all it left behind was the sick sense of all these things building up again. "I will never be through," he said, and that time he heard it, the sullen, selfish anger of his youth. "I keep thinking one of these times you'll come back with your Kepeshkmolik unmasked, ready to run, and it will be the last I see of any of you."

Mehen scowled. While Mehen had traveled to the Shadovar camp where Farideh had been held, a few months prior, the Westgate spymaster had told him there was a dragonborn man, Kepeshkmolik Dumuzi, looking for Mehen. From what little Brin had gotten out of Mehen, he didn't know the other man and he wasn't looking forward to finding out what he wanted. Once a month or so, Mehen would search the kinds of taprooms and inns that might be friendly to a wandering dragonborn, looking for information.

"First," Mehen said, "where I go is no matter. You have all three made it clear that you'll do as you want no matter what I say, and come out more or less fine. You don't need me."

"That's not true."

"Don't patronize me, boy. All our worlds are changing. Seventeen years, and they were my whole world. Seven and a half years, and the grief, the hope, that was my whole world." He shook his head. "I don't even know what I'm for anymore."

When they'd first met, Mehen had had no use for Brin at all. When the dragonborn first suspected there might be something happening between this runaway acolyte and his daughter, he'd been glad to leave Brin behind. And when Brin had arrived in Cormyr where Mehen had been imprisoned—on charges of kidnapping Brin, it had to be said—bearing news that the twins had disappeared, there had been a moment where Brin had been sure that Mehen was going to murder him with his bare hands.

But only for a moment, and after that, the dragonborn had become one of his closest allies and dearest friends—and at times, something like a father.

"Please don't leave," Brin said. "Please don't take her."

"And *that's* number two," Mehen said, shaking a clawed finger at Brin. "She's not a child any more than you are. She'll go where she wants, do as she likes, and having you tell her she ought to go to bed isn't helping your case. You've caged her—she's caged herself. But sooner or later, the cage won't hold. Which of you is going to open the door?"

Brin bit back a protest—he wasn't trying to hold Havilar back, just keep her safe. He knew the ins and outs of Suzail and she didn't, that was all.

And she's always been the one to save *you*, he thought. Now you're putting her in dresses and making her practice in secret.

"I'm going to go talk to her," he said. "If Vescaras and Dahl haven't left, tell them they can chastise me another time." He went back into the bedroom.

Havilar had fallen asleep again, snoring softly as her horns twisted her head forward. She stirred, though, as Brin climbed in beside her and resettled her head against his shoulder.

"We could just run," he said, and a rush of guilt and longing came with it. As a lad, he'd fled Suzail, fled all these machinations for the throne and his great-aunt's scheming ways, and found Havilar. He could run again.

Though it would mean leaving the Harpers in the lurch. It would mean leaving Cormyr's vulnerable grasping for aid. It would mean the war wizards could always come hunting for him.

Havilar didn't answer, pulled down once more by the poison's lingering effects. Brin tucked his head against hers, listening to her breathe and thinking of all the ways this moment might come to ruin.

• • •

THE EVENING FOLLOWED with more questions than Farideh could count, more rude intrusions of magic meant to feel out her lies or weaknesses, her strengths or her truths. If she wasn't forthcoming, the question often came again, just a little changed, and more than once she felt the baby-spider shiver of the spell meant to ferret out evil connections. Every time her heart wanted to beat itself inside out, waiting for Ilstan to realize that Asmodeus had laid his mark upon her. Twice she had to stop to vomit. At some point Brin left, at another Mehen returned. And the tests kept coming.

But whether it was the protection spell's effect or whether Asmodeus's mark didn't count against her, the war wizards left well after the lamps were lit—Ilstan and Devora satisfied, and Drannon annoyed that nothing had come of it.

Farideh stood stiffly and made her way to the entry, where Mehen stood, watching the war wizards go. "You all right?" he asked.

"Fine," Farideh said automatically. "How's Havi?"

"Probably asleep again," Mehen said. "Brin's with her."

Farideh nodded, not trusting herself to say the right thing.

"You look as though you could use something to eat and some of His Lordship's good wine," Mehen said, putting an arm around her and steering her toward the kitchen. There was a roast going cold on the table, pottage and beets besides. Only the kitchen maid was left to keep the fire up. She scurried out when Mehen sat down at the rough table. Farideh watched her go.

"Did you grow up with servants?" Farideh asked.

Mehen gave her a curious look. They didn't often talk about his childhood. "They never seem to bother you," Farideh pointed out. "I'm never sure if asking them to sit down is rude or polite or confusing."

"You get used to it," Mehen said, without answering her question. He poured her a glass of ruby-colored wine. "If I ask you what Helindra said to Havilar, will you tell me?"

Farideh put a little food on her plate. "She offered to pay Havilar a lot of coin to go away, and threatened a lot of trouble if she didn't."

"Did she scare you?"

"A bit."

"Good. Lady Crownsilver's canny as a blue wyrm. Never drop your guard with her."

Farideh took a swallow of wine. "Do you think she's the one who sent the kidnappers?"

Mehen shook his head. "Helindra comes at you with coin and contracts. Not assassins." He blew out a breath. "No one would blame you if you wanted to leave Suzail," he said, watching her carefully.

Farideh thought of the desert under the moon. "Not if Havi's staying." But then she thought of Brin, upstairs, and wondered how long that reason would hold.

Mehen regarded her sadly. "Something will change soon," he promised. "Nothing stands still forever."

• • •

ON A HUNT, Irvel had always thought of his companions as his brothers, linked in a shared goal, a shared excitement, a shared prize.

I have eight thousand brothers and sisters this day, he thought, throwing up his shield to ward off a blow. His horse was lost, somewhere in the chaos, his guardsmen fighting hard against the Sembians that had broken around their rear guard and attacked the royal command.

Spells flashed around him, steel scraped against shields, against armor. Sembian, Cormyrean, there was no dividing which soldier was shouting, screaming, dying. Irvel could only keep his concentration on the men before him, the blades seeking *his* throat, and the officers close by and guarding both him and Baerovus.

He ran the Sembian through and risked a glance at his son—still on horseback, his dun gelding prancing under him, still shooting arrow after arrow into the enemy line. At his side Vainrence and a trio of war wizards summoned terrible storms of magic, powerful enough to make the air thicken and crackle with energy. In the valley beyond, the Sembian army would regret allying with Risen Netheril.

Baerovus reached for another arrow, found Irvel's eyes—

A globe of shadow struck Baerovus's head, rocking him out of the saddle as it passed, hardly slowing. Baerovus's eyes rolled back in his skull. One foot still tangled in the stirrup, he fell into the churning mud, boneless and slack.

Irvel shouted. Another soldier broke through the ranks of the Cormyrean defenders and struck him hard with a pike—missed his head, bruised and bloodied his shoulder through the mail shirt. Irvel turned to throw the fellow off—*Baerovus, Baerovus, he had to get to his son.* Lord Darclant Illance stood between them, catching the pike on his sword and thrusting it away.

"This way, Irvel," he bellowed. "I'll keep—"

A dagger to the throat cut him off—Irvel shouted a war cry and ran the soldier through, seeing his dark eyes widen as the blade breached him. He was younger even than Baerovus. He caught Darclant, who grasped his own throat, blood spilling through his fingers. A healing potion, Irvel thought, but there was no quiet place to administer it—and Baerovus might need it more.

"Back to the palace!" Vainrence shouted, his voice carrying through the chaos. Irvel spun—like an island in a storm of clashing bodies and rearing horses, the Lord Warder stood holding Baerovus's slack body. "The bootstick!" he shouted.

Still holding Darclant, Irvel reached down and slid the flat wooden stick from the edge of his boot with two fingers, just far enough to take hold of the top and snap it sharply down. The air around him and Lord Illance vanished as the Weave whined like the overdrawn strings of a fiddle about to break, drowning out the clash of swords, the shouts of soldiers, the folly of Cormyr.

5

RAEDRA STOOD PERFECTLY STILL BEFORE THE MIRROR, STUDYING THE purple silk gown with a dispassionate eye. She couldn't help but imagine the murmurs of the nobles at the strings of amber beads trimming the flounces, the lace of gold around the bodice—didn't she know this was her second wedding?

"It's splendid!" her mother, Princess Ospra Goldfeather, said. Half a dozen ladies-in-waiting surrounded her, including Varauna and her mother, Lady Adenia Goldfeather. "You look like a true princess of Cormyr."

What did that even mean? Lovely, Raedra thought. Strong. Quiet. Supportive. Willing to waste funds on frills and frippery.

"Is there a crown?" her aunt Adenia asked.

"Oh, there must be a crown," Varauna said. "You won't look like a bride at all if you have no jewels." She reached out and straightened the full and flowing skirt ahead of the seamstress's assistant with her pins. "And it should stay long—a train. You *must* have a train."

All Raedra could think of was the sheer weight of that much fabric. Already it felt as if it would smother her—even before the jewels. Her first wedding gown had been so heavy—silk and wool for a winter wedding, so crusted with pearls she could hardly move. But how she'd shone! And how happy she'd been . . .

Idiot, she thought unkindly.

"Raedra?" her mother said. "You're being quiet. Don't you like it?"

"It could have a more daring collar," Varauna offered. "A little more . . ." She gestured at Raedra's décolleté.

Her mother pursed her mouth. "I don't think that portrays the right image."

"Varauna, don't be vulgar," Adenia said, fluttering her fan. "This is her wedding day, not her wedding night."

"Who's pretending you're a virgin?" Varauna muttered in Raedra's ear. Raedra smiled, though she didn't feel it.

Raedra's mother sighed. "What is it you *want* changed dear?"

I don't know, Raedra thought, watching herself in the mirror. Everything, somehow.

"It doesn't seem to be the best use of the Crown's coin," she said. "Not for a second wedding."

Ospra Goldfeather pursed her mouth. "Raedra, unlike the last one, this wedding is not only about you and your happiness. We are a nation at war, and people want to see that the Dragon Throne will persist. They want to see that the Obarskyrs are still here, still expecting to hold Cormyr. They want to know that we will outlast Shade, and the swiftest, happiest way for you to remind them of that is to put on this lovely gown, smile, and marry Aubrin Crownsilver for all to see." She sat back, smiling politely. "And in nine months, make sure there's something else to make them rejoice."

"Do you think the war will still be going on in nine months?" Raedra asked.

Ospra kept her smile, but her eyes were so tired. "I'm sure it won't be. But you know well there is always something to tilt the scales. Unhappy nobles. Belligerent goblins. Not enough of this or that." She folded her hands. "Your grandfather is not getting any younger. He would surely like to meet his great-grandchild."

Raedra studied the dress again, keeping her thoughts to herself. At least her parents had given up on the notion of Baerovus meeting the right girl and snapping out of everything that made him Baerovus. Her brother would be king. Raedra would be the mother of the next king. And someone would make a painting of her in this lovely dress, holding the infant king beside her poor odd brother, to hang for all eternity in some forgotten hallway of the royal palace.

"May I see it with the crown?" she asked the seamstress. If she was going to do this, she might as well go all the way.

"Of course, Your Highness." The woman had no more than set the gold coronet upon Raedra's head, but one of the doorguards stepped in, announcing yet another visitor.

"Lord Aubrin Crownsilver," the guard intoned, and Raedra felt a rush of blood she seldom got outside fencing practice. The young lord bowed to Princess Ospra, Lady Adenia—all the proper people, to all the proper degrees in the most proper order.

"Well met," he said to Raedra, with a smile that didn't reach his eyes. "I was hoping I could talk to you."

Raedra stared at Aubrin's reflection in the tall mirror, but there was nothing in his expression that said what he intended. If he tried to end it, here, now, in front of everyone—

"Isn't she lovely, Aubrin?" Adenia asked.

"A true princess of Cormyr," Aubrin said.

Raedra stared at him. "A fortunate thing that we were able to track down the silk."

"Very fortunate," Brin said without blinking.

"What is it you want?" she asked.

"I can't come to see my bride?"

"Of course you can," Raedra said, hearing the steel in his voice and matching it with her own. "Though there are many hours in the day—why this one in particular?"

"Raedra," her mother scolded.

"I have guests, Mother," Raedra pointed out, with a smile. "And the seamstress. Lord Crownsilver knows well—"

"'Lord Crownsilver,'" Lady Adenia scoffed. "What sweet pet names you have for each other." Raedra stared daggers at Brin's reflection.

"Might we talk in private?" Brin asked.

Raedra set her jaw—not here, not now. Not with everyone watching and waiting. "I can hardly move, Aubrin. The pins."

"Come sit with us and admire your bride," Adenia said. "She'll be through soon enough." She gave Raedra a significant look. "And then you can have some private time. No one says it *must* be nine."

Raedra's thoughts raced to think of a suitably polite response to *that* and a suitable excuse to get Aubrin away from her—at *least* until she could guarantee she had the time to think about whatever it was he thought he was going to say.

And then a war wizard appeared in their midst, and Raedra regretted wishing for everything to change.

"You must come," the wizard cried over Adenia's little screech of surprise. Ospra was on her feet immediately. "The prince—the crown prince—there's been an attack. Your pardon, Highnesses, you *must* come now."

Raedra felt her blood drain away, and she stepped down from the pedestal as if she were in a dream. "Where?"

"What's happened?" Ospra nearly shouted.

"Lord Warder Vainrence returned with Baerovus," the war wizard said. "The princes were attacked—a force that slipped by the rear guard. The crown prince teleported back with His Highness's bootstick—but they've not arrived. Something's gone wrong."

Pins or no pins, Raedra ran after them. "Where was the bootstick supposed to send him?" Ospra said.

"The Hippogriff Chamber—right to the Hippogriff Chamber."

"Are they searching?" Ospra demanded. "You can find him, can't you?"

"Princess, they're doing what they can."

"Where is Baerovus?" Raedra said. "Is he all right?"

The wizard looked back at her. "He's . . . injured. They're seeing to him."

As they approached the Hall of the Battlebanners, the war wizard suddenly turned, leading the princesses through a narrow space lined with tapestries. Pulling one aside, he gestured them into the secret passageways of the royal palace. "There's a crowd in the halls, I'm afraid," he said. "They may not know what's happened, but they know something's wrong."

Raedra hitched up the too-long skirts as she squeezed after her mother . . . and felt the weight of the fabric ease. She glanced over her shoulder—Aubrin held her train bunched in both fists, his face as pale as a sheet of parchment.

"They told me I had to come too," he said, voice tight.

Which made Raedra's heart pull all the harder down to her stomach. They slipped through the dark and dusty corridors, single-file, emerging into the Hippogriff Chamber at last. The curtains were all drawn wide to let in what little light the clouds allowed. Her grandfather, King Foril, struggled to his feet as Ospra rushed to him. Until a few months ago, the king had been surprisingly hearty as he approached his eightieth birthday. But a brainstorm one cold winter morning had sapped the Dragon King's vitality and clouded his thoughts. The princess embraced her father-in-law gently, as if his birdlike bones would shatter, but Foril clutched her close.

"An ambush," he said. "They got Baerovus out. Still waiting for Irvel."

"What's happened to him?"

"Foul magic." Raedra nearly jumped at the new voice. The Royal Magician, Ganrahast, stood unmoving, against the wall where the secret passage emerged. "He will not die. But it may be some time before we can properly dispel it."

"Thank you, Ganrahast," Ospra said, her voice shaking. "May we see him?"

The red-haired wizard hesitated, pulling his long beard. "His Highness has some unpleasant injuries. Let them be healed first."

A fat line of tears welled up in Ospra's eyes. "I would *see* my son."

"You will," Ganrahast assured her. "But please, Highness, let the clerics do their work."

"It's Shadovar magic isn't it?" Aubrin said.

"We aren't certain."

"We *are* certain," a new voice said. Lord Vainrence, bloodied and scorched himself, slipped in through another of the secret passages. "Now," he added. "They've sent their arcanists in."

"How many war wizards are there with the army?" Raedra asked. Vainrence raised his brow.

"Plenty, Highness."

"Enough to fend off Shadovar arcanists?"

"You must trust us, Highness," Ganarahast said. "There is the Sembian front, the Northern front. We must have war wizards here in Suzail. We are doing what we can."

"A well-placed arrow will end an arcanist the same as an infantryman," Foril said. "We will prevail." He patted the settee beside him. "Sit, my dears. There is nothing to do now but wait for Irvel."

Chastened, Raedra gathered up her skirts and settled down beside her mother. An arrow might take down a wizard—assuming that wizard did not bear shields and defenses and other protections—but their sharpest marksman lay under the tender care of wizards and clerics, here in Suzail. Ospra squeezed her daughter's hand. The tacking on one sleeve snapped, and it slid down Raedra's arm.

"Come, come, Emvar," Foril said, waving Brin over. "You must sit as well. I'm told they're bringing warmed wine for us while we wait. The gods will not be so cruel as to make it much longer, and you should not fight Irvel for a place."

"Aubrin, my lord," Ospra corrected gently. Foril gave her a quizzical look. "He is Aubrin, not Emvar."

"Did I say Emvar?" Foril said. He sniffed. "Must be all the fuss. Too many worries. Come then, Aubrin, and sit. Has no one called Erzoured?" he asked as Aubrin took the chair beside Raedra. After a moment, he reached over and tugged her sleeve up over her bare shoulder, repinning it there.

"Thank you," she said. She took his hand in hers and squeezed it.

"I'm sure the baron will be here shortly," Ganrahast said flatly.

"Good, good." Foril turned to Ospra. "He's family too, you know. We must never forget family."

Ospra offered her father-in-law a brittle smile. "Of course, my lord."

And there they waited, the warmed wine eventually growing cold in its cups, as Raedra repeated her prayers—to Tempus, to Tymora, to all the gods who might make a difference—and kept her hand in Brin's, too afraid to let go.

• • •

THE CROWN PRINCE didn't return.

"They're saying he was still holding Lord Illance when he vanished," one of Brin's palace contacts, the understeward of the purse, had told him between loudly spoken pleasantries. "The bootsticks aren't enchanted to transport more than their bearer and some clothes. They're thinking it threw him off."

"But they can't find him?" Brin asked.

"Not even a corpse," the man said solemnly.

Baerovus didn't wake up.

"Word is," the cleric's assistant had told Brin, "they aren't sure what took him. Ganrahast has all but locked himself in that chamber. No one wants to cross his path. They don't know if the prince will ever wake, or if he'll be himself when he does."

His Harper contacts buzzed with information—most of it dire. "Raiders are heading south," a contact known only as Garce the Scythe told him. "I need more coin if you want to move quickly."

"How much?"

"Another hundred, and tell your young Lord Tapstorn he doesn't get to throw in with us and still pick and choose who makes use of his country stables."

Brin sighed. "Again?"

"Again," Garce agreed. "Plus, I have some information you might want." He sniffed. "Messy sort, but it might be about you-know-who."

Five days after the war wizard had burst into her fitting, while Brin was still trying to decide what to do with Garce's information, Raedra came to call on Brin in Crownsilver Castle.

"Are you going to hide here forever?" she demanded.

"I've hardly *been* here in the last three days," Brin snapped. He rubbed his hands over his face. "Have they found your father yet?" For a long moment, Raedra was silent, and when Brin looked up, he noticed the hollows under her eyes, the pallor of her face.

"They're presuming my father is dead," Raedra said. "They cannot find him, not even his body." Her voice broke, and she turned away. "They want His Majesty to declare it so, to reestablish the line of succession, but he's holding out. It won't be long, though. Even my mother . . ." She trailed off, shaking her head. "She's starting to believe it too."

"Raedra, I'm so sorry," Brin said.

"The nobles . . . *some* of the nobles say this is a sign we should capitulate to Sembia," she said. "Maybe even Shade. It will only get worse from here." She handed him the case she'd walked in holding. "Here."

Brin frowned, but took the slim wooden case from her. Inside, tucked under a blanket of black velvet was a dagger in a tooled leather sheath, its grip dark with frequent use. The pommel held a ruby of significant size, but no significant quality, and carvings of dragons marked the crosspiece.

Brin's stomach plunged. "This is your father's dagger."

Raedra folded her hands over her skirts. "It's a wedding gift. A gesture. You should start wearing it, as soon as . . ." She gestured as if the words she wasn't going to say were floating in a cloud between them. "We need to get married," she went on. "You can keep . . . her. Send her off to Waterdeep for a few months, and let things settle, and I'll learn to tolerate it."

Brin shook his head. "Raedra—"

"Do you understand," she said, her voice harder, "what's happening here? My father is dead, my brother will not wake, there is a call to cull Baerovus from the line and name a new crown prince. There are a dozen advisors hissing in my grandfather's ears about whether that should be you or me or Erzoured—and one person speaking *his* name is too many." Her blue eyes bored into Brin. "If they don't elevate Baerovus, then you and I *must* be allied. That was the entire point of this marriage, and I won't release you from it."

"The entire point of our marriage was to keep me out of the line and off the throne," Brin said, all too aware of the edge of panic in his voice.

"Aubrin . . . Brin, *gods*, Brin, you know . . . you *know* that these are not the circumstances we came to our arrangement in!"

"You're talking about backing the legitimization!"

"When there are fools trying to put that *villain* on the Dragon Throne, then yes, I am!" Raedra stood over him. "If it comes to it, don't think that I won't take

Helindra's side and talk of Emvar whenever my grandfather is near and make *sure* that there is no call to name Erzoured crown prince. How could you possibly think I wouldn't?"

"Baerovus is not dead," Brin said. "And you are ahead of all of us. And you *swore* I wouldn't come near the throne."

"The king names his successor, and his crown prince is dead—"

"You don't know your father's dead."

Raedra looked for a moment as if he'd never said a crueler word to her. "Don't throw that in my face. Do you think I *want* this? Do you think I'm *happy* this is happening?"

"I'm only asking if it would change if he's not dead."

Raedra shook her head. "Who can say? You find out he's alive, and we can revisit the matter." She swallowed again, as if it pained her. "I have to go. Wear the dagger. Let people see you're an Obarskyr."

But I'm not, Brin thought. Not in any of the ways that counted. After she'd left, Brin spent a long time considering what she'd told him, what so many people had told him, and Garce the Scythe's messy information.

It's unlikely, he thought. More than unlikely.

Constancia found him sometime later. "You've missed highsunfeast," she said. "And four of your peers have come calling." She shut the door behind her. "It's killing Helindra that she doesn't know everything you know. She'd like you to come down. At least tell her what the princess wanted."

"What if he's not dead?" Brin asked, not looking up from the dagger.

Constancia frowned. "The crown prince?"

"He might not be dead," Brin said, "and then what?" She sat down across from him.

"I know this is hard," she said. "He was a good man and he would have been a good king—"

"He might not be dead," Brin said, feeling surer. "We can't just leave him if he's alive."

"The war wizards found no sign of him," Constancia said. "If anyone could find Irvel, it's them."

"But they've said before, that magic's acting off—the Weave's growing stronger again, but it means parts shift and pull as it comes together. It could throw a spell off. Or the Shadovar mages—spells ricochet all over the battlefields."

"Which means Irvel is as likely in Abeir as in Durpar as in the Cormanthor Forest," Constancia said. "How do you plan to find him?"

Brin hesitated. "I've heard a rumor."

"There are plenty of rumors—"

"A hunter spotted a pair of injured men matching the crown prince and his retainer while he was floating down the Immerflow River, on the north side of the Hullack Forest. Didn't know what to make of it, but thank the gods, he was a Harper agent, and he passed a message through an informer. Gave it to me, because I might know what to do with it."

"Ignore it," Constancia said. "That's nowhere near the battle or the palace. And the war wizards would have found him on the Immerflow."

"We should check it."

"Aubrin."

"What happens if he's alive?" Brin demanded. "What happens if the Crown Prince of Cormyr still lives and breathes, and the line is reordered without him? That flies in the face of all that we stand for."

Constancia raised a slim eyebrow. "Truly?"

"Constancia," Brin said. "Please. Please. We have to be sure. If I'm going to lose everything, I need to be sure." His voice broke on the lump in his throat, and he set his head in his hands.

Constancia sighed. "You want to cross the country in the middle of the war, on the third-hand word of a hunter that the crown prince survived and went for a rafting ride. That is—"

"Foolhardy," Brin agreed. "Selfish? Thoughtless?" He looked up. "But you can't stop me."

"Don't underestimate what I'm willing to do," Constancia said. "I'll tell Helindra. I'll tell Her Highness. I'll knock you out myself."

"Havilar will go with me," Brin said. "Mehen and Farideh will come with her. Please, Constancia, say you'll come too. You'll wonder forever, just as much as I would, if we could have saved him."

His cousin shook her head. "These are the same sorts of pleas that convinced me to let you spend time without guards," Constancia said. "And what happened then?"

"I ran off anyway," Brin pointed out with a wan smile. "I still think Helindra should have been proud of that."

"She'd never tell you. What happens if it turns out your hunter saw some drowning woodcutters?"

"We come home," Brin said. "And I either marry Raedra or become legitimized."

"No more dallying?"

Brin spread his hands. "I won't have a choice, now will I?"

• • •

Lorcan watched over his steepled fingers as the sand dropped grain by grain through the throat of the hourglass. Two days more.

Two days more, and he might need to stretch it—making Farideh wait wasn't making her pull him closer. She could call him down, and she hadn't. She could ask him to come more, and she hadn't. It took longer each time for her to push him away, but she still pushed.

And he hadn't found a good way to corrupt her for Glasya.

Mortals often thought corruption was a simple matter—do something a god doesn't like, and your soul would be tainted and sweet to devils. But the alchemy of souls was far more subtle, far more complex. What corrupted one soul, often wouldn't mar another. Murder corrupted, but punishing someone wickeder might not. The succubi might bring their due to the Hells by sinking mortals in acts of lust—but sex itself wasn't what did the deed. The mind behind the body mattered, the state of that soul.

Let mortals think the world is black and white, the devils said. Let them think they're safe watching a line that never mattered.

And while there were heinous acts that would incontrovertibly subvert a mortal, turning all but the basest gods aside, the chance he could lead Farideh to such an act was as slim as brokering a marriage between one of the bloodthirsty *pradixikai* and a Prince of the Abyss.

Brin and Havilar—something raw there, something fragile. Put the right tool in her hand, and Farideh might make the selfish choice . . .

The image of his warlock kissing the little Tormite flashed through Lorcan's thoughts. He curled his hands into fists. No. Not that.

The thudding of an erinyes's hooves, sprinting down the hall outside, gave Lorcan enough warning to stand from the chair he'd been lounging in, but not much else. His head pounded, his temper frayed, the hourglass was still half-filled—but letting the erinyes see that was reckless. He focused all of that into anger, into sternness as proud Zela, the leader of the *pradixikai*, stormed into his chambers, her dark eyes glittering. Noreia and Leuctra trailed her.

"What is it?" Lorcan demanded.

"There are demons in the Nine Hells," Zela said gleefully.

Lorcan said a string of curses to himself. "The succubi have been here for a century. Take it up with Asmodeus."

"*Not* those useless slatterns," Zela said. "*Demons.* They've breached Stygia."

Lorcan raised an eyebrow—time did not flow in the Hells quite as it did on other planes, but surely it was too early for this sort of nonsense. "Demons. In the Fifth Layer."

Zela smiled wickedly, baring fangs. "We'd like permission to cross over and smash their mad skulls in."

"Why are you telling *me* this?" Lorcan demanded. "Glasya's the one you need to ask, if you want to cross layers."

"The archduchess's seneschals turned her away," Leuctra said. Zela scowled. "Said no one needs to head into Stygia. Don't think they believe it."

"*I* don't believe it," Lorcan said. "Even during the Blood War—"

"We heard it from erinyes from the Seventh," Zela interrupted. "*They've* got permission, and they're commanding *spinagons*."

Lorcan held her black eyes for as long as he dared. "Did it occur to you that Lord Baalzebul is no friend of Prince Levistus? While His Majesty is displeased, there is the opportunity for less careful devils to act out old enmities. 'Demons in Stygia'—what an excellent reason to rampage across Levistus's kingdom in the name of the Nine Hells! You show up there, you risk Glasya's wrath, and I will not answer for it."

Zela's dark eyes narrowed. Lorcan matched her gaze, reminding himself he was master here, no longer the little brother—the half-worthy half-devil—Zela could torment. "We would be certain," she said slowly. "Whatever it takes."

"And I would prefer you were ready for the countermeasures," Lorcan said. "Assuming you're right and the Blood War is playing out at our neighbor's gates, I'm sure you'll be called when your turn comes. Go run your sisters through their exercises and don't bring me any more of this nonsense."

For a moment he was sure she'd call his bluff, tear him limb from limb and crush his skull between her hands. But after a moment, she only turned and stormed off, followed by Leuctra. Noreia lingered.

"Do you want to hear that gossip now?" Noreia asked.

Lorcan eyed her—he didn't, not even a little. But he might need to. "This is what they were talking about?"

"It might be," Noreia said. "Invadiah says some of the succubi have been plotting rebellion. They want out of the Hells, back to the Abyss. There are portals all through that aerie. Doesn't take too many jumps to end up in the Abyss. *Or* Stygia."

The Abyss, the distant layer of the wild demons, the eternal enemies, eternal brethren of the devils of the Nine Hells. Before Lorcan was born, before Asmodeus claimed the godhood, the two forces battled in a never-ending war for supremacy—over what exactly, Lorcan couldn't have said. But his half sisters all longed for the days of endless battle, and it wasn't merely their old lovely forms they missed.

For one thing, they missed the days when the succubi were their foes, not their allies. Invadiah, once the most terrible erinyes serving the Lord of the Sixth, had been demoted by Asmodeus for her failure to serve his plans—what she would have become before, Lorcan couldn't have guessed; there were innumerable lesser devils. But instead she had been made to take the shape of a succubus—a special insult Invadiah and most of the *pradixikai* still seethed over.

"The succubi are our sisters-at-arms," Lorcan said, repeating the phrase like a catechism. "Asmodeus freed them from the turmoil of the Abyss and found them their true place among us. And anyway," he added, "I doubt strongly there are any succubi in Stygia."

Noreia shrugged. "The Seventh Layer devils said there were. At the moment."

"We return to Baalzebul's storied hatred for His Highness," Lorcan said. "And the erinyes' notorious eagerness to join the battle. Go see to your fury."

It's a rumor, he told himself as Noreia left. A ridiculous rumor. The Blood War is over for everyone except shitting erinyes and lunatic succubi.

Lorcan's very blood suddenly shivered with the buzz of hellwasps.

"Well done," the archduchess said from behind him. Lorcan froze. "I knew eventually you would take your sisters in hand."

He dropped to his knees. "Your Highness. I didn't realize you were watching."

"I am always watching, Lorcan. Did your mother never warn you so?"

Invadiah would not have warned Lorcan if he were about to step into the mouth of the Dragon Queen, but Lorcan did not say so.

"What do you think of our Noreia?"

Lorcan swallowed. "She is eager to advance. She chafes under Zela's leadership."

"That is not peculiar for an erinyes. Nor for the *pradixikai*. I am told she speaks often with your mother."

"She may," Lorcan said. "I don't know."

"Do you worry Invadiah will challenge you for her former place?"

No, Lorcan thought, I know she will.

"I concern myself with the here and now, Highness," Lorcan said. A hellwasp buzzed past his ear.

"How quaint," Glasya laughed, a sound that put him in mind of oil overboiling its pot. "Since we are speaking of the *pradixikai*," she went on, pacing around him, "do make certain you keep their reins close. It would displease me greatly to find out you can't contain your sisters. And I don't wish to see you again while I'm displeased."

"Of course, Your Highness. Is there . . . anything in particular they should be kept from?"

"That sounds terribly close to questioning my authority."

"Never, Your Highness."

"That's better. Should anyone *else* ask why," Glasya said, "I'm sure you can think of more interesting topics to speak of." She tilted Lorcan's chin up with the butt of her scourge, so he had to look into her night-black eyes. "Such a strange notion, demons in Stygia. Don't you think?"

Lorcan swallowed. "Very."

She turned, and Lorcan focused resolutely on the floor. "I cannot say Prince Levistus would not deserve such an incursion," Glasya said with not a little acid. "He has been overbold all his days. Even now, wasting his granted Chosen, scheming against my lord father, snatching lost powers from old enemies as though they are his to take."

She hesitated, and Lorcan felt as if creation split with that silence.

"Find something for the *pradixikai* to do," she finally said.

Lorcan stayed, kneeling on the floor, as the hellwasps whisked their queen and her litter out the open window. At least she hadn't asked about Farideh. At least she had not hinted any further about Asmodeus, and his motives.

It would displease me greatly to find out you can't contain your sisters.

Lorcan shuddered. There was nowhere he wanted to be less than Malbolge. Damn the hourglass, he thought, before leaping from the balcony and flapping toward the fingerbone tower.

The scrying mirror showed Farideh alone, still inside the tallhouse, in the spacious bedroom she and Havilar shared. Lorcan nudged the magic that tied her pact to him. She hissed and clapped a hand to where his brand laced her arm. But she didn't move. Lorcan narrowed his eyes and pulled harder, making her curse and come to her feet.

That was when he noticed the haversacks, the ordered piles of supplies.

He yanked again on the tether of magic, entirely too hard. Farideh went perfectly still, fists clenched, eyes squeezed tight.

"No, Lorcan," she said, a little loud. "I am busy. It's daytime. It's still raining. I'm not going outside, and I'm not answering the flock of questions I'm bound to get if I do. Ask later."

Like Hell, Lorcan thought. Moments later, he stepped out of the portal.

"*Karshoj!*" Farideh shouted. She sprinted across the room and latched the door. "Gods, at *least* wear that disguise!"

"You're alone," Lorcan pointed out. "And you've locked the door—clever girl. What are you packing for?"

"There are windows," she went on. "There might have been someone on the other side of the room."

Lorcan reached over and flicked the shutters closed. "What," he said once more, "are you packing for? Are you finally ready to leave?"

Farideh stared at him as if she planned to face him down until they both collapsed into piles of bones. "We're all leaving," she finally said.

"We?"

"Havi, Mehen, and I," she said. "And Brin and his cousin. We're searching for . . . someone."

"And your someone?"

She looked away, and he feared the worst. "Brin's future father-in-law."

That was not the worst, Lorcan allowed, but it wasn't good. "How did you lose the Crown Prince of Cormyr?" he demanded.

Farideh kept avoiding his gaze. "Put your disguise on. You're already making me break my promise to Brin—don't make it worse."

Lorcan narrowed his eyes. Not a step in the direction he preferred. But more than anything right now, he needed her to listen to him, to trust him, to do what he wanted. He spread his hands and cast the spell that made him look human, wincing as the magic took hold. "Better?" he asked.

She folded her arms, but looked back at him—looked him right over. That *was* better. "What am I supposed to tell Brin?"

"Who said you have to tell him anything?" Lorcan asked. "Doesn't the Crown Prince of Cormyr have his own people to hunt him down?"

"They can't find him."

"But Brin can?"

"He has an idea," Farideh said. "I suppose we'll see."

"And where exactly does this 'idea' take you?"

Farideh blew out a breath. "Into the battlefields." She uncrossed her arms. "We're wandering out into the battlefields looking for someone that everyone else says is dead, because if we don't find him, Brin has to be king or some nonsense. Whatever you're going to say next, I promise, I've already thought it."

"Now that doesn't sound like a trip you're excited for." Shit and ashes, Lorcan thought. It was the opposite of safe.

"It's fine," Farideh said. She considered Lorcan again. "Do you think you could find the crown prince?"

"If war wizards can't manage, how would I?" She doesn't want to go, he thought, watching her face, the way she moved her arms. Lorcan reached over and ran the back of his finger over her cheek. "Darling—"

She pulled away. "You can't . . . you can't come around while I'm with them. The way you . . . have been."

"You can hardly ask me to just sit by and twiddle my thumbs while you stroll among the armies of Shade and Cormyr, following a 'friend' who doesn't seem to be very keen about your best interests."

"Brin's not—"

"The one who's essentially trapped you in this tallhouse so he can string your sister along?" He bent a little so she had to look him in the eye. "The one who's not going to take it well at all if he sees you channeling the powers of the god of sin?"

Farideh said nothing. She didn't want to go—that was plain. She wanted a reason—any reason at all—to stay behind. Lorcan studied her still expression. "Maybe you should stay," he said. He ran a hand down her arm. "For safety's sake."

Farideh scoffed. "Alone? That would go over well."

"Mehen knows about Asmodeus now," Lorcan pointed out. "He could be convinced it's safer if no one else knows you're what you are. And it's not as if you'll be *alone*." He smiled. "I could stay here too."

She looked away, flushing. "That would *definitely* not go over well."

Lorcan clucked his tongue. "You really don't have to tell everyone everything, you know?" Stay, he thought, as if he could will her to do so. Stay and be safe where I can keep an eye on you. Where I can figure out Glasya's edicts and Asmodeus's and . . .

Farideh sighed and sat down on the edge of the bed. "And so . . . what? I'll have your company once every eight or ten days?" She gave him a level stare. "Did you think I wouldn't notice the way you space them out?"

He'd hoped. "I have other matters to tend to," Lorcan said. "And it's not as if you're available all the hours of the day. I have to make do with what I'm offered."

He sat down beside her and pushed her hair behind her ear, drawing his fingertips over her cheekbone. "If you're alone, those hours tend to grow." He leaned close to her ear. "And we can discuss what sort of company you'd like to have."

Farideh shut her eyes, and for a reckless heartbeat, Lorcan smirked. She bit her lip. He reached to turn her face, to kiss her hard and seal her decision. Then she turned herself and said, "Havi needs me. I can't abandon her."

Lorcan dropped his hand. Recalculated. "Maybe Havilar should stay too. It's not as if it's safe for her either."

Farideh sighed and stood. "She won't. Brin needs her."

"And Brin gets what Brin wants?" Lorcan said. She scowled at him.

"Swap your names, and how is it different?" she asked.

Lorcan laughed. "When was the last time I got anything I wanted?" He stood and moved nearer to her. "You want to give me something I want? Don't go. Give me a chance."

Her eyes searched his face. "A chance to do what?"

Lorcan hesitated—what was the right answer to *that* question? A chance to put things back the way they were. A chance to make sure she didn't reject her pact and leave him. A chance to keep his masters happy and both Farideh and him alive.

"I'm trying to make things right again," he finally said.

Farideh didn't blink. "Then tell me what Asmodeus wants," she said. "Tell me what I'm waiting for. If I'm so important to you, that shouldn't be hard."

Lorcan fought the urge to twist her words back on her. "I've told you everything I know."

"And have you found anything else out?"

"This isn't the sort of thing you look into," he said. "Trust me, darling."

She turned her face. "Go home, Lorcan. I'm sure I'll see you soon. Eight days, right?"

Lorcan's temper swelled. In the old days, in the first months of her pact—before Sairché, before the Sundering, before all of this mess—he would have turned it on her, raged and stormed and made her fear him. Made her realize that she was the one making this happen, that she was the one who had to fix it.

But whether it was the fact that in her darkest hour Lorcan had turned from Farideh, or the fact that he'd come crawling back, his mouth full of apologies; whether the blessings of Asmodeus had woken something in Farideh, or Lorcan had softened and the thought of terrorizing her put him off—whatever it was, something had changed.

And so Lorcan would have to be cleverer than his old self had been, because Farideh could not be allowed to leave Suzail.

Down in the lowest level of the fingerbone tower, Lorcan set his hand on the lock to the storeroom. Sinews strong as steel slithered out of their sockets, retreating into the lock and freeing the bone door. It wasn't a pleasant plan, he thought, and if she ever found out, he'd have to have a stunning way of twisting it to his advantage. But he needed to be sure Farideh stayed in that tallhouse, whatever she decided.

At the edge of his mother's armory, on a series of shelves, lay pewter cases stacked three high—Lorcan shifted them around, looking for the proper one. Contagions gathered from every layer of the Hells—plagues vile enough to wipe out armies, sicknesses strong enough to lay heroes low. A coward's weapon, Invadiah would have said. The answer to his problem, Lorcan thought. He plucked one out—the Infernal runes pressed into a lead seal spelling out the contagion inside. *Shaking fever*. Severe enough to keep her in the tallhouse. Mild enough not to hurt her permanently. Perfect. No one could be upset. He slipped it into his pocket.

He'd infect both of the twins—straight away. She and Havilar would wake, already ill—ill enough to warrant a pause in this reckless plan. Mehen wouldn't drag them across the wet and violent countryside while the fever gripped them. They might be well enough to walk, but the shaking would take them if they did much more.

In the uppermost room, Sairché dozed behind her barrier, too bored to stay awake it seemed. Perfect, he thought. The scrying mirror found Farideh fast asleep in bed. She stirred and rubbed her branded arm as the scrying mirror's magic used her blood to find her, but she didn't wake. Absolutely perfect, he thought. One eye on his sister, he opened the portal and stepped into Toril, into the dark corners of the tallhouse's bedroom.

But there, he realized, his plan was not so perfect after all: Havilar wasn't in the bed beside Farideh.

Lorcan closed his fist around the lead vial, calculating how badly this would fall out. If one twin was sick, shouldn't both be sick? Shaking fever passed quickly from person to person—why Farideh and not Havilar? How quickly might they think of Lorcan?

More important, what would Asmodeus do if both Chosen weren't safe and sound?

Havilar isn't Chosen yet, Lorcan told himself. And if she wasn't here, she was likely somewhere else, very awake and in the company of her little lordling. He flexed his wings in agitation. There was nothing for it but to make the best of a bad situation.

He traced a measure of the contagion across Havilar's pillow with the tips of his fingers, more around the doorknob, the candle beside the bed. When she returned, enough would remain to infect her. Lorcan eased around the bed and kneeled beside his warlock.

He tipped the remainder of the liquid onto his index finger and set the empty vial on the bedside table. Farideh's breath hitched as something stirred her sleep, and he froze, waited as she drifted down again. He eased her lips apart, smearing the sickness over them and across the tip of her tongue.

He considered, for a reckless moment, waking her. No Havilar meant a far better setting than the sodden garden . . .

But then she'd wake and wonder, and surely come around to pointing fingers at Lorcan. She grimaced and wet her mouth in her sleep, swallowing the bitter liquid. A weight came off Lorcan's shoulders, and he flicked his wings again in the close space.

"Sleep well, darling," he whispered.

Clink.

Lorcan startled. The vial—it wasn't on the table. He dropped to the floor, his head against the boards. The vial had rolled to a stop in the dust, deep under the heavy bed.

Beshaba shit in my eyes, he thought. He twisted, his wings in the way, trying to get his arm beneath the ornate bedframe. He transformed into a human, biting back the grunt of effort and pain and dropped the extra inch against the floor. His arm slid up to the biceps, blocked by the carved edge. His fingers grazed the vial, rolling it farther into the dust.

He cursed and cursed and cursed. Lorcan lay a moment, staring up at the room's painted ceiling, listening to Farideh's soft breath. She couldn't be left to find the vial . . . but if he couldn't reach it, then neither could she. The dust beneath the bed meant no one was moving it, cleaning beneath. The vial would stay there until Suzail fell and the shades burned the tallhouse down.

And it wouldn't take much luck for Lorcan and Farideh to be far, far from here when that came to pass. This would work, Lorcan told himself, tearing the portal open once again. Everything would be all right, and he'd have plenty of time to figure out how to take the next step without falling into the dragon's mouth.

6

FARIDEH WOKE AT THE SOUND OF THE DOOR LATCH, THE FEEL OF HAVILAR sitting down on the bed, her boots dropping to the floor—*thud, thud*. Farideh blinked, her eyes burning even in the dim light of the sun rising behind thick clouds. Her head felt as if it were made of lead.

"If Mehen asks," Havilar whispered, "I was here all night long."

Farideh tried to agree, but her voice wouldn't come. She swallowed against a swollen throat.

"That's a fair deal," Havilar protested. "It's not like I've told him *or* Brin about all the times you snuck out to see Lorcan—or even that those were *his* bootprints in the garden." She leaned over Farideh. "Besides it's going to be ages before we can . . . Holy gods," she said. "What's the matter with you?"

Farideh shook her head. Her eyes burned. Her throat ached. Her skin felt raw. She sat up, and the effort of it made her arms tremble under her. "I don't feel well," she whispered.

Havilar scooted back to the edge of the bed. "You don't look well." She reached forward, as if to test the skin of Farideh's forehead.

The shaking came again, up her arms, then all through her, as if she were bitterly cold. But if anything, she was warm. "G-get M-Mehen, p-please."

Whether Havilar raced off and returned even faster with their father, or Farideh only imagined it, dozing in between, she couldn't say. She seemed to blink and then there was Mehen's smoothly scaled hand holding her cheek. "Havi, get water and tell the nearest doorjack to fetch someone."

"I don't feel well," Farideh said.

"You'll be all right," Mehen assured her, and pulled the blankets up from where she'd kicked them away.

She seemed to blink again, and there was a woman, with her dark hair cropped short as a boy's, leaning over her, a medallion of Tymora dangling from her neck in front of Farideh's face. The blankets were kicked down to the foot of the bed again. The healer held open one of Farideh's eyes.

"I can't be sure," she said. "I've never examined a tiefling before. Are you sure this is all . . . approved?"

"Lord Crownsilver will convey his highest regards," Constancia said.

"Oh!" the healer said. She dropped her voice. "This is . . . is this *her*?"

"What's the matter with her?" Mehen said.

The healer felt Farideh's throat, her pulse in her wrist. "Is she usually warm? It seems as if they would be."

"*If* she were human," Constancia said tersely, "what would you say?"

The healer dropped Farideh's wrist. "Shaking fever." Mehen cursed.

"What's the cure?" Constancia asked. "What does it cost?"

"It's not worth curing," the healer said dismissively. "I don't know what god would bother."

"*Tiamash*," Mehen snarled. Constancia set a hand on his arm.

"The patient is worth curing," she said.

"Oh, that's not it," the healer said. "The disease—it won't kill her. Only a very bad case in a very weak person will do that. She's young. I assume she's healthy? And . . . well, I have no idea how severe it is, given that she isn't human—her skin might always be so hot, her pulse might always be so quick. Who knows?" She shrugged. "But even a bad case, she should be fine after a month's bed rest."

"A *month*?" Constancia cried.

"You should quarantine the house, for at least a day or two."

"Havi's had it," Mehen said. "As have I. Sent Farideh to the neighbors' right away and she never came down with it. *Karshoj*."

Blurry memories of Criella, the village midwife's little cottage, sleeping on a mat by a strange fire. Slipping letters scrawled on dry leaves to Havilar through the window, and getting swatted when she was caught. She closed her eyes again.

"Brin and I, too." Constancia looked at Mehen. "But the servants. We'll have to delay. Until the afternoon—see if anyone else has it."

"There's a tea you can brew to help when the fever gets too high and to calm the shaking," the healer said. "The fever will crest and fall regularly until everything returns to its balance—let her sweat, but if she starts to act mad or wild, someone should give her the tea."

"Can she travel?" Mehen asked, as if he knew the answer.

"Oh, I shouldn't try it," the healer said. "Sailing, maybe. Perhaps if you could afford a berth in one of the better ships across the Inland Sea? Although I hear it's growing less and less safe. Pirates," she said.

Constancia thanked her and walked her out the door, while Mehen pulled the blankets up once more. Farideh sat up, and he tucked Havilar's pillows behind her so that she could rest against them, her horns curling over their edge.

"If I could have known, I would have let you just catch it right alongside your sister," Mehen said.

"It's probably better," she said.

Mehen shook his head. "Brin'll go anyway. He's bound and determined. We have to find a way to convince him to delay a few tendays—"

"That isn't going to work," Farideh said. "Just . . . leave me here. I'll stay in bed. Give the tea to the maids or the cook or something. I'm sure it's not a v-very . . ." She clamped her mouth shut as she started shaking all over again. Mehen watched her grimly.

"Try again. We're not leaving you behind."

Farideh waited until the shaking passed, until her muscles relaxed and she could ease into the pillows once more. "It *is* probably better. Who knows what would happen if . . . things took over . . . while we were in the middle of traveling?"

Mehen's nostrils flared, his tongue fluttering behind his bared teeth. "Is that worse than having it take over in the middle of Cormyr's capital?"

"I can handle it here. I've been handling it. If everything is quiet and peaceful and . . . stable, I can handle it. But if you take me out into the middle of the war—"

"You might not be able to." He rubbed his hands over his face. "If I leave you here, and something happens . . ."

"I'll be fine."

"Not to you." Mehen looked up at her. "It's going to be dangerous. I don't want to take *either* of you, but if it comes to it . . . Havi won't stay behind."

"And Brin won't reconsider," Farideh said. "And you can't leave him either. It's all right."

"He's not my son," Mehen said. "But he doesn't have anyone else."

Farideh sat up and took her father's hand. "Maybe he'll spare the coin to make certain we can stay in touch. Make sendings. It's better than nothing."

He gave her a sad look. "I've been thinking a lot about what comes next—and you or your sister may well leave someday soon. But I don't want to part from you like this. I don't want you thinking we're going off merrily and leaving you behind."

Maybe you should, Farideh thought. But Mehen's expression didn't change. She leaned forward and hugged him. "I know," she said. Because even if she didn't fit, even if she made the wrong choices and broke all their hearts beyond repair, they were still her family. "I almost wish I'd had it when you and Havilar did."

Mehen snorted and rubbed her back. "You wished it back then too. Felt left out, if I recall, and cottage-crazed. But sick as it might make you, you'll be better off than you would have been as a girl." He stroked her hair. "I'll get them to make you a bowl of broth and send someone out for that tea."

Farideh sniffed and shut her burning eyes. "Will you come back after?" she asked. "Keep me company until you have to leave?"

Mehen chuckled. "And tell you stories of the Battle of Arambar's Gulch?"

"That was Havi's favorite," Farideh said, smiling. "I liked 'Clever Nala and the Ten Thousand Shadows.'" She felt herself dozing again. "And you'd say she would be proud to have such clever descendants, even though we're not."

She felt Mehen's jaw ridge brush against the crown of her head as she started to nod off. "You are," he said. "You always were."

Farideh woke again to someone shaking her foot, sometime later when the light was fading outside. A lamp shone on Havilar crouched at the foot of the bed.

"You're not supposed to be here," Farideh said hoarsely.

"What are you going to do?" Havilar said. "Tattle on me, rattlebones? How are you?"

"I think this is how corpses feel," Farideh said. "Do you remember being this sick?"

"Not much—I forget about it. I remember getting yelled at for trying to talk to you, only Mehen couldn't yell. And the shaking part—that's the *worst*. No blades for a month." Her tail scraped across the carpet with an agitated sound. "I can't believe you're not coming," she said sadly. "I was sort of looking forward to it. Like old times, for once."

"I can't get up to tattle on you, I certainly can't ride a horse."

Havilar snorted. "Mehen says there'll be sendings. At least we can talk."

"No swats for leaf-letters," Farideh said weakly.

"Did you get swatted? Ugh—Criella *and* shaking fever. *That's* the worst." Havilar smiled. "I still think Mehen might change his mind. He doesn't want to leave you."

"What will you do then?"

All the cheer went out of Havilar, and she watched Farideh, worried, worried, worried for a moment. "I don't know," she admitted. "What should I do?"

Convince Brin it's a bad idea, a dangerous idea, Farideh thought. It's not your fight. Stay. Don't go.

"Just stay safe," Farideh said. "Please, please, please stay safe."

Havilar bit her lip. She came around the bed, holding a silver chain in her hand. The medallion of Selûne that Tam Zawad had given Farideh so many years ago. Havilar tucked one end behind Farideh's neck and fixed the clasp.

"No," Farideh protested. "You might need it."

"*I'll* be with Mehen and Brin, and *pothac* Constancia who will *definitely* chop up any devils or whatever who show their faces," Havilar said. "*You* need it." She planted a kiss between her sister's horns. "If you die of this fever, I will *never* forgive you."

It was an old joke, but Farideh didn't laugh. She squeezed Havilar's forearm. "If you die because you decided to fight a Shadovar army by yourself, I'll never forgive you either."

"As if it matters," Havilar snorted. "I'll be back before daybreak. You'll see."

• • •

HELINDRA'S RECEIVING ROOM was sweltering, the fire built high to stave off the chill the rain brought, despite it being the heart of summer. Brin kept his collar laced, out of spite, more than anything. Helindra stood close to the fire, just beside the portrait of her younger self, waiting for Brin to crack. They'd been sitting like that for long, uncomfortable breaths—long enough for Brin not to care anymore what intangible benefit he lost by speaking first.

"It's an *errand*," he said. "For the Crown. I can't say anymore."

"You can't," Helindra said, "or you won't?"

"Both."

Helindra stepped from the fireplace, tapping her way to the chair beside Brin. "I recall, once, you were a sweet child. An obedient child. You used to ask your father's permission to sit quietly beside him. What happened to that boy, Aubrin?"

"I'm fairly certain you trained it out of me," Brin said. "You wanted my obedience to you, obedience to my duty, and the willingness to turn on any and everyone else." He set the cup of wine down. "And I was *never* that boy. You can't have it all ways, Aunt Helindra."

"With a less mouthy child, I could have. Your mother's bad blood, I'm sure."

Brin clenched his jaw, but he stood and helped his elderly aunt to sit. "With a less cold-hearted caretaker, perhaps I might have suited. You never gave me a reason to love you."

"Food and shelter, an education, and a place within the royal palace," Helindra said. "Yes, yes, I've been terribly cruel. Are you taking your doxy with you?"

"Havilar," Brin said, "Constancia, and Mehen will accompany me."

"Of course you're taking my Constancia," she said. "What about the spare?"

"Farideh isn't well," Brin said. A pang of guilt stopped the thought that Farideh had thrown another stone in his path—she hadn't done anything to get sick. "She'll be staying in the tallhouse while we're gone. I want your word, your binding word, that you won't try and turn her out. The tallhouse is mine, and she is my guest. She stays there as long as she likes."

Helindra sniffed. "Why would I turn her out? That only makes it look as if I care. As if she's a problem that can't be dealt with in a civilized fashion. Honestly, Aubrin," she added. "We're not *Ambershields*, for heaven's sakes."

"I want your solemn word."

Helindra eyed him a long moment, then smiled. "You have my most solemn word, the tiefling will not be removed, nor asked to leave, by myself or any agent of the Crownsilver family." She brought the signet ring she wore on her right hand to her thin lips and kissed it. "Satisfied?"

No, Brin thought. Not at all. "Why did you say it that way? Are you planning to force someone else to 'remove her'?"

"Don't jump at ordinary shadows. I leave room for the Crown to do as they like. If she does something to break the law? If Raedra decides she's done trying to wait you out? If the war wizards wish to have her moved to someplace less conspicuous? Well, you can hardly ask me to account for all of that. I'm an old woman, not an archwizard."

Brin stared back, sure he was missing something, sure Helindra had outmaneuvered him. Wondering, too, if he ought to wring the same sort of promises from Raedra before he left . . . But no—they had to go, and soon. The longer he delayed, the harder it would be to track Irvel, and the more likely it would be that someone would detain him.

"Thank you," he said finally. His great-aunt inclined her head. Brin stood. "You must excuse me—we're leaving first thing in the morning." Helindra reached out and took his hand in her own gnarled one.

"Do be cautious, Aubrin," Helindra said. "They say it is a layer of the Hells come to Faerûn between here and and the borderlands."

Brin froze and gave her a practiced, puzzled look. "Who said I'm going to the borderlands?"

Helindra patted his hand. "If you think anyone had to, Aubrin, you are slow as well as impudent. Stay safe."

• • •

BRYSEIS KAKISTOS WATCHED as Havilar and the others packed up their bags and loaded horses in the dark hours of the morning. She watched as Farideh's fever built and broke, built and broke. If there was any time to test her, it was now.

Not the least because now the twins were separated and Bryseis Kakistos would have to decide which to follow. After so many months in the tallhouse where her great-great-granddaughters had had the courtesy to remain for the months while she gathered her strength and searched for the answers, such an inconvenience grated. She'd followed Havilar for long enough to make her later search simpler, and drifted back to the tallhouse to wait for the fever to crest once more.

The ghost shifted, made her eyes focus on the plane before her. The room she stood in was empty, but a line of mortals passed by the door, one after another like drops of blood falling off an altar—pass . . . pass . . . pass. She drifted through them, noting the bags, the packages. The servants, all leaving. Bryseis Kakistos swept through the house, up through the floors, through the dust and mouse droppings and horsehair packed between. She found the bedroom, where two more maids stood, crowding the doorway.

Beyond, Farideh moaned softly.

"It's not right," the maid on the right, a middle-aged human with curling brown hair, said.

"It's what Lady Crownsilver ordered," the one on the left said.

"She's ill."

"It's a fever—she'll survive."

"What if she were your daughter? Would you leave her alone, fevered and shaking?" The older maid shook her head. "She can't even get herself downstairs safely."

"If she were my daughter, I'd have the proper shame to have done something about it, long before she was grown and fevered," the other maid said bluntly. "Don't know how you can lie down with a tiefling and be surprised by what comes of it."

The first maid glared at her companion. "Did you think her mother might have had the taint? No way to know."

Bryseis Kakistos drifted through the two maids, sending the chill of the grave through their hearts. Even if she agreed with them in a sense—the twins were nothing but an error—Farideh and Havilar were still her progeny. They were due a measure of respect, stolen though it might be.

"Have to make sure the jacks all turned their mattresses," the first maid said. "Tuck her blankets back around her and make sure there's a pitcher nearby." She looked at Farideh once more and shook her head. "Poor lamb."

The second maid watched her go, then turned back to Farideh with nothing but distaste written on her face. She threw the blanket lazily over the tiefling woman. Bryseis Kakistos watched the woman's eyes light on the amulet tangled in Farideh's purplish-black hair. She glanced at the door, reaching for the bit of silver.

Bryseis Kakistos was not gentle as she slipped into the distracted woman's mind. The maid's thoughts twisted as if trying to escape the ghost's presence, but she was no match for the Brimstone Angel. The ghost forced the woman's consciousness down, as if forcing her into dark, cold water, and much as if she were drowning, the woman's consciousness struggled violently, then went still.

A thrill went through the ghost as she flooded the maid's body. It had been ages since she'd succeeded in possessing someone so completely—since before she'd been torn apart. But even as she flexed the maid's hands, dreaming of what she could wreak with a physical form, the effort of it drained her strength as steadily as a knife slash to a waterskin.

Farideh's skin was pale and clammy, her eyes drooping and unfocused. The fever gripped her hard, but the protection spell still crackled and snapped as Bryseis Kakistos drew close. She grimaced—no hoping that sickness might weaken the magic that shielded Farideh from the eyes of devils and the powers of Bryseis Kakistos.

So close, she thought, and yet so far.

"Can you hear me, Bryseis?" the ghost asked.

Farideh rolled toward her, her eyes suddenly focusing. "What mockery is this?" she said, in a voice that was all-too-familiar to Bryseis Kakistos. "Mirror and magic," the trapped fragment of Bryseis Kakistos's soul mumbled, unencumbered by the living soul it hid behind. "What mockery is this?"

"One we can remedy," the ghost said. "What is the secret of Asmodeus?"

"Asmodeus . . ." Farideh mumbled. "Don't trust him . . . He doesn't lie, but he does . . ."

"I know that," Bryseis Kakistos said. "*We* know that. What is the secret? One of us knows how to defeat him—is it you?"

Farideh tossed again. "Ask Caisys . . . he knows too much . . . Alyona . . ."

Bryseis Kakistos drifted back, away from the tiefling. Caisys had been one of the warlocks she'd brought to the coven that had helped raise Asmodeus to godhood—a loyal enough follower, but not one whose ambitions had ever risen to match Bryseis's. He would have been happy enough fornicating his way across the multiverse and never again daring anything greater. He wouldn't know anything about Asmodeus's apotheosis—the soul piece was thinking of something else.

And Alyona . . .

The name fizzled in her thoughts, lost in one of the missing fragments, no doubt.

"There is a weakness in the god of sin," the ghost tried again. "We know it. We can punish him for his treachery. We can unseat him."

Farideh stilled, smiled. "You're forgetting things," she said sadly, and Bryseis Kakistos wasn't certain it was her own soul fragment that spoke. "I told you this was dangerous. Who trucks with the god of sin? Who tries to outwit him?"

Bryseis Kakistos slapped Farideh across the face with the maid's hand, hard enough that she lost control of that arm, leaving it to dangle, slack and meaty at the body's side. A red welt rose on Farideh's cheek, and the glazed look returned to her eyes. No, the ghost thought. No, no, no.

"What is the secret?" she all but shouted. But the fragment of herself and whatever might have stirred with it were both gone, drifting once more in the cocoon of Farideh's self.

Calm, the ghost told herself. Patient. But already the edges of her soul were fizzling and fraying, overtaxed by action and anger. She would have to try again, after she'd rested, after she'd had time to regain herself.

The soul piece hadn't known what she was talking about—because it was addled as well? Because it wasn't a conscious part? Because it just didn't know? Bryseis Kakistos had no way to tell yet, and little time to spare. The farther away Havilar got, the more difficult it would be to track her down.

Who trucks with the god of sin? Bryseis Kakistos thought. Who tries to outwit him?

The maid's consciousness stirred.

Havilar first, Bryseis Kakistos decided, turning the maid toward the door. The mind inside wriggled and bucked, and the ghost had little choice but to loose her failing grip on the feeble creature, slipping out of the body.

But before she did, she took what strength she had left and focused it tightly on a cluster of veins at the base of the woman's skull, pinching the center one just enough to slow the blood. As she faded from the room, from the plane, casting her consciousness out into the ether, Bryseis Kakistos felt a petty sort of triumph. When the maid dropped dead in a few hours, her crimes against the ghost and her line would be avenged. A pity she would never know it.

7

29 Flamerule, the Year of the Nether Mountain Scrolls (1486 DR)
Suzail, Cormyr

FARIDEH STIRRED TO THE SOUND OF KNOCKING, BUT AN ETERNITY SEEMED to yawn before the knocks became real, and not a fevered dream, and by then, they were quite insistent. She crawled out of the bed, her arms shaking with the effort. Her skin still felt raw and aching with fever, as if someone had scraped away the outermost layer, and the touch of the dressing robe's fabric rasped against it. She ought to lie back down.

But the knocks became violent and frenzied enough that she imagined the whole tallhouse shaking under her feet—someone might be in trouble. Someone might be hurt and looking for help. She only noticed the pulse of the Hells matching the pace of the knocking as she reached the door, yanking it wide—and dimly, she realized if it were trouble, she was about to bring the war wizards right back to the tallhouse.

Rain-chilled air swept in. The man on the other side of the door seemed a tower in armor, stretching up to the storm clouds. She blinked carefully—that was the fever, still burning in her brain. She dropped her gaze from the water streaming down his helmet to his chest, to the purple dragon emblazoned there.

"Well met," she heard herself rasp. The man stared at her, as if in shock. Behind him someone made a sharp little sound, and Farideh realized there was a woman in his shadow.

She was lovely in such a Cormyrean way—so lovely. And so sharp, Farideh thought. The woman stared down Farideh as if she could slay her with a gaze. If she hadn't been so tired, Farideh thought, she might have blushed under that stare. Another lady, dark-haired, stood beside her, holding a canopy over her head and staring at Farideh.

"Well," the woman said in clipped tones that belied a barely leashed fury. "You're a brazen one aren't you, just . . . answering the door, simple as that, all tumbled about."

Farideh swallowed against her aching throat. "I have to. No one else is here. Would you rather stand on the doorstep?"

The woman flushed. "Just tell Lord Crownsilver I'm here to speak with him."

"I told you, I'm the only one here," Farideh said. "He's gone."

"Gone? Gone where?"

Farideh rubbed her head. "He and Havi and Mehen and Constancia and . . ." The servants—flashes of them passing through the room while she lay sick and shaking, watching her and walking away, leaving the water and bread by the bedside and cursing Helindra and walking away. Farideh looked up at the woman. "I should warn you. I'm ill."

"Havi?" The woman somehow went even stiffer. "Ah. You're not . . . her."

"No. I'm Farideh. She's my sister. My twin." She frowned at the woman. Who in Cormyr knew Havilar? Her head pounded harder, her unwanted powers surging with every throb. The woman's face slipped through her memory, refusing to hold still. "Do I know you?"

The guardsman cleared his throat. "You are in the presence of Her Highness, Princess Raedra Obarskyr."

And at that Farideh did blush. "I didn't realize—"

Farideh suspected Raedra Obarskyr never did anything so vulgar as roll her eyes, but in that moment, she also suspected she mightily wished to. "Never mind. We've had our little comedy of errors." She pursed her mouth again. "If my betrothed is not here, then . . . I suppose I will just . . . He didn't say where he was going?"

"East," Farideh said. "To find the prince."

Raedra's mouth tightened. "The crown prince is dead."

"I don't think he believes that."

"Well, then more the fool him," Raedra said, with an anger that made Farideh remember that this was her father they were talking about.

"I'm sorry for your loss," Farideh said. "I think Brin means well." The princess looked away.

"Tell Lord Crownsilver, when he returns—*if* he returns," Raedra said, "that I do not care what he means or what he says he means."

The throb in Farideh's head grew sharp as a stake through the back of her skull. She kept her eyes locked on Raedra, tried hard not to flinch as the powers of Asmodeus grabbed hold of her mind. The princess kept speaking, but the roar in Farideh's ears snatched away the meaning.

". . . and *then* tell him he can do it again," she said ferociously, as the colors of her soul bloomed in front of Farideh's eyes as if she'd stared into the sun—purple and gray and yellow, "with the opposite end. Good day."

She turned on her heel and stormed off, the guard and her lady with the canopy sprinting after. Farideh started to shake, the fever unwilling to share its hold on her. She leaned against the doorjamb and watched the flickering lights of the guard, the princess . . . the lady with the canopy, whose soul lights were intertwined with spots and threads of deepest shadow.

Farideh blinked—she'd seen those marks before . . . but always on people who served the goddess of loss, Shar. The noblewoman looked back at Farideh, no sign of her alliances in her curious gaze.

"W-wait," Farideh said, but it came out a broken whisper. The Sharran lady disappeared into the Princess of Cormyr's carriage, and Farideh could only imagine what terrible things were about to happen in the Forest Kingdom.

• • •

DAHL STALKED THROUGH the streets of Suzail, Brin's note crushed to wet pulp in his fist. At least he'd never have to read it again—*I cannot say for certain when I'll return.*

Where is your stlarning head? Dahl wanted to shout. Running off, into a muddy, bloody battlefield that stretched from here to the Great Stlarning Glacier, to find the crown prince's corpse was a fool's errand—a fool's *fool's* errand—and Brin should have been wise enough to know it. Even before Dahl had left the inn, he'd made the sending to Tam—they needed to cut Brin out, now, pull him back to Waterdeep if possible, and get his missions under another Harper's command.

Under, the High Harper's reply came, Dahl's command. Which had sent Dahl sprinting through the rain and up the Promenade, in the hopes of catching Brin before he left. He kept an eye out for him or his carriage the whole way to the tallhouse. No sign.

The iron gate slammed back against its latch, and Dahl realized the doorguard was gone. "Oghma's bloody papercuts," he muttered, and hammered at the door himself. There was no answer. He tried again, and again. Nothing.

Dahl muttered a few more curses and kicked the boot scraper. If Brin was gone, Dahl would need the notes that had to be hiding in his study . . . or *somewhere* in the tallhouse. He considered the street beyond the stone fence, the pouring rain. Stormcloaks pulled high on every passer-by. Guards tucked under the eaves. Nobody watching too closely.

Thank the gods, he thought, as he slipped around to the back of the tallhouse. Cursing and stomping around like an idiot—be only fair if you got nabbed.

Dahl dropped over the garden wall, landing in a flooded flowerbed that sent mud splashing up his breeches. He cursed and waded out of the foxglove, stamping his feet in the water swirling over the paving. Stlarning Brin, stlarning rains, stlarning—

A woman stood in the middle of the garden—one of the twins—dark hair and white shift plastered against her body and steaming faintly.

"Well met," Dahl called. She was breathing hard—whichever of them it was—and shaking as if the rain chilled her through. And steaming—definitely steaming. "Farideh?"

She looked back over one shoulder, turning slowly, as if any faster would send her tumbling. "Mother of the moon," Dahl said. She looked like a ghost, all the blood sapped out of her skin, her eyes red-ringed and weeping. "What happened?"

"It's s-so *h-hot*," she said plaintively, the words shattering on her chattering jaw. "I can't . . . I can't . . ."

Dahl pulled his cloak off and threw it around her, over the soaked nightgown, over her goose-pimpled arms. "You're cold," he assured her, even though she tensed as if she would throw it back off. He held an arm around her shoulders "Come on. Where's Brin?"

"They left," she said, stumbling as he steered her into the parlor room. She was burning through the cloak. "To find the prince."

The tallhouse was silent and lifeless as a tomb. Farideh all but collapsed onto the settee, still shuddering violently.

"They left you alone? With a fever?"

"It c-comes and-nd g-goes . . ." she said, the words still fighting to get out of her. "I have to make it break. The rain . . . I have to find the princess."

Dahl cursed under his breath. She was burning up, and clearly delirious. "Stay here."

Down in the kitchen, he threw open every cabinet, one by one, raking out their meager contents, and swept the shelves. This might be burdock, that might be elm bark. Nothing was labeled and everything smelled faintly of fennel—he wouldn't know whether he was giving her something to break the fever or just seasonings in water.

"Where are all the servants!" he shouted at the empty tallhouse.

"You have to tell the princess." Farideh's urgent voice behind him made Dahl leap. Still shaking, still red-eyed and frantic looking. And chilled—the cloak trailed behind her on the stone floor where she'd let it drop, and the gown clung close and clammy to her skin.

Dahl looked over her horns. "Put the cloak on!"

"There's a worshiper of Shar holding her canopy and she doesn't know," Farideh went on. "You could tell her—then I wouldn't have to figure out how to see her. But it has to be soon. Now."

"Gods' books, put the cloak on," Dahl said, snatching it off the floor and tucking it back around her. He steered her over to the table. "Sit down, lay your head on the table. I'm finding you something to break the fever. Where are the servants?"

"Brin's aunt took them away," she said, her reply muffled against the arm beneath her head. "The cleric left something for the fever. A tea. But I can't find it."

"You saw a cleric? What do you have?"

"Shaking fever."

"They left you here alone with shaking fever." Dahl cursed again, suddenly remembering a wave of the illness laying him, his mother, half the hands, and most of the neighbors low when he was ten or so. "What is Brin *thinking?*"

"If they'd taken me, it would have been worse."

"And if they had stayed, it would have been better. Listen—what's the tea look like? Where have you searched?"

"I don't know." The shaking had passed, and she spoke smoothly now. "Mehen sent the doorjack for it . . . I drank a cup before they left. It wasn't in the bedroom. I couldn't find it here. It wasn't in the garden," she said with a little laugh.

Dahl grit his teeth. "Why is it every time I run into you, *somehow* you end up delirious, and I have to take care of you?"

Farideh lifted her head from the table. "Who's delirious?"

"You have to stand in the rain so you can tell a princess that there's a Sharran holding her canopy?" Dahl reminded her.

"*Yes*," she said. "Princess Raedra was here and the fever triggered the soul sight. One of her ladies-in-waiting is teeming with shadow marks. If the war wizards haven't spotted her, I'm not sure who could." She laid her head back down. "And the last time 'taking care of me' meant starting a *pothac* argument about whether the first time was something you were sorry enough about, so don't get too indignant there."

Dahl blinked. "There's a *Sharran* in the palace?"

"Worse—riding in the princess's carriage."

"Why was Raedra here?"

"Looking for Brin."

A door shut somewhere in the tallhouse. Dahl's hand went to his sword. "Stay here," he said to Farideh. But she was already up and moving toward the stairs. Dahl hardly had time to reach her before the shaking seized her again and nearly buckled her leg under her.

"You're sick," he told her, steering her back toward the table. "Just *be sick*."

"W-what if-f it's k-k . . . *k-karshoj!*" Farideh dropped back onto the bench.

"If it's the kidnappers, then I will lure them down here, and you can exhaust yourself slinging missiles at them. Deal?"

"Please," a new voice said from the stairs, "don't . . . don't attack me." A middle-aged woman with graying brown curls peeping out from under the hood of her stormcloak stood in the doorway, hands high and a basket hooked over one arm. "I've only come to drop off some food, make sure she's well enough. The cleric said it wasn't too severe, and we was ordered back to the castle." She eyed Dahl, hands still held high. "You're that Waterdhavian drow lord's equerry, saer, aren't you?"

Dahl decided the parts of the question that made him want to curse balanced out with the parts that made him feel for Vescaras. "I am. He sent me to collect some documents from Lord Crownsilver, only I've missed him, and I found the house empty and his guest delirious and soaked to the bone." He was sure Farideh glowered at him then. "Who's ordered you away?"

"The Lady Crownsilver, saer," the maid said. "She says if Lord Crownsilver's not in the house, then we won't be paid. Ordered everyone back to the castle or the country house." She shook her head. "I've had the shaking fever—won't get it again—and I don't care what her ladyship says, it isn't right to leave the girl ill and alone, even if . . ." She looked at Farideh for the first time. "Even if they brought a bit of trouble for the family."

Dahl did not say what he thought about the price of the Crownsilvers' good name. "Can you make her the tea she's supposed to drink and get her into something dry? Lord Ammakyl needs a receipt he left with Lord Crownsilver by mistake, and I need to fetch it."

"Of course," she said.

"Keep her busy," Dahl murmured to Farideh. She gave him a funny look, but he left the kitchen as if he were a man on a pressing errand and sprinted up the stairs. Brin's study was locked, but not so securely that Dahl couldn't pick it. He ignored the ledgers and actual receipts on the desk, and the locked drawers—they only served to distract from what was hidden in the room.

A bookshelf sat against one wall, dusty and disused as though it were only there for show. Dahl dropped to the floor and counted six fat volumes of Cormyrean history from the end. He pulled the leather-bound tome from its spot and laid it on the floor. The dust remained undisturbed, a clever illusion.

Inside the front cover of the book was a coded list—Brin's street-eyes and how to contact them. Marjana had had a similar list, woven into a series of false love notes kept at her bedside. Dahl skimmed the jumbled letters and wondered if the two Cormyrean agents—who did not, by necessity, know each other—had managed to overlap contacts. Whoever killed Marjana had to have known what she was, which might mean Brin was in danger as well.

Marjana had been watching a number of people, scattered throughout the city—most of them in places where Lord Aubrin Crownsilver had no reason to be. If there was indeed a Sharran plot in place, it would be hard to puzzle out how it could touch both Marjana and Brin.

Until Farideh spotted a Sharran waiting on his bride-to-be, Dahl thought. He shoved the book under his jerkin and, taking a piece of parchment from the desk for pretense, he hurried back downstairs, passing the shut bedroom door. He could hear the maid's voice from behind it, apologizing again for leaving.

Dahl paused in the entry—Lord Ammakyl's equerry ought to leave without another word. If he dawdled or—worse—insisted on staying, the maid would surely get the wrong idea and refuse to leave—or maybe call the watch. Instead he pulled the door open, intending to slam it hard enough to be heard in the upstairs bedroom.

"Well met?" a voice said from the other side. Dahl startled. A dragonborn man with dark gray scales and a row of bright silver piercings across the scaly ridges of his brow stood on the doorstep. Where Mehen was built like an ox, the dragonborn eyeing Dahl and fluttering his tongue nervously against the roof of his mouth was slim and long-limbed, sinuous as a silver dragon. A sturdy long sword hung, peace-bonded, at his side.

"Yes?" Dahl said, wary.

"My name is Kepeshkmolik Dumuzi," the man said, his Common accentless but stiff, "and I am looking for someone. Another dragonborn, and if you please, I was told he might reside here? He goes by Mehen, with no mention of his clan. Perhaps you know him?"

Dahl hesitated, glanced over Dumuzi's shoulder. Not a few people were standing in the street, murmuring to one another, eyes on the dragonborn.

"He's not here," Dahl said. "Can I leave a message?"

"It's personal," the dragonborn said. "When will he be back?"

"I'm afraid I don't know. He's gone on a journey of sorts. I suspect it will be a month or two at least." Piercings meant Djerad Thymar, Dahl recalled. The city that had exiled Mehen. "Are you a friend of his?"

Dumuzi sighed. "We have never met. Will he come back to this house?"

"If he comes back, yes."

"In a month or two?"

"Or more."

Dumuzi sighed again, and whatever his intentions toward Mehen, Dahl had to feel a little bad for the dragonborn—if Vescaras and Farideh stood out in Suzail, a dragonborn might as well be a sideshow. "There's a bit of a fashion these days," he said, "for dragonborn guardsmen. If you need to wait. I'm sure you could find employment."

Dumuzi looked at him as though he'd suggested he might caper naked in the streets for coin. "I am Kepeshkmolik," he said. "Thank you most kindly for your assistance. I hope I may return the favor some day."

"Well met, then." Dahl had nearly shut the door when Dumuzi spoke up once more. "What does he look like?" When Dahl didn't answer quickly enough, he clarified. "Clanless Mehen. What does he look like?"

Not a hunter's question, Dahl thought. There was a plea there, a sort of embarrassed quality, as if the dragonborn knew he shouldn't be asking such an indulgent question.

"Like a dragonborn," Dahl said, at a loss. Dumuzi glowered at him, and Dahl tried again. "Um, big. Very tall, very broad. His scales are a sort of bronze, but dull . . . so I guess yellowish-brown? Intimidating."

Dumuzi's nostrils flared as he sighed again, and shook his head. "Thank you very much, saer," he said, in a way that made Dahl suspect he hadn't answered the question at all. Putting it aside for the moment, he gave the door a stiff slam, then crept into the front parlor and crouched down behind a screen, Brin's codes open on his lap.

One leg had started to fall asleep by the time the maid finally finished and left. He unfolded himself stiffly and hurried back upstairs to find Farideh, dry and dressed and propped up in the bed, her wet hair braided and the blankets folded down.

"I thought you'd left," she said.

"Of course not. There are Sharrans in the palace, remember?" He pulled a chair closer to the bed. "What are we dealing with? A servant? A guard?"

"A noblewoman, I think," Farideh said.

Dahl frowned. "You're *positive* she's a Sharran."

"There isn't any mistaking it." Farideh blew out a breath. "You could get into the palace. You could just give Raedra a note. I'll write it even—I'll take the responsibility."

"Getting into the royal palace isn't simple," Dahl said.

"Neither are *you*," Farideh said. "So think of something."

Dahl considered. "They're starting to make arrangements for the crown prince's funeral. There's vendors and servants coming and going. I might be able to slip in with them. Where were the doorjacks quartered?"

"Upstairs," Farideh said. "Why?"

"We're going to hope they left some livery behind." He gave her the torn receipt and took a scribe's kit from his satchel. "Here—write the note. I'll see if they have what I need."

There was only a tabard with the Crownsilver's crest, kicked under the neatly made bed. Dahl hoped his own breeches wouldn't draw too much attention against the fine—if rumpled—uniform. He folded it neatly as he could and slipped it into the satchel. Downstairs, Farideh was fanning the drying ink with one hand.

"Can I leave these here with you?" Dahl asked, holding up Brin's documents. "I'll be back for them, assuming I'm not thrown in the dungeon."

She nodded at the small table beside the bed. "I expect I'm not supposed to ask what they are. 'Nothing interesting,' right?"

"You want to read them, you'll have to make them into Common first," Dahl said. He paused. "Did Brin ever bring anyone here? Someone who might have been a contact?"

She shook her head, and handed over the note for the princess. "You and Vescaras are the only Harper folks I've seen. Why? Is something wrong?"

"Several somethings," Dahl said. "Beginning with the fact that Brin has fled the city."

"He'll be all right," Farideh said. She smoothed her hands over the blankets in a nervous way.

"They'll *all* be all right," Dahl said. Except for Farideh. "That maid's not coming back, is she?"

"Doubtful. She spent half of the time explaining why she shouldn't have come this-s t-time." Her lips pressed white as another tremor took hold of her.

"Lie down," Dahl said. Watching Gods, he thought, you can't just leave her here—fevers and kidnappers and gods knew what next. "Is there someone else in the city? Someone who could come and sit with you?" Farideh gave him a dark look that not even Dahl could misread. "Lorcan?" he tried. "Could you call Lorcan down?"

She sighed and shut her eyes. "He shows up when he feels like it. You can leave me by myself, you know. Especially if you're coming right back for those uninteresting documents."

"Kidnappers," Dahl reminded her.

"Sharran in the palace," she returned, eyes still shut. "Stop arguing with me and go."

Dahl scowled at her. "When I come back and you're not here because those kidnappers took advantage of the fact you haven't got so much as a doorguard and figured you're close enough to being Havilar for their empoyer, I am not rescuing you."

"No one asked you to," Farideh pointed out. "And if you don't go soon, I will not come rescue *you* when Shadovar teleport into the palace right on top of you."

You *cannot* leave her here, Dahl thought. Not hardly able to walk. Not without a guard of some kind . . .

"Do you know if Mehen was expecting someone called Kepeshkmolik Dumuzi?" he asked.

"Another dragonborn? Not that I know of. What did he look like?"

"Dark gray scales. Bit skinny."

"Oh," Farideh said. "Maybe. I mean, he has a type." She bit her lip. "Mehen would have said something. He'd have to have. Did . . . this Dumuzi say anything . . . about why?"

"No," Dahl said. "But he's definitely not a kidnapper, and I don't get the feeling . . . You don't have a dragonborn brother or something right?"

Farideh snorted, as if he'd made a joke. "No," she said, noting his confusion again. "I am almost positive I don't."

Dahl smiled. "I would bet you a silver piece you do. Maybe you don't want to think about your father and some lonely dragonborn lady but—"

"Dahl," Farideh said. "Mehen doesn't sleep with women. So he doesn't get eggs on them. Keep your coin. He's not my brother."

"Oh." Several memories, snippets of knowledge seemed to reorder themselves at that revelation, as if Dahl had just realized he'd been looking at the world with his head thrown back. "'He has a type,'" he said, and cursed under his breath.

"Don't feel bad," Farideh said. "Most humans don't notice. Like they don't notice Sharrans—"

"Watching Gods, all right! I'm leaving!"

Dahl hurried from the tallhouse, annoyed and worried and embarrassed all at once. You're going to have to come back, he thought. You can't leave her like that. He scanned the Promenade from the steps.

Kepeshkmolik Dumuzi stood in the lee of the building opposite the tallhouse, an adventurer's club all shut up in the early hours. He was counting coins in one scaly hand. Kepeshkmolik or not, Dahl thought, he could take a little pay.

"Well met, again," Dahl said, coming to stand beside him. He held up a silver piece. "If you wouldn't mind watching from the doorstep for an hour or two, you can consider that favor discharged."

• • •

THE SERVANTS HANGING the new banners had to stand on a pair of precarious ladders to reach the anchors, handing down the purple and gold and red gonfalons celebrating the marriage of an Obarskyr and hauling up the gray-and-purple blazon of the fallen crown prince.

Because he's dead, Raedra told herself, watching the second gonfalon drawn up the wall of the Royal Court's public entrance. Your father is dead. You will never see him again.

It didn't bring the flood of tears it should have—there was only an empty, hollow feeling in her chest, as if someone had plucked out something vital and forgotten to replace it. As if she still had to find the thing that fit into the hole she had there so that she could realize her father's death had happened.

She shook her head and turned from the changing decorations. Either you're cold or you're mad, she told herself. But at least it isn't both.

King Foril came to stand beside her, leaning heavily on a carved wooden cane, and trailed by a gaggle of courtiers—and Ganrahast. These days, always Ganrahast. The Royal Magician considered her stonily. She made a polite curtsy to her grandfather— he reached out and took her hand in his gnarled one, squeezing her tight. "My dear, my dear," he said, his voice thick. He leaned against her as he considered the banners.

"They were Emvar's," he said, his grief echoing through the words, as if it had made Foril into a cavern, another empty thing. "They said we should make others. But these . . . these will do. Irvel would have appreciated the honor—he always loved his uncle. Always."

"I'm so sorry, Your Majesty," she said.

"Child, I'm the one who should be sorry." He squeezed her hand down to the bone. "They told me I shouldn't go to war—'let your son go instead, he is nearly king.'" He shook his head. "I don't think Irvel ever understood what it was that war brings upon a man. I have been a long time hiding from it, shifting alliances, twisting borders. And don't give me that 'Your Majesty' business, not now."

"Granddad," Raedra said softly, too softly, she hoped, for the courtiers to hear. Among them, her erstwhile granduncle-in-law, Lord Turin Huntcrown and her soon-to-be granduncle-in-law, Lord Pheonard Crownsilver, Helindra's younger brother. Two men before whom she did not want to show weakness of any stripe. "It's just protocol."

"It's a travesty at a time like this, cheeky bird," he said, and Raedra smiled at the old nickname. "Have you been to see your brother?"

"This morning," Raedra said. And it had not driven the tears from her either. The bandaged man lying in the bed, tended by healers and clerics, fed and washed and made to piss through what means, Raedra didn't dare ask for her brother's own privacy—well, that was Baerovus, and yet it was not. "I will go again after I sit with mother. She was sleeping when I went earlier."

Foril patted her arm. "It's good, how you see to your family. How you understand . . ." He trailed off, looking up at the banners. "These were my brother's. I never thought I would grieve the way I did that day. Such a fool, such a fool."

Raedra hugged the king of Cormyr as he'd wished, as if he were just her grandfather, and didn't care what the watching nobles thought. "You should rest, Granddad."

He sighed. "I have to hear grievances from the nobility now," he said. "It's not all silks and polish and hunts, being king." He gave her a stern look. "Being queen, either. How is . . . Aubrin?"

He'd nearly said Emvar, she was sure of it. Raedra smiled sadly, remembering the addled tiefling's words and wishing she could slap sense into Aubrin. "Most grieved. He's gone to the Crownsilvers' country home, to recover himself." She shot Pheonard a steely look. "Isn't that right?"

His hazel eyes flicked nervously to Foril. "I hadn't heard, Your Highness."

"Whatever for?" Foril asked. "He should be here. He should be with *you*."

"We grieve in our own ways . . . I must go," she told Foril. "Please excuse me, Your Majesty. Your Lordships." Ganrahast met her eye, and she nodded at him. Whatever his faults, he was more loyal than anyone to her grandfather, and would keep the vultures at bay.

"None of that, cheeky bird." Foril kissed her forehead. "Go and see if your ladies can make you laugh."

Raedra curtsied again, but she stayed where she was, watching her grandfather walk away, trailed by sycophantic noblemen. Ganrahast paused, watching Raedra.

"Where are your guards, Highness?" he asked.

"I'm sure they're around," Raedra said.

"Raedra," the Royal Magician said sternly. "Now, more than ever, you need to keep close to your guards. We've lost one Obarskyr too many this tenday, and two more . . ." He trailed off. "War Wizard Barcastle is watching you this afternoon. Should you need anything, simply ask for her. Go draft some guards from the shrine and have them escort you back to the palace, please."

Raedra said nothing, but once Ganrahast had turned to follow Foril, she passed the long hall hung with mourning banners and entered the Shrine of the Four Swords as directed.

Another banner hung from the center of the circular room. Over benches pushed together and draped in black cloth, her father's ceremonial armor lay, in place of his body. A dozen nobles stood around the display, sniffling and weeping into their handkerchiefs, and crowding the close space. Several stopped Raedra to give their condolences, and she had to fight her way through them to the guard station off the center room.

Four Purple Dragons stood guard over the four Swords of State and the makeshift shrine to the fallen crown prince. One, a grizzled fellow on the edge of retirement, saluted as Raedra entered. His comrades followed suit.

"I need an escort back to the palace. Or a sword to carry," Raedra added dryly. "Your choice, lionar." The Purple Dragon regarded her gravely. The next shift was coming, another Purple Dragon explained, could she wait a few songs until then? Raedra settled herself on a bench and accepted a mug of mulled wine from the guards.

The Four Swords of State rested on a simple wooden stand, out of the way while mourners paid their respects to the fallen crown prince. Ansrivarr, the Blade of Memory, the greatsword taken up by the first king of Cormyr. Symylazarr, the Font of Honor, on which all oaths of fealty to the Dragon Throne were sworn. Rissar, the Wedding Blade, on which she and Lindon had sworn their vows.

And Orbyn, the Edge of Justice.

Raedra eyed the keen edge of the long sword, the blade of kings. The blade that had slain Thauglorimorgorus, the Purple Dragon, the Black Doom of the Forest Country. The blade that had slain Lindon Huntcrown.

Some mornings, when Raedra woke too early, she would come down to the Shrine of the Four Swords and sit quietly across from Orbyn's plinth. She never visited Lindon's grave, but here she could grieve a little without anyone asking her what she was thinking.

At Orbyn's side, the jewel-studded hilt of Rissar winked merrily in the flickering lights, as if it were laughing at her. Normally, it rested in its own antechamber, off to the right of Orbyn's, and Raedra didn't have to look at the short sword or consider whether she had broken the vows she spoke over it, whether Rissar had failed her and Cormyr by failing to catch the falseness of her wedding. Whether Lindon's death had been the curse or the blessing of the Wedding Blade.

"Highness?" A Purple Dragon, a hard-faced younger woman, leaned over her. "The new watch is here. Shall we return you to your quarters?"

They walked from the Royal Court and back to the royal palace, passing servants and nobles and guards and war wizards—some sniffling, some red-eyed, some sobbing openly and wantonly. Raedra stared ahead, still hollow, still empty of tears.

Your father is dead, she thought again. Your brother lies, a broken vessel. He may never wake. They may never take those banners down.

Her heart ached, as if she were trying to squeeze the tears from a stone.

When Lindon died, she'd been just as hollow, just as hard. But that time she'd spilled all her tears out at the beginning—the moment she knew she'd lost him. She'd huddled in the dark of his room and wept and wept and wept without ever making a sound. Streams and streams of tears, a river of snot, a most unladylike mourning, all into the folds of her nightdress. Perhaps she'd poured all her tears out that night, because when Lindon had finally died, she had only sat, calm and quiet, and after, everyone said her heart must be made of ice.

And now they'll say it all again, she thought, reaching her rooms. Maybe they were right. The Purple Dragons stationed themselves just inside the door.

A flurry of maids and jacks darted throughout the rooms—carrying bright arrangements of flowers away, folding up her cheerful summer dresses and hanging new-made mourning in their place. Hiding every sign that this month had been meant to be a joyous one in the House of Obarskyr. Raedra eyed the dark red roses on the table beside the windowsill, and wondered how they'd ever come by enough to look suitably somber. The shade was far from in favor, with Shar's dark empire ever on the horizon.

"Oh!" one of the maids squeaked, spotting her. "Oh, Your Highness!" Every maid in the room froze, deer before a lioness—every maid but Nell.

"Your Highness," her lady's maid said, curtsying deeply. "You have my—nay, you have all of our deepest condolences. The crown prince was dear to all of the Forest Kingdom, but dearest to his family and there is none within Suzail who would gainsay that."

"Thank you," Raedra said. Every maid's eye was rubbed red and puffy. "Your kind words are a balm."

"You also have our deepest apologies—we'd intended to be finished before you returned. We never meant to have the room in such disarray—"

"It's quite all right," Raedra said. "If my father's death and my brother's current state aren't enough to relax protocol, what is?" She smiled wanly, and the little squeaky maid—Everly? Eveline?—burst into fresh tears. Nell guided Raedra into one of the chairs near the window, and offered to send one of the jacks for warmed wine and honeyed bread, and another for her retinue.

Raedra thanked her—the woman's nervous energy set her on edge. Something to do, some way to *help* would ease that, even if Raedra wanted nothing to eat and no one to talk to. She wondered, distantly, if Varauna had wept, and imagined her first applying the paint to make it look as if she had, most delicately, and then imagined her weeping as messily and thoroughly as a mourner in a play—beating her breast and tearing her hair, all dramatics.

Raedra's mother had wept that way—though only once the doors were closed, and before Ganrahast had brought her the means to sleep through the night. The Royal Magician had offered Raedra the same potion, but she'd turned it down. The idea of not being able to rouse if someone should come hunting for her . . . well, that was where too many of her nightmares began.

The wine and bread came, carried in by a jack in sore need of a comb and a press for his tabard. She didn't comment on it—if Foril called her 'cheeky bird' in front of courtiers, and the maids could clean while she sat and watched, then Raedra wasn't about to dress down a mourning fellow who hadn't pressed his tabard right.

"Thank you," she said, as he set the tray on the table beside her.

"Of course, Your Highness," he said. He lingered a moment too long, and Raedra looked up to see him pull a folded note from under his tabard. "This came for you as well. It seemed very urgent."

Raedra took the note, frowning at him. "Are you new?"

"Yes, my lady," he said.

"In the future," Raedra said, unfolding the letter, "when some noble hands you a note for me and tells you it's urgent, it isn't. It's an ill-advised attempt at a love note or some other nonsense. If it's urgent, they will hand it to . . ."

She trailed off. It wasn't a love note. It wasn't a scrap of flattery or sloppy blackmail or someone's cousin's brilliant business venture.

I must warn you, the scrawl of ink read. *When you visited, I saw the mark of Shar on one of your ladies-in-waiting. It may be nothing, but I have never seen that mark on anyone but a villain, and you should be sure.*

Raedra's blood turned colder than a mountain stream. "Who gave this to you?" she demanded of the jack.

The servant didn't answer. He wasn't beside her. He wasn't in the room. He wasn't a servant, she thought, remembering the rumpled tabard and the uneasy way he spoke. "Where did he go?" she shouted. "Where is that man?"

The maids all looked at her as though she was losing her mind.

"Find him," she ordered. "Find War Wizard Nyaril and fetch him here immediately."

"Yes, Your Highness," the lady's maid said. She sent two of the younger girls out, and they squeezed past Varauna, Florelle, and Sulue with hurried curtsies.

Raedra froze, eyes on them all.

Florelle gave her a quizzical look. "Is everything all right?"

"Truly, Florelle?" Varauna demanded. "How could *anything* be all right?"

Raedra's heart felt as if it were going to pound right up her throat and out her skull. She shook her head and took a step back. Which of them? Any of them? They were supposed to be safe, they were supposed to be vetted and approved and cleared because there were not supposed to *be* Sharran agents in the palace ever again.

"I need a moment," she managed, her head buzzing like the drone of a hornet's nest. "Please tell Ilstan I'm in my . . . bedchamber when he gets here?"

Sulue gaped at that, but Raedra didn't care. Let them talk. Let them talk and talk and talk. She couldn't sit there faced with a woman who was supposed to be her friend and would stab her—and probably the other two—right through the heart, given the chance. She went into the bedchamber, shut the door, and barred it. Sat in the middle of the bed, her skirts hiked up to her knees like a girl.

Ilstan might be seconds, or he might be hours. He'd want to check with her parents about which families this might indict—ye gods, she hoped it wouldn't be

Florelle. Her father and Raedra's went stag hunting in the autumn, nearly every year. It would kill him if they turned out to be—

Raedra's lungs stopped working. The blood rushed away from her head as if someone had suddenly sliced her heart out.

Irvel wouldn't know. He was dead. It couldn't kill him, he was dead already. He wouldn't know about the Sharran. He wouldn't thunder through the palace, demanding how this had happened again. He wouldn't hug her in his stiff fashion. He wouldn't be here at all.

Raedra tried to breathe. Tried to calm herself. She couldn't leave this room gasping and panting and looking like a madwoman, she thought, not today. It only made her breath come harder. She stood and headed toward the little secret door, stepped into the passage that led to Baerovus's room with it's strange little traps and hoped she wouldn't be interrupting her brother while he—

The sob tore free of her at that, the first of too many. Baerovus couldn't comfort her and she couldn't comfort him. She sat on the threshhold of the secret passage, squatting down among her skirts, and rested her face in her hands as she finally cried, for Irvel, for Baerovus, for herself. For Cormyr.

8

29 Flamerule, the Year of the Nether Mountain Scrolls (1486 DR)
Suzail, Cormyr

THE HALL GLOWS GOLDEN, THE SOFT LIGHT OF A SETTING SUN. EVERY SURFACE is layered with cups, goblets, flagons, and every vessel holds a promise. One has the antidote, and the rest contain more powerful poison.

Adolican Rhand hounds Farideh. Wherever she turns, the wizard is waiting, watching. She reaches for the powers of the Hells, but they won't come. She doesn't remember imbibing the poison, only knows that it's there, eating through her veins, stalking toward her heart. If she does nothing, she'll collapse, any breath now. If she chooses the wrong cup, she'll die.

"Choose," Rhand says. Someone coughs. "Stay alive."

She looks past the vessels, past Adolican Rhand. Havilar leans against a column, blood running down over her chin, spattering the marble floors. Rhand chuckles.

Farideh searches the cups, frantic, frenzied. Havilar is dying, and only one of these will save her. Liquors bright as liquid jewels splash against the floor as she knocks aside the ones she's sure are poison—but is she sure? Can she be sure?

She spots a tiny chalice, buried in the shadows. Its bowl is no bigger than a thimble, filled with emerald liquid. Enough for one, and she knows in her heart of hearts that this is the antidote. She cups it carefully, afraid to spill a drop.

She turns, and Havilar is lying on the floor, her blouse soaked in blood, her breath still. The archdevil stands over her body, watching Farideh. He points his ruby rod at Havilar, and she opens her eyes.

"I can give you many things," he says. "All you have to do is stay alive."

Farideh woke with a great gasp of air that scraped her raw throat. A shudder went through her, setting off another bout of shaking. She clenched the sheets in her fists until it passed and left her panting. The dancing light of a candle filled the room. Lorcan, his handsome face human, and his black eyes serious, leaned over her.

"Well," Lorcan said. "That answers that question."

"How long have you been here?" Farideh asked.

"A few breaths." His hand caressed her forehead, her cheek. "Fever?"

She closed her eyes, her head still spinning. "Shaking fever. I can't go anywhere, so don't ask, please."

He clucked his tongue. "Did they put Havilar in another room?"

"They put her on a horse," Farideh said. "Will you pour me some water?"

Silence. Farideh opened her eyes and pulled herself up to lean against the pillows. "The pitcher's by the washbasin," she said.

Lorcan blinked. "Of course." He took the mug from the bedside table and filled it. "Havilar's gone with Brin? Is this not a . . . contagious sort of fever?"

"She had it ages ago," Farideh said. "When we were little. You can't catch it twice." She gulped the water down, cooling her throat. Lorcan was still staring at her. "I told you that once. About the leaf-letters and staying with Criella."

"Of course," he said again. "So she just left you? Mehen didn't mind?"

"I told him to go with her," Farideh said. Then, "They've all left. Even the servants." She handed him the mug again and he refilled it. "I'm surprised you're not more pleased."

Lorcan smirked back at her, all his annoyance hidden away. "On the contrary. I'm merely concerned about your well-being. And frankly, in Havilar and Mehen's position, I can't fathom coming to the same conclusion." He sat down on the bed beside her and handed her the mug. "Leaving you all alone like this."

"Last night you thought this was a fantastic idea," Farideh pointed out.

"Things change," Lorcan said lightly. He shifted closer to her, his mouth sly and soft. "Remind me why it's fantastic."

One moment, they were alone and the space between them was all Farideh could think of. The next, the room was full of assassins.

Three of them, two men and a woman, all clad in featureless black, stepped free of portals. A moment of puzzlement—eyes flicking to Lorcan—and the woman shot a blow dart at the disguised cambion, sinking it into the back of his neck. Lorcan snarled as he came to his feet and wrenched the dart free. He shook off the illusion, skin flaming red, wings and horns unfolding from his flesh, and drew his sword.

Another moment, the assassins reassessing. The cambion wouldn't take poison easily.

Farideh grasped the powers of her pact. Flames filled her hands, and marks of Hellish magic scorched her arms, while Glasya's dark blessings shivered over her silhouette, making her look as if she could vanish into the shadows at the slightest wish. A bolt of energy peeled off her hands, streaking toward the woman with the blowgun. It shattered an invisible shield around her, shards of brittle magic raining down around her.

But the assassins were quick. The woman was opening another portal. One of the men grabbed Farideh by the arm, twisting it painfully and pulling her toward the swirl of magic. And the second man—

The second man stood behind Lorcan, who was bent double over a blade, eyes wide.

The powers of Asmodeus flooded Farideh. She didn't try to stop them.

• • •

ONCE DAHL WAS free of the palace, he tore off the tabard he'd stolen from the laundry once he'd gotten inside, and stuffed it under his cloak with the Crownsilver one, before moving as swiftly as he could into the busy streets. If there weren't Purple Dragons chasing him, there would be soon, and he needed to be far from where they might grab him and question him. Anyone in the streets would see just another man in a weathercloak, making his way to the market—albeit with a grin that was probably puzzling to any passerby.

Dahl didn't even try to hide it—that had been exhilarating. He'd been out of the field for nearly two years, and while everything that had happened in the Shadovar internment camp had convinced Tam that Dahl was ready to go back out into the world, breaking into the royal palace of Suzail, alone and unarmed, and putting a message into the hands of the princess herself . . . well, *that* was a feat worthy of the Harpers of Waterdeep.

Gods' books, Farideh had better be impressed. "I trust you"—as if she'd asked him to carry a receipt for wine across the city. As if he hadn't had to bluff his way past eight sets of guards, change disguises, and walk right into the princess's private quarters.

Or maybe, a little voice said in his thoughts, she trusted you could do just that.

Unbidden, he thought of the line of writing written on his soul, of Farideh speaking the words: "*Vur ghent vethsunathear renthisj* . . . I don't think Oghma is done with you yet."

He ducked down an alleyway and waited, watching for Purple Dragons. Oghma wasn't the sort of god whose paladins made it into chapbooks—all stiff and noble and bound to law and honor. But Dahl was hard-pressed to think of a reason his former masters would accept that he was still grinning over breaking into the royal palace like a common sneakthief. The kinds of acts asked of a Harper agent were not the kinds of acts that the law of paladins respected.

And if Farideh was right, if Oghma might be willing to take Dahl back, then perhaps he shouldn't be smiling after all.

He arrived back at the tallhouse without incident. Dumuzi still sat on the front steps, his peacebound blade in its scabbard laid across his scaly knees.

"Any trouble?" Dahl asked.

Dumuzi considered him. "I wouldn't say so. People staring, but I can't guess why. Maybe because they're blackguards. Maybe me." He stood, shifting out of the way of the door. "You think they'd be used to seeing one of us if Verthisathurgiesh Mehen lives here."

"You'd think," Dahl agreed.

Faint footsteps beyond the door caught his ear. Dahl scowled. "Gods blast it." He opened the door. "Farideh, go back—"

But it wasn't Farideh. A man clad in black leathers leaped back as the door opened, a bare dagger in his hand. Dahl pivoted, barely missing the blade lunging for his gut. The assassin twisted, stabbing at him again—

Kepeshkmolik Dumuzi caught hold of the man's wrist and twisted. The assassin held tight to the dagger, but the attack took enough of his attention. Dahl punched him across the jaw. The assassin turned from the strike reflexively, and into the dragonborn's arms. Dumuzi wrapped an elbow around the man's neck and squeezed.

Dahl dropped to his knees, blocking the man from the sight of passersby. "How many others? Show me on your fingers," he demanded. The assassin smiled, even as his face started to purple. "How many others?" he demanded again. The assassin went limp in the dragonborn's grip.

A scream came from upstairs.

Dahl ran for the bedroom. But as he reached the stairs, another man clad in black came streaking past him, his eyes wide with terror. He didn't slow for Dahl, didn't even seem to realize the Harper was there. Dread uncoiled through Dahl's heart.

In the bedroom, Farideh knelt shaking on the floor, the rug beneath her charred, and the air tingling with used-up magic. A body lay before her: Lorcan, his black blood staining the charred fibers of the rug.

She looked back at Dahl. "H-help," she managed.

Dahl cursed and took the healing potion from the pouch at his belt, thinking what a waste it was to use on the cambion, knowing that Farideh would never forgive him if he withheld it. He poured half down the cambion's throat, half over the belly wound.

Lorcan's back arched, his screams unholy. Farideh gripped the half-devil's face, and Dahl looked back at the doorway. A moment later, the cambion coughed and sat up. Farideh fell back against the foot of the bed, shaking still.

"Such a good thing you were here," Lorcan rasped. "Many thanks, paladin."

"Same kidnappers?" he asked Farideh. She nodded.

"Th-three. T-telep-p-orted." She clenched her jaw tight. Dahl helped her to her feet and back to bed.

"'Same' kidnappers?" Lorcan demanded.

"Your pardon?" Dumuzi said from the doorway. Everyone turned to face him, and if the presence of a tiefling and a half-devil fazed him in the slightest, it didn't show. "But someone should go for the guard before the man downstairs wakes, and I doubt it should be me."

• • •

Lorcan stepped from the portal once more, into the fingerbone tower, all his anxieties flooding through the false calm he'd forced himself into while with Farideh: Havilar was gone. Someone was trying to kill or kidnap her and attacking Farideh in the process. Farideh was sicker than he'd meant to leave her, and all alone. And godsbedamned Dahl was in Suzail.

Lorcan headed straight to Sairché's corner, the frantic buzz of a hundred catastrophes finally starting to hum together into a proper plan. Sairché stood, pressing against the oozing wall as Lorcan came to a stop at the edge of the barrier.

"We have a deal," he reminded her. "I protect you, you protect me. We both protect them."

Sairché watched him. "True," she said carefully.

Lorcan plucked a ring from the chain he wore around his neck, a garnet on a bronze band, slipped it on and waved it over the barrier's surface in a zigzag. The magic fizzled. "We have a problem."

"What," Sairché said, "did you do?"

Lorcan ignored her and crossed to the scrying mirror. With her protection spell intact, and no blood to draw on, he couldn't find Havilar herself. But Brin had no such protection and sure enough, Farideh's twin rode beside him, her horns almost—but not quite—hidden under a voluminous hood.

"Farideh," he said, "isn't with her."

"How is that new?" Sairché said. "I didn't know that one existed until Glasya told me."

"It is *different*," Lorcan said, "and you and I both know exactly *why* it is different." He shot her a significant look. "Before it was about keeping a spare Brimstone Angel. Now it's about keeping Asmodeus happy before he knows he might not be happy. I will bet this entire chain of rings that she's another of his Chosen."

Sairché stepped carefully out of the space that had been her prison for the past months, as if she didn't quite trust that the barrier wouldn't rebuff her. "Where is she?"

"A day's ride into the Cormyrean frontier," he said. "Headed for the northern front in a permanent cloudburst on a fool's errand."

"And you want me to . . . ?"

"You have to protect her as much as I do, and you're not saddled with the *pradixikai's* latest bull-headed insanity, the archduchess's current, *wise*, and not at all terrifying demands, or Farideh and . . ." Lorcan bit off the rest—he didn't need Sairché knowing about *all* his troubles. "You need to get out there, and stick close to her. Don't let her know you're there, and don't do anything unnecessary, but she needs to come out of this *alive*, whatever the cost."

Sairché gave him a withering look. "And how do you expect me to do that?"

Lorcan let the disguise he wore drop, wings and horns unfolding. "By learning a very uncomfortable spell."

Sairché wrinkled her nose and sighed. "Let me think of something better. That plane is so chilly, and I have no interest in mucking through the rain, pretending to be human."

"Think quickly," Lorcan said. He blew out a nervous breath.

"Poor Lorcan," Sairché said. "Heavy is the head that wears the crown."

"Watch your tongue or you'll get this crown back. And all its attendant troubles." He watched Havilar's horse slip on a patch of slick grass as it climbed a hill. "Do you remember when you intended to broker Farideh's pact to another collector?"

"Are you intending to sell her and get away from His Majesty?"

"You told me that they wanted her specifically, but never why." His memories drifted to a cavern deep beneath the Nether Mountains, to a library buried there, to Farideh, possessed by the ghost of a Netherese arcanist and the consciousness that peeked out while she drifted in a dead man's memories. Of the languid voice that called him Caisys.

"Is she the Brimstone Angel reborn?" he asked.

"Don't be stupid," Sairché said. "If she were Bryseis Kakistos, Asmodeus would have made sure she died long ago. Don't you listen?—Bryseis Kakistos was not favored by the end of her days and certainly *not* in her afterlife."

"Unless he couldn't find Farideh," Lorcan pointed out. "And no one *could*, but for an accident with an imp."

"Well he's found her now," Sairché said. "And she's still breathing."

"So why were your collectors willing to pay so much for her pact?" Lorcan asked, dreading the answer.

Sairché hesitated. "She's not the Brimstone Angel reborn . . . but that doesn't mean people don't believe she could be. Bryseis Kakistos's soul has been missing from the Nine Hells for nearly fifty years—plenty of people are curious where she's gone to."

"Do you think that's why Asmodeus wants her protected?"

Sairché peered at him, as if he'd gone a little mad. "Why on all the spinning planes are *you* asking why Asmodeus is doing something?"

Lorcan shook his head. "Because none of this makes sense. I feel as if I'm being led into a trap."

"We are *all* being led into traps," Sairché said. "This is the Hells, dear Brother."

• • •

Wizard of War Ilstan Nyaril studied the three noblewomen seated at the far side of the room. Florelle twisted her handkerchief in both hands, her eyes on the patterned rug. Sulue watched her companions fearfully, as if either might suddenly turn into a terrible beast and tear her apart. Only Varauna watched him back, with that odd balance of imperiousness and lasciviousness of which only Varauna was capable. Magic shivered over all three of them, carrying out the edicts of his spell. Hunting for the traitor that had somehow slipped in, under all their noses.

Under *Ilstan's* nose.

He might not have been the one to approve of Raedra's retinue, but he *was* the war wizard who stood guard over her most often. He watched the spell collect and shift, like bees swarming, and hoped it would come to nothing. If anyone should have stopped this, it was him.

"Why is it," Wizard of War Glathra Barcastle had asked him years ago, "Her Highness has requested your assistance seven of the last eight tendays?"

"I don't know," Ilstan had lied. "We get along."

Glathra had folded her hands together and leaned forward in a way that made him think of nothing so much as an angry tutor. "You were there the night the Traitor was caught."

"Yes."

"In what capacity?"

Ilstan frowned. "I was standing guard at their door."

"You weren't . . . giving the princess any extra assistance."

Ilstan gave Glathra a level look. "If you're asking if I'm her lover, I'm not. I wasn't then. I'm not now. I haven't been at any time in between." He shrugged. "We get along. She's . . . particular. That's all I can tell you."

Glathra watched him a moment more, and if she were using magic to divine the truth of what he'd said, she was so skilled Ilstan couldn't tell. "You're a young man, Ilstan. No one would fault you if you found yourself bound by nature. It's the way of things, after all."

"In another time and another place, perhaps," Ilstan said. "Where she wasn't the Princess of Cormyr, and I weren't a war wizard, and we had not met under such inauspicious circumstances, and a hundred other things. If she asks for my presence, please assume it is simply because I can do my task well."

"And what of her? What if *she's* the one feeling attached?"

"That is something you should discuss with the princess," Ilstan had said, quite properly.

He glanced back at Raedra, at the stony expression on her lovely features. She hadn't so much as moved since he'd started, her eyes locked on each of the noble-women in turn—one of them had betrayed her, far beyond the usual court games.

"Are you nearly through?" Varauna called. "This is quite dull."

"Nearly," Ilstan said. He looked down at the letter on the table once more.

"There is no date," Raedra had said. "Find out which of them it is, and we should be able to narrow down the day by who was with me. Who sent the note is as important as which of them is the traitor."

A buzz filled Ilstan's ears—the magic suddenly swelled, the buzz becoming a roar, becoming a howl, becoming a tone like a choir holding a note.

Without within, the old man's voice said, *and which is which? You are the one who can find the key and pluck it free . . .*

The sound abruptly ceased. The old man's voice trailed away, and the spell collapsed. Ilstan's hands were shaking.

Raedra set a hand on his shoulder. "Are you all right?"

Ilstan nodded automatically, swallowed. "The Weave snagged," he said, straightening. "It's fine."

It wasn't fine. It shouldn't be fine. But while his hands might have shaken as if the spell had sapped all of his strength, his heart felt calm and peaceful as it had each time the voice had spoken out of the ether with cryptic statements and enough power to make his spells slip. As much as it ought to scare Ilstan, it didn't. And as much as he ought to have told one of his superiors, he hadn't. Not the first time, not this—the fourth—time.

Ilstan took a moment to set all of that aside before he looked up and considered the halo of night surrounding Sulue. "It's Lady Thundersword."

Raedra pressed her mouth shut. "You're *sure*?"

"Completely," he said. "Highness, again, I am so sorry this happened. We should have stopped it."

Raedra shook her head. "We don't know *what* has happened," she said. She watched Sulue, the noblewoman's fearful eye on her dearest companions, suddenly blatant and forced. "But we *will* know," Raedra said sadly. "We will have to know everything."

. . .

THE GHOST FLOWED into the sleeping man's body, taking advantage of his dreaming state to ease into his mind. She felt his consciousness panic, struggle, but only for a breath. Strange things happened in dreams, after all.

Bryseis Kakistos moved slowly, carefully—this wasn't a possession to be violent with. She was still watching, testing after all. Even if she wanted to hurry, there wasn't a need.

The man's thoughts moved around her. By the time he woke, he'd hardly be aware of her presence at all, his mind convinced moment by moment that the ghost was simply a part of itself. She'd always been there. The voice that she spoke with was his. It would make it easier by far for him to rationalize if Bryseis Kakistos had to take control of his body herself.

A memory jolted through the ghost—Pradir Ril, that sad little boy, always on the edge of treachery, his arms and legs contorted as her magic forced him forward, made the cuts that spilled his blood, the final symbol of the rakshasas' misbegotten on Asmodeus's altar. Bryseis Kakistos smiled to herself, remembering the knife in his reversed right hand, remembering how he'd tried to stab her too. Never realizing that his fury just fed the ritual. Never realizing she'd already succeeded.

What success? she asked herself. She didn't sit at the right hand of Asmodeus. She didn't wear the crown of a Lord of Hell. She'd been cheated, poured down only a measure of the strength a Chosen of Asmodeus should bear. Fractured and scattered and kept from her rightful reward.

The memory floated away, Pradir Ril becoming a dream of a man in a scruffy beard, cracking acorns under a stone, the man whose body she'd crawled into, scrabbling to pick them all up. The old man reached up and scratched his head, where the stumps of small horns protruded. Interesting, Bryseis Kakistos thought, settling down deeper still, and recognizing the call of stranger blood pulsing all around her. Very interesting.

PART II

ORBYN
THE EDGE OF JUSTICE

. . .

The blade that shines brightest in the Hall of Gazes is the Edge of Justice—here it ends the tyranny of Thauglorimorgorus, there it stops the heart of a traitorous nobleman. Stitched in silver thread, its oldest depiction hangs at the far end of the passage, a tapestry said to have been embroidered by Queen Engrane, Duar's first daughter-in-law: King Duar Obarskyr at battle with Magrath the Minotaur, the pirate who would have ruled Suzail. The king, embroidered all in gold, springs like a lion toward the ragged beast, Magrath's death leaping ahead like a bolt of lightning. In most works the blade has already done its deed, but here, the moment before Cormyr is saved, it is clear that justice flows not only through Orbyn, but in the blood of the Obarskyr.

. . .

9

THE WIZARD SHIFTED IN HER SEAT, EYES DARTING FROM MEHEN TO Havilar and back to Brin. "That's my final offer," she said, in a tone that suggested it wasn't at all.

"And twenty gold is yours," Mehen said. "Plus three again for any days over." Brin fidgeted with the dagger at his belt, clicking it in and out of its sheath nervously. Without looking over, Havilar stilled his hand under her own. The wizard—a thin, steely-haired woman called Desima—was their only option for a caster in the caravansary. But Mehen had plenty of experience bargaining with sellswords—even Havilar could see that Desima would come down.

Provided Brin didn't tip their hand.

Desima studied Mehen a moment. "Twenty-five. And you cover the components I expend."

"Twenty-five and we'll cover half," Mehen said. "Fifteen now, the rest and the expenses when we find our quarry."

Desima's pale eyes flicked over Havilar again. "Deal."

She didn't offer Mehen her hand when she stood, and only nodded sullenly when he told her where and when they'd leave from. Brin let out a breath when she went upstairs to her rooms. "I was sure we were in trouble there," he admitted.

"Wizards don't come sit out in the wilderness for their health," Mehen said.

"She was looking for someone to hire her," Havilar agreed. "And she was looking desperate."

"Should make up for the cleric," Mehen said. Constancia had protested they didn't need another healer, that they certainly didn't need a priestess of Waukeen, the Merchant's Friend, and there was no reason, by the lions of Azoun, that they needed to pay *that* kind of coin.

The priestess, a human called Moriah, simply grinned and jingled her coin purse when Constancia scowled at her afterward.

"I *like* her," Havilar declared. Moriah, Desima, a man called Crake, and a dragon-born named Kallan rounded out their hires. Enough, with luck, to make it through the Hullack Forest to where Brin had heard the crown prince had last been seen.

Mehen grunted, and scratched his empty piercings. "How much are you planning to tell them?"

"Little as possible," Brin said.

"They're going to be curious."

"Let them be. If we don't find him . . ." Havilar met Brin's eyes, every sleepless night written clear on his face. "There's no point in spreading rumors."

"We can tell them we're looking for your wastrel brother," Havilar said. "Or better, let's just drop *hints*."

Brin made a face. "They don't need a reason. They have coin."

Mehen chuckled and stood. "Sellswords pretend the reason doesn't matter. But that doesn't mean they're not all nosy as a crow in a silversmith's window. Think of a story." He considered his half-flagon of ale and wrinkled his nose. "I'm going to go see if Constancia's sorted out the horses. Don't dawdle too long."

Havilar grinned into her own ale—it was *not* an appropriate time to be happy, but she was. Suzail at her back, the world at her feet, glaive in her hand, and Brin at her side—even Mehen being bossy. It felt like old times.

Except Farideh wasn't with them.

And behind his ginger beard, Brin's expression was tight and troubled. He clicked the dagger in and out of its sheath a few more times.

"You're going to dull it," Havilar said. Brin gave her a wan smile and took one of her hands in his instead, rubbing a thumb slowly over her knuckles.

"Sorry. I'll be all right when all of this is sorted out."

Havilar put an arm around him. "So if we find him—"

"When," Brin said. "Please say 'when.'"

"*When* we find him," she said, "he'll still be king next, but you're still in line. How does that change things?"

"It doesn't," Brin admitted. "It keeps them from getting worse." He sighed and smiled unevenly. "If he doesn't come back, if Baerovus doesn't wake, then the line to the throne is *decimated*. King Foril will absolutely bring up my father's legitimization again, and people probably won't fight it nearly as hard."

"Right," Havilar said, even though she still didn't quite understand that part. They all agreed that Brin's father was his father, and they all seemed to agree his father's father was the old crown prince. The extra step seemed like a lot of nonsense.

But it kept Brin off the throne. And so long as that was true, somewhere on the horizon was a life she'd like a lot better than this.

"So we'll find him," Havilar said. "And maybe he'll be so grateful he'll call off your wedding?"

"Maybe," Brin said in a way that meant "No." He rubbed his hands over his face. "Can we stop talking about this? I promise it will all be fine."

"All right," Havilar said, even though she'd heard that so many times before she'd lost count. Give it time, give it time—one part of Suzail that she'd never shake. "You never told me where you got the dagger. It's not new—was it your father's?"

Brin didn't meet her eyes. "No. It's Irvel's." He hesitated. "Raedra gave it to me, as a wedding gift." Havilar's stomach twisted, even as he added with a little scoffing sound. "More like a costume piece."

"You're carrying a weapon she gave you?"

"It's not like that," Brin said. He looked up at her. "Honest it's not. I should have left it behind, but it seemed . . ." He turned the dagger over in his hands. "I don't know, it seemed the right thing to do. Not," he added hastily, "because Raedra gave it to me."

Of course, Havilar nearly said—would have said, if they were still in Suzail.

"I don't like it," she blurted. "It just seems like if someone's going to give you a weapon, it ought to be me. And I can't afford anything as nice as that," she added with a little laugh. She looked off the way Mehen had gone.

"Havi." Brin turned her face gently back toward him. "She cannot hold a candle to you."

Havilar smiled, but her heart wasn't in it. "She gives you much better presents."

Brin kissed her softly. "*Don't* laugh: you have her beat. You gave me myself back." Havilar rolled her eyes, but it was still sweet . . . sort of.

"I ought to go help Mehen. Do you think we can use one of the sendings before we go?"

Brin frowned. "We don't have that many of the kits."

"I know." Havilar sighed. "I miss her, though."

"She'll be fine," Brin said, even though that wasn't the point. "Go see what Mehen's up to. I'll see you tonight." They kissed once, and Havilar left under the sidelong gazes of the taproom's guests, and headed for the stables.

Down in her bones, she felt the twinge of worry that there was no chance they were going to find Irvel—and even if they did, that it wouldn't make any difference. For all Brin insisted he couldn't just leave Cormyr again, Havilar didn't see why that was so. But she'd stopped trying to get him to explain it—every time he seemed more frustrated that she was asking. She sighed—she'd never understand Cormyr.

Which made her wonder if she'd ever understand Brin again.

She turned up her hood as she stepped out in the rain. "So bored," she murmured to herself, as if she were casting one of the expensive sendings. "Brin is gloomy. Mehen is 'at his task.' Constancia is awful. Still raining. Still waiting. Probably better than being stuck in the tallhouse," she allowed. Was that twenty-five words? Why *was* it twenty-five words? She wondered if Desima knew, and if she were the sort of wizard who would tell Havilar or who would simply tell her she didn't understand.

"Hey, boss," a friendly voice called from the back of a covered wagon. Moriah and the two sellswords crouched in the relative shelter, cards piled in front of them. The priestess, her auburn hair wrapped around her head in thick braids, scooped up the deck, smiling at Havilar. "Care to join us?"

Care to share a little more gossip, Havilar thought. Mehen was right, mercenaries were a nosy lot, whatever anybody said—and Havilar had to include herself. She climbed up into the cart's bed and found a spot between Moriah and Kallan. Crake grinned at her in a way that made Havilar think of Lorcan.

"Sort out the wizard?" Crake asked.

"Well enough," Havilar said. "She'll cover us if we find too much in the wood. What are you playing?"

"High Dragon."

Havilar shook her head. "I'll just watch. Haven't got coin to spare."

"Coin spent invites more coin in," Moriah said.

"Don't listen to her," Kallan said, leaning back against the wagon wall. The dark-gray dragonborn nodded at Moriah. "All it does is invite more coin into her purse."

"Your ready sword there seems to have plenty of coin," Moriah said. "What's he doing out in the rain and danger?"

Havilar sighed. "Family business." Which was true, she thought, and no one could say it wasn't.

Moriah shuffled the deck. "Any particular family?"

"His," Havilar said, smiling back. "What's a cleric of Waukeen doing in the battlefields taking mercenary coin?" Moriah grinned at her.

"Fortune favors the bold."

Crake chuckled. "You sound more like a Tymoran."

"I'll give Lady Luck her due," Moriah said. She kissed the cards lightly. "Only fools don't. Fools and dragonborn," she allowed, smirking at Kallan.

Kallan snorted and turned to Havilar. "The knight says that the clanless one's your father. You're not from Djerad Thymar."

"He is," Havilar said. Then amended, "He *was.* Then a village on the frontier. Then Cormyr." Kallan's silver eyes considered her for a long moment. Havilar eyed his smooth, scaled face—no piercings. "You're not from there either."

Kallan grinned. "Good guess. I'm Yrjixtilex," he said, naming what sounded like a clan. It meant nothing to Havi. "Your father like being a bodyguard?"

"He likes Brin. Mostly. Is that why you came to Cormyr?"

Kallan shrugged. "Better than this. Bodyguards get to stay inside most of the time."

"So what brings you along?" Crake asked, dark eyes boring into Havilar.

"What do you mean?"

"I mean, she's getting paid to heal, Kallan and I are here to cut down goblins and Shadovar."

"You're here to back me up," Havilar corrected.

Crake gave her an appraising look that set her nerves on edge. "Well, that sounds fun. You're pretty for a devilborn."

The hairs on Havilar's neck stood on end, a prickling rush down her back. "And you're rude, even for a human."

"Oh hush up, you spoilt boy!" Moriah said. "Does that *ever* work?"

Crake smiled at Havilar. "We'll have to see."

The sellswords laughed and teased him, but Havilar felt a strange tension come over her, and the urge to run, to lash out at the human, was sudden and intense. She rolled her shoulders—you could always tell creepy. That was it.

"Havi!" Mehen barked. Havilar nearly leaped from her skin. Her father stood at the open end of the wagon, glowering as if he'd been waiting several breaths for an answer. The sellswords watched her, as if it were her turn to reply.

"Come and help me load the horses," Mehen said, slowly, as if repeating himself. "We're leaving in an hour." Havilar climbed down out of the wagon, careful to avoid meeting Crake's eyes again.

• • •

Farideh finished the pass with a thrust of her short sword into the empty air of the garden, and nearly dropped the weapon as her arm gave out. Good enough. She'd stopped counting how many times she'd run through Mehen's exercises, but her arms felt like wet leather, her heart was galloping in her chest, and the rain no longer seemed capable of washing the sweat from her brow.

Farideh threw her head back, letting the rain course over her. The shaking fever had finally run its course, leaving behind the faintest tendency to tremble when she overexerted, but that too was fleeting. A solid hour and a half, and only now her arms couldn't hold the sword steady. She smiled. Mehen would be proud.

She bit her lip. The exercises were through, but Farideh wasn't. She seized hold of the powers ready to surge through her. Flames raced over her, hissing in the rain, and she stood there for a moment, letting them burn.

Could other gods see her when she stood like this? Was there some god who might snatch hold of the lightning storm and spear her with a bolt where she stood? End this waiting, watching, worrying once and for all? She felt the wings of fire unfold around her and spread her arms, half-daring, half-hoping.

But the only thing that fell was the rain. Her arm started to shake with fatigue.

She sheathed the sword and swore she'd dry and oil it—just as soon as she dried off herself. That, Mehen would be less pleased with, she thought, but she went up to her room regardless.

For the past month, Farideh had kept mostly to the tallhouse, her days monotonous enough that she wondered sometimes if *this* were the true curse of Asmodeus. She woke, she ate, she read the books from Brin's library. She trained. She cast the Chosen magic before it overtook her. She ate again. She read. She slept. She fixed dinner. She drank a little wine. She went to bed. Some days Dahl came by, and some days Lorcan did. Some days she coaxed a little conversation out of Dumuzi. Some days when the rain was heavy enough to give her a little more cover, she braved the markets.

But mostly, she waited.

Truth be told, it was comfortable as often as it chafed. She'd started to think of the tallhouse as hers, its fires hers to stir, its stores hers to maintain, its rooms hers to tidy. She'd catch herself humming while she washed dishes or hung laundry, and chuckle at the absurdity. This wasn't her life.

It might be Havilar's though—would they stay here, in Suzail, in the tallhouse, if everything worked out? She imagined visiting them, keeping to the front rooms, when she knew by now, so many of the tallhouse's little secrets.

She wondered where she'd be visiting from.

Dried and dressed in fresh clothes, Farideh went down and poked her head out of the door. The dragonborn was sitting on the steps, sword across his knees. From dawn until dusk, he sat at his post, and then he'd come in and go to sleep up in the jacks' quarters on the top floor. He woke before Farideh nearly every morning. He never spoke to her, unless she spoke first.

"Dumuzi? Do you want something to eat?" she asked.

He looked back at her. "Already?"

Right, Farideh thought. The dragonborn wouldn't be hungry for a while yet. "Never mind. Do you want company?"

"I'm fine. Thank you."

Farideh shut the door, and with it tried to close out the lingering discomfort Dumuzi left her with. She couldn't shake the impression he disapproved of her, nor the worry that Dahl might be wrong about him, that the dragonborn might have come for nefarious reasons.

"Has he *done* anything?" Dahl had asked one day. He'd brought her tea after searching Brin's papers once more. "And do you know a fellow called 'Garce'?"

"No," Farideh had said. "That's just it, he doesn't do *anything*."

"Garce?"

"Dumuzi." She sighed. "I don't know a Garce. I don't know anyone, except you and Dumuzi."

"And Lorcan," Dahl had said, passing her a teacup. "I was just *asking*."

Lorcan, who was a different puzzle altogether. Everything between them seemed to have overturned, scattering fond feelings and bad—she didn't know how to put things back together anymore, and Lorcan seemed perfectly happy to let it remain that way. If he pushed her in any direction, the slightest resistance made him back off. Half the time she was sure he was playacting every hint of affection, and the other half she was sure he was more smitten than she was. She wished a little that he'd push or pull a little harder, steer things again, make it clear what came next, so she didn't have to decide.

Don't wish that, she thought, heading into the kitchen. But what else was going to happen? He was a devil, after all. It wasn't as if they were going to find a little house of their own.

Embarrassed, she shook the thought from her head and rummaged through her stores—an apple, the last of the morning's porridge, a scraping of butter, and a heel of bread that had been stale since she bought it. She tried to bite the edge off and only scraped her mouth. She'd have to go to the market again, later, when it wasn't so crowded. Her stomach growled at the threatened wait.

The brimstone wind of a Hellsportal stirred the loose hairs around her braid. Lorcan stepped into the kitchen, looking like a human and carrying a basket over one arm.

"Well met, darling," he said. "I thought you might like something to eat."

Farideh frowned at the basket as he set it down in front of her. "You made me highsunfeast?"

Lorcan smiled. "A little treat. You don't have to make that face," he added. "I'm not such an extraordinarily bad fellow."

"Thank you," she said. "It just doesn't seem like something you'd do."

Inside, a stack of handpies, all crisp and flaky and golden brown, sent up a lovely, warm scent. Farideh's mouth watered. "Gods. Thank you," she said, taking one out. She broke the top off of the handpie and was glad she did.

A piece of crockery stuck out of an unidentifiable paste of meat and vegetables. Something wriggled beneath the surface. "You didn't make this."

"No," Lorcan admitted. "But it's nearly the same. The thought that counts."

She set it aside. "If you're going to make someone fix food for me," she said, "pick something that actually eats. It's full of potsherds and maggots."

Lorcan watched her steadily. "That . . . is . . ." He cursed. "Shitting imps."

Farideh's gorge rose. "Don't feed me things made in the Hells," she said. "Please."

Lorcan swept the handpie back into the basket with the rest of it. "I get credit for the attempt at least."

"It was a nice thought," she allowed. "Don't do it again."

He sat down beside her. "You know there are plenty of places I could take you that wouldn't care if you were a tiefling, so long as you had a little coin."

"I don't have a little coin if I'm not here," she said. I don't have much more than a little here, she thought.

Lorcan waved that away. "Coin is a trifle."

"Right." Farideh went to scrape the last of the porridge out of the pot. "I've seen what it costs. One soul, for all the gold you could want."

"Only if you're very unimaginative." Lorcan was quiet a moment. "What do you see when you look at yourself with the soul sight, darling?"

Farideh flushed. "Nothing."

"Nothing at all?" he asked.

"I suppose that's what it looks like when Asmodeus claims your soul."

"You really haven't been paying attention to how this works," Lorcan said after a moment. Farideh turned, bowl and spoon in hand. "Being the Chosen of

Asmodeus doesn't mean he's got your soul. You have to give that up yourself—or have it pulled out of you, but trust me, you'd have noticed. You have a piece of his power within you—that's all."

Farideh frowned. "That's not . . . Sairché said she'd take my soul, but then that she couldn't because it was Asmodeus's."

"She didn't say that," Lorcan pointed out. "You said that. It's subtler though. Asmodeus has . . . marked you. Meaning if another devil tries to claim you, they're treading a very dangerous line. And another god would have to be willing to get into the attendent pissing match that comes of conflicting claims. Sairché can't claim your soul without stepping on Asmodeus's feet. She could do it—she's entitled to by the terms—but it wouldn't end well for her, snatching a soul from Asmodeus's hand."

"But if he doesn't have my soul, why would he care if Sairché finished the job?"

Lorcan's smile flattened out. "It's politics. Very complicated politics."

"Try me."

"How about instead," Lorcan said, taking her hand, "we set aside matters of the Hells and Asmodeus, stupid imps, and what you could do to earn coin, and let me buy you some food meant for mortals. Doesn't that sound better?" Farideh had to admit it did. "Go and get your cloak."

Dumuzi pushed into the kitchen, eyed Lorcan, eyed Farideh. Cleared his throat. "Yes?" Farideh said.

"You have visitors."

"Your paladin?" Lorcan drawled.

"You agreed to be civil with him," Farideh warned, heading for the door.

Lorcan caught her by the wrist and tugged her back. "I assumed that meant you'd be a little kinder to me." He pulled her down on his lap, and Farideh blushed. She glanced over at Dumuzi.

"He's probably here to go through Brin's papers again. You don't even need to set eyes on him."

"But *you* do."

"It isn't the Peredur," Dumuzi interrupted. "It's the war wizards."

Lorcan's grip on her tightened. "Stop it," she murmured. "I have to . . . Don't come out. Wait here." She considered him. "If something goes awry, I'll warn you."

Lorcan looked as if he'd like to stop her, but he let her go. "Be quick. You're hungry."

In the front room stood Ilstan and Devora, the tall man and the red-haired woman from the other day, still in their dark cloaks, waiting for Farideh. "Well met," Ilstan said. "Princess Raedra would like to speak with you. But not as you are."

Farideh frowned. "What is that supposed to mean?"

Ilstan held up a wand. "It means I need you to hold still for a moment, goodwoman."

He didn't wait for her assent or tell her what he meant to do. A little chant that seemed to make her ears numb, a fine powder that smelled of pine sap and char and crab apples cast over her skin, and the wand whipping past her face before she could so much as step backward. Her skin itched fiercely where the powder landed on it, and then all over—as if the powder had burned through her blouse and breeches and bodice. Her head suddenly felt as if the top of it had been sliced off—a sharp pain and then a terrible, strange lightness. The air in her mouth seemed to expand and she wriggled her jaw without meaning to. Something rocked her off-balance, tilting her forward onto her toes.

"Finished," Ilstan said. "That should be better."

"What did you do?" Farideh demanded. "What happened?"

"It's just a disguise," Devora said, standing. "You can imagine the tongues that would wag if we brought the double of Lord Crownsilver's mistress in to see the princess."

Farideh settled back onto her heels—but it felt wrong, terribly wrong. She looked down at her booted feet, then back over her shoulder.

Her tail was missing.

"What have you done?" she said again, her pulse racing.

"It's temporary," Ilstan said, smiling. "And minor—I made it to be as uninvasive as possible. But we can't have a tiefling escorted into the royal palace, you understand?"

"What have you done? What—"

Ilstan took hold of her gently, steered her toward the mirror hanging over the fireplace. Her face stared back, but altered. There were no horns breaking from her brow. Her eyes were no longer silver and gold, but brown and blue, and ringed with white. Her hair, no longer held back by her horns fell forward, its purplish cast lost and simply black.

Her mouth fell open as she reached up and touched her suddenly smooth and flat forehead. "Wh-what . . ."

"It's temporary," Ilstan assured her again. "Just a disguise. Pretend you're wearing a mask—that's really what it is. A mask of magic."

"All right," Farideh said, trying to catch her breath. "All right." She rubbed her wrists. "And it will go away?"

"By tomorrow morning at the latest. Now . . ." He looked her over. "Is that the best thing you have to wear?"

Farideh shook her head, baffled. "Yes. No . . . Havi has a gown. I suppose."

"I'd suggest you go and change," Ilstan said. "Wizard of War Abielard would be happy to help you."

"That's not necessary," Farideh said, turning on her heel, her thoughts still buzzing. She passed Dumuzi in the hallway, without looking up at him. "I have to go to the palace," she said, going upstairs.

She thought about Brin's repeated warnings. She thought about running. She thought about locking the door. But there was no way the war wizards would let her go. If the princess wanted to talk to her . . .

Talk, she reminded herself, pulling on the blue dress. Just talk. She laced up the gown and checked herself in the mirror. It didn't fit as well in the bodice as it might, and she grimaced. The strange face in the mirror grimaced back, and she fled down the stairs, wrapping her weathercloak over her dress.

She stopped at the door and turned to Dumuzi. "If I don't come back, please tell Lorcan to exercise a little restraint," she said in a rush. He frowned at her, but she didn't wait for a reply.

Farideh rode wedged between the two war wizards, in a carriage so plush she found herself wondering if this was what the inside of a lady's velvet purse felt like. She pulled her cloak closer around her and imagined disappearing into the padded bench. It already felt as if her tail had, and she shifted, trying to find a way to sit that didn't feel so strange.

She glanced over at Ilstan and it struck her that *this* captured Cormyr in so many ways—wizards and royals deciding where she should be and how she should look, hiding her from sight but wrapping her in luxury as if it made the difference. She fidgeted with her cuffs.

Beyond the war wizard, the high gray wall of the palace rolled past the left window, shining against the heavy clouds. The carriage turned into the gates, and Devora nodded at the guards who approached. They backed off immediately, and the carriage rolled on, into the castle's courtyard.

Ilstan climbed down ahead of Farideh, then held out a hand to help her down from the carriage. Farideh briefly wondered what would happen if she simply refused to move. You can wait out Asmodeus, you could probably wait out Raedra. The thought made her temper flare. She took a deep breath and climbed from the carriage herself.

"Let's get something clear," she said. "I don't appreciate having spells cast on my person without warning or explanation." The muscles at the small of her back tightened, but there was no tail for them to twitch. "I'm sure you can imagine how unpleasant it is having someone remake your whole appearance on a whim."

Ilstan looked surprised. "To be truthful? I assumed you'd be pleased."

Of course he did, and she ground her flattened teeth. "I'm not," she said. "You may have the right, but I'd appreciate a word of warning next time."

He still looked surprised. "Very well." He gestured ahead to where Devora waited. "This way, if you please."

Farideh walked, Devora in front, Ilstan following, through a door and down a long, high-ceilinged hallway. Other war wizards passed, servants and Purple Dragons. Each eyed Farideh surreptitiously, but not a one stared the way she was sure they would have if she hadn't worn the disguise.

The war wizards steered her first down a narrow hallway lined with tapestries depicting kings and queens and powerful wizards in battle. Dragons and shadows and armies of knights. Then up a stairway and the red-haired war wizard suddenly turned, straight into a bare wall. At her touch, a panel of the wall lit silver, and swung inward. Ilstan hurried Farideh into the dim corridor beyond.

"The palace has many secret passages," Ilstan said, sounding apologetic. "Her Highness would rather we took precautions."

The hallways wound through the palace, down stairs and back up, lit only by the globe of greenish light conjured by the redhead and the slants of light coming through small holes drilled through the stone here and there. Farideh wondered what lay behind them, but didn't dare slow down.

At last Devora stopped and opened a door in another wall, the carving of a rampant owlbear over it, illuminated by the light of her globe. Ilstan nudged Farideh through the passage and into a small sitting room beyond. There were no windows to it, but a fire had been built up in the hearth, and small silver globes hung from the walls.

"Sit," Ilstan said, gesturing at the padded furniture. "Would you care for a small drink?"

"No," Farideh said, still standing. She looked up at the painting hanging over the fireplace, an elaborate portrait of two women standing on either side of a sleeping lion—one dark-haired and holding a sheaf of grain, one blond and cradling a sword.

"It's not a very good painting," Ilstan admitted. "Bit . . . modern."

"How long will we wait?"

Ilstan shrugged. "As long as it takes. You should sit."

Farideh stayed where she was, considering the painting, until she heard the click of a latch behind her. She turned and found the Princess of Cormyr staring at her.

"Well met," she said. "Thank you for coming." She pushed a loose curl of blond hair back behind one ear.

"You say that as if I had a choice," Farideh replied. "How can I help you?"

Raedra studied her without bothering to hide it. "I received your note. How did your agent get into the palace?"

Farideh shook her head. "I don't know. I didn't ask. I just knew if anyone could manage to get you that information, it was him. Did you find her? Was I right?"

"Yes."

Farideh cursed to herself. "I'm sorry, Your Highness. I hoped I'd imagined it."

Raedra came a little closer now, into the circle of furniture placed beside the fireplace. "What is it you thought you'd imagined?" she asked. "How did you spot her?"

"It's a skill I have," Farideh said carefully. Ilstan and Raedra both watched her, still as statues, clearly unsatisfied with that thin explanation. "It's like a spell," Farideh went on. "I can . . . see the state of mortal souls."

Raedra looked back at Ilstan, who was frowning. "Is that a spell?" she asked.

"Not one I'm familiar with, Your Highness," he admitted. "But she isn't a wizard, remember."

131

"Of course." Raedra turned back to Farideh. "A warlock." The princess folded her hands neatly over her skirt. "Aubrin said you were trapped. In Baator."

"In the Nine Hells."

Raedra arched one sleek brow. "That is what I said." She gazed at Farideh as if waiting for her to retort, then refolded her hands. "I suppose it was very terrible."

"Yes," Farideh said, though not in the way she'd meant. Sairché had trapped them in such a way that she saw none of the Hells themselves—every horror came of the absence, the seven and a half years that life on Faerûn had gone on without them.

"And of course it's none of your fault," she said, one delicate hand flicking the idea away, as if anything could be so simple. "You just *happened* to end up enmeshed with devils, as one does."

"It's none of my sister's fault," Farideh said evenly.

And at that, Raedra looked away. "You have my gratitude. Whatever it is you have done, you've uncovered a traitor none of my customary precautions revealed. Without your . . . talents," she said carefully, "there is every chance I would be ransomed or enchanted. Or dead. How may I repay you?"

Farideh hesitated, long enough that Raedra smiled uneasily. "Please do me the kindness of not saying 'Break your betrothal to Lord Crownsilver.' You may wish it, but it is a more complex affair than you realize."

"If I wanted that," Farideh said, "I could have left the Sharran in your midst."

Raedra narrowed her eyes. "Quite right. But you must name something."

Farideh considered. If anyone could order the return of Brin's servants, it was Raedra . . . but as much as that should be what she asked for, the thought of losing the privacy that the solitude afforded her sent a pang of grief through her. Or perhaps it was the thought of losing Lorcan—he couldn't come around with servants crowding the tallhouse.

"Gold?" Raedra suggested. "Jewels? A writ to adventure?"

"Someone tried to kidnap Havilar," Farideh said. "Three times now. The last time they thought I was her."

Raedra colored. "How unfortunate."

"Was it you?"

"Absolutely not. That's a coward's act."

"Would you find out who it was," Farideh asked, "and get them to stop? That's what I want."

Raedra considered her, so long and so boldly that Farideh had to look away. "That's what you're due," she said finally, "as a guest in Cormyr. Now, what do you want for your assistance?"

"I don't need anything else."

Raedra's mouth tightened. "Tell me your name again."

"Farideh."

"Farideh," she said, sitting down in the needlepoint chair, "if you were attacked in Lord Crownsilver's home or holdings, that's not merely about you. That is an attack on Lord Crownsilver, and by association, an attack against me. What will people say if they were to find out? They'd assume that it was my doing, an act of jealousy—a tremendously *sloppy* act of jealousy. Even if I didn't see it as my duty to the laws of Cormyr to sort out whatever villain has gotten it into their mind to insert themselves into Aubrin's and my personal affairs, I see it as a personal affront, and it will be dealt with. Thank you for bringing it to my attention."

Which meant that Ilstan hadn't, Farideh thought. "You're welcome," Farideh said. "Do you know who it might be?"

"I have a very good guess." Raedra smoothed her skirts again. "Now if you don't tell me something I can do to even the scales, I shall choose the least practical piece of jewelry I own and bequeath it to you, whether you like it or not."

Farideh smiled, unable to help it, and thought a moment. "I don't have the easiest time getting to the markets for food. People don't like bargaining with a tiefling, and I end up short. Can you have someone bring me food? I'd pay for it—"

"Someone will be by the tallhouse tomorrow morning with an assortment of items. Please tell them if there's anything specific you require then, and it will be taken care of in the next delivery." She hesitated. "You saved my life."

"I'm glad," Farideh said, unsure of what Raedra was waiting for her to say.

"Would you do it? Now?" Raedra asked. "Your spell, I mean. Can you tell me what you see in me?"

"I can't see much," Farideh said. "And I don't know what a lot of what I do see means."

"Still." Raedra refolded her hands. "I'd like to know."

Farideh glanced at the war wizard in the corner, once.

The powers didn't pain her as much when she called them herself, but still the sensation of thin claws sliding through the back of her skull and into her brain made her flinch. When she opened her eyes again, the lights of Raedra's soul bloomed in the darkness, like the aftereffects of staring into the sun.

"What do you see?" she asked.

"Purple," Farideh said. "Flashes of gold. A vein of scarlet."

"Shadows?"

"Everyone has shadows," Farideh said. "But there are shadows and there are Shar's marks. You don't have any more or less than most people." But this time there was something else, something new—the sureness that Raedra wasn't going to corrupt easily. The shadows made a softness around the red vein, as if beneath the shape of her soul was a bruised patch, a reminder of a time when she'd been a much sweeter prize for a devil. There was no digging at that bruise now—the gold flashes armored it. If a devil wanted her, it would take time. Effort. You'd have to lay something drastic in the balance.

Raedra was watching her as if waiting for an answer. "I'm sorry, what?" Farideh asked.

"I said what are you looking at?"

Farideh shrugged. "I get the impression you're not someone people ought to underestimate."

Raedra raised an eyebrow. "From purple, gold, red, and shadows?"

"And from talking to you," Farideh said.

Raedra stood, as if she meant to end the meeting, but she stopped, pursed her lips. "Would you sit with my retinue? Make sure you don't see anything else among them, or the maids or . . ." She shook her head. "I'd be very grateful. It would only be a few hours and I'd compensate you properly."

"Highness?" Ilstan said. "I've already made certain of the others. You're in no danger."

Raedra didn't look back at him. "I would be *sure*. Between the two of you, I think that's possible. Ilstan will come back for you in seven days," she said to Farideh. "The mourning will be over and I'll have a good reason to have such a gathering. And no one will wonder at a new face."

There was no mention of the disguise spell—of course it would be cast again. The princess bade her farewell, and the war wizards walked her back out through the dark passageways and into the light once more. A break in the rain let a little sun through the clouds, and the wet cobblestones steamed.

"Would it be all right if I walked back?" Farideh asked.

"Get the sun while you can?" Devora said. "That seems fair."

Ilstan frowned. "The rain will start again."

"She's not made of sugar," Devora said. She pointed toward the gates, where more Purple Dragons stood. "Go on." Farideh hurried out, turning over what had been said and what she'd agreed to. If playing at domesticity was absurd, what was being a secret advisor to the Princess of Cormyr?

Havilar would be furious, Farideh thought.

She walked down the Promenade without garnering a single comment—certainly no whispers, no gasps, no taunting children. She let go of her cloak, and stopped at a stall to buy some handpies. The older man waved away her coin. "End of the day," he explained. "Discount for pretty girls taking stale wares." He gave her a friendly wink, told her about the daughter he had who was her age, and added an extra one to the pile, tying a cloth around them. Farideh blushed the whole while.

She ate one as she walked back to the tallhouse. Maybe the disguise wasn't the worst.

"Here," she said, handing two of the pies to Dumuzi. He blinked at her.

"Was everything all right?"

Farideh shook her head. "I suppose. Strange, but no trouble. Anything here?"

"The devil left."

"Oh." Farideh considered the remaining handpies. "Do you want another?"

"No, no thank you." Farideh nodded to herself and turned to go inside. Maybe he'll come back, she thought. Maybe she ought to use the ritual she had to call him back.

No, she told herself. You don't want to do that.

"Should I have come?" She turned back to Dumuzi. "I was thinking, I shouldn't have let you go. That something might have happened."

She sighed. "Whatever Dahl has told you, I'm not a complete invalid. I can take care of myself."

Dumuzi nodded once. "You were raised by Verthisa . . . by Clanless Mehen," he amended. "And you aren't sick anymore." He hesitated. "Do you even need a doorguard?"

Farideh looked at him a long time. "What is it you want?" she asked.

Behind his teeth, Dumuzi's tongue fluttered nervously. "Help," he said. "Answers. I would stay," he added quickly. "If it's all the same to you. There aren't many better places to wait in this city."

Are you planning to hurt my father? Farideh wanted to ask. Are you here to drag him back to Djerad Thymar?

Are you my brother?

"Suit yourself," she said instead, and went back into the lonely tallhouse.

10

THE MAN SITTING ACROSS THE TABLE FROM DAHL DIDN'T LOOK LIKE THE sort of contact he expected from the agent they often called "High Cormyr." Not a noble, not a merchant, not even the servant of such a person, Garce the Scythe was ragged as a tinker, half-drunk, half-mad, and completely paranoid.

"What'd you do with the other fella?" he said, after Dahl had explained things.

"He's gone," Dahl said calmly. "He'll be back, but in the meantime, he's left me instructions to carry on with your mission."

"A mission you don't even know the details of," Garce said, fixing him with a wild eye. "Convenient."

Dahl cursed and glanced around the gloomy Nightgate Inn, the only place he could convince Garce to meet him, and the only inn outside the city walls. Not a soul was paying the slightest attention to Dahl, all sunk in their own gossips and troubles. He rolled his right sleeve up past the elbow, and set his fingertips on the skin there. "*Vivex prujedj*," he murmured, too quietly—he hoped—for even Garce to make out. A tattoo of a harp and moon in blue inks burned up through the skin.

The tinker might not have understood the trigger phrase, but he knew well enough that something magical had happened, and he leaped from his seat. Dahl had to all but throw himself over the table to stop the hand reaching for a weapon. He held the Harper tattoo in front of Garce's face.

"See?" Dahl said. "See? He and I work together. Which means you and I work together, all right? I don't know details, because our friend didn't write them down. He wrote your name and a few others. I know you're working in the north, between here and Arabel. I know enough of what's happening out there to be sure you're going to need my help soon if you don't already. Tell me what we're doing."

Garce eyed the mark. "Anyone could have one of those."

"Have you got one?"

"I work with you, not for you," Garce spat, but he settled back down. "When's he coming back?"

"Can't say," Dahl said.

"You kill him?"

"Of course not."

"Did he run away from his wedding?" Dahl raised his eyebrows, and the tinker folded his arms and tilted his chair back. "Yeah, I guessed who he might be. Is that what happened?"

"No," Dahl said, even though it was halfway to a lie, so far as he could tell. "It's another mission."

"More important than this one?"

"You tell me," Dahl said.

Garce kept his eyes on Dahl as he waved the serving girl over. "What are you drinking?"

Whiskey and an ale, Dahl thought. "I don't drink at meetings like this."

"Two ales," Garce said. When the woman had walked off, he added, "Don't want to stand out, do you?" When the server returned with the flagons, and had walked away, Dahl leaned forward.

"I know you're smuggling something."

"Never smuggled in my life."

"I know it's been costing our friend a fair pile of coin."

"Doesn't spend anything he doesn't want to."

"I know whatever it is, no one seems to have put their finger on it."

"'Cause I don't flap my gums to any and all."

"And you're afraid you'll be shut down," Dahl said. "But I also know that our friend doesn't go in for schemes of wealth and glory. He's an honorable fellow at his core, and he wouldn't work with you if you weren't the same sort. So what is it, and how does it aid Cormyr?"

Garce sucked his teeth, watched Dahl as if waiting for some new sign to come burning out of the younger man's forehead—a mark of his true alliances. Dahl sighed.

"I can't help you if you don't tell me," Dahl said. "And if you came to meet me here, I know you need aid. So what is it you're smuggling?"

"It's not smuggling. Not exactly. So if you *are* with the Crown, you've got no grounds to shut it down."

"Duly noted," Dahl said. Another lull. "If you're not going to tell me, how about you tell me what it is you need? Because the notes I *do* have make it very clear you're getting coin and more from our friend on a regular basis."

"Until he ran off," Garce sniffed. "You name it, I can probably find a damned use for it."

"Coin," Dahl said. "Food?"

"Ayup."

"Weapons?"

"Some."

"Horses? Spell components?"

"I *told* you, I can find a use for it all."

Realization dawned on Dahl. "You're moving refugees."

Garce's face darkened. "Keep your voice down." He looked around the taproom. "Shade finds out there's great groups of people moving through the forest, they've got targets they don't even have to work for." He made a face. "Not to mention how too many nobles feel about the unwashed masses pouring into their shining city."

Dahl blew out a breath, wanting to curse. How many people were in on this plan? How many points of failure were there? How much had Brin been funding the system?

"How well is it working?" he asked.

"Two hundred to the city in the last month? Another hundred on their way this tenday? Our friend probably has better records."

"Who else knows? It can't just be you."

Garce drank deeply from his ale. "Nay. We need more supplies, and with the trade roads overrun, they don't come cheap. You get me what I need, and we'll see about other agents." Dahl had no idea where he was going to get any of it, but agreed that he and Garce could meet here again, next tenday.

"At the least, I need waybread and bandages," Garce said, as Dahl stood up to leave. "Get me that, and maybe we'll talk about the rest of the agents you want."

Dahl paused. "Did you ever know a woman in Suzail called Marjana?"

"No." Garce narrowed his eyes. "Why? What'd she say about me?"

"Never mind." Dahl said his farewells and wound his way through the tavern. Not a perfect meeting, but at least he'd gotten *some* information out of Garce. He'd have to see about Vescaras fronting the coin for those supplies—

". . . the Dalelands are completely overrun," he heard a man saying as he left the tavern. He stopped in the courtyard before the door, where a few merchants lingered beside a laden cart. "They say there's no one left to reinforce them—that Myth Drannor can't even keep Shade back from Harrowdale any longer. They'll be driven into the sea before Marpenoth."

Dahl's blood turned cold and still in his veins, leaving his head feeling numb and cut off from the rest of him. Harrowdale was supposed to be safe, he thought. Harrowdale wasn't in Shade's path.

It's gossip, he told himself. It's travelers exaggerating things they've heard along the road. Pick your feet up. Walk back into the city. You have to meet with Vescaras.

What part of him managed to get his feet moving, Dahl couldn't say—fear seemed to disconnect his thoughts from the rest of him. His family lived not a day from the center of Harrowdale, New Velar. Anyone marching on the city from the west would pass right by the little farmstead, and what army would leave the fields of wheat lying, the stores undisturbed, his family safe and sound.

You don't know what's happened, Dahl reminded himself as he made his way through the city gates and up the curving Promenade. Shade had been staying to the south. They'd been avoiding Myth Drannor, the bastion of the elves' power, and therefore steering well clear of Harrowdale. They had no reasons to turn north. Harrowdale was supposed to be safe.

The Witch-Duke's Bride was a far posher tavern than the Nightgate Inn had been, with polished wooden paneling and artful hanging lamps. An enormous glaive-fish hung mounted over the doors to the kitchen as if leaping over the lintel, looking startled that there was no longer any sea for it to land in. Dahl spotted Vescaras in the corner, near the servers' door, and strode toward him.

"Don't sit," Vescaras murmured. "Everyone here knows enough to know you're my servant."

Dahl scowled at him and made a stiff bow. "Any luck?"

"Not much. You were right—she stopped performing here, even though the pay was very good."

Dahl had spent the last month decoding the documents Brin's street-eyes had recovered from Marjana's rooms. The lists of contacts hidden in fake love letters. The notes on her observations secreted into the notes of sheet music. The names of eighteen locations—only half of them now picked out of an unnecessarily complicated cipher—scratched into the wooden sides of the box that held the parchments. Marjana had been afraid enough to forgo the usual symbols and codes—and Dahl felt as if he were trying to learn another language just unraveling what she'd left behind.

"We'll have to check every place on the list," Vescaras said. "You still think this is about Sharrans?"

"The business in the palace says yes," Dahl replied. "And I don't think Marjana would go to this trouble over much else."

Vescaras made a noncommittal noise, and sipped his drink, a small glass of something amber. "How did you fare?"

"Better," Dahl said. "High Cormyr's been a busy boy. We're going to need coin though—a goodly amount." Vescaras scowled up at him. "We can talk about why later," Dahl said. "Someplace quieter." He shifted to the balls of his feet. "Have you heard anything about the Dales?"

Was it Dahl's imagination, or did Vescaras avert his eyes at that? The half-elf raised his glass to the light. "The trade roads are more or less shut down. You can't get past Wheloon going east, and there's no chance of heading north." He sighed and gestured to the seat opposite himself. "Sit. Do you want a drink?"

"I thought equerries didn't drink."

"I'm a wine merchant," Vescaras said. "All my servants drink." He waved to the fellow standing near the cellar door, and signaled for him to bring a second round. "Besides, as everyone just saw, you're a very hardworking fellow with a magnanimous lord."

"You know something," Dahl said, feeling as if his stomach was going to invert.

"I don't," Vescaras admitted. "I wish I could say differently, but no one knows anything. And it's going to try and drive you mad, so this is me trying to forestall it." The server returned with two more glasses of the amber liquor. "Evereskan zzar."

Dahl's gorge rose. "I don't drink zzar."

"It's very good zzar."

"I've had some bad experiences. If it smells like almonds, I don't want it."

Vescaras sighed and sipped his own. "Fine. Why don't you go, take the night off? Get yourself whatever swill will take your mind off of things. You can't change whatever's happening, and you certainly can't do anything about it tonight."

"We have too much to do."

"Hells, visit one of the taverns on the list if it makes you feel more like you're managing." He finished the glass. "But, Dahl, I do mean it—there's nothing more you can do."

Vescaras was right. Or he might have been right—that was as near as Dahl could allow, even with a whiskey in his belly and an ale in his hand. He looked around the taproom, the first name on Marjana's list. He couldn't, after all, make a sending to his mother and tell her that she needed to gather everyone up and run for the hills.

But if he was wrong? If he sent them out into the wilderness? If he sent them running in the direction of the Shadovar forces?

"I hear," a grim-faced woman with a scar down one cheek said to her neighbors, "that the only way to get up to the Dales now is to sail around the Dragonmere and come up through New Velar. The entire countryside is beset with armies."

He wondered if the woman knew from her superiors . . . and what would his mother even think hearing his voice from out of the ether? She didn't know he was a Harper. She didn't have any reason to think her youngest son—surely still in far off Waterdeep—had information that she, looking down into the valley from the farmhouse's enviable perch, couldn't have.

"Can't even do that," a man scoffed. "Blockades are settling in, sure as the sunrise. Heard it from a trader out of Procampur."

Dahl eyed the man and downed another whiskey. If a blockade settled in the harbor of New Velar, then there would be nowhere to run, not really. The Shadovar could cut off the Dales completely, and even if it was just to close in on Myth Drannor and its legendary power, thousands of people would die. He finished another ale. Or they wouldn't, because there would be no blockade, no march north. There was no way to know without the intelligence, which Dahl had no access to in Suzail.

When the tavernkeeper came back, Dahl told her to leave the bottle. She gave him a skeptical look that he met with a stack of coins.

"I think you've had enough."

Dahl laughed. "Trust me. I haven't. Leave the bottle. Take the coin."

She set the bottle of whiskey, three-quarters empty, on the bar. "Take the bottle," she said, "and get out of my taproom until you're sobered up."

Dahl wove through the tables and patrons, picking up more disheartening snippets. Shade had taken Arabel, definitely this time. Shade had Crown Prince

Irvel locked up in their secret laboratories. The Purple Dragon had returned from beyond the grave and circled his former kingdom like a vulture around a dying horse. Shade had wiped Shadowdale off the map and turned the legendary wizard who lived there into a shambling, undead blasphemy.

"Otherwise," he heard them say, "we'd surely have an easier time of it."

Dahl wondered if the speakers had any idea what was happening in the world beyond the taproom, beyond Cormyr, beyond the heartlands of Faerûn. Some days the reports he studied made it feel as if the entire plane were falling apart, from the Spine of the World down to Durpar, from far off Kara-Tur, to alien Laerakond. Anyone with the powers of the Sage of Shadowdale would be in high demand, when not even the gods could seem to stop this upheaval.

This is how the world ends, Dahl thought, tipping back the bottle. And you can't stop it.

Ah, there it is, he thought bitterly, standing in the rain in the middle of the Promenade. The tide of melancholy, the fear he knew he'd just shackled himself to, unable to fight his way free of it. He couldn't solve this, couldn't save them. Couldn't stop imagining Shadovar infantry gutting his mother in the doorway, cutting down his nieces and nephews, burning down the farmhouse with everyone in it while his granny called them filthy names.

This is how the world ends, he thought, swaying on his feet, and this is how you lose the little esteem Vescaras has for you. Because if he so much as breathed wrong, Dahl was sure he was going to lose the fingerhold of control he still had. The terrible images kept skipping through his thoughts. His throat closed around a lump. He poured more whiskey on top of it. There was no going back to the Dragon's Jaws, not like this.

He thought of the other names on his list—taprooms and festhalls and inns. He hadn't seen anything in the first one. He wouldn't see anything in the others, he thought. Sharrans liked their secrets, and they could certainly hide from the likes of Dahl.

He stared down at his feet, glued to the cobbles, and let the rain drip off his head.

But they can't hide from Farideh, he thought.

Dahl considered the Promenade stretching off to the west, away from the Dragon's Jaws and toward the tallhouse. He went to take another sip of the whiskey, then thought better of it. This could work. If he could manage to be a little soberer.

"Well met," he muttered to himself, in practice. "I have a problem, and I think you can help me."

He passed the bottle off to a vagrant, shoved the thoughts of Harrowdale and Shadovar down deep, deep, deep. If she started an argument about the drinking, he didn't have to bring it up. And if he failed and it all came out and he wept like a babe, well, at least she'd already seen *that*, and she didn't hold it against him the way Vescaras was sure to. And the time Farideh had seen him come undone was worse—he'd been caught in a memory of losing his paladinhood, reliving every awful, heartbreaking moment, and all Farideh could see or hear was Dahl, pleading for answers, pleading for a way to fix whatever had broken his life.

If he was upset about his mother and his family and got too emotional, well, that wasn't worse, was it? Of course not. She already knew exactly how much of a weeping mouse he could seem. It would take a lot to beat that.

"If you come with me to this taproom," he practiced turning onto the Promenade, "and help me find a Sharran . . . I will buy you an ale."

And then you can ask her what she sees when she looks at you, he thought.

No. No, no, no. That was the last thing he needed right now: an answer he didn't want as to why Oghma and Farideh hated him.

She doesn't hate you, he reminded himself as he came to the door. For even though Dahl knew that much when they were together, apart he felt surely he'd remembered wrong. And you like her well enough, he added. He knocked. You are friends enough to ask for this favor, that's certain. She's not going to think you're too stupid to manage. The door opened.

"Well met," he said. "I have a . . ." Dahl stopped. The woman who opened the door wasn't Farideh, and though she struck him as familiar, he was sure he'd never seen her before. Human, long dark brown hair, tall enough for her to look Dahl in the eye. Slim. A dark-blue dress—the sort of thing fashionable Cormyrean women wore, with a snug bodice and a wide, slashed skirt—but she wasn't Cormyrean, not judging by the ample plunge of bronzed skin that collar showed off. He met her eyes—mismatched, brown and blue; he would have remembered that—and . . .

"Oh Watching Gods," Dahl said. "Farideh?"

She didn't blush so hard in a human's skin. "Please don't say anything."

"Why are you . . . What happened?" he managed. "Is it *permanent?*"

There was no mistaking the disgust in that look. "*No.*" She ran a hand through her hair, as if she were trying to push it back where it normally fell, held back by horns that weren't there. "War wizards. The princess wanted to talk to me about that note. It hasn't worn off yet."

"Well," he said, "you certainly don't stand out like this. I mean, in the bad way. I mean . . . You know what I mean."

She stared at him coolly. "No. What do you mean?"

"Don't take it like that," Dahl said. He leaned against the doorjamb. "I mean no one's giving you trouble. You can go to the market like that, get a fair deal. If you wanted."

"What do *you* want?" she asked. She narrowed her eyes at him. "Are you drunk?"

Dahl wondered if she'd caught him looking at her breasts. If it would help to point out he didn't realize it was her, or if it was too late and this was all going to sound wrong anyway. "Yes, I am drunk, but I have a mission . . . a thing to do. Come with me to this taproom."

Farideh looked startled, and it was odd how *obvious* that was on her face. "Sorry?"

"I'm mostly sure that there are more Sharrans in the city," Dahl said, lowering his voice. "But I can't find them." He told her about Marjana's notes, about the puzzle he was trying to unravel. "If you look—the way you did for Raedra—maybe you could spot them?"

"Oh," she said. She folded her arms under her breasts. "I . . . Look, I would be glad to help, but I've had such a long, awful day. I don't feel like going out."

"It's not going out," Dahl assured her. "It's preventing the collapse of a kingdom and the success of a wicked empire. You love that, so far as I can see." At least that got a smile out of her. "I'll buy you a drink. Two if you spot my Sharran. And . . . I'll call truce. No more arguing. I'll be perfect company, I promise."

Farideh's gaze flicked over him. "Are you going to keep drinking?"

"Not while I'm working," he said, and he held out a hand.

• • •

THE SHELTER THEY'D built couldn't keep out the rain. Havilar lay on her damp bedroll, listening to the *drip-drip-drip* of it leaking between the pine branches and splashing against a cookpot. At least no one wanted for water. She turned over, toward Brin, tucking her arm under her head to accommodate her horn. He had managed to fall asleep, although Havilar knew if she so much as prodded him, he'd wake. So she only lay there, listening to the course of his breath, glad at least that *he* was getting a little rest.

Havilar had lost count of how many days had passed since they'd left Suzail, but the time was written in the layers of mud embedded in her clothes, in the tattered edge of her stormcloak, in the awful, itchy patches the damp left on her legs. It had been so long since there'd been a town to stop in, even though she was sure that they hadn't gotten all that far. The rain just slowed everyone down, and down, and down, the mud sucking everything out of them.

She laid a hand on Brin's chest, and his eyes opened. "What?"

"Nothing. Go back to sleep." He smiled and laid a hand over hers, and Havilar shifted so her cheek rested on his shoulder. Too many days to count, and still there was no sign at all of the crown prince. And Havilar's doubts were growing stronger and stronger, almost too strong to batter down. They wouldn't find him, not with what little they had. If the war wizards couldn't, then neither could they. And then what happened?

She dreamed of fire and a huge, empty landscape. Of a man laughing that sent shivers through her, and the smell of burned meat. Her glaive kept changing into some sort of staff, then into a snake, then she was holding Brin's hand as they crossed the burning plain. Then it wasn't Brin, but a tiefling woman with small, sharp horns like a mountain goat's and their hands melted into each other, and Havilar couldn't tell where she ended and the strange woman began . . . the shadows of strange, cackling creatures, all armed and armored, surrounded the two of them, and Havilar felt suddenly sick to her stomach. *You have to be brave*, the woman said. *Don't let her lure you in—*

A hand on her shoulder made Havilar sit bolt upright. Beside her, Brin startled awake. Crake stood over Havilar with a lopsided smile. "Your turn."

Brin settled back down, as Havilar buckled her armor back on and took up her glaive. "It's a quiet night," Crake said. "You'll have an easy time."

"I'm sure," Havilar said, not looking at him. She still felt as if she were going to vomit.

"I've been meaning to ask," Crake said, "since you're his lordship's dear darling and all." Havilar pushed past him to the watchpoint, but Crake followed. "What is it we're looking for exactly?"

"A friend," Havilar said. "Someone lost."

"Does he have a name?" Crake asked. Havilar sat and scanned the forest beyond, listening to the rain's patter so that she could hear the sounds that didn't fit with it.

"Is his name Crown Prince Irvel?" Crake asked. Havilar scowled at him, and the human gave her a cheeky grin. "Come on, sweet. I'm cleverer than I look."

"So what if it is?" Havilar said.

"If it is," Crake said, sitting too close beside her, "I think some renegotiations are in order. We're not going to find him—yon war wizards couldn't, everyone knows that, and so we're not getting paid that part of the reward." Havilar fought the sudden, intense urge to elbow him in the face. She rolled her shoulders as if she could shake it off—Crake was obnoxious, but she didn't need to hit him.

"And you don't need to be slogging through the mud for a deluded fool who clearly doesn't appreciate you enough." He reached over and pushed a strand of hair off her face.

Havilar's hand shot up and grabbed hold of his wrist. "If you ever touch me again, I will split you like a log."

Crake pulled his hand back, studying her face in a calculating way that made her skin crawl. It was as if someone else's eyes were watching out of the rakish sellsword's face. Then he blinked and another cheeky grin curved his mouth. "I was going to make you a very similar offer, actually."

Something rustled out in the woods. Havilar went absolutely still, sweeping the dark night with her sensitive eyes. Not sensitive enough, she thought. The shadows were too deep, too dark. The moon was smothered behind a blanket of clouds, and the glow it sent out was only enough to see shadows. There wasn't enough light to see, not even—

"There," Crake murmured. He pointed off into the gloom of the forest, off to the left. "At least four. Hrast—gnolls."

"How can you . . ." Havilar stopped herself. No time. She turned and prodded Constancia with the butt of her glaive. "Gnolls," she said when the knight stirred, and Constancia was up as if she'd never slept at all.

"To the east," Crake said, still looking out. "Four. Maybe five."

"More than that," Constancia said. "Gnolls surround. Take out the first group." She shook Mehen, then Kallan and Moriah awake as she spoke. She looked around. "Gods blast it, where's Desima?"

"Let's go," Crake said, taking Havilar's arm. "We can see what we're up against. Give the others time to prepare." He gave her a wicked grin. "Knock these dogs down and gain the glory."

Havilar wrinkled her nose. "Don't crowd me," she warned, shaking off his grasp. And glaive in hand, she slunk out into the night.

The forest crowded in on her, branches like reaching hands, brush like strangers stumbling into her path. She went smoothly, carefully, toward the patch of trees Crake had pointed to, picking out the way in the moonlight suffusing the clouds. As she reached the edge of a brier, she heard barking, growling voices. She slipped around the thorny barrier, until it was thin enough to see past.

Crake was right—five gnolls hunkered down in the clearing, watching over the pine bough structure, looking as if they were waiting for a signal, their spotted fur peeking out around scraps of armor scavenged from their victims. One had a glowstone cupped in its hand, its light enough to trace their wet noses, the edges of swords—

And Crake as he leaped right in and plunged his blade into the one holding the glowstone.

Havilar cursed. The glowstone's freed light made the battle much clearer.

To all of them. Four gnolls all turned on Crake, teeth bared, and still he wore that godsbedamned smirk. A disgust so visceral and violent hit her, and for a moment, she considered standing in the shadows, letting Crake fall.

Karshoj, Havilar thought. Where had *that* come from? She pressed through the brambles, glaive up, and caught one of the gnolls in the back, throwing them into confusion. One of them—a female with a jagged, bald scar across her snout, swung at Havilar. In the gloom, she nearly missed it, and twisted awkwardly under the sword.

Something *popped*.

Something fundamental, something that shouldn't have broken. Havilar could feel that much, but not the pain that should have come. Not the weakness. Not her shoulder, not a knee. She scurried backward, gaining the space to check herself.

Instead she saw, hanging in the air, a pair of devils no larger than barn cats. Ruby-red and winged like bats, they raced toward her attacker, claws outstretched. The gnoll who'd attacked her was so startled she didn't start screaming until the first creature had torn out her eyes.

Havilar shrieked and, all instinct, chopped her glaive through the nearer one. The blade severed its back and one wing, and the little devil burst into a cloud of flames and an ear-splitting screech. Havilar didn't watch. She turned and sliced toward the second devil, as it turned to see what the fuss was about. One well-placed strike, and it, too, died and returned to the Hells.

Panting, panicking, Havilar looked to Crake, and the last gnoll. The sellsword had lowered his weapon over another fallen beast and was staring at Havilar, looking puzzled and furious. He pursed his mouth, an expression that didn't seem suited to his face.

"Crake move!" Havilar shouted. But it didn't matter. The gnoll was already too close, too prepared. The sword came around Crake's neck and sliced deeply into his throat, spraying blood across the battleground.

Crake never made a sound. Never stopped staring at Havilar.

The last gnoll knew well enough to run then, but a bolt of shimmering power caught him in the back. Desima stood at the edge of the clearing, glaring at the fallen scout. She looked down at Crake and muttered a curse under her breath.

"Lords of the bloody Nine," she spat. "What happened?"

"He . . . he just stood there," Havilar said.

And the devils. The devils that appeared out of the air. They'd attacked the gnolls, she thought, the eerie shiver of her dreams trailing up her spine. They came for *you*.

This is how it starts, she thought, wishing Farideh were there to confirm it.

"Stay quiet," Desima said. "*Don't* move." And then she vanished.

11

26 Eleasias, the Year of the Nether Mountain Scrolls (1486 DR)
Suzail, Cormyr

THE BRIGAND'S BOTTLE MIGHT HAVE BEEN THE MOST ORDINARY INN IN all of Suzail, but to Farideh it felt as alien as stepping onto another plane. Dahl jerked against her arm as she stopped just inside the doorway.

"Everyone here is human," she hissed. Every single face in the taproom—from the merchants haggling over their ales to the beggars spending their alms to the young nobles in their cloaks, clearly enjoying a dip into the rougher parts of Suzail. Dahl looked over the room as if it hadn't occurred to him.

"To be fair," he said, "so are you for the moment."

She followed him across the room, aware of every eye that tracked her—a paltry fraction. Dahl had a point. To these people, she was nothing of note. Dahl guided her to a table in the corner of the taproom where a group of tipsy card players was calling it an early night. While Dahl called for two ales from the keghand, one of the players took Farideh's hand and helped her slide onto the bench that wrapped the table, pressing a quick kiss to her knuckles before she could snatch her hand back.

"I don't think I should be here," Farideh said to Dahl as he slid in beside her. "And you said you weren't drinking."

"It's to put in front of me. People don't just sit in taprooms, watching folks. And you *should* be here—how else are we going to manage this?"

"What if the spell wears off?"

"When did they tell you it would wear off?"

Farideh shrugged, studying the taproom, marking the exits, noting dangerous-looking people. "Before tomorrow morning."

"That's plenty of time." Dahl leaned in close—very close—and smiled at her. "Ready for your first Harper mission?"

Farideh drew back. "What are you doing?"

"We're crafting a cover," he said. "So when people look over here, they don't notice anything interesting. So relax. Look around." Farideh turned to the taproom, but she was still so aware of Dahl, leaning so close to her. "When people look over at this table," he said, "we want them to see a man and a woman, out for a drink. The man is clearly more interested in her than she is in him—he keeps on talking, but she's looking around like she wants a way out. But here's an important piece: is anyone making eye contact with you?"

A man in a blue cap with a small smile behind his trim beard. "Yes," she said. "Then look at me," Dahl said. "And smile, and say something."

Farideh turned and met Dahl's gray eyes. "Does it matter what I say?"

"Tell me who's watching."

"The sailor standing beside the bar."

"Good." Dahl grinned at her. "Now he knows our lady's not in any trouble—she's just bored. Though not *quite* bored enough to want to be whisked away. He'll have to wait for another evening, a few more tendays of our fellow being an *utter* clod. Ready to search?"

Farideh pushed an errant strand of hair out of her face and nodded. She made herself lean a little closer to Dahl—it would look right, she told herself. She closed her eyes and concentrated on the powers of the Hells that fed the soul sight, the gifts of Asmodeus.

It was enough to twist the powers: pain seized the back of her skull, and she gave a little gasp without meaning too. Farideh didn't hide her discomfort—maybe that would add to the ruse. She considered the room, while Dahl murmured a steady stream of nonsense—comments about the weather, the rising cost of feed, what Vescaras drank.

"You look Rashemi," he said suddenly, "has anyone told you that?"

Farideh turned back to him, surprised. He was leaning so close. She slid away without thinking about it. "Sorry, what?"

"Rashemi," he said again. "You know—from Rashemen?" He studied her a little more, the scrutiny incredibly distracting. "Or maybe . . . Mulan? A little Durpari? It's hard to say. But it should be easier to say, right? If the . . . other parts aren't there."

"The devil parts?" Farideh said irritably.

"I thought we called a truce," Dahl said. "I'm just saying, if they take away things like your horns and your eyes, you should be able to guess where your parents were from. What do you think? Have you got a guess?"

Lorcan's long ago words came back to her: *There aren't many likely options.* If she was the descendant of Bryseis Kakistos, there were only a handful of people who might have been her mother or father. "I think it doesn't matter."

Dahl shook his head. "That's . . . I can't imagine," he said, "not knowing where I came from. I mean, my family's been on the same farm for two hundred years. They've been in Harrowdale since anyone can remember. I just can't imagine anything else."

Farideh tried to imagine what it would be like to know anything beyond herself and Havilar and Mehen. Even Mehen's family in Djerad Thymar was as far off and mysterious as the dragonborn of ancient Abeir in his bedtime tales. And as for her blood relatives . . . there was only Bryseis Kakistos, the Brimstone Angel, the Nightmare of Vaasa.

"Do you think I could be Vaasan?" she asked. Dahl looked her over again.

"Maybe," he said. "Vaasan and something else. You're a bit darker than a Vaasan, but your cheekbones and nose . . . Why Vaasan?"

"I have an ancestor who was Vaasan. At least that's what Lorcan said."

"That sounds ominous," Dahl said.

"It's a really far-off ancestor," she assured him.

Farideh went back to considering the jumble of merchants and shopkeepers, apprentices and farmhands and sellswords. Their dappled souls came in every hue she could imagine, speckled with shadows—some faint, some deep and dark. One flickered with the half-written glyph of a god's blessing. A few she lingered on, long enough that the sense of what might sway them came to her—this one was so proud, the chance to clear a slight from her name would make her bend; that one was so consumed by hungers of the flesh that Farideh had to look away.

But none of them were Shar's.

She checked a second time, then a third, before at last she turned back to Dahl, her head pounding. "None of them."

Dahl seemed to deflate at that. "*None* of them? And definitely not any of the staff? Definitely not the tavernkeeper?"

"No," Farideh said. She covered her eyes with both hands, blocking the light. "Sorry."

He muttered a curse and sighed, and stood. Farideh waited, braced for the inevitable argument. Dahl said nothing and nothing . . .

A clay cup settled on the table before her. Dahl slid the whiskey over to her. "Here."

"I didn't find them."

"You tried. And I forgot it gives you a headache." He took up his own cup, toasted her.

"You said you wouldn't drink anymore."

"I'm fine," he said.

"You're drunk."

"Well it's not as if we have Sharrans to contend with, is it?" he said. "You're welcome for the whiskey. And the ales." He took another sip and shook his head. "If I see Brin again, I'm going to wring his neck."

"What's he done now?"

Dahl shrugged as if he couldn't tell her. "Harper things," he settled on. Then, "He was awfully sharp with you the day we arrived. That new?"

Farideh sipped her own whiskey, just enough to warm her mouth. "He's still angry. About what happened." She scanned the taproom again—it was easier than meeting Dahl's eyes. "I suppose I can't blame him. If not for me, none of this would have happened." She took another sip of whiskey, trying to loosen her suddenly tight throat.

Dahl snorted. "Look, let's be honest here." He turned in his seat to face her fully. "This was always going to happen to him. The richest royal family in Cormyr, and they don't have a soul in the line of succession until you get to the Lady Crownsilver? There's not a chance on Tymora's wheel that they're going to let a legitimized bastard's son run away into obscurity. If he hadn't come back, the war wizards would have been sicced on him. Don't let him tell you otherwise."

Farideh smiled. "Thank you." She wrapped her hands around the cup and sighed heavily. "It's sad. We used to be friends—and I don't have that many to spare. But then he and Havi . . . well, I became less a friend and more . . . an obstruction." She glanced at Dahl and then at the whiskey, her head pounding and her heart squeezed tight. "Gods, this makes you gloomy doesn't it? It was ages ago anyway. I should let it go."

Dahl smiled. "You know what's funny? I've known Brin for longer than you have now."

Farideh's throat tightened a little more. "That's true," she managed.

"This is the thing about Brin," Dahl proclaimed. "When he's feeling pressured, when he thinks people are trying to block him, he acts like a real cock."

A snort of laughter escaped Farideh before she could clap a hand over it. "Sorry," she said. "I don't hear a lot of Common cursing."

"You curse all the time!" Dahl cried.

"In *Draconic*," Farideh said. "You wouldn't say that in Draconic. It would sound . . . literal." She chuckled once. "But yeah. He's being a real cock."

"Because he's made himself an unenviable mess. It means all that noble upbringing, all that training to maneuver and manipulate and bully comes right out, and for all that he insists he's not like them, he's exactly like them. And I suspect he hates it."

Farideh gave Dahl a sidelong look. "Say something nice about him now. Be fair."

"He's not here." But when she didn't speak again, he sighed. "Fine. He's loyal—almost to a fault. I have never once worried about Brin turning traitor, and with as much turmoil and scheming and divided loyalties as Cormyr tends to accumulate, that's a tremendous asset." He finished his whiskey. "Also, he doesn't leave folks behind if he can help it—that's beyond loyal. It's *almost* insane." He got a distant look for a moment. "It definitely makes *my* life trickier, but I can't complain. Then *I'm* being a real cock." Farideh laughed. "Is that enough, or do I need to praise his taste in clothes too?"

"You've thought about that a lot."

Dahl shrugged and picked up the flagon of ale that was just for show. "It goes well with doing what I do."

"It makes me wonder what you say about me when I'm not around."

"I will *tell* you, right to your face," he said. "You are *maddening*. You never just listen—you've got to come up with your own answer instead, even if it's exactly what I told you already. And you could give Brin a run for his coin, the way you try to rescue everyone. But," he said, as she started to reply, "for someone who agrees she's made several extremely foolish decisions, you can be incredibly astute, and I am man enough to admit you make me feel like an idiot at times. Also, you look very nice in that dress." He waved at the keghand and gave her a triumphant grin. "There: one criticism, two compliments."

Farideh's face ached with all the blood in her cheeks. "That first one is half of each."

"Greedy," he said and signaled for two more ales. "Check again for that Sharran?" She called up the soul sight, her head still pounding, and scanned the taproom. There was nothing to see, and she was too aware the whole time of Dahl's gaze on her. *You look very nice in that dress.* She fidgeted with the cuff of one sleeve.

"Nothing," she said when she'd made a sweep of the room. She let the soul sight fall and saw the man beside the column opposite their table watching her. She turned to Dahl and smiled. "Should we go?"

The keghand set two ales on the table, and Dahl handed him more coin. "Suffer through my company a bit more," he said. "Here."

She watched him sip from the flagon of ale. You can't take care of everyone, she reminded herself. "What are you really doing in Suzail? Is it this?"

"Partly," Dahl said. "An . . . acquaintance of mine died. I'm here to see to her things. And this," he said, with no small significance, "is one of those things."

Not an acquaintance, she thought. Another Harper. "So you're fully . . . with Tam again?" she asked, carefully. "Well done. And I mean that," she added, before he could get upset at her. "You can't pretend I haven't always thought you were very clever."

"Yes. Well," Dahl said. "I'm not clever enough to figure out what this is."

"It might be nothing."

"It might have been nothing," Dahl allowed, "but then you found a traitor in the princess's chambers." He frowned at the taproom a moment, before turning to her. "Can I ask *you* something?" he said. "How is it you can do this?" He nodded to the taproom. "See people's souls, the marks of gods. I always thought warlock magic was meant more for . . . you know, fighting. Corrupting. Not that you," he added, "corrupt things. Just . . . you could. If you were a different person."

Farideh looked away. "It's . . . meant more for that. For finding people who could *be* corrupted." She took another swallow of ale. "And I *don't* use it for that."

"I didn't say you did," Dahl said.

Farideh stopped herself—it had been too long a day, and they'd agreed to stop arguing. And to be fair, he *hadn't* said she used the soul sight to find corruptible people. She drank a little more ale.

"What do you see when you look at me?" Dahl asked abruptly. "Do I look corrupted?"

Farideh kept looking out at the taproom. "You asked me before not to look. So I haven't. But I don't think so."

"And if I asked you to look again?" he asked. "Would you?"

Farideh sipped the ale. He'd been so insistent before that she not look, not tell him what else she could read in the letters on his soul. "How much have you had to drink?"

"I'm not *that* drunk," he said, affronted. "I can hold my ale."

And your whiskey, she thought. "You didn't want me to before."

"I changed my mind."

"Ask me when you're definitely sober." He started to protest, but she stopped him. "Dahl, I'm not looking while you're drunk, even if you're not *that* drunk. Ask another time."

"I will ask," he said stubbornly. "I want to know." He settled back against the seat and drank his ale. "Maybe that's something you can't imagine—having a god jerk you around with cryptic messages and cruel acts."

It nearly made her laugh, but she stopped herself. She wasn't explaining *that* to Dahl. "Why did you want to be a paladin?" she asked. "I mean, in the first place."

Dahl regarded her warily. "Why shouldn't I have? I liked books. I liked learning things, finding answers."

"But why a paladin then? I mean you can do those things in all sorts of ways. Why aren't you a wizard? Or a scholar? Or a courtier or something?"

"Why aren't *you* a wizard?"

Farideh laughed. "Do you know I learned a little from a wizard? Garago—he lived in our village. Not magic, not quite. But sums and things. History. How to read a scroll, but that was it."

"But not even rituals?"

"He didn't do ritual magic. He was . . . a little odd. I think he ended up in Arush Vayem because something *magical* happened to him. I don't know if he could have taught me magic if he'd wanted to. He didn't always remember things, and there were times you knew not to go visit Garago, because he was in a black mood, slinging spells at ghosts." She smiled wanly at her flagon. "But he was nice other times. Lent me books."

"Better than most wizards I've met," Dahl said.

"Well, my tally's up two horrible wizards—assuming we count the arcanist—and two very nice ones," she said. "So I'll hold off judgment." He chuckled. "So what's the real answer?" she asked. "Why did you want to be a paladin?"

Dahl shifted as if uncomfortable. He looked off at the innocent tavernkeeper. "I liked to read," he said slowly. "And I liked swinging a sword. And I liked being around people who weren't puzzled by that. And I loved Oghma. So it all fit, for a time." He picked up his flagon before adding, "I thought about some of those other things—a wizard or a priest or maybe bookseller. But . . ." He shrugged and looked back at her, maybe a little sheepishly. "I know where I'm from. My father wouldn't have really understood giving up farming for books alone."

Farideh rested her head on her hand. "Does he understand your being a Harper?"

"No, he . . . he died. Two years ago. Of a heartstop. He, um"—Dahl cleared his throat—"he thought I was a secretary in Waterdeep at the time." He looked down at his ale. "Which he didn't really understand either." He sank into a gloomy silence, and Farideh's stomach twisted, like it was pulling down her heart. He finished off the ale in a great gulp.

"There's rumors," he said, suddenly, almost frantically, "that the Shadovar are marching on Harrowdale. But I can't make heads or tails of what's true and what's not, and I can't find anyone who knows and I can't leave the city. So."

"Oh Dahl," she said. He shook his head, as if to cut her off, and she bit back her sympathies. She looked away, out at the taproom. A man in dark leathers was watching them from one of the heavy lumber posts, but then there was no cover to keep anymore. She watched Dahl from the corner of her eye, perversely reminded of the time Dahl had confessed the story of his fall from grace with Oghma—the feeling that she had to say something, or that there was something *right* to even say, pulled on her nerves. But anything she could say seemed faint or false or the sort of thing that would just irritate Dahl. She saw him look over at her, still frowning.

"You know I can tell you're doing that," Dahl said. "You're looking right at me."

Farideh colored. *Karshoj.* She'd forgotten again about the disguise spell. "Sorry," she said quickly.

He smiled at her crookedly. "You do that, don't you? Now I know. Now I'm going to watch for it."

"I'm sorry," she said again, and she no longer had any idea what to do with her face. She looked down at the table. "I was trying to decide if it was better to tell you I'm sorry about your father, and I doubt he thought poorly of you—even if it felt like it—or if you didn't really want to hear that now, because it's long past and you didn't want to bring it up in the first place. But I am sorry about your father." She folded her hands under the table. "I'm not trying to irritate you."

"You're not irritating me," he said.

"You have to call a truce to spend more than a few minutes with me. I irritate you."

"Everyone irritates me then," Dahl said. "Anyway, I'd rather be out with you than Vescaras. Or Brin. Or *Dumuzi.*" She didn't say anything. "Thank you," he added. "About my father."

She nodded, looking again out at the taproom. The man by the post was still watching. Farideh's nerves itched, the unseen shadow-smoke trying to coil from her frame. He looked away, without really looking away.

"I do know what that's like," she said, keeping her eyes on the man. "Not knowing what your father really thinks of you. Not knowing if he appreciates who you are. What you want."

"Mehen adores you," Dahl scoffed.

"He adores Havilar," Farideh corrected. "And I know he loves me, but I also know he probably wishes I were more like her. *She*, he understands." She wrapped her hands around the flagon. "I would bet your father loved you as much. Even if he didn't understand."

Dahl said nothing, and so Farideh kept her eyes on the taproom, wishing she had let it lie. She hardly knew how to talk to anyone anymore, after so long alone. She sighed quietly. The man by the post turned away again.

"I think we should leave," Farideh said.

"Why?" Dahl said. "Do I irritate *you*?"

"There's someone watching," she said quietly. "There aren't any Sharrans here, and if there are, you are certainly in no shape to deal with them anymore."

He scowled. "I could manage. Who's watching?"

"The fellow by the post. He's been looking over for the last quarter hour at least."

Dahl looked without looking—he was still steady enough for that. "Might just be an admirer."

Farideh blushed. "I doubt that."

"Maybe he's admiring me. You don't know." He frowned at the table. "All right. We go. Just a breath." He took the ale she'd hardly touched and drained half of it.

"Come on," she said, standing. She reached up to take her cloak off the peg.

A man came up out of a door she hadn't noticed, a cask under one arm and another hauled up on his shoulder. "Found them!" he called to the tavernkeeper as he backed the door open. "You have to tell the keghands to stop moving things around down there—I have a *system*, gods blast it."

Farideh stopped, one hand on the cloak. The cellarer hadn't been in the room when she'd looked before. She summoned the soul sight and sure enough, the cellarer's form became pocked with dark vortices, as if the touch of the goddess had rotted him. He looked over at Farideh, with a mild, puzzled expression. Farideh went cold.

Dahl set a hand on her shoulder, and she jumped. "What's wrong?"

"The Sharran," she murmured. "The cellarer is the Sharran."

Dahl's eyebrows flew up. "Are you sure?"

"It's him, it's definitely him."

That was when Ilstan's spell peeled off of her with a crackle and a snap, and she was suddenly the only tiefling in the taproom, scintillating with a failing disguise spell and with every eye upon her.

• • •

Lorcan watched the inn's taproom through the surface of a mirror, the busy noises of the customers tinny and distant through the scrying's magic, and utterly unimportant. Lorcan focused on the young couple in the back corner—Farideh, without her horns and with a human's eyes and hair, and Dahl. The Harper sat close—too close—murmuring in her ear while she looked around the taproom. A sudden grin split her face and she turned to look at him, laughing—and even if the human scowled at that, it wasn't honest. His eyes were laughing too.

Something deep inside Lorcan sheared off like an iceberg.

He reached for the scourge pendant.

Behind Lorcan the portal set into the marrow-weeping wall split, sending a faint shudder through the fingerbone tower. He whipped around, fire flooding his hands. A human woman with steel-colored hair and damp robes strode toward him. "You need to come."

"What's happened?" Lorcan demanded.

"A pair of godsbedamned imps showed up," Sairché said through the human's mouth. "And there are *gnolls*. You need to come right now."

"Beshaba shit in my eyes!" Lorcan shouted. He glanced back at the hateful image in the mirror, as Farideh turned back to the room, as Dahl's eyes drifted down to the scoop of her collar. He stormed toward the portal. "If this is anything short of an emergency," he snarled at his sister, "I will make sure you never leave that doomed little plane."

Sairché said nothing as they passed through the portal—and that put Lorcan on edge more than her sudden appearance. He stepped through the passage and into a small clearing in a dense forest. Havilar stood, clutching her glaive, amid the scattered corpses of five gnolls and a human man.

Lorcan stopped, staring at the corpse. Not a human.

"Where did you pick up a—"

"Not the issue," Sairché said. The air was thick with the brimstone smell of Hellsportals, and the forest echoed with shouts and the hoots of more gnolls.

"What is going on?" Havilar cried. Lorcan forced himself to smile at Havilar. "Well met. I hear you're having some trouble with imps?"

Havilar looked at him as if he were completely mad. "How do you know Desima?"

Lorcan kept smiling. Beside him, Sairché was stiff as a rod. "Well you don't think I'd leave you all alone, do you?" he said. "We're allies, remember? And if I have to watch over your sister in Suzail, someone else clearly should be here with you."

"She's a *spy*?"

"She's an ally," Lorcan said. In the distance, a gnoll screamed.

"They're getting closer," Sairché noted.

Lorcan didn't break his gaze. "She said a pair of imps appeared. Did you call those?"

"How would I call an imp?" Havilar turned on Desima. "Maybe she did it. Did you . . . you tracked us down. You pretended to need work. You're . . . Who in the Hells are you?"

"Just an ally," Sairché said, still watching the border of the clearing. The calls were coming from all sides, it seemed, echoing through the ancient forest. "You should get her out of here."

"I'm not going anywhere!" Havilar cried.

"Imps," Lorcan reminded Havilar. "Did they say anything?"

"No!" Havilar said. "They just . . . showed up and attacked and . . ." She looked out into the darkness. "I have to go."

"You have to tell me everything," Lorcan said. Sairché cast a straggly branch of lightning from her wand into the shadows. "Did you hear anything? Smell anything? See anything?"

Havilar's gold eyes looked from him to Sairché in her human disguise. "Felt something," she said, as if she wished she hadn't. "Like something snapped. I thought . . . I thought I got hurt, but then . . ." She looked back at the dead man and then at Sairché. She shook her head, as if she couldn't do this. "It's starting, isn't it?"

Perhaps. Or perhaps the imps were an overture from another devil. Perhaps this was how Invadiah made her move, or perhaps this was all a trick of Sairché's. "It might be," Lorcan allowed. "Which means you need to be careful."

Two gnolls broke through the brush. Lorcan moved to pull Havilar out of their reach, but the tiefling woman turned, glaive in hand and shock nowhere in sight. The blade shot out, faster than Lorcan would have imagined, spearing the creature through the hollow of its throat and sending a spray of blood through the rain. The second gnoll raised its dull blade over her. Another fork of lightning arced past, crackling so close to Havilar's scalp that Lorcan caught his breath. The gnoll convulsed, Havilar's glaive swept up into its belly and it screamed.

"Shit and ashes, Sairché!" Lorcan cried. "What did I *just* say?"

"Sairché?" Havilar straightened, glaive still ready. The pit of Lorcan's stomach dropped.

Lorcan stepped in front of his sister now, the requirements of their deal making it impossible to do anything else. "Havi, think this through. She's the only one who saw what happened—do you want the blame for that fellow's death?"

"They'll believe me."

"Brin and Mehen will." Havilar stiffened, glanced at Sairché. "She's not ideal," Lorcan went on. "I know that. I wouldn't have sent her if there were any other devil I could trust—no, not trust. I don't trust her, and I wouldn't ask you to either. Not completely. You're not stupid."

Havilar didn't move, eyes flicking from Lorcan to Sairché and back.

"Whatever just happened," Lorcan said, spreading his hands, "you're right: it's beginning. We don't know what you'll end up with, and we can't say that you won't be safer far, far away from everyone. Someone needs to stay here, someone who can pull you away if need be."

Havilar shook her head. "Not her. *Not* her. *Karshoj* . . ."

Voices in the distance shouted for Havi, for Desima, for Crake. "Havilar," Lorcan said, "you don't need to trust her, but you need to trust me. She can't hurt you again. And she's the only one who I can guarantee won't hurt you if these powers turn out to be stronger than your sister's." Mehen's voice shouting for his daughter, all too near.

"Choose, Havi," Lorcan said.

Havilar swallowed. "Fine. Fine. For now."

One down, Lorcan thought. "Good girl." He turned to Sairché. "I trust you can manage from here?" Before she could answer, he opened the portal again, returning to the fingerbone tower, the scrying mirror, and Farideh.

. . .

AT THE ROYAL palace, the clouds broke just wide enough to let the moon shine through, even though the patter of rain still rattled against the windowpanes of the prince's sickroom. Raedra sighed.

"At least you're sleeping through this wretched weather," she said. "I think I might go mad at the sound of rain some days." She reached over and brushed her brother's hair off his forehead with the edge of her ring fingernail. "Everyone seems to be inside nearly all the time, soaked through the moment you step outside. I asked after the horses for you. Only Bitter and Solace have rainscald—you know they love the rain, silly things.

"Granddad has a cough, and wouldn't you know? So do Turin Huntcrown, Stossian Ambershield, and Pheonard Crownsilver. Unbearable toadies, the lot of them.

"Oh, I know Mother would have words if she heard me say that—but I'm right. And she's . . . sleeping." Raedra tucked Baerovus's hand back under the thin gray blanket, pressing his palm between her hands briefly. She sighed again. "Rover, if you can hear me, we're not giving up. None of us is giving up. Promise you aren't either . . ." She swallowed against the sudden lump in her throat.

"You're going to miss the funeral as well," she said. "Mother's through making plays and excuses. The only one who still believes Father's alive is Aubrin. And if he doesn't come back soon—"

The door opened, and the cleric's assistant scurried in, trailed by a dark-haired man of middling years. Erzoured, the "Baron Boldtree." Raedra schooled her expression into a mask, though it meant little. Erzoured knew exactly how she felt about him.

"My lord," she said.

"Your Highness," Erzoured said. "You're up late. I hope you're well— well as can be, that is."

"I was hoping to have a private moment with the prince."

"Is he not crown prince yet?" Erzoured asked.

"Give His Majesty time to grieve. There's no need to declare it when the line is clear."

Erzoured shrugged. "Unless he decides not to declare Baerovus. One couldn't blame him—it's all a terrible tragedy. Not that our Rover can't pull through—stubborn rascal." He reached over and gently tousled Baerovus's hair, a perfect gesture of avuncular warmth. The cleric's assistant smiled, and Raedra thought she would scream.

Emvar Obarskyr had not only fathered Halance Crownsilver—sometime after, he had taken up with a merchant's daughter, Solatha Boldtree. He had died before Erzoured was even born, and Solatha had brought the child to court nine months later, claiming the crown prince's descent. And when King Foril had ascended the Dragon Throne, still full of grief for his brother's death, he'd broken with centuries of tradition and made Erzoured an Obarskyr, officially.

"We do not leave family out in the cold to beg for scraps and status," he'd said. But whatever wrong he'd meant to right, it seemed too late. Erzoured was nothing but a blackguard, with an eye for the throne and not a care at all for those who stood between him and it—family or not. Raedra had been watching him from amongst those in the audience chamber the day Helindra Crownsilver had presented her long-lost grandnephew as Emvar's lost scion. If Erzoured had dropped dead, there and then from utter rage, she wouldn't have been surprised.

"Why do you hate him?" Baerovus had asked her later. "If things had been different, he would be crown prince, would he not? Isn't he just jealous? It seems everyone is jealous."

But there was jealousy that ate at the soul and was cause for worry, for pity, and there was a jealousy that drove a man to act violently. And Raedra was all but certain Erzoured would come after Baerovus, dagger first.

"Isn't that why I have Purple Dragon guards?" Baerovus had asked.

"He's tried to kill Aubrin," Raedra said. "At least twice now." The second time, Brin had retreated to her rooms through the secret passages, bleeding heavily from a stab wound. It was the first time he'd spent the night with her.

Baerovus had goggled at her. "Then he should be arrested."

But they wouldn't find evidence, they never did. Erzoured was careful, terribly careful. And patient.

Erzoured gave Raedra a sad look, and more than anything she wished Baerovus did not lay between them. "You poor thing. So much tragedy for such a delicate creature. First your father, and then your brother. Now I hear your betrothed has run away to war."

Raedra regarded her cousin coolly. It doesn't matter how he prods at you, she reminded herself. It is only out of spite. "An Obarskyr is never delicate," she said. Erzoured's eyes tightened. "Have you come to visit, or to see if the truth is as dire as the gossip?"

He smiled thinly at her. "I'll leave you and your brother alone, and come back another time. It's clear strong feelings have you addled."

"Erzoured," she called. He turned in the doorway. "Have you heard? Someone has sent a set of kidnappers after Lord Crownsilver's tiefling friend."

He gave her a slippery smile. "Well done, Raedra. Have you gotten rid of her?"

"Please. She's nothing for me to fear—do you turn out all the jacks who claim a lady's eye faster than you do?" Erzoured's calm faltered—after all, Raedra knew he'd done exactly that.

Raedra smiled sweetly at him. "Rather, I think this is someone who wants to harm Aubrin. Someone who'd like to find something they can hold over his head. Since he is my betrothed, that means they are seeking to hold something over my head by proxy. And I don't care for threats."

She stood and moved around her brother's bed. "However," she said, "I can always make an exception. You see, the person who hired these kidnappers, these killers? He underestimated the tieflings. He's lost quite a few men and with nothing to show for it. One attempt is a tragedy. Two is a pattern. And three?" She dropped her voice. "I think we could call three a conspiracy against the Crown. And that *is* something we all know I'll happily threaten a man over."

Erzoured's sharp eyes searched her face, hunting—no doubt—for a sign of weakness, a sign she was bluffing. "Well," he said after a moment, "I suppose we shall all hope that there are no further attempts. Although I hear it's immaterial, since Lord Crownsilver hasn't gone to war at all has he? He's fled Suzail with his mistress."

Raedra smiled. "He is on an errand for the Crown. Nothing to concern yourself with, Cousin."

A sharp, barking cough interrupted Erzoured's reply. The King of Cormyr, leaning heavily on the shoulder of Ganrahast, came into the sickroom. Erzoured and Raedra stepped apart, and Raedra made a little curtsy. Foril waved her off, breaking into another bout of coughing.

"Granddad, you should be in bed," Raedra said.

"Haven't the time," Foril said. "Well met, Erzoured." He grasped his nephew's hand. "So glad you finally came."

Erzoured gave Foril a thin smile. "Anything for family."

"How's our boy?" Foril asked, leaning past Raedra to look at Baerovus.

"Still asleep," Ganrahast said. "But we haven't exhausted all our options. And at times . . . at times it is the mind and the spirit and the body's need to sleep so deeply. It may be that Prince Baerovus knows best."

"He so often does," Erzoured quipped, and Raedra bristled.

Foril nodded, considering his grandson with a far-off look. He moved toward the young prince, leaning on Raedra's arm as he passed. She took hold of him and helped him to the bedside. The king laid an age-spotted hand against Baerovus's bearded cheek and sighed heavily.

"He's too young," Foril said.

"He'll be fine," Raedra assured him, even though she wasn't sure if she believed it anymore. Baerovus might be locked in this deathlike sleep while he recovered from the attack that had laid him low, or he might be trapped within this dead body, waiting only for release. They couldn't know. She glanced up at Erzoured, who watched Foril like a hawk.

"Granddad," Raedra said. "Don't you think you ought to be resting? Surely nothing is so important that it cannot wait for you to recover?"

"My dear," Erzoured said, "you clearly don't understand matters of state."

She glared at him. "Does the king not have his officers of the court, his advisors, his courtiers for a reason?"

Erzoured smiled. "I think His Majesty knows how to rule the kingdom. Do keep me apprised of our Baerovus's condition," he said, adding a little bow for each of them. "Your Majesty. Your Highness."

"Fare well, Erzoured," Foril called after him. He patted Raedra's arm. "You're a good girl, Raedra. Emvar will be a lucky fellow." He sighed. "I know how it feels," he said to Baerovus. "These mornings it seems as if I simply cannot wake myself. As if sleep is where I belong."

Terror arced through Raedra. She reached for her grandfather's hand and squeezed it so hard his rings of state bruised her palms. "Keep waking up," she said. "Promise me you'll keep waking up."

He gave her a fond grin. "So long as I am able, cheeky bird. I swear it. And perhaps you're right. After all, I must hear the nobles and their grievances tomorrow." He looked to Ganrahast, who nodded once. "I do wish the gardens were dry. They tell me the damp will only make the cough worse. A fire, a goblet of warm wine, and a book it must be."

Raedra hesitated. "Could I help? Could I hear the grievances for you?"

Foril made a face, shook his head. "Don't involve yourself in their troubles, my dear. Those fellows will think it is making a statement, and you haven't the temper for it." He sighed. "Of course, neither does Baerovus."

Raedra felt the blood drain from her cheeks, but only said her good-byes as Foril and Ganrahast left the sickroom once again. She smoothed Baerovus's hair off his forehead once again. "Which is worse," she murmured, "that you wake and have to face all your fears, or that you don't and we'll have to see exactly how ugly the nobles can be?"

12

A SLIVER OF SILENCE FELL OVER THE TAPROOM, AS THE PATRONS OF THE Brigand's Bottle turned toward the sizzle of failing magic, the sudden appearance of a tiefling in their midst. Farideh's heart sped, and she had only enough time to register Dahl's horrified expression before chaos roared all around her.

The table of drunken young nobles were immediately on their feet, trying to draw swords around the heavy furniture. The two women seated beside Farideh leaped up with a shout—one hurled her flagon between Farideh and Dahl. Farideh scrambled back, releasing the Harper.

"Door!" he said.

But the path to the door led through more shouting people. The nobles kicked over their table, wresting swords free with slurred battle cries. The keghands were herding fleeing people toward the doors.

"Devil!" a man screamed. "Devils sent by Shar!"

"A tiefling, you dunce!" she heard a man bellow. "Ilmater's wounds, don't you know anything?"

But for every voice that cried for calm, five more shouted to knock the devil down.

She stumbled as she made for the side door, too aware of the shadow-smoke leaking off of her. There were too many people in the way to run, and too many people watching to use the powers that slipped her through the planes. She clambered over a table, past an old woman staring wide-eyed at her. One of the serving girls grabbed at her, succeeding only in yanking her cloak off her shoulders.

Another hand grabbed hers and she pulled against it out of instinct. But there was Dahl, kicking an empty chair out of the way. He pulled her in front of him and shoved her toward the side door. "Go," he said. "Fast—Purple Dragons."

"What befalls?" a stentorian voice boomed out. "Stand aside and down steel, in the name of the king!"

She was nearly to the exit when the cellarer seized her by the hair. Farideh twisted, menacing him with a hand suddenly pulsing with the unholy magic of the Nine Hells. The cellarer cried out, a new crop of screams burst out around them, but Farideh pulled free and bolted for the door. The last few feet, a hand found her back—but before she could turn and cast the spell at her latest attacker, Dahl shoved her through the exit ahead of him. "Come on!" he said, grabbing her by the hand and drawing her down the alleyway ahead of the taproom's workers. At the end of the alley, he scanned the street. The Purple Dragons had come out the front and were rushing toward them.

Farideh held Dahl's hand tighter and pulled hard on the powers of her pact. The steps she took toward the mouth of the alley, instead brought them through a sudden rent in the fabric of the plane, and when they came free, it was across the street in a farther alley. She kept running, the tattoo of footfalls pursuing them. She leaped them across to another alleyway—halfway down that one, Dahl pulled her to the left, down another dark passage that twisted through the block of buildings. When they could see the road again, he stopped, short of the streetlamps, peering out into the light and breathing hard. Farideh fell back against the stone wall. Her head was pounding as she wiped the rain from her face.

"Oghma's bloody papercuts." Dahl slumped down the wall. "What in the Hells is wrong with people?" Footsteps made him straighten, flattened both of them against the wall. A young guard sprinted by, back toward the inn.

"Did you come out all right?" he asked softly.

"Well enough."

Dahl took his cloak off and draped it clumsily around her. "You stick out the other way now. It should go faster if they can't tell they're looking at you." Farideh pulled the cloak straight and tied it.

By the time they reached the tallhouse, winding through the darkest streets, Dahl was soaked to the skin, and the ales he'd drunk had clearly taken their toll as the urgency faded.

"Where's Dumuzi?" he demanded, leaning against the wall.

"Asleep, likely," Farideh said, unlocking the door. "He's not a statue." She glanced back at the dark and rainy street, thinking of the man beside the post, lurking in the shadows. "Come inside."

Dahl straightened, almost overbalanced. "I have to go talk to Vescaras."

"I think you should stay here tonight."

He stared at her for a long uncomfortable second, and Farideh readied a flurry of arguments to deflect his inevitable assertions that he was fine, he wasn't drunk, he could certainly find his way back through Suzail to the inn he was staying at with a blackguard at his heels.

"I might have given you the wrong impression," he said, a little delicately. "It's not . . . you're an admirable woman, and I like your company. And I meant what I said before, it's just I didn't mean—"

"Dahl," Farideh said, feeling as though she would be better off stepping inside and slamming the door. She looked past him, out at the street. "Mehen's room. I meant you should sleep in Mehen's room. It's dark. It's raining. And you are too drunk for me to feel all right about sending you off when there are Sharrans and other shady folks around."

"Oh!" Dahl cried. "*Oh!*" He laughed, sounding relieved. "Sorry, I thought—"

"It's fine." Farideh quickly stepped into the tallhouse, hanging the cloak on a peg. Her face was burning. "It's upstairs. On the left."

"Could you even imagine?" he went on. He went to the stairs and missed the railing, nearly tripping. Farideh caught his arm and helped him up the stairs, eyes still on their feet. "I'm not tired," he declared.

"Then just lie down and stare at the ceiling."

At the top of the stairs, Dahl dropped to the ground, pulling her with him. "I just want to sit," he explained. "It's been a long, long, long day."

Farideh sighed. "It's ten feet to the bedroom."

"I'm not tired," he said again. His eyes focused on her face with not a little effort. "I think I need another drink."

"No, you don't."

"No, see, I won't sleep otherwise. Because everything's going wrong. I have to get back and I can't—Do you ever wish you could just go home? Where you grew up? And maybe everything would be the same?"

"Everything changed the day I left," Farideh told him. "I can't go back."

"What if you could?"

She was quiet a long moment, remembering the little village of Arush Vayem, the people she'd left behind. The ones who'd driven her out without a moment's hesitation. "I wouldn't. It wasn't a pleasant place."

Dahl looked at her the way he had when she'd said she didn't care where she'd come from. "I'm sorry."

"You sure you don't want to go to Mehen's room?"

"I would go back, but I can't get to Harrowdale," he said. "I can't leave yet, and even if I did, I can't get there."

"You definitely can't get there tonight," Farideh said. She tried to haul him up by the arms, but it was like trying to move a bag of fish, heavy and loose.

"I have to do something, but I can't do anything because no one knows anything. So what do I do? I get stlarning drunk."

"I know," she said. She went into Mehen's room and took the pillow and a blanket off the bed. Before she came out, Dahl was already dozing. She laid the blanket over him, and stuffed the pillow under his head. "Go to sleep."

Her hand brushed his stubbled cheek as it came away, and it bothered her more than she would have guessed, this unconventional intimacy. *You look very nice in that dress.* The way he'd stared at her all evening, his arm around her back. He'd laughed and liked her company.

It's an act, she reminded herself. A cover. He'd laughed like a pardoned man at his misunderstanding. Dahl is Dahl, she told herself, opening the door to the main bedroom. You're lonely and—

Lorcan stood in the middle of the room.

"*Karshoj!*" Farideh shouted. She pressed a hand to her pounding heart. "You scared me."

"Did I?" he said, cold and terrible. "You're home late. Where have you been?"

"Out," Farideh said. "It's not that late."

"Out with Dahl," Lorcan said, as if the words could damn her.

Farideh sighed and rolled her eyes. "I still have the pact. It didn't even come up *once*, and for that matter, neither did you. There's nothing for you to be angry about."

"You're deciding what I get to be angry about now?"

"No, I'm telling you what you *didn't* see."

"Maybe I ought to ask Dahl. He's here, isn't he?"

"Passed out in the hallway. Do you know what I did tonight? I sat in a taproom next to Dahl and looked for people who were bound by Shar. All he wants me for is to make his job easier."

"He certainly looked like he wanted something more," Lorcan said. "And that was hours ago."

Farideh nearly retorted that he most certainly did not want anything else, but the comment hit her in the stomach in a way she wasn't prepared for. "I don't want to be here right now," she announced. "Let's go somewhere."

Lorcan went completely still. "Why don't you want to be here?"

"Because I'm tired of Suzail, and not tired enough to sleep," she said. "And I'd like your company." She stood close to him. "Rashemen," she said suddenly. "Take me to Rashemen?"

"Why Rashemen?"

"We haven't been." She slipped her hand into his. "Come on. Please."

He stared at her as if there were things she wasn't saying, as if he couldn't parse them out. But he took hold of the ring that hung from the chain around his neck, held her hand tight, and blew through it, summoning a whirlwind that pulled them from the plane.

Rashemen stretched, a wide and windy land rippled by hills and mountains. The dark shapes of needle-leafed forests trimming the land like swaths of velvet. In the distance, a city of lights and stone buildings sparkled in the darkness, but from where they stood, Farideh couldn't see a single other habitation. But the land felt nothing like quiet—it seemed to throb beneath her feet, as if it were alive.

"Why Rashemen?" Lorcan asked again.

"I wanted to see it. Do you know anything about it?"

"Enough to know you have nothing to be interested in," he said. Then "They will not make you a witch, if that's what you're thinking."

"It's always the pact isn't it? I don't want to be a witch. I don't even know *how* to be a Rashemi witch."

"The spirits trapped in the land choose you."

The ground under her feet, thrumming with magic as if it had a pulse of its own. She looked back at Lorcan. "You're trouble enough."

A wicked smile curved his mouth. "You have no idea." His arms encircled her waist, his body blocking the chilly wind. "Tell me the truth. Why Rashemen?"

"I wore a spell today. I looked human."

"I saw."

"And someone thought I was Rashemi." She wrapped her arms over his, wondering if there were taprooms in the lit city, if there were princesses or Harpers or wizards alongside the witches. "You left."

"I had things to do," he said.

"Other warlocks?"

"I've lost all my warlocks, darling. You're the only one left." He pressed his mouth to her neck. "But you'd never leave me, would you?"

Farideh considered the roll of hills and the sparkling village on the horizon. She hugged Lorcan's arms closer around her. "No," she lied. "I can't imagine that."

* * *

HOURS LATER, LORCAN tapped his fingers against his upper arm, as the erinyes Nisibis flayed the third of the cultists. Opposite him, the leader of the cell watched blank-faced. Sairché had granted them five years of favor to gain the agreed-upon souls, and they'd squandered them all. Hopefully, the slow murder of half the group would inspire the others to put their backs into the new quantity. Sulci, with her missing eye and shock of yellow hair, raised the club. She broke the man's leg bones—upper then lower—his arms chained wide.

Lorcan stifled a sigh and stared at a spot over the cult leader's head. He had hardly stepped back into Malbolge from wide and windy Rashemen but an imp was on him, reminding him that this deadline had passed. It did not do to be tardy, not with mortals who thought themselves invincible. But such retributions were at best tedious, and for Lorcan now, an uncomfortable reminder of his own torture at his sisters' hands.

Nisibis looked up at him and smiled cruelly, as if reminded of such torments. Lorcan gestured at her to keep on with the whip.

"There are six?" he asked Leuctra beside him, nearly shouting to be heard above the man's screams. She nodded. "Lords, but it does take a long time." The club came down on his back, and his legs sagged, and Lorcan wondered idly how long Dahl would last against a fury of erinyes.

"It motivates them better," Leuctra said. The freshest of the *pradixikai's* ranks and new to leading a fury of three, Leuctra would have been the one holding the whip before Lorcan had taken on his mother's mantle.

She had, he remembered. She had broken his ribs, before.

Sulci bent down and grinned fearsomely in the man's face. "Had enough?"

A trill of horror went through Lorcan, and he shut his eyes. Yes, he thought, remembering.

The man's answer was unintelligible, but cruel Sulci laughed. She looked to her fury leader, and Leuctra nodded once. It had gone on long enough. The club crashed down on the man's head, smashing it open like a rotten squash and sending brain and blood spattering across both erinyes, their leader, and Lorcan.

Lorcan grimaced and looked down at his ruined shirt. Beside him, Leuctra raised a cool brow but said not a word. Enough, Lorcan thought.

"Take your time," he said. "But I have places to be. I'll come remind the survivors of the new agreement when you're through." He met the cult leader's eyes again, hoping it would leave the right impression, as Nisibis stalked toward the remainder, choosing her next victim, Lorcan blew through the portal ring, returning once more to the fingerbone tower.

Sairché had not returned, but he called up her image in the scrying mirror. The group of travelers moved along a trail in that deep, unforgiving wood, the steel-haired wizard toward the back, and slowing further. Soon, he thought. He waved a hand over the mirror, replacing the forest with the tallhouse kitchen, where Farideh, looking exhausted, sorted through a basket of food.

Last night, he'd been sure he was losing her, but then she'd been the one to insist they go halfway across the continent to be alone. You never give her enough credit, he thought. She doesn't give up so easily. She hadn't left him to the erinyes' tender mercies after all.

He turned to face the marrow-weeping wall where the portal was set, intending to return to Suzail, and abruptly all the air went out of his lungs. His vision darkened. His knees buckled, slamming him prone on the floor like a supplicant. Dark forces held him there for what felt like an eternity before releasing him enough to inhale.

You've been very busy, a voice like ground glass said. *Yet you accomplish little, cambion.*

Lorcan scrambled for the voice to give an answer. What had Asmodeus asked of him but to keep Farideh alive and quiet?

I had admired your initiative with her twin, the King of the Nine Hells went on. *But now that we see what that meddling protection is capable of . . .*

The god of sin's terrible voice trailed away. For a second eternity, there was only the darkness and the sound of Lorcan's breath against the bone-tiled floor.

Such a fearful thing, Asmodeus said, and did not say. Those were not the tones of the god of sin, and there was nothing in creation that terrified Lorcan so much as Asmodeus's voice suddenly with another's words, suddenly without the ferocious melody of his voice.

And such a simple thing, he went on. *Depending on where you stand. But then it always does depend where you stand.*

The magic holding Lorcan didn't lessen. He wished he would die, but knew down to his marrow, Asmodeus would never allow it, mad or not. A heartbeat, perhaps two, and the god of sin spoke again, the sound of an avalanche compressed into Lorcan's ears.

You have two Chosen to watch over now, Asmodeus said, briskly as a typhoon. *Make certain neither falls too much under my daughter's interest.*

The absence of the god was as violent as his arrival, Lorcan's senses assaulting him anew. His muscles fought him as he stood, as if they didn't trust that Asmodeus had truly gone. What was that? *What was that?*

No. He straightened. Lorcan had not survived the brutal hierarchy this long by worrying about the things his betters told him, by word and deed, to ignore. He wiped his face—blood trickled from one nostril.

Behind Lorcan the portal set into the marrow-weeping wall split open.

"There is absolutely no reason for all that rain," a woman's voice said.

"You're late," he snapped at Sairché. She tensed all over, and her skin burned bright red, sending her thick hair up in a plume of smoke and leaving the glowing lines of tattoos across her scalp. Sairché let out a held breath and stretched her wings.

"It hasn't *stopped* raining since I set foot on that doomed little plane," she said. "Every shitting fire they build is fit for a gelugon—*I'm* freezing."

"So you settled things?" Lorcan demanded. "Is she calmed down?"

"Calm as one can hope for. More like she's spooked—but she's quiet, and no more imps. Which is excellent, because that shitting paladin holds no love at all for her as a sweet-faced innocent; she won't wait for explanations when she's the Chosen of the god of sin."

"You can handle a paladin," Lorcan said. Much better than he could—he slapped that thought away. "Is that all?"

"She's going to tell the little nobleman, sooner or later," Sairché said. "And *he's* bound to tell the paladin. Which may mean I'll be finished up early, because I don't see that one reacting calmly. If I have to kill her, I'll have no choice but to come home."

"Your deal with Farideh is still in effect," Lorcan pointed out. Lorcan rubbed the center of his forehead, easing out the pinch of tension. First, time had crawled past, now it seemed he hadn't enough to get anything at all done.

"I'll make sure to blame the dead demonborn before I run off," Sairché drawled. She sat down on the little bench that had been her perch for so many months. "It's not as if they can tell the difference down there."

• • •

DAHL WOKE TO Dumuzi standing over him, the sun through the great window over the door glinting on his silver piercings. Dahl shut his eyes and his head started spinning—Farideh, the tallhouse, the obscenely long staircase came back to him. The taproom, the Sharran. Harrowdale.

"How late is it?" he asked, his voice rough.

"Late," Dumuzi said. "The sun is well up."

Dahl forced himself upright, stomach lurching. He cursed. "What were the gods thinking when they made whiskey?"

"That you might drink it in small tastes," Dumuzi said. "She's in the kitchen." He went down the stairs, leaving Dahl staring up at the ceiling and cursing himself. There was too much to be done for him to have a hangover. He should have gone back, told Vescaras what they'd found. He should have stayed at the Brigand's Bottle and kept a close eye on the cellarer. He should have recalled enough of Marjana's notes to figure out where the cellarer lived and taken the opportunity to search for evidence. He cursed again and hauled himself up.

Downstairs, he nudged the door to the kitchen open. The room was warm, and a sour, beefy odor pervaded it. Farideh stood over a large basket, spreading its contents out over the table, item by item. Eggs, greens, apples, a small wheel of cheese, a tangle of beans. She took a loaf of bread out of the basket and broke the end off, inhaling deeply. "Gods," she murmured, as if there were nothing so pleasurable on the plane.

Dahl snickered and she looked up. "Do you two need a moment?" he asked.

"If it means I don't have to share? Yes." Her voice was rough too. "Do you know how long it's been since I've had bread that wasn't stale?"

"Clearly a while. What *is* that smell?"

Farideh nodded at the hearth, and the pot shoved deep into the coals. "*Yrisfexirji*," she said. "It's for hangovers. I thought you'd need it."

Dahl would have protested, except for the fact that the mere sight of the food on the table threatened to upend his stomach. She hooked the pot out of the fire and ladled a cupful out while he sat down, pushing the groceries to the side.

"Do I want to know what's in it?" he asked, when she set the cup in front of him. It smelled worse up close, but blessedly—curiously—his stomach held.

She tucked a bit of hair behind her ear. "Not if you're stomach's unsettled. But Mehen takes it when he's drink-sick, and I can guarantee he gets sicker than you. It's not terrible," she added, when he gave her a skeptical look.

Dahl took a tentative sip and gagged—the brew was spicy in a way that numbed his mouth, pungent and bitter with unfamiliar herbs and speckled with beef fat.

"It's a little terrible," she conceded. "Are you feeling any better this morning?"

"Obviously not, if I'm willing to drink your poison."

"I mean about Harrowdale. And things."

Dahl stared into the depths of his cup. "What are the chances we can just agree never to talk about last night again?"

"None," she said after a moment. "To start with, the cellarer—"

"I mean, I said things I shouldn't have. I was over-familiar and I'm not convinced I held my tongue about things I had no business telling you. It won't happen again, and I would appreciate it if you didn't gloat about it." He sipped the broth again and winced, before looking up at her. "Just . . . take pleasure in the fact you've seen me laid low, and know if our places are ever reversed, I will hold my tongue."

Was it his imagination, or had she grown stiffer? "Fair," she said. She turned back to her groceries. "You ought to drink it all in one go. Sipping's just prolonging your suffering."

He held his breath and knocked the rest back. His stomach coiled and threatened to rebel, but he kept it down. He set his head on the table. "If I have to taste that again—"

"Don't drink so much next time," Farideh said, a little tartly.

He scowled at her. "We're not talking about it, but you could probably guess if you tried that I got some dreadful news yesterday. I had my reasons."

"And so you have your results," she returned, without looking up.

"The truce is ended, I see."

Farideh rubbed her eyes. "I'm tired," she said. "I was up late. And *you* are not being pleasant. What are you going to do about the cellarer?"

"Hopefully? Break into his rooms and find proof of what he's up to."

"And take it to the Dragons?"

Dahl hesitated. "Not yet. He's not the only one, I suspect. Either the Crown and the war wizards know, or they don't, and I don't want to unmask myself with half the information. Speaking of which, would you be willing to help me again?"

"Of course," she said. Then, "Maybe you should think of a different cover."

"I'll work on it. I need to get back. Vescaras . . . Well, he can deal with it, because he's the one who told me to go drinking. I'll see you later." He stood and started to leave. "Thank you," he said. "For letting me stay and for the . . . *yrtifexri*—"

"*Yrisfexirji*," she corrected. She smiled. "You're welcome."

Dahl had to admit as he walked down the Promenade that the brew seemed to have made a small difference. His head ached, and he felt weak, but he didn't shake, and his stomach had calmed to a faint nausea. He bought a potato cake to eat while he walked, and it settled further.

Vescaras was not pleased. "I was fairly convinced you'd met Marjana's end," he said once they were closed in their rooms again. "Moreover, do you have any idea how it reflects on me when my equerry stumbles in at midmorning, looking like he slept in a gutter?"

"A stairwell," Dahl corrected. "I found a Sharran, by the by. In the Brigand's Bottle. Farideh picked him out."

Vescaras raised an eyebrow. "Did you corroborate it?"

"I didn't find evidence of what he's up to yet, if that's what you mean." Vescaras shook his head. "Gods' books, why would she lie?"

"I don't think she's lying," Vescaras said. "I think she might be too eager to give you the answer you want—there's a difference."

"You *clearly* don't know Farideh," Dahl said. "Let me look at Marjana's notes again. We can head out—"

"Tonight," Vescaras finished. "I have business and I'd appreciate a little more cover before I take my very identifiable self down to that particular crossroads. Go sleep it off."

By the time Vescaras was ready to leave, the sun had long been down and Dahl was left with only a scummy feeling in his mouth and a powerful thirst.

"I'll hit his room," Dahl said, as the two Harper agents approached the Brigand's Bottle. "You keep him busy—"

"Don't be ridiculous," Vescaras said. "I'd stick out like a shifter in a sheep pen in that taproom."

"And I'm the one who fled from there yesterday night," Dahl said.

"Perfect: You left her cloak. You're going back for it."

"She started a bit of a riot when that spell fell off. Broken glasses, thrown tables. Why in the world would I go back to that?"

"You have coin?"

"A little."

Vescaras pulled a small stack of gold coins from his coinpurse and handed them to Dahl without ever breaking his stride. "Start low, and pay them off. Apologize a lot."

"Watching Gods," Dahl said. "I don't need to borrow—"

"Call it your wages then," Vescaras said. He very resolutely didn't look at Dahl. "By the way, I actually need an equerry tomorrow afternoon. And you are not my first choice, but you *are* my equerry at the moment. And your hand is legible."

Dahl cursed to himself, but pocketed the coins. "Low Cormyr's notes say all the employees live in the building directly behind the inn, save the innkeeper, the potjack, and two of the serving girls. It's three stories, five rooms on each floor. Ten of them work at the inn, and six of those were working yesterday when we left—two keghands, a serving girl, a cook, a scullery, and the cellarer. The other four may well be in bed at this hour. The cook, the scullery and the serving girl are women, so you've got at least three rooms to search." They paused a block away from the Brigand's Bottle. "Look for one that's spare—tidy, *bleak*. If he's Shar's, he's not going to have a lot of luxuries."

"Unless he knows how to keep a cover."

Dahl shook his head. "We're not talking about an agent like you or me. We're talking about a zealot. Even if you go out and pretend you're not adhering to the goddess of loss and secrets' dogma, you're not going to be naturally inclined to flout it in private. You dedicate yourself to a single god like that, it leaves a mark, and even if he's drinking and laughing and debauching like a full-hearted Cormyrean in public to keep his cover, in private, he's trying to make up for it. Just trust me on this one. Start with the bleak room."

Dahl headed down the road to the taproom, leaving Vescaras to slip into the shadows and find some other proof that the cellarer was indeed a Sharran, as well as any hint of what his orders were. Mentally running through all the places he would look and hoping Vescaras's list looked the same, Dahl returned to the taproom.

Despite the fact that the night was still young, the taproom was much less crowded than before—at least five tables were completely empty. The serving girl nearest the door—the same one who'd snatched Farideh's cloak—spotted Dahl and fled across the taproom toward the back. Dahl hurried after her, and reached the doors to the kitchen as she led a harried-looking older woman out.

"There," the serving girl said. "That's him. That's definitely him." The innkeeper eyed him, up and down.

"Might we talk in private," Dahl said, aiming for apologetic. "I've brought coin."

The innkeeper eyed him another moment, then beckoned him over to the same corner table where he and Farideh had watched the taproom. As they crossed the room, Dahl saw the cellarer come up with another cask of ale. Good. The innkeeper sat and so did Dahl.

"I've got a broken table, six broken glasses, and half my business down for the night," the innkeeper said. "All because you and that devil's child were up to something."

"I'm terribly embarrassed about what happened earlier," Dahl explained. "My friend just wanted to get out, have a drink. That was the only reason she was disguised—neither of us were up to anything further."

"There's at least a dozen taverns and taprooms in this city that are happy to show off tieflings—should have headed there." She pinned him with a stern glare. "So why didn't you?"

Dahl reached into his pocket and fished out three of the gold coins, setting them on the table. "She wanted to come here," he said. The innkeeper looked skeptical, and didn't even glance down at the coins. Dahl added another two to the stack. One eyebrow quirked.

"Do you have any idea how much it costs to repair a table?" the innkeeper asked. Dahl smiled. "It's not five gold."

"Exactly," she said. "Who are you that you're coming down *here* with a disguised tiefling and a pile of gold to make me forget her?"

"Nobody," Dahl said. "Just a fool who's managed to deeply embarrass himself."

"Not good enough. Who are you?"

"He's that Waterdhavian lord's manservant." Dahl turned to see a young man standing behind him. It was the doorguard from Brin's tallhouse, the one who'd been so nervous about Vescaras. "I told you I knew him."

Oghma's bloody papercuts, Dahl swore to himself. So much for anonymity. "He *cannot* know I was here," he said quickly, trying to think of a way out of this. "No one can know I was here."

"Because you were up to something," the innkeeper said.

Think, think, think! Dahl pursed his mouth, looked back at the doorguard-turned-keghand. "Because," he said, "nobles—no matter the city—care about appearances first. Did she turn you out?"

"Lady Crownsilver? Aye. Recalled the lot of us, sent the extras to the country house. But the battles are getting too near, and they had to evacuate. She only needs so many doorguards, she says." He shrugged. "'S a fair point."

"But she could have left you employed at the tallhouse," Dahl said. "It's not like she doesn't have the coin to cover it. It's not like you wouldn't have had a use still."

"How do you know so much about my nephew?" the innkeeper demanded.

Dahl drew himself up. "I'm acquainted with Lord Crownsilver and his household."

The younger man gasped. "Oh Watching Gods. You were here with Lord Crownsilver's mistress weren't you? That's why you're acting so shifty!"

Dahl started to retort, but then the innkeeper's expression had changed dramatically. She leaned in, jaw slack, eyes wide, hanging on Dahl's next words. The doorguard slid in beside Dahl.

"It can't be," the innkeeper said, in a tone that begged Dahl to contradict her. "Word is she left the city with Lord Crownsilver."

"It's not her," Dahl said, hoping his slowness sounded like reluctance. "She's . . . her sister."

The innkeeper looked to the doorguard and he nodded. "Quiet one. Same look though." He smiled at Dahl. "Glim legs."

"Lord Ammakyl doesn't think I ought to be socializing with 'lesser races,'" Dahl went on. He could work with this. "Or lower classes."

The doorguard sniffed. "Of course he doesn't. High-nosed elf."

Dahl didn't correct him—it was better than assuming Vescaras was drow. "So you see," Dahl said, "I can't have been here. The appearance of it . . . well, I'd be thrown out in the street. And I don't have a kind aunt to take me in."

"Maybe you ought to give it up," the doorguard said. "Nice legs or not, there's more and more refugees turning up in the city every day. Not enough work to be had, unless you can train up as a Purple Dragon in a hurry. Keep the job you've got."

"Don't listen to him," the innkeeper said. "You love that girl. Don't give that up for some highborn lord's vanity."

"I—what?" Dahl said.

"I saw how you were looking at her—you can't deny it. Not to me," the innkeeper whispered, a changed woman. "That's what you were up to, isn't it? You were meeting in secret, since your lord doesn't approve. That's why he can't know." She gestured at the table. "That's why you're handing over all your wages to keep things quiet." She gave him a triumphant grin, and swept the coins into her hand. "I'll keep your secret," she said, tapping her ruddy nose.

Dahl kept his expression as still as possible. What way had he been looking at Farideh? And how angry would she be when she found out what people thought? He glanced across the taproom and at the cellarer helping the second keghand fill flagons. It had to be done.

"Thank you," he said. "You've made my life much easier."

"But don't bring her back here," the innkeeper said. "I don't much care what makes you happy, but my customers don't want devilborn around."

"I've gotten some suggestions," Dahl said, racking his brain for the names from his list. "The Golden Goblin? The Dragon's Last Drink? The Mouse and Dove? Teneth's?"

The innkeeper snorted. "The last two are festhalls, so I wouldn't take her there by surprise—wait until *she* suggests it. But Teneth's especially welcomes all sorts, should you find yourselves interested. The Dragon's Last Drink is a mite fancy for a servant's wages, and I don't know they'll take kindly to a tiefling, but you hand over enough coins, they might not care." She made a face. "The Goblin is a swillhole and little better than a brawl in a mud pit. Don't take her there."

"Many thanks," Dahl said, with what he hoped was a self-effacing sort of smile. He slid out around the table and made his good-byes. He pulled the doorguard aside, as his aunt went back to her business. "What's your name again?"

"Arven, saer," he said. "I didn't mean to unmask you back there."

"Worked out for the best, didn't it?" Dahl said. He slipped the young man a gold coin. "I'd appreciate your silence too."

"You don't need—"

"I also need a little information," Dahl said, apologetically. "You see, my lord sells wine. I found this place looking for taprooms that might have a market for his wares. I figured if he asked where I was, I could tell him it was business. Only your cellarer . . . I don't think he liked my friend."

Arven made a face. "Uwan. Doesn't surprise me. He's a pleasant enough fellow, but if you get him talking . . ." He glanced behind Dahl, to where the cellarer had been working. "It gets ugly. And that's all I'll say."

Like Hell it is, Dahl thought. "If Lord Ammakyl comes around, I'm going to be in a great deal of trouble if I'm right—I don't need Uwan there unmasking me, and I don't need him to know he could. Would you keep an ear out? Tell me if you hear him making undue complaints about me or my friend?"

Arven chuckled. "Are all Waterdhavians so coy? 'Your friend.' Heh." He grinned at Dahl. "He mutters one word about your ladylove, I'll let you know. Where do I find you?"

"Leave a message with her at the tallhouse," Dahl said. "She'll get it to me. And if you notice anything else—anything that might help me work around him, I'd be happy to make it worth your time."

"Of course," Arven said, eyes alight with the promise of adventure. "A good night to you, saer."

Dahl collected Farideh's cloak and left the taproom, setting himself up at the street corner, where he could see the front entrance as well as the side alley, in case the cellarer came out. With any luck, the innkeeper and the doorguard were spreading the tale of Lord Ammakyl's equerry and the twin of Lord Crownsilver's mistress among the staff, and the cellarer would have no notion at all that the Harpers were onto him.

He leaned his shoulder against a wall, rocking back and forth as if he were a little drunk. All but accidentally he'd managed to craft a brilliant cover. Cormyreans, they said, gossiped as though it were ordered by an Obarskyr. The more taprooms he and Farideh visited, the more likely it would be that the people working there would expect the star-crossed lovers to turn up, hiding from the equerry's lord. The rain started up again, and Dahl wondered who was going to be more annoyed at this plan: Vescaras or Farideh?

He thought back over the evening, from going to the tallhouse and Farideh opening the door in that dress to the walk to the taproom and the fact that he couldn't seem to stop saying cloddish things to her the whole way. The taproom and the vague memories of things he said, one arm around her back—was one of them why she was so prickly that morning? Or had it gotten worse?

He remembered suddenly, the stab of embarrassment, Farideh cutting him off as he tried to let her down—last night would have been a terrible time to shake things up. There was no pretending her severity didn't sting, even if he agreed with her.

Dahl looked up at the tenement. What was taking Vescaras so long?

A moment later he had an answer: the flash of a mirror reflecting candlelight from one of the windows. A signal. Dahl swallowed a curse and made his way to the other building as quickly as possible while still affecting a drunk's gait. He shinnied up the narrow gap between the inn and the tenement, and made his way across the shadows of the roof, to the flashing window.

Vescaras pried it open and hauled him in quickly. "Did you bring your ritual book?"

"Of course," Dahl said. "You find anything?"

"Plenty, though we'll need to sift through it." He pointed to a series of papers, laid out on the bed. "Sewn into the mattress. But they're all coded."

Dahl crouched beside the bed and pulled out his ritual book and a pouch of components, then a few rolls of parchment. He grimaced. "I've only got enough to copy three."

"How much time?"

"Not enough to do three," Dahl said. "I don't want to be here when he gets off work." He sorted through the sheets, eyeing the spacing of the text, and chose the one that looked most like a list—lots of items meant lots of ideas.

"You were right," Vescaras said as Dahl unrolled the parchment beside the coded vellum. "But you were wrong too."

"About what?" Dahl asked, taking out a powdered ink and another pouch of metallic salts. He fished out a quill and laid it across the unrolled parchment.

Vescaras's hand dropped in front of Dahl's face, and something smoky and floral went up his nose. Dahl jerked away and saw a waxy plug of scent in his hand. "What is that?"

"Avarine," Vescaras said. "This fellow may be a humble cellarer *and* a Sharran, but he's allowed himself at least a little luxury. And fortunately, too."

"Why is that?"

"Avarine's obscenely expensive, said to have 'potent' qualities, and—outside of Netheril—it's extremely hard to come by. Which means he was in Netheril sometime, recently enough that this hasn't gone rancid." He closed his hand around the perfume. "There's no doubting Marjana stumbled onto something very serious here."

13

30 Eleasias, the Year of the Nether Mountain Scrolls (1486 DR)
The Hullack Forest, Cormyr

THE HULLACK FOREST STOOD SENTINEL ALL AROUND THEM, DEEP AND silent and eerie. Old stories kept rising up in Brin's thoughts: foolhardy adventurers who wandered into the wood looking for lost comrades, only to be torn down by the werewolves those comrades had become. The angry ghosts of elves, wandering since the days of the empire of Cormanthyr, locking humans into the bodies of trees to die slowly over eons. Great pits and caves where hungry monsters hid, waiting to leap out at passersby.

And the trees. Brin looked up at the towering pines and beeches. This far into the forest they grew so close together, the rain that drummed against the canopy high above came down in fat drops, here and there. The forest seemed to watch him, in a way that made him think of Helindra. *Just what do you think you're doing here?*

Brin blew out a breath. This was the right thing to do. If Irvel was alive, they couldn't leave him, clinging to a rock in the Immerflow.

If he's still alive, Brin thought, then why has no one found him? Why has he not managed to find his way out to a village or a waystation or even the army of the West's encampments along Calantar's Way?

If it wasn't the Hullack that ended Irvel, it might well have been the army of Shade, the bands of goblins and gnolls and other monsters they'd driven out of the Stonelands, stirred up and ready for war. Aunkspear was razed, Knightswood taken, and the beasts hammered at Fair Arabel. If Irvel had landed in the Immerflow and came up the western bank . . .

The sinister presence of the Hullack all around Brin made him wonder which would be worse.

It's just a forest, Brin told himself, eyes on Constancia walking ahead of him. If you only find his body, then at least you'll be sure. At least no one will wonder.

And then you can run, Brin thought before he could stop himself.

He dropped back to walk beside Havilar and Desima. The wizard eyed him with a stern, grandmotherly glare, but slowed her pace further to let him walk beside Havilar. Not that Havilar noticed—she kept her eyes on the ground, lost in a gloom. When he spoke her name, she leaped as if he were one of the Hullack's ghosts.

"You all right?"

She blew out a breath. "I've been better." She caught his free hand in hers. "I keep thinking about Crake."

Why? Brin nearly demanded. She'd avoided the sellsword, complained about him repeatedly. "It must have been upsetting," Brin said, even though he'd said it before already. "Seeing him die like that."

"I should have done something."

"What could you have done?"

The words were out of his mouth and he could already hear her retort: *Hit the gnoll, silly.* But Havilar only shook her head. "I think I might have . . . distracted him."

Brin recalled the sellsword's leer and the fact that he'd wished from the start they'd left him behind. "That's not your fault."

Havilar said nothing, and it agitated him. He was worried for her and worried for him and worried for Cormyr, and all of them together was enough to make him crack. He rubbed his eyes. She's not doing anything on purpose, he thought. "It will pass," he said, and squeezed her hand.

"Do you think I can talk to Farideh when we stop?"

"Havi, we've only got the one sending kit left. We need that for when we find Irvel." *If,* he thought, if, if, if. "You can talk to me."

"I know," she said quickly. "I just wanted to talk to her."

Brin grit his teeth. "Well, sorry. You've just got me."

Havilar rolled her eyes. "Don't take it like that. You have too much to worry about already." She sighed. "How close do you think we are?"

"Four days until we reach the Immerflow," he said. "And then I have no idea at all what it will take before we find Irvel. If we find Irvel."

Havilar slipped her hand in his. "When," she said. Then a moment later, "If we don't, what happens?"

Brin pursed his mouth, watching Constancia's back. "If the crown prince is dead, then the line becomes Baerovus, Raedra, and Erzoured. And if Baerovus has died, then it begins with Raedra. There is no possibility that Foril will leave my father's legitimization to molder if that's the case. I'll be made an Obarskyr, and I will have to stay in Cormyr and . . ." He trailed off, and she squeezed his hand. "What do you think about just . . . leaving?" he murmured. "Heading—I don't know, do you want to go back to Tymanther? We could go there. Or somewhere else—Kara-Tur? Waterdeep?"

Havilar frowned at him. "If you're willing to run away, why are we doing any of this?"

"Because I don't want to. But it's not going to change," he said, feeling the edge of panic slicing up his nerves. "Cormyr doesn't change like that—it can't. And I can't just . . . if they lay the crown on me, I can't throw it off."

Havilar stared at him. "You're already your father's son—nothing anyone says changes that. And he's his father's son, too. Why does a king agreeing it's so mean that suddenly everything's unsalvageable?"

Brin shook his head—this might be one thing Havilar couldn't understand. "Because my responsibilities change. It's the difference between leaving your own children to starve and not rescuing every urchin you pass."

Havilar scowled at him. "Think of a better example."

Brin winced. "Sorry. Sorry, that was . . . I know this doesn't make sense. But can you just trust me that it does? That this is how things are for me? For us?"

"Yes," Havilar said, and she squeezed his hand again. "Although if you have to stay and be not-quite-crown prince, I don't see how that means *everything's* gone belly up. You can still be *you* and be in Suzail. You can still be you and be king, for that matter."

Brin snorted. "If I became king, I guarantee Cormyr would have a civil war in a year."

"You wouldn't be a rubbish king, you know," Havilar said. She bumped against his shoulder affectionately. "Maybe you'll make things change a little."

Brin held her hand tight, but didn't try to explain that changing Suzail was a prospect better left to ambitious gods than mere mortals. Since Havilar had returned, he'd become increasingly aware of how much the veneer of noble manners he'd affected had grown into a second skin—and how much he didn't like himself that way. If he stayed, he wouldn't change Suzail, but it was likely Suzail would change him.

• • •

HAVILAR SLICED HER dagger through the base of the mushroom and added it to her pouch. When Moriah had spotted the clusters of golden cones among the mossy roots of some pine trees, Havilar had leaped at the chance to hang back and pick them instead of heading on to their planned campsite. She needed a few moments alone, even if she was sure Mehen wouldn't give them to her.

But her father had only studied her with a worried expression, checked to see if she wanted company, and when she'd declared she would be fine, reminded her to keep her glaive unharnessed.

Now that she was alone, Havilar wasn't sure how to feel about that either. Mehen had let her go, Brin had let her go, Constancia had eyed her in a way that almost surely meant she hoped Havilar fell into a ravine on the way back. She uprooted another few mushrooms. Stupid Constancia.

She wondered if she ought to tell Constancia about Brin's urge to run.

Havilar sighed. "Fari, oh dear gods, why couldn't you have come too?" She sighed. "Everyone's acting mad," she said, as if through the sending spell. "And I think I'm going maddest. I hope Lorcan was right." She counted the words again, and added, "*Henish.*"

Nothing further had happened to her in the days since the imps had appeared and Crake had died. Truth be told, she felt better since he'd left their company.

"Desima" told the others a story of too many gnolls, and of course, no one had known better than to believe her.

"I don't have to protect *you*," Havilar had told Sairché shortly after.

"If you think I've forgotten that for even a moment," Sairché had replied, "you greatly underestimate my intelligence and my current position." But at least she did nothing Havilar would have expected from the devil who'd trapped her for the better part of a decade. She was still Desima so far as anyone else could have seen, although she was suddenly two steps from Havilar all the time. When she'd moved to follow Havi to the mushroom patch, Havilar had made a very clear gesture with the dagger that she wanted some peace.

The air behind her *popped*. Havilar spun, dagger in hand, and there were the two imps, hanging in the air, watching her.

Glaive on the ground, she thought. She swiped at the nearer one with her dagger. Get it back before—

"No, no, no!" the little red devil said, flapping out of her reach. "None of that!"

"Broken planes, Lady," the other said. "You're going to clear the Hells out of imps if you keep this up."

"I will!" Havilar snatched up her glaive. "Don't think I can't."

The imps looked at each other. "You're an odd one," the second imp said. "Didn't anyone tell you? Put the weapon down." Havilar did not, but she didn't swing as the imps landed on the forest floor, well out of her reach, their stinger-laden tails curled over them, as though they were curious cats.

"I'm Dembo," the second imp said. "That's Mot."

"If you're going to try and kill me like you killed Crake," Havilar said, "you won't find it easy."

The imps traded glances again. Mot shrugged. "What's a Crake?" he asked Havilar.

"The man who died when you came before," Havilar said. "Did you put a spell on him or something?"

"We didn't kill anyone," Dembo said. "We weren't even here until just now."

"Those were *other* imps," Mot said. "You sent them back. They won't be coming around for a while."

Havilar pulled her glaive nearer. "So what do you want?"

"No, no, no," Dembo said. "The question is what do *you* want?"

"We're here to do your bidding, Lady," Mot said. It made a florid little bow. "By His Majesty's grace."

Havilar's stomach twisted and her heart started to pound. "I don't need anything you can help me with."

Dembo folded his arms. "Contrary to what *some* people may have told you, we are *excellent* at helping."

"And when we're not," Mot said, "we are *excellent* at finding someone who can."

Dembo looked over at him. "Well, mostly. I mean, there's limits."

"But we know people," Mot assured her. "We're very important."

Havilar looked from one to the other. "I'm not evil," she almost shouted. "I don't need help with devil things."

Mot snorted. "Who said evil?"

"We don't pick what you ask for," Dembo said. "You order, we act. That's the deal. You want us to pick mushrooms, we can pick mushrooms."

"The sky's the limit!" Mot declared.

"Well, no," Dembo said. "You can't have the sky. But what else do you need?"

Havilar hesitated, thoughts whirling. She wanted to tell them there was nothing desperate enough to require a devil's help, nothing she couldn't fix on her own. She knew whatever she asked for might be twisted into something evil if she asked all wrong.

But then she thought of Brin's drawn expression, the repeated assertions that she didn't understand.

"I need to find someone," she said. "Someone magic can't even find."

"Well, that's no surprise," Dembo said. "This place's magic is more churned up than the rulership of the Sixth Layer." Mot tittered, and it set Havilar's teeth on edge.

"That's what I need," she said. "Can you do that?" The imps considered each other, murmuring in soft Infernal, which made Havilar's skin crawl.

"Hang on." Dembo vanished with a *pop*. Mot sat down on his haunches and grinned up at her.

"Are we doing all right," he asked, "would you say?"

Havilar frowned. "You haven't *done* anything yet."

The air split with a gust of brimstone and heat. A massive creature bounded through the rent in the plane, dragging Dembo behind by the chain he was holding. Havilar scrambled back, got her glaive up, searching for the weak spot.

"Sit!" Dembo shouted. "Sit!"

The creature stopped in front of Havilar and dropped onto its backside with a heavy *whump*. Its eyes glowed eerily red as it studied her, and the iron cage of a muzzle kept daggerlike teeth at bay. It yawned, and a pink tongue lolled between the bars.

"It's a dog," Havilar said, dumbfounded.

"Nessian warhound," Mot corrected. "Purebred."

"Here," Dembo said, dropping the chain in her hands. "This is what you need. Give it something that smells like who you're looking for, and it'll hunt them to the ends of the plane. *Don't* take the muzzle off."

The warhound scratched an ear with its hind leg, then looked around the forest.

"Why?" Havilar asked, feeling numb.

"Because it's just a puppy," Dembo said. "It doesn't know any better. It'll gorge and get sick and *we* don't want to clean it up."

"Also, it will eat the person you're looking for," Mot added. "Unless you want that?"

"If she wants that, we should get something different," Dembo said. "The puppy's going to make itself sick, and then we'll be in trouble."

"I don't want it to eat anyone!" Havilar shouted. She eyed the warhound. It made a little yelpy bark and thumped its tail on the ground. "Does it have to eat people?"

The imps exchanged glances. "Lady, it's a *devil*-dog," Dembo said. "It doesn't *have* to eat anything."

"It just *wants* to," Mot added. He looked around. "That fellow you wanted to know if we killed, you might be able to get rid of him by feeding it to the puppy?"

"Not *all* of him though," Dembo said severely.

Havilar's gorge rose. "He's not . . . I don't want . . ." She laid her head in her hands. "You didn't kill him?"

"Pretty sure," Dembo said.

"We'd remember," Mot said. "We're good rememberers."

"Anything else?" Dembo asked.

Havilar considered the enormous dog. "What's its name?"

"Dunno," Mot said. "Don't speak hellhound." He ducked low, peering under the dog. "But it's a bitch."

She ought to send it back right now. The puppy yawned and snorted and spat a little tongue of flame. Havilar's eyes widened.

"Right," Dembo said. "Don't put it out in the hayloft or anything either."

"It will work," Mot assured her. "We're very good at helping." With that, both imps popped out of the plane.

Havilar scrambled back, wrapping the chain around a slender beech tree and shoving a thick stick through the links to lock it. The puppy followed her around the tree, ears perked. Havilar darted beyond the chain's reach. The puppy pulled against the chain, once twice. Then it spotted the remainder of the mushrooms and gave them a great whuffling sniff. Its tail wagged.

Havilar folded her arms around her knees, trying to wrap her thoughts around what she'd done, what she was going to do next.

Wondering what she was going to say to Brin to explain all of this—she'd asked for the hellhound for a reason after all. It would be worse to forget it.

The hellhound flopped down and rolled around in the remains of the mushroom bed, and for a moment Havilar thought she might cry. She wished Farideh were there.

Havilar snatched at her haversack and took the remaining sending from the bottom of the pack. Emergencies, she thought, were emergencies. With shaking hands, she pulled out the vials of components and unrolled the ritual.

"Fari?" she said, as the rush of magic swelled around her. "It happened . . . Sairché's here, watching. I have some imps and a hellhound thing that's supposed to find Irvel. I don't know what to do."

The air crackled. "*Oh gods, Havi,*" her sister's voice cried. "*Oh . . .*" She stopped, as if keeping herself from wasting precious words. "*You have to tell Mehen. I'll tell Lorcan. Don't talk to Sairché, she's trouble.*"

"Lorcan *sent* Sairché," Havilar started, but Farideh couldn't hear her and kept talking. "*Don't listen to devils. Stay safe, I—*"

The magic's limits cut off whatever she was going to say, but she'd said enough. Farideh was right—Sairché was an enemy, no matter what agreements she had, and the imps weren't to be trusted. Unless she wanted to wind up damned. Havilar sat back, hugging her chest and staring at the hellhound. The only thing she knew of that would find Irvel, dead or alive.

If she was willing to listen to devils.

She sat in the dirt for a long time, thinking.

"Stay here," Havilar told the hellhound and headed up the path.

As she entered the camp, Brin looked up from beside where he was trying to coax damp branches into a fire, and every last scrap of her uncertainty crumbled away.

Mehen and Kallan stood, butchering a brace of hares. "I think you can cut up a gnoll faster than a hare," Kallan teased.

"Nobody needs to eat gnolls when I'm done," Mehen answered. He looked up as Havilar stopped beside him, her head feeling as if it were going to float right off her shoulders. "Did you get the mushrooms?" he asked.

"No," she said. "I think I need some help."

The ridges over Mehen's eyes shifted. "With mushrooms."

"Yes. Please. Can you help me?"

Mehen glanced back at Kallan, looking puzzled, but as soon as Havilar turned back toward the hellhound, he was following close behind. Havilar shot a look at Sairché and jerked her head toward the path. That was all the invitation the cambion was getting.

When they were out of earshot, Mehen said, "This isn't about mushrooms is it?"

"No," Havilar said. What would he do when he found out? Would this be as bad as Farideh's pact, or worse or different? A hellhound wasn't Lorcan, but she'd have a lot easier time saying no to a hellhound since it couldn't talk back.

"Is it about Brin?" Mehen asked, a moment later.

"No. It's . . . sort of."

"I'm not prying," Mehen said. "You're old enough to have a relationship with a man, you're old enough to solve your own problems there."

"I know," Havilar said. "I can."

"Good. Though if you need to talk to me, I'll listen."

"It's fine. Except . . ." She stopped beside the boulder just before the little clearing and turned back to Mehen. "I don't want to bother you if you don't want to help, and you don't want me to bother you, but I think that Chosen of Asmodeus stuff started up."

"What?" Mehen roared.

"There were imps and then they brought me a hellhound and it's up there." She pointed to the clearing, and her arm was shaking. "And"—she looked over Mehen's shoulder, to Sairché standing stock-still six feet behind him—"Lorcan sent someone to watch me, and it's Desima, and I think you both ought to come see what we're dealing with. Now."

Mehen looked over his shoulder at the wizard, reaching for his falchion. Sairché's hand was on her wand. "I don't want any trouble," Sairché said.

"Now," Havilar said again. She continued on to the clearing, to where the hellhound lay panting on the remains of the mushroom patch. When it spotted Havilar, the dog sat up and barked once, sending out a puff of flames.

"Karshoj," Mehen swore.

"I think it can find the crown prince," Havilar went on, "only I don't know how to say so to Brin; he's going to be so upset." She shook her head. "All right, but maybe—maybe—it won't be so bad if it's disguised, right? We can tell him it's just a dog that can track. So that's why you're here," she said to Sairché. "You can disguise yourself, then you can disguise it."

"Perhaps," Sairché said, sounding cautious. "What are you willing to trade?"

"You can keep breathing," Havilar offered. She turned to Mehen. "That's Sairché. She's the one who tricked Farideh and trapped us."

Now the falchion was out and Sairché scurried back, against the trees, wand sparking. Havilar stepped between them. "Stop," she said. "We need her." She looked back at Sairché. "Can you do it?"

The cambion's eyes flicked over Havilar, disgusted. "Yes. But it won't last. They grow quick. It's a dog's size today. In a month it will be the size of a pony, and by winter it will rival a draft horse."

"Havi," Mehen said. "No."

"It's the only way," she said. "Otherwise . . . Otherwise I don't know what to do."

"You can't lie to Brin about this," he said. "About any of this. He deserves to know. He deserves a say in what we do."

Havilar shook her head. "He's going to be so upset," she said. "And maybe he was always going to be upset, and maybe that's for the best, because I hate all of this so much and I just want to go back to how things were."

"Hush," Mehen said, and caught her up in his arms. Havilar buried her head in the crook of his neck, and fought tears. He'd think she was such a little girl. Mehen hugged her tight, cursing a soft stream of Draconic. He pushed her back, and took her face in both his hands.

"I don't care if I'm not supposed to be giving you advice, you take this advice," he said. "Don't do foolish things because Brin might be upset. You're a grown woman, but so is he a grown man. He can handle his own feelings when you come down to it. All right? It might last, it might not, but *don't* think you can drag things out by keeping secrets from him.

"And I'd say *don't* deal with devils, but I suppose this is one of those times no one could help." He tapped his tongue against the roof of his mouth, all nerves. "Karshoj."

"Will you go get him?" Havilar asked. "I'll stay here and keep an eye on them."

"What *is* it you think I'm going to do?" Sairché demanded. "If I leave, I had best have a very excellent reason, and a dragonborn with a sword is not that."

Mehen's hold on Havilar tightened. "I'll get him," he said. "But don't take your hands off the glaive."

Havilar gave him a weak smile. "You don't have to tell me that." He headed down the path, glancing back twice, before picking up his pace. Havilar turned to Sairché.

"Can you do it now?" she asked. "And get out of here?"

Sairché eyed her suspiciously. "Aren't you supposed to be guarding me?"

"Look," Havilar said. "I can reason with Mehen on this. For now. But Brin? Brin's not going to care what you can do or cannot do. If he doesn't try to kill you himself, he'll sic Constancia on you. And if you hurt a *hair* on Brin's head, I'll kill you."

"I wouldn't if I were you," Sairché said. "It might be pleasant in the short-term, but you ought to think of me as a very thin defense against a much greater army. Do you *want* a much greater army at your door?"

Havilar shook her head. People might think she was stupid, but gods, they could be dense themselves. "Are you going to make that army vanish? You can't. So I'd rather have them at my door, than go to *theirs*. Who wouldn't?" She hefted her glaive and watched the hellhound rub at the muzzle. "Besides, right now? I think they like me better."

• • •

"Say something?" Havilar asked, but Brin found he couldn't oblige. The enormous dog lying on the other side of the clearing wagged its tail twice, thumping the ground. It might look like nothing more than a mastiff, but the tree behind it was charred in places from the hellhound's burning breath.

Brin shook his head mutely.

Havilar bit her lip. "You have his dagger—do you think it smells like Irvel still? I mean, we could try it, and see if . . ." She looked over at Mehen and trailed off. "Oh. It's the other thing, isn't it?"

The other thing. Brin nearly laughed at that, vague and sanitized. *The other thing* sounded like a coy way to talk about a relation's mild deviance. Not the fact that the love of his life was the Chosen of the archdevil god of sin. The rain drummed against the leaves above him, and for the first time in days, Brin felt as if he couldn't hear anything else.

"You have to get rid of it," he said finally. "Kill it."

"It's a solution," Havilar protested. "And it's a *puppy*."

"Then it should be easier." Brin dragged a hand through his hair. What would come of Lord Crownsilver hunting down the crown prince with a hellhound of all things? What would happen to Havilar if that got out, or worse, if she was right, and people discovered she was the Chosen of Asmodeus. "How did this happen? Did Farideh do it? Did she mark you somehow? Corrupt you?"

Havilar's brows rose. "Excuse me?"

"Come on—do you want to pretend that the Hells don't follow your sister?"

"Look, you might be mad at her—be mad at her, she's done enough to earn that—but don't make up ridiculous stories. Do you really think for a second Farideh would force something like this on me? No—that she'd *let* it happen if she could stop it?"

"I don't *know* what Farideh would do anymore, and frankly, neither do you!" Brin turned to the dragonborn. "Are you just letting this happen?" he demanded.

"Point me to the part I can change," Mehen said. "We watch, we wait, we move carefully. That's the only way to deal with gods."

"We take her to a temple of Torm," Brin said. "And then—"

"And when they can't get rid of it?" Mehen said. "Because who says Torm can decide to undo another god's decisions? Are they going to hand her back all apologetic?"

Brin faltered. "They might. She's not evil. You're *not* evil," he said to Havilar.

Havilar regarded him soberly. "Neither is this. We leave the muzzle on. We give her something that smells like Irvel, and the imps said she'd find him no matter where he is. We just have to keep hold of the chain."

"I cannot believe you're even suggesting this," Brin said. "It's a *hellhound.*"

"Well, what do you plan to do?" Havilar said. "Wander around the Hullack until you can't take it anymore and then run? I don't *want* to run, Brin. I want to go back to my sister. I don't want to spend my life listening to you wonder if you did the right thing or not. And I'm *not* living out my days in Suzail as Lord Crownsilver's mistress. If the right thing is finding Irvel, then let's do it."

"Not like this." He ran a hand through his hair. "I cannot believe Desima helped you disguise it."

Havilar glanced at Mehen. "She's pretty understanding," she said. "Brin, I know why you don't like this—"

"Do you?" he demanded. "Because frankly this whole mess doesn't seem to faze you half as much as it should. You're the Chosen of Asmodeus, and it's not a crisis—it's a boon! A handy solution! Farideh's the Chosen of Asmodeus, and she's not a defiler, a destroyer—she's a sweet innocent who we left alone in my tallhouse! I'm so sure she won't get into any trouble and have devils running all over Suzail! A stlarning helloune—"

"Gods *damn* it, Brin!" Havilar shouted. "You told me you would fix this. You told me all you wanted was to be with me. But it's been *months* and *nothing's* changed. You're still engaged, we're still in Cormyr. I still have to stay locked up and cowled and hidden because an entire city is saying *awful* things about me. How is that *fixed*?"

"I'm trying!"

"It feels a lot more like you're perfectly happy with your titles and your house and your princess. And if you don't find Irvel, you keep all of that."

"I am giving up *everything* for you—"

"Don't you *dare* put that on me, Brin Crownsilver," Havilar shouted back. "I never asked you to do anything but tell me the truth and be yourself."

"And what if that *is* myself? Hmm?"

All the anger fled Havilar's features, and the way she looked at him made Brin's heart ache. "It's not," she said, simply. "I know it's not."

Everything was spinning out of control. "Get rid of it," Brin said again, turning back to camp, all of Havilar's accusations ringing in his ears. He hadn't fixed things—that was true. He hadn't done enough to make Havilar feel safe and comfortable in Suzail, but what was he supposed to do? He couldn't change the whole city. And, fine, he didn't have the best plan for finding Irvel—

No. He was completely planless. Every step was a leap into the darkness, in what he hoped was the right direction but knew deep down was just another leap away from Suzail. He didn't have a plan at all, and everyone else would hang for that fact.

Constancia was waiting like a tiger to pounce on him as soon as he returned to camp. "What happened?" she demanded.

"I don't want to talk about it," he said.

"Stoic is a poor look on you, Aubrin," Constancia said. "What did she do?"

But angry as he was—lost as he was—he couldn't tell Constancia about Havilar being a Chosen of Asmodeus. His reaction to the hellhound might be his cousin's reaction to Havilar, after all.

"She . . . found a way to track Irvel," Brin said quietly. "A dog."

Constancia frowned, puzzled. "She found a dog? In the Hullack?"

"Looks like a mastiff," Brin said. "But I don't think it will work. It's . . . gods only know what it is or whose it is." He wondered how foolish it was to hope Havi would kill it—she's stubborn if you push her, he thought. Just like you. "I don't know how we're going to find him," he confessed. "I'm worried even with the Harper's information this is a wild goose chase."

Constancia patted his shoulder. "You know what this is."

"Bad luck," Brin said.

"This is Torm guiding you," she said. "You have a duty—accept it. Make peace with who you are, who you were born to be. You cannot change the past, and you can't make yourself into someone who isn't meant to lead Cormyr somehow."

"I suppose," Brin said, but that was a lie too. Havilar and Mehen came back and gave him his space. Desima returned with bundles of herbs, knowing better than to meet his eyes. He went to his bedroll early, sunk in his worries. If Torm had meant for his duty to be ruling Cormyr, he thought, staring up at the canopy of leaves, then he could have made Brin better suited to being king—more patient, more sure, more silver-tongued. Taller, Brin thought bitterly. If Torm had wanted so badly for him to be Raedra's consort, Torm could have kept him from ever meeting Havilar, or kept her from coming back. A thousand small shifts, and he would never have landed here, in the Hullack, with a hellhound chained a hundred feet away.

Yet here he was.

So it can't be your duty, he reasoned. One way or another.

Which hurt in its own way. Brin *wasn't* suited to rule—not as king, not as prince-consort, not even as the Lord Crownsilver—but that didn't mean he wanted to leave Cormyr to its own devices, especially in its darkest hour. Havilar was very right about that—if he ran, it would be the act of a petulant child, and he would regret it all his days.

Maybe your duty, he thought, on the edge of sleep, your destiny is to be the one who takes the steps that need to be taken. Who bends the rules and ignores the expectations and makes sure things don't fall apart. He thought of Garce and the refugees.

Things that needed to be done. Did Torm's gifts only come when he stood there, on the edge that others feared to approach? He rolled his eyes at himself—gods, that sounded dramatic. But a little right.

He crawled out of his bedroll and picked his way among his comrade's sleeping forms, around the coals of the fire. Desima sat watch, beside the filmy lines of a conjured sentinel. She regarded him coolly as he lay down alongside Havilar. Havilar stirred as he wrapped his arms around her, and mumbled, "What? What happened?"

"I'm sorry," Brin whispered. "I'm sorry. I lost my head. I didn't even ask if you were all right, I—"

She reached back and cupped the back of his head. "It's all right," she said sleepily. "It's just a fight. I was sharp with you too."

He buried his face against her hair. "We should try the hellhound. It's the best option we have so far. But after, it has to go back to the Hells."

"Agreed," she said, rubbing his cheek. "After."

14

30 Eleasias, the Year of the Nether Mountain Scrolls (1486 DR)
Suzail, Cormyr

YOU SEEM IN A POOR MOOD," DRANNON COMMENTED, AS THE CARRIAGE rattled the short distance up the Promenade to Lord Crownsilver's tallhouse. Seven days had passed, as swiftly as the brimful streams in the countryside, and Ilstan'd had no luck at all convincing Raedra this was an unnecessary step. "Sick as I am of being told to see to mischievous devil-children?" Drannon asked.

"Just tired," Ilstan said. Drannon didn't know about Raedra's plans, shouldn't know about Raedra's plans. Both because Her Highness's secrecy and safety was paramount, but also because he didn't want to admit that she trusted a tiefling warlock over a wizard of war.

That's not what's happened, he told himself. Raedra's frightened and she *is* right—Farideh saw the traitor where you missed it.

Not even his superiors faulted Ilstan for not shaking down the timid-seeming daughter of an established noble family. There'd been no reason to assume that the preliminary tests weren't enough, and the headache caused by running such a sweet young lady through the more thorough studies without cause wasn't worth it. Until it was.

Sulue was a changed creature, staring silently at the walls of her cell. Refusing to speak, even to her tearful parents. They begged Ilstan to tell them this wasn't their daughter, this was a trick of Shar, a terrible doppelganger of their sweet-natured Sulue. But he couldn't—she was the lady herself, no creature in disguise, and her tremulous insistence that "Secrets are meant to be kept" didn't waver, no matter what the war wizards did. Ilstan had excused himself from the continuing interrogation. Sulue was a traitor, he reminded himself. She wasn't one of them.

At the tallhouse, he stepped out into the rain, not bothered by the downpour. Drannon lingered behind, crafting a cantrip to keep dry, so Ilstan forged ahead to knock on the door. The tiefling opened it by the time Drannon reached his side, looking harried and upset.

"Good morning," she said.

"Is everything all right?" Ilstan asked.

"Yes. Sorry, I was . . . upstairs. Come in. Would you like a cup of tea or something?"

Ilstan ducked through the doorway. "Well met," he said. "And no thank you. This shouldn't take long, and they're waiting for you at the palace to get started."

She pursed her mouth. "That sounds ominous."

Ilstan considered her drab blouse and tunic, the patched breeches, the unbound hair. Nell would come after her like a general into battle. "Only a little," he said with a smile. He raised his wand. "Would you mind, goodwoman?"

Farideh spread her arms and took a deep breath. "Ready."

Why she made such a fuss over the spell, Ilstan couldn't fathom. The magic swirled around her, hiding the tail, the heavy horns, the disquieting eyes, and her beastly teeth. Smoothing Farideh out into something much more acceptable, even pretty. Once they sorted out the clothes—

The spell suddenly surged again, a wave of magic rolling through the fabric of the Weave. Ilstan snatched at it, trying to stop the spell from twisting away. Beside him he sensed Drannon, attempting the same. He managed to keep it from hitting Farideh—instead, a ball of magic formed out of the ether and slammed into the wall, leaving behind a covering of cloth-of-gold and a delicate painting of shepherdesses and their flocks on the hillside beneath an elven ruin.

The traitor no one knows is lurking, the strange voice murmured. *And the savior no one trusts . . . neither side is simple . . . but we must prevail.*

"Ilstan, man!" Drannon's shouts snapped Ilstan from his reverie. The older war wizard stood, inches from the taller man's chin, staring up at him, furious and fearful. "Are you well?

"Fine," Ilstan said.

"Mystra's misbegotten children," Drannon swore. "I thought you'd gone spell-mad for a moment." He sneered at Farideh and the splotch of glittering wall beyond her. "Godsbedamned Weave is supposed to make things *simpler* they say. Well, praise be to Mystra, that's the fourth spell I've seen go awry this month."

"It's . . ." Ilstan rubbed his head. Farideh was watching him closely. "It's just taking time to get used to," he lied. "Things are still coming together."

"Well, they can come together faster," Drannon said. "We've a war to win. And a warlock to deliver to Her Highness. Let's go."

Ilstan followed Drannon and Farideh back to the carriage, replaying in his mind the strange voice's words and the feeling of the magic swelling his spell, powerful enough to turn the tiefling into a beauty to rival the Princess of Cormyr for a solid tenday, had he not been able to shift the focus.

He ought to be afraid, Ilstan knew. Now, more than ever.

• • •

In the owlbear room once again, Farideh felt tense enough to snap. The princess's maid had pulled and pinned her hair into a confection Havilar would have coveted and painted her face in soft colors that made Farideh feel as if she ought to melt away into the painting of the two women standing over the lion that hung above the fireplace. Farideh focused on the dark-haired woman's blue eye as the maid pulled the strings of a corset tight around her, all the while Havilar's sending echoing in her thoughts. She might be able to scrape together enough to make a sending of her own, but without any knowing who was nearby her sister, it might make everything worse. She could only wait.

Raedra came in, looking pinched, and the pulling mercifully stopped so the maid could curtsy. Farideh didn't dare move. "Well met," she said. "Is this necessary?"

"If you're going to join my retinue, you must look the part," Raedra said. "I've decided we'll do best if we tell them you're Aubrin's cousin. There are a handful of Crownsilvers in Athkatla, you will be one of them. You've been sent to Suzail to . . . gain some polish. Your name won't suit—it doesn't sound human."

"Because it isn't," Farideh said.

"Fair," Raedra said. "You'll be Asmura Crownsilver. If anyone asks, you're a third cousin, once removed. You arrived only three days ago, and we were introduced when I went to Crownsilver Castle to discuss the Crownsilvers' revels around the wedding, and I invited you to join us. Let them do the talking—they're all very entertaining, so it shouldn't be hard. When they ask you questions, your best tactic is to demur and turn it on them. I won't call them off if they get too intrusive. That would be noticeable."

"I can manage, thank you," Farideh said. The maid pulled a purple gown over Farideh's head—the ease with which it slipped past her ears and over her arms startled her. No horns to catch, she reminded herself, as the maid fastened a line of buttons down her back.

Raedra sat in the needlepoint chair, and sighed. "Someone should get rid of that painting."

"Too modern?"

Raedra waved a hand as if that were a minor crime. "It's meant to depict two princesses of Cormyr: Tanalasta and Alusair, the daughters of Azoun the Fourth. Who is supposed to be the lion in the middle—the dead one."

"Oh," Farideh said. "I thought it was asleep."

"Because it's a *terrible* painting."

The maid closed the last button, and Farideh took a deep breath to assure herself she still could, looked down and realized the collar scooped low enough that Mehen would have lectured her roundly about exposing such a vital spot, had it been armor. She tugged the collar up. The maid tugged it back.

"Alusair was called 'the Steel Regent' and ruled the damned country for thirteen years," Raedra went on. "Tanalasta was a brilliant political mind, and look at them—they look like maidens in a Greengrass play, all flimsy and fawning. *And* the lion looks like a drugged bear. But it was a gift to my grandfather from an Akanulan envoy, and he felt they'd made the effort and t'would be rude to destroy the Netherese-loving genies' stupid gift. At least here no one has to look at it."

She drummed her fingers against the chair's arms. "There's a much better portrait of them in the Hall of Gazes. Are you finished, Nell?"

Raedra stood and flicked her eyes over Farideh. She sighed again. "The hem," she spat. "Blast, I forgot—you're a bit taller than me. If anyone asks, it's the fashion in Athkatla and you didn't know any better. Did you bring a necklace, Nell?"

"Yes, lady." The maid draped a gold chain around Farideh's neck, and the disguise was complete enough for Raedra. She thanked the maid, and led Farideh out into the corridor. A pair of guards fell in behind her, eyeing Farideh's attempt to follow. Farideh fought the urge to cover her low collar again.

"Oh, my dear knights," Raedra said, stopping cold. She turned to the guards. "This is Lady Asmura Crownsilver, my betrothed's beloved cousin. She's just arrived in Suzail. I completely forgot to mention she'd be joining us." She smiled winsomely, and held out a hand to Farideh, like a girl beckoning a playmate. "She's coming along today and—if you please—we wish to have a little space." She smiled impishly. "There's much I need to apprise her of, if you catch my meaning."

The guards traded glances but let Farideh pass, and the princess folded the tiefling's arm around her own, although her lovely face didn't warm. "That's . . . uncanny," Farideh whispered, once they were a good distance from the guards.

"You show them what they want to see, and no one fights you," Raedra said. "Although, they may just paint you like a Greengrass maiden when you're dead and gone."

"Or a sleeping bear," Farideh added. She glanced back at the guards. "Do they always follow you?"

"Of course," she said. "Two in sight at all times. Plus a war wizard, sometimes two—although often, if it's not Ilstan, they'll conceal themselves. I am well-acquainted," she added, "with kidnapping attempts."

Farideh pursed her mouth. "Did you settle that?"

"One hopes," Raedra said grimly. "Come along."

Raedra's retinue was already waiting for them in an enormous ballroom. A table and chairs had been set up to one side, with small treats and bites of fruit, a pitcher frosted with condensation. Three maids stood by, as well as two more Purple Dragons. A war wizard, a stern-looking older woman, stood by the door. She raised an eyebrow at Farideh as she followed the princess in, but Raedra gave the woman a significant look, and she made no move.

"Well met," a blond man lounging in one of the chairs called. "Where have you been, and *what* have you brought us?" Friendly as he sounded, there was no mistaking the distrust in his expression. The two women beside him were giving Farideh similar looks. Every one of them was dressed in padded leathers and holding a foiled rapier.

"This is Lady Asmura Crownsilver," Raedra said. "Fresh from Athkatla. She is Aubrin's third cousin, and she's quite fed up with being locked in the castle with

Hellish Helindra. So I rescued her." She smiled back at Farideh, a warning look in her pale eyes.

"Well met." Farideh made an awkward curtsy. No one's expression softened. Raedra introduced the three nobles in turn—Maranth, Varauna, and Florelle—the maids, the Purple Dragons and Pelia, the war wizard by the door.

"Are we . . . sparring?" Farideh asked, puzzled.

"Fencing," Raedra said. "Come on, we have armor for you too." She went behind a screen set up in the corner, one of the maids hurrying over.

"Why am I in a dress if we have to put on armor?" Farideh hissed.

Raedra gave her a puzzled look, as the maid unbuttoned her gown. "Well you can't walk *in* wearing fencing gear as if you *rode* here dressed that way." A second pair of hands went quickly down Farideh's stays. "That would be bizarre," Raedra said.

Farideh kept her eyes locked on a gap in the screen, while the maid quickly stripped her out of the gown that Nell had gone to such pains to get her into, and pulled on a set of similar leathers, with reinforced bracers and a high metal-plated gorget.

"Varauna *will* try to upset you," Raedra warned, in a soft voice. "She's terrible when she wants to be, but when it counts, she's good to have on one's side. Florelle will act as though she is exactly as snobby as Varauna, but she'll be the first to try and befriend you, guaranteed. Maranth will act like a guard dog—but if Varauna gets too rough, he'll be the one to pull her off. Pay none of them any mind."

That was easy enough for Raedra to say. As Raedra and Maranth took up their foils, Farideh called up the soul sight, only to be interrupted by Varauna.

"Oh, I did love your dress," Varauna said. "It was my absolute favorite fashion last summer."

"Thank you," Farideh said, realizing a half second after she'd started speaking that it wasn't a compliment. Beside her, Florelle tittered, and Farideh felt herself blush. Her temper swelled—and behind it the powers of Asmodeus woke. No, she thought. Don't give in. "Perhaps you can give me the name of a good dressmaker while I'm here."

"I have a *private* seamstress," Varauna said, as though Farideh were simple.

"She does a very good job," Farideh said.

Varauna looked past Farideh at Florelle, looking appalled. "It's like Sulue all over again."

"Is it?" Florelle asked. "Or is she clever enough to know how to get to you?"

"Don't be a twit, Florelle."

Farideh took the moment to consider Maranth, retreating from Raedra's attack. The lights of his soul left a sort of trail as he darted forward and back, streaks of olive green and gold and blue. The smattering of shadowy parts, though, made no pattern, and held none of the depth and emptiness that the missing noblewoman's had.

He's afraid of being stifled, Farideh thought without meaning to. He's afraid of being made into . . . an uncle? A grandfather? There was only a sense of the stern, unforgiving man who loomed over Maranth's life—

"Asmura!" Varauna snapped. Farideh startled, realized that Varauna had meant her.

"Sorry," Farideh said. She nodded at the fencers. "They're very good."

Varauna shot Florelle another look. "We were asking if you're enjoying the city," she said enunciating carefully.

"It's hard to enjoy in all this rain," Farideh said. She watched the Purple Dragons beyond Raedra and Maranth—it was easy to study them without looking as if she were prying. Neither showed the marks of Shar.

"What did you do for fun in Athkatla?" Florelle asked.

Farideh hesitated. What did nobles do for fun? "Riding," she said. "Hunting. Some . . . swordwork—"

"Oh ye gods," Varauna said. "Our mothers aren't here—what do you do that's interesting?"

I turn into a burning angel, Farideh thought, and let a devil kiss me. I stare down the Chosen of Shar and challenge undead arcanists to mortal combat.

"Do you play cards?" Florelle asked. "That's what we're doing tomorrow."

Farideh smiled hesitantly. "I . . . haven't had anyone to play cards with in a while, but I can learn. I have a little Wroth deck for playing patience games with."

Varauna's eyes went wide as gold pieces. "*Wroth?*"

"Where did you learn *Wroth*?" Florelle said.

"A friend from Waterdeep," Farideh said. "They're nothing, really."

"Did you bring them?" Varauna asked, in hushed tones.

"No," Farideh said. "I didn't think—"

"But you brought them to Suzail," Varauna said. "You have to bring them next time. We'll play cards, too, in case anyone comes in. And you can tell our fortunes."

Raedra lunged forward, planting the tip of her sword on Maranth's padded vest. "Ha! And that makes five."

Maranth smirked at her. "Bring your long sword next time." Raedra chuckled. She crossed to the table, taking the cup the maid held out for her. "Thank you. Are you enjoying yourself, Asmura?"

"Very well," Farideh said, trying not to look as tense as she felt, "Your Highness."

"Did you *know* she reads Wroth cards?" Varauna demanded.

"I don't—"

"I see you've found the way to Varauna's good graces," Maranth said. "Tell her how glowing her future will be and you'll have a fast friend for at *least* a tenday." He turned a hollow smile on Farideh. "Maybe you could ask them about your cousin and what he's up to."

Farideh glanced at Raedra, but the princess was suddenly very interested in the bottom of her cup.

"What do you think of dear Aubrin, Asmura?" Maranth asked.

"I haven't seen him in some time. He was a boy when I last knew him."

"But what do you *think* about him?"

"I think . . ." Farideh shook her head. "He has many good qualities—he cares very deeply about his family, his friends. He's braver than he believes himself to be, and he's . . . a good person to have on your side." She fixed Maranth with a hard stare. "But he's also not the boy I knew. So I can't say how much my opinion counts for."

"Would you let your sister marry him?" Raedra suddenly asked. Her face held no hint of the answer she wanted. "You're more distant cousins than he and I are. Would *you* marry him?"

"I don't *let* people marry each other, Your Highness," Farideh said, wishing she had a tail to lash. Her stomach twisted. "If they loved each other, then it wouldn't be my business. I want my sister to be happy, and she deserves that. But I wouldn't marry him, no."

"Why not?" Maranth demanded.

"Because he's not my type," Farideh said sharply.

"Neither are you his," Varauna said dryly. Maranth glowered at her.

"Florelle?" Raedra said. "Come on." The willowy lady took her position, sword drawn and soul sparking. Farideh leaned forward, intent on studying Florelle.

"Have you met her?" Maranth asked, in a low voice. "Aubrin's mistress?"

"I haven't," Farideh said, feeling her pulse in her throat. "He'd left before I arrived. I hear she went with him."

Maranth shook his head. "I cannot believe Aubrin would do anything so vulgar. An errand for the Crown—everyone *knows* that's what it is—and he brings his monster-doxy along?"

Farideh felt her cheeks growing hot, the powers of Asmodeus churning up toward her heart. She kept her eyes on Raedra, on Florelle. The noblewoman shimmered with curling lights of pinks and violets and bile-yellow. No light-swallowing shadows. Raedra lunged forward and managed to hit Florelle twice, one above the hip, once mid-belly.

"I've seen her," Varauna said.

"Liar," Maranth retorted.

"I *did*." She leaned in toward Farideh, dropping her voice. "I was coming home—very late— about a month ago. Don't ask what I was doing—"

"*Who*," her brother corrected.

"Shut *up*, Lord Tightbreeches," Varauna snapped. "Just because you can't even get a fellow into bed when your hand's down their purse . . ."

Farideh kept watching Florelle. She wants status, Farideh thought—and this time she clung to the knowledge instead of fighting away from it. Anything to not hear Varauna.

She wants to be someone, she thought. She wants to have security and power. Dominion over *something*. She would fall so quickly, if one were just careful to offer—

"Anyway," Varauna went on. "Who comes down the Promenade but Lord Aubrin Crownsilver, a-horseback?"

"Could have been anyone in a cloak," Maranth pointed out.

"Anyone who rides with a knight of Torm and a dragonborn by his side? It was definitely him. And who's riding behind but a tiefling. It must have been her."

"Five!" Florelle cried, throwing up her blade. "Honestly, Raedra, I don't know why you bother with us." She came over to the table. "Your turn, Varauna."

"A moment!" Varauna said. "I'm telling Asmura something." She gave Farideh a sharp smile and whispered, "Such an *ugly* thing. She surely has a spell on him or something."

"Who?" Raedra asked, coming to stand near them.

For a moment, the nobles were quiet.

"Varauna thinks she saw Aubrin's mistress," Maranth said after a moment.

"Ah," Raedra said.

"*Very* ugly," Varauna said again.

Farideh felt her cheeks burn, and wanted more than anything for Varauna to be bruised and hollowed by Shar's blessings—but only normal shadows dappled her.

"Well, she's a tiefling," Florelle said. "I doubt *you'd* have many fellows to hurry secretly home from if you had horns and a tail. Those teeth."

"Beyond *that*," Varauna said. "She's taller than him, by almost a head. And such a beak of a nose—"

"Enough!" Farideh snapped. Every eye was suddenly pinned to her, but she didn't care. "Does it *matter*?" she demanded. "What do you gain by pretending how she looks is a point to be won? Monstrous or beautiful, she's still there. It's not as if being a tiefling is something she's *done* to you."

No one spoke for a tense awful second, and Farideh was ready—so ready—for whatever comment or jab or insult they might throw at her. She wanted a fight, wanted an argument. But Raedra was the one who spoke.

"She's there," Raedra said, all coolness. "And that *is* the problem."

"What do they do in Athkatla?" Maranth drawled. "Take bugbears to their beds? It must be extraordinary for you to think it's no matter that a lord of the blood has a tiefling lover."

"Do you have one of your own?" Florelle asked, attempting Maranth's drawl. "Is that what it's about?"

"*Do* you?" Varauna asked, a little too much interest in her voice.

"No," Farideh said. "I don't have a lover." She kept staring at Raedra, furious that she had brought her into the middle of this, furious that there was no escape except with the princess's leave. Furious that Raedra just stood there and let her friends insult Havi—and insult Farideh too, even if they didn't mean it. If she cared so deeply what happened to her guests—

"Wait," Varauna said. "You don't have a tiefling lover, or you don't have *any* lovers?"

"I don't have a lover," Farideh snapped.

"Because you left them in Athkatla?"

"Because I don't have a lover—why?"

"*Never?*" Varauna all but squawked. "How is that *possible?*" Maranth swatted at her, and she smacked his hand back. "Even *Sulue* knew how to ride a man, for heaven's sake. Don't pretend this is normal."

Farideh flushed. "The opportunity hasn't presented itself. Exactly."

"There's a point where it's not the opportunities' faults," Varauna said, "but your fault for not seizing them. And what have they done to you but shipped you to Suzail when there's a veritable drought of fellows on." She clucked her tongue. "That's just tragic."

"If nothing else," Maranth said, "there is a surplus in the city of tieflings who'll take coin. Sounds like your type after all."

"Asmura," Raedra said. "Come on." She gestured to the floor with her rapier.

"I don't use a rapier, Your Highness," Farideh said. And I don't spar with people I want to hit, she thought. Raedra narrowed her eyes.

"There is an array of weapons available to us," she said crisply. "What *do* you use?"

"Short sword," Farideh said. "But I wouldn't wish Your Highness—"

But already the war wizard was bringing forward a pair of blunted short swords. Farideh took it, her pulse speeding. "Do you use the short sword?"

"My brother was trained to it, as it happens," Raedra said. "So I learned, to help him practice." She swung the sword, testing the weight. "It's not my favorite weapon, but I can handle it."

Which was when Farideh realized Raedra might be just as angry with her as she was with Raedra.

"What are the rules?" Farideh asked.

"The sword touches you from the forearm up, it counts as a point," Raedra said. "Five points to finish. You strike the head or neck, you forfeit." She held the blade up in a ready posture. "You let me win, I will *never* forget it."

Never in her life had Farideh been so glad she'd been practicing with her sword. Raedra might have favored a rapier, but she was nearly as quick with the short sword, and it took all of Farideh's focus to stay ahead of the blade. The first two touches came quickly, Raedra's expression grim and fierce. Farideh leaped back, out of reach.

"I am not interested in being humiliated," Raedra panted. "I am not acquiescing. I am not telling *my* friends not to defend me—"

"Who was defending *you?*" Farideh said, keeping her voice too low for the others to hear. "They were mocking *her*, there's a difference."

"Not such a difference." Raedra sprang forward and nearly caught Farideh's arm.

"What do you think this is," Farideh demanded, "a game she's playing with you? Do you think you win something if you remind yourself of all you have that she and I don't?" She lunged, and Raedra caught the sword on her own, shoving Farideh back. "Do you think you matter even a moment to how she feels about him? Because let me tell you, you don't."

Raedra shot forward again, striking Farideh across the shoulder, but leaving her guard open. Farideh jabbed her with the practice sword—a strike that might well have pierced her belly had the blade not been blunt and the armor so thick. Raedra cried out, and Farideh swung the sword down on her upper arm, before skipping out of reach.

"I don't think she or you understand what's at stake here," Raedra said. "You think this is a little romance, a story where something that passes for 'true love' wins all, but we're not talking about star-crossed lovers, we're talking about king-doms and families and politics. We're talking about a story where the kingdom falls into chaos because the hidden prince runs off with his half-breed mistress." She reached with the blade, scoring a hit on Farideh's elbow.

Farideh lunged forward, smacking the blade into Raedra's ribs. "Don't *call* her that!"

"What should I call her?" Raedra whispered, taking the sword in both hands. "Ugly devil-child? I hear she's pretty stupid as well."

The powers of Asmodeus surged at that—no, no, no, Farideh thought, and shoved them down. "Then what shall we call your brother?" she said, savagely. "I'm sure they have names for him too. Do *you* stand there and smile while they call him odd and addled and neutered? Or are you the one who says it loudest?"

Raedra's last remnants of restraint seemed to snap, her lovely features contorted around a screech. She leaped at Farideh, leaving a split second where her guard was wide as she pulled the weapon back for a strike hard enough to bruise. No time to retreat, Farideh threw herself against the princess, shoulder first. Raedra kept her feet though, and wrapped an arm around Farideh's neck.

"Take it *back*!" she snarled.

"You first!" Farideh twisted and slammed her fist—and the sword in it—into Raeda's jaw.

The Purple Dragons were close around them before Farideh realized what she'd done. One grabbed hold of her by one arm, yanking her from Raedra's reach. Raedra touched her bleeding lip.

"I'm sorry," Farideh said, as the war wizard rushed forward. She looked from one guard to the other, picturing dungeons, unwelcome spells, gleaming swords. The powers of the pact crawled up her spine. "Oh dear gods, I'm sorry—it was an accident." She dropped the sword and reached to help, but one of the guards blocked her. Raedra didn't stop them.

"You forfeit," she panted. She pressed on her lip and winced. The war wizard grabbed her face and Raedra swatted her away. "It's a fat lip, Pelia, not an assassination attempt."

Still, not even Raedra could stop the war wizard from applying a quick healing spell. The princess held still for it, eyeing Farideh, who didn't dare move.

"You make a compelling argument," Raedra said finally. She crossed over to the table, where the three nobles were staring at her and Farideh.

"Are you all right?" Maranth demanded.

"Fine," Raedra said, calmly, taking up her cup. "Asmura still needs to learn the rules better."

The Purple Dragons returned to their stations, still eyeing Farideh. The war wizard didn't move. *She knows,* Farideh thought. *She knows and you're about to be in the dungeon and who is going to come for you? Who will speak for you?* She imagined Lorcan trying to charm a pack of war wizards, and her stomach twisted. She'd lost her head for a moment, in the worst possible way, and there was no chance that this wouldn't rain down on everyone—

Raedra drained her cup. "I think I've had enough fencing for the day," she announced. "I'm going to retire." She pursed her mouth, as if testing the healing. "Asmura will you walk with me? I feel we have more to discuss." The nobles all kissed her cheeks and said their farewells, not a one knowing how to leave things with Asmura.

Raedra smiled, but it never reached her eyes, and as they left the ballroom, she made no pretense that they were friends. Farideh followed through the constant, winding corridors, trailed by the guards and the war wizard. They were not returning to the room with the painting of the princesses.

But at least, Farideh thought as they climbed a second staircase, they were not heading down in the direction of the dungeons.

Finally, Raedra turned down a long, wide hallway, hung with paintings and tapestries—enough nearly to cover every inch of the walls. A hundred eyes seemed to look down on Farideh. Battles raged, dragons died, martyrs fell to fierce blades. The whole history of Cormyr played out in gilded frames and faded yarns, washed in the gray light of a dozen windows that interrupted the art.

"No one will think you are a noblewoman if you gape like that," Raedra said. "They're only paintings." She gestured at the guards and the war wizard to stay where they stood.

The war wizard frowned. "Princess, I don't think it's wise—"

"As if you cannot blast her into ashes from a hundred yards, Pelia," Raedra said. "If the Royal Magician has something to say about it, tell him to come and be quarrelsome at me." To Farideh, she said nothing, only walked into the hall of paintings, leaving Farideh to follow.

Raedra stopped a little more than halfway down, looking up at a painting of a strikingly beautiful woman in jewels, holding a stiletto in one hand and a rose in the other.

"I'm sorry," Farideh said. "I didn't mean to hit you."

"Of course you did," Raedra said, sounding weary. "What was I doing but dragging your sister through the mud and asking you to bite your tongue? *I* would have hit you—I did nearly hit you—so I must concede, it was invited." She looked askance at Farideh. "*Do* they call her stupid?"

"Yes," Farideh said. "She's not, not really. Just flighty. She gets things mixed up sometimes." She looked up at the beautiful woman. "But she sees things other people don't. And she's brilliant with her weapon." Raedra said nothing. "I didn't mean those things. About your broth—I mean, the prince."

Raedra nodded, absently. "Do you want to see the portrait of the two princesses? The better one?"

Farideh glanced back at the trio of protectors, each one ready to leap to action if Raedra gave the slightest sign. "Do you want to know what I saw?"

"In a moment," Raedra said. She crossed the hallway, and at the other side of a window indicated a large painting of two women, side by side. Where the painting in the dark little room had been gauzy and sweet, all pastels and soft lines, this was rich and detailed and stern. The brown-haired woman here was turned in profile, one hand on a stack of books, the other arm cradling a baby in swaddling. The blond woman wore armor with a cream-colored hood, one hand on her sister's shoulder and one holding a shield emblazoned with a purple dragon.

"It's not accurate," Raedra said. "Tanalasta died in childbirth. And some say they never really got along that well."

"I see why you prefer it," Farideh said. She leaned forward, eyes locked on the woman's warm brown eyes. "What was her name again? The Steel One?"

"Alusair. It does look like her."

"How do you know?"

"She haunts the palace," Raedra said, as if it were the most normal thing in the world. "I've only seen her once—after one of the revels they held before my other wedding. I don't think she likes me much—I've never been scowled at like that before, by the living or the dead. But maybe she knew better about the wedding."

"You were already married?" Farideh asked. "What happened?"

Raedra looked at her, surprised. "No one told you that? I can't believe Aubrin . . ." Raedra trailed off and shook her head. "It seems like the sort of detail one would tell one's mistress, if one were trying to make a case. Maybe she didn't tell you."

Mistress. It had such an ugly sound, the way Raedra said it, like a disease, an infestation. A *mistress.*

Raedra sighed. "Baerovus and I used to come up here, play a silly little game called Tribute. We'd take turns choosing which piece we would want as a gift, until we chose them all. Or I got bored."

Farideh frowned up at a tapestry of a woman holding a shining sword, surrounded by bestial-looking orcs. "That's . . . a game?"

Raedra paused. "My brother's a little particular." Whatever friendliness had crept into Raedra's manner fled, and she suddenly became formal and not a little defensive.

"Which did he pick first?" Farideh asked.

Raedra was silent a moment, before she beckoned Farideh down the long hall. She pointed up at a painting of a cool-eyed man in full armor, holding a shining greatsword. If someone had folded the board it had been painted on in half, it would match perfectly side to side. "Faerlthann the First King, and Ansrivarr, the Blade of Memory," she said. "He liked how tidy it is." She bit her lip. "*Likes*," she corrected. "He likes how tidy it is."

Farideh's chest tightened. "Is he doing any better?"

Raedra stared up at the dead king. "The same. Every day, the same." She folded her hands. "I always let him choose this one," she said briskly. "My first was either the princesses or Azoun the Second killing the Purple Dragon."

Farideh frowned. "Why did he kill a guardsman?"

Raedra snorted. "No, no. *The* Purple Dragon." She took Farideh's arm and led her back down the hall to a painting of a man astride an enormous dragon's skull, his sword nearly to the hilt in the creature's violet-scaled crown. At their feet a man in voluminous robes raised his hands, spangled with magic, a second lay supine, clutching a chest wound.

"Thauglorimorgorus," Raedra said. "*The* Purple Dragon. He ruled the Forest Kingdom before the humans arrived, before we built Cormyr. He returned once to take it back—it took the king, two High Wizards—Jorunhast, that's him with the beard; and his teacher, Thanderahast who's there rolling around on the ground—plus a whole company of soldiers to kill him."

She waggled her fingers at Farideh. "Some say it wasn't enough, and if an Obarskyr ever doesn't sit on the Dragon Throne, Thauglor will return again and reclaim the Forest Kingdom."

"But he's dead?"

"Well one never can tell with a dragon," Raedra sighed. "Better to keep an Obarskyr on the throne anyway. Speaking of—" She glanced down the hallway at the Purple Dragon guards and sighed. "Are they safe?"

Farideh nodded. "None of them is in service to Shar. Neither are your friends, or the maids." She paused. "You might watch out for Florelle, I think."

"Florelle?" Raedra said, incredulous.

"I get the impression that she might be swayed to do a lot of things if it meant she gained a little power."

Raedra chuckled. "That describes half the noblewomen in Suzail. I should expect you to warn me about Varauna before Florelle."

"No—Varauna . . ." Farideh hesitated, the noblewoman's sharp, unkind words replaying in her thoughts. "She's likely the safest of them all. She's . . . *satisfied* in a way the others aren't. And regardless of anything else, Maranth clearly dotes on you. They're safe," she said again. "You're safe."

"Thank you," Raedra said. "That is a burden from my mind." But she didn't walk back toward the guards, staring instead for several breaths at the dying black dragon in the painting. "Would you come again?" she asked. "In a day or so? There are others . . . I will tell Varauna she must keep her tongue about your sister. About you." She looked at Farideh, clearly embarrassed. "You're not ugly, you know. She was only trying to gain attention."

Farideh smiled, an empty thing. "I know what I am."

"You might come again," Raedra said once more. "If nothing else . . . I owe you a better measure of hospitality."

"That isn't necessary," Farideh insisted. "And your war wizards—"

"Are very good at what they do," Raedra finished. "But they cannot spy the Lady of Loss's mark on a person, and they're sure Varauna is going to ruin me. You will come. Please?"

Farideh swallowed a sigh of her own. "Do I have to wear the dress?"

"I'll find something with a more suitable hem." Raedra assured her, and set off for the guards before Farideh could protest that wasn't what she meant. The Purple Dragons and Pelia whisked Raedra off, down the corridors.

"Should I follow?" Farideh called.

"That isn't necessary." Farideh's heart leaped, and her pact poured Hells' magic through her veins, carrying the soul sight with it. She spun—ready for ghosts, ready for kidnappers, ready for more sharp-tongued nobles—and found Ilstan standing behind her with a pleasant smile.

"My apologies. It seemed faster to just make the jump, so to speak." Ilstan's soul lights flickered like a hundred candles in a drafty room—silver and blue and violet and gold. But in the center of that glittering mass was another shape—a glyph, the sort of glyph she'd seen impressed upon the souls of Chosen. She couldn't read it, but she knew it was the mark of a god, a claim placed upon this soul, their blessed agent in the world of Toril.

But Farideh was sure she'd seen that same glyph before: emblazoned on the heart of the god of sin himself. Ilstan's smile didn't waver as he took her by the arm.

"You'll want to change," he said. "You can't go out in fencing gear." He gave a good-natured chuckle. "That would look very odd, indeed."

• • •

"I NEVER THOUGHT I'd see the princess disguising a tiefling and squiring her around the city," Pelia Rowanmantle said as she and Ilstan headed toward the Royal Magician's tower as the sun set. "Utterly bizarre. Whatever she's doing, certainly we could do it just as well."

Ilstan kept his eyes on the path, his expression as blank as he could manage, but the memory of Farideh, jumpy and staring on the ride back to the tallhouse, nagged at him. "The tiefling is the one who identified Lady Thundersword's true allegiances. It's a safety measure."

"Hm," Pelia said. "The same tiefling who punched her in the mouth? Very safe."

"An accident."

"None of her retinue has ever struck her. Not even Lady Thundersword."

"None of her retinue has had work as a bounty hunter," Ilstan said, though privately he was just as appalled as Pelia. Raedra had brushed the whole incident off when he returned from dropping Farideh back at Lord Crownsilver's tallhouse.

"She slipped," Raedra said. "And she wasn't holding back the way the others do."

"With all due respect, Highness," Ilstan said. "They hold back for a reason." But she'd waved him off and gone to sit instead with Baerovus. He wondered what Farideh had told her.

"Have you brought it up with Ganrahast?" Pelia asked.

Ilstan blew out a breath. "He has more important things to be concerned about."

"At this point?" Pelia said. "With the crown prince lost and his son comatose? Anything that touches the life of an Obarskyr is something to be concerned about."

They reached the Royal Magician's tower, but as Pelia passed through the door, Ilstan was seized with a dizziness so sudden and overwhelming he slammed into the tower's stone wall.

How is a devil like a wizard? The voice from the ether rang all around him like the pealing of a bell. *Neither is a god—until they are . . . we all snatch and scrabble . . . we know it can always be lost, ah yes . . .*

"Ilstan!" Pelia shouted. The vertigo vanished and with it the strange voice. But unlike before, it didn't leave Ilstan at peace. He dropped to a crouch and was sick all over the path and Pelia's slippers.

"Ye gods, man!" she cried, leaping back. "What's the matter with you?"

I don't know, Ilstan thought. But it was rapidly becoming apparent that he needed to figure it out. This wasn't a hiccup in the Weave. This wasn't a spell going awry.

But the moment Ilstan said something, Ganrahast would pull him aside, for safety's sake, and Cormyr couldn't spare another war wizard. A devil, a wizard, and it can always be lost. He squeezed his eyes shut.

"It's fine," he said. "Just . . . a spot of vertigo."

"Go lie down," Pelia said, though by her look, it was clear she didn't believe Ilstan. He hurried back to the palace, his thoughts ringing with warnings of gods and devils, of keys and locks, of traitors and saviors and all that might be lost. Too many fingers pointing to the same trap, the flat eyes that widened at him, that wouldn't stop staring. She'd made him uneasy as he conveyed her back home—was this why?

He hardly knew where he was going, until he passed between the guards standing outside the prince's sickroom.

Raedra looked up as he came in, the haze of his vision making her seem as golden and glowing as a solar in the sunset. Her pale eyes flicked over him.

"Ilstan?" she said. "Whatever's the matter?"

"You cannot send for her again," he blurted.

Raedra stiffened. "I beg your pardon."

"The tiefling. Farideh. Your Highness." The manic feeling ebbed in a jerky uneven way, but that sureness that something was wrong, that the voice meant the tiefling, remained. "There's something . . . I can't be sure what she might be up to."

"She's up to nothing at all," Raedra said. "*You* already assured me of that much." She peered at him, over the sleeping prince. "Are you well?"

"Of course I'm well," he snapped. Raedra raised an eyebrow and through his sureness Ilstan realized the Purple Dragons near the door had moved closer. "My apologies. I've just . . . I have a terrible feeling . . . What did she tell you?"

Raedra folded her hands. "That you are correct about Lord and Lady Goldfeather, Lady Ambershield, Nell, and the four guards that attended us. And Wizard of War Rowanmantle, as well," she added coolly. "She also complimented several aged paintings of variable quality. But I'm sure Ganrahast is well aware of all of that."

Ilstan heard the rebuke she didn't speak. She didn't have to.

"Is there something you've found?" Raedra asked. "Or is it only this feeling?"

"I've overstepped," he said. "I . . . I beg your forgiveness, Highness."

Raedra smoothed Prince Baerovus's blankets unnecessarily, and did not meet his eyes. "She will return again, tomorrow. If you find something more concrete than a feeling, I'd be happy to hear it, but otherwise . . ." She cleared her throat. "You will keep your opinions to yourself, War Wizard."

Ilstan bowed his head. "Of course, Your Highness. Your pardon." He slipped from the room, feeling as though he'd managed to fail both the princess and the intrusive voice.

15

30 Eleasias, the Year of the Nether Mountain Scrolls (1486 DR)
Suzail, Cormyr

D AHL BLEW OUT A NERVOUS BREATH, SCANNING THE PROMENADE BEFORE the tallhouse as though it would make Farideh step out of the cobbles. "How long has she been gone?"

"A few hours," Dumuzi said. Then, "She told me not to go with her."

"She would." Dahl drummed his fingers against the punnet of blackberries. *I have good news and I have bad news,* he imagined himself saying. Possibly. Depending on how mad she really was about the other night, maybe it was all bad news. "So you've just been sitting here since?"

"You are all so very nosy about what I do," Dumuzi said. "I ate a meal. I pulled some weeds from the flower boxes and the garden. I was going to fetch a book from the library when you showed up."

"What's in Brin's library?" Dahl scoffed. "Mountains of chapbooks?"

"Lot of history books. Books about planes and devils." He was silent a moment. "I just finished one about trade in the Heartlands. It's interesting."

"Is it?"

"You don't do things like we do," Dumuzi said simply.

A carriage rattled up to the iron gate, unmarked by any family's crest. The coachman climbed down, but before he could reach the door, the rider inside opened it and stepped out. The tall, dark-robed war wizard from the previous night smiled pleasantly at Dahl and Dumuzi, then helped Farideh from the carriage.

She looked human again, and worse—she was cinched into a purple gown that made the blue one look demure. Her hair had been pinned up in a pile of braids and curls, displaying the long column of her neck, and if he wasn't mistaken, she was wearing a little paint. She spoke to Ilstan briefly, her blue-and-brown eyes averted, then came up the walk with a stormy expression.

"If you say a *word*," she told Dahl, "I will kill you." She frowned at the blackberries.

"A gift," he said holding them out. "An apology. I was an ass the other night—"

"I thought we weren't going to talk about it," she said, pushing past him, but she took the blackberries as she opened the door.

"There's . . . more," Dahl said. He nodded at the pegs by the door. "I got your cloak back. And you were absolutely right—the cellarer is an agent of Netheril. That's the good news."

"You say that like there's bad news coming."

"Maybe." Dahl hesitated. "I got your cloak back by letting the innkeeper at the Brigand's Bottle believe we were unlucky lovers hiding from my hidebound employer. And I'm wondering if you'd mind keeping that ruse up, because I have seventeen more possible Sharrans to flush out. Also," he added, "I'm fairly sure she's going to spread that gossip around like it's tilling season. So . . . I might need to do better than blackberries."

Whatever Farideh'd been expecting him to say, that clearly wasn't it. "I thought . . . you said you were going to think of a different cover."

"Circumstances changed. And all things considered, it's a *very* solid cover. If the Sharrans talk to each other and note they've seen us in more than one place, well, of course they have, we're trying to stay ahead of Vescaras. All you have to do is come with me to the places on the list," he said. "Sit there, let me buy you a meal or a drink. Pretend you're enjoying my company. Thwart some Sharrans."

"Lorcan . . ." She sighed. "He wasn't happy the other night. He's firmly convinced you're going to talk me out of the pact or something."

Dahl snorted. "Has he *met* you?"

"You're trying to talk me *into* this, so don't play to my stubbornness so quickly." She chewed her lower lip, deep in thought. "Would you help me with something if I help you?"

"Name your price."

She beckoned him down the hall and into what turned out to be the tallhouse's library. It wasn't much of a library, that was certain, but at least it was dedicated to being a library, and not a sitting room or gallery or second parlor, the way so many nobles did. Only a little bigger than the entryway, and lined ceiling to floor with shelves and packed with books and scrolls. Farideh plucked a bit of foolscap from the narrow desk, scratched a stylus across it with careful, forceful strokes. She considered the finished product, then handed it over to Dahl, the ink still wet.

"There: What is it?" she said. "What do those say? And before you tell me to use the ritual, I have. It didn't work."

And whatever Dahl had been expecting, the row of glyphs on the parchment scrap wasn't it. Oghma, Mystra, and lost Deneir, he swore to himself. "What in all the planes are you doing with Supernal?"

"Is it very bad?"

"It's not bad . . . it's just *odd*," he said. He considered the feathery markings. "Supernal's just a strange tongue all around. They say it's the language of the gods."

"Which gods?"

"*All* of them," Dahl said. "Only *no one* said that until after the Spellplague. If it showed up before, no one identified it. They say all the gods and their angels—or whatever they *do* have—speak it, and that if they want you to understand, you will. But if they want it to be a secret, you'll hear Supernal's true sound."

Farideh furrowed her brow. "If it sounds like whatever language you understand," she said, "then how would you know it's another language at all? Aside from"—she waved at her drawings—"those. I mean lots of languages use the same letters. Draconic and Loross, for example."

Dahl gave her a sidelong look. "For example," he said dryly. "But these aren't real letters. They're *glyphs*. Each of these is—purportedly—a whole word. A picture to represent a concept, but abstracted. And 'purportedly,' because you're right. That's the thing that makes the whole idea hard to swallow—when people claim the gods or their messengers speak to them, they speak whatever tongue those people speak. And so, does the god speak the common tongue, or Dwarvish, or Evereskan Elvish, or Damaran? Or is it some magical language that sounds like whatever your thoughts know best? Or is it just a case of a fellow having an off-dream and calling it 'linguistics'? Where'd you come across Supernal?"

Farideh pursed her mouth. "Chosen," she said. "They have these marks on them when I look. These are from the Chosen in the camp, and this one"—she pointed to the first symbol—"is on the princess's favorite war wizard."

"And you don't know who chose him."

She met his eyes. "I have a bad feeling. But it could be a bad god and he might still be a decent fellow." Farideh took the paper from him and tucked it into her pocket. "You don't choose the god, the god chooses you."

Dahl nearly retorted—what evil god would waste power on a good person? But he stopped himself. He knew that tone in her voice and he needed more than anything for Farideh to feel agreeable right now. Besides, it might just amount to a bad feeling.

"Good point," he said instead. "You don't have enough information to justify throwing him to the rest of the war wizards' mercy. It doesn't sound like Raedra's particularly gentle with potential traitors."

"I don't think she'd do anything like that."

"Tell that to the noblewoman rotting in the dungeons. Just figure out what it says. If he's Chosen of the Unicorn Queen or something, you don't have to say anything at all."

Farideh bit her lip. "It just seems like something she ought to know. That *he* ought to know. I don't even know where to start looking."

Dahl blew out a breath before he spoke. "Well," he said, "you have one very good source at hand: Lorcan."

"Lorcan?" Farideh said, surprised.

"Devils are supposed to speak it too. Ever since Asmodeus became a god, he makes the devils ape the angels. If the whole thing's real. If it's not a bunch of devils letting folks believe crazy things." He considered the glyphs again, wondering if this was what she saw when she looked at him—too risky to ask now. "Whatever Lorcan can't or won't tell you, I'll help you look for. But it's not going to be an easy thing to find.

"Why don't you tell me about the rest of your day over evenfeast? And I can regale you with tales of how incredibly boring it is to be a wine merchant's equerry."

Of the list, he'd decoded eleven names now. Four were festhalls—better saved for down the line, both to preserve the cover and figure out a way to convince Farideh it wouldn't be so bad. Of the seven left, three would be unperturbed by a tiefling. The last four ranged from the shabby Keen Raven to the luxurious Dragon's Last Drink. A good place to start, he thought.

As it happened, Farideh was not taken by the Dragon's Last Drink. She had never, it was plain, been in an establishment so fine—never seen a menu, never sat at a table with her feet on a plush carpet. Even in the clutches of Adolican Rhand, she had not looked so ill at ease, and Dahl felt a little guilty for insisting. He ordered wine and dinner for the both of them. The dining room was a maze of tables and carefully placed vases—heavens knew where they got so many flowers. Dahl glanced around the room as though he were hunting for the woman who'd taken their orders—lots of nobles, lots of wealthy people. He recognized a very few. This wasn't Waterdeep after all, where he could pick out a family's features with fair success.

A man strode in dressed in a swirling black stormcloak, with a trim beard just starting to show a little gray. The owner was quick to greet him and take his cloak and those of his guests, though the owner's smile was unconvincing. The man looked over at Dahl and Farideh.

Dahl nodded at Erzoured Obarskyr, breaking his gaze swiftly and surely. That was one nobleman he could pick out of a crowd, and one whose attention he didn't want.

"Switch chairs with me?" Farideh pleaded.

Dahl turned back to the table. "What for?"

She looked very pointedly at the tall vase of flowers to her right. "I can't . . . It's blocking my view and I can't shake the feeling someone is lurking."

"No one is going to sneak up and stab you in a place like this." But he traded seats with her anyway. She took a nervous gulp of wine and reassessed the dining room from her new perspective.

"So," he said, "what do you think the Sharrans are up to?"

She blinked at him. "Is that a test? Am I supposed to unveil myself with the answer?"

"Do we need to explicitly remake the truce? I'm on your side and I have never once suspected you'd give yourself to Shar." He sipped his wine and thought about what Vescaras had said. "Tempting as it may be."

"What is that supposed to mean?"

"It means," he said, nudging her glass toward her, "you've lost a lot and grieved a great deal. That's when you're meant to give Shar her due, to ease you through it. That's when her followers are made."

"You've given her worship?"

"Of a most . . . begrudging sort," he said.

Farideh laughed. "Sorry. I've seen the way you worship Oghma. Is there anyone you don't worship begrudgingly?"

"That's not begrudging," Dahl said. "Oghma just irritates me sometimes. I *told* you. Everyone irritates me sometimes."

Farideh smiled and looked down at the tablecloth. "Fair." Then she sighed. "You know, it's all . . . almost fine. This feels almost normal and I start to forget. But then . . . all of a sudden something will happen, someone says something, I remember something. And I realize I'm not eighteen. I'm twenty-five. There are a thousand, thousand things I'm never going to do, never going to catch up on." She gestured at the table with a wild little laugh. "Do you know this is only the second time in my entire life that I've been alone in a taproom with a man who wasn't my father? And it's fake."

"And it's not a taproom," Dahl said. "To be fair."

Farideh rolled her eyes. She picked at the tablecloth. "Maybe I owe it to her, but I don't think I could spare Shar any worship. Not after . . ." She trailed off, and the horrors of the internment camp filled the silence in Dahl's thoughts. "Mehen would kill me anyway," she added with an entirely unconvincing chuckle, and finally took a solid sip of her wine.

"I never understood that about dragonborn," Dahl said, skirting the topic. He knew all too well the signs of a confession that burst its way out, that you wished you'd held your tongue over. "The gods are *there*. There's no arguing it. What's to be gained by ignoring them?"

Farideh was quiet a long time. "I grew up on stories of how my father's clan survived in Abeir under the cruelty of the dragons there, of how they threw off those shackles, raised armies out of slaves and won their freedom at terrible cost. His great-great-great-great-great-great grandmother, Khorsaya Who-Would-Be-Verthisathurgiesh, killed the favored offspring of Emycharianatris, the Jewel-Born Empress, with a bowl of her own fermented blood and a knife carved out of her father's thighbone and magic. Drugged him and then stabbed him through the gullet. The gods had nothing to do with it."

A shiver ran over Dahl. "Gods' books. He put you to bed with that?"

Farideh shrugged. "It's what they lived with."

"But the gods weren't *there*. They say they literally didn't appear in Abeir. They can't fault them for that."

"It's not a fault," Farideh explained. "I mean, the dragonborn did the unthinkable alone. They don't feel like they need gods, and they don't really trust them because the gods demand worship in exchange for things they feel they've already done for themselves. Like putting yourself in a yoke without a clear payment—it's too much like things were on the other side. People *do* worship gods, here and there, as I understand it. Young people, mostly. But they're considered rather strange."

She sipped her wine. "Makes me wonder what the Chosen of Djerad Thymar think about their circumstances."

Dahl frowned. "They don't worship gods—*mostly*—why should they see many Chosen?"

"As I said, they're Chosen. Not Choosers."

It was, altogether, a way of considering things that Dahl hadn't ever encountered. And while in his heart of hearts, he didn't think it true, wanted to dismiss it out of hand as wrong, it piqued his curiosity. He thought of Dumuzi saying, "You don't do things like we do." He wondered if Oghma would appreciate him digging into that sort of knowledge, and then wondered if it mattered.

"So what do you think?" he asked. "About gods?"

She turned away, looking embarrassed. "That's kind of personal."

"I bet I can guess." She didn't egg him on, but then, she didn't stop him. "'Mehen would kill you' so he's raised you not to venerate anyone. But I also know you've mentioned that at least your village's midwife was a priestess of Chauntea, so you didn't grow up completely unaware. And the way you say 'they're Chosen, not Choosers' makes me suspect you've recognized this much: whatever you think of the gods, they're there and they might not be ignoring you."

"More or—*karshoj!*" Farideh's eyes suddenly widened at something out of Dahl's sight.

"Sharran?"

"Worse. Get—duck, or get up or something!" she hissed.

Dahl sprang to his feet just as a woman in a lavender gown, buttercup silk peeking through the slashes of the skirt, came rushing up to Farideh. Several ropes of pearls hung around her neck, and a pair of peacock feathers bobbed from the knot of her brown hair. Dahl stood straight, hands behind his back—equerry, he thought.

"Asmura!" the woman cried, clasping Farideh's hands and pulling her to her feet. "How delightful! What are you doing here? Aren't you dining with the Lady Crownsilver?"

"Well met, Florelle," Farideh replied. "She . . . took to her bed. Ill."

"Did she?" the woman said skeptically. Then, "Oh, never mind at all, I don't blame you. She's a beast, and everyone knows it. Are you alone?"

"Yes," Farideh said, too quickly.

Florelle's gaze swept the little table, the two glasses of wine, two place settings waiting for two meals, and then made its way up to Dahl. "Asmura," the noblewoman said chidingly. "Perhaps we were a bit hard on you, but I hope you're not so stubborn as to lie when the truth is plain. Who is this?"

Farideh looked up at Dahl. He gave the woman a placid smile. "I'm Lord Vescaras Ammakyl's equerry, your ladyship. I'm afraid I've had to interrupt his lordship's dinner with an urgent business matter. He's stepped out momentarily to take care of it. But he could not leave the lady to seem abandoned, so I must suffice."

"Lord Ammakyl of Waterdeep?" Florelle asked.

"Yes, my lady."

"Well," she said to Farideh, with a knowing smile, "I see you were holding back."

Farideh blushed. "We're old friends, he and I."

"Of course." She lowered her voice, though not nearly enough to hide what she said next: "You know Varauna will be *thrilled* if you come with tales of a Waterdhavian half-drow's bedchamber. Just a thought." Dahl bit his tongue.

Farideh turned a deeper shade of scarlet. "Yes, well, I should see you tomorrow or the day after. Her Highness asked me back."

"I'd heard you were back in favor," Florelle said in a conspiratorial way. "A Crownsilver to the core." She dropped her voice again. "Have you met the Baron yet? He's over by the windows. I would introduce you, but Raedra does not care for him. She cannot possibly fault *you* for making yourself known though."

"Thank you," Farideh said. Florelle gave Farideh a very stiff, fluttery sort of embrace, kissed her cheeks, and with many reminders to have a good story and bring her Wroth deck, Florelle flounced off to a farther table. Farideh all but fell back into her chair and reached for the wine glass.

Dahl suppressed a laugh. "What was *that*, Lady Asmura?"

"I forgot. Raedra told them all I was Brin's distant cousin so they wouldn't wonder why I was in their midst. I didn't think I would possibly run into anyone from the palace." She rubbed her hands over her face. "Thank you. That was quick of you."

"Except now you have to make up a story about sleeping with Vescaras."

She gave him a dark look. "Asmura doesn't like him that well, as it happens."

"She shouldn't," Dahl said. "He's pompous and he drinks zzar."

Farideh sighed. "I suppose this is going to be trickier now."

"Nah," Dahl said. "As it happens, Lord Ammakyl *is* in Suzail doing business, and he does run off at odd times to see to things, because he likes to hold the reins himself, so to speak. So you just keep getting jilted. Tragic."

"Terribly," she said. "And you have to play my nursemaid instead of meeting your scandalous tiefling lover."

"At worst, they'll assume I'm juggling the two of you," Dahl said. "No—at worst, we'll have to recruit Vescaras for a few rounds to clear up the story."

"Is he going to be upset about rumors of 'Lady Asmura'?"

"He won't show it," Dahl said. "That would be 'terribly brightcoin.' Besides he's always got some lovely lady or another on his arm—and so far as I've seen, he hasn't managed in Suzail. So really, he ought to thank you."

Farideh smiled and rolled her eyes. "It's the back doorguard, by the way. I saw him just before Florelle intruded."

At least it hadn't been Erzoured, Dahl thought. That was a headache he didn't need. Dahl spotted their dinners approaching from behind Farideh, born by a pair of young women garbed in scaled green skirts that bared their legs. "You saw *nothing*," he advised. "Here: offer me a seat in the most magnanimous way you can so everyone will think you're a gracious lady and I can eat some of this pheasant."

• • •

IN THE HELLS, before the scrying mirror, Lorcan stood, toying with the scourge pendant and watching Farideh laughing as Dahl escorted her out into the rainy evening, watching as they found cover under an overhang in an alleyway at the edge of the streetlamp's light, talking and joking and waiting until the spell that hid her shimmered away. Waited and picked at the tangle he didn't want to deal with as it grew more snarled by the moment.

• • •

SOME HOURS LATER, after they'd finished their dinners, after Farideh's disguise spell had worn off, they left a second taproom of a tavern called the Sweet Nymph, where bawdy servers and watered ale had tested both Farideh and Dahl's nerves. It took nearly two full hours before Farideh spotted a bedraggled-looking serving maid coming in, her hand seeming to vanish into a patch of nothingness as she scratched her nose.

"If that is what passes for a sweet nymph in Cormyr," Dahl quipped as they strode off into the rainy night, the ale clearly enough to make his tongue thick, "then I do not want to know what a bad one is. Are you up for one more?"

Farideh's head ached dully, but the thought of returning to the cold tallhouse, to the unbearable quiet, to Dumuzi avoiding her . . . "Yes," she said, taking Dahl by the arm. "But I need a bit of a break before I look again."

"Do you mind a walk? The . . . oh, what's on the list? . . . Golden Goblin's on the western side. Rough enough they won't care if you're a tiefling. Far enough, you'll get your break."

The rain had stopped being quite so cold as summer wore on, and the heat of the day meant it fell warm and steady. Outside the stuffy taproom, the air was clean and close; beside her, Dahl smelled of whiskey and bay.

"So what do you think they're up to?" Farideh asked. "The Sharrans. You never said."

"Gods only know," Dahl said. "I certainly don't. Not yet."

"Is it something to do with the jobs they've taken? Are all the places taverns and inns?"

"Maybe. All the ones I could pick out have been taprooms, inns, and festhalls, but all sorts. The only thing they have in common—"

"Festhalls?" Farideh interrupted. "You never said festhalls."

"Didn't I?"

"You said 'taverns and inns,'" Farideh said. "I am sure you said taverns and inns."

"A festhall's *practically* a tavern and an inn," Dahl hedged. "There are *rooms* for rent."

"And people for those rooms."

"It will be exactly the same thing as these other places. You have to look at the dancers *once*, and we're probably looking for the girl who cleans up, or the fellow that hauls the barrels. Besides it's not as if they have anything you've never seen before."

"Oh for the gods' sakes!" Farideh pulled her arm out of his and crossed them over her stomach. "It's not the dancers." It wasn't and it was—she had no interest in watching Dahl watch the dancers. "I'm going to stand out."

"But you won't, that's the—"

"Dahl," she said sternly. "I've been in a festhall before. I've been in a few."

"Really?"

Farideh shook her head. "Bounties. People think you won't come after them in a place that's meant to be private. But every time, they nearly slipped us because the flash and flourish can tell I . . ." She hugged her chest tighter. "They pull me up in front of everyone and say things to make me blush, and I don't like it."

"They're not going to do that," Dahl said. "If they did it before, don't you think it had more to do with your being a tiefling than anything else? That's not going to matter this time, one way or another."

"They never grabbed Havilar."

"Because she always has an enormous polearm in one hand. Anyway, that's not today." He hooked his arm through hers once more. "And if it comes to it, and you'd rather not, I'm not going to drag you. But be honest? It's going to be better than the Sweet Nymph."

The Golden Goblin, on the other hand, was not an improvement on the Sweet Nymph. A smoky tavern with a low ceiling, lit by the eerie gold radiance of an enormous goblin statue over the bar, the Golden Goblin was crowded with people. The tension of angry men nearly stopped Farideh in her tracks.

Beside her, Dahl suddenly moved more cautiously, keeping between her and the bulk of the taproom. "Sure those festhalls are the worst?" he murmured.

"If we don't find them quick, we can go." She steered him toward an empty table with a decent view. They'd hardly slid into the bench when a keghand plunked two flagons of ale on the table and stood glowering at them until Dahl handed over a small stack of copper nibs.

"At least the ale's better," Dahl said, after a heavy sip.

Farideh didn't touch hers, but scanned the room despite her aching head. She'd been in enough low taverns to know one where folks came to fight. The Sharran didn't appear, and she avoided lingering too long on any one person. She blinked the powers away, and realized that a few folks were staring at them and whispering.

"Come here," Dahl said, pulling her closer. "Pretend you're spoken for."

The smell of bay and whiskey found its way through the pipesmoke. Farideh tensed. "That is absolutely *not* what they're whispering about."

"Farideh, most of the tieflings in this city are here for one reason. Chances are good they think you're here for that one reason too. Act like you're spoken for or at least paid for."

Farideh felt herself flush, more at the mistake than the implication. She scooted a little closer to Dahl, uncomfortably aware once more of his arm around her back, his hand just above her hip. Uncomfortably aware of the scent he was wearing. She stared at the crowd so she didn't have to look at him, looking at her.

He cleared his throat. "Well done," he said. "Your fellow takes you out and we end up at a place like this. It's like I'm not even trying. It's almost like I'm ashamed. You'd be mad, wouldn't you?"

"I wouldn't know," Farideh said.

"I suppose Lorcan only takes you to the finest of places."

That made her blush in earnest. "Gods, why would you say that?"

"What?" he said. "You go out places with him. And if you're going to pretend you're not lovers—"

"We're *not* lovers," she said hotly. "Not that it's any of your business."

Dahl's eyebrows rose. "Sorry." He looked out at the crowd. "Just, he doesn't kiss you like an acquaintance is all."

Farideh shut her eyes and cursed at Lorcan silently for making such a show of that moment in the internment camp—whatever he said to the contrary, he wouldn't have done it if Dahl hadn't been standing there watching.

Which she had been surer of when that had been the only kiss, when it had only *been* a kiss. They weren't lovers, and they wouldn't be—even if she faltered, Lorcan would not.

She wasn't foolish enough to believe Lorcan was being genuine.

"Lorcan is Lorcan," she said. "He does what he does because it suits him. I suspect in that moment, it suited him to unsettle me and to remind you that he wasn't really gone. He's *not* my brightbird," she added, and picked up the ale. It was sour and yeasty, but strong enough to warm her mouth.

"Good," Dahl said lightly, as if he were trying not to stir her up. "You could do a lot better."

He means it as a compliment, Farideh told herself, eyes locked on the crowd. But it wasn't—what exactly was she passing up for Lorcan, after all? She'd known since she was thirteen that she'd be a spinster, barring something extraordinary.

Only she'd always assumed she'd have Havilar with her. She gulped the ale and felt the powers of Asmodeus simmering along her nerves, bitter and angry and humiliating. Runaway princes falling in love with tiefling bounty hunters. Very extraordinary. She drank a little more as if the ale could cool them.

"It might surprise you," she said, a little tartly, "but there isn't a lot of demand for a tiefling with a bent nose, a weird eye, a warlock brand, and an eight-year gap in her memory."

"Lid for every pot," Dahl quipped. "There are at least six men in this taproom who I would wager fair coin don't care. I'm not saying you should go home with any of them, mind." He frowned. "That one . . ." Farideh followed his gaze to a fellow leaning against a post. The same man who'd made her nervous in the Brigand's Bottle.

"*Karshoj.*"

"Might be bad luck," Dahl said. "Might be he frequents low taverns for other reasons."

"Might be he's one of those kidnappers."

"I thought your princess had sorted it. Don't stare."

"I'm not staring at him."

Dahl turned her face toward his, and Farideh's stomach clenched. "You *look* like you're staring. You'll tip him off, and you'll wreck our cover."

"I'm angry at you," Farideh reminded him. "I don't think it will do a thing to this stupid cover."

"Well, if you keep looking like you want to shank me, you might find yourself having to entertain other offers."

"With my fists?" she said sweetly.

Dahl snorted. "Better than your rod."

Farideh slouched down against the bench, and very deliberately set her head on Dahl's shoulder, where she could still see the man. "Better?"

"That . . ." Dahl said. "Yeah, all right. That works." He shifted his arm behind her, and held her a little tighter. The man by the post laughed at something on the other side of the room, something that didn't seem to exist, and Farideh shut her eyes, breathing the smell of bay.

"You smell nice," Farideh said. "What is that?"

Dahl shifted. "It's just a little scent."

A smile tugged at the corner of her mouth. "*Very* fancy. Did you do that for me?"

"No." Dahl scoffed. "No, no, no. Gods." He reached for his ale. "I mean, yes, in the sense that I haven't had a chance to visit a bathhouse in too many days and it's probably more pleasant for you to sit next to me this way. So . . . you and everyone else in Suzail. Don't worry."

"Right," Farideh said. She eyed the man by the post and wondered why she imagined, even for a moment, that Dahl would have said anything else.

But she had imagined it—there was no denying it. Just as there was no denying there wasn't a Sharran in the Golden Goblin, that the man beside the post wasn't an unwelcome admirer, or that she wasn't incredibly distracted by Dahl's arm around her back. You're acting like a fool, she told herself. And he's going to realize it. Don't do something stupid because you're lonely and Lorcan's making you mad.

Varauna's words ran through her thoughts. *There's a point where it's nothing to do with your opportunities and everything to do with the way you squander the opportunities you're given.* Did this count as squandering? Was there anything to squander? He hadn't just said no—*No, no, no. Gods.* As if there weren't anything more ridiculous in the wide world.

A lid for every pot, she thought, but he's not yours. And you never wanted him to be yours. So stop being dreary.

But she didn't move her head.

The man beside the post finally set down his flagon, picked his stormcloak up and strolled past their table. Farideh tucked her fingers into her sleeve where her rod was hidden. He did not stop to look at them, but as he passed back into the crowd, he brushed against a much larger man's shoulder. An accident—a foolish accident in a place like this. A change cascaded over the beefy man he'd bumped, bunching his muscles, readying him for violence.

Then he caught the first man's eye. Froze. Tensed. Readied.

"We need to go," Farideh said, standing. Not a tavern brawl, something more organized and as primed as people in the taproom were, it would spill out to all corners. She threw her cloak on and pulled Dahl to his feet. Even Farideh didn't think she could stop it.

"Well, there's a pair of horns I'd like to mount" a voice behind her said. The beefy man stood there, leering down at her. He smiled, his teeth like tombstones, broad and long. "You taking other fellas' coin?"

Dahl stepped between them, before Farideh could stop him. "She's with me."

The man looked Dahl over, the practiced eye of a brawler. "You pay extra, so you can feel like a la-di-da noble? Bent over an ugly tiefling?"

Farideh squeezed Dahl's shoulder down to the bone, as he tensed. "He's baiting you." One punch, one spark, and everything came down. The Purple Dragons would come, and gods only knew what came next. "We're leaving." The man moved to stand between them and the door.

"How much is it," the man asked, "to take the Hells' leftovers?"

"How much do *you* cost?" Farideh asked calmly. "What's that man paying?"

Amusement flickered in the fellow's pale eyes. "You can't afford it," he whispered.

Farideh let the rod slip from her sleeve, dark smoke seething from the crystal at the tip. "Neither can you," she said. The man narrowed his eyes.

He held up both hands, a gesture of surrender, but that smirk in his eyes wasn't gone. "Maybe take your custom over to Pyter there. You share Lord Crownsilver's perversion for ugly tieflings, eh Pyter? Maybe 'cause your mother looks like a bull that's had a run-in with a barn door."

If he couldn't goad Dahl or Farideh into punching him, the bearded young man behind them made a good mark. He leaped to his feet and dived past Farideh with a roar of incoherent rage. Suddenly, every person who'd come to the Goblin looking for a fight had found one.

Farideh ducked a hooked punch, and drove her elbow hard under the sternum of a strange man who tried to grab her around the waist, before slamming the heel of her palm into his philtrum. She ducked as another man launched at her attacker, and came up close to the man who'd instigated things. He gave her a bloody smirk, a gap now in his tombstone teeth.

"The Baron wins eventually," he whispered, before another fist crashed into his cheek.

Dahl grabbed hold of her arm, favoring his bruised fist. "Come on!"

But there was no easy leaving. They turned into the wall of Pyter, all rage and repulsion, his fist pulled back.

Enough—Farideh held tight to Dahl and twisted toward the window, pulling hard on the powers of the Hells. The blow connected, she dragged the both of them through the fabric of the planes, through wall and window and out into the rainy street. People scattered, shouting as the pair of them stepped free with a gust of brimstone, Dahl stumbled into her, rocked by the blow, and Farideh caught him before he hit the street.

And then a pair of strong hands caught her. More hands yanked Dahl from her grasp. A wad of cloth in her mouth nearly gagged her, a bag came down over her head. Ropes on her wrists and ankles. The rod plucked free of its hiding place. *Karshoj, karshoj, karshoj*—She kicked someone and heard a strange man grunt and gasp, and others laugh. Someone cuffed her through the bag.

Calm, she told herself. *Martifyr.* There was hardly enough air to breathe, snot and tears streaming down her face from the effort. Wait, wait—they were carrying her somewhere. Hopefully Dahl too.

Farideh didn't have to wait long before she was set down and the hood and gag removed. She was in a carriage, a very fine carriage—at least as luxurious as the one that Raedra had sent for her. Her hands were still tied behind her back, and the man sitting opposite her regarded her in a way that didn't suggest he was going to untie them. Sturdy in the way old soldiers were, with short-cropped hair and the trim beard noblemen in Suzail seemed to favor, the first threads of gray marring it. The chain around his neck was gold, as were the rings on his hands. He studied her rod with faint disgust for the cracked and cloudy amethysts, as the man who'd deposited Farideh closed the door, and something heavy was loaded on the roof.

"If you're going to bring our private affairs to the princess's attention, good-woman," the man said, "you should at least let me in on it."

The powers of the Hells surged up through her, setting every bruise ablaze with pain. "You want to tell me who you are and where my friend is before I burn this carriage down?"

The man gave her a thin smile. "Your, ah, friend is with us. On the roof, securely tied, and presuming you don't do anything foolish, he shall be fine." He waved out the window and the carriage started moving. "Don't worry. The cart springs are the best you can buy. I am Erzoured Obarskyr. They call me the Baron Boldtree, when they're feeling polite. I suppose your friend Lord Crownsilver would call me 'Uncle,' not that we have the sort of family that encourages such things."

"But the sort that encourages sending kidnappers after a lover you don't like."

"I'm sure your sister is just as charming as you are. I don't much care to like or dislike you. Though you haven't done yourself any favors by killing and injuring my men."

"Maybe you should have hired better kidnappers," Farideh said.

"To be clear," he said, "none of those were mine. I left it to someone who did not think his plans through very well. As you can see, when I make an attempt to kidnap someone, I succeed."

The carriage jolted over a missing cobble, throwing Farideh against the carriage wall. She struggled up again, without any help from Erzoured. Thuds from above—was that Dahl breaking free or being dangerously jostled? "Where are you taking me?"

"Why, home, of course. Much more comfortable, isn't it? And we'll have a chance to talk. Because while your sister seems an excellent piece by which to steer Aubrin's actions, you, my dear, seem to have Proud Raedra's ear. Quite a feat."

Farideh cursed to herself. "I don't know what gave you *that* impression. She asked me to take care of something and I have—"

"Don't be modest," Erzoured said. "For Raedra to have stepped in to stop something as beneficial to herself as kidnapping your sister means she must hold you in very high regard indeed. Trust me," Erzoured said when Farideh scowled. "She is my dear cousin, after all."

Farideh frowned. "So you're . . . the old crown prince's other son?"

"His *true* son," Erzoured said. "My father promised my mother he would come back to wed her. If he hadn't been killed by a Sembian ambush, I would be crown prince now—or king. Your friend's father was nothing but a by-blow from a foolish dalliance with a married woman. He should have stayed a Crownsilver. As Aubrin should stay a Crownsilver."

"I don't really have any say in that," Farideh said.

"No," Erzoured agreed. "But Raedra has a little. She might have a great deal more. And she also has a say in whether or not her marriage to Aubrin Crownsilver continues apace. I see several ways we can all be a great deal happier."

"You want me to tell her not to marry Brin?"

"I want you to encourage any doubts she has," Erzoured corrected. "I want you to remind her she can do much better if she's simply patient."

"You?"

"Heavens no," Erzoured said. "*I* can do much better."

Farideh frowned. "You want to be king, but . . . wouldn't she be queen before you? Regardless of whether Brin's in the line or not?"

Erzoured's expression tightened, and Farideh realized this man was far more dangerous than she'd expected. "Do you think I'm not acutely aware of the line of succession? I'm also acutely aware of the fact that Cormyr has, in all its history, had only six queens regnant—and one abdicated, one died within a year, one was widely contested at the time, and one is renowned for going spectacularly mad.

"It is not a great feat to convince the right people that—especially with the threat of Shade and Sembia all around us—Cormyr is in need of a king, not a queen, nor for the right people to then apply the right pressures—even to Raedra. She will see reason."

Farideh thought of the sight of Raedra's soul, the sense that she was not a ready prize, that she would flare out before she broke down. "Much luck with that."

"I don't need luck," Erzoured said, as though he were reminding her. "I need you to do your task. You will, of course, be handsomely rewarded in a discreet fashion—"

"I'm not interested."

Erzoured raised an eyebrow. "We're talking about more coin than you can imagine, goodwoman."

"And I don't want it."

That rage flickered through him again. Farideh drew up the soul sight, wondering if she'd see the empty pits Shar's touch left behind . . . but no. Every bruised, broken patch of light was only Erzoured's. If he dealt with any god at all, they did not claim him now. Which was strange, as dearly as he wanted the throne. No—that wasn't what wafted off of him like a pall of smoke. He wanted power, wanted recognition and inclusion and acceptance, and the throne was a symbol, a means to an end. Someone should have made use of him by now, so what did—

Farideh shook the thought from her head. This was getting out of hand.

"Then perhaps you'd prefer," Erzoured said, as the carriage drew to a stop, "the assurance that Princess Raedra, the war wizards, and the Purple Dragons won't be made aware of what you truly are."

"They already know I'm a warlock," Farideh said.

"That may be. But the men who survived that third attempt tell me that you also managed to nearly burst their hearts with fear, that you caught fire like a haystack and sprouted burning wings." Farideh kept her face expressionless as Erzoured smiled. "I don't consider myself a scholar on the scale of our Royal Magician, but I don't believe I've ever heard of magic quite like that from a warlock weak enough to be of no concern to the war wizards. You've hidden something, somehow. They'd be very interested to know that." He rapped on the door.

"Do consider carefully," he said, as the man who'd stood beside the post opened the door and hauled Farideh to her feet.

Another fellow cut the ties and shoved her toward the wrought-iron gate, while the other yanked a burlap bundle to the cobbles. Both leaped back onto the carriage, clattering off into the rain. The man gave her a jaunty salute and tossed her rod onto the ground as they left.

Farideh tore at the knots of the ropes around the cloth, ripping aside the rough cloth as Dahl fought out of it, gasping. A dark lump of a bruise stood out on his temple—Farideh pushed his hair back, checking for blood, for fractures. He swung at her hands, as if fighting off an attacker.

"It's me!" Farideh cried. "It's me." His eyes focused on her, darted around the street.

"Oghma's bloody papercuts," Dahl panted. He touched the bruise, gingerly, then untied the rope around his knees. "If you tell anyone . . ."

"I will tell them the truth," Farideh said. "You were overtaken by Erzoured Obarskyr's private toughs." She helped him sit up and then stand.

"Are you stlarning joking?" he demanded. "What have you been getting into?"

Nothing, Farideh thought. Everything. And how much worse would it get now? Raedra had made it quite clear she wasn't going to discuss her betrothal, not with Farideh. She scooped her rod up.

But you can't let Cormyr figure out you're the Chosen of Asmodeus, she thought. The immediate danger might be gone, but the course of Hellish powers pounded along her nerves.

"Come on," Dahl said. "Let's get inside."

The air was thick with unfallen rain, and as his hand settled on the middle of her back, the smell of bay floated on it. Farideh stopped dead and turned. "I'll be fine. Go home."

"Like Hells," Dahl said.

"He's not coming back," Farideh said, looking toward the door instead of at Dahl. "He wants me to talk to Raedra, and I can't imagine he'd jeopardize that by hurting me before I can."

Dahl frowned at her, as if he couldn't believe that. As if he could tell there was something more—that there had to be something more. "All the same."

"Dumuzi's here."

"I could be too."

For the barest of moments, Farideh nearly agreed. She nearly told him what she'd been thinking, curled up next to him. She nearly admitted she didn't want to be alone, and to her surprise, she didn't want Dahl to leave at all.

"I mean," Dahl added, "I could sleep in Mehen's room, of course. *Actually*, in Mehen's room this time. I'm not . . . We're clear right? I don't want to confuse things, or—"

Farideh laughed and looked up at the rain clouds. Gods, that stung, but she'd needed it. "Go home, Dahl," she said. "You have to report to Vescaras."

She went into the tallhouse, turned the lock, and stood leaning against the door for a long time. Through the door to the front room, she could see the patch of wall that Ilstan's spell had struck, the gilt still glittering in the light of the streetlamps through the windows. It was hard to believe that had only been this morning.

Go to bed, she told herself, even though no part of her was eager for sleep. She climbed the stairs, wondering how lunatic it would be to take her sword out into the garden in the middle of the night, and burn off some of this mad energy.

Dumuzi came partway down the stairs to the servants' quarters when she reached her bedroom door, sword in hand.

"Well met," Farideh said.

He nodded once, and she unlatched the bedroom door. Then, "How did it go?"

Farideh considered the doorknob in her hand and thought of Florelle and Erzoured, the fight and the flowers, of Dahl's laughter and his hand on her cheek. The feeling of being close and comfortable chased by familiar, complete loneliness.

"It was all right," she said. "Good night."

She shut the door and started unbuttoning her boots, when a *crack* made her leap to her feet, flames pouring into her hands as the portal opened. Lorcan stepped out, in the skin of a human, and she shook the flames out. "Gods, you scared me. Is Havi all right?"

"Well met to you too," he said. "Havilar's fine. How's *Dahl?*"

Farideh scowled at him, and pulled off her boots. "I thought we were done with that."

"I thought you were done with him."

"Are we really having this ridiculous argument again?" Farideh demanded, even though a little part of her wanted to protest that maybe it wasn't so ridiculous.

It's ridiculous, she told herself firmly. Just because you got all wistful and dreary doesn't mean you're fond of Dahl.

"We are if you're going to keep telling me one thing and then acting another way." He came closer, and the Hells twined up Fariden's bones, nervous and hungry. "I saw all of it."

"Including the part where I was kidnapped?".

"Don't change the subject."

"That's well within the subject of you spying," she said. "He doesn't want me, all right? Not that it matters, not that it's any of your *damned* business."

"That's not what it sounded like last night," he said.

Farideh gave him a level look. "Do you think for a moment I don't know exactly what this is, you and I? It's just a game you're playing. You kiss me and so I stay. If you wanted this to be anything more than that, you've had a hundred chances. You made it a game every time. Didn't you tell me once I need to decide what I want from this agreement?"

Lorcan's dark eyes bored into her. "I said you didn't ask for another agreement. You still haven't."

Farideh felt her cheeks burn, the first tatters of shadow-smoke curl off her frame. "I already know the answer."

"Oh do you?"

"Please. If you want me to believe you're suddenly sweet and mine and *interested*, then you could do a lot better—"

Lorcan's mouth stopped her, her last words smothered in his kiss. He pushed her up against the wall, her horns forcing her head down, but he twisted with her. He pinned her there, pressed against her, and though a part of Farideh ran through a list of all the ways she could or should fight him off, she was too stunned to do any of them.

"Tell me the answer," Lorcan murmured. She felt his fingers unpicking the stays of her bodice. "Say you don't want this. Tell me this is a game."

She pushed his hands away. "Lorcan—"

"Oh say it," he dared, pulling the loosened bodice down. "Or just admit it—I'm right, you want me to be sweet and yours and *interested*." He kissed her neck roughly. "Is this the answer you want?"

Yes, Farideh thought. Yes, yes, yes. She wanted him—and what better option did she have, even if this was just another game? *There's a point where it's nothing to do with your opportunities and everything to do with the way you squander the opportunities you're given.* Every nerve of her body seemed to hum, and her arms kept trying to cling to him, pull him closer.

But gods above, he was dangerous. He was toying with her. And some part of her wished profoundly that he smelled of bay. She looked down at his hands, parting her blouse, and her heart was suddenly galloping.

But it was Lorcan who jerked away. "What the shitting Hells are you doing with that?"

Farideh looked down at the amulet of Selûne lying between her breasts. She cupped the amulet in her hand. "Safety?" she managed. She rubbed her thumb over the amulet's spiral.

"Take it off," Lorcan ordered.

Farideh reached back, her thoughts racing too fast to separate into things she ought to listen to and things she ought to ignore. She unfastened the clasp and cupped the amulet in one hand. Even in the dim light of the entryway the silver shone as if it reflected the full moon. If she spoke the trigger word, it would bind a fiend from harming her for an hour—powerful magic. Even Lorcan was afraid of it. She looked up at Lorcan. You cannot let him be in charge here, she thought.

"*Vennela*," she said.

The amulet's magic crackled over Lorcan, and he yelped as it bound him. "Gods damn it!" His wings spread, as wide as the room would allow. "And I'm the one that makes it a game?"

"You remember how this works?" Farideh asked, never looking away from him. "You hurt me, it hurts you." She wrapped the chain around her left hand, tucking the amulet under the chain. Lorcan eyed her, warily. "You're right—I still want you—but I am not an idiot because of that. I'm not handing over the reins to you because you can make . . ." She stopped herself. "It's never been a secret that I want you. It's never been a secret that you're trouble. So if suddenly, something's changed and we're heading to bed together, you have to mean it."

Lorcan stared at her for so long that Farideh started to worry she'd gone about this all wrong. You don't want to go through with it the other way, she told herself, even though it was such a lie. She had sense enough to know even this much was a bad idea, even this much was a gamble. She imagined him storming off, she imagined him catching her up, she imagined the tirade he was about to unleash—and chased them all off. She was ready for any of it.

"Don't hurt me and it shouldn't matter," she said, unable to bear the silence anymore.

Lorcan pulled her near, a little sharply, and they gasped in tandem as the amulet gave a measure of Farideh's pain to the cambion. He leaned down and bit her ear gently. A shiver ran through her, and she hooked her fingers in the waist of his breeches. For a brief, frantic moment, she wished she'd let Havilar tell her everything she could remember, no matter how embarrassing it might have been at the time.

"It's going to hurt a little," Lorcan murmured. "Should be interesting."

16

THE SUN ROSE, AND BRIN WAS ALREADY AWAKE, ALREADY DRESSED AND armored. Already attending a morningfeast of porridge over the fire. Constancia woke early, and he wanted to be ready. Beside him, Havilar sharpened her glaive, the *skirring* of the whetstone against the blade threatening to lull Brin into a sort of trance.

Constancia will understand, he told himself. She won't like it, but she'll accept it. How many times, after all, had he done something that went against Constancia's suggestions or even her orders, and in the end, she had accepted every time that Brin would make his own decisions, his own mistakes?

He did not let himself consider if the hellhound would be a mistake.

Havilar's whetstone stopped. Brin watched Constancia rise from her bedroll, feeling fourteen again and nearly ready to vomit. She frowned—first at him and then at Havilar as she came to the fire. "What conspiracy is this then?" she said.

"We need to talk," Brin said. "Come walk with me?"

Havilar didn't follow—he'd insisted she couldn't. The hellhound lay in the opposite direction, but the trees of the Hullack Forest felt no friendlier, no safer. Brin found he couldn't say a word until Constancia broke the silence when they'd made it out of sight of the camp.

"What is this about?" she asked.

"I want to use Havilar's plan."

"The dog from nowhere? Do you really think it's going to manage—"

"It's not a dog," Brin said, stopping. "It's a muzzled hellhound. So yes, I do think if anything can manage, it can."

Brin had never before seen Constancia so surprised. For a long, terrible moment, she merely stared, mouth agape. "You're joking," she said, with a finality that did not make it so.

"I'd like if you came with us," Brin went on. "I think that's safest and wisest—we don't know what shape he'll be in, and I can't say I wholly trust the hound."

"Stop," Constancia said, her hands shaking as she held them up, as if she could ward off the words. "I have all but raised you, Aubrin. I have defended you from threats uncountable. I thought I taught you right from wrong, the ways of the world. You *know* better! Taking gifts from a devil so that you can escape your duty? This is *everything* you were raised to abjure!"

"This *is* my duty!" Brin said. "Albeit wrapped in an unpleasant package."

"No—this is you trying to run without running! This is you—yet again—refusing to accept what you are, *who* you are. That you can't have everything you wish for."

"What would you have me do?" Brin demanded. "Your crown prince—your future king—lies somewhere in the Hullack Forest, perhaps unable to escape. Do you really intend I leave him here because the only way to save him means taking an enemy by the hand? Not even an enemy—you can hardly claim a hellhound is out to take my soul!"

"I can't," she agreed. "But I can argue that Havilar might."

Brin's temper lit. "Don't be ridiculous."

"Doesn't it frighten you even a little that Havilar has even the capability to come to you with a beast of Baator on a leash, and offer it up as a simple solution to all of your problems? Doesn't that ring *any* warning bells in your mind?"

"Why?" Brin said. "Because it's the sort of thing Aunt Helindra would do? Does it remind you of orders she's given? Like convincing me I ought to propose to Raedra? Like trying to tell me everyone would be better off if I broke it off with Havilar?"

Constancia shook her head. "You think those things come from Helindra, you're worse than a fool. They are true, they are right, they mark the path you ought to be on. *She* is handing you a *hellhound*—how can you defend her?"

"Because she's the only person who isn't trying to manipulate me. And whatever is happening to her, I'm on her side—not the least because I know she's on mine."

Constancia barked a short mocking laugh. "How else do devils work?"

"She is not a godsbedamned devil!" Brin shouted. "And she's done a greater service to Cormyr than anything you—or anyone else for that matter—has managed when it comes to finding Irvel. So you will not say a word to her, and *that* is an order, because I am *not* a boy you can chastise—I am your lord."

Constancia drew back, her earlier shock mild and meek beside what took her now, and guilt squeezed Brin's chest.

She swallowed as though it pained her. "I will not say a word to her, Your Grace," she said softly. "Because I will not follow you any farther."

Now it was Brin's turn to be shocked. "What?"

"You are on your own, Aubrin." A line of tears glistened along Constancia's lids, but her stern expression never faltered. "You want to cast aside everything I taught you to venerate? Your duty, your sense of righteousness, your dedication to Cormyr, to the Crownsilver name? Then you give me no choice—I must cast *you* aside."

All of Brin's confidence crumbled around him. "You're not serious. You can't. You can't."

Constancia stepped toward him and pressed a kiss to his head. "Torm grant you what you're looking for," she said.

Brin watched her go, unable to find the words that would stop her, unable to truly believe it was happening even though he knew there was no doubt he could hang tight to. He'd spent so long up until that moment fearing Mehen would abandon him—but never Constancia.

Is it worth this? he wondered.

But nothing was that simple, he thought, finally trudging back to the campsite. It wasn't all about Havilar or about Brin or about Raedra or Irvel or any of them, but the way they fell into the treacherous web that threatened Cormyr at its weakest.

Constancia was gone when he got back to the fire. Everyone was awake now, watching him as though he might shatter.

"Brin," Havilar started.

"It's fine," Brin said, not because it was, but because it couldn't be anything else. "She made her choice. And we've made ours." He met her golden eyes. "Go get the hellhound."

· · ·

Farideh drowns.

Ice crystals trail the stroke of her arms—she knows the water is cold more than she feels it. Tiny lights swarm around her, and there's no way to tell where the surface is. She swims one way, doubts herself, then tries another, her lungs about to burst.

In the dark water, a darker, monstrous shape swims. A dragon? A hydra? A ghost? Any moment now, it will close on her. Any moment now will be her last.

The water behind her turns colder still as the creature brushes past her back. In the same moment she spies the door, a dark portal in the rock face. She swims with all her strength, feeling as if the water is growing thicker and thicker. In the watercourse, she'll be safe.

The water is still cold, the dark complete. And now a current pulls Farideh down an endless tunnel. She grabs at the rock and her fingernails tear free, her palms are shredded and bloodied. When was the last time she breathed?

The water buoys her upward, against the ceiling, and suddenly the rock gapes. Farideh's thrown up, high enough to gasp air, enough to catch the hands that reach for her. Dahl pulls her out of the freezing water, into the air. She wraps her arms around him, an anchor. He takes her face in his hands, and all the fear and adrenaline seem to vanish. But then he speaks.

"Stay alive," he murmurs. "Stay alive."

Farideh pulls away, studies Dahl's face. But when she looks over his shoulder, the archdevil is there, watching, waiting. Smiling in a way that turns her blood as cold and fast as the watercourse.

Farideh woke, sucking in air as if she were drowning again, hands clutching at the swamp of sheets. The gray light of early morning made the room seem as if it should feel colder. The bed certainly felt bigger. Emptier. Farideh sat up, pulling her knees to her chest, and pressed a hand to her eyes. She sighed, and counted off on her fingers.

"Havi, I've done either the most foolish thing ever or maybe the wisest option I had. But either way, you were right: it's tremendous fun."

Mostly, she amended, stretching and slipping into her dressing robe.

It wasn't the nightmare Criella had threatened it would be—in fact, at points last night, Farideh had wondered if the old midwife had any idea what she was talking about, or if maybe it came down to who you went to bed with. Whether because of what Lorcan was, who he was, or the menace of the amulet, it had been pretty *karshoji* good. But then he'd left.

In the cold light of day, she could hardly believe she thought he'd do anything different. Even if he'd made her feel amazing, even if he'd been almost gentle, even if he'd seemed for a moment like he was as lost in her as she was in him, he was still Lorcan.

"I don't sleep," he'd pointed out when she'd held tight to his arm, asked him to stay. "What am I supposed to do?"

"I just . . . I don't want to be alone."

Farideh poured cold water in the basin and washed her face, trying not to cringe at the memory of her own plaintive voice, at Lorcan's absolute befuddlement. They were done after all—unless *that's* what she was asking for?

It was what she settled for.

Clean and dressed in the blue gown, she went down to the kitchen and found Dumuzi still there. "Well met," she said. "I suppose it's earlier than I thought."

Dumuzi gestured at the kettle on the fire. "Tea. But I did not make you anything to eat."

Farideh poured herself a cup of tea, and added a spoon of honey.

Dumuzi cleared his throat. "That was not the Peredur last night, was it?"

Farideh stirred a vortex in her tea and felt a blush creep up her neck. "No."

"Are you going to tell him?"

Gods, no, Farideh nearly said. But the thought stopped her—she'd see Lorcan again, that was certain. And while she wanted to insist that last night was an oddity, she also knew if Lorcan suggested it wasn't, it wouldn't be. And she wasn't ashamed of it. So why wouldn't she tell Dahl?

Because you wouldn't, she thought.

"If it comes up," she said to Dumuzi. The dragonborn's nostrils flared in a skeptical way. Farideh found herself studying him, looking for traces of Mehen. Dumuzi stared back, his tongue fluttering behind the gap of his teeth.

"Are you my brother?" When he didn't answer, she reluctantly amended, "Are you Mehen's son?"

"No." Dumuzi poked the eggs on his plate. "He and my father were clan-mates. I'm *kosjmyrni*."

Farideh shook her head. "I don't know what that means."

"My mother is Kepeshkmolik. It's her clan I belong to."

"So, you're cousins? On your father's side?"

Dumuzi wrinkled his brow ridges, making the moons shift and threaten to crash into one another. "Perhaps. Many, many, many times removed."

And is it Kepeshkmolik or Verthisathurgiesh that's sent you after Mehen? Farideh wondered. She sipped her tea. "Mehen doesn't talk much about his life before," she said. "Does your father talk about Mehen?"

Dumuzi laughed once to himself. "No. No, not really. But other people do."

"Why is that funny?" Farideh asked.

Dumuzi's tongue fluttered again. "Does Mehen really never talk about Djered Thymar? About . . . the Lance Defenders? About why he left?"

Farideh stopped. "About Arjhani?" she asked flatly.

Dumuzi gave a shrug, but he wouldn't meet her eyes. "About all of it. About any of it. There are . . . there are people who think Pandjed made the wrong decision. I just wondered."

Farideh didn't move, the memory of a long-ago summer—a slim bronze drag-onborn, Havilar with a dummy glaive in hand—so present she thought she might smother in it. "Do you know Arjhani?"

A sharp rapping came at the door. For a moment, Farideh and Dumuzi sat, each watching the other, unmoving.

"War wizards again?" Dumuzi asked.

Farideh cursed to herself. It was—it would have to be. She stood, and thought about promising Dumuzi the conversation wasn't over. But she found she had no room at all in her heart for Arjhani.

The air outside was warm and thick with the falling rain. Ilstan stood on the doorstep, the red-haired war wizard Devora beside him.

"Good morning," Farideh said. Ilstan nodded at her with a tight smile as he entered. The muscles at the small of Farideh's back tightened.

"I heard you had quite the evening out, 'Lady Crownsilver,'" Devora said in a knowing way. "Though I hear it's Lord Ammakyl and I hear it's the equerry."

"How . . ." Farideh started. Devora merely shrugged, looking like a cat full of cream.

"My coin's on the equerry," she said. "He's a bit rough around the edges, but there's a spark there—"

"We are not here to gossip, Wizard of War Abielard," Ilstan snapped, mercifully releasing Farideh from the expectation of a reply. He pulled his wand out. "If I have your permission, goodwoman?"

"Ye gods, Nyaril," Devora said. "Who pissed in your porridge?"

"If you don't mind," Farideh said, "could you make it last through the evening again?"

Ilstan lowered the wand. "To what aim?"

"I have errands," Farideh said. "It's much easier to get to the market and such if I don't have to worry about what people think of how I look."

"What sort of errands?"

"Oh for the gods' sake, Ilstan!" the other war wizard said. "She wants to meet her lover. Just cast the bloody spell."

Ilstan never stopped scowling through the spell, nor the ride to the palace. Farideh called up the soul sight, and looked Ilstan over. The rune remained, sharper and brighter than before, but no more understandable.

"Do you read Supernal?" Farideh had asked Lorcan as he dressed the night before.

"Not if I can help it," he said. "Why?"

She leaned over the edge of the bed and hooked the skirt she'd worn. She fished the foolscap with the glyphs on it from her pocket, and held it out to him. "What does it say?"

Lorcan buckled his belt, frowning at the paper. "Where did you get Supernal glyphs?"

"What does it say?"

Lorcan eyed her warily, but sat at the foot of the bed, leaning over the sheet. He tapped each down the line. "Chauntea"—the one she'd marked on Samayan, the boy from the camp. "Shar"—on the Nameless One. "Asmodeus"—on the ghost who'd enchanted the comb. His finger stopped on the last one, and he frowned. "I don't know that one."

It was the glyph she'd seen on Ilstan, the one she'd seen on Asmodeus in her vision.

"*That* doesn't say Asmodeus?"

"As I said"—Lorcan pointed to the sigil to the left, a latticework of sharp strokes—"that says Asmodeus." He studied the last glyph more closely. "Where did you see it?"

Farideh hesitated. "It's on a fellow in Suzail."

Lorcan raised an eyebrow. "A *fellow*?"

"One of the princess's war wizards," Farideh said. "I'm trying to decide whether I ought to tell her about it. They're the marks," she added, "that I see on Chosen."

He gave her a puzzled look. "Why did you think it was Asmodeus's?"

Farideh hesitated. "I saw it on him," she said. "I had a vision, in the internment camps, and I saw Asmodeus. Then I saw the glyph. I assumed that meant the fellow was a Chosen of Asmodeus, but I suppose it means something else."

Lorcan didn't move, didn't so much as blink, but something about him seemed to shift, as if he'd suddenly turned to stone. He considered the scrap of paper again, then very deliberately tore the right half of the paper away, and the symbol with it. He crumpled the torn section into a ball and handed back the rest of the page. "You ought to stop worrying about this."

"Why is that?"

"Because nothing good comes of delving too deeply into Asmodeus's interests."

Nothing good comes of hiding from them either, Farideh had thought. But she'd only nodded. If Lorcan didn't know what the sigil said, there was no point in cajoling him anyway.

Which still left her without an answer to the question of what to do with Ilstan. As they descended the carriage near one of the palace's smaller entrances, Farideh asked him if he was feeling all right.

"A headache," he said tersely.

Not a normal headache, Farideh thought. She had to tell him. "I know of people," she said carefully, "who've become taken by strange feelings recently, and—"

Suddenly the light flared. Ilstan's hand shot out and grabbed Farideh by the shoulder as he gasped. She turned to steady the taller man, and noticed how his eyes had glazed over.

... *be a fool* ... she heard a man's voice whisper ... *a weapon, a tool* ...

"Ilstan!" Devora shouted. Ilstan straightened, eyes wild. He wet his mouth, blinking hard as his compatriot came to stand beside him.

"He just stumbled," Farideh said. "I don't know what happened."

The redhead shook her head. "That's three times—one with me, one with Drannon, one with Pelia. Go to Ganrahast, right now."

Ilstan stared at Farideh for a long terrible moment, and she felt certain that he knew she'd heard the voice too. "Yes," he said. "You're right. Give my apologies to Princess Raedra." He turned, heading off toward the other end of the palace, his already ungainly gait shaken.

"Don't get any ideas," Devora said. "It's only protocol that two escort you."

She led Farideh through the winding passages of the palace, back to the windowless room with the painting no one liked. This time, Raedra was already there, waiting, with a decanter of chilled wine and a plate of sweetmeats. Nell stood beside the screen, brushing the lint from a dark blue gown.

"Well met," Raedra said. She gave Farideh an impish smile. "I wasn't sure you'd come."

"Of course. I promised." Nell sat her down and started yanking a comb through her hair.

"But you were out late," Raedra sang. "Tell me you enjoyed yourself."

Farideh froze—Erzoured's threats coming back to her once more. She looked back at Devora, who shrugged. "At least tell me how much you know?" Farideh said.

Raedra drew back. "Well that makes it sound *dire*. All I know is that you went to the Dragon's Last Drink with a man who was not very convincing about being there for his lord's benefit." Her eyes flicked up to Devora and back. "What am I missing?"

"Nothing," Farideh said. Nell yanked her hair up into a knot and slid a pin through it. "It's just . . . It's personal."

"Not in Cormyr it isn't," Raedra said dryly. She poured a little of the wine for them both. "Tell me." Farideh took the glass warily—it wasn't an order, though it could have been. Raedra raised her eyebrows. "There is no chance you're going to top Varauna's tale of the two brothers she was juggling for sheer depravity, nor Florelle's dalliance with a certain Huntsilver heir for blind passion she would rather we forget. Maranth will always surpass you for missing the obvious opportunity, and I will hold the crown forever and ever on willful idiocy in matters of the heart. You cannot shock me. Out with it."

Farideh took a very deliberate sip of wine. It was sweet and mild, with a faint herbal scent. This wasn't a conversation she could imagine having with anyone except Havilar. But Havilar was on the other end of the kingdom, dealing with her own problems.

A spike of worry went through her thoughts—she's fine, Farideh told herself. Lorcan said she was fine. He's making sure of her.

Maybe he wasn't such a bad fellow after all.

"I suppose," she said, eyes on the wine, "I have a lover now."

Raedra clapped her hands. "Well done! The equerry?"

"No. Someone else."

"His lord?"

Farideh searched for a safe way to put it. "An old friend."

"My, you *were* holding out. So you went out for evenfeast with one man, while pretending to go out with another, and then slept with your secret bright-bird—is that it?"

"He's not . . ." Farideh glanced back at Devora. "He's not someone who's any-body's brightbird. I don't think." She gulped more of the wine. "I've known him a long while. I should know better."

"But he's devastating, isn't he?" Raedra said, plucking a sweetmeat from the tray and popping it in her mouth. "And charming—they're always charming, those fellows. Never fails."

"Up, please," Nell said, plucking the wine from her hand and herding Farideh behind the screen. Farideh blew out a breath, as Nell unbuttoned the gown.

"They're positively traumatic in your youth, those fellows," Raedra called. "Before you know better."

Even after everything else, Farideh felt her cheeks burn. "I didn't exactly have the chance," she said weakly. An awkward silence descended.

"My apologies," Raedra said. "I forgot."

Farideh swallowed. "It's fine." Nell came around and cinched her bodice tighter, tight enough to make her gasp. "Is that what you meant?" she called back to Raedra. "About 'willful idiocy'?" The dark blue gown slid over her head with disconcerting ease. "Was it . . . someone devastating?"

Nell's hands stilled on the buttons. Beyond the screen, no one spoke. No one so much as breathed. Farideh shifted so that she could peer between the panels of the screen.

Raedra sat staring at her wineglass. "Yes," she said. "And no."

Nell's hands flew up the buttons again, giving Farideh a little time to wonder what she'd prodded and how to make amends. When she stepped out, Raedra was still looking at her glass.

"Truly," she said, without looking up at Farideh, "has no one told you about my first husband?"

She said the word in the same sort of way she said *mistress*—like it was something fearful as the ghosts she said wandered the palace. Farideh glanced at Nell, but the maid was folding the discarded dress with elaborate care. Devora only had eyes for the painting of the two princesses.

"No," Farideh said. "Only you, the other day."

Raedra sighed and looked up at the ceiling, as if it held a window to another time, another place. "Lindon was devastating," she said finally.

"Handsome as the Sunlord. Kind and witty and everything you could ask for. A graceful dancer, a spirited conversationalist, an excellent horseman. He never treated me like a prize or a stepping-stone or a foolish girl. He surprised me when no one else could. And I loved him, every inch of him, inside and out." She pursed her lips, closing off a tide of old sorrows, and Farideh's heart ached.

"What happened to him?"

"I killed him," Raedra said simply.

"Was there an accident?"

"No." The princess gave a bitter little laugh. "Not one moment of it. I knew what I was doing. That's why it worked."

"Highness," Nell started. "Please don't—"

Raedra held up a hand. "Nell, I don't need you to smooth it out for me." She looked to Farideh. "I was . . . choosy in my youth, you see. I broke a lot of lords' hearts, because . . . well, frankly, I knew I could do better and everyone around me reminded me of that fact continually. My parents hadn't figured out yet that Baerovus would never get the throne an heir, so they let me follow my heart. Lindon was the only one who captured it.

"We were married for two tendays. Two blissful, lightning-storm-electric, thrilling tendays of utter, utter goblin-shit." She smiled at Farideh, a brittleness that she'd hidden suddenly bare. "Because he was never mine. Not for one moment."

Farideh's stomach dropped. "Another woman?"

"I wish," Raedra said. "I got up to use the chamber pot one night. Only the maid had left it on the other side of the room." She looked away, up at the painting of the princesses. "I think of that. Often. What would have happened if she'd put it back beside the bed instead? I might be dead now. Cormyr might be fallen. Or I might still think I was happy. Who knows?

"So I found it, used it, and headed back to bed, back to my husband's side.

"Only I tripped in the dark, on the clothes we'd left strewn about as we made our way to bed. I tripped, and I fell, and I landed against his writing desk. And I knocked out a piece of moulding, a part of the trim along the floor. There was a little—a little pocket there"—her voice hitched—"and inside there were the letters.

"He wasn't . . . he wasn't *anything* he'd seemed. I read them all." Her voice hitched again, but she mastered it. "He was always supposed to catch my eye, always supposed to win my heart, always supposed to marry me. They planned every *bit* of it," she spat.

"Who?"

"The Church of Shar. He belonged to the Lady of Loss."

Farideh couldn't imagine how deeply that must have cut—her closest companion an agent of her country's worst enemies. She found herself thinking of Lorcan and Asmodeus, and stopped herself. "What did you do?"

Raedra's lovely face twisted in a mocking smile. "I sat there, and cried my heart out, as quietly as I could. I wept and wept and he never woke. He never even stirred. It was like I wasn't there. Then I washed my face and dried my eyes. I went to the door and I told the guards there that I needed as many war wizards as they could muster in a hurry, because there was a traitor in my bed. Two went off, two came in along with Ilstan and stood over him—that woke him quick. So they held him—naked as a newborn, mind—and while we waited for the war wizards, I read the letters to him. I watched his face and I wished he would have looked confused or surprised. Even scared. But he only looked angry. He told me it was a scheme, a trick to destroy us and how could I believe in it?" She stared ahead, as if she were staring into the past. "I told him I didn't have to believe in things like this. That was what war wizards were for.

"And then, at least, he was a little afraid."

The way she said it made Farideh's stomach turn. "What did they do?"

"Made sure he was a traitor," Raedra said, in a voice that brooked no more questions down that line—that said to Farideh, Raedra knew and wished she didn't. "He was still a nobleman, so he was granted death by Orbyn, the Sword of Oaths. Foril and my father wanted to make it private, to spare me, but I wanted it clear that I was not a cow-eyed girl the Shadovar could use as a pawn in their game for the plane. I sat beside my father. I watched them take Lindon's head. I never blinked. I never looked away. I will never forget that day. And I will never forgive myself, because a part of me loves him still. But at least I—and the Shadovar—can be sure: there is nothing and no one I love so dearly as Cormyr.

"So" Raedra said, her tone suddenly wry once more, "you shall never beat me for willful idiocy in matters of the heart. I don't suggest you attempt it."

Farideh thought of the raw-looking patch of Raedra's soul, of the difference between the way she'd seemed that first time at the tallhouse and when she'd brought Farideh here to thank her. *You saved my life.* Of Erzoured's insistence that Raedra could be persuaded and the rumors Dahl had mentioned about Shade.

"It sounds like whatever mistakes you might have made," Farideh said, "you certainly know better. They'd be fools to try again."

"And yet they have," Raedra said. She stood and held out a hand to Farideh. "Come along. There's more than a few people I want you to meet, and if we dawdle, you'll end up changing back in the midst of it." She looked back at Devora and frowned. "Wasn't Ilstan with you?"

"He was, Your Highness," the war wizard said. "But he . . . He had to meet the Royal Magician in his tower."

Raedra frowned. "Ganrahast is with the Sage Most High. I passed them on my way here."

Devora smiled, never once looking at Farideh. "I'm sure they'll find each other."

Farideh walked beside the princess. Raedra's schemes and Erzoured's and the Crownsilvers' and the war wizards'—no wonder Brin was fit to collapse. Add in Havilar in the wilds, the mark on Ilstan's soul, and Lorcan, and Farideh could hardly hold it all in her head.

They hovered at the edges of the court, watching a string of nobles airing grievances, Farideh hunting for even the smallest holes in them.

"Anything?" Raedra asked.

"They're afraid," Farideh said. Which was dangerous in its own way—afraid and used to being safe and in control made people do desperate things. She rubbed the middle of her forehead.

"If I saw something," Farideh said, "something that wasn't to do with Shar, but which might make a difference or might just be someone's private matter, would you want to know?"

Raedra was silent a moment. "It would depend on the someone."

"Ilstan," Farideh said. "It's probably nothing, but I can't be sure. Not without more information." She swept the court again. "I need to find a book about Supernal in order to tell you whether Ilstan's in trouble or not. Some god has him in mind, but I don't know who."

Raedra nodded to herself. "That can be arranged. Not today or tomorrow. Soon. It will have to be soon."

Farideh frowned. "Promise me, please. Don't do anything until we're sure. He's never seemed anything but loyal to you."

"Of course," Raedra said swiftly. "I'll find out where such a book might be. We may need to scour some libraries, but we'll find it."

Farideh wet her mouth. "Could I bring a friend?"

Raedra smirked. "Your not-quite-brightbird?"

"No. The, um, equerry."

The princess laughed. "Well, it's nice to see Florelle wasn't entirely off the mark."

"It's not—There," Farideh said, pointing at a scribe standing beside the far wall whose soul looked moth-eaten with the goddess of loss's attentions. But as Raedra sent the guards for him, Farideh found herself wondering where the line fell between the wicked devotees and the blameless blessed.

• • •

THE HELLHOUND SNUFFLED at Irvel's dagger. She looked over at Brin and growled, baring teeth as long as iron nails.

Havilar yanked on the chain. "No! Bad puppy! No growling at Brin!" The hellhound made a little whining bark and turned back to Havilar, tucking her enormous head against Havilar's stomach. She rubbed the dog behind the ear. "It's all right. You're learning."

"How is this going to work?" Kallan muttered. "Untrained tracking dog in the rain on a cold trail?" The hellhound swung its head toward the dragonborn sellsword. Sairché's disguise spell still made the hellhound look like an ordinary mastiff—albeit a very big one.

"We're just trying it," Brin said, never looking away from Havilar.

Havilar held the dagger out again. "There's another smell," she told the puppy. "Another man. *Not* Brin, Find *him*."

The hellhound sniffed at the dagger again, longer this time. Long enough that Havilar was uncomfortably aware of five sets of eyes on her, waiting to see if this plan would work.

The hellhound lifted her head, scenting the air. She swung around so sharply the chain nearly yanked free of Havilar's grip. The hellhound threw back her head and made a squeaky little howl.

Moriah clapped a hand to her mouth, giggling. "Oh, tell me it's not cute," she said at Kallan's dark look.

The hellhound suddenly broke toward the north, nearly tearing Havilar's arms from their sockets. Havilar held onto the chain, running as fast as she could after the hellhound, who strained against her leash and muzzle. Behind Havilar came the crash of her companions running through the thick forest.

"Stop stop stop stop!" Havilar shouted. Suddenly the hellhound turned and whipped around her, and before Havilar could leap aside, the enormous dog had ducked between Havilar's legs and heaved her up onto its back. Havilar caught the black fur, thick as steel wool in both hands as she teetered on the hellhound's back. The puppy bucked and twisted, settling Havilar into place. "*Gods, gods, gods!*" Havilar shouted. "Stop! Sit! Be a good puppy!"

"Loyal Fury, Havi!" Brin cried behind her. Mehen and Sairché were close behind, and the sounds of Moriah and Kallan moving through the woods were far off. "What are you doing? Get off it!"

"Do you think I got up here on purpose?" Havilar shouted back. She nudged the hellhound's flanks, as if she were a horse, tugged gently on the fur as though it were reins—the puppy turned . . . then caught sight of her tail, and snapping at it, turned again.

Havilar managed to catch the chain up and get the hellhound's attention pointed toward the rest of her friends. "She's too strong. I can't hold the chain when she runs." She bit her lip. "I can ride her. Could you follow?"

"No!" Brin cried.

"You're likely to hurt its back," Mehen pointed out. "It's not full grown after all."

"They're meant to be ridden." Everyone turned to Desima—to Sairché—standing with her arms folded tight at the back of the group. "That's what they say," she amended. "The mounts of Hellish cavalry, ready to ride as soon as they can run." The hellhound sneezed, shook her head, scattering sparks. Mehen stomped them out. "Of course," Desima added, "they're *probably* trained first."

"How much weight could she carry?" Havilar asked.

Desima gave her a withering look. "I don't train the things."

"Brin," Havilar said, "climb up and see if she'll bear us both. We can ride ahead, the two of us. Make camp and let everyone catch up."

"It's a big forest," Mehen said. "We might lose you."

Brin's eyes held hers, and for a moment, Havilar was sure he was going to tell her to get down. She held tighter to the dog's fur.

"You should take Desima," Brin said. "She can send out a signal from where you get to. Maybe something to get us there quicker. We'll catch up."

Havilar's chest squeezed. "What if we find him?"

Brin gave her a crooked smile. "Then you have some time to convince him to talk Raedra out of the wedding." Havilar slid off the hellhound. "Or," Brin added, lightly, "he'll be dead and you'll have time to think of where you want to run to."

"Stop that," she said. She kissed him and hugged him tight. She took Irvel's dagger from Brin. "Let's think of a way for you to ride next," she said. "This is your adventure anyway."

"I know when I'm beat," Brin said. Havilar gave the hellhound the scent once more and climbed onto her back, trying to keep the enormous dog steady.

Mehen helped Sairché onto the back of the hellhound, pulling her near enough to hiss. "I haven't forgotten. You harm one hair on her head and—"

"And worse threats than you will make sure I suffer far worse than you could stomach," Sairché finished quietly. "Don't worry, goodman," she added in a tone that Havilar knew could only make Mehen worry. "I'll take very good care of her."

The hellhound gave another squeaky howl and took off running through the Hullack before Mehen could change his mind, and Havilar for one was very glad. They'd find Irvel yet, she was sure of it.

• • •

VESCARAS KNOCKED, BUT Dahl's concentration never left the map of Suzail spread out on his still-made bed, the scraps of foolscap with the six unbroken codes repeated over and over. The other Harper opened the door anyway, leaning in.

"How'd your efforts last night prove?" Vescaras asked. Dahl considered the asterisk of ink he'd made where the Sweet Nymph stood, near to the eastern wall.

"Two more," he said. "I've got their . . ." He rubbed his eyes. "Their information over there." He waved at the desk. "One that didn't bear out, but that might have been due to the brawl."

Vescaras sighed. "Who did you hit?"

"I didn't hit anyone who wasn't trying to hit me." The memory of his fist colliding with that sneering bastard's jaw. "I hit one person who wasn't trying to hit me," he amended. "And he deserved it anyway." He looked up at Vescaras. "Not that it matters. You would have hit him too."

"What did he do?"

You share Lord Crownsilver's perversion for ugly tieflings, eh?

"Never mind. It's not relevant." He looked up—Vescaras was wrapping a bandage around one hand. "What happened to you?"

"Card game went sour trying to feel out High Cormyr's network of nobles," he said.

"Ask the wrong questions?"

"Forgot to lose." Vescaras came into the room, looking over the maps and the notes. "Are you still decoding that?"

"Yeah. It's a mire. The first layer's expected, but Marjana changed the second code twice in the middle. I got the first two groups unpicked, but it's trial and error to get it started." Vescaras raised an eyebrow. "I have to start guessing and see if it matches any taverns or inns or things in the city. So far, I haven't guessed right."

Vescaras picked up a scrap of paper. "So you're just going to run through every rune in the . . ." He paused. "Are you sure they're taverns?"

"Why?" Dahl asked, dreading the answer.

"Because you started translating this one into 'Kraliqh,' which is the name of the man I got myself trapped beside all night. Arvel Kraliqh, second son of Lord Kraliqh of Arabel who sent him to their Suzail house before the Shadovar army came through. Not a bad source of intelligence about Arabel—which is well and mightily buggered, by the by—but not one of Brin's."

Dahl stood and snatched the paper back. "Noble familes?" No, he thought. Noble houses. That was what they had in common—they were all locations. Places the Sharrans had infiltrated. "Do you think you could find out if he had any new staff in the last . . ." How long had the others been in Suzail? "Two years or so?" Dahl finished.

Vescaras snorted. "He has. Everyone has. A jack or a scullery decides they'd rather adventure. A maid gets pregnant or comes into a family farm. Your neighbor lures your cook away when he tastes the poached salmon. The Kraliqhs have a new servant, no doubt. Just remains to figure out who it is."

Dahl cursed and dropped back down at the desk to puzzle out the remainder of the list. It wouldn't be hard to find out who it was—send Farideh in with the disguise spell on, pretending that she's Asmura Crownsilver, Vescaras's dear friend and maybe more. Dahl could stay in the Dragon's Jaws and draft contracts for his lordship's wine sales.

"Farideh's free tonight," he said. "We were supposed to . . . She'll have the disguise on, and by the way I may have let some noblewoman think you were having dinner with her like that at the Dragon's Last Drink." *Cormaeril*, he wrote over the second line.

Vescaras was silent a moment. "Keeping in mind that I am not Khochen," he said. "Are you all right?"

"Long night," Dahl said. *Goldfeather. Greatgaunt.*

"Did you sleep?"

"Maybe a little. I don't remember."

"And you're all right?"

There was nothing in the world he wanted to do less than talk about his gods-damned feelings with Vescaras. He half wished Khochen were here instead—he hardly had the choice not to talk to Khochen.

"I'm fine," Dahl said.

Huntcrown, he translated. *Crownsilver.*

"Son of a barghest," he muttered. This was going to get very complicated.

17

5 Eleint, the Year of the Nether Mountain Scrolls (1486 DR)
The Silent Room, Suzail, Cormyr

DAHL LOOKED UP AT THE ELABORATE EDIFICE OF THE SILENT ROOM, THE seat of the Church of Oghma in Exile. "When you said we were going to a library, you didn't mention it was a Temple of Oghma."

"I didn't realize," Farideh said. She was enchanted as she'd been before, the red-haired war wizard's spell leaving her looking like a rather untidy, but very pretty noblewoman. "Raedra's sages said the book we need is in here. Is it all right?"

"Fine," Dahl said mechanically. He shook his head. "Please stop calling her that. She's not your neighbor over the fence. They take that sort of thing terribly serious."

"What am I supposed to call her?"

"Her Highness," Dahl said.

"Will you two stop gawping and lollygagging?" Her Highness called from within the door. "I haven't got all day."

Dahl mounted the stairs with a certain apprehension. He hadn't set foot in a temple of Oghma in the better part of three years. Guilt at his absence and anger at the god's silence murmured in his thoughts like disagreeable advisors.

It's not Orthodox, he told himself. It won't be anything the same. They won't recognize who you were. He stepped over the threshold and felt as if he were entering a dragon's lair.

Beside him, Farideh must have had similar thoughts. He heard her exhale noisily as she stepped inside, as if she'd been holding her breath.

"Did you think you were going to burst into flames?"

"I don't know," she said. "I can count the number of temples I've been in on one hand. The way some of you go on, the priests might have rigged a spell whatever the gods think."

Dahl took her arm and folded it around his. "I doubt Oghma has such opinions, and if anyone is going to act like that, it's the Church-in-Exile, you have me and you have Her Highness." Raedra walked ahead of them, garbed in a gray and pale blue gown and flanked by a pair of Purple Dragons. "What is that supposed to mean, 'some of you'? Are all humans alike now?"

She shot him a dark look. "You have said *very* similar things in the past."

"I have *never* said anything remotely like 'you ought to be burned alive'—don't be ghoulish." They passed through a second set of doors, into the library and sanctuary. "Besides, I think you have a blanket apology for anything I said to you prior to the Year of the Nether Mountain Scrolls. I was a git."

She was quiet a moment. "You weren't that bad," she allowed.

On the either side of the temple's nave, rows and rows of bookshelves lined their path to Oghma's altar. Polished marble tiles lined the floor, making a road of pure white to the god, lined with lecterns and tables two-thirds of the way down. The sounds of a harp drifted down from somewhere above.

The books—gods, the books. Dahl had been in libraries more spectacular than the Silent Room's, but it had been a long time, and there wasn't a library on the face of Toril that didn't hit Dahl like a really good whiskey. The sight of the soaring shelves of books eased a well-worn peace over him, the smell of old inks and parchments sweeter than a love song. A shiver ran down his spine.

As Raedra passed, sages and loremasters looked up from their texts and bowed deeply. She nodded as she walked, never stopping, and Dahl had to like her a little for that—he would have hated to be in the midst of a book and find himself forced to make small talk because of custom and tradition. Indeed, most of the sages they passed dropped immediately back into their studies.

Raedra came to a stop beside the last of the tables, beside a small, older woman using a magnifying glass to read the very tiny text of a very large book. She wore the blank scroll of Oghma, embroidered on her indigo robes.

Raedra cleared her throat, and the loremaster leaped. She blinked owlishly up at Raedra, at the Purple Dragons. "Your Highness!" she gasped. Someone shushed her.

"Well met," Raedra said, as the woman struggled up from behind the heavy table to make her bows. "The Sage Most High sent me. I'm looking for books on Supernal."

The gray-haired woman blinked at Raedra. "*Books*, Highness?" she said. "You'll find you're being a bit optimistic there."

"Pardon?" Raedra said.

"Such an oddity, Supernal," she said. She moved past Raedra deeper into the library, and the three of them followed. "'The milk tongue of angels, the secret breath of the gods.' Poetic, but imprecise—Waldbrudge never does say how an angel could possibly have a milk tongue, having never been anything but whole. Still, his is the central text—you cannot make a study of Supernal without it." She stopped abruptly, peering up at the princess. "I'm very surprised Sage Eveningstar sent you. I trust you gained a very long lecture about the quality of true scholarship and why Waldbrudge is a dilettante at best. What is it you want Supernal for?"

Raedra gave an artless shrug. "A fancy," she said.

At the end of the long shelves, just past the bust of an old Turami woman in marble, the loremaster stopped, scanning the shelves. "Hrmph," she said. "I see Loremaster Margull has been here. He does not feel Waldbrudge is appropriately vetted, and untested knowledge . . . well, you know." She sighed. "There are secondary sources which will discuss aspects of the language here. You'll want those. But the Waldbrudge will be in the Unspoken Chamber with the other untested."

"Could you get it for me?" Raedra said sweetly. "It's very important."

The loremaster shifted. "I ought not. It will start trouble with Loremaster Margull."

"Perhaps I should come with you," Raedra said. "I suspect Loremaster Margull would have a difficult time arguing about a book's merits when it is in the interest of the Crown."

The old woman snorted. "I see you are unacquainted with Margull. Very well, Your Highness. Follow me, please."

"Search for those secondary mentions," Raedra said suggestively, elbowing Farideh as she passed.

Dahl pulled a title from the shelves at random. *Languages of the Fiendish.* "Do we know if this Waldbrudge book has what you're looking for?"

"Not in the slightest," Farideh said. She plucked a book down, skimmed it, replaced it. "This is going to take forever."

"Nah," said Dahl, stepping up on the edge of a shelf to reach one of the higher ones. He pulled down a fat green leather book. *Planar Entities and Their Weaknesses.* "This is nothing." Farideh hitched her skirts up so that she could crouch down low. "Did you have a nice time with Vescaras last night?"

"Not particularly," she said, flipping through a book. "I don't make a very convincing noblewoman. But I found the groom."

"Vescaras said you left early."

"I was done."

"Left early, holding your arm."

She snapped the book shut, and pushed a strand of hair behind her ear. "All right—I had to talk to Lorcan about something."

"Did you ask him about the glyph?"

"Obviously he didn't know this one."

Dahl went back to searching. He did not tell Farideh he had spent the prior evening alternating between being bored enough to march down to the Golden Goblin again and find that lost Sharran himself, and worrying about what was bound to happen to her without him there.

It was with a mix of relief and annoyance that he found the answer was "find another Sharran and go home early."

"She walked down into the kitchen and into *the cellar*, simple as you please," Vescaras had said, as though Farideh had gone digging through Lady Kraliqh's closets. "Blundered in on the grooms and jacks playing cards. You can imagine the lies I had to spread about Athkatlan customs to cover for her."

Aside from the Sharran, Vescaras had found two of Brin's noble connections and resecured their involvement with the refugees. "You can send Garce to Lady Illance again," he said. "And Lord Tapstorn—although he apparently takes issue with folk from Arabel coming under his roof, whatever that's about." He'd rubbed his eyes. "And the gods damn us: Marsheena's army is moving south again. The rain and Arabel has them slowed, but they're heading this way, tearing up the countryside as they go."

"I suppose I'll have to do the same again," Farideh said. "How many nobles was it?"

"Six," Dahl said. "Kraliqh, Greatgaunt, Goldfeather, Huntcrown, Cormaeril, and Crownsilver. Although, we may well have let the wizard blast blindfolded on that one. Helindra won't even crack the door for Vescaras, and she knows you're not her relation."

"Maybe I could get in myself," Farideh said. "Tell her I want to discuss Havi and Brin or something."

"And wander around the castle in the meantime? Don't. We might not need it."

"You know I'm not just some sort of dowsing rod," Farideh said, yanking another book down. "I don't have to have one of your tattoos to be useful."

"You're very useful," Dahl said. "So useful that if something happened to you, I . . ." A little burst of dread hit him, an echo of his fears for Harrowdale. "I wouldn't be able to replace you," he finished. "So don't."

Beneath him, Farideh drew a sharp breath, and he braced for another argument. But she was looking down at the book on her lap. It lay open to a printing of a tiefling woman holding a baby by its ankles before a statue of a grotesque-looking devil. Around her, a dozen other creatures stood arrayed, all mostly human, but clearly none completely so.

"It's just nastiness," Dahl said quickly. "Don't mind it."

"No," Farideh said, touching the very edge of the printing with a strange mix of reverence and revulsion. "That's . . . her. That's my Vaasan ancestor."

Dahl crouched beside Farideh. "The Toril Thirteen and the Brimstone Angel," the caption read. The tiefling woman's horns were short and sharp, forked like a mountain goat's and her feet were drawn as cloven hooves, but her face was human and implacably lovely.

"This is why I have a pact," she murmured. "This is why Lorcan has a use for me." She looked up at him. "This is where I came from, I suppose."

Dahl leaned over her shoulder. *Sacrifices . . . murders . . . Apotheosis of the King of the Nine Hells . . .* Gods' books. Everything bad you expect from a tiefling warlock, and then some more. Farideh stared at the drawing as if Bryseis Kakistos had her by the heels, instead of the doomed baby, and Dahl's stomach dropped.

"At least you didn't get her feet," Dahl said.

"Don't tease."

"It's not teasing," Dahl said. "That's the only thing you could possibly have to worry about, so far as I see." He reached over and closed the book. "That woman isn't your family. She's not your destiny. She's not where you came from any more than my mad great-uncle who's not to be left alone with the sheep is, where I came from. It's not all about blood."

"But a little," Farideh said. "Enough."

"Well, if your plan is to follow in her footsteps and be a warlock wicked enough to warrant some sage writing about you, you're doing a terrible job. Starting with trying to rescue your sister's rival and her favorite war wizard."

"She's hardly Havi's rival," Farideh said.

"'Adversary'?" Dahl pulled down another book. "'Challenger'? I doubt very much Brin laid a bit of that to rest before he ran off."

"Maybe things will be different now," Farideh said, not looking at him.

"Or maybe Brin will flick her nose enough that she throws you in the dungeon the next time you forget to bow. *How* are you getting away with that?"

"Getting away with what?"

"You're supposed to always bow when a royal comes in. That's the law."

"That seems inconvenient," Farideh said. "What if you were in the middle of something? She comes in sometimes while her maid's fixing my hair—am I supposed to bow while someone's yanking on my scalp?"

"Cormyr's full of rules that don't make sense," Dahl said. "Commoners can't wear more than one kind of feather in their hats, adventurers need special permission to hunt monsters, and if a king gets resurrected, they castrate him like a yearling and throw him out of the country, and his benefactor gets executed—gods only know what *that's* about."

"And Waterdeep's laws all make perfect sense?"

"I don't know," Dahl said irritably. "But you bow to a princess. That's just what you do."

Raedra returned soon after, bearing a book as long as Dahl's forearm and as thick as his wrist, bound in faded blue cloth. "Here we are," she said. "Although I suspect it's more than you bargained for."

Dahl opened it, the pages so fine and delicate they shuddered as he breathed. He dropped down beside Farideh, turning pages and pages of a long-dead sage's scrawlings, his hand in Common, blotted and shaking, his Supernal glyphs, painstaking and lacy. Each was tagged with its purported translation, words flowing in and out of categories without apparent rhyme or reason. On the open pages: a mix of verbs and flower names, plus "snow," "sand," "Turmish," and "elbow, or perhaps joint, connection, break?"

"A step in the right direction," Dahl allowed. "Many thanks, Your Highness."

Raedra cocked her head at him. "Tell me your name again?"

"Dahl, Highness."

"Dahl. You're that jack that no one hired, aren't you." She laughed. "Oh, you ought to have said. I would have remembered him."

Farideh pursed her mouth. "I thought he might like his privacy. Your Highness."

Raedra gave her a funny look, and laughed once more. She looked back over her shoulder. "Shall we claim a table, or—"

Suddenly, the red-haired war wizard sprinted up the aisle. "Your Highness, you must come. It's urgent." She glanced down at Farideh and Dahl. "They said I must bring you to the palace immediately."

Raedra held herself very straight. "Of course," she said, the faintest hesitance in her voice. "I shall return shortly," she told Farideh. "Don't leave without me."

The Purple Dragons and the war wizard ushered Raedra out of sight.

"Do you think everything's all right?" Farideh asked, craning her neck to see down the aisle.

"I think the country's at war and there are Sharrans in the palace," Dahl said, eyes on the Waldbrudge. "There are a thousand reasons they've recalled her, but she's probably fine."

He brushed the onion-skin pages over, considering the fragile-looking glyphs. *Angel. Solar. Planetar. Mistake. Error.*

"Is this . . . do you see this when you look at me?"

Farideh set the book she was holding into the pile they'd made of potential sources. "It's not like that."

"What is it like?"

She sat back, tucking her legs under her, beneath the wide swirl of skirts. "Do you want to know this? I mean, do you really want to?"

"Of course."

"It's just the whole business upsets you—you know it does. What if it's not the answer you want?"

"Like what if it says 'Stlarn off, Dahl, I can do better, signed Oghma'?" he said. "I've lived my life thus far assuming that's exactly what He'd say. Anything better is a blessing, anything worse . . ." He gave her a wan smile. "Well, if it's worse than that, at least I know I have to give up once and for all."

"You're not happy being a Harper?" she asked. "I mean, you're fairly good at it."

"It's . . . I like it. And when I'm not"—he sighed again—"ruining things, I suppose I'm good at it. But once you know what it is to channel the favor of a god who loves you completely, loves what you love completely . . . it's hard to give up on."

She bit her lip, and he wished she wouldn't. "All right," she said. "Come a little nearer." Dahl settled onto his knees, on the edge of her skirts. Her gaze shifted, drifted, as if she were looking at something an inch off his face. He watched her pupils darken and she edged a little nearer, her knees brushing his, her eyes darting back and forth, as though reading lines of a book.

"'Does . . . Does the salmon demand the tide?'" she started. "'Does the owl's wing unfurl the gale? My priest may name the spinning plane. The plane has never spun for him. Does the owl's wing unfurl—'"

"You said that already."

"I *know*," she said. "It repeats itself. Quite a bit. But it does it in Draconic, too, so I have to assume it's meant to. It's like a poem, or something." She frowned, worried. "Are you sure you want to hear this?"

More than anything, Dahl thought, though he had never in his life been so nervous. "Do it," he said, and shut his eyes.

Farideh paused a moment. Then began again.

"Does the salmon demand the tide?
Does the owl's wing unfurl the gale?
My priest may name the spinning plane
The plane has never spun for him.

Does the owl's wing unfurl the gale?
It is the gale that folds the wing
The plane has never spun for him
And still the wise seek the axis

It is the gale that folds the wing
So turn your face into the wind
Be still, be wise, seek the axis
The Harp shall be your truest guide

So turn your face into the wind
My champion, my wayward son
The Harp shall be your truest guide
From heav'ns to Hells the plane will ring

My champion, my wayward son
The path's well trod, the hunting's poor
From heav'ns to Hells the plane will ring
Reflect, and after, my priest speaks

The path's well trod, the hunting's poor
You may yet name the spinning plane
Reflect, and after, my priest speaks
Where the salmon demand the tide."

The hairs on Dahl's neck stood on end. He opened his eyes. "That's it?"
"That's all."

He cursed. He cursed and cursed and cursed. Another stlarning riddle. Of course. And nothing—not a single thought in his head—on how to solve it. She watched him with what he was fairly sure was pity, and he smiled tightly back at her. "Well it figures. 'You are doing everything wrong. Go back to being a Harper. Find a fish.'"

"If it helps," she said, "the Draconic . . . It translates a little different. Maybe it's a clue."

He didn't answer. She was right—he didn't want to know and now he did.

"'Axis'" she went on anyway, "is *optivich* in the other lines. It doesn't mean a literal axis or 'a center point.' It means 'the point where things change.' A fulcrum. Something that makes everything shift. Maybe . . ." She leaned close again, peering at the air near his jaw, eyes skipping along unseen text. He wondered if he'd be able to see her do that with her eyes the way they normally were. "'Hunting' is another one," she murmured. "It's not necessarily hunting like you're tracking down a deer, but . . . searching for something. Looking for signs." She looked up, seemed to realize how near she'd moved, and straightened.

"Anyway," she said. "Now you know."

"You must think I'm ridiculous," Dahl said.

"I have thought a lot of things about you, but never once that." She reached over and patted his hand. "If Oghma doesn't want you around, it's his loss."

Dahl turned his hand, so that her palm lay across his. "Thank you."

A shadow fell over them. Dahl looked up to find a startlingly tall man garbed in a war wizard's severe robes.

"Ilstan," Farideh said. "You've just missed Raed— Her Highness."

"I know," he said, his face pale, his words choked. "I've been sent back to tell you she isn't returning. You should head home."

Farideh stood. "What happened?"

"It's a matter for the royal family at the moment."

"Is she all right?"

Ilstan hesitated. "It is a matter for the royal family at the moment." He turned to leave, but Farideh darted around him. Dahl took the opportunity to slide the book of Supernal up the back of his jerkin—without a royal, it might be bound for the Unspoken Chamber again.

"Did Brin find the crown prince?" Farideh demanded. "Is that it?"

"No," Ilstan said. He swallowed hard as though it pained him. "King Foril is dead."

• • •

"THERE IS ABSOLUTELY no way they don't know what this is," Sairché muttered to Havilar, after she'd disguised the hellhound once more. "No one is this stupid."

The "black mastiff" whined and belched a little burst of flames, surprising herself. Sitting, her face was almost level with Havilar's shoulders.

"How is she getting bigger when she doesn't even eat?" Havilar asked.

"It will get bigger still. They're the size of draft horses fully grown." She wrinkled her nose. "And it's going to want to eat eventually. You can't stop that."

"Would a rabbit do?"

Sairché laughed as if Havilar were a child making an accidental joke. Havilar scratched the dog behind the ear. It was hard to picture the puppy turning into anything wicked. Clumsy, yes. Driven by instincts, most definitely—the last two nights she'd howled and fought the chain, trying to follow the scent into the lightless forest.

It doesn't matter, Havilar reminded herself. She's going back to Mot and Dembo when you find Irvel. They were three days closer to their quarry. She hoped. Every morning she'd climb on the hellhound's back and ride until it grew dark. Then Sairché would take a ring from her pocket, powerfully enchanted to call to a second ring around Mehen's neck, and speed the rest of the party to where Havilar and Sairché waited.

"I still don't like you," Havilar had told Sairché.

"You are breathing," the cambion had replied, "and that is literally all I care about."

If they didn't find Irvel soon, Havilar thought, this entire plan was going to come apart. Brin would find out about Sairché or Mehen would lose his patience or Havilar might. The hellhound would get too big or maybe eat someone.

We'll find him, she told herself, idly scratching the hellhound under the chin. She wondered what Irvel was like. Whether he'd treat her like Helindra had, or the shopgirl, or maybe more like Brin.

"We *must* be getting close." Havilar turned at the voice—Moriah, wearing an oddly beatific smile. "Perhaps I should ride with you instead today. Your fellow might need healing."

"Desima" sniffed. "Or dispelling. Or protection. Or Heavens know what."

"If we're close, Brin ought to be the one coming along," Havilar said. "He'll recognize Brin, and besides, Brin can heal."

"But well enough?" Moriah asked. There was a coolness to her, a chiding quality that didn't match her earlier joking.

It's this place, she told herself. It's what's happening to you.

"You seem awfully eager, priestess," Sairché drawled. "I wonder what it is you're hoping to gain."

Moriah turned that cool smile on the wizard. "I've been wondering the same thing about you, *baatezu*." At the unfamiliar word, Sairché stiffened.

Brin came up, swaddled in his cloak. "Are you ready?"

"I was just saying you ought to come with me today," Havilar said. "In case we're close."

"And I was offering my services," Moriah said. "You did pay me to perform healings."

Havilar slid a hand into the hellhound's thick fur and thought about how quickly she could pull her glaive from its harness.

Brin sighed. "That is a good point."

"You can heal," Havilar said. "Give her Desima's ring. Give her the ring and then when we get there, if he needs more healing than we can do, she can just jump to us." She made herself look at Desima. "That's reasonable. Go ask Mehen for it."

Moriah blinked at her. "Very reasonable," she said. She turned to go. Sairché watched her with a look that would have melted glass. She handed the simple gold band over to Havilar.

"Be careful," she said, before joining the others.

"What was that about?" Brin asked when she'd left. "I thought you liked Moriah."

"She gives me the creeps," Havilar admitted. "I don't know. Desima's right—we don't know what we'll need. I still think the answer is you."

Brin sighed. "We'll see, I suppose."

They would, Havilar thought, pulling herself up on the hellhound. The beast had been whining and pawing at the dirt all night, ready to run again, her quarry near enough to taste. Brin climbed behind her, his arms around her waist.

Havilar unhooked the hellhound's chain, and without another order, she sprang off into the woods, fleeter than any horse. The sounds of their companions were soon lost in the maze of ancient trees, as the enormous hound bounded through the Hullack, stopping now and again to sniff the air. It was all Havilar could do to keep her seat, her legs clamped hard around the dog's sides, her hands knotted in its fur.

By the time they broke through the brush into the clearing, she was convinced that she couldn't manage another moment. And then the hellhound stopped.

She skittered suddenly, whimpering and scrambling back as though the clearing dropped away in a sheer cliff. Havilar clung tightly to her fur, and Brin's arms in turn wrapped her like steel bands. As the hellhound retreated into the apparent safety of the broad clearing's edge, Havilar followed the dog's fearful gaze.

A temple.

It was old, almost crumbling into the forest in great blocks of stone coated in thick moss. A tree grew out through the roof, its roots leaving a ripple in the stone wall. The rear of it abutted a tall bluff of gray stone. As broken down as it seemed, a sense of stillness, of peace pervaded the entire clearing.

"There," Havilar said, as they climbed down. "He's in there."

The hellhound whined and whimpered, pacing along the invisible edge of the dilapidated temple's hallowed ground. Havilar scratched her behind the ears. "Good girl," she murmured, and hooked the chain around a tree root, while Brin started toward the temple in the distance. "Wait here."

• • •

RAEDRA REACHED HER grandfather's room, that hollow, crumbling feeling taking over her chest. Someone had turned Foril onto his back, folded his hands over his chest and smoothed his hair.

Ganrahast, she thought. The war wizard sat beside the dead king, his face drawn with grief. The Royal Magician had already been a young man when Foril was born, and now the magic that saturated every part of Ganrahast's life made him look as if he might have been another of Foril's sons. Raedra's eyes flooded at that—sudden and overtaking. She wiped them quickly as the war wizard looked up.

"While he slept," Ganrahast said. "The underjack found him."

Raedra crossed the room, willing herself to take each step although her whole body rebelled at it. If she didn't look, it wouldn't be so. If she turned and went back to her rooms and her retinue, everything would continue the way it always had been.

It can't, she thought laying her hand atop her grandfather's. Still warm, though cooler than flesh should be and without the support of blood and firm muscles. The wrongness shook her, but she couldn't take her hand back. She kneeled down on the rug beside him. Everything keeps changing, she thought. It all keeps going.

"Was it painless?" she heard herself ask.

"He never cried out," Ganrahast offered. "He slept . . . I suppose that is the easiest death one can ask for."

The sort of death meant for King Foril of Cormyr, who had not been made for the Dragon Throne. Not dead in battle, not by assassins, not giving out in a lover's arms, but quietly, alone and in bed, of age and the damp in his lungs. Raedra thought of the Hall of Gazes, of the portraits ranging down the corridor of kings and queens, and wondered what her children's children would make of her grandfather. Would they call him weak for raising up his brother's bastards? For stalling the inevitable war against Shade and Sembia until it broke out in the current disaster? Would they see the wisdom in that stalling while the country rebuilt, and the kindness behind calling Erzoured and Halance his trueborn nephews? Would anyone see how much strength it took to hold together a realm still reeling from the catastrophes of a century ago—especially when Foril had been the second son, meant to support his dear brother's reign?

So much of that would depend, Raedra realized as Erzoured came in the door, upon Foril's successors.

"Well met, Cousin," Raedra said. "You arrived swiftly."

To his credit, Erzoured only looked shocked. He might have dreamed of this day all of his life, but clearly he harbored at least some fond feelings for his uncle and king. He moved to the foot of the bed, looking somber.

"Was it quick?" he asked.

"Peaceful," Ganrahast said, never looking up at Erzoured. "He died while he slept."

"How long?"

"An hour," Ganrahast said. "Perhaps two."

Raedra's mother flew into the room, a tornado of silks trailing courtiers. Whether tears for her husband, her son, or her father-in-law reddened her eyes and streaked her lovely face hardly mattered, especially when the normally composed Princess Ospra burst into tears anew. "Oh gods!" she cried. "No. No, no." She kneeled on the rug beside Raedra, and cupped Foril's cheek. "Was it peaceful?" she asked.

Raedra put an arm around her mother, as Ospra asked the same questions, a litany for the dead. She caught the eyes of the Purple Dragon guards, and jerked her head at the gaggle of courtiers. "Ask them to wait, please. They will have their turns."

Erzoured's gaze pinned her, challenging her—was she going to throw him out as well? Raedra ignored him, and turned back to her mother. Foril would have wanted his nephew to stay.

"It was coming," Ospra said. "It was always coming. But . . . I would have liked so much to bid him farewell. To tell him how dear he was, how much I loved him."

Raedra's eyes flooded, and she wiped them quickly. "He knew, Mother."

Ospra hugged Raedra tight, tucking her daughter's head against her shoulder. "Oh, my dear darling," she whispered. "I hope you're ready for what comes next."

Over Ospra's shoulder, Erzoured watched, his expression a still and somber mask.

• • •

"Irvel!" Brin shouted, sprinting toward the temple. The seal of a waterfall crashing into a still pool marked the door—a temple of Eldath, goddess of groves and sacred pools, though one long since abandoned to the Hullack and its own peculiar peace. He pushed through the doors. "Irvel!"

The space inside echoed with the crash of a waterfall, spilling down the corner where the temple abutted the cliff face. Everything within was slick with patches of moss, and a tree grew through what remained of the roof.

"Irvel!" Brin shouted again. A faint sound—a groan, a cry came from the back of the temple, near the altar. Brin hurried across the sanctuary, slipping on the moss. The stench of death rolled against him as he approached the altar, and terror slipped between Brin and his sense of himself, as if he was peeling away from his own mind.

"Irvel," he said, growing dizzy.

The crown prince lay behind the altar, curled beside the sacred pool that filled the corner of the temple. A wound festered in his side, black and seeping through the fabric of his shirt. The skin visible on his face and neck, his hands and the arm bared by his torn sleeve was bruised and mottled. He turned at the sound of Brin's voice, his eyes focusing on nothing at all.

"Baerovus, lad, where are you? You shouldn't be here," he rasped. Brin dropped his sword and fell to his knees. A fever, an infected wound and blood rot—gods damn it! He laid both hands upon the wound—Irvel screamed once as Brin touched the gash, shut his eyes, and tried with all his might to still his mind and open his heart.

"Loyal Torm," Brin intoned, "aid this servant of your justice." The god's presence flickered somewhere beyond—but no flood of strength poured into Brin, no cascade of light. Havilar came to stand beside him, her sleeve held over her nose.

"Oh gods." She fidgeted with the ring, twisting it into glowing. "Moriah! Come on!"

"Loyal Torm," Brin said again, shaking, "aid this servant of your justice." Irvel clutched almost blindly at his arm. "Loyal Torm!" Brin shouted. "Aid this servant of your justice!" Nothing—no ring of the whetstone, no hand of the god.

"Moriah!" Havilar screamed. "Moriah get over here!"

"Loyal Torm," Brin cried. "Gods stlarning *hrast* it, listen to me!"

Irvel smiled up at Brin, his eyes focusing on the younger man's face for just a moment. "Hal," he said, reaching a trembling hand toward Brin. "Where have you been . . . ?"

Irvel's hand hand fell against the stones as his last breath fled him, the peace of Eldath, the dark silence of the Hullack Forest restored, as the Crown Prince of Cormyr died.

• • •

THE COURTIERS COULD not be kept at bay for long, and not an hour had passed before the room was close and crowded with too many stewards and understewards and lords and ladies. Raedra watched them all—half-wishing they would go and leave them all be, half-hungry for whatever bits and scraps of information could be gleaned from the appearance of their mourning.

Ospra clutched her hand tightly, and Raedra patted it. How many times had they thanked someone for their kind words? How many times had someone asked if it had been swift, if it had been peaceful? The day was growing late, and with every passing breath Raedra felt as if she were growing heavier and heavier. All she wanted was to retreat, to hide, to mourn in her own time.

The heads of the Silver families arrived, thoughtfully dressed in somber mourning and with only a single retainer. Helindra leaned on Pheonard's arm as she entered, a faint hollowness to her eyes—even Helindra Crownsilver could cry. Behind her, strapping Lord Oskar Truesilver entered, his eldest daughter, Laendra, standing stiff and demure at his side. Little Lady Roatha Huntsilver entered, draped in a miniature version of a grown woman's gown and clutching the hand of her twin brother, Glorin. Her mother, Pelarra, a sternly beautiful woman of a certain age, pushed Roatha forward, the girl's dark eyes locked on Raedra as if she were a phantasm. Raedra nodded at each as they approached, patted Roatha's pile of blond curls.

"You have House Crownsilver's deepest sympathies, my dear," Helindra said, bowing over Raedra's hand. "A pity Aubrin isn't here to offer his own sympathies."

"I'm sure he will return soon," Raedra said, another answer that was all but rote. If he did, if he didn't, her grandfather would still be dead. Her father would still be gone. Her brother would still be trapped in his sleep. And the tiefling would still be an issue.

Raedra blinked—how long had it been since she'd left Farideh sitting in the library with the equerry? Surely someone had conveyed her home. Raedra took Lord Truesilver's proffered hand, accepted his condolences, and thought about how nice it would be to have some wine and talk to one person who didn't look at her and see a piece in a grand game, who she could hardly count as a piece of her own. Today, she wanted out.

But there was no escaping—not even for a few breaths.

"When will they announce it?" Lord Truesilver asked.

"It's already been done," another said.

"The succession will have to be addressed," Pheonard Crownsilver said. "The people will demand it."

"And soon," the understeward of the regalia added.

Even though her eyes were reddened and swollen, Princess Ospra's gaze could have cut glass as she turned toward the straw-haired man speaking. He and Pheonard stood near Erzoured, Raedra noticed. Helindra, seated in a narrow chair, eyed her brother coolly. This wasn't Helindra's play, Raedra realized.

"Baerovus is king," Ospra said. "There is nothing to address."

"Your pardon, Highness," the understeward said, without an ounce of shame. "But your son is in no condition to rule. We are in the middle of a war that is overtaking all our resources—a crisis of succession could destroy us." He turned to Pheonard and Erzoured. "It might be best if we just presumed the prince will not be well, and crowned a king down the line."

Erzoured's eyes darted to Ospra, and he gave her a frown. "My good man, this is hardly the time to discuss the matter."

"Pity Crownsilver's not here," the High Chatelaine said.

"Crownsilver isn't an Obarskyr," Erzoured retorted. "Not officially."

Ospra squeezed Raedra's hand tight, but Raedra stood, all her grief shoved to the side. You cannot flee it, she thought. Cormyr needs you.

"*I* am," she said. The men turned to look at her. "Or did you forget Irvel has two trueborn children?"

The understeward gave her a pitying look. "Your pardon, Princess," he said. "We only wish to spare you the discomfort of dealing with a populace in need, dare I say it, of a king."

"Spare me nothing," Raedra said. "To begin with, Baerovus still breathes. He will be king, and to suggest otherwise is to spit upon the traditions of Cormyr and toe the line of treason. The line of succession stands firm. Unless, goodsirs, you are openly discussing flouting it?"

Pheonard looked abashed. "Of course not, Your Highness." The understeward looked as if he were rapidly reconsidering his impressions of Raedra.

"A regent," Ganrahast spoke from the other side of the room. Suddenly it seemed that every courtier in Cormyr was hanging on this conversation, and Raedra felt as if she were standing on the edge of a cliff, looking down. "If the king cannot rule, a regent is appointed, until he can be crowned. Or until there is no question that he cannot."

The understeward sent the smallest, most secretive glance at Erzoured, who had gone very still—save for a muscle, pulsing at his jaw. "Very well. Who shall be named as regent?"

"The next in line," Ganrahast said, as though nothing were more obvious. "With the blessings of the prince's next of kin." He nodded to Ospra. "Of course."

The princess stood, as if unfolding herself from her grief, and all at once it was plain to see why Ospra Goldfeather was thought to play the game of court better than any of her contemporaries. She smiled at the understeward.

"I don't know where you've gotten this mad idea that Cormyr has never had a queen before, but rare as they may have been, it doesn't change things. Baerovus will be king when he wakes. And if he does not, Raedra will be queen." She stepped nearer to the understeward. "Whichever fate comes to pass, you shall not be here to see it, saer. You are dismissed." She glanced back at Ganrahast. "I agree. Raedra should be regent."

Raedra held still as stone, eyes on her grandfather's bloodless face, feeling as though it were all happening to someone else, someone she was watching from a distance. She wished it would slow down.

"You will have the war wizards' support," Ganrahast said. "As well as mine."

"You have my house's support, Your Highness," Lord Truesilver said.

"The Crownsilvers stand in favor," Helindra said, ignoring the look Pheonard shot Erzoured. Raedra turned to the baron, and her cousin smiled politely.

"How anyone could doubt you were made for such a role is far beyond me," Erzoured said. "No one, of course, is asking for my blessing, but you know, dear Raedra, that you have it."

Pelarra nudged her daughter. Roatha's mouth worked for a moment. "The Huntsilvers agree. Also your dress is so pretty." She looked back at her mother and whispered, "May I have something to eat?"

"You all have my gratitude," Raedra said, aware of every eye on her. There was no other choice in that moment. "I shall endeavor to be a worthy substitute for your true king. But today is for mourning." She looked back at Foril's body, feeling the heaviness on her heart fading as she stepped back into the world of the living, where she was needed.

18

5 Eleint, the Year of the Nether Mountain Scrolls (1486 DR)
The Hullack Forest, Cormyr

THE SPLASH OF THE WATERFALL IN THE CORNER WENT ON AND ON, A perverse reminder of the inevitable passage of time. Irvel was deader by the moment, and Havilar couldn't move.

Brin looked up at her, his hands covered in the stinking blood of the dead crown prince, and Havilar's heart broke.

"It didn't work," he said.

"I'm so sorry, Brin," she started.

"He's gone."

"Maybe Moriah . . ." Havilar trailed off. She had no idea if the priestess was powerful enough to perform a resurrection, and besides she hadn't come.

"We have to bury him," Brin said, reaching to fold Irvel's arms.

"We have to make sure the others can find us first," Havilar said, pulling him up, away from the crown prince. Brin didn't fight her as she walked him back out into the clearing. The hellhound was bounding back and forth along the edge of the temple's magic.

"I triggered the ring," Havilar said. "They should be here soon." They should have been there *already*, she thought. "Maybe Moriah can resurrect him."

"No, she can't." Brin stared at his bloody hands. "No one can." He looked up at the cloudy sky. "I should have listened," he said, sounding numb. "Gods damn me, I should have listened to you. If we'd left, if we'd gone the moment you suggested, he would have been alive. He could have been saved."

"Wait for Moriah," Havilar said. How hard was a resurrection? She'd seen it done only once—it seemed simple. Expensive, but simple, and no one would let her forget that Brin had enough coin to drive a person mad.

"What if she was right?" Brin said. "What if Constancia was right? Torm refused me because I refused my duty."

Havilar rubbed a hand over his back, watching the woods. "That seems awfully petty for a god. Maybe we were just too late? Maybe everything will be all right anyway."

Brin shook his head, over and over and over. Suddenly he was breathing too much.

"Put your head between your knees," Havilar said.

"They'll push the legitimization," he said. "There's no way they won't." He held up his bloody hands, seemed to recognize them for the first time. "Oh gods."

The puppy started snarling at the wood. Havilar shushed her, searching around. "The river's through those trees. Come on, let's get you clean. Stay here," she told the hellhound. She walked with Brin down to the muddy banks of the Immerflow. Here the river slowed as it straightened, deepened—easing around a flotilla of boulders. Havilar could imagine Irvel catching hold of one, forcing himself to swim to the next and the next until he could pull himself up the bank.

Brin stared at the rocks, and she wondered if he was imagining the same thing.

"I need to tell them. Tell them that he's dead," he murmured. "I really want to be alone for a moment." Terror arced through Havilar. She took his face in both hands.

"Brin, it's *not* over. We can make this work. We can fix this. I love you," she added, as if it were the magic words to keep him safe and sane.

He gave her a wan smile, his hand over hers. "I love you."

But what could they do? Havilar thought as she trudged back to where she'd left the puppy. How could she fight something when she couldn't even understand the rules?

All that was left was running—and running would haunt Brin forever, and mean she couldn't go back to Cormyr. Running meant nothing if the war wizards came after them.

She was so lost in her worries, she did not notice the hellhound until she let out a long, low growl. Moriah stood at the edge of the woods, just out of the chain's reach.

"About time!" Havilar said. "Where have you been? Where are the others?"

Moriah smiled. "He gave you gifts, didn't he?"

That strange prickle ran up Havilar's spine again. "Who? Brin?"

"They were supposed to be mine," Moriah went on. "I should have known he would know how to escape even this deal." She tilted her head. "You don't even know what you have. You think Crake was just a fool who said all the wrong things."

Havilar took a step back. "What did you do to Crake?"

"You didn't like being around him," Moriah said. "No—more than that. His presence was a *violation*. Your whole body rebelled at him, didn't it?"

Havilar didn't look away. "I don't know what you're talking about."

"He was a tiefling too—did you know that? Not the current sort, the older sort. The kind *he* tried to swallow up. But even a god can't decide what mortals summon up for their pleasures or others' pain." Moriah's dark eyes glittered in a way that eyes should not. "It was the Abyss in Crake. That's what made your skin crawl, that's what made your bones itch. A gift befitting the Chosen of the king of devils."

"I didn't kill him."

"Of course you didn't," Moriah said. "Because for all your wildness, girl, for all you'll accept the aid of the Hells and the presence of an enemy, you have *honor*." She shook her head slowly. "This isn't the fight for you."

The puppy's growl deepened, and the air *snapped* again—Mot and Dembo tumbling out of the air. Havilar didn't stop watching Moriah—the priestess only raised an eyebrow at the devils' sudden appearance.

"Are you *finally* done?" Mot asked. Dembo spotted Moriah and cursed.

"What in the name of churning Maladomini is *that?*" Dembo cried. The imps scrambled backward to hang in the air on either side of Havilar, behind the hellhound.

"Do you know her?" Mot asked. "Because she's not what you think she is. I bet." He wrung his tiny hands. "Unless you know what she is?"

"I got that she's not just human."

Moriah smiled at her. "But am I worse than making agreements with devils?"

"Whatever you heard, lady," Dembo snapped, "we're better than *you.*" He swung around to Havilar. "What do you need? You need something or we wouldn't have come."

"Something good," Mot said. "Something you can't do yourself."

Havilar looked over at the crumbling temple. "Can you resurrect someone?"

The imps looked at each other. "Maybe," Mot said. "But . . . not for free. Not *that* for free. We'd get in trouble."

"You said you could solve problems for me," Havilar said. "This is my problem. I have a dead man who needs very much to not be dead."

"Right," Mot said. "But there's problems and there's *problems*. Mucking with souls, that's getting into formalities and you don't want that."

"Don't do it," Moriah warned. "Devils will always bring you to ruin, no matter how clever you think you are or how stupid you think they are."

"Who are you calling stupid?" Dembo shouted.

"An imp cannot resurrect a mortal," Moriah went on. "No matter what they say. Leave the crown prince to his grave. Leave your young man to clean up his own mess—what do you think you owe him when he's been the inconstant one? When he can't even tell a woman he swears he doesn't love that it's all over? You have the whole world, your whole life ahead of you, and you've lost too much time already."

Havilar clutched her glaive tighter. "I love him," she started.

"And that's how devils claim you," Moriah finished.

"Oh, you should know about devils," Dembo said. "Where are your imps, huh? Huh?"

"Dembo," Mot said. "Maybe we shouldn't—"

"No!" Dembo snapped. "We got told to take care of this one. We don't have to take care of *all* of them. When you get down to it, they're all still mortals anyway, so nobody can say we don't know our place." He spat at Moriah's feet. "Leave our Chosen alone, lady."

"Yeah," Mot said, a little weakly. "Unless . . . you want to do the resurrecting?"

"Lords of the Nine she will!" Dembo snapped, and with another pop he was gone.

"Oh," Mot said. "Oh, oh, oh. This is going to be very good or very bad."

Havilar didn't look away from Moriah. "You're a Chosen of Asmodeus too."

Moriah sneered. "In a sense."

Then you shouldn't listen to her, Havilar thought. But why her and not the imps? Why any of them? She squeezed the glaive tighter and wished Farideh were there.

The imps don't make you feel like your skin's crawling off, she reasoned. And you need to save Brin.

Dembo returned, panting, in a little gust of flames and burning air. A heavy gold chain dangled from his tiny claws. He dropped it over her head.

"There!" he spat. "*That* will fix your problem. One emergency resurrection fit for a mortal—no strings. It's windfall from some temple sacking. Don't go blabbing that we gave it to you."

"That *he* gave it to you," Mot chimed in.

"And *don't* listen to this *crazy* witch," Dembo said. "Because we are very good at helping."

"Do you want us to take the warhound?" Mot asked.

"No," Havilar said. "I still need her."

"Fine," Dembo said. "Call us when you need something else."

"And think of smaller things," Mot suggested. "Just saying."

Moriah's eyes were colder than the river's flow as the imps departed, back to the Nine Hells. "You're making a mistake," she said. "I can offer you a much better trade."

"To resurrect Irvel?" Havilar asked. Moriah's mouth hardened. "Did you kill Crake?"

"A gnoll killed Crake," she said, but a cruel smile played at the corners of her mouth, and Havilar made up her mind.

"Stay," she told the puppy. "Don't let her out of your sight." She closed her hand around the amulet and headed back into the temple.

• • •

IRVEL OPENED HIS eyes, feeling as though he had slept for an eternity, dreamed for an eternity, and wasn't quite ready to wake up. The sound of running water came back to him, the cold rock underneath. The smell of rot and death. He sat up, surprised that nothing hurt, but not quite recalling why it should hurt . . . and found himself facing a young tiefling woman kneeling beside him and clutching a soot-streaked gold chain. She looked so completely terrified that Irvel's first instinct was to smile.

"It's all right," he said, and his voice cracked. "I don't bite."

She kept staring at him. "But are you all right?"

Irvel touched his stomach—that's right, he'd caught the sharp edge of a cracked boulder as they'd been carried down the river. Despite his best efforts the wound had festered, and then blood rot had quickened up his veins. The smell was him.

"Did you . . ." He pulled the torn and tattered, stained and spattered shirt away. The flesh was whole and smooth. How? "Did you use my healing draft?" Why hadn't he?

"No, I used a, um, an amulet. You didn't have anything like that."

Irvel blinked, and remembered pulling the healing potion free, the cold of the river sinking into his bones. Clinging to poor Illance and pouring the draft down his throat. But then it hadn't been enough. He'd dug the grave with a broken piece of the temple's roof, just beyond the river's reach.

"I'm Havilar," she said.

"Well met," Irvel said. "Did you come with the war wizards?"

"No," she said. "I came with Brin."

"Aubrin?" Irvel said. "Aubrin *Crownsilver?*"

A soft cry came from the back of the temple. Irvel looked up to see Aubrin rushing toward them. "You're alive? You're alive."

His cloak was soaked with mud, his cuffs spattered, and Irvel could not remember seeing his daughter's betrothed looking more like a man he'd call his brother-at-arms than in that moment. "Well met, son," he said, wishing Hal could see this.

A flicker of memory, the sense of standing beside Halance Crownsilver or something like him. The memory of being beside his father, but wholer somehow, stronger.

Aubrin pulled him to his feet. "Well met, my lord." He looked to the tiefling woman. "What happened?"

"I used an amulet," she said. She wet her lips as if to speak again.

"To heal him," Brin said. "You *healed* him with an amulet."

Irvel looked around the temple once more, feeling lighter than he had in years. "It's a good thing she did," he said. "I suspect I didn't have much longer." He smiled at the young man, but Aubrin didn't smile back.

Crownsilver blood, Irvel thought. So serious.

• • •

"To HEAL HIM," Brin said, staring at Havilar as though it would seal the words against her mouth. "You *healed* him with an amulet."

Havilar knew Brin wouldn't like that she'd gotten the amulet from the imps, not any more than he'd liked using the hellhound—but in both cases the end result was so much better than if she hadn't. She nearly said as much . . . but Brin's stare closed her mouth.

"It's a good thing she did," Irvel said. "I don't think I would have lasted much longer." He bowed his head to her. "You have my utmost gratitude, goodwoman."

"The rest . . . the rest of our party will be here shortly," Brin said, getting his footing again. "We have a little trail rations if you're hungry."

"Famished," said Irvel, striding ahead. The amulet seemed to have consumed all traces of injury and infection from him. "Can't wait to get to a proper village, have a proper meal."

"Havi, what did you do?" Brin breathed as they followed, letting Irvel get ahead.

"I brought him back," Havilar said.

"Did you not hear me?" Brin demanded. "You *can't* bring him back."

"I did, though!"

"No, I mean the law doesn't allow it. A resurrected Obarskyr goes to the end of the line of succession—now I *will* be king before Irvel. He's as good as dead to us."

"*Karshoj,*" Havilar said. "Are you *listening* to yourself? Maybe he won't be king, but he *does* get to see his family again." Brin had the decency to color at that.

"You're right," he said. He rubbed his hands over his face. "Forgive me, that was . . . I'm reeling a little, is all." He watched Irvel cross the clearing. "We can't tell him."

"I think he ought to know."

"He might want to," Brin said. "Or it might upset him—you *don't* resurrect nobles in Cormyr. And he'd ask where you got such magic, and I can't imagine he'd like the answer any more than I do."

Havilar scowled at him. "I got it from devils, but I didn't have to do anything and no one lost their soul."

"This time."

"This time is all we're talking about," Havilar said. "Fine—we keep it to ourselves. You can be a *little* happy I fixed this."

Brin shook his head. "Promise me you won't take anything else from those imps. That you won't make any more agreements."

"I haven't *made* any agreements." At least, she didn't think she had . . . But Farideh hadn't thought she was doing what she'd done when she'd made an agreement with Sairché. "I'm not going to promise *never,*" she said. "They've been useful twice, and what if they're useful again? But I will be more careful."

"No," Brin said. "Never. I think you owe me this much."

Havilar stopped, as startled as she'd be if he'd slapped her cheek. "I owe *you?* When you can promise me you won't run away or marry *her* or never ever make your mind up, then you can wring promises from me about not saving you."

Brin pursed his mouth. "Havi—"

"Watching Gods!" Irvel had stopped within sight of where the puppy was chained. "Is this your dog? What a beast he is!"

"Oh," Havilar said. The hellhound was still where she'd chained it, but Moriah was nowhere to be seen. "We have a big problem."

• • •

THE PRIESTESS WAS harder to control than her fellow had been, but Bryseis Kakistos had not wasted her time possessing the mortals. She had grown slowly stronger— strong enough to resist the priestess's efforts to shake her loose. She kept to the shadows, hiding the priestess under a blackberry bramble. Waiting for the crowd of adventurers to reach Havilar and Brin and the newly raised prince, listening to them curse Moriah's name and call for her. The woman called Moriah shuddered and wailed within her own mind, but Bryseis Kakistos paid her no attention. There was too much at stake.

She watched as they camped, as her great-great-granddaughter argued in hushed tones with her unworthy young man, who was furious about a used sending. They stood so close the ghost was tempted to flow into his mind, to get as close as she dared to her missing soul piece. Close enough to kill the young woman, close enough to seize her soul as it tried to flee, and bind it to her own . . .

No, she told herself. You are not that strong anymore.

Had she ever been that strong? Bryseis Kakistos couldn't remember, only the sound of a wail that pained a heart she would have claimed she didn't have, the feeling of a ghost struggling in her grip like a piece of living air.

You are not that strong, she told herself.

Why couldn't they both have been fevered? she thought. For simplest of all potential plans was the one where she asked the missing part of herself how Asmodeus could be brought down, and it answered. If she could only make the girl ill, so much trouble could be avoided.

The ghost crouched in the blackberries, waiting and thinking. After the sun rose, and the lot of them had gone, crashing back through the underbrush toward civilization again, Bryseis Kakistos forced the priestess to her feet.

The temple resisted her, but the blessings that repelled fiends and other fearful things, that blocked the prying eyes that might disrupt the peace of Eldath, were not meant to keep away the likes of Bryseis Kakistos. On the stones before the altar, a viscous mix of fluids, the remains of the diseased corpse that had just walked away, puddled in the cracks and shallows.

It became harder to force the priestess's feet as she realized what Bryseis Kakistos intended. One step, another—the ghost made the woman's knees buckle so she fell to the flagstones, forced her head down, down, the tip of her tongue trailing in the filth.

PART III

ANSRIVARR
THE BLADE OF MEMORY

. . .

The painting is simple—among the oldest in the palace. Faerlthann First-King in his armor, the greatsword clasped before him, point down. There is no great art here, nor need there be: here is the first king of Cormyr, the first sword of Cormyr, the first steps toward the Forest Kingdom's greatness and that is art enough. And in the great blade, which did not stop the massacre that led to Cormyr's founding, a reminder of the kingdom's frailty. Ansrivarr coronates all sovereigns of Cormyr, and reminds each that to survive, sacrifices must be made.

. . .

19

10 Eleint, the Year of the Nether Mountain Scrolls (1486 DR)
Suzail, Cormyr

L ORCAN HAD NOT TRAVELED FROM THE NINE HELLS TO TORIL WITH THE intention of sloshing down a crowded thoroughfare, but Farideh hadn't given him much of a choice. It was that, she said, or sit and wait for her to return, unless he wanted to go home. He did not want to go home, and he did not want to wait—the last time, that blasted dragonborn had come and annoyed him, and besides there was nothing to do in the tallhouse. If he was going to be bored, then better to be bored with Farideh, who could at least be provoked into entertaining him.

"I doubt you're willing to concede," he said as they walked, she cowled and cloaked, he disguised as a human, "but darling, you don't exactly have a plan here."

"No," Farideh admitted. "I'm going anyway."

Lorcan considered this. She was insistent that she was going to meet with Lady Helindra Crownsilver, Brin's great-aunt, who was the one who'd recalled all the servants in an attempt to get Farideh to leave, in order to ask about said servants, and she did not plan on telling Helindra why.

"Tell *me* why," Lorcan said. "What's so important?"

Farideh kept her eyes on the cobbles before them. "There's a plot," she said finally. "I think it involves one of her servants."

"A plot against who?"

"The Crown," she said.

"Well, there you are. Let them succeed and Havilar's problems are solved! Maybe they'll take out this great-aunt while they're at it." Would that count as a corrupting act? he wondered. It seemed likely. Especially if she let things continue in the hopes that the Lady Crownsilver or the princess would be killed. She could twist a lot of things into deeply unselfish acts, but Lorcan felt sure this time it would be impossible.

"Absolutely not," Farideh said. Then, "How is Havilar? Is everything all right?"

"Fine," Lorcan said. Was it fine? He couldn't remember when he'd talked to Sairché last. Time seemed to speed by on this plane, while in the Hells, Lorcan was dragged from cultist to archdevil to imp without end. If he had a moment, he came to Toril, to Farideh.

He couldn't pretend that sleeping with her would corrupt her, not to Glasya. But if Glasya's spies were watching, it would look enough like he was trying. He couldn't imagine Selûne appreciated the uses he'd found for her amulet, after all.

As they approached a huge gated manor, Lorcan raised an eyebrow. "Well. I see what your sister sees in the Tormite."

"If it were that, Helindra would have paid her off already." Farideh started toward the gate, but Lorcan stopped her.

"Why in the world would she see you?"

"Because," Farideh said, as if it were patently obvious, "I embarrass her. She wants me gone, not standing at her doorstep."

Lorcan nodded at the doorguards. "Do *they* know that? Come on, darling, let me show you how to embarrass a noble family."

It was not hard to guess that Helindra Crownsilver had more than one young man living in her household—nephews, grandnephews, grandsons, cousins, it hardly mattered. And at least one of them would be a rake, or feared to be a rake. Or maybe too quiet, too odd. One of them would leap to mind when a suave fellow leading a tiefling woman wearing a hood implied that he was missing coin for services rendered and very tired indeed of extending Lord Crownsilver credit. The doorguards could call him out, or he could call the Purple Dragons.

Or—exactly as he'd hoped—they would rush the two of them inside, calling for the Lady Crownsilver, who'd had quite enough of that young man's nonsense.

"Are you mad at me for letting them think you were a coinlass?" he asked once they were ensconced in a little parlor, quite crammed full of overthought furniture. Farideh hadn't blushed, then or now. She crossed to the fireplace, examining the row of portraits over it.

"Everyone in this town thinks I'm a coinlass," Farideh said, not looking away from the pictures. "If you want to be shocking, you're going to have to try harder."

That made him smile. "I could think of some terribly shocking things to do with you on this sofa."

She looked back at him, calm as could be. "Shocking to who?"

And *that* made him laugh. "Oh, have I bored you already, darling? Lucky for you I have plenty of other tricks to shock you with."

She didn't blush, but she smiled, as she turned back to the portraits. Lorcan frowned at the paintings—the first four were done in the same hand, four siblings approaching the same age. Late teens, he thought, early twenties. The last was the same age, a young man with hazel eyes, but while the painter had attempted to mimic the previous portraits' style, it was not the same hand. Much younger, Lorcan thought, and he wondered why they'd bothered.

"Have you used the soul sight on this Lady Crownsilver?" he asked.

"I'd rather not."

"So how are you going to get what you want?"

"I already know what she wants," Farideh said.

"You know what she *says* she wants," Lorcan pointed out. "Come on, darling, you know there's a difference." He nodded at the portraits. "Which one is she?"

Farideh tapped the frame of a young woman with pale, imperious eyes and dark hair. "It was a long time ago," she noted.

"Proud, I suspect," Lorcan noted. "Shrewd. Not the sort of opponent you ought to come up against without a plan. Where did you find out about this plot?"

"Harpers," Farideh said mildly.

Lorcan narrowed his eyes. "Harpers? Or Harper?"

"It's more than just Dahl involved, if that's what you're getting at."

Lorcan studied her—the set of her shoulders, her unwavering focus on the portraits, the tip of her tail flicking at the rug. Closed, he thought—but because Dahl was something he ought to worry about or because she was getting tired of him questioning her? "Come here," he said.

She came and sat down beside him, and his annoyance cooled a little. He brushed the hair off her cheek, and she did blush at that—Lorcan smiled. So odd.

"Why aren't the Harpers handling this?" he asked. "Where's Dahl?"

"I have no idea where Dahl is," she said. "They're not handling this because they don't know *how* to handle this. Helindra won't talk to them, and they can't get inside. They can make a guess, but it's not a good one—the servants don't want to talk about the family."

"So it's your problem?"

"I can do something about it," she pointed out. "So yes."

Lorcan considered her graceful neck and wondered how complicated it would be to use Dahl to corrupt her. Whatever she truly thought of the Harper, he clearly had a way of inspiring her into rash actions. But then he'd have to find a way to convince Dahl to take appropriate steps. Possible. Not pleasant.

Lorcan sighed. He knew the answer, and it was no answer he wanted: Havilar. If anything could lead Farideh to do something unforgivable, it was finding Havilar in peril. But if he did anything to put her into peril, Farideh would never forgive him.

And all that aside, if he managed to corrupt Farideh, to gain Glasya her soul, well and truly and without technicalities, then Farideh would certainly react—fleeing to the mercies of some greater god or off the edge of a cliff, it hardly mattered. Lorcan had come to realize that Glasya's demands would make him disappoint Asmodeus.

Better to look busy, he thought, running the back of one finger down her neck, and be prepared with multiple responses. Her breath hitched and Lorcan smiled.

"We'll have time after this, won't we?" she asked.

"As much as you like."

The door opened and an elderly woman, the imperious girl from the portrait tumbled down the long slope of life, strode in, leaning heavily on a silver-tipped walking stick. A coal-black gown covered her from neck to wrists, and a swath of amethysts hung around her throat so dark they made Lorcan think of Glasya's terrible gaze. More gems adorned her rings, humped like carbuncles over her thin fingers. Her pale eyes had lost none of their cold ferocity, as she looked Lorcan up and down like a gutted fish someone had left on her sofa.

"I trust since you were *kind* enough not to name which Lord Crownsilver you're accusing that we are early in this . . ." Farideh stood, and Helindra trailed off as she seemed to recognize the tiefling. Her eyes narrowed. "I see. My dear niece, Asmura, come to call."

"Well met," Farideh said. "And I'm sorry. That wasn't my idea."

"Was it your idea to play the part on the arm of that Waterdhavian merchant lord at the Kraliqhs' brightstarfeast? You may not be the initiator, but you are as culpable as dear Raedra in this. Sit down like a civilized person."

Helindra took the chair beside the fireplace, and Farideh sat back down on the sofa. "This is my friend," Farideh began.

"My dear, my time is short and my mind is quite filled with more important matters," Helindra said. "I don't care who he is, since I presume no one under my care owes him coin. Tell me what you want."

"There's someone on your staff that I need to find. A Sharran traitor."

Helindra's eyebrows rose. "I doubt that very much."

"So did the Kraliqhs."

Helindra tapped her fingers against the walking stick. "So this is Raedra's errand then? I suppose it is too much to ask to wait until we've all had our proper mourning, when Netherese are involved." She sniffed, and reached for the velvet rope behind her, one eye still on Farideh. "Is that why she's been so incautious, bringing you into the royal palace? Because you're her aide in this?"

"In a sense," Farideh said. "How did you find out?"

"A niece I've never heard of is flouncing around Suzail, I make certain I know who she is and why my good name is being risked. Tell me what you need."

"All the servants you've hired in the last two years, somewhere I can observe them. They don't need to see me, if you'd prefer."

Lorcan watched the old woman, waiting for her counterdemand. But she said nothing, only waiting for the jack who'd conveyed them to the room to come back. She asked him to track down a list of people and ask them to go to the main gallery and wait. Then to return when they were all found.

"Now, my dear," Helindra said once the jack had left, "I must ask you to do something for me. I fear that Raedra's ruse will not last. That you will be unmasked—an uncareful word, a bit of dispelling magic at the wrong time." She gave Farideh a very pointed look. "Pressure from someone who might prefer Raedra and Aubrin did not make a match with one another."

"She doesn't want to discuss it," Farideh said. "So I don't bring it up."

"But someone wants you to bring it up, don't they? I'm going to guess you've been approached by someone representing the Baron Boldtree, with a strong suggestion that you join forces?"

Beside Lorcan, Farideh stiffened. The cambion frowned. This was the first he'd heard of any baron, and that didn't bode well.

"Did he tell you that?" she asked.

"Erzoured does not tell me anything," Helindra said. "He does not have to. He tells Pheonard things, and Pheonard is generally a disappointment when it comes to subtlety. Now, Pheonard seems to believe that Aubrin's marriage shan't continue as planned. He is entirely giddy at the prospect, despite trying to seem concerned. I will spare you any attempts to descry what he's holding over you. Like as not, it's nothing I want to dirty my hands with." She regarded Farideh with a steely eye. "But I would encourage you to consider what you stand to lose compared to what Cormyr stands to lose, now that King Foril has left us. Raedra is regent. If Baerovus does not wake, she will be queen. Already the jackals circle, looking for the weakness in her. She needs no further scandal, no further marks against her authority. If the marriage doesn't go forward, Raedra is jeopardized."

"I should think it wouldn't matter," Farideh said. "Not in the middle of everything else."

"As much as I should like to tell you that all of Cormyr is aligned behind its monarch, there will always be those who take whatever chances avail themselves, regardless of the consequences. So for her sake, cement her fond feelings for Aubrin. Be certain that their marriage continues. I will give your sister all I promised—I don't wish her particular ill. But if you choose Erzoured Obarskyr over me, you will find you have miscalculated gravely."

"He's threatened to ruin me," Farideh said. Her tail lashed the sofa's feet. "What do you expect me to do?"

Helindra smiled thinly. "Be ruined," she said. "You do not want the alternative on your head." The jack returned and nodded once to Helindra. "Come along. Let's see if we can find your traitor."

The servants milled in an open gallery off the entranceway—eight altogether. Helindra led Farideh and Lorcan to a balcony that overlooked the space. From the shade of one column, Farideh studied the group, her face tense with concentration. Lorcan gave Helindra a brazen smile. It did not thaw her.

Farideh straightened with a noisy exhalation. "Is that all of them?"

"Every servant taken on in the last two years who is still employed here," Helindra said.

"Problem?" Lorcan asked.

"They aren't there," Farideh said. She squinted again, as if she might find what she missed.

"Then I trust you're satisfied that I am a little more careful with my hirings than Lady Kraliqh," Helindra said crisply. "Marlon will show you out."

"I don't suppose you're satisfied?" Lorcan said as they followed the jack down the stairs.

"There has to be one here," Farideh said.

"Because Dahl's never wrong?"

She didn't answer, lost in thought. She wouldn't leave it here—she never did. Lorcan tapped the jack on the shoulder. "When she thought I was looking for coin from someone, who did she think owed it to me?"

The jack's eyes darted to the stairs, as if he expected to see Helindra waiting there. "I'm sure I don't know, saer."

"Of course you do," Lorcan said. "A bright fellow like yourself in a house that talks as much as this one? It's not Lord Aubrin," he added, "though one might be tempted to assume. Lady Helindra has a son?"

"It . . . It would be unseemly for me to speculate."

"Who would *you* expect to owe coin to someone unsavory?"

"No one, saer," the jack said as they came to the door. "The family pays its debts."

"But if someone were not paying their debts?"

"Marlon," a man's voice called from the path. A middle-aged man with hazel eyes and the same severe features as Helindra Crownsilver was coming up the path, pulling gloves from his hands, while a servant tried to keep up with a canopy to keep the drizzling rain off. He looked Lorcan up and down—the fellow from the last picture, Lorcan realized. Pheonard. "Are we having company? Are you a friend of Naranthe's?" He spotted Farideh behind them. "Ah," he said. "My apologies."

"Lord Crownsilver," Marlon said with a little bow. As he straightened, he gave Lorcan a very significant look, and the cambion smiled.

"Come on, darling," he said, holding an arm out for Farideh. "We have much more interesting things to do." But as they passed, Farideh could not seem to take her eyes off Pheonard Crownsilver.

"Him," she said as they passed through the gates. "He's the one."

"A nobleman in league with Netheril?" Lorcan said.

"He's not . . . he doesn't have quite the same look. But the holes are there. Maybe he's just got different reasons." She bit her lip, deep in thought. "I could swear I've seen him before."

"In the portrait," Lorcan suggested. He tucked an arm around her waist. "Your task is through—now come on. I have to shock you before someone demands me back."

• • •

ILSTAN STEPPED FREE of a door hidden behind a panel at the end of the cellar, followed by a pair of Purple Dragons. Every trap and spell was in place—almost not worth the time to check, he thought as he strode down the passage. The Dragons did not follow.

Ilstan frowned back at them. "I have to check the wards on Faerlthann's Keep."

The guards traded glances. "We don't leave this post," the shorter man explained. "You'll pick up the Dragons at the post near the keep."

"Are you new?" the other, a young man with brown hair, asked amicably.

"No," Ilstan said. "These are simply not my usual duties."

"Right, what happened to War Wizard Abielard anyway?"

"I presume she's attending Princess Raedra in my stead," Ilstan said. "Good day to you." He swept down the corridor and on to his next task before the guardsmen could ask any more questions. When War Wizard Barcastle had pulled him aside the morning after the regency had been announced, Ilstan had been expecting a reminder that his duties had taken on new importance, or perhaps a reprimand that he had not in fact gone to speak with Ganrahast when he'd left Devora with Farideh.

"Princess Raedra will have a different set of guardians," the stout old woman told him instead. "You won't be needed."

Ilstan blinked. "Because she is regent now," he said. It made sense. She was Ganrahast's most important charge now. But the pit of his stomach dropped.

But the war wizard had hesitated, a gulf of indecision packed into that brief moment. "Yes," War Wizard Barcastle had said. "Not to worry, there is plenty for you to do here."

Ilstan had dwelled on that pause for three days now. He had watched the assignments given out—who was tasked with guarding the princess. Always Ganrahast. Always Glathra Barcastle. But the rest . . . they were nothing special.

The headache came on Ilstan, swift and sudden, as he walked back from the building known as Faerlthann's Keep, the original palace of Suzail. He'd felt it buzzing in his brain as he checked the old tower's wards, vital protections against the strangeness of the haunted wing spilling out. The pain felled him to his hands and knees, turned his vision into a scramble of broken images—

An old man watched him, as though he somehow stood opposite Ilstan, buried in the grass . . . *I gave Her my whole life, every part . . . but there is no protecting against all dangers, even when you have the powers of the divine . . . who could predict an archdevil from the heavens' heights?*

It vanished as suddenly as it had come on, and Ilstan sat back on his heels, panting.

She's in danger, he thought. He was sure. That was what the voice meant. Raedra was in danger, and she didn't know it. He had to stop it.

His feet carried him unerringly to Raedra's rooms. As he reached them, he glimpsed her, ushered down the hall by Ganrahast himself, solemn and lovely in muted violet mourning. She looked up at him, and Ilstan nearly called out to her. But as their eyes met, she turned swiftly to speak to Ganrahast, a litany of schedules and names meant, clearly, to deflect Ilstan. He bowed as the regent passed, never once stopping.

She had ignored him completely.

"An armband ought to be enough," he heard Varauna complaining from behind him. She and Florelle came out of the princess's door, dressed in solid black gowns. "I look like I'm either going to raise up a ghoul or turn into one myself when I wear black."

"I think it's proper to show the king respect," Florelle said, a little loftily.

"I'm no sadder for looking ill." Varauna stopped as she spotted him. "Well met, Ilstan."

"Are you well?" Florelle asked. "We've been wondering where you'd gotten to."

Ilstan shook his head. "Do you know why Her Highness has requested I be put on other duties?"

Both noblewomen's faces went carefully blank. "I can't imagine why," Florelle said.

"Perhaps it was the Mage Royal's decision," Varauna said.

"Something's changed," Ilstan said. "She won't speak to me, and I need her to know . . . Something's happening."

"Many things are happening," Varauna said. "If you hadn't noticed."

"That's not what I meant!" Ilstan said, feeling suddenly, unavoidably aware of how easily his spells would tear through Varauna. "She's changed. Something's changing her."

"Perhaps she's just getting a better measure of those around her," Varauna said.

"No, he's right." Florelle glanced around. "Honestly?" she said. "I think it's Asmura. Did you notice everything changed when she started coming around?"

"Yes," Ilstan said. The tiefling—it had to be the tiefling.

"And," Florelle went on, "Asmura's friends with Lord Ammakyl, that Waterdhavian nobleman that everyone says is part *drow*."

Varauna snorted. "Thank the gods, Florelle, I never laid any coin on your having reached the full depths of your stupidity. No one with any brains thinks Lord Ammakyl is a drow."

"I said *part* drow," Florelle shot back. "And last tenday you couldn't stand her."

"I didn't say that," Varauna replied. "I said she was dull and uninteresting, and that she oughtn't have promised Wroth cards if she wasn't going to bring them."

"I doubt her as well," Ilstan said. "I don't think the princess realizes what she's dealing with."

"Then you are both ninnies," Varauna declared. "Sulue betrayed her, her father died, her brother is in a coma, and now her king is dead. Raedra's acting odd? Who wouldn't?" She fixed a sharp eye on Ilstan. "And I would say doubting the *regent's* mind as though she is a child in need of guidance, treads terribly close to the sort of talk the Mage Royal would not like to hear."

"He's questioned *your* presence time enough," Ilstan said hotly. A burst of flames, a word of destruction, a gesture, and she'd be transmuted into something small and harmless.

Varauna pressed a delicate hand to her bosom. "How sweet," she said. "I never knew he cared."

"You need to get Raedra to talk to me," Ilstan said. "It's vital. She doesn't know what she's doing, pushing me out."

Varauna raised one inky eyebrow. "Somehow I think she might. Come on, Florelle. Raedra needs us." The noblewomen walked away, leaving Ilstan alone to master the spells that were dancing on his fingertips.

• • •

TWELVE DAYS AFTER Havilar had decided to act like the doomed heroine of a chapbook, Brin followed Irvel along the banks of the Wyvernwater, trailed by the two remaining mercenaries, Mehen, and Havilar leading the hellhound.

"Is that dog part dire wolf?" Irvel asked him. "I swear it gets bigger every time I look at it."

"Who knows?" Brin said. "Better than some other options."

Irvel's teeth gleamed in the setting sun. "I won't call this a blessing—not given poor Darclant's death. But it's certainly opened my eyes on one matter." He clapped Brin on the shoulder. "Your father would have been proud of you. And I'll be proud to call you my son-in-law."

Brin thanked him, but he doubted anyone knew what Halance Crownsilver would think of his only son resurrecting an Obarskyr.

Or using a hellhound to find Irvel. Or having the Harper contacts to even get that far, for that matter. Bringing along Havilar, wanting her more than the Princess of Cormyr, a woman Brin should have been raised alongside—all of these things would have been too outlandish for Halance Crownsilver to fathom having an opinion about, in life.

At eight, Brin had high hopes of growing into a version of his father—and had only just begun to modify that vision, when Halance Crownsilver had fallen to assassin's arrows, Brin would never be so boisterous. He would never laugh so loud. He would never want to go hunting as often as his father did. But it never occurred to him to think Halance wouldn't always love him and think the world of him.

And now? Now he didn't know.

He couldn't have said what Constancia would think—he imagined seeing her again with Irvel in tow, knowing he had been right and the crown prince had been in need of rescue. He imagined Constancia seeing Havilar and the hellhound she wouldn't get rid of, discovering the truth about the resurrection.

He imagined, too, Constancia not knowing, *never* knowing, carrying that secret to the grave.

The laws about resurrection spells were, as many laws in Cormyr, tortuous and specific, crafted in reaction to ten thousand crises no one wanted to repeat. A resurrected noble lost all of their blood rights. Except a resurrected Obarskyr lost their place in the line of succession. Except a resurrected monarch was immediately deposed, magically neutered, and exiled from Cormyr, their would-be benefactor executed as a traitor.

At least he isn't king, Brin thought.

The sun had sunk beyond the edge of the trees on the horizon, setting the low, patchy clouds ablaze in orange and gold and magenta. It would be dark by the time they reached Hultail—a blessing, Brin thought. They could hide the damned hellhound more easily, forestalling the inevitable questions about its parentage.

He looked back at Havilar, talking quietly as she walked with Mehen, the dog still trotting alongside her. She looked up at him and felt the same divide of loyalties—wanting to take her hand in his and reassure her that he was with her, that everything would be all right; wanting to stay beside Irvel, to make it clear that keeping the hellhound *was* a betrayal.

"She makes me feel safer," Havilar had said.

Safer than you ever could make her feel, Brin thought. They hadn't found Moriah. They hadn't figured out why she'd said the things she had, whether the imps had been truthful when they called her a Chosen of Asmodeus. Between Moriah's betrayal and Crake's, Havilar wouldn't come any nearer to Kallan than she had to, even if Mehen was talking to him. Who knew, Brin supposed, whether he might be next?

Desima, on the other hand, seemed to have become her special companion. The wizard was always hovering near to Havi—unless she had wandered off entirely. Brin had decided if Desima was going to wander off, he wasn't going to wait for her, and to his surprise, Havilar agreed.

"Just look at that," Irvel said, stopping to admire the sunset over the calm lake. "Beautiful. You'd never know Shade was bent on destroying it." He looked down at Brin. "How bad have things gone since I got lost?"

"Bad," Brin said. "There's goblins and Shadovar all over Cormyr. Arabel is safe enough, but so cut off that could change in a heartbeat. We'll have to be careful once we get to the Way of the Manticore."

"Headed for Wheloon, no doubt," Irvel said grimly. "Unleashing their fellows."

Out of the gloaming, a dark shape cut away the blaze of the sunset. A frisson of terror prickled over Brin, even before he realized the shape was a black dragon. All instinct, every one of the party flattened to the grassy ground as the wyrm flew past, winding over the Wyvernwater.

"Holy Beshaba, pass us up," Irvel breathed.

"*Vutha*," Kallan spat. "It would be. Any idea where it lairs?"

Brin swallowed. "I don't know of any dragons around here."

A piercing roar echoed over the lake as the dragon flew toward the King's Forest, off to the west.

"The *vutha* are little better than scavengers," Kallan said. "Maybe it's just drawn to the battlefields."

"Likely," Irvel said, but Brin could hear the past in his voice, the coiled fear of a black dragon, so old its scales had become tinged violet, that lay in the heart of every Cormyrean.

• • •

RAEDRA'S MOUTH WAS already full of angry words when she burst through the doors to the White Stag Chamber, startling the overswords and battlemasters, their lieutenants and aides already assembled there as they leaned around a large table spread with maps. On the far side of the room, Erzoured straightened as she entered.

"They are *clearly* in league with Shade," a man—a Huntcrown—shouted at the suddenly quiet room.

"Your Highness," the Lord Warder said. Fresh from the Sembian battlefields, Vainrence's robes were muddied and streaked with soot. "Lord Ganrahast." The bows came sudden and sheepish, one synchronized dip.

"Why," Raedra said, cold and calm, "is my war council meeting without me?" A pause, time for her to consider each and recall their names.

"Apologies, Your Highness," Oversword Gerain Huntcrown, a narrow-shouldered man with a tendency to spit as he talked, said. "Circumstances are growing dire."

"I thought you'd been sent for," Battlemaster Pierrick Cormaeril said, looking a bit like a befuddled sheepdog with his bushy beard and thick brows. "What was that jack doing if not going to fetch Her Highness?"

"You're here now," said Erzoured. "Shall we catch you up?"

Raedra bit her tongue. This was not the first time such a meeting had convened without her presence. Always with apologies and protestations of innocence. Always with "well, you're here now."

"Start from the beginning," she said.

"Of course, Your Highness," Oversword Elmaina Greatgaunt, a woman of impressive stature and large teeth, said. With a wooden pointer, she gestured at the map, to a city midway between Sembia and Suzail: *Wheloon*. She'd no more than touched the spot when dread unfolded like a beast from the shadows in Raedra's heart.

"The Warden of the Eastern Marches managed to get word to us that he believes that Lady Marsheena's army is headed for Wheloon," Oversword Greatgaunt said. "We believe she intends to breach the walls, to gain reinforcements from the gangs within."

"She's going to unlock the shadow fiends!" cried Oversword Huntcrown.

"Shadow fiends?" Ganrahast repeated. He frowned at Vainrence, who merely shrugged.

"That Shadovar bitch will be the end of us if we don't stop her," Huntcrown went on.

"How do you propose we do that?" Raedra asked.

The oversword regarded her, not a little smugly. "Gather the war wizards. Wipe Wheloon from the map once and for all. Nothing else will stop her."

"As I pointed out," Vainrence said, "we don't have that sort of magic to spare.""Moreover," Ganrahast said, "even if we seize on the repaired Weave, we could easily find that sort of magic going awry. It could burn the whole of the Hullack down and boil away the Wyvernwater."

"Which is all well beside the point," Battlemaster Cormaeril said. "Wheloon has always been a blight on our history. There are upward of three thousand people trapped in that city—and not only could no one prove every one of the original inhabitants was deserving of imprisonment, in fifteen years Wheloon has seen an entire generation of children born. Would you condemn them too?"

"Do you think that mating a Sharran to a Sharran produces a monarchist somehow?" the Oversword snorted. "If it cannot be done by magic, then we must send troops and war wizards to soften Marsheena's blow at least.

"The Army of the Eastern Marches has their hands full at Arabel," Oversword Greatgaunt continued. "The Army of the Purple Dragon remains in Sembia. We don't have the soldiers to spare, either to attack or to aid."

"And we have few war wizards to spare," Ganrahast said. "You've been running through them rather cheaply of late."

"What says our regent?" Erzoured said. His dark eyes pinned Raedra. "Now, if ever, this war council could use some royal wisdom."

Raedra did not look away from his dark gaze. He meant to humiliate her. He meant to make her fumble. And gods help her, she well might. She considered the map spread out before her. "None of these plans will do," she said.

Oversword Greatgaunt laughed suddenly. "Highness," she said, "please. You are not choosing dresses. Lives are at stake."

"Precisely," Raedra said. "They deserve a little consideration." She glared at Erzoured. "Not merely to be used in your games of position."

"Time is of the essence," Battlemaster Cormaeril began.

"How long until the Shadovar army reaches Wheloon?"

Oversword Greatgaunt hesitated. "A day, perhaps two."

"Then unless you have been keeping some magical source to move an army six times its natural speed," she said, archly, "there is nothing to be done that cannot be done tomorrow."

"Highness," Oversword Huntcrown said, the chiding tone in his voice enough to make Raedra wish she could order him thrown over the walls and into Wheloon. "You must choose."

"Am I not enunciating clearly enough?" Raedra asked. "Go home, saers. I will have an answer for you tomorrow."

The war council stared at her a moment, as though she would concede to joking. But when Raedra didn't budge, didn't so much as blink, they took up their things, and muttering to one another, left the room. Vainrence shot Ganrahast a look full of significance, and vanished from the room.

Ganrahast remained, watching Raedra with a stern expression and one raised eyebrow.

"What?" she snapped. "What is it?"

"With all due respect," Ganrahast said, "you are not your grandfather's cheeky bird anymore."

Raedra colored. "Did I give you a different impression?"

"You give me the impression of a young woman who thinks she has to squeeze respect from her advisors like blood from a stone," he said. "Who does not know her own worth or power."

Raedra regarded Ganrahast levelly. "Well," she said finally, "I shall hardly get much done with them acting as though I wouldn't want to interrupt my embroidery with something as crass as a war council."

"Then dismiss them," Ganrahast said. "If they do not respect the Regent of Cormyr, then there is no room for them in her war council."

Raedra sighed. "Grandfather trusted them. They know what they're doing. If I sack them, it will only look as though I don't."

"In his younger days, your grandfather spent most of these meetings prodding them into arguing with one another. 'Let them find the holes in their own plans. They know best after all.'" He sighed. "I'm afraid as things have gone on, he demurred more and more to these fractious voices."

"Do you think I should listen to them?"

"Yes," Ganrahast said. "But then I think you should make up your own mind."

Raedra picked up one of the troop markers. "A pity I wasn't allowed in Baerovus's warcraft lessons," she said. "Is it wrong to hope I stop looking like a fool before he wakes?"

"I have never seen you set yourself to a topic and fail to grasp it swiftly," Ganrahast said. "Given motivation and a suitable tutor."

Raedra considered the maps, tapping the marker against the edge of the table. It was too much to hope that her war council would be those tutors, not after today. She knew that edge, that quiet—they'd want to see her fall first, to learn her lesson about giving them their due before anything else. There was no time for that. She needed a tutor who wouldn't coddle her and wouldn't trip her up—and fast.

"I want to leave the palace," she said after a moment. "*Quietly.*"

Ganrahast tugged on his russet beard. "You know I won't let you go alone."

"I do," Raedra said. She gathered up the wooden markers. "So kindly make an effort not to frighten my friend, please."

20

19 Eleint, the Year of the Nether Mountain Scrolls (1486 DR)
Suzail, Cormyr

F ARIDEH SPRINTED DOWN THE HALLWAY AS THE KNOCKS ON THE DOOR pounded harder. Dumuzi leaned down the stairs. "I have it," she called. "Sorry." She pulled her dressing gown closer around her and opened the door. There was no one at the door. She stuck her head out, into the rain, searched the little yard along the gated path, the street beyond. Nothing.

Farideh cursed at a night of interruptions. She latched the door and turned to find herself standing face-to-face with a robed man with a red beard. She yelped and the powers of the Hells poured down her arms. The man raised a hand, spat a word, and a bubble of force surrounded her, slamming her back against the door. From the top of the stairs, she heard Dumuzi cry out. Without looking back, the wizard reached over his shoulder, hand crackling with a new spell.

"I wouldn't," he said in a deep voice.

"Damn it, I asked you not to frighten her." Raedra stepped out from behind the wizard. "My apologies," she said. "We had to sneak."

Farideh pushed the magic back down, shook the flames from her hands. A moment later the shielding spell evaporated. Farideh looked from Raedra to the imposing wizard and back. Dumuzi hung on the stairs, ready to spring over the bannister. "It's all right," she said. To Raedra, "What are you doing here?"

Raedra pursed her mouth. "I need a favor." She gestured to the wizard. "This is Lord Ganrahast, the Royal Magician, by the way. He doesn't feel I can be trusted to not die."

"Well met," the wizard said.

"Well met." Farideh wet her mouth. "I wasn't trying to hurt her. You just startled me—"

"Better to be safe than sorry," Ganrahast said. "You should know there are four highknights stationed in and around this tallhouse."

Farideh's stomach plunged. "I . . . I have a guest. In the library. Are they going to bother him?"

"Not if he doesn't try to leave."

Farideh opened her mouth to protest, then thought better of it. The Regent of Cormyr and the Royal Magician were standing in her hallway—of course they had guards.

"They won't bother us," Raedra said. "Or your not-quite-brightbird."

Farideh considered the wizard again, every one of Brin's and Dahl's and Constancia's warnings about the war wizards coming back to her. "This is Kepeshkmolik Dumuzi, son of Uadjit," she said, gesturing up at the dragonborn. "He's staying with me."

"Well met," Raedra said. "Now, Ganrahast, I think it best—"

"Before you ask, Your Royal Highness," he said, "I'm not going to sit in the parlor while you discuss things."

Raedra's brows rose. "Are you sure? We may drift to girlishly uncomfortable topics."

"I am one hundred and thirteen years old," Ganrahast said. "I was raised by five extraordinary women. I daresay I could think of 'girlish' things to make you uncomfortable long before you could make me so."

Raedra snickered. "Do you have a large table?"

"In the kitchen," Dumuzi said, coming down the stairs. "Your Royal Highness."

"Go back to bed," Farideh said.

Dumuzi didn't budge. "*I am not taking your coin to sleep,*" he said in Draconic. "*She has plenty of guards and guardians. You should have at least one, since you don't seem to have plans to tell—*"

"Fine," Farideh said in Common. "Assuming it's all right with the Royal Magician? This way."

In the kitchen, Ganrahast plucked a series of maps and several small bags of wooden markers out of the ether. Dumuzi stood against the pantry. Farideh dug out a bottle of wine and several goblets, wondering as she poured what Raedra was thinking. Raedra stared at her all the while. Farideh pulled her dressing gown closer. "If it bothers you, I suppose we could discuss your wizard disguising me."

"My apologies." Raedra set more of the markers on the maps. "I suppose I've gotten used to 'Asmura.' I keep thinking you might take the horns off any moment. But that's my mistake."

Farideh handed her one of the goblets. "What's your trouble?"

"I have a war council I may have . . . insulted. I need to come up with a military plan by tomorrow morning. And you, I recall, have a special interest in old battles and tactics."

"You want me to help you craft a battle plan?" Farideh said. "Are you mad?" She looked to Ganrahast. "Why not ask him? A hundred and thirteen years has to know more than a little about war."

"We all choose where our interests lie," the wizard intoned.

"It's not going to get anyone killed," Raedra protested. "If I'm wrong . . .well, you can be certain my war council will let me know and put a halt to it. And possibly throw the whole country into civil war for the trouble," she added, with that bitter humor she had when she was nervous. Farideh sat at the table.

"I can't promise you anything," she started.

"All I want is for you to tell me if I'm being a fool," Raedra said. She set the markers in place—a red cluster near *Arabel*, a black cluster near *Wheloon*, a line of purple near *Saerloon*, a small grouping of gold in *Suzail* and more scattered through the countryside.

"Wheloon is a prison," Raedra explained. "Fifteen years ago, the Purple Dragons uncovered a shocking number of Sharrans in that city, allied with Risen Netheril and plotting against Cormyr. Walls were raised by royal decree, sealing the city with all of its inhabitants inside."

"All the *Sharran* inhabitants?"

"*All* the inhabitants," Raedra said. "No one wanted to take the chance. It's only recently that people have been saying that might not have been the wisest course. That perhaps the Crown committed a grave error in acting so swiftly. But most people still remember their crimes." Farideh frowned at the city. "So it's dangerous."

"Likely," Raedra said. "But it's been fifteen years. There are children in Wheloon who have never known another world. And *that* is a grave error." She pushed the black markers closer. "Shade's army is making for Wheloon. There's no doubt they intend to take it."

"What resources does it have?"

"Sharrans," Raedra said. She frowned back at Ganrahast. "What was that about shadow fiends?"

Ganrahast sighed heavily. "Rumor and hearsay. It is simpler for the people of Wheloon to be invented monsters—and to be precise, there is no such thing as a shadow fiend. If there are shadow *demons* in Wheloon, I will swallow a wand whole."

"Not much else," Raedra said.

"'Nala and the Ten Thousand Shadows' come to life," Farideh murmured.

Behind her, Dumuzi laughed. Raedra and Ganrahast started at the sound.

"What does that mean?" Raedra said.

"It's an ancestor story," Farideh said. "A kind of dragonborn nursery tale. Nala Who-Would-Be-Verthisathurgiesh freed her family and two others from Morthongiarimyth, the Starshine Duke. She made the dragon fear creatures seeping out of the shadows by playing light off of stones, until he went mad."

"'And lo, the wyrm looks on the plane,'" Dumuzi said. "'In every crevice hides a shadow, by every stone his death is waiting. *Where can I flee?* the Starshine Duke cries in his madness.'"

"'*Only the light may save you,* Clever Nala tells him,'" Farideh finished with a smile. "'*Fly! Fly! into the sun's embrace.*' They're trying to frighten you," she told Raedra. "Shade doesn't gain much from breaching Wheloon—"

"They free their fellows," Ganrahast said.

Farideh shrugged. "Do they care about that? All the Shadovar and Sharrans I've ever crossed paths with think only of themselves or else of destruction. They don't strike me as the sort to gather up lost followers. And," she went on, "if it's a prison, I assume you take care of the food. I don't expect the city is full of well-fed, well-exercised soldiers. It might look like a run for reinforcements, but the kind of reinforcements Shade would get aren't worth the grain it would take to keep them fed. They're trying to scare you by unleashing 'shadow fiends.' I assume she's been heading for Suzail? That's what the rumors say."

"Ever south," Raedra said. "And seemingly everywhere."

"You might consider surrender if Shade rode to Suzail at the head of all your childhood nightmares," Farideh said. "Wouldn't you think?"

Raedra peered at the map, deep in thought. "Lady Marsheena's clever," she said. "She's the one who stirred up the goblins and gnolls and things, incited the Stonelands to pour out and ravage the countryside. Whatever damage a band of goblins can do, the stories are worse. And she always leaves survivors, people to carry the story ahead of her army. We think she's breaking her force as well, so they can attack all sorts of settlements while the bulk of the army captures the Way of the Manticore."

"It's not wise," Dumuzi said. "She gives you time to muster your forces."

"Our forces are defending Arabel," Raedra said. "And holding the line in Sembia. We are quite short of forces." She wrapped a braid around her fingers. "Meanwhile, 'capitulation' is no longer treated like a treasonous utterance."

"Who wants you to capitulate to Shade?" Farideh asked.

"Just mutterings," Raedra said. "The nobles know that whichever of them throws over stands to gain a great deal from Shade—so long as they don't leap for the spoils too early, or care about morals and such."

"*Karshoj*," Farideh spat. "That's repulsive."

"I would agree."

"Can't you call them out? Punish the ones saying that? Why do they get away with being so terrible?"

"They have power in exchange for the services they provide the Crown. Like collecting taxes, protecting the villages and cities where their lands are. Riding out in times of war."

"There are an awful lot of them sitting around the city if that's the case."

Raedra sighed. "It's just the way things work. The majority of the nobles do their duty, but more and more of late wait until they are forced from their comforts."

"That's hardly fair," Farideh said. "Maybe I don't understand Cormyr, but when they keep their wealth and their fancy houses and their lands and their titles, and all the while the people they're supposed to take care of are fleeing gnolls and having their homes destroyed, I don't think it's working very well. Why should they keep those things if they won't do their duty?"

The Regent of Cormyr considered the map, tapping her fingers against the Sea of Fallen Stars. "That's . . . a very good point," she said. She hummed to herself.

"And it would be compelling, to say the least." A small secretive smile played on her mouth. "If I offered you land," she said to Farideh, "do you think you'd march?"

"No," Farideh said. "I don't think I'd do well, a tiefling among an army of humans."

"But if, say, we were all tieflings. Land would be a good reward. Good land, plowed and cleared already?"

"What's your plan?" Farideh asked.

"The refugees," she said simply. "It occurs to me, now, that there's another army in Suzail, who could be ready to march, given the proper motivations." She looked back to Ganrahast. "How many war wizards can be spared?"

"Perhaps one or two. You'll need a few Dragons. And someone to lead the thing."

"Oh, I'll have more than a few captains."

"You won't have time to train them," Farideh pointed out.

"Which is why they can't be asked to do anything too complicated," Raedra said. "They sweep for refugees, help them back to Suzail. Cut down Marsheena's skirmishers." She bit her lip. "We can arm some of them—most of them, maybe. Maybe a benefit for those who bring their own."

She scrawled notes on the maps, asking questions of Farideh and Ganrahast and even Dumuzi, putting scenarios to them, and polishing off her glass of wine, and then a second. Farideh tipped the end of the bottle into her own glass.

"I'm sorry," she said when Raedra had grown quiet and thoughtful again, "about your grandfather."

"Thank you," Raedra said. She set down the stylus, drank a little more wine. "I keep thinking how sad it is that he won't have . . . well, he wouldn't have an ancestor story like that. He was a good man, and not a bad king, just . . . the gods handed him a lot of havoc. It seems like he spent his whole reign trying to fix things that kept falling apart. Maybe that's all anyone does as king, I don't know."

"Sometimes I think that's all anyone can do," Farideh said.

"He listened," Raedra said. "I always noticed that. And he tried so hard to protect everyone. He *loved* his people, his family." She sighed heavily. "Any other king and Aubrin would have gotten a dukedom, a thousand gold a year, and a pat on the head. But Granddad . . . he loved his brother, he loved his nephews. The games of the nobles and the way things have always been done didn't matter."

"He sounds like a good man," Farideh said.

Raedra smiled sadly and drank a little more wine. "He *never* wanted me to rule. Neither did my father. They didn't think I had the temperament." She blew out a breath and wiped her eyes, suddenly overcome. "Gods," she said in a choked voice. "I'm so tired."

Farideh ignored the wizard and the dragonborn, the vast gulf between them and the ever-present specter of Brin. She came around the table and sat beside the regent, embracing her and tucking Raedra's head against her shoulder, beneath the curve of her horn. Raedra stiffened, then relaxed, hugging Farideh tightly.

"If Baerovus doesn't wake up," she whispered, "I don't know what I'll do."

"Scrub Shade from the maps? Make your own ancestor story in his honor?" Farideh said. Raedra chuckled. "I'll help."

"You are the strangest friend I have ever had," Raedra declared, releasing Farideh. "But I'm glad of you."

Erzoured's threats swept through Farideh's thoughts, chased by Helindra's. "I'm glad we're friends," Farideh said. "I don't have many." She hesitated. "Can I ask you something? Do you love Brin?" Raedra's expression closed, swiftly as a slammed door. "I'm not asking," Farideh said, "if you'd break your engagement. I just wondered if you loved him."

Raedra looked over the maps, as if she were searching for Brin among the painted roads and trees. "I could have, I think," she said. "But not now, not anymore. Not when I've seen how selfish he can be, how *foolish*." She sipped the wine. "Not that it matters."

"I'm not going to tell you what to do with Brin," Farideh said. "Only, I think you should know . . . Erzoured wants me to convince you not to marry him."

Raedra's eyes narrowed. "Does he now?"

"And Helindra Crownsilver has told me to make certain you *do* marry him, to save your reign from scandals."

"Pah!" Raedra snorted. "As if she wouldn't be happy to spread scandal if it were any other family's son. Why are you telling me this?"

"Because you should know. Because I don't want to play these games. Because I think either of them could make trouble for me—or you—and I don't think that's very fair." She sighed. "I suppose this happens to you a lot more. Brin always made it sound as if it were like breathing in Cormyr."

"Not quite," Raedra said. Then, "Perhaps for him. He's in a more complicated position. Is he an Obarskyr or not? Is he an heir or not? Where does that put him for the Crownsilvers? His grandmother's husband," she pointed out, "was the eldest son. If he's a Crownsilver, not an Obarskyr, then he's the head of the family, not Helindra. But he's not a Crownsilver by blood—he just styles himself that way because it's what he's used to—and the old lord Crownsilver never named him as an adopted heir—his father's brother was meant to be the heir, but then he was killed. So where does Aubrin belong? I imagine the sort of snares that lie in the path of the throne *are* doubled for Aubrin."

That question again—*where do you come from*? What lay growing in your bones from birth, and what was scribed on your heart by life? Farideh drained her glass and took a little comfort in the buoyant feeling of wine diluting her own cryptic blood.

"It's getting late," Raedra said. "And you have your mysterious guest to attend to."

Farideh looked away. "And my books. I *must* have an answer for you by the end of the tenday—I'm running out of pages."

"An answer to what, pray tell?" Ganrahast said.

Raedra stood, her expression a mask. "A puzzle," she said lightly. "Come along. I need to prepare before tomorrow." She gathered the maps and markers for the wizard to tuck away into the subtle folding of the plane. Ganrahast kept watching Farideh with a thoughtful expression.

"It doesn't seem like the Baron Boldtree to ask for such a boon without a way to be certain that he gets it," he said, almost conversationally.

"He threatened me," Farideh agreed, though she did not elaborate on the threat. Raedra and Ganrahast left the kitchen, and by the time Farideh and Dumuzi had followed them out, they had vanished completely from the tallhouse, the bolt untouched.

"The door works fine," Dumuzi sniffed.

"Do you think it'll succeed?" Farideh asked. "The conscription and everything?"

"Depends on whether they fight like Verthisathurgiesh or like Fenkenbradon," Dumuzi said, not bothering to explain what he meant to Farideh. He bid her good night and headed back up the stairs.

Farideh longed to follow him, to collapse onto the feather mattress and just sleep. The hour was late and growing later. Instead, she fetched another bottle of wine and glasses, and went back to the little library.

"Sorry, I took a little long," she said.

Dahl looked up from his seat beneath the window box. "I heard," he said. "Sounded interesting."

"You could have come out," Farideh said.

"I could have," he agreed, turning another page of the Waldbrudge book. "But my cover's already thin, as it is. I don't need the Royal Magician prying. What did they want?"

Farideh told him about the maps and the armies, about Raedra's war council and the plan she'd drawn together. Dahl raised an eyebrow.

"Do you know when she's going to announce that?"

Farideh shook her head. "It sounds like soon, but she has to make sure of some things first. A few days?"

Dahl set the book aside. "I might be able to help with it. Put some of the refugees in the right frame of mind, anyway."

"Anything will help." She sat down just past him, pouring them both a little wine. "How long do you think we have?"

"A month at best," Dahl said. "It's a wonder to me that you don't see more people fleeing Suzail."

"Where else are they going to go?" Farideh asked. "Who else is going to save them?"

"Well, not the Chosen of Helm, Amaunator, Sharess, Velsharoon, Enlil, or Garl Glittergold," he said. He took a swallow of wine and grimaced. "Damned Vescaras. I used to like Arrhenish just fine."

Farideh brushed the thin page over, revealing a new set of glyphs. *Acorn. To grow. To unseat? To upset? Dweomerheart.*

"Would you give me the drawing?" she asked, holding out a hand to Dahl.

Instead he took her hand in his. "I thought you were going to get this fixed." He rubbed a thumb over the third knuckle of her left hand, the finger that Adolican Rhand had removed as punishment, that Sairché's Hellish healing magic had regrown, corpse white beside its bronzed mates.

"I haven't had a chance," she lied.

He didn't let go of her hand. "How much did Brin and the rest of them leave you with? It wouldn't be terribly expensive."

"I don't know how long they'll be gone," she pointed out. She yanked her hand back. "I have to make a little coin last as long as possible. It's not as if I can go become a shopmistress or a fishmonger or something. If you say 'festhalls,'" Farideh warned, "I will break that bottle over your head."

Dahl grinned. "I wouldn't think of it." He nodded to her hand. "Can I see it a moment? I might be able to do something."

She laid her hand in his, as if setting it into a pile of coals, and Dahl just held it, considering the bleached finger. He had nice hands, Farideh thought.

Suddenly, Dahl pulled her hand across him, dunking her finger up to the knuckle in the inkpot on the floor beside him. She yelped and pulled away, spattering ink across the both of them, and the carpet besides.

"*Henish!*" she spat. "Give me your handkerchief."

"No, wait," he laughed. "Let it dry a little. That ink takes ages to scrub out—I swear I spent half my time in Procampur scrubbing ink off my hands and the other half sharpening swords. So it won't be skin-colored, but it won't remind you of bad times. Unless," he added, "this counts as bad?"

No, she almost said. It wasn't bad. It wasn't bad at all. He had nice hands, and lovely eyes and he smelled of bay again. He was funny and kind and sharp, and she missed him when he didn't come.

But then there was Lorcan. There were a hundred little comments that said Dahl found her strange and inhuman. There was the biting smell of whiskey on him. And there were the seven and a half years of life she'd lost, the years where surely she would have learned how to navigate all of this.

Dahl's smile faltered as the silence stretched.

She reached up and swiped her inky finger over his cheek. "There," she said, "now everyone has to scrub."

"Scorchkettle," he chuckled, wiping the ink off. It left a murky streak through the stubble. He pulled out a handkerchief.

Farideh stood swiftly, scooping up the Waldbrudge book and setting it at the desk. She flipped through another page, hardly absorbing the glyphs as she heard Dahl stand and move to her side.

"Here," he said, setting the page that she'd drawn Ilstan's glyph on atop the open book.

"Thank you."

"It's just a little ink. I didn't mean—"

"No, I'm not upset. It's . . . it's late. I've been looking at these things for ages." She waved a hand over the book and stopped.

The parchment scrap lay on the left-hand page . . . and on the facing page, its symbol's twin.

"Oh gods," she said. She slid the scrap of parchment so that the two symbols lay side by side. "'Azuth,'" she read. "A good god or a bad one?"

Dahl frowned, peering at the glyphs. "That's not right."

"They're the same," she protested. "Down to the last stroke."

"I know, but . . . they can't be." He leaned over her, studying the marks more closely. "Azuth is dead. *Very* dead."

The glyph seemed to shiver under Farideh's gaze. "Who was he?"

"The Lord of Spells," Dahl said. "The god of wizards. He stopped answering his worshipers after the Spellplague. After, they say, the Plane of Dweomerheart was destroyed."

"So he's not bad."

"He wasn't bad when he was alive," Dahl corrected. "And I'd say the gods only know what he is now, but that seems to be more and more like asking for the moon."

Farideh smoothed the parchment scrap against the book. "Did he have anything to do with Oghma?"

"A little," Dahl said. "Allies, more or less. And when he stopped answering, a lot of Azuth's worship came to Oghma instead."

Farideh bit her lip. "Did he have anything to do with Asmodeus?"

"I doubt it. Why would he?"

Farideh smiled at him in a way she didn't feel. "I like to be sure of these things. I've reached my limit with devils."

Dahl considered her, as if he knew she was hiding something. You ought to tell him, Farideh thought. But if she told him about the vision, he'd wonder why she'd had it, why she thought it was anything but a dream, and then he'd know where the soul sight came from. And then he'd be back to thinking she was a monster.

Maybe, she amended. But either way, she preferred this Fugue Plane state to the Abyss that would be losing whatever fondness she'd earned.

Coward, she thought.

"Do you expect Lorcan—" Dahl started. But a sudden sharp pain, prickling at the brand on her arm made Farideh cry out and clamp a hand over it. Dahl reached as if to steady her, but she stepped out of his reach—that would only make it worse.

"Speaking of," she said. "You'd better go."

Dahl frowned. "I'm not afraid of him."

"I didn't say you were," she said. "I just know you're going to make each other very annoyed. He's already annoyed." The fire came again, the old ungentle way Lorcan used to use the brand. "Just go."

Dahl didn't move. "You can do better than this, you know? And I don't much care if he hears that. The pact's not the only answer, just the easy one."

The Hells rode high on the blush that forced its way up her neck. "Oghma's not the only answer either," she shot back. "But you're certainly content to pine over *him*."

"That is *not* the same! It's years of dedication and promise and study. Not a gift from a devil."

"Yes, you seem very dedicated to ignoring that poem, for example," Farideh said. Dahl looked away. "Maybe we all need an easy path now and again. But if you think mine's a lazy choice, you don't know me or it very well."

The sizzle of the opening portal ended their argument. Farideh didn't look away from the Harper as Lorcan spoke. "Well met, darling. Is he bothering you?"

"No," Farideh said. She reached over and shut the Supernal book shut before Lorcan noticed it. "Just a discussion that got a bit heated."

"I see," the cambion said, and she feared he did. Lorcan took her by the hips and drew her close, as if Dahl were not in the room. *Because* Dahl's in the room, she thought, even as the base of her belly grew warm.

"Well, I hope you saved a little of that heat for me," he said, grazing his lips across her jawline. Dahl watched as if someone had just hit him in the chest with a hammer.

"Stop it." Farideh shoved Lorcan back, breaking his hold on her. "Not now."

But Lorcan merely caught her up again, arms wrapped around her from behind. "Of course not *now*," he said in her ear. He looked up at Dahl. "No one likes a gawker, paladin."

"Not your brightbird, huh?" Dahl said.

And what could she say? Whatever she and Lorcan were, the difference would mean nothing. And it shouldn't matter, and it did matter—to both of them, she thought. But after so many heartbeats of saying nothing, Dahl abruptly turned from the room, and left without another word.

"Aw," Lorcan said, releasing her. "Had you not told him?"

"Of course I hadn't told him," she said, feeling the rage of Asmodeus surging up her veins. She tried to remember how long it had been since she'd vented the powers. "Why on all the broken planes would I have told him?"

"Because you're mine and that precludes cozying up with your little broken paladin," Lorcan said. "What were you doing?"

"Research for something."

"Research you couldn't do alone?"

"I'm going to have friends, Lorcan," she said. Her bones felt as if they were turning to fire. "I'm going to talk to men who aren't you, and since I'm *not* your *karshoji* thrall, you don't get to order me not to."

His black eyes glittered dangerously. "Maybe I just have to make sure they aren't there to talk to."

Farideh squeezed her eyes shut and held her breath—the Chosen powers were too strong, too much. She was too angry and there was nothing to do but sprint for the garden and the driving rain, the flames erupting from her as she passed through the door.

Before, she'd made a point of igniting the powers and dousing them as quickly as she could, but this time she let the magic eat her alive, devouring every scrap of her temper and turning it into the terrible pulse of fear.

When she opened her eyes, Lorcan stood just under the shelter of the roof, his expression still, but his whole body tense. She made the flames keep burning.

"I can make threats too," she said. "But I don't want to. I don't want to love someone who threatens me, *hurts* me, so why would I do it back?" She took three steps toward him, watching his wings flick anxiously. "But I could."

She let the fire go out, let the fear fall away. "Swear to me right now that you won't harm Dahl. Ever."

Lorcan swallowed. Blinked. "Or what?"

"I'm not threatening you," she said. "But as I said, I don't want to love someone who threatens the people I care about. So you can swear it, or I'll see who you really are."

Lorcan watched her for such long moments, that Farideh's heart began to plummet. You knew this, she told herself. You knew he was a devil. This day was always coming.

But then he closed the space between them, and planted a kiss on her forehead. "I will never harm Dahl. Happy?"

"Thank you," she said. She slipped her arms around his waist and kissed him softly.

She thought of Dahl's shocked expression. That ship has sailed, she told herself. No—That ship had never been in her harbor.

Lorcan chuckled. "Where's this sudden chasteness from?" He brushed her hair back, revealing her ear and her neck to the humid air. "Let me chase it off."

● ● ●

Lorcan passed through the portal and into the fingerbone tower, his good mood undiminished by the portal's hideous shriek. Everything was humming along. No one could be displeased with Lorcan. Farideh was more tractable than he ever imagined her being—and the price for that peace was one he was glad to pay.

And when she tires of you? he thought without meaning to. A danger, always a danger. But then he recalled the flutter of her heart against his, her long legs wrapped around him. The soft request to stay, just this once.

Maybe she wouldn't tire of anything.

"What in all the layers are you smirking about?" Lorcan startled at the voice. Sairché sat on the floor beside the scrying mirror. The reflection showed a camp beside a swift-moving river, five bodies bundled against the drizzle of rain beneath a ghostly magical sentinel. The shape of a woman, the double of Sairché's human disguise, sat staring out at the river.

"Do you have any idea how long I've been waiting on you?" she demanded. "Where have you *been?*"

"On an errand for Her Highness," Lorcan said. How long *had* he been? "What's wrong?"

Sairché scowled at him. "You need to step in. I still haven't found any trace of the cleric."

Lorcan paused. "Perhaps she simply tired of your company."

"Havilar has no love at all for me, but I doubt she has the sort of mind to make up stories about errant Chosen of Asmodeus just to spite me. Did you find the imps?"

"I haven't had a chance."

"You haven't had a chance, or you've been too busy swanning around with your sweetheart? This is not a small matter."

"Nor is tracking down two imps of an unknown layer," Lorcan shot back.

"I would have done it in hours," Sairché said.

"Yes, well, perhaps you ought to have considered that before failing so spectacularly on Toril," Lorcan said. "Get back to Havilar."

Something thumped heavily against the door. Both cambions reached for their weapons, but the sound didn't come again . . . then a slow dragging. A body, sliding down the bone and sinew door. Lorcan went to it, undid the locks. The weight of Noreia threw the door open the rest of the way.

"Shit and ashes," Lorcan spat. The erinyes looked up at him from one bruised eye—the other had been torn out.

"Help," she mumbled around broken teeth and swollen lips. "Succubi."

"Get her inside," Sairché ordered. Lorcan didn't move. Succubi. Fifth Layer. The Blood War anew. Lorcan didn't want to know.

But Noreia was already shifting onto her side, scooting herself over the threshold, her sharp hooves leaving bloody grooves in the soft tissue of the floor beyond. He shut the door behind her and locked it tight.

"She can't talk," Sairché said scathingly. "She needs a healing if we're going to find out what happened."

"And then we'll *know,*" Lorcan said. Sairché glared at him and snatched the vial he kept on his belt. She poured half of it over Noreia's uglier wounds—the broken arm, the rib poking through her armor, the missing eye—and dumped the rest down her throat. The magic hissed like fat on a fire, but Noreia only gritted her teeth, even as they grew back into her jaw. Her face was still swollen, her skin still raked and raw, but she would not die in the little room at the tip of the fingerbone tower.

"You went to the succubus aeries," Lorcan shouted. "You godsbedamned idiot."

"I went to see Invadiah," Noreia panted. "Those bitches ambushed me." She looked back at her half brother. "Make no mistake—they're up to something."

"Yes," Lorcan drawled. "Succubi taking the opportunity to bloody an erinyes who's where she shouldn't be. Clear conspiracy."

"What are they up to?" Sairché asked, eyes shining.

"Fifty of them are *missing*," Noreia said. "At least."

"You had time to count while they were tearing out your eye?" Lorcan demanded.

"I know how to estimate an enemy's forces," Noreia snarled. "And when I went to Invadiah, she turned me away."

Sairché looked to Lorcan. "Have you spoken to Mother?"

"Not since she asked me to help her topple you," Lorcan said. Indeed, he dreaded the day Invadiah demanded he make good on their deal—if she commanded it while his deal to protect Sairché was still in effect, he would be damned.

"I think she's changed sides," Noreia said reluctantly.

"Invadiah?" Sairché said. "Throwing in with the succubi?" Invadiah had once been the most exalted of Glasya's erinyes—but a failed mission on Toril had led to her demotion, trapping her in the form of a succubus. Considering how much Invadiah had loathed the succubus agent who'd ruined her plans, it was a special punishment.

"Why else would she refuse me?" Noreia demanded. "Why else would she throw me to a pack of those lunatic slatterns?"

"Maybe she's dead?" Sairché said.

"I'm not that lucky," Lorcan said. "What possessed you to head to the succubus aeries?"

Noreia pushed up into a seated postion. "I heard a rumor." She looked from one cambion to the other, as if gauging their trustworthiness. "Those demons that broke into Stygia didn't just rough up the place," Noreia said. "They managed to break into Levistus's storeroom as well. His Highness isn't admitting to anything being missing, but rumor is they made off with powerful artifacts, and he's almost angry enough to melt the glacier."

. . . not the least of which snatching lost powers from old enemies. Glasya's words skittered over Lorcan's thoughts, and he shuddered as though the archduchess had purred them in his ear.

"What sort of artifacts?" Sairché said suspiciously.

Noreia bared her teeth at her little sister. "If I knew that, I would have gone straight to Glasya."

"Don't go to Glasya," Lorcan ordered. Both women frowned at him as if he'd spoken out of turn. "You don't know what's happened. You don't know who to lay the blame on. You're talking about open rebellion, on a level to rival the sort of nonsense countenanced in Cania. And neither of you is Lord Mephistopheles's equal. Don't go to Glasya."

He considered Noreia. "You need to hide. Get off the layer—get out of the plane if you can. Until we have an inkling of what's actually happening, you're a liability. Go to the barracks. Get your weapons and anything you'll need for a long journey. I'll find somewhere, but you come back here in an hour—no longer. Beyond that, I'll hand you to Glasya myself." Noreia growled and grumbled under her breath as she stood, but she complied, still limping.

A slow, wicked smile curved Sairché's mouth. "You *know* something."

"Don't ask," Lorcan warned. "You don't want to hear it."

"You know I do."

"Let's just say I'm not convinced Glasya doesn't already know plenty. Get back to your post. I'll find somewhere to stash our curious erinyes," Lorcan said, crossing to the scrying mirror. His hand went to the scourge pendant he wore, the one imbued with Farideh's blood, but he let it go. When the choice lay between keeping Farideh in line and avoiding the archduchess's interests, Lorcan knew he didn't really have a choice at all.

• • •

"GODS ABOVE," WIZARD of War Pelia Rowanmantle declared as she strode into the tower of the Royal Magician and spotted Ilstan. "I've been looking everywhere for you. You need to come with me."

Ilstan stood. He'd been waiting all morning for Ganrahast to return, to tell him that he wanted an explanation for why he'd been taken off Raedra's guard, to tell him about his fears for her safety, about the tiefling, and perhaps about the strange voice. He had come here most mornings in the last tenday, determined to finally come clean. But every time he had fled from the tower, overwhelmed by a pain in his head and the voice of an old man muttering in his thoughts.

"Is it Lord Ganrahast?" Ilstan asked, hoping and fearing, making himself follow Pelia across the sodden yards. "Is it Her Royal Highness?"

"It's her tiefling," Pelia said. "She's asked for you. Says she won't leave until she sees you or Raedra."

Farideh stood in the Shrine of the Four Swords, looking up at Ansrivarr, the Blade of Memory. Other visitors gave the tiefling a wide berth, eyeing her more than the swords. She realized it—it was plain in the tightness of her shoulders, the stiff straightness of her back, the determination that kept her eyes on the blade before her, and not on her onlookers.

"Good morning," he said, coming to stand beside her, feeling those same eyes suddenly on him. "Would you come with me?"

Her eyes shone with the lamplight as she turned to face him, a miniature sun and moon. "Well met," she said, sounding relieved. She followed him out of the shrine, across the court and down a hall to a little room, hung with a long tapestry of wild beasts fleeing a crowned figure.

"Well," Ilstan said, forcing himself to smile. "What is it you need to speak to me about?"

Farideh studied him for a long, uncomfortable moment, as if she were staring into the core of his heart. She swallowed, as if it pained her. "When I look—you know, when I look for Sharrans—sometimes I see more. Before I came here, I was taken to a Netherese internment camp. They'd imprisoned people there, people who . . . there are symbols on them, the marks of the gods. Chosen."

Ilstan kept smiling, not knowing where this could possibly be heading. "Oh? Her Highness never mentioned." She handed over a scrap of parchment, upon which was drawn a lacy symbol of Supernal.

"What is this?" Ilstan asked.

"Yours," she said. "You've been marked by a god. You're one of the Chosen."

It should have rattled him—Ilstan found he was dimly aware of that fact, but instead a sense of security took him. This was why the voice spoke and why the spells went awry, why his head ached and why he knew that Farideh was no good—

He squeezed his eyes shut, as if to scrub the thought from his mind. She wouldn't tell him this if she were planning to do anything . . . unless she didn't know she was the tool of something wicked . . .

"I should have told you," Farideh said, "the moment I saw, but I was worried it was something fearful, something that might upset you. So I found out which god it was."

"Which god?" Ilstan said. Oh yes—the Voice must have a name. Such things always had names . . .

Farideh hesitated. "Azuth."

A shiver ran over Ilstan. "Magister of Mystra," he intoned. "The Lord of Spells."

"I don't know how," she said, apologetic. "I don't know *why*. He's supposed to have died in the Spellplague." She was silent another moment, her emotionless eyes studying him. "That's . . . why the headaches. Why the voice."

"How do you know about the voice?" Ilstan demanded.

Farideh looked embarrassed. "I heard it too. That day outside the palace, when Devora sent you off. I don't think it's through happening. I think you'll know when the powers come. If they come."

"If?"

"Well," Farideh said, "he's dead, isn't he?"

"You would hope so, wouldn't you?" Ilstan snapped, a burst of irritability. He mastered it, and then smiled at her. "Forgive me. It's strange news to take. Do you plan to tell Her Royal Highness?"

Farideh bit her lip. "She already knows you're Chosen. I promised I'd tell her everything I saw." The truth of things unfolded in Ilstan's heart—the tiefling had frightened poor Raedra, poisoning her with stories of uncontrollable Chosen, unspeakable gods.

"She doesn't know it's Azuth who's Chosen you yet," Farideh said. "Do you want me to tell her or not?"

"You'd keep it a secret?" Ilstan said.

"If you asked," Farideh said. "It's a private thing, I think, what the gods say and do to a person."

Ilstan only nodded—what an odd thing to say. But what part of this wasn't odd? He felt as if down in the core of his soul the truth of it sang, but his mind wouldn't wrap around it, kept focusing on flitting nonsense, on surges of emotion, on bits of inconsequence. He felt as if he were going to faint, but his body held firm.

"Are you all right?" she asked.

"What are you?" he asked.

Farideh gave him an uneasy smile of her own. "I'm just trying to help. I'll . . . find my own way back out." She excused herself and slipped from the room.

Ilstan knew he ought to chase her down, ought to at least walk her from the palace himself, but he simply stood in the little side room, waiting to hear the voice of the Lord of Spells again.

21

28 Eleint, the Year of the Nether Mountain Scrolls (1486 DR)
Suzail, Cormyr

THE RAIN POURED DOWN ON THEM AS IF THE GODS THEMSELVES WERE trying to make the crown prince and his rescuers turn back. The walk from Hultail at the edge of the Wyvernflow River to Juniril, a fishing village halfway down the lake, should have taken three days. Instead, here they were almost eight days out of Hultail—muddied, footsore, battered by two separate bands of goblins, forced off the road repeatedly by flooding.

At this rate, Brin thought, we should reach Suzail by mid-spring.

"Gods," Irvel said. "This place seems smaller every time I pass through here." At the road's bend, a strange building stood on a hill—a tavern shaped like a gigantic helm. "There you are," Irvel said. "Get some rooms for yourselves, while Aubrin and I see to the Santeduls."

"Maybe leave the dog by the stables," Brin said to Havilar.

She pushed the edge of her hood back, looking worried. "What do you think it would take to convince them to let her stay with me?"

"A blind innkeeper," Desima said dryly as she passed.

"If your *karshoji* magic worked better," Havilar shouted, "then I wouldn't have to worry!" She rubbed the dog's shoulder absently. It was nearly level with her own.

"If you're going to keep it, you have to put it in the stables," Brin said. "*Away* from the horses." Irvel called to Brin. "I have to go. I'll be back," he promised.

"Will you?" Havilar said. "Zoonie belongs in the stables, you belong in a lord's fine chambers?"

"You *named* it?" Her cheeks burned scarlet.

"I was getting tired of calling her 'it,'" Havilar said.

"Aubrin!" Irvel shouted again. "Come along!"

"You should go," Havilar said. "Before he starts wondering why we're talking so long."

"I will see you later," he said, a promise. He went to join Irvel, Kallan falling into step with him.

"Mind if I come along?" Kallan asked. "Lord of Cormyr, maybe he's in the market for a bodyguard? I hear we've become fashionable."

Brin frowned. "Lord Santedul is quite old, and his sons are quite staid." He racked his thoughts, trying to recall the family—they were wealthy, but not influential. "A daughter. He's got a daughter who's more interested in wizardry than wealth."

"Nothing says 'eccentric wizard' like a peculiar bodyguard. So can I come?"

Irvel seemed puzzled by the inclusion, but let it lie. They didn't speak much as they walked through the quiet, empty town.

The elder lord Santedul was the only one in the manor, apart from a handful of servants. "My boys have gone to Arabel," he explained. "My daughter to Sembia's line. My sons' wives and children, I sent to Suzail with as many townsfolk as would go—and with them all my horses. We haven't the sort of walls that keep out the Shadovar," he said, all apologies. "And our warrior friends are keeping safe greater treasures."

"We do what we must," Irvel said. "And should Shade come to Juniril, then so will the Army of the Purple Dragon."

Lord Santedul's smile wavered, skepticism bald in his expression. "My heart is so glad to see you alive, Your Royal Highness," Lord Santedul said. "So very glad. After your father's passing . . . well, it was enough to think perhaps our kingdom wasn't so blessed after all."

There followed a moment where the room seemed thinner, less real. Where neither Brin nor Irvel so much as breathed.

"My father is dead?" Irvel asked.

"My apologies, Your Royal Highness," Lord Santedul said. "I presumed you knew. That Lord Crownsilver . . ." He gestured helplessly to Brin with one arthritic hand.

"He was alive when we left," Brin said. "He was alive when last we made a sending."

"Who have they crowned?" Irvel demanded.

Lord Santedul seemed to curl inward. "No one, for the moment. Baerovus is presumed king, but he sleeps from the attack that felled him. He must wake before they can coronate him. Her Highness is regent."

"Well done, Ospra," Irvel said.

Lord Santedul shook his head. "No, my lord. Raedra."

Irvel stood, dumb and stricken. Santedul took him by one hand. "Come, my lord, sit. This is too much news to take on one's feet." He led the younger man to a cushioned chair beside the fire, and rang for a servant to bring something strong to drink.

"We must get back," Irvel said. "As soon as possible. I can't believe I've left her . . . Is she handling it all right?"

Santedul shook his head sadly. "I can't say I know. We don't get many travelers from the south these days, you see? And without Ophira here, I hear no magical news either. But we all know she is an Obarskyr, through and through."

"And headstrong," Irvel said. "And sharp-tongued. And unused to war."

Says the man who pushed into Sembia with Shade on the horizon, Brin thought, a little uncharitably.

"I'm sure she will manage, Your Royal Highness." Santedul blanched. "Your Majesty, I suppose. Good gods, my apologies." He made a stiff and painful-looking bow.

"None of that, please," Irvel said. "As you said: it is a lot of news to take."

The servant brought warmed wine that Irvel merely held, frowning at the floor. Brin drank a little cup while Santedul ordered rooms made up for Irvel and himself.

"If you don't mind," Brin said, standing, "I ought to see to the others in our party. Unless you have the room for all of them, they'll be staying in the High Helm."

Santedul's eyes darted to Kallan, still standing rigid by the door. "Are they all like that one?"

Brin gritted his teeth. "Two dragonborn, a tiefling and a human."

Santedul nodded. "The High Helm is a very nice place to stay. They'll be quite comfortable there."

"I'll go and see to it." He bowed formally to Irvel and politely to Santedul, and left the manor.

"Are they all like *that* one?" Kallan asked as they came back out into the rain. "I was fairly sure he was about to ask if I was housebroken."

"Most of them might think it," Brin said. "They don't ask it, though."

"Well, they ask it, I might just shit on the carpet." He shook his head. "Weird place, this is."

Nausea suddenly overtook Brin. He dropped down on the covered steps of a boarded-up house and put his head between his knees. Foril was dead. So Irvel was king. And if resurrecting the crown prince was bad, resurrecting the uncrowned king was so much worse that Brin's guts threatened to invert at the possibility. Suddenly, Havilar's assistance wasn't just threatening to make Brin's life harder—it could actually get her killed.

No one knows, he reminded himself. No one has to know.

He had to find out when Foril died.

"Are you all right?" Kallan asked.

"Just a lot of things all at once," Brin said. He lifted his head. "You think 'What else could go wrong?' but after a while you think 'Don't ask, because you'll get an answer.'"

"Are these crown prince troubles or a certain tiefling troubles?"

"Both," Brin said, resting his head in his hands. "Just give me a moment."

Kallan did not speak for several breaths. "You know I don't think *he's* going to care much if you do tell him about her," Kallan pointed out. "He seems to think she's charming enough. 'Course, I also think he tends to see what he expects, so you could walk the rest of the way to Suzail holding hands and climbing into each other's bedrolls and His Majesty there might chalk it up to keeping warm in the rain, because why would a man of your status love a tiefling? Assuming," he added, "you still love her by that time."

"It's hardly your business," Brin said. What was he doing telling his troubles to a sellsword anyway?

That stopped him—that snobbish, selfish voice. After all, what were the people he loved most but one-time sellswords? He looked up at Kallan.

"Actually it's probably everyone's business at this point," he said wearily. "It's not as if anyone has any privacy at all like this. So thank you for your concern." He sighed. "I love her. It's just rough right now. She . . . kept a secret from me, and while I know she kept it in order to protect me, it was cruel and foolish to . . ." His own voice seemed to turn over a memory in his head. Oh ye stlarning gods. He leaned back against the door.

"Would you believe I just realized I did the very same thing to her?" He shook his head. "We were parted for a time, a long time, and when I found her again, I didn't want her to know what had happened since. That I was engaged to someone else. I couldn't bear the thought of adding to her worries." He blew out a breath. "But that just made it worse."

"Then it seems she ought to know better," Kallan said. "Or at least that you're justified in reminding her." He sat down beside Brin, under the shelter of the eaves. "That secret have to do with that giant beastie that's suddenly loping alongside her?"

Brin cursed and shook his head. "'Zoonie.'"

Kallan snorted. "What sort of a name is 'Zoonie'?"

"I didn't ask." I should have asked, he thought. "I have a score of good reasons to be mad about that dog," he said. "But the one that sticks is that it makes her feel safe. I don't blame her for wanting to feel safe, but ye gods, it's not as if I'm not here. It's not as if I'm useless. It's just humiliating, you know? Emasculating."

Kallan shrugged. "My granny always said, 'Don't get slap-cheeked over being outrun by a spooked horse.' First, that dog is going to bite someone's face off if they come at her by surprise—you're not. I'm sure you still have a lot of qualities she appreciates. Second, no, I don't know what you're talking about. But I don't go after women, and the men I like, I like them for lots of reasons. Who you rub scales with seems like a piss-poor measure of how much of a man you are." He searched Brin with one golden eye. "Maybe it's a human thing. But I'd still say reconsider. You don't have to be that kind of man."

He shook his head. "I never thought I was. I mean, let's face it, Havilar could kill a person four times before I got a hit in. But maybe deep down we're all exactly the way we're told to be."

"Now you're getting maudlin," Kallan said. "Come on. The walk back will do you good." He pulled Brin to his feet.

"Thanks," Brin said a little sheepishly.

"Don't mention it."

Brin considered Kallan as they walked. "You know Mehen—"

"Is definitely not interested?" Kallan finished. "I've tested those waters. They're cold."

"Tested how, though?" Brin said. "Unless you said 'Well met, Mehen, I think you're pretty fine-looking, let's get an ale,' I can all but guarantee he didn't notice. He doesn't like coyness."

The ridge of Kallan's brow shifted. "So what does he like?"

Brin thought—when it came to his love life, Mehen was private in a very careless way. He didn't talk to Brin about the men he saw or had seen, but then he was never particularly secretive about why he didn't always sleep at the tallhouse. Still, in all the years Brin had known him, Mehen had never introduced him to a brightbird—he had to guess they weren't important enough.

Or you're not important enough to Mehen, that selfish little voice piped up. Brin shoved it aside. If he sounded like that, no wonder Havilar would rather sleep with a hellhound.

"Plain talk," Brin said. "Action. His daughters mean the world to him. I think if a fellow didn't accept that he came second, he'd suffer for it. In many ways. He respects someone who fights well, fights fair when the fight is fair. Stands up for folks who need it." Brin thought. "Don't ask him to go for an ale. He doesn't really drink."

Kallan chuckled. "A lot of us don't, outside home. Do you know what clan he was in? Why he left?"

"No," Brin said. Havilar had told him enough of what followed Mehen out of Djerad Thymar though. "It was something to do with his father. He left someone behind, someone I suspect he's still tangled up on. So maybe it's better if you don't bother."

"Thanks," Kallan said, pushing the door to the High Helm open. "I'll keep it in mind."

Mehen sat alone at a table near the bar, beside two dishes of fish stew. A handful of patrons, including a fair number of halflings, held a scattering of the tables. A bored-looking keghand stood behind the door. Brin waved for an ale.

Kallan hesitated beside the table, then took the seat beside Mehen.

"They've got rooms to spare," Mehen said. "Desima's gone up to hers. Havi's still out in the stables. Here's one for you—" He passed Kallan a brass key, then looked to Brin. "I figured I'd wait and see if you and His Highness needed lodgings here."

His Majesty, Brin thought. The keghand set down a flagon of dark ale that Brin suddenly didn't want. "I'm going to go find Havi," he said. "Be right back."

"Take your time," Kallan said.

As Brin turned, his eyes lit on a figure descending one of the High Helm's many staircases, Constancia, pale and hollow-eyed, her tabard rumpled. Her shield arm hung in a sling.

She stood perfectly still, watching Brin for a moment. Then she rushed to him, pulling him close with her uninjured arm.

"You're safe," she said. "Ah, thank the gods, you're safe. I have been praying and praying and praying. Trying to divine the right path. Asking for guidance." She straightened and cupped his cheek. "I suppose the answer was patience. I should have known you'd come back."

"Maybe that's what made the difference," Brin said. "We found him."

"Irvel?" Constancia said.

Brin nodded. "He's at Lord Santedul's manor."

Constancia stared at Brin as though he were a ghost. "You found him? With . . . that creature?"

"Four days," Brin said. "He was sheltering in an old temple. The protections wouldn't let the war wizards' scrying in."

"Well," Constancia managed. "Well, I'm glad to know he's well. You were right, Aubrin. I beg your forgiveness."

"Don't," Brin said. "We're fine." He thought of Havilar and the resurrection and Foril, and swallowed. "I heard about King Foril."

Constancia looked grave. "So much the better you've found the crown prince. We need to return, and soon." She squeezed his shoulder. "I should have gone back for you."

"It's fine," Brin said again. "I had Havi and Mehen with me."

"Yes, of course," Constancia said, dropping her hand.

"In fact," Brin said, "I need to go talk to Havilar. I'll be right back."

Out in the rain, Brin's panic bubbled up to the surface again, urging him to take to the road, to flee wherever he could reach. He pressed it down, steering himself to the stables. The smell of damp hay and manure laced the air, old and steady, but there were no horses stabled here. Havilar stood at the far end, her back to him. The hellhound was trying to follow her as she backed away from it."

"I know," Havilar said to the dog. "But you can't come inside. You're too big and you'll scare everyone." She rubbed the creature under the muzzle. "If I bring you a fish, will you eat it? Will that make you happy?" The dog whined and gave a short bark. Havilar sighed and sat back on her heels, looking at her fingers. "Fari, I think I got the better deal, but I wish I could speak hellhound. Ask Lorcan if he knows how to." She paused, as if counting the last words of a sending. "I miss you."

"I think you should give her the fish," Brin called, startling her. "But maybe keep her muzzle on." Havilar pursed her mouth and turned back to the dog.

"I was going to come in," she said. "I just wanted to get her settled."

"Can we talk about—"

"I don't really want to talk about any of it," Havilar said. "How was I supposed to know this wasn't allowed? How was I supposed to stop Moriah from running off? How was I supposed to stop Asmodeus—"

"Hush."

"No, *you* hush. I get it—I make things harder for you, but they are not exactly easy for me, all right? And now I'm *stuck* and I don't even have Farideh, so I'm going to talk to Zoonie, if I like, which means, yes, she needs a name." Her attention fluttered, agitated, from the floor to the straw to Brin. She sat down beside the hellhound, who licked her hand. "And honestly, I don't want to make things hard for you. I don't want you to . . . Maybe you're better off without me."

"Foril died," Brin said. "Irvel should be king now."

Her eyes went wide. "Oh gods. I'm sorry, Brin."

An explanation of the changed crime was on his lips, a warning for how seriously she needed to take this—she could be executed. But it failed. What would it accomplish anyway? She already felt guilty and conflicted, and he knew in his heart of hearts he would do anything to make sure the worst didn't come to pass. He sat down beside her.

"I am so *stlarning* scared for you," he said. "For me, for us. These are problems that I can't even fathom how to solve."

"I don't think you can," Havilar said. "I don't think anybody can, not just yet." She sighed and scratched the dog behind the ear. "But maybe you're right, it doesn't help in the meantime. Maybe we are doomed."

Brin's heart squeezed as he put his arms around her, held her close. "Don't decide, please. Not until we get back to Suzail." He hesitated. "I'm not leaving you."

"Yet," Havilar said. "And you know that's true." The dog whined again and licked her hand, its eyes on Brin. "Be nice," she said.

"Why'd you call it Zoonie?" Brin asked.

Havilar kept her eyes resolutely on the stall's corner. "I don't want to tell you. You'll just get mad and think I'm being stupid."

Brin laughed. "I would not. I can't think of a name you would give it that could make me mad." Havilar took a chapbook from her bag and handed it over to him wordlessly. *The Secrets of the Obarskyrs.*

"Oh ye gods," he said. "Is Zoonie short for Azoun?"

"No," Havilar said. Then, "Azoun is a boy's name. I thought she could be Azounarella. But that's too much to say."

Brin smoothed the folded cover of the chapbook. "I like it. Just don't tell Constancia. Who's in the inn, by the way."

Havilar sighed. "Well, I'm glad she's all right, but that gives the stables a leg up over the inn room if you ask me." She patted Zoonie's side.

"Havi, tell me you're going to be able to send her back when the time comes," Brin said.

For a long moment, Havilar didn't answer. "If I have to. But she's done nothing bad, you know. And if she's loyal to me, then she won't. And I can keep the muzzle on her. It's not fair to send her back to that place as if she's doomed by her blood." Brin said nothing, and after a moment, she sighed. "I won't decide until we get to Suzail. And if she does *anything* that endangers us, I'll send her back. Fair?"

Zoonie gave a pitiful whine and butted her head under Havilar's arm. Havilar gave Brin a pointed look.

"Fair," he said.

Suddenly, Zoonie leaped to her feet, to the edge of the chain's reach, letting out a long, low growl. Something moved beyond one of the windows of the stable—a shambling shape, a rustle of brush. Havilar froze, reaching for the glaive beside her. Brin leaped up, sword in hand, and searched for the source among the growing shadows.

"Nothing," Brin said. "Maybe some villager getting a peek." He looked back at the hellhound, at Havilar's drawn expression. "She's part dire wolf," he said. "We'll say that."

"I don't think it was a villager," Havilar said. "I have a very bad feeling that it wasn't a villager."

• • •

The morning was late, but the sun did not make it through the heavy clouds as Raedra stood atop a dais erected in the Promenade, looking down at more people than she could count. In the carriage beyond, she had listened to the cacophony of so many men and women talking—wondering what this was all about. So many voices, she could not pick out a single statement.

They all bowed and fell silent as she stood before them.

"Make me look like a warrior and a queen," she had told Nell. And so her purple gown was covered by a steel breastplate and gorget, her golden hair pulled high into a nest of braids. She was regent, so she wore no crown, but no one mistook her for another.

Oversword Greatgaunt had insisted that she write Raedra's speech to them. Raedra had laid out what she intended to do, deflecting the war council's initial arguments that it was too difficult, too disruptive, and was she even allowed? Eventually, when they had settled into it, smoothed out the rougher edges, only Greatgaunt remained uncertain and pleaded to write her words.

"My dearest subjects," Raedra read, as the wind threatened to pluck the parchment from her hands. "Cormyr has come to dark times, like a child trapped in a nightmare, and we must care for it, guide it back into the light."

One of the women in the front row whispered to her neighbor, a clear sneer on her face.

"You who are Cormyr's hardiest and most trustworthy—" *Servants.* Raedra stared at the page. She actually meant to call farmers and woodcutters, miners and shepherds, *servants*? "Subjects," she corrected, "must surely hear her cry for aid and rise up, heroes new-made . . ."

She searched the crowd. Furrowed brows. Folded arms.

Raedra folded the paper in quarters.

"These are very pretty words that someone has written for me," she said, holding up the paper. "If you'd like to hear them, perhaps I can finish it after I say what

I've come to say. Because I don't think you need to hear poetry and fancy from me. You know what you've lost. You know what Shade has taken and what they seek to take—our land, our kingdom, our very selves.

"Some of you came here having lost your homes, your farms, your livelihood. You defended them, against all odds, until you had no choice but to flee. Some of you have sent your sons and daughters, your brothers and sisters, into the battle-fields, and they haven't returned. They might never return. Some of you may be wondering how I have the gall to stand before you and tell you that *you* have more to give to Cormyr. You are not Purple Dragons. You are not nobles. But it is *you* who will mark the difference between our success and our failure."

They were silent now, the whispers fled. The woman in the front row watched Raedra, skeptical but listening now. Still stiff, still closed off. Listening, but not on her side, not yet.

"Shade would make us into Sembia, if we are fortunate, and the name of the Forest Kingdom would become as tainted as Sembia's has become. We will fall into history, colluders and weaklings, the lapdogs of Netheril forever after.

"Such a fate would break my heart," she told them, "but I will not be the one to suffer—Shade will kill me if they breach Suzail. It will be you, who the Shadovar overtake, and neither you nor I nor anyone truly of Cormyr can let that happen."

They knew it—she hardly needed to say what would happen, but she saw in the way their expressions shifted, the way the whispering woman unfolded her arms, that they hadn't heard the truth from someone of her status. Cormyr was in trouble.

"And so *any* person able to march and carry a weapon who comes to the Royal Court, beginning tomorrow, may swear their oath of fealty. If you do not have arms and armor, they will be given. You will ride the Way of the Manticore, scattering the Shadovar raiders and escorting refugees from their predations back to Suzail. You will be paid as Purple Dragons are paid, your families will be granted the same benefits in the event of your death. When the Shadovar threat is routed, your farms and your villages will be the first that the Crown sees to, and the powers of the war wizards will be given to your aid."

"Fine talk, Your Highness!" a man shouted. "Take it to yon nobles and tell them to get off their arses!" A grumble of agreement rolled through the crowd. Raedra smiled.

"In a sense," she called to the man, "that is why I am here. If the defense of your home does not move you, I offer you this:

"Whichever noble family does not do their duty to Cormyr in the efforts of our defense shall have their lands seized by the Crown," she said, and knew they heard every word. "And those of the common class who take up arms, despite never having sworn oaths to do so, will be allotted a portion of those lands as reward. The finest farm and pasturelands in Cormyr. *You* will have earned them."

A new cacophony of voices, but this time, the tone had changed—Raedra heard now the fear in the first commotion, by the lack of it in the second. She held up a hand and spoke once more.

"As my pretty words said: These are dark times. But they are not our darkest, and it is within our power to bring back the light. It is Cormyr who stopped the Tuigan Horde. It is Cormyr who halted the Shoon Imperium. We have weathered goblins and elves, orcs and pirates, dragons and the Blue Fire. And we have *never* fallen, we have *never* surrendered.

"Carry that news, if you please," she said. "Carry it far and wide—right up to High Prince Telamont's ears if need be, and let him realize that Cormyr is not a prize he can ever win, and I am not an Obarskyr he will *ever* frighten."

A wild cheer rippled through the crowd, their fear overtaken by this promise of strength and action. Later, she thought, they will have questions. They will wonder about the amounts and the guarantees. People had to eat, after all. She'd had the overswords prepare for such things, and planned to hold court after highsunfeast.

The Purple Dragons ushered her back to the carriage. Ganrahast was sitting within it, and she knew better than to wonder where he had come from.

"That was quite stirring," Ganrahast commented. "Did you practice it?"

"No," Raedra said, suddenly flushing. "It was just true and so it all came out. Did it make sense at least?"

"A great deal of sense," he said. "Hopefully it will aid you in this next trial: we must return to the palace."

Raedra's heart leaped. "Is it Baerovus?"

"No." He dragged his fingers through his russet beard. "Let us say Lord Erzoured is not happy with his promotion."

An understatement, to say the least. The moment Raedra stepped into the Hippogriff Chamber, the Baron Boldtree stormed toward her as if he meant to run her down like a charging bull. The Purple Dragons stepped in front of him, but he reached through them to shake a finger at her.

"You have gone too far!" he shouted. "This is nothing but a childish game to you!"

"I can think of a fair few people who make it more of a game, Cousin," Raedra said. "And a fair few people who would be more pleased with being given the command of an army."

"So give it to one of them!" he shouted. "Or is the chance to feed me to the gnolls too good to pass up?"

"No," Raedra said. "It must be you."

"A commoner to lead commoners," Erzoured fumed. "Is that it?"

"No," Raedra said. "An *Obarskyr* to lead commoners. You're right—if I had another choice, I wouldn't send you. Do you think I want you carried back on the shoulders of an army that doesn't know what you're capable of? But we are asking these people to risk their lives where we shouldn't. If they are going to head into the fray, we must reassure them that they *aren't* meant to feed the gnolls. And whether you and I like each other at this point is immaterial: everyone knows I do not have the luxury to waste heirs." She folded her hands. "Nor ignore them."

Erzoured grew very still. "A pity for you," he said, but the venom had left his voice.

"I don't matter at this juncture," Raedra said. "Cormyr matters. They need an Obarskyr, so it's you or it's me and, Cousin, you have much better success convincing old soldiers you aren't missing your embroidery and dresses.

"You'll have a handful of Purple Dragons to help keep order, and Ganrahast can spare two war wizards. They'll fit you with a bootstick, though be wise about its use. You'll probably get some nobles, too, starting this afternoon—I'm hoping a fair few families buy their way out of this with horseflesh. It would be a great deal simpler."

"I suppose you have a list of who should be given charge of what."

"No," Raedra said. "I leave that to you. I said you were in command; I must trust your judgment. But I will tell you this, Erzoured: If you use this opportunity to try and hurt me, if you use it to harm those in your care, I will be just as merciless with you as I've been to these derelict nobles. I don't have the luxury to ignore heirs, and I don't have the luxury to coddle conspirators and blackguards." She smiled. "Now, if you don't mind, I need to take highsunfeast. I would ask you to join me, but I suspect neither of us would enjoy that, and you have preparations to make."

Erzoured regarded her for a long, furious moment, as if too many things were trying to fight their ways out of his mouth. Finally, he exhaled noisily. "You are an infuriating girl. Your Royal Highness," he added.

"Yes, well," Raedra said, with a cheek she felt she'd earned. "I never did claim we weren't related."

• • •

Ten days later, the Dragon's Jaws was shut up tight as the festival known as Chasing the King began. Dahl stood by the window of Vescaras's room, watching for his return as much as the passage of the condemned prisoner playing Mad Boldovar Obarskyr, roaming the streets and trying to survive until sundown when he'd win his freedom. A herd of young children pelted down the Promenade shrieking, "Chase the King! Chase the King!"

Dahl wrinkled his nose. Barbaric practice.

Vescaras stumbled through the door, blood soaking his left shoulder.

"Gods' books! What in the Hells happened to you?"

"Stray bullet," Vescaras said in a strained voice. "Some damned fop wanting to play along without getting too close, whipping a sling around like just *anyone* can manage." He dropped onto the settee with a grunt of pain. "I'm stlarning lucky they were just unpracticed idiots."

Dahl peeked through the hole in Vescaras's shirt back. "Hrast, I think it hit the bone. Can you get your shirt off?"

"Just cut the damned thing. It's ruined."

Dahl pulled out his flask. "Drink it while I get my things." Stlarning barbaric practice, Dahl thought. He hoped Farideh had locked herself in the tallhouse. He could just imagine some idiot using Chasing the King as an excuse to attack a tiefling. He lit a candle and heated the forceps and blade over it to clean them, wondered how many tieflings would end up hurt. He washed his hands in the basin, murmuring a prayer to Oghma and Ilmater, the god of suffering, that everything would go smoothly.

When Dahl came back in with his equipment, Vescaras was looking distinctly gray.

"Gods, lie down." Dahl sliced the shirt from the other spy and folded it under his shoulder to catch the blood. "Did you find out about the Greatgaunts?"

"Five," Vescaras hissed as Dahl poked a finger into the wound, gauging its depth. "A chambermaid, a groom, a cellar jack and two doorjacks since last winter. But the chambermaid was poached from Naranthe Crownsilver and the doorjacks are Suzailian, born and—*tluin and buggering Shar!*" he gasped as Dahl eased the forceps in.

"Hold still," Dahl said. The bullet had gone deep, back to the shoulder blade. He wondered if it had been as accidental as Vescaras claimed. "So it's the groom or the cellar jack?"

Vescaras nodded, his breath held, his face screwed up against the pain. The forceps' grip slipped and a fresh gout of blood rolled over Vescaras's dark skin. "Hrast," Dahl spat.

"Another thing," Vescaras said. "We're trapped. The portal to Waterdeep was closed off last night."

"What? Why?" He pulled, rocking the bullet against its trap. Vescaras answered with a sharp cry. Dahl set his hand around the wound and pushed the shoulder back as he pulled the bullet free. Another gout of blood came out. Dahl pressed a clean cloth to it, while Vescaras swore in a most ignoble way.

"Malfunctions," he gasped. "Too many people have been using it, and they lost four souls to gods know where. The war wizards claimed public safety and shut it down."

"Son of a barghest," Dahl said, still pressing on the wound. "They're saying we've got a month at best before the Shadovar army gets here."

"They've been saying *that* for months." Vescaras winced. "I think they're right this time, though."

"You have an escape plan?"

"Depends entirely on how Shade attacks."

"Well Tam's going to want an answer. Do you want stitches or is this worth a healing potion?" Dahl asked.

"I'm sure your embroidery is very fine, but give me the damned potion. I have a brightstarfeast to go to and I don't want to spend it nursing my shoulder." Dahl passed him the vial, and Vescaras downed it. "Many thanks."

"Of course."

"How about you? Did you get any information about the other Sharrans?"

Dahl shook his head as he poured enough water into the basin to wash his bloody hands. "Nothing. So far as I can tell, they're just waiting for something. But I've got another inn and four festhalls still."

Vescaras made a face. "I see."

"What?"

The other spy shook his head, tipped the vial back again to get the last dregs of the potion. His shoulder was already sealing shut with a faintly silver glimmer of magic.

"What?" Dahl demanded. "I'm not inventing this. Marjana wasn't inventing this."

"No," Vescaras agreed. "But . . ."

"But what?"

"Don't you think it's taking you an awful long time to sort out what you need to know?"

"No," Dahl said. "Not when I have to wait for Farideh to be called to the palace."

"Why? We just narrowed down our suspects at the Greatgaunts' manor without her."

"It's different when we're talking about festhalls and taverns. You don't like sharing the glory?"

"Please." He stood and rotated his shoulder gingerly. "Don't be obtuse, Dahl. You're entirely too clever to pass it off."

"Well, don't be cryptic then," Dahl shot back. "Say what you stlarning mean."

Vescaras regarded him levelly. "I mean, this has gotten well out of hand. Unless there's some truth to all that tavern talk and you have to wait for the right time of the month for her teeth to recede or somesuch, you are not going to get her into bed dawdling like this. And if I have to watch one more *moment* of this idiocy, then *I* will stlarning seduce her."

"She thinks you're a prat," Dahl shot back. "Also, if it matters? I'm not trying to sleep with her."

"No, we've established that you're lagging around taverns pretending it's *so hard* to look for Sharrans. Get yourself together. Not only is it annoying, but it could well jeopardize things."

"I fail to see how," Dahl said. Then, "Anyway, she's got a lover." He kept coming back to Farideh's assertions that Lorcan did such things specifically to make Dahl annoyed—but then she hadn't denied it when Dahl had called Lorcan her brightbird.

It's not your business, he thought. She's not interested in you, and why would you be interested in her? You've already burned that bridge anyway, saying whatever stupid thought came into your head, whatever you were about to do when that cambion showed up.

"*That*'s why you've been avoiding her," Vescaras said.

Dahl blew out a breath. "I have absolutely no interest in talking about this with you."

"Good," Vescaras said. "Look, if you're not interested, you've still got four fest-halls to check and another inn, so get to it. If you are interested, get to it anyway. Shar doesn't care if your feelings are hurt."

"Oghma's bloody papercuts." Dahl bit back a further stream of curses. "I'm going downstairs," he said. "You'd do well to rest and let that healing potion work through." He went down to the quiet taproom—the Dragon's Jaws' usual customers were no doubt in clubs and inns with better views of the festival—ordered an ale, and tried to concentrate on the problem at hand.

Dahl unfolded the map of Suzail he'd sketched on the back side of a discarded menu. Eighteen stars marked the locations from Marjana's list. The ten that he or Vescaras had verified were circled.

Vescaras was right: this was taking too long. But even if Farideh helped him find the last eight Sharrans, what good would it do? Not a one of them had done so much as steal a crust of bread in the meantime.

"Same old sour self," Arven, the doorguard-turned-keghand, had reported. "Except when he was out sick one evening last tenday."

"Sick?" Dahl asked. "Or do you think he was playacting?"

"Sick," Arven assured him, wiping down Dahl's table. "Ten times as sour and rubbing his head. My aunt sent him home. Hey, how's your tiefling?"

"Fine," Dahl had said. "Get me another ale, would you?"

None of the others Dahl had checked in on had taken ill the same night as Uwan from the Brigand's Bottle. None of them seemed to contact one another. The list he'd copied from Uwan's mattress had made it clear he'd been recruited by Netheril. The first half was a list of Cormyrean customs. Or at least the Netherese notion of Cormyrean customs:

Cormyreans do not practice magic. Do not cast spells.

Cormyreans like to talk about others. Have an opinion but maintain lightheartedness. This is social bonding, not an act of accusation.

Do not speak ill of the ruling class, it will draw attention to you.

The second half was even more damning: A list of components. *Half* a list of components, Dahl amended. Five items that—to his knowledge—did nothing. But add a few more? A ritual, a spell, an explosive, or maybe a poison—all depending on what the rest of the list said.

And still none of the Sharrans did anything but haul kegs, guard doors, mop floors, and serve ale.

Dahl considered the map. There had to be something else.

Fifteen of the locations lay within a few blocks of the wall—but three were farther in. Four if you counted the palace where the traitorous noblewoman had hidden herself.

Three taverns, five inns, four festhalls, six noble houses, and the palace. They weren't owned by the same people, they didn't buy the same things from the same suppliers, they didn't have interests in the same parts of Cormyr. They didn't have access to the same people—this wasn't an elaborate assassination plan. They didn't have any pattern at all that Dahl could see.

Maybe I need a Cormyrean's eyes on it, Dahl thought. Maybe if Arven looked at the map, he'd toss out the clear connection that all the buildings were constructed in the reign of Queen Gantharla, and how could Dahl not know that?

A jack in the Dragons' Jaws livery hurried across the taproom to Dahl's table. "Pardon me," the jack said in a low voice, "there's a . . . woman here to see you. At the kitchen entrance." He bounced on his feet. "If you'd come with me, we can hold the table until she leaves."

Dahl folded his map and followed the jack through the hot and bustling kitchen to the open doors at the back. There was a little antechamber there, a place for the employees to hang cloaks and store things. A heavyset guard sat on a stool beside the doors. Farideh stood, cowled and cloaked beside him.

"So do you make much like this?" Dahl heard him ask her as they approached.

Farideh shook her head. "Sorry?"

"My cousin, she has a festhall. She's hiring tiefling girls—can't say for sure she'd take you, but I would if I were her." He offered Farideh a pleasant smile. "Twenty for the first month, plus meals and another gold for each visitor. Might be you make more visiting highborn lords, but I can promise it's safer and you wouldn't have to be out in the rain."

Farideh flushed scarlet. "That's . . . that's not . . ."

"Well met," Dahl said. She looked at him gratefully. "Come on, I have a table."

He turned to head back through the kitchen, and nearly crashed into the jack who'd led him there. "Wouldn't you prefer to conduct your business in private?" he said pleasantly.

"I'd *rather* go finish my ale."

"We can bring it up to your room."

Dahl gritted his teeth. "I understand that things are done differently in Suzail," he said, in the clipped tones of a fine lord's personal servant. "Otherwise, my guest would have felt safe coming to the Promenade entrance. But I do not intend to entertain Lord Ammakyl's business associates from Waterdeep as though they are doxies and dealers."

The jack's pleasant façade wavered. "Let me arrange a private booth then."

The private booth might have been the best compromise for the Dragon's Jaws, but once the screens were closed around them, Dahl found himself wishing he'd gone up to Vescaras's room anyway.

"You've been avoiding me," Farideh said.

"I've been busy," Dahl protested.

"It's all right," she said. "I don't blame you. I came to say I'm sorry."

Dahl froze. Of all the things he'd expected to hear Farideh say, an apology for Lorcan wasn't one. Shouldn't be one, he told himself. She never owed you anything different. It's not your business. "Are you?" he managed.

"I shouldn't have said those things about Oghma."

"Right," Dahl said. He hadn't even thought about that. "It's fine."

"It's not fine," she insisted. "I don't have any idea how hard that is. I don't know what the message means or what you should do with it—you're not me. And if I think it's similar to my own worries . . ." She shook her head with a little smile. "I'm just guessing."

"It's all right," Dahl said again.

She took a little package out of her cloak and pushed it across the table to him. "Here. It's not blackberries. But I thought you might like it."

"What happened to saving all your coins?" Dahl asked, unpicking the twine. She shouldn't have done it, he thought. You shouldn't have let things get to this point.

"I needed to make things right," she said. "And this is how you always make things right."

Dahl unwrapped a bottle of ink the color of ivy leaves. It wasn't large, but the color was lovely. He held it up to the lamplight and it glowed emerald.

"It smells too," Farideh said. "Like rosemary. They had a rose-scented one too, but I thought that might be too feminine."

Dahl stared at her. "You bought me scented ink?"

Her smile wavered. "I can take it back, if you don't like it."

"Fari," he said, "people use scented ink to write love letters. It's not for reports and maps and things."

She turned scarlet once more and her gaze dropped to the table. "I didn't mean . . . I'll take it back." She reached across the table. Dahl slid the ink back toward himself.

"I didn't say I didn't like it," he said. He might never open that bottle for the rest of his days, but he'd keep it. It was sweet of her, and he hated the idea of making her try to return it to whatever shop she'd wrangled it out of.

"You needn't act as if I'm never going to have someone to write love letters to," he added.

She was quiet a moment. "I was going to tell you about Lorcan."

"No, you weren't," he said. "You already told me he wasn't your brightbird."

"He *wasn't*," she said. "And . . . he isn't, I don't think. I don't know. This hasn't been going on for all that long." She looked up at him through her dark lashes. "I'm not trying to talk about it. Just . . . do me a favor and don't tell me I could do better. That's something *you* don't know about."

What had she said? *A tiefling with a bent nose, a weird eye, a warlock brand, and an eight-year gap in her memory.* She could do better, she deserved better—but it was true those were things that might scare a fellow off. Absent her nose, which was completely normal and even a little elegant, and her eye, which was easy to get used to. Especially once one worked out how to tell what she was looking at and when she was rolling her eyes.

"Does he make you happy?" Dahl asked.

Her mouth twisted. "That's a really complicated question."

It shouldn't be, he nearly retorted. But she was ready for that—her jaw tight, her shoulders tense. And what was the point of starting a fight? It wouldn't change things. She wouldn't change her mind, and then Dahl would have to face the possibility that Vescaras might have been right.

"I bet I can top it," he said instead, and slid the map of Suzail across the table to her. "What do these," he asked, "have in common?"

• • •

LADY MARSHEENA'S TROOPS strung themselves along the Way of the Manticore, several score jet markers trailing down the painted path of the map, clustering together as the shade general swept them up, riding back from Wheloon.

"You were right," Oversword Greatgaunt said, laying down a row of smaller markers, chips of marble the size of peas, ahead of the Shadovar. "She drives the Whelunians before her."

"Shock troops," Oversword Huntcrown said.

"A defensive wall," Battlemaster Cormaeril said.

"It's both," Raedra pointed out. She hoped Erzoured would be able to manage sorting the one from the other. The amethyst pyramids to mark his army of volunteers had moved into the Way of the Manticore, heading toward Marsheena. The ranks had swollen quickly with chagrined or sulking nobles and eager refugees. In two tendays, they'd already made great progress and picked up several adventuring companies.

"I am never forgiving you for this," Maranth had told her the evening before they headed out. Raedra poured him a little more wine.

"You were bored," she pointed out. "And to be fair, I was quite certain Grandpapa would buy your spot out with horses or weapons."

"You underestimate how much Uncle Ordmann would like the softness driven from me."

"As if you've any softness," Raedra said gently. "Play nice with your fellow officers."

Maranth snorted. "You mean 'bring you information about Erzoured'? You assume I'll survive that long."

"Don't be ridiculous," Raedra had said. "I wouldn't let them send you out on a mission you'd be killed at."

Raedra considered the jet markers, their proximity to the amethyst ones. "How long do we have before Marsheena reaches Suzail?"

"Depends on the rains," Oversword Greatgaunt said. "I would estimate a tenday."

"The Crown and most of the noble families have been establishing stockpiles since last winter, to prepare in the event of a siege. We could last a month if we're careful."

"That was before we became the haven of every homeless farmer," Oversword Huntcrown said. "We'll be blessed if we make it through a tenday."

"Start tightening your belt now, Oversword," Raedra said. "How fast can we recall war wizards?"

"In moments," Ganrahast said. "If we must."

"We may," Raedra said. "Make certain, if you're able, to let them know we anticipate such an action within the tenday. Any word from Marsember?"

"They beg to retain their Purple Dragons," Battlemaster Cormaeril said apologetically. "They understand the concerns, but fear they may be next."

Raedra bit off a curse. If Suzail fell, Marsember could hardly imagine it would stand against Shade. "They won't manage with their fancy Watch alone? Well then, we're quite short of forces, aren't we?"

No one spoke.

"These are not our darkest times, Your Royal Highness," Oversword Greatgaunt said. "We will prevail." But her own words gave Raedra little comfort. The bulk of her army was still mired in Sembia, no longer fighting toward Selgaunt, but fighting to keep the Sembian army from pressing past Daerlun.

"Where the blazes is Arabel in all this?" Oversword Huntcrown demanded. "Still picking off goblins?"

"Arabel remains sieged by monstrous raiders," Battlemaster Cormaeril said. "And their portion of war wizards are at work trying to seal of the Forgotten Keep, the portal Marsheena's army came through."

"Well, you lot are rather good at sealing portals, hmm?" Oversword Huntcrown said to Ganrahast sourly.

"Your manners, Oversword," Raedra said. "Lord Ganrahast made a decision in the interest of Suzail's safety. A portal is little good when it starts devouring people."

"Your pardon, Your Royal Highness, but with a siege on and our sources for food dwindling, that portal could have come in handy."

"We still hold the harbor," Oversword Greatgaunt reminded him. "We can all get by with a little more fish and kelp in our diet." He reached into the table's drawer and drew out another figure, a dusty little dragon made of jasper that she set on the town of Hilp.

Raedra's stomach dropped. "Another one?"

The oversword nodded. "It's sweeping closer. Always at night."

"Another of Marsheena's ploys," Raedra said. But the oversword didn't look convinced.

"It would be very clever," she allowed. "But controlling a black dragon of that size . . ." She looked to Ganrahast.

"Difficult," he agreed. "Not impossible, but very difficult for the level of spell-casters she has on hand."

"Do you mean to tell me, Oversword," Raedra said, a bit archly, "that you think Thauglorimorgorus, the Purple Dragon, has risen from obscurity and thrown in with Shade?"

"No, my lady," she said soberly. "I mean to tell you that a black dragon is circling toward the capital, while no Obarskyr sits upon the Dragon Throne, and that your subjects have noticed."

Raedra had no answer to that, at least, none that would suit. Baerovus could hardly sit upon the throne unless he woke, and if people grew anxious enough to start asking if she might take his place, what could she say? She could not agree—the crown was Baerovus's so long as he breathed—but she couldn't disagree that the lack of a proper king was dangerous.

The council departed, off to send messages to overswords and lords far, far from Suzail. Raedra considered the painted map, the markers. The little jasper dragon.

"It cannot be Thauglor, can it?" she said.

Ganrahast stroked his beard. "At this point, I don't think it wise to say no. The gods seem to take too much pleasure in upending us."

Raedra sighed. "We shall have to be more tenacious. I find it works with sour nobles, so why not gods?" Ganrahast gave her a disapproving look, and she smiled. "Do you know where my mother is?"

Ganrahast's expression grew distant, as his magic searched the palace. "Princess Ospra is visiting the temples. She's just left the Shrine of Tempus, headed for the Temple of Good Fortune."

By the time Raedra caught up with her mother, she had finished at Tymora's altar and was heading down the Promenade to the temple of Oghma. Raedra met her there.

Grief had dimmed the princess's radiant beauty, but not destroyed it. Her dresses were still black, touched only by modest jewels to prevent herself from being overswaddled in Shar's dark colors. She smiled wearily at Raedra as her daughter climbed down from her carriage.

"Well met, my dear," she said, taking her hand.

"Well met," Raedra said. Then, "I haven't seen you in so long."

Ospra looked as if she were wilting in the rain. "I'm sorry, Raedra. I haven't been altogether myself, have I?"

"How much of that tincture are you taking?"

"Enough to sleep," Ospra said. "It will not last forever. I . . ." She smiled again, as if by doing so she could banish the grief that welled up in her. "But let me have it for now," she finished.

Raedra tucked herself close beside her mother, the faint perfume of roses surrounding her like a cloud. "Here," she said, "we'll go in this one together."

The loremasters stood and bowed as the two royal women passed through, two princesses who might have been queens, had Tymora thrown a different die. They made their offerings, their ablutions, and laid their foreheads against the altar stone at the heart of the massive library.

Give me the wisdom to keep Cormyr together, Raedra prayed. Please don't let me make a mistake that costs lives.

The two women were shown to a little alcove behind a screen, where they could sit in quiet contemplation in the hopes that Oghma's answers would bless them. Raedra found her own thoughts raced from Arabel to Sembia, to Marsheena to Thauglorimorgorus, and to the darkness that had birthed Wheloon fifteen years ago. She clutched her mother's hand tight, concentrating on the feel of her rings against her palm.

The sound of someone running through the temple jerked away whatever semblance of peace Raedra had managed. Ospra didn't move, her head bowed, her lashes fluttering.

"Lord Ganrahast!" Raedra heard a woman shout. "Lord Ganrahast you must come right away."

"War Wizard Abielard," he said, in that sharp way he had with all his war wizards, "it is hardly necessary for you to run, slap-sandaled through the Silent Room to—"

"I'm sorry, my lord," the war wizard panted, "but Prince Baerovus is *awake*."

22

THE PALACE MIGHT AS WELL HAVE BEEN ON THE OTHER END OF THE world; Raedra and Ospra could not reach Baerovus's sickroom swiftly enough. Already there were nobles milling outside the room, bowing as the princesses were hurried past.

"Do not open that door again until we say so," Raedra ordered the Purple Dragons.

Baerovus sat, propped up by so many cushions he might have been an angel descending on a cloud. As he slept, Raedra had noticed the flesh melting from his already rangy frame, magic and thin gruel not enough to keep up with his body's needs. But awake, his dark eyes sunk into their sockets and his cheekbones stood out like knives.

"Oh, my dear sweet boy!" Ospra cried. She rushed to him, gathering him up in her arms.

"Mother," Baerovus said, his voice rough and tense. "Raedra." He pushed Ospra away, searching her face. "I don't know what happened," he finally blurted. "They've asked if I know, and I don't and they won't tell me. But this is not my room, and I know you wouldn't put me in another room unless there were a reason. Please tell me."

Ospra smoothed his hair. "My darling, you've been asleep. Asleep for a very long time."

"How long a time?

"Two months," Ospra said, folding his hand in hers. "Nearly three."

"You were struck by Netherese magic," Ganrahast said. "We managed to dispel it, but there was damage."

Baerovus swallowed. "Am I all right?"

"We will make certain that you are," Ganrahast said.

Baerovus nodded to himself. "And father?"

Ospra's eyes welled up with new tears. "Your father . . . vanished, trying to escape the same battle. We never found him."

All the air came out of Baerovus in a great rush. His wide eyes found Raedra's, but she could only nod. "No," he said, his own tears rising. "No."

"There is more," Ganrahast said.

"Can't it wait?" Raedra cried. "Give him a chance."

"Your pardon, Highness, I don't think it can." Baerovus looked up at the Royal Magician as if he held a sword to his throat. "King Foril has also passed on. He died last month."

Baerovus covered his eyes, to hide the tears, to hide from the truth.

"Rover," Raedra said. "Stay with us."

"I'm the king, aren't I?" he said in a small, flat voice. "Grandfather's dead, and father's dead, and so I'm the king." He sighed, a long shuddering sound edged with unspent tears. "*Hrast!*"

"Your Highnesses?" a Purple Dragon beside the door said. "I know you asked the door to remain closed, but is there any news we can relay?"

"We demand to see the king!" Lord Turin Huntcrown shouted.

"And I have to see them, don't I?" Baerovus said. "They've already waited for a month. Oh gods. Hrast, *hrast*!"

It was invitation enough for the lords beyond the door. Pheonard Crownsilver, Turin Huntcrown and more than a few others crowded the door. They bowed, those who could enter. But Baerovus only nodded, his eyes locked on his feet beneath the covers, his face blank of comprehension. As if he were sliding back within himself, trying to escape this waking nightmare.

"Out!" Raedra barked. "Everyone but Lord Ganrahast and Princess Ospra needs to leave."

Pheonard gave her an oily smile. "With all due respect, Princess, that is King Baerovus's prerogative. You are not regent any longer."

Raedra nearly told the Purple Dragons to take hold of him, just to call his godsbedamned bluff. But Ganrahast's warning came back to her: *You are not your grandfather's cheeky bird any longer.*

"A fair point," she conceded. "Your Majesty," she said to Baerovus, with a deep curtsy. He wouldn't look at her still. "Would you like these people to leave you alone for the moment?"

Baerovus glanced at Ospra. "I should be talking to them, shouldn't I?"

"You're king, my lord," Raedra said sweetly. "Who you do or do not speak with is your prerogative. Do you want to talk to people right now?"

Baerovus gave a small shake of his head. Raedra gracefully interposed herself between her brother and the courtiers. "There you are, my lords. I'm afraid the king would prefer to rest. You may call on him another time."

Pheonard gave her another oily smile. "Of course, Your Majesty. We'll be waiting."

The first arrows, Raedra thought as Lord Crownsilver left, *in a very long war. And now you have far less to fight them with.*

But for the moment, all that mattered was Baerovus. Ospra hugged him close again, clutching his head to her shoulder. He looked up at Raedra.

"If I must be the king," Baerovus said, "then I want a law that you cannot call me 'Your Majesty' or 'my lord.' Ever. It sounds as if you're someone else. I don't care if it's protocol."

"I will only do it if it makes those bastards listen," Raedra said.

"Raedra!" Ospra said disapprovingly. "Choose a different word."

"The word I'd like to use is *far* more uncouth," Raedra said. She sat at the foot of the bed. "Rover, we don't have to talk about all of it now. But you must have a coronation. It can be small and quick. They can do it right in this room—"

"No," Baerovus said. "I really must insist I go back to my own room. As soon as possible. Now. Preferably."

"Of course," Raedra said. "Just give them a chance to make it ready for you."

Baerovus winced. "They've touched everything, haven't they?"

"They know better," Ospra said. She released him, and Baerovus pulled his knees up to his chest, laying his head against them. "We could do the coronation in the Royal Court," Ospra said. "We *ought* to do it in the Royal Court."

Baerovus tensed all over, and Ospra pursed her mouth. If there were a place in all of Suzail that Baerovus liked less than the Royal Court, Raedra had not been there with him. So many people, so many rules about where one could sit or go, and when one could speak—and then everyone tried to twist and bend them so that he couldn't be sure what he was supposed to do or not supposed to do. It overwhelmed him.

"Perhaps we ought to do it in the stables," Raedra said. "Make it clear it's the king's prerogative."

"Raedra," Ospra chided.

"I should think there would be a lot of complaining about that," Baerovus said, missing the joke. "Everyone would wear their good shoes and be surprised there was muck. And then I shall be known as 'Mad King Baerovus' for certain." He lifted his head, setting his chin on his knees. "But that will surely happen anyway."

It nearly broke Raedra's heart.

"What about the Hall of Gazes?" she said. "It's proper enough—who can complain at the king swearing his oaths before the portrait of Faerlthann First-King?" She laid her hand on his ankle. "And it is narrow enough, so that we *must* limit the guests and cannot swarm you easily."

"I like it," Ospra said. "Eccentric, but well-reasoned. And deeply symbolic with everything else happening."

"What else is happening?" Baerovus asked.

"We'll worry about that next," Raedra said. "But keep in mind, you have us beside you. And you are king—you may always decide what you need to have done."

Baerovus eyed the edge of the covers. "All right," he said, and Raedra knew he didn't believe her. Rules, after all, were rules.

"Raedra has been a very good regent for you, Baerovus," Ganrahast said from his corner, and a strange pang of grief hit Raedra. "You can rely on her."

"I always have," Baerovus said, taking her hand and squeezing it.

• • •

"Lords of the Nine," Sairché muttered from their hiding place behind a row of rocks at the top of the rise north of the village of Gladehap. "At this rate we're never getting out of here."

"Is it still there?" Havilar murmured.

"Winging around like an imp on a string," Sairché said. She slid back down to sit beside Havilar and Zoonie. Havilar slunk low around the bracken to where she was in sight of Brin and the others where they'd camped beyond another rise, and signaled with a thumbs down. Whoever was visiting Lady Marsheena on a bat-winged veserab, they were still there.

The road out of Juniril had flooded before they could leave, the bogs around the road turning into lakes and sodden islands. Lord Santedul had been pleased—Shade would hardly come slogging through the bogs to capture a fishing village—but the only way out had been a fishing boat across the Wyvernwater and then too many days picking their way through the trail-less hills and moors and abandoned farms, toward the Way of the Manticore and the road back to Suzail. Twice they'd run into goblin bands, which was to Havilar a welcome distraction, but it slowed them down. Too many times, they'd been forced to detour and delay by parties of Shadovar soldiers heading the same direction. As much as Havilar knew she wasn't the only one itching for a proper fight, she had to concede that giving them a chance to spot Irvel would be very bad indeed.

And then they'd finally come close to the road, to the village of Gladehap, which Irvel had waxed long and nostalgic for. "Loveliest little place you've ever set eyes on," he said. "Pretty little dell, charming green. Shops," he added, with a smile at Havilar, "with all the very nicest wares. Ospra and I used to come up here when we were young, let Baerovus toddle around the picnic field."

Of course, when they'd come to Gladehap there was no one there, except Marsheena's army, camped on the picnic field and rifling through the little boarded-up houses.

"We should move quickly," Mehen had said when they'd retreated far enough to be sure the lookouts wouldn't spot them. "Get around them while we can."

But Irvel had shaken his head. "We wait. The path they take to Suzail is critical."

"We'll risk them beating us there, Your Majesty," Mehen said. "We could bring critical information to Suzail if we hurry."

Irvel pointed up at the hawk circling overhead. "They know. Let's see if we can divine anything they can't."

So they watched and they waited and then a veserab came diving into Gladehap. The creature, which looked like nothing so much as a flying lamprey to Havilar, had been tethered by a long lead and flew in circles around the encampment, shrieking to itself.

"Does your sweetheart think we're dealing with a Prince?" Sairché asked. "Or just another grasping lackey?"

"I don't know," Havilar said. She and Brin were avoiding each other, circling each other, one advancing and the other evading, like two opponents on a sparring circle. Irvel and Constancia kept Havilar from approaching him, just as Desima and Zoonie seemed to make Brin keep his distance.

Sairché raised an eyebrow. "So are you through with him then?"

Yes. No. Havilar scowled at Sairché. "All I said is I don't know if a prince rode the veserab. Why should it matter?"

"Because a Prince of Shade is no one we want to be anywhere near," Sairché said. "They're powerful shades, all of them, and some degree of lunatic enough to throw in with the goddess of loss and utter destruction in order to reclaim an empire, so I don't imagine there's much hope they're going to ignore the Crown Prince of Cormyr sitting a hundred and fifty yards away." She shot Havilar a withering look. "'Why should it matter?' Honestly, it's a testament to the laziness of your plane that you've survived this long without caring about local politics."

Havilar stuck her tongue out, and patted Zoonie's side. The hellhound rubbed at the muzzle with one paw, and Havilar wished she could take it off—it probably chafed terribly. But there was absolutely no way she'd do that now. Constancia had insisted on telling Irvel what Zoonie was, and Havilar was a little glad that Brin was still mad at his cousin about it.

But Irvel didn't seem to care—since Juniril and finding out about his father's death, there was a grimness to him that made Havilar miss the man who saw good signs in all manner of ordinary sights. "We take what weapons the gods give us," he'd said. "If it gets us to Suzail faster, I don't care if it's part veserab."

Havilar was wondering what it would take to steal the veserab now circling the Shadovar army, when Zoonie rolled up onto her feet, ears pricked. Sairché drew her wand. Havilar shifted into a crouch, glaive in hand, and eased forward enough to see around the line of bracken.

Tattered, bruised, sunken-cheeked, and sallow as a corpse, Moriah stood on the other side. Her breath came in a faint wheeze, her eyes bright and fevered. Sores covered her bare arms and one marred her cheek.

Sairché's wand lit. "Stay back." Moriah's eyes fluttered, but she didn't move.

"Moriah?" Havilar said, easing a little nearer.

Moriah took three swaying steps forward. Havilar pulled back the blade to strike—whatever Moriah was, she wouldn't harm Havilar. But the priestess's leg buckled and she fell forward without even lifting a hand to break her fall.

Havilar crept just near enough to see her reddened, lifeless eyes, the still blades of grass beside her parted mouth. "She's dead."

"I can see that," Sairché said. "Get away from her—she's riddled with *something*."

Havilar peered at the corpse—the same sores that had been eating at Irvel's skin when they found him. "She followed us all the way from the Hullack like this?"

Soft footsteps approached and Havilar turned toward them, weapon raised. Brin stepped around the ferns. "We found Moriah," Havilar said grimly. Brin smiled.

All the hairs on Havilar's neck stood on end, and Zoonie let out a low growl.

"Well met again, Havilar," Brin said, but it wasn't Brin looking at her. It might have been his body, his face, his features, but the voice, the cold malevolence in his eyes was the same as whatever had looked out of Moriah. What had looked out of Crake, Havilar realized. It looked over at Sairché, dismissively. "*Baatezu*," Brin said. "I see you haven't scurried back to your master yet. Pity for you. Put the wand down or I'll unmask you."

Sairché lowered her weapon. "Who are you?" she asked, peering at Brin.

"Get away from him," Havilar said, squeezing her glaive. But there was nothing to hit—it was Brin and something using him like a shield. Her heart started racing.

Brin clucked his tongue. "None of that now. You had your chance to come along easily, and you didn't take it."

"All I recall is you telling me not to trust devils."

"You never let me finish. Let's finish, Havilar."

"First get out of him." Havilar heard the tremor in her own voice.

"It's quite simple," the creature in Brin said. "You have something I need, locked deep inside you. First, I would be certain it is there and, to do that, I need you—Havilar—to get out of the way. Ideally, I would have found a way to possess *you* or the priestess would have had the sort of tinctures to lock you aside. Ideally, you would have been eager to aid me, but that moment has passed. So I need you to get very close with dear Moriah's mortal coil and find a way to give yourself a fever, and get nice and addled for me."

"A fever?" Havilar said. "That might take days."

Something else smiled at her, twisting Brin's face into an unfamiliar mask. "I can wait. I've waited a long time already. And when someone chooses not to aid me . . . I like to make sure they regret it. Touch the body."

Havilar didn't move. Brin stretched out his right hand, considering it. He took hold of his own index finger, met Havilar's eyes, and wrenched it back with a sharp *crack* of bone. She clapped a hand over her cry of horror.

Brin smiled. "He means *nothing* to me. Do you understand that? I will cut his body apart, bit by bit, and all the while . . . he's still here. He'll know it's your obstinance that's killing him slowly, and he'll feel every bit of it."

"Don't do it," Sairché said. "You can fix a finger." She tilted her head. "You can't fix betrayal."

Brin smiled. "But you can repay it. Touch the body, or we see how well he handles a broken leg next."

Havilar clung to her glaive as she crouched down beside Moriah's oozing corpse, swallowing against a lump in her throat. If she took the glaive to Brin, it would only hurt him, not the ghost. Crying out would alert the Shadovar. She glanced across the field to where Constancia and Mehen crouched behind an emptied henhouse. Constancia stared straight ahead in a way that Havilar knew meant she was focusing very hard on what lay to her side—on Havilar and the hellhound no doubt. The way the bracken grew, they couldn't see Moriah, but they could see Brin and Havilar, if she stood.

"If his plight doesn't move you," Brin said, "there is always your own. I'm prepared to kill you and hold fast to your whole soul if need be. I've done it . . ." He trailed off, as if he forgot what he was saying, then blinked his eyes hard as if the ghost was reaffirming its control. "Touch the corpse."

"Brin, I am so sorry about this," Havilar whispered. In one swift move, she straightened, keeping her grip near the base of the glaive, and swung the flat side of the blade into Brin's head. He gave a hideous, horrible grunt, and toppled over. Sairché cried out.

"Get back," Havilar advised, as she turned to the sound of Constancia's booted feet, the sound of a blade being drawn.

She dropped the glaive, hands raised high. "Ghost!" she hissed, as loudly as she dared. "Turn it! Turn it before he wakes!"

For a moment, she thought that Constancia wouldn't stop in time, that the paladin's blade would take her. Beside her, Zoonie coiled as if to spring. Mehen was rushing across the gap to tackle the knight.

But Constancia looked down at Brin as he stirred, that alien malevolence shining through his eyes for the briefest moment.

The ghost contorted his face in terror. "She killed Moriah," he whispered. "She was going to kill me. Constancia, help."

The paladin's expression hardened. Her hand went to the gauntlet symbol welded to her armor. "By Loyal Torm I cast thee back to Kelemvor's mercies," she intoned. A bright light swelled around the symbol, surging down Constancia's hand as she slammed it against Brin's chest. The air went out of him in a *whuff*, his eyes bulging, and he screamed in two terrible voices, twining together. The something that smelled of mildew and brimstone and ice streamed out of his nose and mouth and ears, thick as blood and swirling in a strange cloud over him. Brin stopped screaming, went slack.

Shouts. A trumpet's blare.

Constancia's eyes were ice. "Get him on that stlarning animal and run."

Glaive in the harness—Havilar hauled Brin up and over Zoonie's shoulders, pulling herself up behind him. Up the rise, through the forest—if they glimpsed the hellhound, there was no way the Shadovar wouldn't chase it. The hellhound lurched forward, then yelped as another weight settled behind Havilar.

"You are *not* leaving me behind," Sairché said as Zoonie started forward, into the brush again. An arrow *zinged* past them. The shouts of the Shadovar soldiers came nearer—at least a dozen. She glanced back, past Sairché—a score. Were the others running?

"If ever there was a time I needed to pull you back—"

"You're not pulling me anywhere," Havilar snapped, as Zoonie hauled herself up onto the rise. Havilar turned and shoved Sairché off the hellhound's back and onto the grass. "And I'm not taking our wizard. Throw spells at them, and run if you have to."

"You little fool!" Sairché shouted. "Where are you going?"

"To distract them," Havilar said grimly. She leaned over Brin's slack form and spoke in Zoonie's pricked ear. "Can you make a lot of fire?"

Zoonie yelped twice and then a third, deeper bark that sent a plume of flame out over the brush. She shook her head, raining sparks.

"Good girl." Havilar wrapped the chain around her fist and one arm around Brin. "Let's go."

Freed of the extra weight, the hellhound bounded down the steep slope, darting between the trees. The others were hurrying up the same slope, off to Havilar's left, and as she passed, she heard Constancia shout at her, but she paid it no mind.

Zoonie raced toward the Shadovar soldiers—all ordinary men and woman armored in black—jaws sparking through the muzzle. She darted near enough for Havilar to glimpse the whites of one terrified soldier's eyes as he scrambled to a stop. Zoonie snarled at him, and bounded toward the road.

Havilar couldn't understand the shouted orders, but a blaze of blue-black magic seared through the air past her head, and when she glanced back, a solid half of the soldiers—including their wizard—were chasing her. Zoonie stopped, prancing in a circle, as if she wanted to dive back into the attackers racing toward them. Another blast shot past Havilar.

"Go!" she shouted, tugging on the chain. "Lead them off."

Another fiery bark, and the hellhound ran for the road—it was all Havilar could do to hold tight to her and to Brin. They broke out into the road. More shouts—another band of Shadovar soldiers had stood at a blockade there. Havilar cursed and nudged the hellhound to go faster, farther. From up on the ridge, a smattering of burning hail rained down on the Shadovar. She was far enough ahead they might not catch her. A swarm of arrows zipped past—

She felt the first arrow's impact in the back of her shoulder before the pain registered, knocking the wind from her and abruptly sapping the strength from the arm around Brin. She gave a wordless cry as pain burned through her. The second didn't hurt nearly as much, buried below the first.

Run, she thought. Run, run, run.

A whirl of shadows—a gray-skinned man suddenly stood in the road, one hand upraised. A pulse of energy, cold and airless, slammed against them and Zoonie's legs went out from under her as she scrabbled to a stop. Havilar clung to Brin as they were thrown free. The arrows *snapped* beneath her, driving another cry of pain from Havilar.

"Well, well," the shade said. "What a strange little spy."

Havilar clambered to her feet, sliding the glaive from its harness. Her vision swam as she did, but she kept herself firm—this was no time to faint. Dimly she heard Zoonies's pained whine. She stepped between Brin and the shade, and he smiled.

"You're going to die one way or another," he said. "But come with me first, and I promise it will be swift."

Havilar shifted her grip, focusing on him instead of the screaming pain in her back. "Better fools than you have tried."

The shade's smile widened as he drew his sword, shadows unfolding from the blade.

He darted forward, so fast that Havilar didn't have time to think, only move. The sword's strike rattled her glaive—once, twice. She caught both, and sidestepped a third before slicing the blade down toward his shoulder. The shade seemed to blur, to skip across her vision. Devilslayer cut through the empty air and the sword came at her from the right now.

Twist. Swing the butt of the glaive up—the shade stumbled back. But he was coming at her again, and Havilar's feet danced backward before she could tell them to. Her vision prickled, a thousand tiny lights flashing around the edges, and her ears ached with Zoonie's whines. She lunged forward with the glaive, forced the shade back—away from Brin, away from Zoonie.

Gods, gods, any minute those archers would be here. She slashed at him, quick as the glaive would move, but he only retreated. He's wearing you out, she thought. *Henish.* Her shoulder was screaming, pain all down her arm. Her grip was weakening.

The shade attacked again, his blade so quick it might have been made of shadow and air. But it struck the glaive's shaft with the joint-shaking strength of steel.

Any moment now, she thought. You have to end it.

She dived forward, past his guard, and managed to pull the glaive's heavy blade up into the joint of his arm. But the sword came around her side, slamming into her ribs. The air exploded from her lungs. A lightning bolt of pain exploded across her ribs, tangling with the pain from the arrows. Havilar hit the road.

The shade came to stand over her. "Now. Will you come give Lady Marsheena and Prince Yder your audience?" he said. He twirled the sword that still leaked shadows. "Or shall we continue?"

Havilar couldn't draw breath enough to answer. She looked past the shade, at Brin struggling up from the ground, at Zoonie trying to regain her feet—

A dark shape plummeted out of the sky, larger than any hawk. Sairché, red-skinned and bat-winged once more, hit the shade square in the shoulders with both feet, driving him hard into the ground. His head slammed against the road, stunning him. Sairché checked the fingers of her left hand, then wrapped her fist around the silvery ring there and punched him hard in the back of the skull. A burst of light exploded outward. The man screamed, an unearthly sound, as the radiance seemed to scour the shadow from his body. Sairché pulled the dagger from her belt and plunged it into his back, before stepping off of him.

"Listen, you little mongrel," Sairché said, coming to stand over Havilar. "I don't care *who* you're the Chosen of, don't you push me off that shitting hellhound again. I have *one* job here, and it should be simple! If you so much as look cross-eyed at another Netherese soldier, I swear on everything you hold dear, I will drag you back to the Hells, back to that shitting stasis cage and I will feed the trigger ring to the godsbedamned Dragon Queen and let you guess which head got it!"

She pulled a small vial from her pocket, checked it, and dropped it on Havilar. Then she retied the chain she wore about her neck, resuming the appearance of an older human woman. "Drink the potion, get up, and let's get out of here."

"You're not coming with us."

For a terrible moment, Havilar was afraid it was the strange ghost again. But when she lifted her head enough to see, it was Brin—only Brin—rising to his feet, the holy symbol of Torm grasped in his whole, shaking hand.

"Well," Sairché said, "I suppose that little ruse is ended."

"Quite right," Brin said. The symbol in his hand took on a faint shimmering. Sairché sneered at him. "As if that's worked for you lately."

Brin never took his eyes off the cambion. "Havi," he asked, "did you know?"

"Brin," she managed. She pulled herself up onto her hands, and nearly vomited from the pain. Zoonie was opposite her, standing with one hind leg tucked up, one front leg bent.

"Did you know?"

"She has arrows in her back and a rack of broken ribs from trying to save your pitiful self," Sairché said. "Drink your bloody potion." She stared back at Brin. "And then get up: we're leaving."

Havilar shook her head. She'd rather wait here for the Shadovar archers.

"No, you aren't. You're right," Brin said. "Torm hasn't been answering my prayers the way I'd have hoped. But this one's been enchanted with something extra."

A ball of burning light struck Sairché between the shoulder blades, knocking her forward. She spun around to face Constancia, storming across the road toward her.

"And Torm seems to like her fine," Brin finished.

Sairché threw herself out of the reach of Constancia's sword, nearly tripping on the dead shade in the process. The knight advanced, but the devil was quick. Sairché pulled the ring from her finger and, with a last glance at Havilar, blew through it, casting a whirlwind that sucked her out of the plane and back to the Nine Hells.

Constancia's sword sliced through the air where she'd been, landing with a *clank* against the paved road.

"Havi!" she heard Mehen shout. "Havi!" He was running down the hill toward them, sword out. Kallan and Irvel behind him. Havilar's arm was shaking.

Constancia turned, sword on the dragonborn. "Stay back. Your daughter's been in league with devils."

Mehen didn't slow. "My daughter is *injured.*"

"Constancia," Brin said. "Put your sword down. The devil's gone."

"One devil's gone. And what did she do but run you straight into our attackers?"

Havilar's arm buckled, no longer able to hold her, and her vision closed briefly. She woke to Kallan tipping a healing potion into her mouth, Brin close beside, while Mehen shouted at Constancia.

"Havi," Brin said, smoothing a hand over her cheek. "Did you know she was Sairché?"

Tears flooded Havilar's eyes—how could she have thought it was a good idea to keep it a secret? It seemed so obvious that it was always going to get away from her.

"I didn't have a choice," she said. Then, "I didn't think I had a choice."

"Will you all hush!" Irvel shouted. "Someone's coming."

Havilar jolted upright. "Archers. There were archers—"

An arrow landed with a meaty *thwack* in the dead shade's thigh. Another clattered to the pavement. Another grazed Brin's arm.

"Move!" Mehen bellowed. Havilar scooped up her glaive. Zoonie barked and tried to follow.

"Havilar, come on!" Mehen shouted.

Sairché's healing potion still lay on the ground where she'd left it. No one else had seen it, so no one else had fed it to her. Havilar snatched it up and jammed the end of it through the muzzle's cage and into Zoonie's mouth. The dog balked, but Havilar held the vial firm. An arrow hit Zoonie in the hindquarters, and she leaped out of Havilar's grip on new-healed legs. Havilar sprinted after, chasing Mehen and the others toward the trees, toward cover.

Then over the rise, another army appeared, and her heart nearly stopped—how could they be expected to outfight yet another enemy?

And then she saw the fireball scream out of the hands of the dark-haired woman hanging in the air beside the lead riders and slam into the ground at the center of the Shadovar archers.

Pikemen ran ahead of the riders and it was all Havilar could do to get out of their way. Mehen caught hold of her and pulled her close. A rain of arrows fell from the sky, sent this time by Cormyrean bows to clear the way for the pikemen. The riders came up the sides, closing the paths into the woods.

Another rider, a man in a purple tabard, came forward and reined his horse in beside their little party. Zoonie gave a low, rumbling growl. He was dark-haired and a bit thick, like a dock worker or a butcher—all muscle with a layer of softness.

"Cousin," the dark-bearded man said, with a little smile. "How very fortuitous."

"Erzoured," Irvel said, chillier than Havilar expected. "What are you doing here?"

The man gave Irvel a grin that put Havilar entirely too much in mind of Lorcan. "Winning your war, Your Majesty," he said. "Shall we help you home?"

· · ·

THERE ONCE WAS a wizard who wanted power beyond all mortal reach, the strange voice murmured to Ilstan. He couldn't stop it. Azuth had been murmuring at him since he woke.

Ilstan would never have said he was afraid of the Royal Magician, but as Ganrahast considered him from the other side of his desk, the war wizard was put uncomfortably in mind of an obscenely intelligent hawk, biding its time. He kept his expression still, and hoped it didn't show that he was listening to someone else as well.

Such stories always end poorly, the voice murmured.

"Obviously," Ganrahast said, "I am deeply disappointed that you didn't bring this to my attention yourself."

I tried, Ilstan wanted to say. It wouldn't matter. "Who told you?" he asked. "Was it Her Highness?"

But luckily for the wizard, the Lady of the Mysteries took a shine to him and became his queen . . .

"That isn't important. What is important is that we know what we're dealing with. I cannot allow a war wizard with divided loyalties to stand in a position where the royal family could be compromised." His dark eyes seemed to sharpen. "We are only recently aware of the . . . Chosen situation." He said the word with not a little disgust. "But from the sound of it, you may need some time to yourself as things sort out."

She granted him powers—such powers—until he was no longer a mere wizard but a god in truth . . . A god dedicated to his lady and all who wore her crown . . .

"Sorry," Ilstan said, aware he'd let the silence hang. "Sort what out?"

"There is no being certain what will happen," Ganrahast said. "You are developing some sort of powers—and I suspect it is that and not the remade Weave that is the source of your recent . . . spell-slippage."

He forgot what it was to be human. What it was to not wear the god's mantle. He forgot what it was to crave power.

"I don't have the luxury of dismissing you from your post for the duration."

"You wouldn't!" Ilstan cried. Ganrahast raised his eyebrows. "My apologies, Lord Wizard. I . . . I am useful still. I think . . . I think Princess Raedra may be in danger."

And so he was not there when her rivals came for his queen.

"I think you have become entirely too concerned with Her Highness," Ganrahast said bluntly. "Why did War Wizard Barcantle allow you to remain so frequently on her guard?"

"She requested it," Ilstan said lamely.

"Well, she isn't requesting it now," Ganrahast said.

Down, down, the wizard fell, from the heights of the heavens to the depths of the Hells, the fabric of the very planes tearing as he passed . . .

"As I was saying, I don't have the luxury of dismissing you until your business is settled. We are short-handed in the most extreme fashion. You must remain in Suzail. But I will be having you sweep the tunnels."

"Is that really the best you can use me for?" Ilstan asked.

And perhaps, then, it was a fitting punishment, for the wizard who forgot what it was to want, that he landed broken at the feet of one who was nothing but want incarnate.

"It is the best holiday I can provide for you," Ganrahast said, standing. "You will keep me abreast of anything that changes." He exhaled once. "They say you're favored by Azuth. Is that true?"

"I don't know," Ilstan said. "I only know what I was told."

Ganrahast sighed. "I never thought I'd see the day where we must take the word of a tiefling warlock on matters of the gods of magic."

"Maybe you shouldn't," Ilstan said. He shook his head. "You shouldn't. She shouldn't be here, I'm sure of that. It started with her—"

"War Wizard Nyaril," Ganrahast said, cutting off the younger man. "There are a thousand actual threats you could be concerning yourself with. The motives of a tiefling whose spells are trifling and whose aid has thus far been a benefit to all of us are not one. Now, if you please." He gestured to the door.

Ilstan left the Royal Magician's tower and wandered the palace halls for a time, listening to the muttering voice and wondering what would come next. In the Hall of Gazes, he stopped beside a window, looking down into the Royal Gardens. There was Raedra, standing beside Baerovus, between the king and a pack of advisors, while Baerovus shot arrow after arrow into the bull's eye of a target. Too far to hear what they were saying, but he could see Raedra's earnestness and the advisors'—the war council, he realized—discomfort. It was raining after all. And a normal king would be pleased to be inside, sitting behind a table, discussing things.

The rain slicked Raedra's gown down against her.

He remembers now, too late, what it means, the perils and the potentials.

She has not brought Farideh back in tendays, Ilstan reminded himself. Or had she? Why would she tell him? Why would any of them tell him? They were all avoiding him, every war wizard in the palace. He walked down toward the gardens, he needed to warn her.

By the time he reached the gardens, though, the lot of them were returning, passing through the halls muttering about dry clothes and warm wine, and where had summer gone? Ilstan bowed as Baerovus and Raedra passed. The young king stopped.

"Well met, Ilstan," he said. "I haven't seen you around."

"Her Highness has no use for me," Ilstan said. Raedra's expression didn't flicker.

"Of course she does," Baerovus scoffed. "She has to have war wizards and highknights and Purple Dragons, same as all of us."

"Would you excuse us, Rover?" Raedra asked.

"Of course." Baerovus nodded to Ilstan. "Well met."

"Are you better?" Raedra asked.

"You've been avoiding me, haven't you?" Ilstan said. "You cast me off."

"No," Raedra said. "I asked that you not be made to guard me while you were compromised. I think that's entirely reasonable."

"I have never been compromised," Ilstan said, even as the god rambled in his thoughts. "I was *dedicated* to you, and you threw me away."

Raedra stiffened. "I'm sorry I've given you the impression I haven't cared. Other things have been on the forefront of my mind. But this is all sounding a bit like you think I owe you something more than I do. You are Cormyr's war wizard. Not *mine*."

"Is that *all*?" Ilstan demanded. "How can you think that's all I am?" He took a step toward her, fists balled, magic crackling around his knuckles.

Two highknights materialized beside Raedra—Ilstan had no idea where they'd been or how they'd appeared so swiftly.

"Leave," Raedra said coldly. "Right now. And be glad I did count you as a friend."

Two Purple Dragons marched him from the palace—what would happen now? Would Ganrahast recall him? Would Raedra change her mind? Would he be made to wander Suzail, waiting for Azuth to grant him something, anything that might change things? He could think of nothing else to do, so he did just that, walking circles in the rain. Passersby marked his dark robes, the purple dragon stitched on the hood and breast, and gave him a wide berth.

He found himself standing before Aubrin Crownsilver's tallhouse. Staring up at the windows. Wondering where the tiefling was. Her dragonborn doorguard spotted him, bared his jagged teeth like some kind of animal. Ilstan made himself invisible and stayed where he was.

Then she came out.

Cowled and cloaked, Farideh hurried up the Promenade, heading east. Toward the palace. Ilstan followed her, Azuth's rambling voice a dull buzz in his thoughts. This was it, he thought. This would be how he caught her.

But she continued on past the palace, down the Promenade. She wove through the crowds and carts, tucked deep into her robe, until she reached the Silent Room.

In the temple of Oghma, Farideh hesitated before stepping into the sanctuary. She looked around and withdrew a pair of books from under her stormcloak. Ilstan watched as she left them surreptitiously on a table before heading deeper into the temple.

Ilstan wove into the bookshelves, letting his invisibility drop. He kept pace with the tiefling, staying near enough to hear her apologize and introduce herself to an old loremaster near the middle of the library.

"Would you have anything about Azuth in your library?" she asked.

The voice of the god went suddenly silent in Ilstan's head.

It's not just Raedra you have to worry about, Ilstan thought, no longer able to hear the edge of madness in his thoughts.

23

2 Uktar, the Year of the Nether Mountain Scrolls (1486 DR)
Suzail, Cormyr

ROVER?" RAEDRA CALLED THROUGH THE DOOR, TRYING TO IGNORE THE pair of war wizards almost standing on her skirts. "Rover, you either have to come out, or let someone in."

"I do not," Baerovus called back, his speech quick and agitated. "If I'm the king, then I may do as I please, and I don't wish to hold court today. Tell them to come back tomorrow."

Raedra bit back a curse. "Will you let *me* in?"

A pause. "Go around the other way, and I'll meet you."

"Stay here," she told the war wizards before she slipped into the passageway. "Give us a moment."

"Highness," the first, a bearded man, said. "He *must* come out."

"And he will not, if you try and drag him," Raedra said, climbing into the passage. "So give me a moment."

Baerovus opened the secret door, his eyes hollow and his expression tight. "I already know," he said, helping her over the traps, "that everyone thinks I'm acting like a child and being difficult on purpose. But I can't. I can't do this, not today. And people keep saying I need to stand my ground, and so I'm standing my ground on this. You can't make me hold court."

"You're right," Raedra said. "But I don't think you should be so hasty. Your advisors are very upset. They can't do much without their king."

"They don't even listen to me," Baerovus said. "I've said a hundred times that they need to make you crown princess, and everyone always changes the subject to some other nonsense."

"You can't make me crown princess," Raedra said gently. "It sends the message you won't have heirs."

"But I won't," Baerovus said. He dropped onto a couch as if his legs couldn't hold him any longer. "It would make no sense for me to marry. I'm not interested. This is the right thing to do, and no one will do it. They just keep trapping me in rooms with women I don't want to talk to."

"You could just pick one to marry and give it a try," she said. With the line so slim, Cormyr needed Obarskyrs. "You could marry Varauna and both be very happy continuing exactly as you are."

"That is a terrible idea. She teases me horribly." He sighed and ran his hands through his hair. "Why did he have to die? I knew going to war was a bad plan. And what if I die too? They're going to insist I ride out eventually. Kings do. You need to be crown princess."

"You don't *need* a crown princess," Raedra assured him. "If you don't have heirs, then the crown will pass to me regardless. A long time from now." She sat down beside him and wrapped her arms around her brother, hugging him tight. "I know this isn't what you want. I know this is overwhelming and frightening and . . . it would have been nice if Father had had a nice, long reign to follow and you could rule over fat farmers and distracted nobles." She let him go and squeezed his shoulders. "But right now, your people are frightened too. You need to go out there and look like a king."

"I don't look like a king."

"Put your crown on," Raedra said. "I'll pick out some clothes for you. Walk into the audience chamber and let people talk at you for *one* hour. Look thoughtful, and I shall sit beside you the whole time, in case you must give an opinion and want to talk it out. Then retire. That's all you have to do today."

Baerovus shook his head. "What's that supposed to do for them being scared?"

"You'd be surprised. If you give them a little, their imaginations will fill in the rest." She smoothed his hair. "But if you give them nothing, the same thing will happen."

At the close of an hour, there were still petitioners who wished King Baerovus's time, but it was all Baerovus could do not to sprint from the court. Raedra watched him go. They could work up to a longer stretch, she thought. They'd done it for other things—dinners and balls and social engagements. Before the war, Baerovus could muddle through several hours of strangers, provided he knew what was coming and had a quiet place to retreat to when it was through.

The Dragon Throne loomed lonely beside her, and Raedra swallowed a sigh. For all she felt as though she'd been thrown into the harbor in her court dress at the beginning of her regency, by the end she felt as if the gods were snatching back a sort of paradise.

"Do you think he will ever accustom himself to it?" Princess Ospra stood beside her daughter, her deep black mourning untouched by any spot of color, and her pallor unaided by paint.

No, Raedra thought. He will only learn to suffer through it. "With time all things are possible," she said.

"He has you," Ospra said.

Raedra smoothed her own gray skirts. "I know you don't want me propping him up—he has to learn it for himself, but—"

"No," Ospra said. "I'm not unfeeling. Your father and I had hoped the right pressures would shake Baerovus from his strangeness, but it's clear to me that they only entrenched it. If there was any chance to change him, we lost it." She stared after her son, looking as if a stiff breeze would scatter her. "I do not wish he were still sleeping," she said. "Only it seems as if it would be kinder to everyone. They say the Shadovar have stalled near Gladehap. Perhaps Erzoured has a use after all."

"Perhaps," Raedra answered. In truth, she did not worry so much about the army of Lady Marsheena as she did the Sembians to the east. The shades made a more fearful image. The eastern army was stronger, and pushing back the Army of the Purple Dragon every day.

"Have you heard anything from Aubrin?"

In truth, Raedra had not thought of Aubrin in the last four days. "Not a word."

War Wizard Pelia Rowanmantle strode up to the princesses. "Highnesses," she said with a little bow. "His Majesty has locked himself in his rooms again. Do you think one of you could persuade him to come out and eat something?"

"I'll go," Ospra said. She embraced her daughter. "You have a rest."

Raedra walked to the Shrine of the Four Swords, taking up her customary place across from Orbyn's gleaming blade. People in the shrine spotted her and whispered to one another, but Raedra paid them no mind. They could say whatever they liked—it would not change the truth, and it never could.

"Highness," a gruff voice said. She looked up at Oversword Gerain Huntcrown as he bowed, leaning on a wooden cane. "May I join you?"

"If you wish," she said.

He sat beside her, and for a long time neither spoke. "They say you come here often," he finally noted.

"Often enough."

"But never Lindon's grave."

Raedra regarded him cooly. "I daresay I wouldn't be welcome—his parents still think he was framed, do they not?"

He shrugged. "They're parents. I dislike accepting my second cousin twice-removed was a Netherese agent; I can't imagine it's any easier when it's your son." He tapped his cane against the floor. "I've heard that you insisted he not be sent to Wheloon. You did them a kindness they'll never realize."

Raedra traced the edge of Orbyn with her gaze. "That's hearsay. The only choice they gave me was whether it would be public or private. I didn't choose for his sake."

"For Cormyr's," the oversword agreed. "So why do you visit Orbyn still?"

"I can guess what they say. Is it because I'm a soft-hearted girl who regrets such a rash action? Because I'm a cold-hearted hag who's obsessed with the instrument that destroyed the only man who could ever have loved me? Because I'm contemplating beheading Aubrin?"

"I think," Lord Huntcrown said, "because you mourn him, but also because you remind yourself that when we serve the Forest Kingdom, our choices have consequences. Lindon chose the promise of power over his noble duty. You chose your duty over love." He tapped his cane once. "Forgive me. Perhaps you fancy the design of the hilt. I came here to tell you . . . you should know, Highness, that while I disagree with your methods, I cannot pretend they have not been working. I hear Lord Ezoured's army has been successful at clearing Calantar's Way to Hilp. Not a few of the refugees they've claimed were fleeing Wheloon. Perhaps destruction would have been rash."

"Thank you," Raedra said.

"In fact, I intend to suggest to His Majesty that you join us permenantly. Perhaps you can have Aubrin's oversword title? It's not as if he's using it at the moment."

Raedra smiled to herself. "I am quite sure my mother would die of shock. But I will join you regardless." She sighed. "And hopefully we'll discover soon what's become of Aubrin."

"Very soon," the oversword said grimly. He dropped his voice. "Word is that Marsheena marches on Marsember."

Raedra turned to him, startled. "Marsember?"

"Through the Hermit's Wood perhaps, down the Wyvernflow." He shook his head. "They're marching like there are demons on their heels. Word is Yder Tanthul marches with them."

Raedra set her eyes upon Orbyn's blade again. It had been a long time since a king had wielded the Edge of Justice in battle. Shade circled Suzail, like a flock of buzzards, like the dark dragon that screamed at sunset and flew over the armies, scattering rumors in its wake. *She is trying to frighten you,* Raedra reminded herself. *She is aiming for surrender.*

Forcing Baerovus to take up Orbyn might be the only way to wring such a thing from Raedra Obarskyr.

• • •

FARIDEH DEALS THE Wroth cards in a semicircle—Paeryl, the Mother; Tethyla, the Dark Lady; the Ancestor; the Companions; the Rising Dragon; the Adversary.

The cards slide away from her, making room for another row—Iolaum, the Arcanist; Loskor, the Harvester; the Rising Dragon; the Godborn; the Adversary. *The deck in her hands is always full, no matter how many rows she deals.*

"Darling," Lorcan says, "what are you looking for?"

She doesn't know, but it's here—it must be. The Companions; the Godborn; the Adversary; the Reaver; the Sentinel; the Herald. *The last is a Harper, his instrument in one hand, a blade in the other, looking back over his shoulder. It looks like Dahl.*

"Darling," Lorcan says again, "they're only cards; they can't steer the future. What can one mortal manage after all?"

She deals another row, unfamiliar cards coming up: the Traitor—*a red-haired succubus hovering over a city that is unmistakably Neverwinter.* The Tomb—*a library lost in a deep cavern, with a strange mummy holding a book standing in the middle of it. The Fiend in the Shadows—a dark-haired wizard with bright blue eyes, a wicked smile on his painted face, a goblet in one hand. The Handmaiden—a gray-skinned girl with glowing eyes, her hands folded as if in prayer. The Unspeakable—Brother Vartan standing at the Chasm's edge, a box in his arms, hideous tentacles waving swords all around him.*

She turns the last card—the Adversary. Only now it looks, not like an angel chasing a devil, but like a young tiefling woman with one gold eye and one silver, wreathed in flames that form wings that curve around her. She holds the rod out, parallel to the ground, drawing grasping souls out of the Nine Hells. Their spectral hands clutch at the air.

Lorcan plucks this last card up, holds it before Farideh. "What one mortal can manage with the powers of the Hells," he amends. "How very fortunate you've been."

Farideh blinks, and it's not Lorcan, but the archdevil watching her. He waves a hand and the Wroth cards scatter. "Stay alive," he says. "Remember what goals we have in common, and we can all be very happy, Farideh."

Late that night, the dream still plucked at Farideh's thoughts, and if she were being honest, she would rather have walked into the internment camp, into the lost library of the arcanist, into the Chasm of Neverwinter, rather than into Teneth's with Dahl on her arm. The festhall loomed over them, a shining edifice of painted plaster nymphs around a stained-glass window of a red-haired woman. Every thought demanded she dig her heels in, turn and go back out into the rain. She focused instead on nothing at all, letting Dahl's determined steps lead her into the first of the festhalls.

"Look," he'd said before they left, "if you don't want to go—"

"We have to go. That's four Sharrans we'll be missing, and we can't find the pattern."

"Right," Dahl said. "But technically *I* don't have to be there, if you'd rather. I was thinking, you could turn up early tomorrow, pretend to be applying for a job. Two of these places have tiefling dancers—"

Which would be worse, Farideh couldn't guess. The idea of strangers looking her over, evaluating how much still more strangers would like to stare at her—it made her want to find a very small room and shut the door. But was that so much harder than sitting next to Dahl, wondering whether he liked looking at the strange women around them—humans or tieflings or anything else? Was it worse than the persistent awareness of him while he pretended to be her not-so-secret lover?

Too late, Farideh told herself, as they crossed into the wide doorway.

An alien sort of peace came over Farideh, a warm security that made all the fear and chaos still roiling through Suzail drop away as if it never existed. She did dig her heels in then. The soul sight overtook her, out of instinct, and she swept the scattering of people around them for Chosen. "What was that?" she breathed.

Dahl laughed. "Gods, you're jumpy. It's a temple, too. Well, a sort of lay-temple," he amended. "Or a lay-shrine—I don't know how Sune categorizes these things."

A young woman wearing gossamer-thin golden scarves approached them with a little bow. "Welcome back to Teneth's," she said, eyeing Farideh curiously. "Is Lord Crownsilver . . ." She trailed off and shook her head. "My apologies. I mistook you for someone else."

Shock burned up Farideh's neck. "I think you meant my sister," she heard herself say. Havilar had come here? Havilar and *Brin*.

The young woman inclined her head once more. "Then welcome to Teneth's and the blessings of Sune Firehair on you. Before you enter, please make your ablutions." She gestured Farideh to the left, Dahl to the right. Farideh held tight to his arm.

"You just have to wash," he murmured.

"I know what ablutions means!" she said. "I don't want to be here." Even more than awkward, it felt like an invasion, an intrusion. Not only a place where Farideh had no idea what she was meant to say or do, but a place where Havilar came to keep her secrets. The shadow-smoke started leaking off her arms.

"Hey," Dahl said, turning her face toward him. "This is the simple part. Splash some scented water around, and I will buy you so much whiskey on the other side that you won't care where you are."

The young woman narrowed her eyes at him. "What was that?"

"She's just nervous," he explained. He handed over a stack of coins. "That door?" The young woman watched him go, a troubled expression on her face. She dropped the coins into a tall amphora behind her.

"Come with me," she said, taking Farideh by the hand.

They passed through another pair of doors and into a tiled room. At the center was a deep, steaming pool, where at least a dozen women lounged. Around the outer edge, stone basins caught streams of water—the whole room smelled like cedar and sandalwood and lavender. And bay—it hit her like she'd walked straight into a laurel bush. No one was dressed and everyone looked up as she came in. Farideh's tail started lashing under her cloak. The young woman led her over to one of the basins and took her cloak, folding it and tucking it into a niche. She washed Farideh's hands in the scented water, and cupped more of it up to rinse her face, before handing her a towel.

"Do you want to be here?" the young woman asked.

Farideh stared down at the water. What was she supposed to say to that? "Of course."

"Because you don't seem comfortable," she went on, "and I don't feel comfortable escorting you in with a fellow whose plan is to force whiskey on you until you don't care where you are. Say the word, and I'll show you the back way out and him to the no-nonsense."

"The what?"

The woman gave her a serious look. "Don't be shy about asking for the guards, now."

"Oh!" Farideh said. "No, no not like that." She dried her already dried hands again. "I am nervous. I don't belong here really. Definitely I don't belong here with him," she added, before she could stop herself.

The woman frowned. "Why is that?"

Farideh looked down at the basin. "I'm not his type, let's say." Except she was supposed to be, that was the cover—gods, where was her head tonight? "I mean, I don't think it's going to last much longer. I'm not the girl you bring home to your mother."

The young woman gestured for Farideh to sit, and she washed her feet in the stone basin, planting a kiss atop each, and Farideh found herself thinking it would be less strange to be fighting Erzoured's kidnappers again. She locked her eyes on the fresco on the wall, panel after panel of silver-haired women and their myriad lovers, and tried to ignore how many of the other women were watching her.

The woman finished and pinned Farideh's hair loosely on top of her head, then helped her out of Havilar's dress and into the pool. Farideh kept looking at the fresco. She didn't want to guess what the other women were thinking—whether they were gawking at her still and whether it was because she looked like a monster or because she was just built awkwardly, whether they were remembering Havilar.

No one said anything uncomfortable to her. No one got out of the pool or made a fuss. Farideh started to relax. She sank down in the hot water, nearly to her chin. A shiver of pleasure ran down her back to the tip of her tail. She wondered if public baths were like this. She wondered if Dahl's side was the same, if he was stewing in the same scented water. If they were going to make him shave.

The young woman came back after a while and helped her out of the water. She dried her wet skin while Farideh fought the urge to snatch the towel back and do it herself. The soft singing that accompanied the act made her suspect this wasn't just for Farideh's sake.

When she was dry, the young woman put her in a sleeveless, robelike dress, belted at the waist with a similarly gauzy gold scarf. The young woman frowned and touched the warlock brand on Farideh's upper arm.

"It's fine," Farideh said. "I can cover it up."

"Does it hurt?"

"Not always," Farideh said.

The young woman looked troubled, but she didn't give Farideh anything to cover up further with. "Come with me."

They went out through another door, which led into a wide room and still more doors. More people milled around here, sipping drinks, flirting with more men and women in the golden scarves. Farideh felt her tail start to lash again—she didn't see Dahl.

The young woman didn't lead her to Dahl, but over to a woman wearing a full golden dress, trimmed with ruby-colored beads. She was older than Farideh and—surprisingly—taller, her dark hair threaded with silver, but her cheeks smooth. Farideh found herself awash in relief that she was there. Before she could sort through the source of it, the woman had taken Farideh's hands in hers.

"Be welcome," she said, "Blessed of Sune."

"I think you mean someone else," Farideh said apologetically. The woman smiled, and Farideh's heart fluttered.

"Renda tells me you have doubts about your worth," she said. "Sune does not—there may be those she shows obvious favor, but all are worthy of love."

Farideh started to protest that that wasn't the problem, that she didn't need to say that sort of thing. But while in another's mouth those words would have been humiliating, platitudes that skimmed right past the reality of Farideh's life, when this woman spoke them, they struck her straight in the heart. Tears flooded her eyes, and she gripped the woman's hands hard.

"To love someone is a brave act," the woman said. "It is a bravery that we should all seize, even when the costs seem high. But love is an action, not a reward, not a magic spell. You can love someone who does not value you, and you must remember that it does not change your value. And it cannot change them."

"It's not like that," Farideh said. Was it? Not with Dahl. But Lorcan . . . she looked up into the woman's pale eyes and took hold of the soul sight. All around the air erupted with streamers of red and gold and fuschia. A glyph spread across her chest, bright and sharp as a tangle of veins. She was Chosen.

"Fari?" Farideh turned to see Dahl standing there, wearing a similar robe and a worried expression. For a moment, she had the urge to tear her hands out of the Chosen's and throw her arms around him. She took her hands back and clutched her hands into fists instead. "Is everything all right?" Dahl asked.

The woman stared at Dahl a moment and smiled. "Yes. I think everything's just fine. Enjoy your visit."

This is the Chosen's doing, Farideh told herself, unable to look away from Dahl. She could almost believe it.

"I didn't know about the robes," Dahl said before she could say a word. "Although you look nice."

Farideh's hand went to the brand on her shoulder. "Thank you."

"What was that about?"

Farideh shook her head. "They were just worried about me. I think the first woman thought you might be coercing me. The one in the gold dress is a Chosen," she added. "If you got any strange feelings off her."

Dahl gave a short, strange laugh. "Well that explains some things." He did not take her by the arm this time, but slipped his arm around her waist and escorted her through the large doors. "She's Lady Gaelyse Cormaeril—or she was. She bought Teneth's outright less than a year ago and remade it like this. Got herself disinherited, which frankly seems to have added to the place's charm—it's not just for nobles or for commoners." He looked around the open room. "Everyone gets to look like they're playing the chorus in a Chessentan melodrama."

The room beyond the doors looked more like Farideh had expected—a high-ceilinged space with a large stage surrounded on three sides by tables. More lovely women and men in gold scarves roamed the floor or sat with customers. Over the stage, a graceful couple wrapped in impossibly long sheets of tissue-thin silk dangled acrobatically in nothing but clouts. Farideh stared, struck by how impossibly beautiful their bodies were.

A young man led them to a table high on the edge of the room, with steep walls all around it. Their view of the stage and the floor in front of it was unimpeded, but no one could peer in from the corners.

Another man set a pair of goblets on the table, full of something sparkling and citrus-scented. He winked at Farideh. She took a long swallow of the wine.

"This place is so *karshoji* odd," she declared.

"Better than the Golden Goblin?"

"Better," she allowed. "But odder."

"So would you rather have a stranger give you a bath or try and punch you in the face?"

Farideh finished her wine. "I'd need a minute to decide."

He laughed. "Was it *that* bad?"

"I know what to do when someone tries to punch me in the face," Farideh pointed out. "I have no idea what to do when they dry me off in the name of Sune. What's our plan here?"

"There's eight acts to the show. Every other one is dancers. Those plus the strollers should be the bulk of the staff. After that we track down breakskulls and cleaners, and then . . ." He paused. "We'll find them before that."

"If we don't?"

The couple on the sheets of tissue hung near the ceiling, fabric twined in complex knots around their torsos and hips. Suddenly, in tandem, they dropped, spinning like maple seeds. Mere feet from the floor they stopped and the crowd erupted.

"Then we have to think of a reason for you to plausibly search the private rooms," Dahl said clapping. "So you're applying for a job or you're looking for a companion."

Farideh pursed her lips, sure as she'd ever been, that it wouldn't be one of the talent. Dahl took her empty wineglass. "I'll get you another drink."

"Not whiskey," she said, as she let the soul sight slide into her mind once more.

The acrobatic couple took their bows, the shades of their souls blooming with bursts of red and gold. On the crowded floor, it was hard to spot the strollers among the patrons. She searched the riot of souls for Shar's dark markings for several moments before releasing Asmodeus's strange blessing. Teneth's was packed—with lonely people, with friends, with couples. There was an edge to them, an intensity to their merrymaking as if they were trying to keep the end of the world away with ale and wine, laughter and grasping hands.

But then there was Gaelyse Cormaeril, the Chosen of Sune, moving through the crowd. As she passed, Farideh could almost see the wake of peace she left—the patrons loved and were loved, and that meant something. There was still beauty in the world, despite Netheril, and that meant something. Lady Cormaeril passed Farideh and favored her with a small smile, and a nod. Farideh watched her walk along the railing, knowing she ought to fight against the Chosen's powers—they weren't real. But they were a comfort.

Dahl returned, passing the Chosen of Sune as he did, and Farideh smiled, knowing it was a problem that her heart stuttered and her stomach tightened, and not wanting to care. If everyone else got to throw themselves into Teneth's mix of madness and divine grace, why couldn't she?

You know the answer to that, she thought as he spotted her and smiled back. She tried to make herself think about Lorcan.

"Apparently," Dahl said, sliding in beside her, closer than before, "we're supposed to wait for someone to come to us. Any luck?"

"No," she said. The curtain opened again, this time for a flock of women garbed in bright feathers and masks. "I don't think it's someone on the stage."

The dancers began moving, a sinuous dance to a pounding drumbeat. Farideh considered each, too briefly for the impressions of their vulnerabilities to come through. A scarf here, a crest of feathers there—bit by bit the birds shed their plumage, stripping down to just the masks, but always moving, moving. The young man from before brought another glass of the sparkling wine and a flagon of ale, lingering a bit until Dahl gave him a rather pointed look.

"Why don't you wear your hair up more?" Dahl asked.

"It's hard to pin it around the horns. I need someone else to help. And Havi . . ." Her chest tightened again, and she reached for the wine. "I haven't heard from them in months," she said. Lorcan's periodic assurances did nothing to calm her—he was taking Sairché at her word, little better than guessing, in Farideh's mind. "I have no idea anymore whether I'll ever have someone to pin my hair up again."

"The war wizards *have* to be keeping tabs on Brin."

"Maybe," Farideh said. "But they have to be doing a lot of things. And ultimately, they're only people and there aren't a lot of them. If they set Brin aside until they *need* him, no one's going to be upset. And Brin's not Havi." She sipped her wine. "Gods, you didn't even buy me whiskey and I'm getting gloomy," she quipped. "Sorry."

"You're all right," Dahl said.

"Our birthday was two days ago," she admitted. "And I have no idea where she is."

"Your birthday? Why in the Hells didn't you say something?"

Farideh watched the dancers wheel. "Because it's not blackberry season anymore. What would you have done?"

"Blackberries are for getting drunk and passing out on your stairs," Dahl said. "Everyone knows that."

Farideh smiled to herself. "And scented ink's for saying boorish things?"

"No, that's Wroth decks," he said. "Or warlock rods. But don't worry—the appropriate gift for giving the wrong gift is a flagon of ale, so you can make it up to me later."

Farideh looked at him, puzzled. "What rod?"

"Your rod. That's why I gave it to you." He looked down at his drink again. "I would have stayed, explained it. But you were sleeping."

"You've never given me . . ." Farideh stopped—she had been sleeping, long ago, just before she left Waterdeep for the first time, when the sound of Lorcan talking to another man had awoken her. A delivery boy, Lorcan had said. And he'd given her the package containing her rod, with its cracked and cloudy amethysts, its peeling gold leaf.

A gift, he'd said. But not from who. Where had he gotten it? "You ask the right people the right questions and all manner of things come to you."

"You were the delivery boy," Farideh said, feeling like such a fool.

"Well, I take it Lorcan didn't pass on my good wishes," Dahl said. "Don't know why I thought he would have."

The same reasons I thought he'd find me a new rod, Farideh thought. *He knows how to make you think he's saying what you want. And if she brought it up, what would he say but that it was so long ago. Why in the world did she still care?* Still, her anger made the powers of Asmodeus simmer.

"You gave me a new rod," Farideh said, "after everything that happened?" After they'd fought, after he'd sneered at her pact, after she'd embarrassed him. After she'd been sure that they'd never see each other again, and it was for the best.

Dahl cleared his throat, and watched the dancers. "I thought . . . well, I assumed that you had the pact just for . . . selfish reasons. Power and . . . well. But when I watched you destroy your first rod because someone might have been using it to find Havilar, it was a little hard to keep myself convinced. I thought it made a decent peace offering."

Farideh made herself turn back to the stage, a sudden lump in her throat. "Gods. That's . . . that's so thoughtful."

"Yes, well. Consider it a birthday gift. Eight years early." Farideh laughed, and the lump dissolved. "What did you do for your birthday then?"

"I went back to the Silent Room," she said. "Read books."

"You didn't want company?"

"I wasn't sure you'd be interested in the topic." She considered the dancers, the shapes of their souls overlaying their bare bodies. Bursts of red and gold spangled them all, the blessings of Sune.

"Try me."

Farideh blinked away the soul sight before turning to him. "I saw something in the camp," she said. "When I had the wizard's finest. I saw Asmodeus, and there was a Supernal glyph on him."

Dahl's eyes widened. "Well," he said after a moment, "that makes sense, I suppose. He's a god and all."

"But it didn't say 'Asmodeus,'" Farideh went on. "It said 'Azuth.' And I want to know why." She looked away. "Maybe I just made it up."

"You made up a symbol in a language you don't speak that happened to be the name of a dead god you'd never heard of?" He sipped his drink. "Did you find an answer?"

"No," she said. "I found possibilities—gods who were trapped in the Nine Hells, gods who made deals with archdevils. Nothing about Azuth specifically, though. And nothing that seems like it would make a Supernal glyph on Asmodeus."

Dahl frowned at his ale. "Maybe you have it backward. Maybe Azuth has something over Asmodeus."

"You mean Asmodeus is indebted to Azuth?"

"Could be? I mean, if the mark's not meant to identify him as who he is, maybe it's more like cattle. Or Chosen," he amended. "Or," he went on, "maybe it's because Asmodeus *is* Azuth. Maybe he killed the archdevil and took his place."

Farideh wrinkled her nose. "That doesn't seem right."

"Maybe," Dahl said, eyes dancing, "Undead Azuth is the tenth lord of the Hells. Asmodeus's master."

Farideh fought back a smile. "Maybe," she said, "Azuth survived because he saw Asmodeus doing something filthy and extorted him."

"If it's Asmodeus, it was probably something *good*."

"Maybe," Farideh said, dropping her voice, "they're lovers."

Dahl broke into laughter. "That's a better answer than you're likely to get," he said. "If the gods haven't told anyone where the connection lies, they may well have an interest in keeping it quiet." He sipped his drink. "Although that's something we haven't considered with the Sharrans," he said, all mock earnestness, "maybe this is all an elaborate attempt by Shar to get Asmodeus's attention away from Azuth."

"Romantically?"

"She could do worse."

Farideh chuckled and considered the dancers as they started weaving around one another in elaborate rings. "How would that even work?"

"The gods work in mysterious ways," Dahl said. He leaned over, moving near enough to see what she was watching. "Trust me. Is it one of the dancers?"

"No." Farideh turned back to Dahl. "She'll have to dazzle him another way." She swept the room again as the curtain closed. She still felt sure it wouldn't be a performer, but that sureness's source was muddled—because what was a Sharran doing dancing naked for a crowd? Because the performers all looked so happy? If it wasn't going to be one of the performers, then who?

Farideh let the soul sight drop, a pattern forming in her mind. "A cellarjack," she said. "A doorguard. A serving maid at a shorthanded tavern." She looked back to Dahl. "A cellarer. A groom who dices with the pantry jacks. A scullery. Who else? What am I forgetting?"

"Another scullery and an armsman," Dahl said. "And a cellarer and sometime keghand. Why?"

"They're all people who go down in the cellars and basements."

"The doorguard?"

"The back entrance to the Dragon's Last Drink. If it's like the Dragon's Jaws, the workers have to go down that way to get in. He'd have to stand guard there some days. The groom doesn't fit, but that's where I found him. In the cellar, because he dices with the cellarjacks." She searched the walls. "Does this place have a lower level?"

"Yes," Dahl said slowly. She started to stand, expecting to head for it, but Dahl stopped her. "The lower level is where the rooms are. The rooms people rent."

"And probably our Sharran," Farideh said. "And maybe whatever he or she is interested in." She shook him off. "If you didn't want people to think you're sleeping with me, then you should have thought of a different cover."

At the back of the room, a wide staircase descended beneath a plastered archway. A pair of women in gold scarves came up, one replaiting her auburn hair.

Farideh headed that way, glad for the distraction, for the clear purpose. They'd search for the Sharran or anything out of the ordinary, and she wouldn't have to worry about Lady Cormaeril or Dahl or why he was asking about her hair. At the base of the stairs, the hallway split in two directions at a statue of a woman and a man writhing sensuously on a pedestal. In both directions the hall was lined with doors—mostly shut. The faint sounds of couples trying to forget the encroaching army came through the heavy doors. Farideh turned left, searching for anything out of place.

"We were probably meant to pay up there," Dahl said. "Or 'tithe' I suppose."

"Do you have the coin?"

"Of course I brought the coin." Farideh peered around the next corner. More doors, heading down to a fountain that burbled merrily against one wall.

"Well, if they ask, we didn't realize and we'll give them the coin."

"Right." He edged past her, searching the doors. One stood open, and Farideh peered inside—a bed, another little fountain with a ewer and basin beside it, a vase of flowers, and a small table and chairs. It looked like an inn room, only passed through a temple, which she supposed was accurate enough. But there was nothing extraordinary to it. Dahl continued down the hallway.

"Stairs," he said. They wound around and down into the earth, to another row of doors that bent around beneath the upper hallway. Farideh tried not to think too much about all the stone and dirt above them.

"Why would you crawl down into a cave to take a lover?" she whispered.

"The rooms are warded," Dahl said. "You come here for privacy."

Which was likely why Brin and Havi had come, Farideh realized. "Did you know Havi and Brin had been here?"

Dahl glanced back at her. "You didn't?"

"No," Farideh said. "She doesn't talk about him much. At least not that part. Did he tell you?"

"I guessed," Dahl said. "They weren't in the tallhouse—you're in the bedroom. He wasn't taking her to Castle Crownsilver or the palace—that would be mad. So they were going to one of the inns or festhalls that hasn't got a problem with tiefling clientele *and* was nice enough for someone like Brin who's gotten used to clean linen and lack of mites *and* was associated with the right families, such that he wasn't going to fall neck deep in the midden heap by taking his lover to an establishment owned by one of Raedra's friends. I hear the owner takes Sune's dogma very seriously—regardless of whether the Cormaerils can afford to upset the Crown or the Crownsilvers. It was the most likely."

"Right," Farideh said. Why did that bother her so much?

They came around another bend—this one ended with a slope downward and an iron-banded door. "Interesting," Dahl said. He pulled the handle, but it caught. "More interesting."

"Can you pick it?"

"With the lockpicks I managed to sneak out in this getup?"

Farideh bent her head. "Pins," she reminded him.

Dahl set a hand at the base of her neck, and fished a pin out of the knot of her hair. "Clever," he said. He nodded back at the corridor. "Keep watch, all right?"

Farideh turned back the way they'd come, cursing Sune's Chosen under her breath.

A few breaths, a sharp curse, and the latch clicked open. "Let's see what we've found."

A wooden staircase led down into a stone-lined room. Against one wall were crates of wine bottles and casks of ale; on the other a rack with several bolts of the fine linen that made robes, a weighted dummy, and a broken ring on a chain. The air was cool and faintly damp and a pair of glowbaskets hung overhead, illuminating the space up to the wall of iron bars and the passage beyond. Farideh walked over and stuck a hand between the bars—the faintest breeze stirred against her fingertips and eddied the hem of her dress. "I think it's a tunnel," she said.

She looked back at Dahl, who gaped as if someone had just told him the secrets of the gods. "Tunnels," he said. "They all sit over the tunnels—how could I have *forgotten* the tunnels?"

Farideh tested the bars—the middle section was hinged, but locked tight. "Smuggling?" she said. "Where do the tunnels go?"

"Everywhere," Dahl said. "It depends on the—"

The door creaked open, and Dahl sprang at her, pulling her into the farthest corner of the room. A stack of crates hid them from the stairs, but if the intruder came even a step farther, they'd be in plain sight. Farideh pulled Dahl closer, right up against her, right up against the crate behind her—it wouldn't be enough.

"We got lost," he said quickly. "We didn't pay. We're a little drunk."

"Right," said Farideh.

He hesitated for the briefest of moments, his gray eyes considering her mismatched ones. And then he kissed her.

It was not a small kiss, not a chaste kiss—there was no need to fear he wouldn't believe they were lovers, impatient and impassioned. But to be certain, Farideh pulled Dahl closer, her arms around his neck, and Dahl grabbed hold of her hips. To be certain, she angled her hips into his, and he lifted her up onto the crate. To be certain, his hand slid up her thigh and she drew her leg up his.

What are you doing? a little voice in the back of her thoughts screamed, over and over. What are you doing?

She knew better than to say *being certain*.

"Oy! Brightbirds!" a man's voice shouted. "Can you hear me? Get out of there."

Dahl broke away, the look on his face nothing short of battle-shocked. "We're in the middle of something!" he shouted back.

"Take it upstairs or take it home." The man—dressed in a jerkin with a red rose embroidered on it—grabbed Dahl by the shoulder and spun him around. "Sune's blessings on you and all that, but not in the wine stores. Whoever left the door unlocked is getting a talking-to from me for disappointing Mistress Gaelyse, and no mistake."

Farideh grabbed hold of the soul sight. The flecks of red and gold that seemed to cling to those who spent time in Gaelyse Cormaeril's sphere were there . . . but they orbited around the dark patches of one of Shar's own. She squeezed Dahl's shoulder hard, and when he turned back to her, still a little wild-eyed, she whispered, "Him."

Dahl gave her the slightest of nods. "Fine!" he said. He turned back to the man and Farideh slid off the crate. "Are you the one I throw coin at or what?" he demanded.

The man made a face at him. "You can take that attitude right out the door. You should be grateful Gaelyse welcomed you in, you and your . . ." His eyes met Farideh's and he faltered. "'Lord Ammakyl's equerry and Lord Crownsilver's mistress's twin,'" he said as if reciting the epithets from a card. He laughed once, looking a little wild-eyed himself. "The door *was* locked wasn't it? You've puzzled it out."

"Look," Dahl said, "yes, I picked the lock. I didn't realize how expensive things were. I concede. Get us a room."

The magic of the pact soaked Farideh. The man wasn't fooled. He'd been warned about them, and not because they were spendthrift lovers.

"Were you planning on telling Gaelyse?" the Sharran said, sounding frantic, desperate. " 'Cause you can't stop them. There's no reason to upend the turnip cart here. Things are finally going all right. And now the attack's gone to Marsember—there's a chance it doesn't even matter."

"I think she'll understand," Farideh said. "You're not like the others."

"I'm not," he said. "She saved me. I was alone, all alone. And I'm not when I'm here, when I'm with her. Do you see?"

"She'll understand," Farideh said, not understanding, herself.

He looked at her as if she were so very young and foolish. "But will the Lady?"

"There are many ladies you can serve," Farideh said. "It doesn't have to be Shar." A terrifying moment, but then the man only nodded to himself. He trudged up the stairs.

Dahl shot her a look of utter disbelief. "Well done," he said. "Suppose we're finished." Farideh watched the Sharran—this was too simple.

At the top of the stairs, the man turned the lock. "I can't risk it," he said. "I can't let you tell Gaelyse." He drew the daggers from the sheaths at his belt, advancing down the stairs, his expression a grim mask.

24

N EVER CORNER A WILD ANIMAL BIGGER THAN YOURSELF." MEHEN'S advice came back to Farideh as the Sharran advanced down the stairs, swift as a displacer beast, broad as a bear. "Especially if it knows you're out to kill it."

The man lunged at Dahl, daggers first. The Harper skipped back, shoving Farideh out of the way, and ducked under the man's swipe. One fist shot out, hitting the Sharran in the ribs. The blade came down again, and Dahl just managed to twist out of the way. A line of blood appeared down the back of his shoulder. He cursed and slammed the back of his fist into the man's cheek. The Sharran shoved him off, throwing Dahl against the crates.

The Hells surged up into Farideh's nerves, into her veins. "*Adaestuo*," she hissed, and a bolt of bruised-looking energy streamed out of the air before her hands. It broke against the man's chest with an angry sizzle, and he cried out, dropping one dagger to slap at the dark flames. He looked up at Farideh, surprised. He hadn't thought she was dangerous—the powers of Asmodeus sank their fingers into Farideh at that realization, urging her to show him how dangerous she could be.

We need him alive, she reminded herself.

"I don't want to hurt you," she said. But the Sharran had already shaken off his surprise, the dagger cutting a long arc toward her. She twisted out of his reach, back and back. Her heel struck the stairs and she pulled hard on the boiling energies of the Nine Hells, drawing a rain of brimstone missiles out of the ether. Two struck him, shoving him back again—others hit the linen bolts and caught fire. The Sharran paused, aghast at the destruction.

"Gaelyse won't like that," he said.

Dahl shoved the weighted dummy into him.

The man let out a grunt of surprise and pain, and stumbled but didn't fall. Dahl sprinted past him, up the stairs to Farideh and reached for the lock—

"Won't get far without a key," the Sharran called, limping toward them. A cut on his head oozed blood, where the dummy's wooden head had crashed into him.

"Break the door," Dahl said.

"It's too big." Too many of her spells were too dangerous in the storage room— the little fires in the linen were smoldering still, sending smoke drifting through

351

the room. The wrong spell and they might all three end up dead. She pointed two fingers at the cask of wine the Sharran was passing instead. "Assulam."

The cask burst open, an explosion of wood and ruby-colored wine. The Sharran yelped, and leaped away from it, covering his face. Dahl pushed Farideh toward the farther side of the room, and ran around the Sharran's back. He snatched up a wine bottle from one of the open crates, and swung it like a club at the man's back. The Sharran lashed out with the dagger, and Farideh hit him with another bolt of energy. The man howled, a shriek of frustration and rage and grief. He threw the dagger end over end at Farideh. It sliced past her ear, clanging off her horn.

She heard Dahl shout, his cry breaking off into coughs. The Sharran cried out as Dahl struck him again across the back with the wine bottle, and sliced the dagger across Dahl's upper arm. The wine bottle shattered on the stone as Dahl leaped back, clutching the cut.

The Sharran looked from Farideh to Dahl, blood streaming down his face from the cut on his scalp. Farideh edged around to the left, but he tracked her with his dagger, every step. He wasn't going to let them leave—they might unmask him, to Gaelyse, to the Sharrans. But his breath came labored, his eyes full of blood. He had to know that he wasn't a match for the two of them at this point.

"Give me the knife," Farideh said. "We're not going to kill you."

The Sharran took a step back, alongside the wooden stairs. He crouched down, laying his remaining dagger on the ground, as if in surrender . . . but then he yanked a pendant from his neck with one hand and with the other pulled an oilcloth from something hidden beneath the stairs. The scent of something oily, something like pitch, assaulted Farideh's nose. Dahl started forward, but in the same moment, the Sharran pressed the amulet to whatever lay in the shadows. When he straightened, his face was full of sorrow.

"They can't find out," he said. The smell of pitch, the sizzle of magic, built in the little room. Farideh caught Dahl by the back of his robe.

"Gods' books," Dahl spat. They were going to die.

The pact's powers raced up her frame, fast enough to force the trigger word to tear a passage in the planes out of her. She pulled Dahl through the vent, out into the tunnel beyond the iron bars. Her feet no more than touched the stone floor but she cast the spell again, and again. The third time she stepped free beside an intersecting passage and veered hard as she pulled on the powers, her heart pounding hard enough to burst. She was already off balance when she stepped out, back into the stone-lined tunnel, and the explosion went off.

A wave of wind lifted her off her feet and tossed her against the floor. The rough stone ripped through her skirts and skinned her knees and shins, her palms and one forearm, her cheek. It threw Dahl on top of her, the weight of him driving all the air out of her lungs. A high-pitched howl wailed in her ears—that and the pain, she had no other senses.

Then she managed a great heaving breath—there was that. And there was Dahl, struggling up onto his hands and knees. She didn't dare move, not yet. But he shook her, frantic, rolled her onto her back, and somewhere beyond the howl she could hear him shouting her name. She opened her eyes, saw his mouth shape a curse. His arm was bleeding, and he had a fat bruise on his forehead. He was still shouting something at her.

"Are you skullscorned?" she asked, even though she couldn't hear herself. "You look skullscorned."

Whether he could hear her or not, a look of utter relief came over him, and he gathered her, bleeding and battered, into his arms.

Which was how the war wizards found them, not long after.

• • •

RAEDRA COULD NOT have been asleep for long when the blast woke her. The windows in their panes rattled, the stones grated on each other in the walls. For a moment, she was sure that Lady Marsheena's army had come to Suzail, despite the abrupt reports that arrived several days earlier that said she was attacking Marsember.

Raedra was out of bed and to the window, but there were no other blasts. In the distance, people screamed—to the southwest, away from the gates. The Purple Dragons burst into her room.

"Highness, are you all right?"

"What happened?" Raedra demanded. They didn't know. Only the sound, the rumble of earth. An explosion, surely, but where and why? Raedra threw a dressing gown over her nightdress. She'd have visitors soon.

Sure enough, Ganrahast came to the door. "Safe?" he barked.

"I'm fine," Raedra said. "Baerovus?"

"I've come from there. He slept through it."

"Lucky thing," Raedra started for the door, but Ganrahast held up a hand.

"It was an explosion in the tunnels, nothing expected and nothing that can be addressed just yet," he said. "My people are searching. We'll find the source. You should stay here—there's nowhere safer than the palace."

A retort was on Raedra's lips, but he vanished. The palace had seen assassinations enough—it was platitudes and nothing more to insist that she'd be safe. She considered asking the Purple Dragons to fetch Nell—she ought to be dressed in case something was afoot, but if the maid had managed to sleep through the noise, she ought to remain. Instead she sat down again at her writing desk, considering the reports from Marsember and Sembia.

Dire, she thought. Just as dire as it had been when she'd finally given in and fallen asleep. Marsember was sieged, and underprotected. The Army of the Purple Dragon held their position at Saerloon, not advancing, not retreating. The Stonelands were still a nightmare of monsters and unattached raiding parties—Arabel was only just getting some semblance of control back, which spoke not at all for the many villages and hamlets and farms that had been razed or abandoned. She set these aside once more, and Erzoured's notes with it. Marsember was the priority at the moment—Marsember and what Marsheena would do next.

A frantic fist battered her door. War Wizard Devora Abielard stood on the other side, her bow hardly more than a stumble.

"It's your tiefling, Your Royal Highness," she said, quite out of breath. "They caught her in the tunnels, near the bomb with a man. Drannon and Pelia are questioning her, and—"

"Where?"

Raedra followed Devora down the corridors, down the stairs, her thoughts a whirlwind. Farideh had been where the explosion had gone off—Farideh whose shoulder she'd wiped her tears on, who'd heard her fears and her hopes and her secrets. Memories of Lindon, of Sulue, of Aubrin even, dragged themselves up the chain of her thoughts—you let them close, they betray you, she thought. Her stomach was in knots by the time Devora opened the door to the windowless little room, her temper ready to explode.

Farideh looked up from a wooden chair. Her wrists and ankles had been cuffed to the chair by leather straps. Her face was a mess of scrapes and bruises, her lower lip split, and her dark hair full of stonedust. Someone had put her in a prisoner's rags. A candle burned on the table beside her, flickering in the draft from the open door. The two war wizards looked back at Raedra as she stopped in the doorway, and bowed to her.

"Your Royal Highness," Drannon said. "Can we help you?"

Raedra held Farideh's gaze. "What in all the broken planes were you doing in the tunnels?"

"As I said," Farideh said in a weak and scratchy voice, "fleeing an attacker."

"A Sharran, she says," Pelia supplied.

"A Sharran?" Raedra said. "And you didn't tell me?"

"It wasn't my place," Farideh said. "I didn't have enough information."

"If you had any information," Drannon said, "you should have brought it to us."

"It wasn't my place," Farideh said again.

"Well whose stlarning place is it?" Raedra demanded.

"Highness, we can manage," Pelia started. But Raedra didn't move—if Farideh was going to use Raedra's acquaintance to an advantage then Raedra was the one she could answer to.

Farideh wet her mouth. "Because there are Harpers involved."

The war wizards both stiffened. Raedra folded her arms—the jack who no one hired, she thought. He would be the man in the other room. "Did he set off the bomb? Darl? Dahl?"

"Dahl. No." Farideh said. "They say that they'll know everything one way or another. Is that true?"

Raedra didn't waver, even though the memories of what that meant surged up in her thoughts. "Very true."

"It's not mine to tell," Farideh said. "But I'd rather try and tell it than let him get hurt for trying to help you." She told Raedra of the dead Cormyrean Harper, of the coded list of eighteen locations—festhalls and inns and taverns and noble houses. She told her of visiting the first of these, of spotting a man as corrupted as Sulue had been, of the Harpers' discovery of letters that proved his connections. Raedra's stomach knotted further still. Farideh told her of sculleries and cellarers, of guards and wenches, and Pheonard Crownsilver. She told her about the breakskull in Teneth's who loved Gaelyse Cormaeril so hopelessly that he died trying to keep his secret from her, the broken logic of a soul undone by grief and loss and Shar's promises. She told Raedra how the bomb smelled of pitch and magic, the smell of a lightning storm. She told her how she'd used the magic of her warlock pact to escape, carrying the Harper with her, how the explosion had lifted her from her feet and deafened her. She hadn't seen the remains of the storeroom, the collapse of the rooms above it. She didn't know what it was meant to do. She didn't know when it was meant to be triggered.

"Please let him go," Farideh said.

"Everyone leave the room," Raedra said. The war wizards traded glances.

"Highness—"

"Leave the room," she said once more. "And kindly tell your fellows what we've learned. See if you can speed up the Harper's questioning."

Farideh's eyes were flat and unreadable, her horns an alien crown. Raedra chastised herself for being rattled by it—she's not Asmura, she thought. Asmura doesn't exist.

Farideh broke their gaze first, looking shyly away at the floor. "Are you all right?" she asked.

A spike of guilt went through Raedra's chest. She wasn't the one who'd been within sprinting distance of an explosion. "No," Raedra said. "People are dead. More people are in a complete panic over what in the Hells just happened. There are Sharrans planning on blowing my city up from the inside out, and you knew, and you didn't tell me."

"I didn't know all the facts," Farideh said. "I still don't. They're likely to change now, since one of the bombs has gone off. They'll have to know the war wizards will be suspicious."

"Here are the *facts*," Raedra said. "Marsheena has attacked Marsember. The siege is ongoing and Marsember's not going to win it, and what did I do but chastise them for being quakeboot hardjacks when they insisted on holding on to all their troops? I can hardly sleep for thinking about what would have happened if they'd obeyed. And now I'm reading accounts of warriors who can pass through the shadows—maybe Oversword Huntcrown's shadow fiends aren't such a fancy, and I was *wrong* about Wheloon. Not that it matters, I have no power anymore, and yet I spend every waking moment trying to keep Cormyr together and my brother from collapsing into panic. Now the entire city is in a panic, I am at my wit's end, and you didn't tell me there were Sharran agents in the city!"

Farideh watched her for a breath, solemn and still. "No," she agreed. "They asked me not to, and I kept my tongue, because it was more dangerous to tell you these people *might* be agents of Shar and they *might* be in these places and they *might* be up to something. If I'd known about the bomb, I would have brought it to you immediately. You have to believe that." She shifted in the chair. "Is there any way I can convince you to let me out? This wasn't made for people with tails."

"How do I know you're not one of them?" Raedra demanded. Tell me, she thought. Tell me how to be sure.

"After all of this, do you really think I'm in league with Shar?"

"You might be," Raedra pointed out. "I don't know anymore."

Farideh's mouth tightened. "Well, then you have to face that you *won't* know. I can tell you I'm not. I can tell you who I am. I can repeat what really happened for the tenth *karshoji* time. But I don't have any damning letters on me." She shifted again, wincing. "So you're stuck deciding if I'm too dangerous to live free or just an ally who was in the wrong place."

The dilemma of Wheloon, Raedra thought. What was safest was not necessarily most just. There were a thousand things she didn't know about Farideh. Any one of them could be what ended her, ended Cormyr.

Or what saved them.

Raedra kneeled beside the chair, unbuckling the leather restraint at Farideh's ankles. "In future, I expect to be told about *anything* related to the presence of Netherese, Sharrans, or—for safety's sake—any other enemies in Cormyr's borders. Clear?"

"I'll do my best," Farideh said. "I'm sorry I didn't tell you. I wanted to be sure." She rubbed her freed wrists as she stood. "And . . . maybe some other things that weren't so noble, to be fair." She bit her lip. "Dahl isn't a danger either."

"The war wizards don't much care for Harpers these days," Raedra said dryly. She sighed. "I'll pull them back. But he has to tell us *everything* first." She pursed her mouth. "Are you all right?"

"Someone healed the worst of it before they started."

"Good. But that isn't what I meant—"

Raedra hadn't been aware of the door hidden in the stones of the wall until it swung open, and Ilstan unfolded himself from its narrow confines. Panic flooded her, all the worse for the recognition that came alongside of it—he was familiar and yet he wasn't anymore.

"You're not supposed to be here," she started.

Ilstan shook his head. "I'm sorry, Raedra," he said, as if he meant it. "It's for your safety. You have to believe that." He pointed his wand at Farideh. "I have to kill you," he said. "I'm sorry."

Three darts of vibrant blue shot out of the end of the wand, striking Farideh in the chest, one after the other. She cried out and fell against the far wall. She threw up a hand, slinging a ball of sizzling, hungry energy at the war wizard. It broke against his shield, never touching him, and even as it did, Ilstan was casting another spell, a fireball building around his wand.

"Ilstan!" Raedra screamed. He didn't look up, his eyes haunted and shining peculiarly blue. As the fireball broke free, rolling across the room, Raedra leaped through its path and tackled the wizard. The flames scorched her, singeing her dressing gown and burning one arm. She heard Farideh shout again. She drove her shoulder into Ilstan's chest, knocking him back, breaking his concentration. He shoved Raedra off.

"Stay back! You'll be hurt."

"Drop your wand," Raedra ordered. "She's not an enemy."

"She is the Knight of the Devil!" he cried. "The Lord of Spells wants her dead. It's over your head, Highness."

He'd gone mad—Raedra ran for the door, to call for more war wizards before he killed Farideh. Ilstan released another spell, another bolt of blue flames.

Fear, as deep as the night she'd lost Lindon, as fierce as the cry of a dragon, sank its claws into Raedra's gut. She looked back at Farideh, and saw a nightmare of flame and shadow, wings of fire reaching from her back.

"I don't want to kill you either, Ilstan," the creature said. "So put your wand down and let's talk this over."

Don't do it, Raedra thought, a frantic animal voice she couldn't speak. Ilstan took a faltering step backward, toward the hidden door. She dared to look back at the terrible angel of doom—

Within the halo of flames, Farideh held one shoulder, as if it pained her. Her shift had burned through where the missiles struck. She was leaning against the stone wall, as if she couldn't stand.

A flash of light—Ganrahast appeared, and a heartbeat later, Ilstan vanished. In the midst, the flames around Farideh extinguished, and she collapsed to the floor.

"Where are Wizards Rowanmantle and Weirgate?" he demanded.

Raedra found she couldn't quite speak. Farideh lay on the floor, staring up at the ceiling. Ganrahast had woven a spell over her, wrapping her in the same barrier he'd used in the tallhouse. Yes, Raedra thought. Take it away.

Her burned arm started throbbing, a pain that seemed to tap directly into the middle of her brain, and all the rest of her fear evaporated.

"She didn't hurt anyone," she managed to say. "It's Ilstan. War Wizard Nyaril. He's gone mad. You have to stop him."

"We will," Ganrahast said. "But I'm afraid I can't ignore a burst of Infernal magic that large."

"You can." Raedra eased herself back to her feet. "She was defending herself. And me." For the first time, Ganrahast seemed to realize that Raedra's arm was burned. He stormed to the door and threw it wide. "Cleric!" he snapped at the Purple Dragons there. "And find War Wizards Rowanmantle and Weirgate. I would have a word with them." He waved a hand over Farideh and the tiefling visibly relaxed as the barrier vanished.

"Your Royal Highness, you are to return to your rooms and accept the guards placed on you. Kindly do not dismiss them—I don't care what they may see or overhear, Shade is making for Suzail and I will not risk another Obarskyr. You, goodwoman," he said to Farideh as she stood, "will make use of the cleric that arrives and then you will return to your home."

"Ilstan's trying to kill *her*," Raedra said.

"All the more reason she should not be anywhere near you," Ganrahast said.

A protest, a counterorder rose to Raedra's lips . . . but then the memory of that horrible, gut-wrenching fear stopped it. She didn't want to be anywhere near Farideh while the fear of that dread threatened her. What had that been? *The Knight of the Devil.* Farideh met her eyes.

It's fine, she mouthed.

"Send her two highknights," Raedra said, as the clerics hurried into the room.

"Highness—"

"Two highknights," Raedra repeated. "Until you catch your wayward war wizard. And I want as many Purple Dragons as can be mustered to root out these purported Sharrans—every one that the Harper and she can list. We'll have our work cut out for us tonight."

• • •

FARIDEH WAS AWARE of the highknights only as faint disturbances in the shadows to either side. They were there, certain as coursing hounds, but silent, nearly invisible as they blended into the still-busy streets.

The imminent fall of Marsember had clearly become common talk during the evening. Folks carrying bundles of belongings, heading for the waterfront, crossed paths with folks up early, nailing boards over windows, and still more people trading goods in the shadows of the alleys. Farideh's heart was in her throat.

She had revealed herself in front of Raedra and Ilstan, and possibly Ganrahast. The Sharran had identified both her and Dahl, and made sure they not only couldn't get more information from him but that every other Sharran agent in the city knew he'd been found out. She'd told the war wizards that, along with all the locations and names she knew of.

"There's also Pheonard Crownsilver," she had said.

Drannon raised an eyebrow. "What's he done now?"

"He's . . . not allied like the others," Farideh said. "But I think he's connected." Pelia had made a frustrated little sound, but made a note.

"Might as well cross him off," Drannon had grumbled. "We'll never pin him down."

Neither made any effort to explain that to her, nor did they tell her what they planned to do next. She asked for Dahl, and was told they'd let him go just as soon as they had all his information as well. Could she see him? That wasn't necessary, they told her, and left her to wait for the two highknights, who steered her straight back to the tallhouse.

He'll come find you, she thought, as she opened the door. He'll be all right and he'll come back here . . . unless you're through, now that the Sharrans are the war wizards' problem.

Dumuzi was waiting for her, pacing the entryway. "There you are!"

"Here I am," Farideh replied. "What happened now?"

"What happened is I woke up to that explosion and you weren't here, and I had no idea where you were," he said, his Common slipping into a clatter of Draconic. "Not that it's my business, not that it's any of my business, except that you've paid me to guard you and we're all but clutchmates. Where were you?"

"Being blown up," Farideh said. "I'm fine."

"And the Peredur?"

"Dahl's fine too. Everything's all right. We need to lock the house up. Every door, every window." And even then, would it make a difference? Surely Ilstan had the powers to get through ordinary locks.

"What trouble?"

"Tonight, someone has the wrong idea about me," Farideh said. "And then there's a siege coming, so we can start getting ready for that too."

The moons over Dumuzi's eyes shifted. "I thought they had gone to Marsember instead."

"Marsember is about to fall," Farideh said. "Suzail is next."

They went through the house and latched every window and door. In the kitchen, Farideh took stock of their food stores, while Dumuzi brought every pot and pail out to the garden to catch the rainwater.

"I've never been through a siege," Dumuzi said. "I've never been through a war, really. Ash giants don't count much. They never get anywhere near Djerad Thymar."

"Did you have to fight them in the Lance Defenders?" Farideh asked. She knew every dragonborn had to serve at least two years in the city's defense.

"I haven't done my service yet," Dumuzi admitted. "Next year."

Farideh shut the doors to the pantry and went to the firewood stores. "How old *are* you?"

"Fifteen years."

A laugh escaped her. "Sorry," she said. "All this time . . . I assumed you were older, or we were agemates at least." But dragonborn grew faster—and Farideh had eight years missing. By the complex math of their two races, they probably were closer. She smiled at him. "So you really aren't Mehen's secret son."

"I told you I wasn't."

"But we're all but clutchmates? We're not the same age. We don't have the same father." Dumuzi's tongue fluttered behind the gape of his teeth. "Dumuzi," she said, "what are you doing here? Who are you?"

For a long moment he didn't speak, and Farideh was sure he was going to walk away again, avoiding the question as he'd done before. "I was sent to tell Clanless Mehen something. It's for his ears first." He snapped his teeth shut and parted them again, a flash of nerves. "I should not have said we were all but clutchmates. That was . . . inaccurate. Overly familiar."

"But why did you say it?"

A silence, a terrible yawning silence, where the answer seemed to coalesce despite Farideh willing it not to. "Because," Dumuzi said, "I'm the son of Verthisathurgiesh Arjhani."

Farideh sat down, the powers of the Hells stirred up and loose. "Well. I see why you kept it to yourself."

"Wait," Dumuzi said. "I say we are clutchmates for reasons . . . I spoke unguarded. *Thrik omin' iejirkkessh*, you know?" She didn't. He snapped his teeth again, clamped them shut, his eyes locked on hers. "But I say that, because I think you know like I do how my father disappoints. Fifteen years ago, he left my mother sitting over their third clutch—my clutch—knowing that the first two hadn't ripened. He didn't come back for six months. He was with you, wasn't he? Arush Vayem, the village on no one's maps."

"Turns out he wasn't really with us after all," Farideh said. "You won."

Dumuzi shook his head. "Let us agree that Arjhani is with no one but himself when it comes down to it. I've had fifteen years to learn that much. I'm sorry," he added, "I should have said when I agreed to stay."

"Don't be. I wouldn't have let you stay if you'd told me at the start."

"He hurt your father very badly?"

"Worse," Farideh said. "He hurt my sister."

She wanted to ask him what Arjhani wanted with Mehen—no one else in Djerad Thymar would have sent Dumuzi to find her father. She wanted to tell him to leave, to take his message with him. Down in her bones, she couldn't make herself believe Mehen could say no to Arjhani. She wondered what Havilar would do—she had been completely mad for the dragonborn glaivemaster, and when he'd vanished one winter morning, tiny Havilar's grief had been perhaps the thing that threatened to break Mehen.

It might not matter, she realized. The Shadovar army was nearly upon them, and she had no idea where her family was.

"It's late," Farideh said, standing.

Dumuzi stood as well. "Right, I'll—"

"Just get some sleep," Farideh said. "We have guards tonight."

Up in the bedroom, Farideh locked the door. She took the rod out from under her pillow where she'd tucked it and turned it in her hands. It shouldn't have surprised her that Lorcan lied about getting it for her. No, she thought. Not lied. He never lied. He just let her misinterpret things the way he wanted her to see them.

Gods—a half-mad Chosen out to kill her for unknown reasons, the army of Shade ready to turn on the city, her family missing, and this is what she worried about. She wondered if they left that part out of the ancestor stories, if Khorsaya and Nala Who-Would-Be-Verthisathurgiesh were secretly worrying about lovers and whether their friends would still be their friends when their trials were finished.

Her ritual book sat in the drawer of the dresser, beneath a blanket and beside the ruby comb she'd taken from the internment camp. She could call Lorcan from the Hells with the spell within it, leave Suzail and be safe somewhere else. She might convince him to bring Dumuzi, to bring Dahl too—after the rod, he owed him that, owed Farideh that, she thought, pulling the ritual book out of its hiding place, along with the bag of components. Was there any other way she'd definitely be safe from Ilstan?

It would be good to see Lorcan too, she thought, kneeling down on the floor to mark the circle of runes. Sort her thoughts out. Remind herself why she'd chosen him. But also make it clear that his stunt with the rod wasn't all right, wasn't how things should be going forward.

And what was forward? she thought. Dahl's hands on her hips came back to her, her skirt pushed back.

She sat back on her heels. There was absolutely no way she could tell Lorcan about that. Chances were good Dahl would never bring it up again—or worse, he'd bring it up only to make sure she knew that it shouldn't be brought up, it was a mistake, a misunderstanding. They should never speak of it again.

Gods, what she wouldn't give to worry about shadows and dragons.

She stretched to correct the stroke of one of the far side's runes, and as she did, her foot kicked out, striking the rod and sending it rolling across the room and under the bed.

"*Karshoj*," Farideh cursed. She went to the bedside, peering into the dusty darkness. She brought the candle down beside her, shedding enough light to see where it had come to rest beside a horrifyingly large lump of dust. She lay down, flat on her back, and with the tips of her grasping fingers managed to inch the rod out by the pointed amethyst. She wiped it clean with the sleeve of her blouse and lay for a moment on the floor.

Lorcan had lied about the rod, she thought.

He'd lied about the rod, and worse, he'd lied about it when Dahl had been trying to smooth things over. He'd let her think that Dahl found her wicked or worse. *Maybe I just have to make sure they aren't there to talk to*—and she'd been so furious he could suggest such a thing. But he'd been doing that for ages. He didn't trust her.

She thought of Dahl's mouth on hers—

Finish the circle, she thought.

As she pushed herself up from the floor, the candlelight glinted on something silver buried in the dust. She leaned back down and reached for it, but it was farther in than her arm would go. She took the rod and swung it around, into the pile of dust. It hit the bit of metal with a *clink*, knocking it from the dust and into her reach.

It was a silver tube as long as her finger. The remains of a lead stopper clung to its open mouth, and a seal halfway down bore a single word of Infernal. She turned it over, her stomach knotting—along one edge of the lead seal a fringe of half-hidden Dethek runes protruded, the vial's original label. With one thumbnail she picked at the lead, until it peeled away, revealing the contents of the vial: *Shaking fever contagion.*

• • •

Lorcan entered the fingerbone tower, fleeing more cultists' punishments, more sly exchanges with rivals, more nonsense of the purebred Hellish variety than he could stomach. He headed for the tower, for the scrying mirror and the portal. For Farideh. He thought of the hourglass in the palace of Osseia—he had no idea how long it had been since he'd seen her, but he found more and more that he didn't care. She wouldn't leave, and the more time he spent with her, the surer he was of that—and the more Glasya would think he was seeing to her tasks, the less he would have to bother with his erinyes half sisters, who barely tolerated him, and the more pleased overall Lorcan would be. A perfect solution, Lorcan thought, opening the door to discover Sairché watching the scrying mirror.

"Shit and ashes," he said. "What now?"

"Nothing particularly," Sairché said. "Only the paladin found out and I wasn't going to stand around while she slung her god's blessings around." She shot him a dark look over her shoulder. "I told you so."

The mirror's surface reflected Brin, amidst a small army, riding horseback between a blond man with a newly trimmed beard and said sour-faced paladin. Havilar wasn't in sight.

"She's riding somewhere at the rear," Sairché said, anticipating his question. "This lot's just more interesting for the moment."

"What happened?"

"I told you. I got unmasked. The little Tormite set his cousin on me, and here we are."

"Brin knows? Is that why she's riding at the back?"

"That," Sairché said, "and she's kept the hellhound."

Lorcan cursed to himself. What sort of ridiculous powers granted imps that brought hellhounds? "You need to go back."

Sairché laughed. "Hardly. This is much safer."

"Get her out of there."

"She'll kill me first. This is fine. Unless," Sairché said, turning to him, "you just want me away so you can run off on another little tryst. How are things? Have you asked the dragonborn for his blessings yet?"

"I figured I'd do better bringing him your head on a pike first," Lorcan said. "You had one job."

"And I told you, right from the start, what the conditions were: I don't trifle with paladins."

Something slammed bodily against the door—once, twice. The door buckled. Sairché leaped back. She grabbed the portal ring. "Go," Lorcan said grimly. "Get back to Havilar."

Sairché triggered the portal just as the locked door came down. Four wasps the size of large dogs flew through the broken entrance, their mandibles clicking in an agitated way, their sword arms slashing against one another. A fifth entered, dragging Zela by her hair, and dropped the battered and poisoned erinyes at Lorcan's feet. Lorcan wondered how many of the insect-demons Zela had destroyed for them to bring her so low.

"Where is the erinyes called Noreia?" the largest of the hellwasps buzzed. "She is wanted."

Lorcan smiled blandly, pressing down all the terror that tried to rise up at the sight of five hellwasps, at the sight of Zela helpless at their feet. "Noreia? What is it you want with Noreia?"

"The queen wants her," the hellwasp said. "You will tell us where she is or you will suffer like this one. She did not have answers, so you must have answers."

Lorcan had answers—many answers. He'd been prepared for this moment since Noreia first came to him, beaten by succubi. "Which one is Noreia?" he said. "Remind me."

"Ninth among the *pradixikai*," the hellwasp droned. "The fury leader of Faventia and Fidentia. Offspring of Fallen Invadiah and Ilcanorr of Luthcheq."

"Oh *Noreia*." Lorcan smiled. "I can recall speaking to Noreia. She seemed to mean to head to the succubus aeries. Have you checked there?"

Before the hellwasp could respond, the floor beneath Lorcan's feet seemed to vanish, and for a brief, vertiginous moment, he fell farther than ever possible. Seconds later his feet hit the floor again—a different floor, a wooden floor. Chalked runes traced a circle nearly his height in diameter. Farideh kneeled opposite him, over her open ritual book.

Any other time, he'd have been wildly pleased.

"Shit and *ashes*—what do you think you're doing?" he shouted. "Send me back. I'm in the middle of something that can't get much worse, but you've done an excellent job testing that."

Farideh didn't flinch, didn't so much as blink. She stood and held up a small metal vial. The vial he'd thought lost forever. "What is this?" she asked.

And Lorcan realized that things could indeed get much, much worse.

"How in the Hells should I know?" Lorcan said, as calmly as he could. "Darling, this is *not* a good time. I am in the middle of something very important and you may be *killing* me by yanking me out of it. Send me back now, and I will talk to you about this later."

She lowered the vial, her face devoid of any expression. "You can go whenever you like," she said. "All you have to do is answer one question truthfully: Did you give me shaking fever?"

Lorcan's heart nearly stopped. "That's what you made the requirement?" She nodded, her eyes shining. "Darling, this isn't a simple question."

She folded her arms around herself. "Then explain it. Go ahead."

"I don't have time."

"Then answer the question," she said. "Did you give me shaking fever?"

"You are acting like a *child*—"

"No, Lorcan," she said. "*You* are the one acting like a child. I'd made up my mind, and you didn't like it, so you *poisoned* me to get your own way."

"I was protecting you."

She shook her head, as if she couldn't believe him, as if she didn't want to believe herself. She unfolded her arms and looked down at the rod in her hands. "You're never going to love me are you?"

Panic rushed through every part of him. "Is that a *problem*?" he said as if it could not possibly be. As if this weren't worth considering. He didn't love her, he couldn't love her, it wasn't safe for anyone to love either of them, so why was she asking him this?

Farideh swallowed, a wry sort of smile on her face. "Oh, I think it is."

"Darling," he said, his calm splintering, "I do not have the luxury to stand here and discuss your hurt feelings. There are hellwasps in my chambers—Glasya's personal minions—who want to talk to me or possibly tear me into little pieces. Break the circle. Make yourself a cup of tea. We will talk about this later."

She only shook her head. "I'm not asking you to discuss my hurt feelings. I'm asking you to answer the question. Did you give me shaking fever?"

"It's not a simple question," he shouted.

Farideh laughed. "Oh, isn't it? I suppose you'll be standing here awhile then." The shadow-smoke started to waft off her, her temper rising. "You can't even be straight with me when all the proof is right here!"

"I have been *nothing* but good to you."

"You *poisoned* me," she said. "You've tried to kill my friends. You bully me. You make me feel like this is the best I'll ever be, because it suits *you*. You abandoned me in that camp." She broke then, covered her face with her hands, and caught her breath. When she looked back up at him, her eyes were shining with tears. "You can't even help it, can you? I figured you'd always be a little wicked, but . . . I'm still a game."

"You don't know what you're talking about," Lorcan said. There was a chance here, he thought, growing frantic. She doesn't want this to be true. If she was crying, there was an opening, a regret. He had to do something quickly, or else Glasya would be enraged when he came back. "Please break the circle," he said, softer. "I will explain everything. Later."

But Farideh only shook her head again. "Did you give me shaking fever?"

He closed his eyes. No escape. "Yes."

As the portal magic surged around him, he heard a sob escape her. She'd known the answer, but she hadn't wanted it.

"Then we're done, you and I," she said as the Hells drew him back into their terrible embrace.

He landed, reeling, terrified—but not of hellwasps. What did she mean *done*? They weren't done. They couldn't be done. He should have said something different—there had to be something else. He could go back to her, make it right.

The drone of fiendish wings pulled his attention back to more pressing matters, and to the creature that stood in the hellwasps midst: a succubus with bronze wings, midnight hair, and an air of violence that put the rest of her kind to shame.

"Mother," Lorcan said coolly, mastering all his turmoil.

"Where is Noreia?" Fallen Invadiah demanded.

"Noreia?" Lorcan said, as if the hellwasps had not asked him the same thing.

"Tread lightly, Lorcan. I have Her Highness's blessings."

Lorcan cursed his luck. It wasn't the answer he'd intended to have when Glasya came calling, but he'd been prepared for it nevertheless. "She is in Avernus," Lorcan said. "Cooling her heels, as it were, and waiting for Her Highness to, ah, have a use for her."

"And so she has a use," his transfigured mother said. "As do you: take me to Noreia."

• • •

SAIRCHÉ RETURNED TO the same grassy knoll she'd fled from some days before. The Shadovar army had left the little village of Gladehap behind, a ransacked mess, and Havilar was long gone. Let her be gone, Sairché thought. No one said that she needed to watch out for that one—so far as she could see, she wasn't even supposed to know Havilar existed, let alone was Chosen. Equal odds of angering Asmodeus, she thought. It's not as if she was the one being given orders.

Anyway, there were far more interesting things afoot.

Sairché went to the hollow where she and Havilar had hidden, watching the Shadovar army. There was no sign of anyone about. Sairché twisted the ring on her smallest finger, opening a pocket in the plane. She took from it a shallow dish, a flask of alcohol, a pouch of herbs, and another pouch of powdered blood. She mixed these in the dish, pouring the alcohol over all of it. She drew her wand and the edge of the fireball was enough to ignite the mixture.

She drew a shield of magic around herself. Now to wait.

The ghosts came in ones and twos, drawn to the smell of blood, the warmth of the flame, the lure of magic. The dead of Gladehap, the villagers who'd remained behind when the Shadovar came, they were first. The archers who'd fled their posts, and then the shade she'd killed. The echoes of the dead, they touched the barrier she'd crafted, recoiling from it's snapping magic.

The one she wanted came last, materializing as the spell forced her to—a tiefling woman, patched and rotting as she seemed to waft in and out of the plane. She glared at Sairché with silver eyes that seemed to glow.

Sairché smiled. "Well met. I think have a great deal to discuss." She beckoned with one finger and dropped the shield of magic. "Why don't you come inside, O Brimstone Angel?"

25

THE WAR WIZARDS WERE PROBABLY GENTLE WITH DAHL, IF EVEN A fraction of what he'd heard was true. Over and over, they asked him their questions, casting their spells to coax out any hint of a lie. Over and over, Dahl answered, leaving aside the details they wanted most—how did he come by the list? What other Harpers were in Suzail? What other missions was he involved in?

He tried to tell them the names of the Sharrans, but over and over they diverted him back to Teneth's, to the explosion, to Farideh.

"You can't possibly think she had anything to do with that," he said. The woman questioning him, a matronly, no-nonsense sort, merely repeated the question.

"Think, Goodman Peredur: How did she manage to get you away from the explosion so swiftly?"

"If she'd anticipated it," he said, "I would think we would have gotten a great deal farther."

The prickle of magic crawled over him. "Answer the question please."

The door flew wide, stopping eerily just short of the wall, and a towering man with a long auburn beard and a furious expression stormed in. The war wizards all leaped to their feet.

"A list," the Royal Magician said, "of every purported Sharran you have discovered and their location. Now."

Dahl rattled off the ones he knew—from Uwan at the Brigand's Bottle to the dead man now buried under Teneth's. A map appeared, the war wizards marked the locations Dahl named, while Ganrahast stared, unblinking, at him.

"What about Pheonard Crownsilver?"

"What about him?"

"He wasn't on your list. He was on the tiefling's."

Dahl blew out a breath. "Castle Crownsilver is on the list. If she's identified Lord Crownsilver—" Then she went in there by herself, he thought. "—I would trust her," he finished.

The Royal Magician made a sharp gesture, and the bindings at Dahl's wrists and ankles opened. "Go home."

"You want me to promise not to leave the city?"

Lord Ganrahast looked back at him. "I'm afraid you don't have much of a choice, goodman. As of an hour ago, the gates to the city are closed—Shade is days away." He left, the other war wizards following behind. A trio of Purple Dragons surrounded Dahl, escorting him out of the little room and through the winding corridors of the palace.

"Where's Farideh?" Dahl demanded.

"Who?" the man beside him asked.

"The tiefling woman I came in with."

"Being questioned," the man said.

"No," his comrade, a thick woman said. "They already sent her home."

"Did they? I saw the princess come, and then the clerics. Then the princess leave and Ganrahast—but the clerics were still there."

A trill of worry went through Dahl, the memory of Farideh lying on the stone floor of the tunnels, bleeding from a hundred small cuts, bruised and dazed. They wouldn't let her die, he reminded himself. Raedra wouldn't let her die.

You don't always have that choice, he thought. A healing too late was a healing wasted on a corpse. They came to the exit, the gate at the side of the palace.

"Take me where she was," Dahl said. "Let me make sure."

"Not a chance," the woman said. "We've got other orders. Good night and go home." They shut the gate behind him.

His brain felt as if it were on fire, and how much was from a war wizard's wand he'd never know. The Sharrans were handed off, with their plans only partly unveiled. Shade would be at the city gates any day now. Oghma wanted his attention. And he couldn't find Farideh.

If they didn't let you die, Dahl told himself, they won't let her die. If Raedra was there, Farideh was safe. He repeated it over and over as he jogged to the Dragon's Jaws. He had other orders, more critical things to do than worry.

Vescaras came back to the inn just as Dahl did. "Give me your best manners," he said, closing the door behind them, "because I've just come from the Huntcrowns' manor and you'd better be grateful. What a belligerent bunch of snobbish—"

"The Sharrans aren't our problem anymore," Dahl said. "Take it to the war wizards." He sat down on the settee, his head still buzzing.

Vescaras frowned. "What happened to you?"

"The war wizards grabbed us. Thought we were involved in the explosion at Teneth's."

"I went past—the whole building's tilting over. Were you anywhere near there?"

The man's expression as he triggered the bomb flashed through Dahl's mind—the sorrow, the fear, the fury. Farideh lying unresponsive on the ground. "Yeah. That's what the Sharrans are doing. They have explosives," Dahl said. "In the tunnels. I'm not sure what they're for—aside from killing anyone too close."

"Were you too close?"

"Almost." *Almost*—if it hadn't been for Farideh's spell, they would have been dead. He kept thinking that, all the ways that things could have gone wrong, all the things he'd done that had led to the Sharran cornering them in the storeroom. If they hadn't gone down there, if he'd just somehow hidden them better. If he'd been quieter about kissing her, maybe the Sharran wouldn't have noticed.

He covered his face with his hands—nearly dying, being questioned by the war wizards, finding out they were *days* from an attack and without an easy escape route, and now Vescaras was *right*. There was no possible way he could have kissed her more quietly. If that Sharran hadn't interrupted them, he would have kept going.

"How close?" Vescaras said. It took Dahl a moment to remember he was talking about the explosion.

"We were standing in front of him when he activated it."

"Watching Gods!"

"She got us away. Barely. The . . . warlock magic. And now Shade's about to turn for Suzail and I have to leave a message for Garce about it and maybe Pheonard Crownsilver is a Sharran." No—you left that to the war wizards. He lifted his head. "Also, I don't know where Farideh is."

Vescaras stood and pulled a bottle of brown liquor out of his dresser drawer, poured a few fingers for Dahl. "Here. Drink it and go to bed. I'll see to Garce. I'll find out a better timeline for Shade's arrival. I'll swing by the tallhouse and make sure Farideh's there."

"I can manage—"

"Dahl, you stood within spitting distance of an explosive device that took out half the foundation of a multistory building. If there weren't a kraken's load of protective spells on the structure, it would have collapsed completely. You're in shock. Stay here and rest. Because I suspect strongly we'll need you to stop being in shock tomorrow."

Dahl downed the whiskey, and after Vescaras left, he drank another. But it didn't sit right in his stomach and when he tried to lie down, he stood right back up. He couldn't sleep—no part of him would possibly sleep. He pulled his boots back on and left the inn.

Shock, Dahl thought dismissively. How many times had he nearly died? He couldn't have shock over this one. He walked several blocks up the Promenade before he realized that he wasn't wearing his cloak—that his cloak was still in whatever remained of Teneth's entry room—and that he was heading the wrong direction. He'd meant to go to the tallhouse, to ask if Farideh had returned. To broach the subject of what happened in the storeroom.

He stopped, but didn't turn. That's a terrible idea, he thought, as the rain picked up. She has Lorcan. She doesn't like you. You don't fancy tieflings.

How had his own thoughts gotten so out of his control that he could believe that and kiss her up on that crate like the world was ending?

Maybe because the world is ending, he thought, looking up at the rain clouds. He sighed and looked back down to the street before him. To the Temple of Oghma, seat of the Church-in-Exile waiting like a patient dragon on the opposite side of the Promenade.

Does the owl's wing shape the gale? . . .

Fine, he thought. *Fine.* It's not like I don't have anything *better* to worry about. Let's do this. Two whiskeys softening his resolve, Dahl entered the Church of Oghma.

Ten years had gone by since Dahl was a paladin, but he remembered the approach to the altar, the steps up the dais, as though they were the path to his childhood home. Before him, other worshipers followed the Church-in-Exile's ritual, laying their foreheads against the altar stone. Dahl washed his hands in the font and handed the acolyte beside it a silver piece, but he did not touch his forehead to the altar. He stepped to the side, away from the approach, glaring up at the smiling statue of Oghma as he did. He lay down on his stomach, on the cold tiles, cushioning his head with his hands and blocking any view beyond the floor.

Lord of All Knowledge, he prayed. *Binder of What Is Known: Make my eye clear, my mind open, my heart true. Give me the wisdom to separate the lie from the truth. Give me the strength to accept what is so—*

What was he doing? This was such a waste of time, and he had things to do. Real problems to solve. Except how could he solve any of them when his thoughts wouldn't run straight?

He concentrated on the backs of his eyelids, on trying to pull his thoughts in further. *Lord of All Knowledge*, he prayed. *Binder of What Is Known: Make my eye clear, my mind open, my heart true. Give me the wisdom to separate the lie from the truth.*

He hadn't been lying about trying to sleep with Farideh, he thought without meaning to. He wasn't, or to be fair, he hadn't realized he might be. He wasn't such an idiot as to pretend he wasn't a little attracted to her. A lot attracted to her. But wanting to do something and trying to do something were not the same thing.

Give me the strength to accept what is so, he chanted firmly. *My word is my steel, my reason my shield. And I shall fear no deception, for the truth remains.*

And it wasn't idiotic that he hadn't realized it anyway—it had crept up on him while he'd been thinking about other things. While he'd been worried about Sharrans, he'd been staring at her ears.

And Oghma has made me a lantern in the gloom, he chanted, fast enough to overrun his errant thoughts. *A compass in the wilds.*

So many nights spent staring at her, trying to look like a besotted fool while she hunted for Sharrans. So many nights staring at the side of her head, the shape of one ear or the other. Small and round and strikingly normal. Human. The way her earlobe pointed a soft line to her jaw. It was not something to notice, but it was something to look at. After the spell had worn off though . . . he started to notice: her ears were exactly the same, with and without the war wizard's interference.

Her ears were the same and her jaw was the same, her nose and her lips and her legs and her little quips and the face she made when she was worried about something. The way her mouth would quirk before she smiled, as if she were trying to rein in her reaction and then giving in. The way she surprised him. The fact she could win an argument with him. And holy gods: when she wore those gowns with the low collars—

Lord of All Knowledge, he prayed furiously. *Binder of What Is Known: Make my eye clear, my mind open, my heart true. Give me the wisdom to separate the lie from the truth. Give me the strength to accept what is so.*

What is so, he thought, is that you have gotten completely wound up over a girl you can't have. She was with Lorcan. She was still a tiefling—and what did he imagine doing? Taking her back to Harrowdale and trying to explain that? Gods' books, if he showed up at the tallhouse trying to unburden himself that would be bad enough. He remembered the look she'd given him when he'd confessed to letting the innkeeper at the Brigand's Bottle believe they were lovers. That, all over again.

Everything was perfectly clear, he told himself, until you started forgetting the very thing you'd agreed on. Until you let everything get muddy.

That was what he missed most about being a paladin. The rules were clear and you knew when you were right and when you were wrong, and Dahl didn't have to worry so much about being wrong, at least until he fell . . .

The truth nestled in the middle of that sorry defense struck Dahl as hard as if he'd run a plow into the stony heart of it.

He'd followed Oghma because he'd loved knowledge, loved learning, loved books. But he'd become a paladin because he liked being right. Which wasn't the same thing. To be right meant clinging to what you already knew. To be right meant turning from the wild splendor of the unknown. To forsake the potential of knowledge for the comfort of one's own ego.

Every nerve in his body hummed with the realization, feeling like a shiver that rolled over him from head to toe, all at once. And the middle of Dahl's mind glowed like a lantern in the gloom, each nerve shifting like the needle of the compass to point the way back home. He forgot to breathe.

You came back.

Dahl couldn't have said if it was his thought or the god's, only that it was there, and it was true and he thought he would weep onto the cold marble floor. Here was the answer. Here was the truth: Dahl had fallen because being a paladin harmed him, harmed Oghma, harmed knowledge. There were other ways to find that grace.

My champion, my wayward son.

How long he lay on the floor of the temple, Dahl couldn't have said— it felt like an eternity he'd only just begun to savor. The presence of Oghma receded as gentle as the tide, and Dahl lay perfectly still, holding in his mind the sensation, the memory of the sound, the light, the voice. Eventually the cold floor intruded, and it was hard to ignore exactly how uncomfortable he was.

Dahl stood and dusted himself off. Beside the font, a new acolyte stood. "You were there a long time," he said, with a nervous smile. "Did you find what you were looking for?"

No, he nearly said, but he caught himself, startled by the answer.

"As much as I could have," he replied. "Thank you."

He nearly put it out of his head—why would he have said no? He'd spent almost a third of his days trying to find what had happened, and though he suspected he'd never know which moment was the one that had tried Oghma's patience, the subtle presence of the god was as good an answer as any. It *was* what he'd been looking for—moreso than the specific crime, more so than an absolution. Oghma had not forgotten him. He had not rejected Dahl whole cloth. There was a place for Dahl to stand here, which was almost more than he could have asked for.

So why "no"?

The rising sun broke through the clouds—he *had* been there a long time. He reached the Dragon's Jaws and kept walking. If he was worried about Farideh, she would certainly be worried about him. But even as he reasoned that much, he knew he was already walking, coming up with excuses after the decision was made.

The strange calm that clung to him even after Oghma's presence had left, carried him across the anxious city, up to the tallhouse. He rapped on the door before he noticed the black-clad guard standing in the bushes by the gate. Before he remembered it was just after dawn.

"Who's there?" Farideh called through the door.

"It's me. It's Dahl."

Farideh cracked the door, one silver eye peering out, then opened it wide enough to pull him inside. She was wearing a nightdress and a dressing gown, her hair braided and fuzzy as if she had been tossing and turning. Her eyes were red and puffy—she'd been crying.

"Oh, thank the *karshoji* gods," she said. "They said that they'd let you go, but I didn't know and I didn't dare leave to come find you."

Dahl forgot to breathe. The middle of his mind took on that same warm glow for a moment, as every nerve shifted like a compass needle.

"Ilstan's gone mad or something," she said. "He tried to kill me, right there in front of Raedra. There's highknights outside. For now. They've locked the gates—did they tell you that?—and the Shadovar army are coming. I'm so glad you're all right." She stopped, searched his face, the flat color of her eyes shifting. "*Are* you all right?"

The path's well-trod, he thought, maybe a touch giddy, the hunting's poor. You can't see what you aren't looking for. And so you never found it.

"I'm having a really strange night," he said, feeling as if the words were going to change as they came out of his mouth.

She frowned at him. "Do you need to sit down?"

He opened his mouth, but whatever he was going to say went out of his head. Everything he meant to tell her—about Oghma, about the war wizards, about where Vescaras was—dissolved on his tongue.

She beckoned him into the front parlor. The nearer sofa had been pushed out of the way, and in its place was a pile of bedding before the fireplace. A chalked circle of runes lay just outside of the strewn blankets. "Did you sleep in here?" Dahl asked.

"My room was . . . I didn't want to sleep there. Not now." She folded her arms around herself. "If this is about the storeroom, you don't . . . you don't have to tell me . . . Look, please don't tell me that you didn't mean that. It's fine. I know. You don't have to say so and right now I would really rather not have the reminder that—"

"I figured it out," he said. "About Oghma."

That surprised her. "You solved the riddle?"

Dahl laughed. "No. Not that. At least, not most of it. A little. I meant why I fell."

Her eyes widened. "Oh gods."

"I like being right. Sometimes I think I'd rather be right than be happy. I guess I started wanting to be right more than I wanted the truth. I stopped loving learning in favor of being right. So that's why Oghma took it all away. Better to hurt me once, I suppose, than let me keep hurting myself. At least this way I kept thinking, kept searching. Kept learning even when I was doing everything I could not to. A sort of kindness."

"Doesn't seem kind," Farideh said.

Dahl laughed—he could imagine Farideh telling the god that right to his face, holding Oghma accountable for every moment of grief he'd given Dahl. He laughed until he lost his breath—you stlarning *idiot*, he thought a little wildly. How could you have missed this?

"Sit down," Farideh said, pulling him by the arm toward the other sofa. He tugged her back, drawing her into an embrace.

"I'm in love with you," he said. "I am so in love with you."

Farideh went stiff. "No, you're not," she said quickly. "You're shaken up, you're tired, you're—"

"In love with you," he said.

"In the middle of a war," Farideh finished. She pushed away from him. "And you smell like whiskey. You can't be in love with me. You don't like tieflings."

"Clearly I do. I like *you*. I love you." It was true, true as the glow of the god in his brain. He cupped her cheek. "The moment I met you, I couldn't stop thinking about you. Do you know that? I never thought about why."

"Because you hated me. You're shaken up."

"I never hated you," he protested. "You irritated me, but everyone irritates me. Except you, now. I found out about Oghma and I walked over here without even thinking about why—not because I have no one else to tell, but because I wanted to tell you. I just want to *be* around you." He stopped, hearing the way he was rambling and catching the words before he embarrassed himself. But there wasn't any stopping it. "And I'm not going to lie: I'd really like to . . . revisit what happened in the storeroom. I'm an idiot—I've been thinking about you naked and it's taken me this long to realize, I'm *really* fond of you."

She blushed, looking as shocked as if he'd just spoken in tongues. "There are things you don't know," she said. "You'd change your mind."

"I doubt it," Dahl said.

"Just trust me, you would."

"Try me."

"This isn't a dare!" she cried. But he didn't move. "I will probably always be a warlock—"

"Good. It's saved my arse a time or two."

"I slept with Lorcan. A lot."

"I already knew that. I don't care." He shook his head. "I mean, I wish you wouldn't. And don't mistake me—I hate him and I still think you can do better. Maybe I'm better. I still love you anyway."

"Dahl, you're not thinking this through."

"You're not arguing very well," he returned. "*None* of these are things I didn't know. None of these are things that change my mind." A thought occurred to him. "If it's because you don't think you can love me—"

"I didn't say that."

"You should say it, if it's true. It still won't change my mind, but gods, I ought to know."

Her tail slashed over the carpet. "It's not about *you*."

"Then why? Just tell me."

"Because I'm one of the Chosen of Asmodeus!" she shouted. "You cannot possibly love me."

Outside, the rain came harder, rattling against the windows. Someone in the street was crying for spare arrows for the city's defense.

"That's not true," Dahl scoffed.

But even as he spoke, he could hear her saying *They're Chosen, not Choosers.* She was so sure that it didn't matter what a Chosen thought of the god, so certain that Chosen could come from faithless and nonworshipers, because that was what happened to her.

"It *is* true. That's where the soul sight comes from," she told him, tears spilling down her cheeks. "I have the wrong blood, the wrong ancestors, so I have the wrong *karshoji* god's attention. When I say it's dangerous, I don't mean because of bigots or jealous former lovers. I mean there is a very real chance that you could gain the notice of Asmodeus, and I won't let that happen. You can't love me, and I can't let you."

If ever there was a good, logical reason to pass up a woman, this was it. But it wouldn't be true, and Dahl wouldn't be happier for it. The calm that Oghma's presence had left around him was fading, and Dahl's chest was starting to feel tight. Farideh was staring at him as though she was waiting for the end of the joke.

Or maybe for him to leave her behind.

"I already love you," he said. "So unless Asmodeus has forms I have to declare, it's already true and he already knows it. Stop telling me what I can think."

And whichever it was—disbelief or fear or something else altogether more complicated—she had a point: the Shadovar were coming and the world felt like it was ending. Dahl didn't feel like wasting any more time.

He kissed her softly—the way, he thought, he should have kissed her in the storeroom, and it occurred to him, as he drew her close, that he might still owe her an apology for taking advantage of the circumstances so abruptly.

But as slow as he tried to stay, she matched him, urged him on. There was much more he needed to say to her, needed to ask her, needed to hear from her—but not a god in the Heavens or the Hells could have reasonably asked Dahl to think straight when she held him like that.

From heav'ns to Hells the plane will ring, he thought and he didn't care if that was what Oghma had meant, it was still apt.

She pulled away, held his face in her hands. "This is so dangerous," she murmured. "And complicated. It's always going to be complicated."

"I don't care." His mouth found her neck, the soft place just under her ear and she gasped. Harpers and pacts and Chosen and gods—complicated didn't begin to cover it. But she'd said "former" lover and so everything seemed simple. "It's worth it. You're worth it."

"If you're drunk, I will never forgive you," she said. And he laughed—he'd never been so sober in his life. Her fingers slid through his hair, cradling the back of his head. "So," she said, the faintest tremor in her voice, "you thought about this. Have you got a plan?"

"I have a couple plans," he said. "I mean, if you're amenable . . . ?"

The color of Farideh's eyes shifted—she was looking into his. She bit her lip. "Very," she said. "But we have to be in the circle—we can't risk it. Come here."

"You always have to change things," he teased. She kissed him again—very amenable, he thought, light as air—but then she pulled away sharply.

"Circle," she said, her breath rough. "In the circle. Come here."

And the world might or might not have been ending, but for Dahl Peredur it suddenly felt as if it had at least turned the right way around.

• • •

THE GATES OF Suzail were shut tight by the time its newest army returned, with the Crown Prince of Cormyr and Lord Crownsilver riding beside their command a tenday later. A bad sign, Brin thought, eyeing the line of archers whose bows were trained on the approaching army. Shade hadn't beaten them to the city, but they couldn't be far behind. As the archers spotted the Purple Dragon standard, they lowered their weapons.

"A fine sight," Irvel said. "I didn't think I'd ever see it again."

"I'm glad you can, my lord." For his part, Brin found a mix of dread and relief in his own heart. This was his home in so many ways, but in so many others it was the last place on Toril he wanted to be.

Irvel had insisted the war wizards not report his return just yet. Baerovus was awake, they had learned, and on the throne. Give him some dearly needed practice.

"Is that the wisest course, my lord?" Brin had asked. "Are you planning to leave Baerovus on the throne?"

"Heavens, no," Irvel said. "But better he sees he can manage it when his time comes. We'll be home in no time at all, and then we'll sort it out."

That Baerovus needed practice while Raedra needed rescue had not been lost on Brin. Irvel doted on his daughter, but he never seemed to appreciate the fact that she wasn't a child any longer.

The guards over the gate grumbled at their approach. "Gates aren't supposed to be opened, my lord baron," one called down to Erzoured. "By order of the King."

Erzoured grimaced. "I have infantry and refugees. Open the door or I'll have your head."

"Open the gates," Irvel called, grinning. "By order of the King."

The guard's eyes widened. "By all the Watching Gods," he swore. "Open the gates!"

Erzoured gave Irvel a sour look that the crown prince did not notice. For once Brin was in sympathy with the baron. But the gates opened and the army ambled in, flush with triumph. There were a hundred refugees with them, most of them armed and armored now, extensions of the army that had marched out. Mounted officers, mostly nobles, led their soldiers to muster points along the wide Promenade. They might be home, but the war wasn't over. Not by a shot.

Brin reined his horse in, watching the procession for the others. Constancia rode up beside him on a prancing bay. "High-stepping fancy-legs," she snorted. "Times like this, I mourn for Squall."

"Aubrin!" Irvel called, halting the crowd. "Come along."

"A moment," Brin called back, climbing from his horse and handing the reins to a palace groom. There—Mehen and Havilar, and Kallan as well, walking beside the covered wagon that held the hellhound. He'd found her weeping into the dog's fur the night before they reached the city, preparing to send her back, and though he knew he'd regret it, Brin had convinced Irvel that Zoonie should be allowed in—*hidden* and muzzled and under the guard of war wizards.

He dismounted and strode over to them. "I have to go to the Court. I assume you'll be at the tallhouse?"

"Do you need someone to come with you?" Mehen asked.

"Aubrin!" Irvel called again much closer. "You can't shy from the glory this time, my boy." He looked up at Mehen and Havilar, still grinning. "Don't tell me you're shooing off these brave souls? You three must come as well. You've done such a service for Cormyr.

Brin imagined Havilar in the middle of all those courtiers. At Raedra's feet. "I don't think that's wise, Your Majesty."

"Nonsense. I insist. Come along before I drag you." He clapped Brin on the shoulder. Mehen gave his charge a dark look before following after.

Havilar pursed her mouth. "So I get to see the court after all."

Brin thought about telling her to run for the tallhouse, to stay by Zoonie's side. But the court would remain, the whispers would increase. Raedra would still hang over them.

Kallan put an arm around Havilar's shoulders. "Whatever happens, you saved him. They can't say anything about that."

"Want to bet?" Havilar said.

"Don't worry," Kallan said, releasing her. "You've got quite the pair of shields in Irvel and Brin. He won't let any harm come to you." He grinned at Brin before following after Mehen.

"Cheeky bastard," Brin muttered, even though he ought to be right.

"He's not so bad," Havilar said. "Although, gods above, I wish he'd just *tell* Mehen he's interested in something else. It's going to be embarrassing when Mehen realizes we *all* knew before him."

"I told him to," Brin said. He held out a hand to Havilar. "What do you say? Can I be your shield?"

She pursed her mouth again and looked to the covered cart. "All right."

They had to rush to catch up to Irvel and Erzoured. A crowd was growing around them, but the sight of the two war wizards marching at their lead was enough to make people move out of the way, whispering as they passed. Havilar's tail lashed the tiles. Brin squeezed her hand tight.

Baerovus sat on the Dragon Throne, looking as if it were made of red-hot pokers. The circlet he wore pushed back on his head as if he couldn't risk catching sight of it. Princess Ospra sat beside him, still in dark mourning colors, and Edwin Morahan, the Lord Magister, stood before him, his helmet under one arm.

As Irvel came into sight, the reactions of the individual nobles were lost in the scream that came from Princess Ospra. Brin would never have thought his future mother-in-law could look so uncomposed. Beside her son, she looked a shell, a woman walking through a shadow world, trying to find the way out.

And as her husband walked into the court, she climbed free, and weeping in relief, she leaped at him.

Irvel embraced her, nearly wrapped himself around her. "My love, my love."

Perhaps it wasn't such a bad thing that they'd brought him back, Brin thought, a sudden lump in his throat.

"Are you here?" Ospra breathed, holding his face. "Are you real?"

"As ever," Irvel laughed.

"You're alive?" Baerovus cried. He looked around the Royal Court. "If he's alive, then I am not king."

"You were coronated," the stunned Lord Magister noted. "You're king."

"I shouldn't have been," Baerovus said. He ripped the circlet from his head. "I abdicate. I abdicate because there is a better claimant—that's allowed, it's in the laws."

Irvel winced, but it was followed by a fond smile. "All right, Son. We'll sort it out." Baerovus nodded once, then descended the stairs and bowed to his father.

"I'm glad you're alive. And not just because . . . I mean, I missed you." Irvel pulled him into an embrace with Ospra.

A flash of light and suddenly Ganrahast stood there, with Raedra beside him. Raedra had no more than materialized but she was running to her father. "How?" she cried. "How? Dear gods, you're alive!" She threw her arms around Irvel. "How?"

"A very good question," Ganrahast said.

"Your very wise and clever betrothed," Irvel told her, with a gesture back at Brin. For the first time, the Obarskyrs seemed to notice Brin standing there, with his friends. Raedra crossed to him, and to his surprise hugged him close.

"Thank you," she said, burying her head against his neck. Brin let go of Havilar's hand for the moment, hugged Raedra back.

"I told you," he said lightly. Raedra released him with a chuckle, and wiped her eyes. Then she spotted Havilar, and a strange sort of fear seemed to take over her features. She stepped back from Brin and folded her hands against her gray skirts. "You must be Havi."

Havilar didn't move, didn't speak. Her glaive was still in its harness, and her hands kneaded the air as if missing it. "This is Havilar," Brin said. "She made sure we didn't lose your father. It was a close thing."

"Don't be fooled," Irvel said. "She's a delightful girl."

Raedra smiled at Havilar tightly. "You have my many thanks," she said. She looked away. "I suppose . . . we shall have to get to know each other better."

Every eye in the court was on them. Brin swallowed. "Havi, you need to bow."

Havilar looked at him, horrified. "You can't be serious," she whispered. "I don't want to."

"It's protocol."

"So I get to come" she said, "only to make a show for them?"

Raedra stepped forward. "It's a show no matter what we do," she said. "Just make a little curtsy, and I'll embrace you, and we can figure this out in our own private time."

Havilar's mouth made a hard line. She dipped in a curtsy but as she rose she stepped back, away from Raedra and Brin. "I think I've already figured it out. Excuse me." She fled the Royal Court. Mehen shot a look at Brin.

Raedra grabbed Brin's hand. "Don't move." A heartbeat passed, and Mehen scowled at him, and hurried after Havilar. Raedra sighed. "Aubrin, what did you do?"

Listened to all the wrong people, he thought. "I need to go."

"Don't go now," Raedra said. "She's mad—let her be mad. Give her a chance to not worry about you and your feelings." She let go of him. "Besides, we have much more critical issues at hand."

Ganrahast suddenly loomed over Brin. "I don't know how you managed it, Lord Crownsilver," he said, sounding frankly stunned. "But you have my apologies. And my curiosity."

"It's luck, that's all," Brin said. "Someone told me the right information, we followed it. Used the tools we were given." Every part of him wanted to chase after Havilar.

"A good thing, my lord," Ganrahast said. "We are dearly in need of more tools." He turned to Irvel and Baerovus. "Perhaps all of you ought to come now to the war council—we have many plans to make firm."

Brin started to excuse himself, but Raedra turned on him. "You as well, Oversword," she said sharply. Then softer, "Marsember is on the brink of falling. We cannot be next. Do not abandon Cormyr just to have your head handed to you because you rushed into a lovers' quarrel."

Better a quarrel than a decision already made, Brin thought, but then he thought of the archers, the army of refugees, the Shadovar forces camping out in Gladehap. Would he make the difference? There was no knowing. But if Shade took Suzail, it hardly mattered if Havilar thought he was a cad or not. The image of her facing the shade warrior with arrows protruding from her shoulder flashed in his mind. The memory of Sairché dropping out of the sky . . .

"Lead on then," he said to Raedra.

• • •

AVERNUS, THE LAST Outpost. Avernus, the Field of Blood. The first layer of the Hells stretched in every direction farther than Lorcan could see. Gray and jagged ridges of cooled lava, the plain torn by rivulets of magma and chasms that might have fallen all the way to Nessus, to the feet of Asmodeus. Beneath Lorcan's feet, the crushed bones of a thousand years of demons crunched into gravel as he followed Noreia, thrashing against her chains.

The cave where he and Sairché had hidden Noreia in was not hard to find—nor was it a difficulty to discover where Noreia had moved to once they'd left her. There were uncountable places to hide in Avernus's broken landscape, but none were permanent.

Beside him, Invadiah, former leader of the *pradixikai* and mother of the squad of erinyes now assiduously ignoring her, landed lightly upon the skull of something that had once been enormous, horned and fanged. "The trophies of the Blood War," she mused. "They say when Asmodeus forced the Abyss into the depths of Chaos, Lord Bel shut himself in the heart of the Bronze Citadel for decades, threatening to fall upon his sword."

"He seems to have gotten over it," Lorcan said.

Invadiah only shrugged, a secretive smile on her lips. Noreia cursed and screamed and threw Sulci off her feet as the smaller erinyes tried to hold onto the chains that bound her.

"You tit-sucking coward!" she screamed at Lorcan, which was completely unnecessary. What had Noreia expected? He wasn't going to die for an erinyes' sake.

"What has she done?" Lorcan asked in an idle way as the erinyes lashed another chain around their sister. The succubi, the raid on Stygia, Glasya's careful disinterest in the forces of the Abyss breaking through to her worst enemy's kingdom.

"It's better not to ask these things," Invadiah said. "Glasya doesn't like when you delve too deep into her business uninvited." The succubus with his mother's faint features grinned at Lorcan, the smile of a tiger about to lunge. "Though perhaps she intends to remedy that."

Lorcan shuddered. They had come to Avernus by portal. The Lord of the First, Bel the Risen General, had quickly agreed to Glasya's innocent request. Finding Noreia had taken perhaps a day—this could be finished and he could get back to Farideh very soon. She would understand—she wanted to understand, he was sure. He watched as two furies of erinyes fought Noreia into exhaustion.—eager Leuctra with one-eyed Sulci, and quiet Nisibis; tall Lutetia with dark-skinned Neferis, and Gaza with her silken black hair.

"Shall we go?" Lorcan asked. "I can't imagine Her Highness is all that interested in playing out her business for Lord Bel to observe."

"Lord Bel will not give an imp's right stone," Invadiah said, a feral look in her eye as she watched her daughters slowly destroying one of her own. That, more than anything, made Lorcan want to run—as an erinyes, Invadiah had been proud of her fierce and ferocious daughters. While she never shied from punishing them, never hesitated to kill if the point was there to make, it had always left her furious. After the Ascension, she didn't have daughters to waste.

As a succubus, her punishment for failing Glasya nearly a decade ago, Invadiah was certainly as violent, certainly as calculating, but there was a wildness there that promised everything Lorcan knew about surviving in his mother's presence was useless now.

"Perhaps," she said, "he will even be pleased, should he watch closely enough. How is Sairché?"

"Quite mad," Lorcan said. "But she doesn't claim your mantle anymore, and if you want it from me, you have only to ask."

Invadiah laughed, a sound like waves crashing against a rocky shore. "Oh Lorcan. That isn't how this works."

"Why don't you open the portal?" Lorcan said to the hellwasps that hung around him.

"That is not the orders," the hellwasp buzzed. "We are to continue east at this juncture."

They crunched across the surface of Avernus. In the distance, devils roamed, watching them pass, gauging their strength. Invadiah carried papers of safe passage—they could not be harmed without those devils suffering the ramifications of flouting an archdevil's orders—but the presence of Glasya's hellwasps kept them from coming close enough to demand the papers. The *pradixikai* cemented it. Still, they watched.

Ahead the land rose up, a sudden mountain of sharp cliffs and, carved into the face of it, a temple of colossal columns, reaching nearly to Avernus's churning orange sky. The finial of each column was carved with the faces of dragons, their chins tucked down. Five faces, each rotated slightly from one column to the next. The ground sloped down to the temple's entrance, a cavern large enough to set Osseia in its mouth.

"The cambion should lead the condemned through to Dis," the hellwasp said. "That is hierarchy."

"No," Invadiah said. "It will take more than a mere cambion to drag one of the *pradixikai* through the layers." Her wings flicked. "You should have them do it."

It was close to an order, but far enough that the erinyes complied. Lutetia took the papers of safe passage from Invadiah, never meeting the succubus's eyes. Sulci and Nisibis took the chains that hung from Noreia's shoulders, Leuctra claiming the one that ran from her wrists. Neferis and Gaza marched ahead, weapons drawn, papers in hand. Invadiah's hand fell on Lorcan's shoulder, stopping him when he tried to follow.

"Watch and learn, Lorcan," Invadiah said. "And be glad, indeed, you owe me a favor."

As the erinyes approached the colossal temple, something rumbled within, something moved. The shadows shifted and then every inch of the opening was full of a dragon.

More than a dragon, Lorcan thought, stepping back from the approach. Five terrible heads the size of pit fiends—red and black and white and blue and green—ducked through the entrance and spread, opening like the petals of a nightmare flower. A roar, a scream, a roll of thunder—multiplied by five and then doubled and redoubled until Lorcan was sure that his bones would crumble into dust.

Tiamat. The Dragon Queen. Guardian of the Gate to the Second Layer. Latest Vassal of Asmodeus.

You wish passage to Dis, a voice in his thoughts spoke. Invadiah's hand squeezed his shoulder as though she were trying to dislocate the joint. Only the hellwasps seemed unperturbed, zipping back and forth.

Lutetia strode forward and held up the documents of safe passage. The green head lowered, peering at the scroll with one lambent eye. The green's nostril flared, and then the head raised up high, plummeting like a boulder to snatch Lutetia in one great gulp.

Lorcan watched, his horror all hidden as the four other heads chose from the erinyes arrayed before them. The white head snapped Gaza in half. The blue head rattled lightning from its jaws, stilling Nisibis before slamming her against the ground and tearing off her leg. Sulci managed to stab the black head with her dagger, but to the Dragon Queen it must have felt like a mosquito's bite, and the fearsome horned head seized Sulci and slammed her against the cliff face, smashing her skull. The fearsome red head had time to consider Noreia, frozen in her chains, before it dived down and snapped her up, tossing her once in the air and swallowing her whole, chains and all.

Neferis, alone spared her sisters' fates, scrambled back up the bone-strewn rise, unable to look away. "Lucky one," Invadiah said as she reached them. "You'll go far."

The Dragon Queen, her sacrifice taken, hauled herself from the temple-cave, the ground trembling with each terrible step. The red head, its muzzle smeared with Noreia's blood, lowered itself to Invadiah and Lorcan's level. Not a muscle of Lorcan's body moved. Like a vole before the fox, he thought, like a deer before the dire bear. He was nothing to the dragon goddess, less than nothing. Something to be eaten and obliterated, nothing more.

But the head of the red dragon remained, two feet from Lorcan's farthest reach.

Invadiah withdrew a second scroll, a second set of orders for safe passage—the true ones perhaps—and held it open for Tiamat.

"Your assistance is invaluable, Your Eminence, and the Archduchess extends her deepest regards and a renewed welcome to the Nine Hells. As evidenced, I hope, by the quality of her offering."

Whatever your mistress is trying to rid herself of, the Dragon Queen's avalanche voice echoed through Lorcan's skull, *it will uncover itself. Secrets are not meant to stay secret.* She leaped into the air, landing as lightly as a raven coming to roost on the crown of the strange temple. *Keep your hand upon the rightward wall. Unless you wish to drift into my domain, and play by my rules.*

"Many thanks, Your Eminence." They passed through the cavern, one hand against the rough, rocky wall. The air was thick and fetid with the smell of death and dragons, and in the shadows to their left, a shifting, depthless darkness threatened.

"Somehow I think she might question if Asmodeus's protection is an improvement upon Lord Bane's," Invadiah said, sauntering along toward the distant light and clamor of Dis. "I suspect she did not realize His Majesty would insist she be useful to us."

"Guarding a gate in exchange for a piece of her own kingdom?" Lorcan said. "That seems simple enough."

"The guarding," Invadiah said. "And the eating. Nothing devoured by Tiamat returns. Every piece down to the soul is consumed." She smiled at her son. "We'll take the long way home, I think. It will give you time to consider what a gift you've been given."

So into the clamor of Dis, Lorcan walked, trying hard not to wonder what exactly Noreia had stumbled upon, and whether or not he'd stumbled on it too.

26

FARIDEH WOKE FROM A DREAMLESS SLEEP, FEELING RESTED AND PEACEFUL. No archdevil's words echoed in her thoughts, and she did not feel as though she'd run from wolves for the last hours. She lifted her head from Dahl's shoulder, blinking and vaguely disoriented. It had been such a long time since she'd slept without the nightmares.

"You," he said, just a little smug, "went out like a torch in a puddle."

It made her feel suddenly, oddly shy. She turned her face into him. His hand moved up her back as he pulled her closer, and her heart felt full enough to burst. It felt as if she could get drunk off the smell of him. He moved under her, and she realized her tail had wound itself around his ankle.

"I guess I was sort of worn out," she said. She pulled her tail away. "Sorry."

"It's adorable," he assured her. He gave a nervous laugh. "I didn't bore you to sleep, I hope."

"No," she said. "You have very good plans."

He laughed. "Can I have that in writing?"

She pushed up on one elbow and smiled. "You haven't . . . Have you sobered up?"

"I *wasn't* drunk," he said, testily. "And I didn't change my mind. You want to get rid of me, you'll have to just do it yourself."

"I don't want to get rid of you," she said. She traced the indentation between two ribs. "I love you." He laid his hand over hers. The light through the gap of the drapery had grown brighter, the noises from the street more insistent. "I suppose we ought to get up. I don't really want to."

"I would lie here with you until the city comes down around our ears," Dahl said. "But I am famished. How about I see what you've got to eat, and you go get dressed?"

"Don't go wild," Farideh said. "We don't have remotely enough to sustain us through a long siege."

A rapid knocking came at the door. Farideh sat bolt upright, clutching the blankets back up to her chest. She snatched at her nightgown as Dumuzi came striding down the hallway.

"Wait! Don't!" she cried pulling the shift over her head. It caught on one horn. The dragonborn turned, taking in the scene.

"*Chaubashk vur kepeshk karshoji!*" he cried. He turned as if he were going to storm off, then turned back, eyes on the ceiling. "This is what doors are for! And rooms that have them!" Dahl unhooked the sleeve from her horn, and Farideh yanked the nightdress down. The knocking came again, and Dumuzi opened the door.

"Well met," Farideh heard Vescaras say. "Is Farideh in?"

Dahl winced. "Ah. Right." He reached for his breeches, and Farideh threw her dressing gown back on and went to the door.

"Well met," she said to Vescaras. "Is something wrong?"

Vescaras smiled at her, even though he looked positively exhausted. "Dahl was worried you didn't make it out of the palace. I said I'd come by and check to make sure you were all right." He paused. "Goodwoman, I don't mean to speak out of place, but I think you ought to know that he's . . ." Vescaras cleared his throat. "Dahl's a good man, a good agent. And I suspect he's going to go on refusing to tell you he thinks well of you—"

"He's here," Farideh said, the nobleman's discomfort more than she could stand. "He's here. He's . . . You don't have to convince me of anything."

Dahl came up behind her, still buckling his breeches. "Did you find Garce?"

Vescaras's jaw dropped. "Are you stlarning kidding me? What happened to resting?"

"I rested," Dahl said defensively. "And I'm feeling a lot clearer, which was the goal anyway. I'll tell you later. Did you find Garce?"

"I found him. He's dead. They fished him out of the harbor yesterday morning."

"Son of a barghest." Dahl turned to Farideh. "Can we use the library? I'll still fix some food."

"Of course." She turned to go and he pulled her back, kissed her cheek.

Farideh climbed the stairs, aware of a lightness in her, a giddy feeling that was completely mad considering they were on the brink of war. As if something vital had clicked into place.

Then she opened the bedroom door, saw the remains of the binding circle, and the middle of her heart tore wide open.

It seemed as if the previous night had happened a thousand years ago—until she stepped inside the bedroom and it rushed back at her. The vial lay under the chair where she'd thrown it. A pile of silver dust waited beside the circle of runes, where she'd grabbed one too many items in her rush to get downstairs and spilled the component. She stopped in front of the circle, the same place she'd stood when she realized that Lorcan was going to break her heart if she didn't break it first.

Under that giddy lightness, her soul ached.

He poisoned you, she thought. It was all the worse for knowing that Adolican Rhand had done nearly the same thing, lacing her drink with something so she'd be tractable. It haunted her still. He knew that, he didn't even consider that. And you were a fool for ever thinking he would.

As much as she was a fool for thinking that she hadn't just doomed Dahl. *Maybe I just have to make sure they aren't there to talk to.* There was no way at all that Lorcan wasn't going to come after Dahl.

Lorcan promised, she told herself. He promised he wouldn't harm Dahl. But that was before. That was when she'd insisted that Dahl wasn't a rival, wasn't a threat. Not even the gods knew what would happen now.

And under all of that, a part of her wanted to weep for what she'd done to Lorcan.

Gods, she thought, sitting down at the foot of the bed. You idiot. Gods, gods, gods. Who *are* you?

A sharp rapping came at the door. Dumuzi poked his head in.

"I'm sorry," he said, sounding flustered. "You surprised me, that's all. What happened to the devil?"

Farideh covered her face with both hands. "I told him we were done. And then I don't know."

"I doubt he'll like this turn of events."

"Thank you, Dumuzi, I was assuming he'd be delighted."

The dragonborn sat down beside her. "You are not my clutchmate," he said a moment later. "But you have to tell me if you're being careful. You aren't married. You could get gravid. I hear it happens to humans like *that*." He snapped his thick fingers. "And then what happens?"

"My children will be clanless?" Farideh said dryly. Dumuzi had the grace to look abashed. "I've been counting my days since I was thirteen. It's nice to have a use for it finally. Not that it's your business. Now go away, I have to get dressed."

Dumuzi left, climbing the stairs to his own room at the top of the tallhouse. Farideh considered the abandoned circle a moment more. She thought of Raedra, of what she'd said about her dead husband. *I will never forgive myself, because a part of me loves him still.* She loved Lorcan, but he was going to keep on blithely hurting her.

And Dahl makes you happy, she thought, pulling drawers open. In his own strange way. She dressed in her leathers, and felt as if she were in her own skin for the first time in ages. When she came downstairs, Vescaras had left, but Dahl was still in the library, bent over a map of Comryr and rocking on his heels. Her pulse quickened. Oh, he makes you happy, she thought.

"Problems?" she said.

Dahl shook his head. "Garce died like Marjana," he said. "The other Cormyrean agent. The one who made the list of Sharrans. Knife in the back, multiple times. Dumped in the harbor, somewhere on the east side, based on where they found him."

"You think he was killed by the same person."

"It makes sense. What I don't know is why. They didn't know each other, him and Marjana. He had nothing to do with the Sharrans or anything else she was watching over."

"What was he doing?" Dahl straightened as if he suddenly remembered he wasn't supposed to be telling her all of this. "I already know plenty," she pointed out. "Maybe I can help."

"Smuggling refugees into Suzail," Dahl admitted.

"Maybe he was smuggling more than that."

"Not Garce," Dahl said. "He wasn't in it for coin." He hesitated. "He was one of the good ones."

"Maybe he crossed paths with someone who *was* smuggling."

Dahl shook his head. "None of the Sharrans have done anything like smuggling . . ." He trailed off. "The tunnels. The tunnels are for smuggling. So they have to go outside the city—they must. Maybe through the sewers. And if you knew a certain good-hearted nobleman in Castle Crownsilver, you could bring people right into the city without worrying about other nobles getting riled about the rising population of homeless farmers."

"But Brin left," Farideh said. "So he found another path in?"

"He wouldn't tell me where," Dahl said. He put his hands behind his head, squinting at the bookshelves as if the secret were there. "Garce never trusted me. They must have been terribly careful—paying off the right guards, getting the right war wizards on their side. Or maybe Brin somehow got permission to switch off the wards and traps and things."

"Traps?"

"The Crown knows about the tunnels—they use them too. But there are limits. You can't just have whoever wishes, traipsing in and out of Suzail. They'd lose cartloads of coin in tariffs and you'd never know where any of the goods came from. There are traps throughout, and most places with access to the tunnels do like Teneth's—put in a wall of some sort only the owners can open."

Farideh bit her lip. "But if you had a powerful explosive . . . you could clear a path."

"A path to what, though? And how does that relate to Garce?"

Farideh looked down at the map of Cormyr, at the little farmsteads scattered over the countryside as little crosses and family names. Hundreds of people driven ahead of Shade. She imagined them all, huddled in the tunnels, creeping toward the light. A shiver ran over her.

And then she imagined them, not frightened refugees, but Shadovar soldiers.

"A path to the exits," she said. "If they could clear the path from the exits of traps and guardians and things, they'd have a way to bring the Shadovar army *inside* the walls."

"You couldn't," Dahl said. "They'll seal them from the inside if they haven't already. But then . . . the seal won't be against people inside trying to get out. The spell will be made for incoming forces, not outgoing. It will almost certainly be weaker on the inward side—why waste magic balancing it?

"There will have to be maps," he said. "They've got to have a plan—eighteen people and they're going to need to be cautious about where they place the explosives." He ran a hand through his hair. "I need to go."

His stomach growled and Farideh laughed. "Eat first. The war wizards have almost certainly already beaten you to whichever Sharran you're thinking of shaking down. Then maybe I can come with you."

Dahl smiled at her. "You *are* much more fun than Vescaras. Why didn't you tell me about Pheonard Crownsilver?" he asked as they headed into the kitchen.

"Because something is funny about him," Farideh said. "He's up to nothing good, that's for certain. But he isn't like the others. He's tainted but . . . I don't know." She took out the half loaf of bread and a wedge of yellow cheese. "I'm not convinced he's one of them."

Dahl took a knife to the bread. "You went by yourself."

Farideh hesitated. "I went with Lorcan. About that," she said, "he's going to come back, sooner or later. I made him promise not to harm you, before. I don't know what that's worth, but—"

"I'm not scared of him," Dahl said.

"Well good." Farideh leaned against the table beside him. "But that's not what I'm talking about: I don't know if this means the end of my pact with him, and to be honest, I hope it doesn't." She'd thought about this, all the long hours of the night. "I can't afford to have the whole of the Nine Hells trying to claim me right now, and I at least know what to expect from Lorcan. At least . . . I did. Before. You have to let me figure out if I can keep things simple."

"You want to keep us secret."

"I want to not bring it up until it comes up. And I want you to promise that if he doesn't try to hurt you, you're not going to try and hurt him."

Dahl reached over her, moving so that he stood with one hand on either side of her, leaning on the table. "All right," he said. "But promise me it's not for good."

"Of course not." She smiled. "Well, that was simple. No argument?"

"Permanent truce," he said, and kissed her.

The front door opened and Farideh jerked toward the noise. No one had knocked. "Just Dumuzi," Dahl said.

But then Farideh heard a voice she knew as well as her own pulse call out her name. She pushed Dahl away and all but ran across the kitchen, yanking open the door.

It was Havilar—standing in the entry, looking up the stairs for Farideh to descend. "Havi!" Farideh shrieked and sprinted down the hallway, colliding with her twin in a fierce embrace. She was real, she was here. Tears streamed down Farideh's cheeks even as she laughed wildly. "You're all right! You're here. You're all right."

"Of course," Havilar said, holding her tight.

Farideh looked over Havilar's shoulder and saw Mehen watching them, smiling. Farideh let go of Havilar and hugged her father. Mehen lifted her off her feet, rubbing the fringe of scales along his jaw against the side of her horns. "Let me look at you." He held her out. "I see that fever couldn't break you." He smiled. "You look well."

"I've been drilling," she admitted. "And . . . I am well. Very well, now that you're home."

Mehen looked past her head and his smile dropped. "Dahl," he said.

"Well met, Mehen," Dahl said from the hallway.

Farideh glanced back at Havilar—she'd been preparing to deal with Lorcan when it came to Dahl . . . but not Mehen. Havilar raised her brows—*what* was there to make *that* face about?

"We were just about to eat," Farideh started.

But movement on the stairs drew Mehen's attention. Dumuzi stopped at the top of the staircase.

"Who in the Hells are you?" Mehen demanded.

"This is Dumuzi," Farideh said quickly. "He . . . Dahl found him. He's been sort of the doorguard. He came from Djerad Thymar."

Mehen turned on the younger dragonborn, reaching for his falchion. "Dumuzi—"

"Clanless Mehen," Dumuzi said, tripping on the epithet. He came down the stairs, hands held up in surrender. "I'm . . . I am Kepeshkmolik Dumuzi, son of Uadjit."

Mehen scowled. "I see," he said, slipping into his milk tongue. "My unwelcome shadow. What does your mother want now?"

"Nothing." Dumuzi's tongue fluttered behind his teeth. "I've searched for you, for so many months."

"And then you decided to take advantage of my daughter's weakened state and set an ambush?"

"Mehen," Farideh said. "That's not what happened."

Mehen bared his teeth. "Tell me what Kepeshkmolik wants and get out of this house."

"Nothing," Dumuzi said again. He looked to Farideh. "Is there somewhere we can speak privately?"

Mehen snorted. "Kepeshkmolik and Djerad Thymar have cut my throat enough times."

Dumuzi took a deep breath. "It's not Kepeshkmolik. My father sent me to deliver a message."

Mehen laughed. "What *sthyarli* did they find to satisfy choosy Uadjit?"

Farideh shook her head at Dumuzi—don't say it, don't say it. "It's . . . not about my father," Dumuzi said hesitantly. "It's about your father. Verthisathurgiesh Pandjed is dead."

Mehen went completely still. "Well," he said after a long, uncomfortable moment. "Well. Who knew the old henish could die? Good riddance, I suppose." But then he looked at his daughters—Farideh found herself wondering what could make a person so glad to lose their father.

"The clan is short of heirs," Dumuzi went on. "Verthisathurgiesh Anala is matriarch now. She's asked Vanquisher Tarhun for permission to overturn Pandjed's expulsions. You are among them. Would you come back?"

Mehen turned and stared at the younger dragonborn, studying his dark eyes. Farideh wondered if he would spot Arjhani in his son's face, if everything would come out when it didn't need to.

"Clanless is forever," he said. "There's nothing for me in Djerad Thymar. Good day." He turned to Farideh, as if Dumuzi had vanished with that proclamation. "Where in all the broken planes did Dorn and Arven get to?"

Farideh told him what had happened with the servants, how Dahl and Dumuzi—and Lorcan, although she was careful to avoid emphasizing him—had been the ones to make sure she got through the fever and no one kidnapped her in the meantime. "And Dahl," she began delicately.

"Did you say there was food?" Havilar interrupted. "I'm starving. Let's see about something to eat." She took Mehen by the arm and pulled him toward the kitchen.

"Go on," Farideh said to Dumuzi. "He'll warm up when he sees you're not after anything." Hesitantly Dumuzi followed Mehen, and Farideh turned to Dahl.

"I'll tell him."

"Would you mind if I'm far, far away when you do? He went for that sword awfully fast for my tastes."

Farideh chuckled. "I need to stay now."

"I know. Do you mind if I come back tonight?"

"I insist." She kissed him and said good-bye. When she turned, Havilar was standing in the hall, looking smug.

"I knew it!" Havilar said. "Gods above, Dahl? You're kissing *Dahl?* What did you get up to while we were gone? Are you sleeping with him? Have you got an understanding?"

Farideh tucked her hair behind one ear. "Yes. It's pretty new, though."

Havilar crowed. "Dahl. Oh holy gods, that's so odd. But perfect. I always thought he was good-looking." She glanced back at the kitchen. "Wait—what about Lorcan?"

"He doesn't know yet," Farideh admitted. Then, "I sort of had an understanding with Lorcan while you were gone, too."

"What?" Havilar cried. She broke into nervous giggles "You slept with *both* of them? *Karshoj!* Who are you and where's my prissy sister?"

"*Don't* tell Mehen," Farideh said.

"Psht!" Havilar snorted. "I won't tell him about Lorcan, but he cannot say a *word* about Dahl while he goes along saying things like 'if you're old enough to have a relationship with a man, you're old enough to sort your own problems.'"

"He said that?"

"He said that." Havilar dropped her voice. "Also, I think Mehen's going to have his own fellow to worry about soon. There's this pretty dragonborn sellsword who keeps hanging around him, talking him up. If he doesn't show up at that door in the next hour, I owe you a gold piece."

Farideh frowned. "Wait, if Mehen doesn't care, then why'd you rush him off?"

"*Because,*" Havilar said, "you *have* to tell me first. I'm your sister."

It made Farideh laugh. "I missed you," she said. "Where's Brin? Did you find the prince?"

Havilar's cheer collapsed. "We found him. Brin's at the palace. I think maybe we're done, though."

For all her sister's relationship had worried at Farideh, that admission punched straight into her chest. "Oh Havi."

"It's just too complicated."

Farideh sighed and tucked Havilar's arm under hers, squeezing her hand. "It's always going to be complicated."

"Well, I've had about my fill of complicated," she said. "I think I've been full since the hellhound showed up."

"I think you need to start from the beginning," Farideh said, leading her back toward the kitchen.

• • •

HAVILAR DUG HER toe into the sludgy mess of the garden and sighed. "I see you got no more sun than we did."

"Do you want to spar anyway?" Farideh asked. She could have used it herself, as a hundred nervous thoughts pecking at her. "We could manage."

"No," Havilar said. "I am so *sick* of mud. Anyway, Dahl will be back soon, won't he? You'll just have to run off."

Maybe, Farideh thought, the shadow smoke threatening to edge out of her skin. "I've seen plenty of him lately," she said. "I haven't seen you in months. He can wait."

Havilar gave her a skeptical look. Farideh folded her arms. "He might not come back," she pointed out. He might have sobered up. He might have changed his mind or remembered that she brought so much trouble and chaos into a relationship. Remembered that she wasn't going to suddenly look like she had under Ilstan's spell.

Havilar snorted. "He'll be back."

"Are you going to bet me another coin you don't have and won't pay?"

"No, because you have no business betting me he won't come," Havilar said, going into the house once more. A knock came from the door and she shot Farideh a triumphant look.

Farideh's stomach tightened.

But as they came into the corridor, Mehen opened the door to a dragonborn man with scales of a dark blue-gray. Havilar grabbed Farideh by the arm and yanked her across the hall and into the library. "Kallan," she whispered. She pressed a hand to her own mouth to stifle her giggles.

"Well met," Mehen said. "Did you have a problem with your payment?"

"Are you sure Mehen fancies him?" Farideh whispered. Her father looked stiff, braced for something unpleasant.

"Who can even tell?" Havilar said. "But I think Kallan *definitely* fancies Mehen. And Mehen ought to fancy him back, anyway. He's funny. You'd like him."

"Well met," the sellsword said. He leaned on the door jamb with one wiry arm. "Nothing like that." He paused, looking Mehen's face over. "Truth be told I'm finding lodgings in short supply. Lord Crownsilver mentioned you were staying here. Thought you might have the space."

Havilar pulled Farideh out of the doorway and peeked out herself. "I wish he would just *say* something. I don't know if Mehen even knows he's flirting."

"*Is* he flirting?"

"Hush up, I know the difference."

"There's room up in the servants' quarters," Farideh heard Mehen say. "But you'd be sharing with our unexpected guest."

"Sounds ominous."

"A hatchling with self-important ideas," Mehen said. Farideh peeked out from behind Havilar. "Nothing more."

"We shouldn't be spying," Farideh whispered.

"From the city, I suppose?"

"Kepeshkmolik."

"Figures. Your kinsman?"

"Hardly."

Kallan grinned. "You could just tell me. Stop me guessing."

"Or you could come up with something more interesting to ask me," Mehen said. "Room's at the top of the stairs."

"Much obliged," the slim dragonborn said. As he climbed the stairs, Mehen's eyes definitely lingered on Kallan. Then he looked down at the twins in the doorway.

"What in all the broken planes are you two doing?"

"Staying out of your way," Havilar said sweetly. "Although I think I might not much longer. He *likes* you, Mehen. You should just—"

"I know that."

Havilar jerked back, visibly startled. "You do?"

"Of course I do." Mehen folded his arms. "Do you think I just hatched? Do you think your lot invented flirting?"

"No," Havilar said. "But I *know* how you do it and *you're* not flirting. He doesn't know . . ." She trailed away. "*Do* you like him? Is that what it is?"

"It's complicated."

Havilar gave him a withering look. "Try me."

"Does that mean you've got an understanding?" Farideh asked, uncomfortably aware of how that, too, made her stomach knot. "He seems nice."

"I hardly know him," Mehen said. "And it's not just about whether I fancy someone. I don't get that luxury."

"Why?" Havilar demanded.

"Because I took in two babies left in the snow," Mehen said sternly. "You two have my heart, never mistake it. After the last time . . ." He broke off, his voice uncharacteristically thick. "I won't do that to you again," he finished. "I don't care if I fancy someone. You'll understand when you're older."

Farideh thought of Dumuzi, of Arjhani and the third clutch and the summer Havilar picked up her first glaive. She didn't blame Mehen. Lock your heart up close and you never get hurt, she thought. As if it were that simple.

"Oh Watching Gods. We *are* older." Havilar set a hand on their father's shoulder. "Mehen, we're not little girls anymore. You've said it, we're grown women. We have brightbirds and heartbreaks of our own. We're not so dumb as to think you've got things different—maybe he's your one true love and maybe he's just some fellow you have fun with for a bit. So that's just a really *pothac* excuse, when you get down to it."

"Also," Havilar added, "I like him better than Arjhani. And he's better looking too. No question."

Mehen burst out with a great laugh, and pulled Havilar into an embrace. "Broken planes, you've grown, my girls." He reached for Farideh, too, and hugged them both close, rubbing the fringe of scales along his jaw against Farideh's head.

"Does *that* mean you have an understanding?" Havilar asked, muffled by Mehen's chest.

"It means no such thing," he said. Then, "I'll think about it. But no more spying." Mehen released them both, one yellow eye fixed on Havilar. "Why did you say 'brightbirds'?"

Havilar pursed her mouth. "Because Fari's going to tell you something, if she ever stops being a *karshoji* blink dog about the whole thing."

Mehen turned to Farideh, and she blushed hard enough her cheeks ached. "If you say 'Lorcan,'" Mehen began.

"Not Lorcan," Farideh said.

"Who?"

She hesitated. What if he didn't come back, after all? "Dahl," she said.

"Dahl," Mehen repeated, looking as if he didn't believe her. He sighed, flaring his great nostrils. "Well, it's not Lorcan, that's something. Dahl, though?"

"Dahl," she agreed. Her heart was thudding in her throat, as if telling Mehen were going to make certain everything came apart. "He makes me happy."

Mehen's severe expression softened at that. "He'd best."

They'd gone to the kitchen to re-assess the food stores, now that there was another mouth to feed when someone else knocked at the door. Farideh shot up from her seat, and Havilar grabbed her arm, pulled her back.

"If you don't let him come in, Mehen's just going to come pester you."

"I will," Mehen said over his shoulder. Farideh laughed, and settled back into the chair. But still, she replayed the inevitable scene in her mind—Dahl coming in, meaning to tell her he'd made a mistake, everything coming out in front of her family.

Dumuzi came through the door. With nowhere to go, and the city sealed tight in advance of the Shadovar attack, Farideh had convinced Mehen to let him stay—and Dumuzi to hold his tongue about Arjhani.

"Your young man is here," Dumuzi started.

"I can meet him," Farideh said, standing again. "I'll bring him back."

"No," Dumuzi said. "Not the Peredur. The Crownsilver. *Her* young man."

Havilar's eyes widened and she grabbed her sister's arm. "Fari, I can't. I can't right now—"

"It's just Brin."

"It's not, though. I made up my mind, but Fari, the littlest thing, and I just know I'll unmake it. I want everything to be all right, but right now . . ." Mehen turned around, watching them.

Farideh squeezed her sister's shoulder. "I'll go and talk to him."

In the tallhouse's front room, Brin looked a wreck, still in his armor and clearly short of sleep. He leaped from the sofa when Farideh appeared, as if he thought she were Havi. But then she wasn't, and he seemed to deflate.

"She's, um," Farideh started. "She's busy. Maybe you should come back another time."

"She's not busy," Brin said. "She doesn't want to see me, does she?" He looked down at his hands, clasped together. "There's really nothing I can say to fix this is there? Ye gods, you must be *loving* this."

Farideh drew back. "How can you say that? I'm not glad—why in the Hells would I be glad? She's heartbroken. She doesn't want it to be like this."

"Oh, please," Brin said. "You've wanted to be rid of me since she and I first got together. You pushed me away, you took her away and left me behind."

Farideh came into the front room and sat on the opposite sofa, her eyes never leaving Brin. "Is *that* what you think *happened*? That I made the deal and left you out so we could leave you behind?" Brin wouldn't even look at her.

"You know what?" Farideh said. "*Karshoji arbrinominak*—both sides all the way back! You *know* I didn't know what would happen."

"But I wasn't someone you wanted to protect," Brin said. "I was fine on my own, right?"

"No!" Farideh cried. "Sairché was going to kill Lorcan. She knew about Havi, she was threatening to give her up to collector devils. She didn't have any idea who you were—and so long as she didn't know, she couldn't hurt you, couldn't use you to get to Havilar. You proud, *karshoji* idiot!"

"Excuse me?" Brin said. "You're sitting in *my house* calling me names?"

"Tell me it's not true," Farideh said. "You happily assumed the worst about me for eight years, and given the possibility that you might have been wrong, you decide it's better to let me be what ruined everything." She stopped, her cheeks burning. "Gods above—is that it? It is easier if I'm the worst, because then you aren't."

"Oh, drop into the Hells," Brin said. He covered his face with his hands. "You were never worse than I am."

Farideh went and sat beside him, rubbing a hand over his back. "You're not the worst. You made the best decisions you could have in bad situations. I wouldn't dare pretend that I wouldn't end up in the same place. Not that that's much of a reassurance." Brin laughed, muffled by his palms. "I know why you were keeping us in Suzail," Farideh said. "At least I think—the tunnels? And Garce?"

Brin looked up. "Ye gods, Dahl. Can't you keep a secret?"

"I figured it out. Through the tunnels under Castle Crownsilver," Farideh said. "But when you left, he had to find a new path, right?"

"There is no telling whether Helindra would be pleased or furious at my rescuing so many fleeing farmers. As much as we all like to pretend the nobles know their duty, they like comforts better. There were already rumblings about Suzail taking on too many of the dispossessed. I skirted it."

Farideh pursed her mouth. "Did you hear about your uncle?"

"Pheonard? I heard they want him for questioning, but not what about."

"You know how Havi . . . can apparently call imps and spot demons?" Farideh asked. "I can see how corrupted people are. Whether a god has a particular interest in them. Your uncle—"

"Is obscenely corrupted?" Brin finished. "That's hardly a surprise."

"He has some of the signs that suggest he's under Shar's influence."

Brin turned to face her. "Shar? That doesn't seem like Pheonard. He wants too much to dance for the Lady of Loss."

"So does Netheril," Farideh pointed out. "Maybe she doesn't mind using an imperfect tool. What's he want?"

Brin frowned. "There's talk," he said slowly, "of what should be done if Suzail falls. Of whether we should capitulate, and what terms would be acceptable. Everyone knows Shade would want a puppet on the throne. A 'governor' like Sembia has. Everyone suspects it would be Erzoured."

"That doesn't seem likely," Farideh said. "I mean, if nothing else were there, he would take it, I think. But he doesn't want another's victory. He's not just looking for the crown, after all." Brin eyed her. "I looked."

"Promise me you won't use that power on me."

"Promise you'll sort things out with Havi," Farideh returned.

"Regardless," Brin said, "of whether Erzoured wants it for himself, there are people who want it *for* him. Like Pheonard."

"Has he staked so much on the baron?"

"Not exactly," Brin said. "Erzoured isn't king because it doesn't *matter* which child is firstborn so much as it matters which heir is claimed. Erzoured and my father are absolutely Emvar's get. But neither was claimed by Emvar—not my father because my grandmother wasn't married to him, and not Erzoured because Emvar didn't know he existed when he died. You can't inherit *just* because of who your parents are—they have to acknowledge you and preferably declare you their heir. It goes without saying, most of the time, but then there are peculiar circumstances. Like Pheonard's."

Farideh frowned. "What does that mean? Because he's so much younger? Is *he* Emvar's get too?"

"No," Brin said. "Helindra's."

"Are you joking?"

"She had a lover when she was sixteen—I've heard it was one of the grooms and I've heard it was a Truesilver and I've heard it was a foreign lord from Zakhara. Nobody knows anymore. Anyway, she got with child, her parents whisked her off to Athkatla, and pretended her mother was in confinement with a 'winter-babe' as they called it. They all came back, Pheonard declared as the fifth child of Britharra and Rence Crownsilver, Helindra was married off to a second cousin who was considered sickly and difficult to match. And officially, that was that."

"So Pheonard might feel he ought to be Helindra's heir," Farideh said.

"Exactly," Brin said. "I suspect that's why he's never much liked me, not since Helindra took over—so long as no one officially decides where I stand, I'm still theoretically a Crownsilver and the direct heir of Narvus. I could unseat Helindra if I'm not an Obarskyr, and then it doesn't much matter if Pheonard is her heir or Everonth, her official firstborn. Of course," he added, "the only thing that sounds worse than running the Crownsilver family is running Cormyr."

"Your family," Farideh said, "is like a chapbook drama come to life. Do you have any idea where Pheonard might be?"

"Too many," Brin said. "And I told them all to the war wizards. I have to get back." He stood. "Will you tell Havilar I'll come see her again?"

Farideh hesitated. "Can you get her in to see the hellhound? She misses it."

"I can do that," Brin said. "I can't say I think I *should*, but I already know I'm not arguing her out of keeping the thing. We could go tomorrow—damn, no. I've got to . . . Day after tomorrow. Tell her I'll meet her after morningfeast, by the palace gates and I'll get her to Zoonie" He sighed. "Will you tell her I haven't given up?"

"I'll tell her," Farideh promised.

Brin hesitated, and then embraced her. "I'm sorry I was a hardjack."

"It's all right," Farideh said. "We all have rough days."

"Months," Brin corrected. "Please, get her to talk to me again."

"I'll do what I can," Farideh said, thinking that it might be simpler to stop the Shadovar army single-handedly. She walked him back to the door.

"Is Mehen going to kill me, do you think?"

"No," she said, opening the door wide. The highknights were still there. "He loves you, and Havi would stop him even if he didn't—she doesn't hate you. Besides, he's . . . got other things to distract him at the moment."

Brin frowned at that, but at the same moment the iron gate banged against it's latch. Farideh looked up and there was Dahl. And all the doubts that circled around her thoughts fled. In that moment, she was certain: she wasn't ever going to want him to stay away. He smiled as he saw her, and her heart thudded in a very different way.

Brin looked back over his shoulder. "Ye Gods," he said. "I left a message that I'd be by tomorrow morning. You didn't have to come hunting for me."

"Well met to you too. I'm not here for you," Dahl said not looking away from Farideh. "Pardon us."

"Come on," Farideh said, once the door was shut. "We can talk in the library for a bit."

"Listen," he said as she reached the library door, and Farideh turned, her heart in her throat. "I've been worrying all day about what you're going to say," he admitted, sounding sheepish. "Is it still too dangerous?"

She heard her own fears in his voice, bit back a laugh. "Come here," she said, and pulled him into the room and into her arms. "How did it go?" she asked, and she kissed him.

"I didn't find out much," he said, pulling her closer. "They rounded up everyone we listed for them, save four."

"Which four?" she asked, between kisses that grew longer and more lingering.

"The Kraliqh's groom, the serving girl at the Sweet Nymph, the cellarjack at the Keen Raven, and Pheonard Crownsilver. Gods' *books*." He pushed her back. "Are they all still here?"

"And more," Farideh said. "A sellsword they met."

Dahl cursed again, and kissed her. "Come back with me to the Dragon's Jaws?"

"I can't," she murmured. "Ilstan."

"Godsbedamned Ilstan."

"Did they sweep the tunnels?"

"For all the good it does," Dahl said. "I don't think they're even properly mapped. I'll ask Brin for more information. Stlarn it—does this door lock?"

Farideh did laugh then, but she took his hands and pulled them from her hips, pressed them in her own hands. "It will," she said. "But if we're gone too long just now, I think Mehen's going to come looking. I told him," she added.

"What did he say?"

"That you'd best make me happy."

He smiled at her, and it was such a nice smile. But then a serious expression crossed his face. "How about you? Did you talk to Lorcan?"

Farideh's happiness stuttered. Lorcan had not come to call since the night before, and Farideh found herself caught between being terribly afraid something had happened to him and relieved that she had a little more time to think of what her next steps were. She hadn't made her choices with an eye to how smooth the aftermath would be.

"Right," Dahl said. He folded his hands around hers instead. "Well," he said after a moment. "I brought a little silver at least. Just in case."

• • •

"I DON'T SEE what the trouble is," Irvel said, as he and Ganrahast considered the hellhound pacing in its pen. They'd spent the morning going over everything he'd missed, updating him on the city's defenses, the scouring for Sharran agents. The hellhound was the last oddity of his journey home, kept locked in a secret room whose only entrance came from the gardens beyond the Royal Court. "It was instrumental in finding me, and she seems to have it trained."

"They can be trained," Ganrahast said in a begrudging way. "I knew a fellow, a war wizard in the court of your grandfather who had one. Kept it on a leash and fed it salted pork. But it never lost the instinct to hunt."

"Good," Irvel said. "So far as I can see, that's the most useful thing about it." The hellhound had worn a track in the dirt with her pacing. "That and the stamina. Perhaps we can breed it to some of the coursing hounds. End up with something a little more manageably sized. Did your fellow ever try breeding his?"

"It had been gelded, as I recall, to curb its tempers. Which did not stop it from savaging him one day."

The hellhound looked up at Irvel with faintly glowing eyes and whimpered. The King of Cormyr flinched. A savaging would take a man's head off with those jaws. "Well, keep it in the pen," he said, "and keep the muzzle on. But let Havilar see it. She dotes on the beast." The Purple Dragons beside the door parted and bowed as Raedra came in. Irvel nodded to her and continued. "Such a charming girl. And quite well-mannered for a tiefling."

"So long as no one asks her to bow," Raedra said, coming to a stop beside him. She made a curtsy, as if for emphasis. "Your Majesty."

Irvel frowned at her. "Blunt your tongue, cheeky bird. Being jealous of someone less fortunate like that is unbecoming. You're still my favorite girl."

Raedra set her jaw in a way that reminded Irvel of her mother. "I should hope. Did you know that she's Aubrin's mistress?"

Irvel started to scoff, to tell her she should listen less to the wild talk of envious nobles. But then he recalled the frequent glances, the hushed conversations, the way Havilar seemed to become more upset the closer they came to Suzail. The way Aubrin had gotten quieter. All those postponements. He blinked.

A mistress was one thing—nothing much. He'd had none, but it was hardly uncommon. A tiefling mistress was another—a deviance, no matter how charming Irvel thought her. A mark against Aubrin and against Raedra by comparison.

"Well, yes," he said, unwilling to admit his ignorance, "but I think it's plain he intends to . . . mature. Leave behind boyish things, and all. He's quite impressed me."

"He found you when no one else could," Raedra agreed. Then, "What kept you from coming back yourself?"

"Raedra," Irvel chided, "don't you think I would have if I could have? You, your brother, your mother—you all mean the world to me."

"Thank you," she said. "But that's not what I mean. What happened to you?"

"I was gravely wounded—I could hardly walk for tendays while I waited for it to heal and someone to find me. How could I have known my sanctuary made a shield against my allies? And then it was infected, then blood rot took me. To be honest, I had no idea at all how much time had passed. Everything's a bit of a haze, until the end—until Aubrin arrived and I realized I was in so much pain! I imagined I saw Halance—Aubrin's father—there, beckoning me."

That part, that memory was so incredibly sharp in his thoughts, set beside the rest of his time in the temple of Eldath—but sharp even beside his memories of the tendays since. He paused, running through it once more—Aubrin's fierce, frantic expression growing hazy even as the delusion of Hal became clearer.

Raedra and Ganrahast were staring at him. "What happened after that, my lord?" Ganrahast said.

Irvel blinked. "I blacked out a moment. And then Havilar was there. She'd healed me. She's a good one," he said to Raedra. "Whatever else is happening."

"Your memory of the moment before you blacked out," Ganrahast repeated, "is Aubrin Crownsilver trying to heal you, and the spirit of his father reaching out? And it's very clear in your mind?"

"Yes," Irvel said. Then, "I must have slept a little between then and waking up. I think I dreamed of Hal and my father and a great towering castle . . ."

Irvel stopped. A chill ran over him. Hal was dead and Foril was dead. And beyond the darkness of death lay the kingdom of Kelemvor.

"What day did they find you?" Ganrahast asked.

"I don't remember," Irvel said. But it hardly mattered—he'd seen Foril there. His father was already dead. By law, the crown prince was the king in all but the most technical matters.

And the king may not be resurrected.

"Perhaps breeding it isn't such a bad idea," Ganrahast said suddenly. "Has she gone into heat?"

"I don't think so," Irvel said. His daughter stared at him, her expression haunted. She knows, he thought. We all know. He reached over and took her hand in his. She squeezed it. The hellhound stuck her muzzled snout right up against the bars, licking the air between them like a dog trying to comfort its master.

"It's a good sign," Raedra said briskly. "Even the denizens of the Hells cannot help but wish for your success."

Irvel stuck out his hand, let the hellhound snuffle it. No, he thought, feeling numb. It knows I don't belong here any more than it does.

27

13 Uktar, the Year of the Nether Mountain Scrolls (1486 DR)
Suzail, Cormyr

GREAT SWATHS OF TIME PASSED, LEAVING ILSTAN NYARIL A RELIC IN their dust. He dreamed of darkness and blue fire, of the edges of the multiverse and the brimstone stench of the ever-dying damned. He moved in the darkness of Suzail's tunnels, searching for the light and always stymied. Perhaps the city had already fallen? Perhaps Farideh had already succeeded.

He looked down at the strangled rat in his hands. Succeeded at what? He couldn't remember.

You may think a god may not know fear, the drifting voice in his thoughts said, *but let the beast of beasts, the end in the beginning's skin pluck his soul out of the center of his power and make it his own. Then, shall they see fear.*

Magic crawled through every vein of Ilstan's body, dragging on his blood as if it came from a rusty still in the Hermit's Woods. It felt as if the Weave were knitting him into itself, as if he'd never break free. He'd tried to use his spells, but the feeling didn't diminish, and the rambling voice only grew louder.

The Knight of the Devil, the voice said. *The Lady of Black Magic. She has* the key. With it the prison unlocks.

"What is the key?" Ilstan all but wailed. But Azuth never said.

In his more lucid moments, Ilstan decided that Azuth was not dead, but trapped. Perhaps imprisoned in the Nine Hells. That was why he spoke of devils and the fall through the planes. That's why he was quiet when Farideh asked to know about Azuth.

Because he fears what she might find, Ilstan thought. Because her master wants to find a way to end him. You cannot let that happen.

He did not hear the man approaching, did not notice him until he stopped before Ilstan's hiding place, tucked behind the ward that kept prying eyes from a certain noble family's business. An older man in trim, simple clothes, his hazel eyes sharp and the air of danger around him. Ilstan held his wand up, brandished like a sword.

"Well met," the man said. "Shall I assume you are the war wizard I hear they're hunting?"

Ilstan didn't speak, didn't move. Ganrahast didn't understand. Raedra had been turned against him. The fact that either of them took the word of a tiefling, of a Knight of the Devil. "She has poisoned all against me," he explained.

"I can see that," the man said. "A very grave situation, if I have the right of it. I've come to offer you my assistance."

"What can you do?"

"Offer a lot of coin," the man said. "Recruit a small army of friends. She's made a fool of me as well, that tiefling lass."

"It's worse than that," Ilstan said. "I think she means to undo Cormyr, undo the very gods."

"That *is* grave," the man said. "I must help you. In fact, perhaps we can help each other. I think, perhaps, our plans might intersect."

I hear the words he says, the god murmured as Ilstan followed the hazel-eyed man, *every one as though he's speaking in my dreams. They are so sweet, sweet as brandied cherries. But at their core they are so rotten . . .*

But here is another fellow who has heard the rot of Asmodeus in her words, Ilstan thought, gripping his wand tight and bristling with more magic than his long frame was ever meant to hold.

• • •

THE PASSAGE FROM the Fifth Layer—Stygia—to Malbolge thawed as they approached the Sixth Layer's shores, the icy canal becoming one of the former ruler's fetid, open veins. Great blossoms of virulent hues and intoxicating scent lined the passage, as if Glasya meant to draw the difference between her domain and that of Prince Levistus into sharp contrast.

"Home sweet home," Invadiah said, alighting from the craft that had carried them through the dark and shifting passage. "And now it's so much roomier."

Lorcan shivered, unable to shake Stygia's unwelcome cold. The battle Zela had come to him demanding to join had left parts of the Frozen Wastes utterly destroyed. "How many succubi fled the Hells?"

"Enough," Invadiah said. "Vain, inconstant things."

"I suppose you'll have your promotion now. Felicitations." Lorcan stepped from the boat onto Malbolge's hungry surface. Neferis followed him, grimly silent. She had not spoken since they left Avernus. The hellwasps shot into the air, making for the distant skull palace.

"Not yet." Invadiah considered her moonlight arms. "I think I'll make use of this form a little longer."

Don't ask, don't ask, Lorcan thought. "It's curious," he said. "The way suddenly the succubi turned traitor. Fled to the Abyss."

"Not all of them."

"That any of them returned seems curious."

"Some have never been happy in the hierarchy. Some have never managed to lose their madness."

"But they have always been canny. Their queen has always had the unruly ones in hand."

"Perhaps she has fled as well? There is no news out of Nessus. They have always been our enemies. Even those who have flown to our side must accept that their kind will face them on the battlefields. It is their nature."

And what is in your nature now? Lorcan wondered. "If I didn't know better," he said, as they approached the palace, "I would think you were talking about the Blood War beginning again."

Invadiah laughed, a sound to go mad by. "Whoever said it ended?"

"Everyone," Lorcan pointed out. "Everyone says it ended. We have not fought demons for a century."

"And demons are predictable in their unpredictability," Invadiah said. "Their princes point and they ravage. No one sane believes that the powers of Asmodeus will frighten them forever. They must periodically be reminded, it seems."

In the skull palace, Glasya perched on her throne, a golden goddess of pain. The hellwasps formed a swarm around her, and two pit fiends stood sentinel at her side. Instead of her usual scourge, she held a short blade across her lap. Fear streaked through Lorcan's heart.

"Is it done?" she asked.

Invadiah, Lorcan, and behind them, Neferis all fell to their knees.

"Very neatly," Invadiah said.

"Do not praise yourself," Glasya said, her disapproval rolling over them like a landslide. "It's most unattractive. What did she take for her services?"

"Five erinyes. Three of the *pradixikai*."

"A pity. But you do not truck with gods by handing them imps and sweetmeats." A pause that yawned like a chasm. "Dear Neferis, you are quite lucky to be spared. Will you give me any cause to wish otherwise?"

"Never, my lady," Neferis said.

"Good. Perhaps you can help me watch over your delicate little brother here. I would hate for something to happen to him. It would be such a trial to get him back."

Lorcan suppressed a shudder over the threat and the promise buried in that statement. She would end him, merrily, and then she'd find a way to bring him back to life. He had fallen entirely too much under Glasya's notice.

"I have a gift for you, Little Lorcan. Come here." Glasya snapped her fingers and one of the hellwasps surged forward. Balanced on its bladed arms was a case of gold, inlaid with cinnabar and marked all over with barbaric-looking runes. Lorcan took it. Inside lay a heavy scepter, wrought of iron around fat unpolished garnets. The heat that radiated from it banished every memory of the chill of Stygia from Lorcan's bones.

"The scepter of Alzrius," Glasya said in her lilting voice. "Keep it safe." She smiled at him, and Lorcan's soul tried to tear itself free. "Perhaps you can use it with your warlock. Give her something to sweeten the deal."

"You are very wise, Your Highness," Lorcan said.

Glasya dismissed them. Lorcan headed straight for the fingerbone tower, ignoring Neferis's attempts to follow him, ignoring where Invadiah went. He was already too far in. He put the scepter in the room with the portal and made certain the doors were locked. Farideh would never see it, never lay hands on it. Whatever it was, why ever Glasya had given it to him, he didn't doubt it was meant to make things worse.

Sairché hadn't returned—good riddance, he thought, taking hold of the scourge pendant he wore, the one enchanted to let him bypass Farideh's protection spell. He waved the trigger ring over the scrying mirror to activate its magic. He'd find Farideh, go to her, smooth things over. He'd have to be careful, very careful for a time, but he could surely manage.

The mirror's surface swirled and shifted . . . and did not settle. No tiefling woman rose out of its murky depths. Lorcan held more tightly to the scourge pendant, willing the spell to take hold. It did not.

Terror crept up Lorcan's throat. She might be locked away in a temple. She might have found a way around the spell. She might be dead. He felt out the bonds of their pact—still there. Alive then, and she hadn't rejected it. It's temporary, he told himself. The panic didn't let go of him.

The mirror flashed a scene that shattered into fragments, then appeared again whole. The bedroom of the tallhouse. Farideh lying across the middle of the bed, her horns curving back over the edge. Her blouse was off, her hair was loose—

"Better?" Dahl asked, leaning over her.

Farideh smiled at him, and Lorcan's blood turned as icy as Stygia. "Much."

"So you *never* sleep on your back?"

"If I'm on the ground, I can roll my cloak up under my neck. But here? I'd gouge the featherbed." He laughed and kissed her. Her arms twined around his neck.

"It's a nice featherbed," he said. "Remind me to thank your sister for taking my bunk up in the servants' quarters?"

Lorcan looked down at the magic circle chalked on the floor—the source of the magic's difficulties. A pillow had fallen from the bed, scuffing the runes and breaking the spell. The runes were neat and deeply marked—not Farideh's handiwork, he thought, his head buzzing.

"You still have to go back up there before Mehen wakes up. Unless you want to face that dragon."

"Mm, I will rescue you from Sharrans and devils and madmen and arcanists, but I will not face down Clanless Mehen."

We're done. She'd meant it. She'd been angry enough. She hadn't given him a chance to explain. And then Dahl had stepped in, exactly as Lorcan had known he would—

Swear to me right now that you won't harm Dahl. Ever. Because she was preparing ahead for this, or because Dahl had been preparing? It can't be her. It was never her. She didn't abandon him to his sisters, she didn't abandon him when Sairché tricked her, she didn't abandon him when he'd broken her heart.

This is fixable, he told himself. Because she thinks she loves you.

But now you cannot kill him, Lorcan thought, forcing himself to look at the couple reflected in the scrying mirror. Now, you need to be very clever indeed.

• • •

Farideh races through the warren of tunnels, searching, searching for the Chosen of Azuth. He's here somewhere, and wherever he is there will be a link to the Lord of Spells, an answer to the question she can't quite puzzle out. The stone passage twists and forks and doubles back. At every crossroads, she can only guess which way is right. She has no idea where she is.

She turns down a corridor and finds herself facing a succubus with copper skin and red curls that twine around her like a mass of live snakes.

Rohini smiles. "Is this what you're looking for?" she asks. The tunnel leads into the snowy village of Arush Vayem, its huts somehow cozier than she ever remembered. Farideh steps toward it, the unavoidable lure of home hooked into her heart. The pendant on her chest, the amulet of Selûne grows cold as ice, cold as the winter in Arush Vayem and Farideh remembers the disapproval of her neighbors, the feeling of being trapped, the certainty that no one could love or trust her. She takes a step back. "No."

"Maybe this?" Beside her, Rohini snaps her fingers. The village erupts into flames, her former neighbors suddenly fleeing devils armed with chains and whips and hooks. "No!" Farideh cries, scrambling back. She bolts into the tunnels, away from Rohini. She remembers Azuth and Ilstan.

The passage ends in a left-hand turn, to the right, a little hollow. Farideh follows the curve and finds herself facing Rohini again. She turns away, toward the hollow. But where a stone wall should be is a portal that opens to a tower room, and herself, snowy-haired but still youthful, standing over a tome that pulses with power. Through the window beyond is a city, her city. She is powerful beyond any measure her younger self can make.

"You could have this," Rohini says.

The amulet grows cold. Power is not free. The older her looks up, meets Farideh's gaze. What would she have to do to have that security, that strength? Who would fall in her path? "No," she says, and turns back the way she came.

Ahead she glimpses the back of an old man as he takes a right-hand passage, his hair long and white, his robes blue and silver. Farideh sprints to catch up with him. She turns the corner and finds herself facing Rohini.

"All I want is your happiness, Farideh," the succubus says, her voice mellifluous and malevolent at the same time. She turns Farideh around, and the tunnel behind

opens into a street, a tidy tallhouse. She and Havilar sit on the front step, laughing and chattering. A man comes up the walkway with a basket over one arm, full of food. Farideh's heart hits her throat. Lorcan in his human skin. She stands and dusts her hands off on her breeches. Takes the basket and kisses him fondly. Havilar laughs and rolls her eyes—they are incorrigible.

"You can't give me that," Farideh says.

"I can give you anything you want," Rohini answers.

"I don't want it." Farideh doesn't need the amulet to tell her to turn away, to hurry down the tunnel. The side passages bloom with more promises—plenty and wealth and safety, admirers and finery and solitude, should she want it. She tries to keep her eyes on the old man, who keeps vanishing just as she almost reaches him.

She turns one more corner and comes face-to-face with Dahl.

"Don't flinch," Dahl teases with a crooked smile. He reaches for her cheek, to ease her near, but she leans in quick and presses her lips to his. Everything smells like bay and brimstone, and he kisses her like time's stopped. He pulls her close, against his bare skin, his hands stroking her back. Another pair of hands cup her breasts. "Darling," Lorcan murmurs, and he bites the edge of her ear, curls his fingers around her flesh. She gasps and reaches back for him. Dahl's mouth skims her neck.

"Don't mistake my position," a beautiful voice says. "I am not opposed to happiness. I am perhaps the greatest champion of happiness. Tell me what you want and it's yours, child."

Then she blinks, and it's not Rohini, but the archdevil, watching. Smiling.

Farideh grabs hold of the amulet, and she's standing beside Asmodeus, watching herself get lost between Dahl and Lorcan. She holds the amulet tight, wishing on some level she'd never touched it.

"I don't want that," she says.

"You don't need to lie to me," Asmodeus says. "I have seen all your secret wants, child. You have wished for every one of these things."

"But I don't want them," Farideh says. There is no world where she can love both Dahl and Lorcan and they are happy. Not without changing them at the very base of their selves, and she shudders to think of it. None of these things she's been offered come freely. Someone will always get hurt.

"What do you want then?" the beautiful voice says.

The Supernal glyph blooms from the archdevil's navel, an incomprehensible flower. For a moment, the tunnels go dark and there is nothing and no one, not even Farideh. The face of the ghost who haunted her in the internment camp flashes in the night, cold and haughty first, then kind and stern. She reaches out to Farideh. "Hold tight to the amulet," she says. Farideh touches her hand and the lights come back. Asmodeus is standing there once more, waiting for her answer.

"Tell me the secret," she says, never letting go of the amulet. "That's what I want."

Asmodeus stares at her, the dark of his eyes bleeding into his beautiful face, opening the orbits like terrible mouths. "I would think long and hard about what you want, my Chosen. The one who gets hurt doesn't have to be you."

"Farideh?" Farideh opened her eyes, gasping for air. She sat up, one hand planted on Dahl's chest. The bedroom, morning, the light coming through the spaces between the boards they'd nailed over the windows. No tunnels, no archdevil. But her breath wouldn't slow.

Dahl sat up and put his arms around her. "Just a nightmare."

Not just a nightmare. Not a one of them was just a nightmare. That had been the god or some part of him. *I have seen all your secret wants, child. You have wished for every one of these things.* She started shaking. It had always been Asmodeus, sifting through her dreams. Taking the measure of her.

Dahl held her tighter as she started sobbing. You're in danger, she wanted to scream. Terrible danger—was the god watching even now?

"You have to go," she managed, hiccupping.

"It's too late," Dahl said. "We overslept—time to face the dragon." Farideh buried her face in the crook of his neck. "Gods' books, are you all right? What did you dream about?"

She ran through the dream—the tunnels, the amulet, Rohini, Arush Vayem and the parade of temptations, Dahl and Lorcan and Asmodeus. The sigil and the sudden darkness. The tiefling woman who led her back out, the ghost from the internment camp, but kinder . . .

The ghost. The ghost had small sharp horns like a mountain goat's, horns like the woman in the print, sacrificing the infant. The ghost had Bryseis Kakistos's horns. Farideh scrambled out of the bed, yanking open her dresser drawer. At the bottom, tucked into a haversack, was a ruby and pearl comb, the gems set to look like poppies weeping milk. The ghost had helped Farideh enchant it so that she could speak to Farideh. Farideh turned to face the room and jammed the comb into her hair, scraping the teeth against her scalp.

There was no one in the room but her and Dahl.

"Fari?" Dahl said. "You're scaring me."

She was scaring herself. She pulled the comb free. "It was a bad dream," she said. "But I think it was a warning too." She remembered Lorcan tearing the Supernal glyph from the piece of parchment. *You ought to stop worrying about this.* What do you tell him and what do you keep secret? she thought. "I was dreaming about Ilstan," she said. "And the tunnels." She swallowed. "And there were devils and things. And Asmodeus. And maybe Azuth."

The mark was on Asmodeus and he didn't want her to worry about what it meant—badly enough to threaten her, badly enough to bribe her. Take all of this away, she thought, the one wish she hadn't been shown. Make me normal.

Maybe he didn't show you, because you don't want it.

Dahl climbed out of the bed and put his arms around her. "Which one is warning you?"

"Please don't ask," Farideh said. "Please—I don't want you to uncover things that should stay hidden. It's already so dangerous."

"What in the name of Oghma, Mystra, and Lost Deneir am I doing here if I can't help you puzzle these things out?" Dahl said irritably.

Did Oghma watch over Dahl at least? Was that why Asmodeus had only offered Dahl to her once? Or because he couldn't give her Dahl, was he in worse danger, something that had to be removed?

And was there anything Asmodeus wanted hidden that was better left uncovered?

"Just hold me a moment," she said. "It will be all right."

The door opened and Havilar ducked inside. "Sorry!" she cried, clapping her hands over her eyes. Farideh snatched her dressing gown off the table and held it up like a curtain. "I would have knocked," Havilar said, "but I only just sneaked past Mehen. Are you dressed yet?"

"No," Farideh said, handing Dahl his breeches.

"Well, hurry it up," Havilar said. "I want to see Zoonie."

"What about Brin?" Farideh said, pulling on her blouse.

Havilar blew out a noisy breath. "I don't want to want to see Brin," she finally said. "But there's nothing for it. Apparently, he has to get a war wizard to open a secret door," she said, turning blindly toward where Dahl stood.

"You can uncover your eyes," Farideh said. "Everybody's decent."

Havilar did so. "Does that sound like *aithyas* to you," she asked Dahl, "or do you think that's true? I mean she's *my* dog."

"Uh," Dahl started.

"She's your *hellhound*," Farideh corrected. "Even if she's perfectly trained, she's still bound to frighten everyone."

"Well, right, but they ought to open the door for *me*. I don't see why Brin has to be there." She tugged on her braid. "We're going to be late."

"And Brin had better be willing to wait for you," Farideh finished. She tucked the rod inside her sleeve, thinking of Ilstan. Havilar watched her.

"Do you think you ought to stay?" she asked. "I mean . . . no one's found Ilstan."

"We'll be quite surrounded by war wizards," Farideh pointed out.

Havilar shot a worried look at Dahl. "Do you want to come as well?"

"He has things to do," Farideh said.

"I really don't at this stage," Dahl said. "Vescaras is ensconced with the Roaringhorns. It's all a lot of waiting before the siege starts. And if I come," he noted, "that means I won't be stuck here with your father trying to scare me."

· · ·

"I just don't see," Queen Ospra said, taking in the chaos of her daughter's sitting room, "why it's necessary."

"The silk stretches around the arrows," Raedra explained. The *zip* of another skirt being torn into pieces cut through the air. "Slows them down and stops them from penetrating too deeply. If they get shot, it will help keep the wound from being mortal."

"Where in the world did you hear that?"

"Baerovus," Raedra said. "The Tuigans did it, when the horde came."

"And how well did it serve them?"

"Well, they didn't die of arrows."

A dozen maids and noblewomen crowded her sitting area, taking the dresses apart and stitching them back together into simple tunics. Ospra in her simple silk velvet looked positively decadent next to the ladies, who had all gone so far as to arrive in things like hunting dresses and fencing costumes. Raedra wore armor of mail and leather, which she had to admit was close to stifling in the crowded room.

"You are dressed as though you are planning to stand on the walls," Ospra said. "Don't think I haven't noticed."

"Am I on the walls?" Raedra asked. "I am indoors, I am guarded, I am far from my people. If I do that wearing armor, you can hardly complain. I shall be safer still, in armor."

"You are being flippant," Ospra said. "You may have liked playing the warrior regent, but you are not Alusair reborn. You are the last hope the Obarskyr line has for an heir. You owe it to your people, as you put it, to make certain that you're in a state to do something about that, when this is over."

"Which will hardly matter if Shade routes us in the meantime."

Varauna sauntered in, dressed in snug leather armor. "Your Highness," she said to Ospra with a little curtsy. "Have you come to join in?"

"Oh, Varauna, not you too?" Ospra groaned.

"You can hardly blame a girl for taking the opportunity to show off her legs," Varauna said. "Especially when *everyone* else is doing it." She scooped up another stack of the finished shirts, and headed back out, up to the city wall where the archers waited for the army of Shade.

"Who is everyone?" Ospra demanded.

Raedra gestured at the room behind her. "Naranthe Crownsilver, Laendra Truesilver, Eloinica Greatgaunt, Marielle Cormaeril, and also Zoene. She's running the shirts to the eastern end of the wall. Florelle is off with Brenna Rallyhorn and Calline Wavegallant, collecting more dresses. And more seamstresses—Florelle's cousin Audrina and Elspeth Scatterstars have started their own little circles, according to Varauna. The maids are from the palace, but also the Crownsilvers, the Braerwinters, the Goldfeathers"—she gave her mother a winning smile—"and I got one out of the Huntcrowns. It seems that a great number of young ladies would like something to do right now."

"It seems a great number of young ladies are enjoying the chance to be scandalous and tear up their good dresses and underthings," Ospra said. "At least this is an improvement on the sorts of gods-awful things your cohort normally dons to bare a little skin." She sighed. "Give me a pair of scissors."

"Thank you," Raedra said quietly.

Ospra tucked an errant blond curl behind her ear. "I know what it is to feel at loose ends. War may be politics and machinations and games of court for years and years, but when it comes down to it, everything is swords and fire."

"You can swing a sword," Raedra said. "I had the same fencing tutor as you."

"I am quite sure the Shadovar will not come at me one at a time, and in good form," Ospra said dryly. She pursed her mouth. "Have your father and Baerovus got these shirts on?"

"First ones," Raedra said.

"Good." Ospra ran her hands over the next gown. "Do we unpick the embroidery or—"

"Leave it," Raedra said. She cut the full skirts away from the thickly padded bodice. "There isn't time. If the men don't like it, they can change with one of the women."

Ospra sighed again, but snipped the skirt into panels. "How is Aubrin?" she asked.

Distant, Raedra thought. "I presume he is on the wall with the others."

Ospra gave her daughter a rather pointed look. Raedra sighed. "Would it be so bad if I didn't marry him?"

"Because he has a mistress?"

"Because he has *that* mistress." Raedra still couldn't shake the image of Havilar in the Royal Court. For a moment, Raedra had thought she was Farideh, and nearly hugged her, too, in her joy. But she was rangier, thin from months of trail rations and muscled from the pole arm strapped to her back. And her eyes were gold and clearly frightened. This woman, Raedra had thought, could kill me before the Dragons could stop her, could ruin me simply by making the wrong gesture in that moment. And yet Raedra might as well have been Shar herself, stepping down from a Shade Enclave onto the Promenade, the way Havilar looked at her with such grief and defeat.

What do you think this is? Farideh's words came back to her. *A game she's playing with you? Do you think you matter even a moment to how she feels about him? Because let me tell you, you don't.* Raedra tore another strip of silk.

"I don't blame you," Ospra said gently. "But please don't think it has the slightest bearing on you. Whatever you imagine people are saying, her presence does not impact you. Whether you marry Aubrin or not."

Raedra recalled her father's dreamy recollections—the fact that he'd woken with Havilar sitting over him, saying that she'd healed him.

She's affected all of us, she thought. One way or another.

"Actually, I need to speak with Aubrin," Raedra said, standing. "If you'll excuse me."

Ospra grabbed hold of her wrist. "Don't do anything rash."

"Nothing like that," Raedra promised. She caught a page careering by with a sharp command, and the boy looped back and bowed in one fluid movement.

"Run down to Lord Aubrin's tallhouse and fetch me the two tieflings," Raedra said in a low voice. "I'll meet them in the Royal Gardens."

"Begging your pardon, Your Highness," the boy said. "But haven't you heard? They're standing outside the court, on the Promenade. Waiting for Lord Crownsilver." The boy dropped his voice further still. "I think he's otherwise engaged. Been half a bell, and no sign of His Lordship."

"Thank you," Raedra said. "Go and track down Lord Crownsilver and bring him back. He's posted at the Horngate. I'll be in the gardens." The boy bowed once more and ran off.

She debated going out into the Promenade herself, but surely her guardians would prevent it. Instead she asked a jack to collect Havilar and her friends, and bring them to the Royal Gardens.

By the time they arrived, Raedra felt as if she were going to snap apart from the tension of keeping herself still. Havilar watched her warily as she approached.

"If you've held Brin back," she said, before anything else, "you shouldn't have bothered. And I'm not taking my glaive off."

"We're to be under attack shortly," Raedra said. "I don't blame you." She greeted Farideh and Dahl, trying to keep the memory of the burning angel from her mind. *She's your friend*, she reminded herself. *Or near enough.* "I was hoping I could talk to you a moment, before Aubrin comes."

Havilar shook her head. "I just wanted to see Zoonie. That's all. You won."

Raedra's stomach twisted. "Do you want to see her now?" She looked around. "Devora?" The war wizard seemed to materialize out of a hedge of lemon-scented greenery. "Can you open the room where the hellhound is kept?"

"Of course, my lady."

Raedra turned to Farideh. "If you'll excuse us, the room is not terribly large. We'll return shortly." She smiled, even though Farideh's worried expression made her think that surely the warlock knew the thought of being in the little space with her made Raedra very tense indeed. "Hopefully, Aubrin will be back by then."

Farideh and Havilar exchanged a glance, full of worry. Havilar sighed and followed Raedra, the war wizard, and the pair of Purple Dragons across the lawn. Devora stopped before a spot in the snowspikes, moved her hands in arcane passes, and a door suddenly creaked open out of the air. The ramp down to the hellhound's pen was gentle, the room lit by frosted windows that led to where only Ganrahast knew. The hellhound lay on the stone floor, more massive than Raedra had remembered. She growled at their approach.

"None of that!" Havilar said. The hellhound barked and wagged its tail, and scattered sparks over the stone floor. Havilar stuck both arms through the bars, utterly fearless, and scratched the dog behind both ears. "Good girl, Zoonie."

Raedra folded her hands together. "I wouldn't say I won. I don't think, in retrospect, we were competing. At least, we were never competing in the same contest."

Havilar let the hellhound lick her cheek through the muzzle. "You're prettier—I get it."

"I mean, he loves you. You love him. He and I are allies, maybe something like friends. If we were fighting, we were fighting for different things—and none of that seems fair since really we were both just waiting for Brin to decide who he wanted to be." She pursed her lips. "People keep acting as though I'm sullied by your presence. The only thing that disgraces me, though, is the fact he couldn't love me in two years as much as he loved you in two months."

Havilar sat back on her heels. For a long time, she didn't say anything at all.

"My sister hates anyone who hurts me," Havilar said finally. "She always has. She thinks I hold a grudge, but . . ." She shook her head, as though there weren't words for Farideh's anger. "But she likes you."

"She punched me in the mouth once," Raedra said. "I said something rude about you."

To her surprise, Havilar laughed. "Are you serious? Oh, Fari."

Raedra folded her hands again. "I know," she said. "About what happened. About my father." Havilar looked up at her, her expression too-carefully schooled. Raedra chose her words as cautiously as she could. "He didn't . . . Brin didn't tell you that wasn't allowed, did he?"

"Brin didn't know I was going to try," she said. "I'm not going to say I'm sorry. It's a stupid rule."

"In this instance, I agree with you very much."

"Are you trying to chase me off?" Havilar asked. "It's not as if I can go anywhere right now."

I am trying to decide what to do, Raedra thought. By the laws of Cormyr, Havilar was a traitor. A traitor who had brought her father home.

"What is it you love about Aubrin so much?" Raedra asked, a question that had puzzled her. Havilar reached through the bars and scratched the hellhound's chest.

"I used to think that Farideh was the only person who was ever going to understand me. And then I met Brin. Not that it matters now," she said. "He doesn't understand anymore, and neither do I."

Raedra sighed, and set her hand on Havilar's shoulder. "Don't do anything rash. We're in the middle of a war."

Out beyond the gardens, horns played four quick bursts, followed by a long note that sent a chill up Raedra's spine. She squeezed Havilar's shoulder hard, looking back the way they'd come.

"Trouble?" Havilar asked.

"Shade is here," Raedra said.

Devora was suddenly beside Raedra, taking her by the arm and speaking a smattering of arcane syllables, the rattle of rain against glass.

"Devora, wait!" Raedra shouted, trying to pull her hand off Havilar. But she wasn't quick enough. The spell tugged all three women through a place that felt like the air before a lightning storm and smelled of wine and wintergreen, and dropped them unceremoniously into the Royal Court. Already there were Purple Dragons stationed at every entrance—and highknights behind every secret one, no doubt. Four at every door and three beside the Tomb of Baerauble, First Royal Magician, at the end of the hall. An extra for the siege, Raedra thought, getting her bearings.

"What happened?" Havilar cried. "Where are we?"

Devora blinked at her. "Oh, son of a barghest—sorry, Your Highness, I mean—"

"I don't care if you've brought her," Raedra snapped. "I want a report from the wall. And the tunnels. Now."

"Yes, Highness." Devora vanished into the air.

Purple Dragons brought her mother, trailed by the other ladies, Florelle and Varauna among them. Florelle rushed up to Raedra. "I'd just got back," she said, tears streaming down her cheeks. "And the horns . . . I feel like I'd thought it wouldn't come after all."

"Oh gods, Florelle, you're not a damsel in a . . . " Varauna trailed off as she spotted Havilar. Raedra would not have thought there was a sight in all the world that would leave Varauna with nothing to say—evidently she was wrong.

"I need to go," Havilar said.

"You can't," Raedra said. "None of us can. Those horns clear the Promenade. If we go out, we risk being shot by archers as combatants." She offered Havilar a friendly smile. "I suppose the gods have a sense of humor after all. We'll be spending the end of the world together."

Havilar did not return the smile. Her golden gaze swept the room, as if she were looking for a way out regardless. But anywhere she looked, there were Purple Dragons and war wizards and more nobles. She took a step back from Raedra and all but bolted for the farthest end of the room, past the Tomb of Baerauble, and down the passage to the Shrine of the Four Swords.

"Gods, Raedra," Florelle said. "What in all the planes happened while I was away?"

Raedra didn't speak. As Havilar passed the tomb of the ancient Royal Magician, Raedra's eyes had fallen on the Purple Dragon standing beside it. A scowling woman who stared at Raedra as though there were no greater disappointment. A woman, Raedra could see quite completely through.

The ghost of the Steel Regent, Alusair Obarskyr, vanished, leaving behind only the certainty that whatever reasons had been given for Raedra to remain locked in the Royal Court, they wouldn't have stopped the Steel Regent, and she was disgusted that they were stopping Raedra.

• • •

FARIDEH DRUMMED HER fingers against the edge of the stone bench, watching the pair of Purple Dragons who remained behind. Wondering what Raedra was going to say to Havilar. Wondering what she'd been thinking when she saw Farideh—did the moment in the war wizards' interrogation room come to mind still? The shadow-smoke started drifting off her arms, and she fought to keep it in check.

"She'll be all right," Dahl said. He stood beside the hedges, examining their leaves.

"I know," Farideh said.

"She will."

Farideh stopped herself from throwing out a list of things that might happen to Havilar—that might be happening right now. "What are you doing?"

"Trying to figure out what this *is*. It looks like boxwood but that lemon smell. They've crossbred something."

"How are you so calm?"

"I'm not," Dahl said. "If I think about hedges, there's a chance I can keep myself from thinking myself into a hole." He cleared his throat. "Where do you think you're headed? When this is all over?"

Farideh looked up at the sky, the patches of blue between the swiftly moving clouds. "Assuming we survive? I have no idea. I'm a little afraid the answer might be Djerad Thymar. Or nowhere." Which she couldn't say was as bad. There were parts of Cormyr that had steadily grown on her, and it surprised her to think that she'd lived in Suzail for longer than anywhere else, save Arush Vayem.

Dahl kept examining the leaves. "Would you consider coming to Harrowdale?"

Farideh turned, surprised. "Is that where you're going?"

"I need to. I have to see if my family's all right. I'd like if you met my mother."

No—If Suzail was a trial, what would Harrowdale be? Dahl's family had probably never seen a tiefling, leaving aside the trip there. The dangers of the road after the battles would only multiply the farther they got from the cities. But, for all her instincts panicked at the thought, the invitation warmed her. "It's been three days," she managed. "Are you sure?"

"Three days since I told you I loved you," he pointed out. "We've been all but courting for months—false or not, I don't think there's much I haven't learned about you by now. You can hardly pretend I'm rushing. Besides," he said after a moment, "I have to go."

Yes—He loved her. It was strange and surreal and dizzying to contemplate, but no matter how she asked, he loved her. And she loved him too—as much as that scared her and as much as it should have terrified her even more. "Have you thought about what your mother would do if she met me?"

"Truly? I think she'd be polite and make you some tea—probably ask if they have tea where you're from—ask too many questions and worry about what the neighbors said or didn't say to you. My granny's the one you ought to worry about." He looked over at her. "I'm not going to tell you that she's worldly enough to never bat an eyelash at her son bringing home a tiefling for dinner. But she's not a bad person. The circumstances . . . I've never actually brought anyone home to meet her. You could be a shade and I suspect she'd be pleased I'd finally met someone."

But how long are you going to be happy? Farideh thought. Whatever Dahl said, everything felt as if it were moving too fast, and she couldn't shake the sense that they would outpace their own strength and everything would crumble apart. For a brief, terrifying moment, it occurred to her that meeting his mother might be a prelude to asking her other questions she couldn't fathom the right answers to, not now.

That is what Asmodeus could offer you, she thought. The power to know the right answers.

Dahl watched her, waiting for a response. And right or wrong, there was only one answer in her heart: She could not bear for him to leave. "I'd like that. Maybe it will keep Mehen away from Djerad Thymar," she added. "Does . . . the invitation extend?"

"Sure," Dahl said, in a way that made Farideh suspect he hadn't considered Mehen or Havilar. "Of course. It's a big farmstead. Both my brothers live there, and their families, and the hands." He sat down beside her. "I suspect my brother will be *fascinated* with Mehen."

"Why is that?"

"He's always had a little streak of adventure—not enough to leave the farm—but he loves going down to New Velar, sitting in the tavern and hearing stories of exotic places. And with Mehen you get the proper mix of 'exotic places' and 'down to earth,' that will keep Bodhar entertained for days and never slow him down. Plus, your father thinks I'm a sour layabout, so he and my granny will have that in common."

"He does not," Farideh said. Dahl put an arm behind her and she set a hand on Dahl's leg. You could be normal, she thought. If you don't bother about Azuth and Asmodeus, you could just be normal.

A boy of about ten raced up to where they sat, to the Purple Dragons standing guard. "The princess?" he asked, breathless.

"She'll be back in a moment," Dahl told him.

The boy made a face. "Only I have to get back to the wall—they need a runner at the Horngate. Will you give her a . . ." He noticed Farideh sitting there, and his eyes nearly popped.

"A what?" Dahl demanded. "A message? A kite? A stiff drink? Finish your thought."

"A message," the boy said, snapping his eyes back to Dahl. "Lord Crownsilver isn't on the wall. He didn't show up to his post this morning. Done a runner. *Again.*"

"What?" Farideh stood. "Where is he?"

"Not at Castle Crownsilver," the boy said. Then he added, hesitantly, "Saer."

Farideh cursed a stream of Draconic. After all of this, Brin wouldn't have run—she felt sure of that down to her bones. He might wish to, but he'd never leave everything hanging, not with Shade on the horizon and not without telling Havilar.

"They never found Pheonard," she told Dahl.

"Go," one of the Purple Dragons, the man, told the boy. "We'll get her the message."

"We have to find him."

Dahl frowned. "Where do we start?"

Farideh shook her head. "He went home from the tallhouse yesterday night. If he hadn't made it, Constancia would have come looking for him." She turned to the Purple Dragons. "Do you know where the princess and my sister are?"

"They'll be back soon," the guardswoman said.

"Now," Farideh said. "They need to be told *now.*"

"Fari, come on," Dahl said. "We'll get back to them."

"I need—" Farideh broke off as a woman in armor approached.

"There you are," Constancia said, no warmth in her gray eyes. "You need to come with me. Aubrin needs to speak with you immediately."

"What's happened?" Farideh demanded.

"It's important," Constancia said. She cut her eyes to the Dragons. "And private. He's in trouble."

From the wall, four short blasts of a horn came, followed by a long hollow note.

Constancia looked up at the sound. "Hurry," she said, as the alarm faded. "We don't have much time." They followed her, out of the Royal Gardens, down a lane between huge manors, and in through a rear entrance to the sprawling Castle Crownsilver. Down, down, staircase after staircase, until they were deep below Suzail.

In the tunnels beneath the city, all sounds of the battle above smothered in the layers of earth. Constancia moved through the passages, unerring, unstopping, and it was all Farideh could do to push aside the remnants of her nightmare and keep pace with the knight.

"What happened?" she asked.

"There is a problem," Constancia said.

"Is it Pheonard?"

"It's not for me to say."

Farideh felt for the rod tucked into her sleeve. Dahl grabbed hold of her shoulder, stopping her as the tunnel straightened out. Constancia kept walking. "Does she seem peculiar?"

"Yes." Farideh said. "She would never come to me for help, and if Brin sent her, she'd tell me why, right off, so I'd know she hadn't decided it on her own."

Dahl cursed. "Mind control?"

"Do you think they have Brin?"

Dahl shook his head. Constancia was almost out of sight. "Come on. Assume it's a trap."

"I'll just confirm it," a man's silky voice said behind them. A spell fell over Farideh, a barrier that pressed her up against the wall. Pheonard Crownsilver smiled at her, his hazel eyes suddenly all too familiar. Behind him, Ilstan stood, swaying on his feet, his wand held high.

"It's absolutely a trap," Pheonard said. "And this time, my dear, you are caught."

• • •

KING IRVEL OBARSKYR, First of his Name, stood atop the city wall, watching the Army of Shade march up the Dragoneye Way.

"Something's not right," he said.

"More siege engines than reported," Elmaina Greatgaunt said from beside him.

"There aren't enough soldiers," Baerovus piped up, closing his spyglass. "They can't have sieged Marsember with so few." Exactly, Irvel thought. The soldiers that marched from Marsember numbered in the hundreds—not enough to bring down Marsember, not alone.

"Watch the other roads," he ordered. "And sound the horns."

Four blasts rang over the city, a warning to clear the Promenade for military action, followed by a long hollow note: this is no drill. Irvel flexed his hand against the pommel of Orbyn, hanging at his side. The catapults mounted on the nearer towers flung their loads of stone against the Netherese's sleek siege engines, their flying cavalry.

This will be over in a day, Irvel thought. So there is something more coming.

The Lord Warder, Vainrence, appeared beside him, several songs later. "Army to the north, my lord."

"Are the tunnels secured?" he asked.

"Secured as we can make them."

Irvel shook his head. "Where are the rest of them?"

"Perhaps more than reported have stayed behind in Marsember?" Vainrence suggested. "Perhaps more than expected intend to test the tunnels." The nearest catapult launched a second stone that narrowly missed one of the distant veserab.

"You rounded all of those Sharrans up?"

Vainrence hesitated. "Almost. What remains should be no trouble for wizards of war."

Perhaps you are merely melancholic knowing you are not meant to live? Irvel thought. He'd hardly slept, spending every moment he could savoring the feel of his wife beside him, the sound and the smell of her. What if he never said a word? What if he kept the resurrection a secret? Ganrahast and Raedra surely wouldn't say.

Which will damn them all the worse when it all comes out—Irvel couldn't imagine such a thing staying silent. There were the sellswords and Aubrin and Havilar and what if he should be injured? Could a cleric spot such a thing? Eventually, it would tumble out, and his enemies would leap on it.

He thought of Erzoured, his army readied behind the East Gate. What would Baron Boldtree do, given the news that Irvel had been dead already?

Perhaps what's missing is something in you, Irvel thought, drumming his fingers against the pommel of his sword.

It didn't start with screams. Someone down the line gasped, then a shout, then a hundred shouts. The screams came next.

Over the hills, a shadow unfolded against the gray clouds, a beast of night and endings, a beast that haunted the dreams of every Cormyrean down through the ages.

The Purple Dragon reared up, whole and terrible as the day he came down upon the Azoun, the Second of his Name, and roared for the blood of the inconstant Obarskyrs.

28

14 Uktar, the Year of the Nether Mountain Scrolls (1486 DR)
Suzail, Cormyr

THE COURT FELT MORE LIKE A TOMB THAN THE HEART OF SUZAIL, PURPLE Dragons and war wizards at every entrance—but maybe it always felt this way. Havilar was hardly familiar with court. She'd found a little corner of privacy in a funny little antechamber off the main room—a round room with four plinths around it. Three held different swords, and one was empty. The Purple Dragons looked askance at her as she sought refuge there, but no one stopped her. One detached from the rest of the guard to watch over her.

They live like this, she thought. Even when nothing's happening, there's a guard watching.

At least she had her glaive, but she knew better than to take it out for anything short of the Shadovar pouring into the court. She wondered if Farideh was panicking in the gardens, and if Mehen was going crazy not knowing where they were. She wondered if Brin was all right.

Havilar heard footsteps and glanced back to see Raedra standing at the brink of the shrine. She turned back to the greatsword. Gods' sense of humor, indeed.

"Would you give us some privacy please?" she said to the guard. As he walked away, Raedra sat down beside her, on the floor, and Havilar could hear disquiet in her breath. "Devora hasn't come back," she said.

"Maybe they found something else for her to do."

Raedra shook her head. "She's supposed to be guarding me. More likely she would have been reprimanded for leaving her post, even under royal order. Something's going wrong."

"Fat lot we can do about it."

"I need to get out of here," Raedra said quickly. "I *can't* stay here. Will you help me?"

"And get shot through for the pleasure? No, thanks."

"I have a plan," Raedra said irritably. "It's . . . maybe a little wild."

Havilar considered the greatsword opposite them. Wild plans, that she was more acquainted with. "What is it?"

"I need to get to the wall," Raedra said. "And then the tunnels. It's one of those places where she vanished from. And besides, there has to be something better I can do than just sit here." She folded her hands against her skirts and blew out a breath. "I need your hellhound. My father said it's fast and strong. It can carry the both of us?"

"Probably. But you can't get it out."

"I can unlock the cage. I don't think Devora closed the door."

"How are you going to get past all these guards?"

"There are passages out of here," Raedra murmured.

"I thought the tunnels were full of Shadovar and things."

"These don't leave the royal complex. You can't get in without already being in. We just need to get to the gardens. But we still have to get past the guards. And any guards in the passage."

"So you need a diversion."

"I'm working on it."

Havilar was about to ask if this diversion ended with her being thrown in the dungeons when the raven-haired noblewoman in leathers crept into the little shrine. "What *are* you doing in . . . Am I interrupting something?"

"Varauna," Raedra said, standing. "Finally. Go fetch Florelle, and do it *quietly*. I need your help." The noblewoman raised her ink-line eyebrows, but did as she was bade. Raedra watched her go, then considered the swords on their plinths, settling on the jeweled short sword.

"Don't you fail me again," she muttered as she took it from its case.

"Are you supposed to touch those?" Havilar demanded.

"I'm allowed," Raedra said, as if she knew the difference and did not care. She went into one of the side rooms and came back with a battered scabbard and belt. The gems of the hilt winked in the lamplight. "Maranth, you ought to have forced me to use the greatsword," Raedra muttered.

Varauna came back with the weepy, blonde noblewoman she'd originally arrived with. Havilar stood, unable to shake the feeling she was being surrounded.

"Listen to me very carefully," Raedra said. "I am leaving the court, one way or another. Something has gone awry and my duty is not to sit on my damned hands and wait to find out what. If you have any love for me, you'll help me, and if you have any wisdom at all, you'll know you can't stop me."

Varauna shot a look at Florelle, but the other noblewoman watched Raedra, rapt.

"I need a diversion," Raedra went on. "Something to draw the eyes of the guards and my mother. Something big enough to warrant whoever is guarding the exit coming out to help. Something they're all somewhat expecting to see." Now Raedra looked rather pointedly at Varauna. "Something like what happened three Greengrasses ago?"

Varauna folded her arms. "I don't know what you're talking about."

"I'm talking about the reason that Pelarra Huntsilver and you cannot be in the same room together anymore."

"She's a viper?" Varauna suggested.

"You tore out a hank of her hair."

"Because she's a viper," Varauna said once more. "And she was an absolute beast to Florelle—we agreed none of us would be in the same room as her. Now she doesn't want to be. I call that a hit."

Florelle had turned deep pink. "Please don't bring that up."

"Start a fight," Raedra said. "A loud one. People will remember, they will assume it's going to get out of hand fast. Don't be too interesting," she added. "You don't want them waiting for all the details. Pick something vague."

"She's an idiot?" Varauna suggested.

"She's a whore?" Florelle returned.

Varauna gave her a winning smile, without any trace of having been insulted. "That should do nicely." Her blue eyes flicked over Havilar. "Are you bringing her?"

"She's integral," Raedra said. "So hold your tongue."

Varauna gave Havilar a pretty smile and held out her hand. "Very charmed to make your acquaintance, goodwoman."

Havilar held her gaze. "I doubt that," she said. "I also don't care." A snort of laughter escaped Florelle, and even Varauna's stiff smile twitched.

"Keep her alive anyway," she said. "If my very best friend comes to harm because of you, you'll have to see how much worse I can manage than pulling out your braids."

"Come on," Raedra said. To Havilar she added, "Stay near me, but not too near."

In the main room, the scions of the royal families gathered together with a handful of retainers, in case the worst should happen. Havilar could recognize the queen, sitting beside a gray-haired man and a woman who could only be his daughter. Helindra Crownsilver sat on a padded chair, her teenaged grand-daughter, Naranthe, beside her. Havilar nodded at Helindra. Raedra took a seat beside the old woman, on one of the collected chairs. Unsure of where she ought to be, Havilar found a place against the wall, just short of the dais. The queen looked up at Havilar with the same pale eyes as her daughter—the same steel in her gaze—until Havilar had to look away. Everyone it seemed was watching her, watching Raedra. Wondering what they'd talked about. She wondered if she ought to look angry or if she ought to pretend to cry—help this plan along. Raedra sat silent beside Helindra, though, so Havilar settled for looking unconcerned. She studied the people gathered in the main room . . . and wished profoundly Brin had been among them, safe and locked away.

He can handle himself, she thought. Then: you have to let him, now.

Helindra's eyes drifted down to the blade at Raedra's belt. "You have the look, my dear," she said, "of someone who is plotting something."

Raedra turned to face her, cool as ice. "Do I? I suppose I am only overcome with worry for my city."

For a moment, Havilar was sure the old woman would call the princess's bluff. But then she only smiled thinly. "Aren't we all?"

"To begin with," Varauna's voice rose through the genteel murmurs, "I would not call you a half-wit—that implies you are not an idiot half the time."

"Amazing you have any time to muddle through such distinctions," Florelle shot back. "One puzzles how you can think through all the rutting and moaning!"

"You puzzle over everything, dear."

"And you're a *slut*!" Florelle all but shrieked. Roatha and Glorin's nurse covered their ears. "As if everyone doesn't know you've already bounced your way through all their beds!" Havilar fought not to wince—she sounded like an actress in a play. And who were 'they'?

Fortunately, Varauna had a better measure of how to respond. The *crack* of her slapping Florelle resounded through the court.

Florelle cried out and touched her bleeding mouth. "What in the Hells did you do that for?"

"Because you're a smug little tart!" Varauna snapped. She reached out and grabbed hold of the knot of her friend's hair, yanking her off balance and scattering pins. She shoved her to the ground and then leaped on her like a wild animal, ignoring Florelle's raking hands.

"Ladies!" Queen Ospra shouted. Raedra stood from her chair and backed toward Havilar. Florelle threw Varauna off her. The raven-haired noblewoman rolled to her feet, scanned the room—assessed her audience, Havilar thought.

"I would pay to see this another time, I think," Havilar whispered to Raedra as they slid along the wall.

Varauna's eyes lit on an empty chair and she heaved it up, as if she were going to throw it at Florelle. The Purple Dragons nearest the two noblewomen rushed forward. Varauna twisted back, and let the chair tumble from her grip—narrowly missing the queen. Ospra yelped and leaped into the older man.

That got the guards moving. One grabbed Varauna, who kicked and thrashed and called Florelle a string of names. Two more grabbed Florelle, who seemed to have lost all her reticence and was ready to knock the teeth out of Varauna's mouth.

Havilar glanced over at the other nobles. Helindra was watching her and Raedra ease along the wall with a narrowed eye. Havilar grabbed Raedra's wrist, pulled her attention to Lady Crownsilver. Helindra gave them an entirely too cunning smile.

Then she grabbed her chest and gave a loud, dramatic cry, falling back into her chair. Naranthe sprung up and caught her. "Help!" she cried. "Someone quick! Help! I think she's dying!"

Raedra fumbled with a panel in the wall as some other woman struck Florelle. The door popped open, startling a man standing there. "Highness," he started, "you need to—"

"Help!" Raedra said. "They're going to *kill* each other." The man looked past her, and the chaos brewing in the court. He cursed to himself and pushed past Raedra and Havilar. The princess pulled Havilar into the little passage.

As the door closed, Havilar glimpsed Helindra, still watching through the crowd that encircled her, a faint glimmer of amusement in her eye.

"You're going to pay for that later, I'll bet," Havilar said as they ran down the passageway.

"Let's start by making sure there's a later." Raedra drew up short by a span of wall where the stonework gave way to clay. Set into the dirt was a ladder. She set her hands on the rungs, and a magical glow lit them. "Come on."

They emerged beneath a monument, a woman with an orc's head in one hand and a short sword in the other. All around were weedy-looking roses. Raedra led Havilar through them, back to the stretch of garden where the lemon-scented hedges and the snowspike bushes lined the green.

The door was nowhere in evidence.

"Gods be damned," Raedra panted. "I was sure . . ." Havilar peered at the snowspike bushes, waving her hands through the air before them. Nothing. Raedra bit her lip and looked back the way they'd come. "We'll have to find a war wizard, or maybe just walk—"

A dark shadow blotted out the patchy sunlight, the massive shape of a dragon wheeling overhead. Both women moved back into the snowspikes as it passed overhead.

"Now," Raedra said. "We have to get up there *now.*"

The creak of the catapults sounded down the walls. They weren't going to get up there without help. And they couldn't get the hellhound to get them up there without still more help. She looked at Raedra. "Will you promise not to tell about this?"

"About what?"

"This," Havilar said. She shut her eyes tight. "I have a problem!"

It took a moment, but then an imp dropped out of the air. Raedra cried out and drew the jeweled short sword. The imp scrambled away from her.

"Piss and ashes!" Mot squeaked. "Be a little more careful!"

"I need you to find a secret door and open it," Havilar said. "Can you do that?"

"You say that like it's *easy,*" Mot said.

"You made it sound like *everything* was easy before!"

"That was before."

"Where's the other one? Where's Dembo?"

Mot flapped up so that he was level with Havilar's eyes. "He got in trouble."

"What does that mean?"

"It means your stupid demands weren't *allowed* and he's not coming back. Ever."

Raedra stared at them, wide-eyed. It was Dembo's own decision, Havilar wanted to explain. She didn't know he'd get in trouble and *he* should have. But the imp was dead, and she felt guilty nevertheless.

"I'm sorry about Dembo," Havilar said. "But I need you to open the door, and you said you were here to do what I needed. So open the door, Mot, unless you *can't.*"

The imp scowled at her. It flapped along the row of snowspikes twice, then kicked out at a spot, striking something invisible there with a hollow *thunk*. He folded himself into the air, disappearing with a pop. A moment later, the door opened from the inside.

"Thank you," Havilar said.

"*Don't*," Mot replied. "I'm too upset." He vanished once more.

The cage responded to Raedra's touch, unlatching like it was alive, and Zoonie barreled out, knocking Havilar off her feet. Havilar took hold of the chain and led the puppy out into the gardens.

"Is it like riding a horse?" Raedra asked, pulling herself up behind Havilar.

"No." Havilar tugged on the chain. "Come on Zoonie, good girl." The hellhound broke into a loping run across the gardens, heading for the East Gate.

• • •

As THEY WALKED through the tunnels, Dahl kept running through possible plans in his head—even without a sword, he could surely disarm one of the six rough-looking sellswords if he could just get his hands untied, and then—

And then you have the wizard to deal with, he reminded himself. Ilstan, swaying on his feet, stared at Farideh, as filthy as a hermit. Just looking at him put Dahl on edge, as if he were looking at something cursed and enchanted. But just as the wizard wouldn't stop staring at Farideh, Dahl didn't dare take his eyes off Ilstan.

"Your plan is so near to completion," Pheonard crooned. The nobleman—the hazel-eyed man in the scarf who'd tried to kidnap Havilar—Dahl could have kicked himself for not spotting that. The sellswords kept their weapons trained on Farideh and Dahl, on Brin and Constancia, on the red-haired war wizard, Devora. A heavy-looking collar closed around Devora's throat, and it left Dahl with a sense of vortex, sucking away all that was vital around the war wizard. One of the sellswords dragged a cart behind, a stack of five boxes atop it, each one belted with strips of metal and topped with a strange little tray.

"Soon Cormyr will be safe," Pheonard went on, "and the Lord of Spells will be free. As soon as his enemies are dealt with."

"The Lady of Black Magic retains the key," Ilstan murmured. "But the lord lives, and I am his champion."

If he attacks her, Dahl thought, still watching Ilstan, you knock her out of the way. Or head butt him. He looked over at Farideh, who was chewing her lower lip as she studied Ilstan, her breath labored with anxiety, her tail flicking back and forth, smacking his heel. Faint shadows seemed to drift off her arms.

Or she head butts him, Dahl amended.

"Loyal Torm," Constancia muttered behind him. "I cannot believe you two fell for that."

"Constancia, not now," Brin said. His eye was blacked and swollen. "*Do* you have a key?" he whispered to Farideh.

"I have no idea what he's talking about," she said.

Ilstan surged toward her, forcing her back against the sellsword's blade. "There is light in the darkness and darkness in the light! I cannot be stopped, O Knight of the Devil! *He* cannot be forsaken!"

"All in good time, saer," Pheonard soothed. "Now, if you please?"

Ilstan searched Farideh's face a moment, before abruptly turning and walking down the passage to its end.

"Are you all right?" Dahl asked.

She gave him a dark look. "None of us are all right."

"Cast?"

She hesitated. "My hands are tied." She leaned against his shoulder, as if they were trying to embrace without their arms. "I have a way. It's not pretty. And I need space."

Dahl nodded once, and kissed the crown of her head. *Lord of Knowledge*, he thought, *Binder of What is Known. If you want your damned salmon sorted out, I could certainly use some hints.*

"Oy!" one sellsword, a broad-shouldered man with a bristly beard, called. He prodded Dahl's back with the tip of his blade. "Separate, brightbirds. You'll be together soon enough."

Ilstan reached into his pockets and flung a handful of powders and a piece of something dusty-looking into the tunnel before them, just at the point where it joined another, larger passage. The Weave crackled around them, swelling to fill the space. The components he'd tossed up vanished into ash and a puff of smoke, and a barrier of silvery magic snapped into the space.

"So you have a madman casting cantrips?" Brin said. "What a clever plot, *Lord* Crownsilver. The war wizards will sniff him out in a hurry. And the next time they won't be alone."

"I don't doubt it," Pheonard said. "In fact, if my plans are correct, there should be a great lot of them just around the corner here." He gave Brin a wicked grin. "Fortunately, I think they'll shortly find a pressing need to be elsewhere. Come along." A blade jabbed at Farideh's back, urging her forward. When they reached Ilstan, he was running his hands over the barrier, pressing them through in places. Beyond, the sound of voices echoed down the passage.

"Praise to Azuth?" Ilstan said, sounding frantic. "Praise to the Lady of the Mysteries? I don't know the words."

"They are in your heart," Pheonard assured him. "They are in all of our hearts. Are you ready for the next step, saer?"

"Are any of us? Some spells tread the line, but when there is such wickedness among us, what can we do? We must fight the wicked with whatever tools we have, even if they be immoral."

"So wise, saer," Pheonard said. "I think to begin with, we should ask the pretender for her help."

Ilstan crossed to Devora, as two of the sellswords nudged her forward. A third man picked up one of the strange boxes from the little cart and came to stand beside them.

"You shouldn't have challenged me," Ilstan said sadly. "I have a sacred duty. You should have known."

"When?" Devora said. "Before or after you betrayed all you swore an oath to protect?"

Ilstan dug a little vial and something like a pile of threads wrapped in a handkerchief out of his pockets. He set a drop of the liquid on one finger, a thread upon the other. He lifted his hands, held them ready. One of the sellswords, a scarred man, reached up and unlatched the collar from around Devora's neck.

Several things happened all together. The sellswords threw themselves against the walls. Ilstan began muttering a spell, the powers of the Weave swelling around him further still. Devora spat a trigger word and half a dozen missiles coalesced out of the stale air and shot straight into Ilstan. The smell of burning cloth and flesh filled the space.

But Ilstan's casting never stopped, never slowed. A chill ran through Dahl. Devora's missiles had no more than struck him when a net of magic seemed to cinch around her, and even as she drew up the magic to cast again, Ilstan's spell stopped her. He reached out and brushed the liquid down her nose. Devora went completely still.

"This man will bring the box down the hall," Ilstan said, as the sellsword behind her untied the rope. He held out a little onyx pendant on a velvet string. "Put this charm on the plate atop it, if you please. That way the magister's prison will begin to weaken, so the signs have spoken."

Dahl bit back a curse. The charm was the same sort the guardsman at Teneth's had used. The boxes were the Sharrans' explosives, the ones built from the list of components. Four missing, Dahl thought, or four dead because Pheonard gave them shelter and took their tools.

Devora's expression became dreamy and placid. She took the charm, smiling at Ilstan as her spells winked out like embers drifting from a fire. "I can do that," she said. "Nothing easier."

"Devora, don't!" Farideh cried.

Dahl cursed beside her. "Suggestion spell," he whispered. "She won't listen to you."

Devora walked through the barrier, trailed by the sellsword with the box. Pheonard beckoned the man holding the collar over, and clasped it around his own neck. He smiled at Farideh. "In case you get any ideas, warlock."

"The others were willing to die for this plan," Dahl said.

"And so they did. The others were zealots and fools," Pheonard pointed out. "I'm merely using the tools that the gods grant me."

"Ilstan," Farideh said, "you need to listen. He's trying to—"

"No," he said, turning on her. "Your words are rotten. I know this now. You have always sought to subsume me as your master subsumed mine. But we will see, we will unlock the door and banish the shadows. Oh yes."

"Devora?" Dahl heard a man's voice call—Drannon, the bearded man who'd come that first day with Ilstan. "What is it? What befalls?" A pause, a terrible pause. "What do you have?" The sellsword ran toward the tunnel, his hand reaching for the barrier.

The explosion ripped past the barrier Ilstan had conjured, throwing the sellsword past like a doll in a rip current. The sound was loud enough Dahl couldn't hear the scream that tore from his throat. His arms pulled against the ropes, wanting to yank Farideh back even as his feet scrambled away from the explosion. But the flames, the smoke, poured past the magical wall without even so much as stirring their hair.

As the ringing in his ears faded, Ilstan's steady muttering replaced it.

"And when the glorious day is won and evil is pressed back into its lair, then what the Blue Fire has burned away will flourish anew." He closed his eyes and started humming softly.

"Nothing easier," Pheonard said. He turned to the sellswords. "Saers, your portion seems to have increased, but I would warn you once again, you'd best move quickly when it counts. Come along, we have much to do."

The tunnel beyond was nothing but blood-spattered rubble. Enchantments held the walls and ceiling, but the floor was a treacherous pass of rocks and body parts. Dahl kept his eyes on the farther edge of the rubble field, imagining the war wizards he'd met in Suzail and wondering which of them he was stepping over.

Lord of Knowledge, take them up, he thought. *Open their souls to the wisdom of the planes forevermore. And find me a stlarning way out.* He could feel the presence of the god, just out of reach, but there. As if Oghma were watching, waiting to see if Dahl was worthy of his earlier gesture, if he had the wits to save himself.

He dawdled over a particularly large chunk of ceiling. "Whatever you're thinking, don't aim it at Pheonard," he murmured. "That collar will dissolve any spells that come near it."

"Sellswords then," she said. "Maybe Ilstan."

"Try and leave their weapons whole."

"I need more space to cast first."

"The two of you are doing an awful lot of chatting," Pheonard called from the other side of the blast site. "I think it's time for our Knight of the Devil to have her turn." The sellswords hauled Farideh up the far side, pushed her toward Ilstan. Dahl scrambled after them. If they cast the suggestion spell on her—

"No!" the war wizard cried. "There is an order to be followed, a pattern to be realized. The Knight of the Devil holds the key, and if the lock is not prepared, it will fall through the planes and nevermore be found."

Pheonard smiled. "Apologies, saer. Perhaps her ready sword should be next then?"

Shit, Dahl thought.

Ilstan nodded thoughtfully. "I have no quarrel with you," he told Dahl, as the sellswords prodded him forward. "Only you have chosen the side of evil." He walked a little way farther and crafted another barrier.

Dahl could hear Farideh's breath grow erratic again—she's reaching for the pact, he thought. The shadows thickened around her as the sellswords forced Dahl past. Keep your wits, he thought. Focus on the sword—you can grab the sword before you follow the order, remember. Remember. If you knock the fellow down, you buy time.

Oghma seemed to press upon his thoughts. He was missing something.

But there wasn't time—Dahl repeated the thought of the sword over and over as Ilstan cast his spell, as sweet oil dripped down Dahl's nose.

"Place the charm on the plate."

The Hells I will, Dahl thought.

He blinked. He glanced over Ilstan's shoulder at Farideh. The sellsword untied his wrists. But still Dahl had no urge whatsoever to follow the order meant to kill him and pave the way for a Shadovar incursion.

Because you know it will kill you, he thought. Gods-stlarning-hrast it. The spell wouldn't force him to harm himself—but Devora hadn't known what the charm did.

Ilstan frowned, so Dahl smiled and took the charm from him. "On the plate?" he said. He shot another look at Farideh and gave her the smallest of smiles, before he nodded. "Simple enough. I'll be right back."

He turned and marched through the barrier, down through the short hallway, hoping for more war wizards. But instead he came into an enormous room. The air was close here, dank with the stink of the sewers—a crossroads of sorts, the meeting place of the sewers and the tunnels. The shimmer of barriers placed over three of the passages provided the only light, the faint suggestion of the purple dragon insignia of the Royal House, glittering in the magic's traces.

"Come back here," the sellsword called. "I can hardly see you."

"I can't see you either," Dahl said. "Where's the plate?" He threw the charm deep into the dark room. It landed with a *clink* near to the exit on the far left wall . . . and a gout of flames roared to life, illuminating columns, rubble, and the startled sellsword.

Dahl rushed him, slamming against the box he held before his chest and knocking the wind out of him. The flames died and the darkness reclaimed the room. Dahl punched blindly toward the man's face, connecting painfully with his jaw. He heard the box crash to the ground, the man draw his sword. Dahl backed away, scooped up a rock from the nearby pile of rubble. He threw it toward the left and heard the sellsword turn.

Again he rushed the man, running full into his back. He got an arm around his neck and squeezed until the man dropped his sword, trying to pry Dahl off.

If you let go, Dahl thought, you die.

The man slowed, stumbled, fell to the ground. Dahl held tight still, until he stopped moving. He grabbed the sword off the floor.

Panting, Dahl called out, "That spell doesn't work when I know it's going to kill me! I've already watched one of your zealots work these things." He scrambled up the rubble heap as he heard Pheonard curse, crouching low in the shadows of a niche hidden there.

Pheonard cursed again. "Get in there!"

The sellswords pushed in, dragging their remaining prisoners. Pheonard himself hauled Farideh forward by one horn. Ilstan cast a spell that caught around a node of rock high overhead, making it glow brightly enough to illuminate the subterranean room.

Pheonard pulled Farideh past the wizard, shoving her to her knees. "Come along, 'ready sword.' You don't want to see what I'm willing to do to your Lady of Black Magic, here."

She said she needed space, Dahl reminded himself, watching Farideh twist against her bindings, watching the shadow-smoke thicken and curl around her. She's saved you as many times as you've saved her.

Then: He lays a stlarning finger on her and you can gut him.

"You can try," Dahl called from the shadows. "I don't recommend it."

Farideh looked up at Pheonard, eyes suddenly glowing. And then she turned into a monster before Dahl's eyes.

• • •

THAUGLORIMORGORUS, THE PURPLE Dragon, reared up, spewing poisonous gas over the ground in front of the wall before launching into the air. He swooped over Suzail, a rain of arrows and the screams of the guards who bore his epithet following him.

If an Obarskyr does not hold the Dragon Throne, Irvel thought, stiff with sudden dragonfear, the Purple Dragon will return. Gods, gods—

"Why is everyone screaming about a wyvern?" Baerovus said. Irvel grabbed his son's arm—get away, you have to get away. "Father?"

"My lord!" Vainrence shouted. "Shake it off! That isn't Thauglor!"

The shadow of the dragon wheeled overhead, returning to its master—Lady Marsheena, mounted on a veserab. It was Thauglor—unmistakably Thauglor. What Cormyrean child didn't know the legend of the black dragon so old its scales were violet?

"It's a phantasm!" Vainrence shouted. "Laid on a very large wyvern! Not a dragon!"

Irvel shook his head. "How can you be sure?"

"For starters, Thauglorimorgorus would have announced himself," Ganrahast said, appearing beside them. "Even a fell wyvern only roars. Marsheena has fought this entire war with the goal of forcing Suzail's surrender, Your Majesty. She is trying to scare us with shadows and nightmares, rumors and superstitions."

And it's working, Irvel thought. The armies were in utter disarray, the catapults silenced. "Can you dispel it?" Irvel asked, and as he asked, he saw the shape of Thauglorimorgorus dim, the shape of an enormous two-legged wyvern shine through, its scales gray and deepnight black.

Ganrahast shook his head. "There are four arcanists down there maintaining the illusion. If you don't believe it's there, you won't see it anymore. But you have to *believe* it's not real, and she's chosen a very potent symbol. Especially now."

A king who slept, a king who did not want to be king, the son and grandson of the rightful crown prince standing by . . .

And now the king who died and came back, Irvel thought. Even if they won, if anyone ever discovered he'd been resurrected, then the presence of the Purple Dragon would poison Cormyr all over again.

"Wily bastards," Vainrence spat. "At least you can still break a phantasm same as a beast." He pushed up his sleeves. "Shouldn't take too long."

Irvel met Ganrahast's eye. "No," he said. "The Purple Dragon falls to Orbyn. Otherwise the fear will linger. The throne is the Obarskyrs'. The throne is Cormyr's." He knew what he had to do. "Is my horse saddled?"

"Father," Baerovus said. "You shouldn't fight a wyvern alone. Especially a fell wyvern surrounded by arcanists. Which is also sort of a dragon, considering the spell. You could die."

Ganrahast's mouth made a firm line. "I don't think it's necessary," he said quietly.

"All I have ever wanted," Irvel said, "is to be sure that my children take the throne of a Cormyr safer and stronger than it came to me. And I find that . . . this is the only way to do that. Or risk some other Purple Dragon, some other terrible threat calling for the throne."

"You cannot go alone," Vainrence said.

"Indeed," Ganrahast said. "What king would ride to battle against a dragon with no armsmen or women?"

"Four archers and two war wizards. For cover," Irvel said. "It's still a wyvern— I've handled worse alone. Let them think King Irvel slayed Thauglor alone." He turned to Baerovus, wishing Ospra and Raedra could have been there, wishing he could make one last true good-bye. He hugged his son tight. "I am proud of you," he said quietly. "I may not have always understood you, but I am proud of you, and I love you." He mussed the younger man's hair, feeling tears crowd his throat. "Should anything happen. Tell your mother I love her so. Tell your sister she . . ." He couldn't go on.

"She is your truest heir, in heart and word," Baerovus finished. "It's all right. I know." He hesitated. "This is just in case, right? Nothing might happen."

Irvel looked at his son one last time. "If anything does, I go glad that I got to see my son sit upon the Dragon Throne."

"Don't look back," Ganrahast advised as they hurried to the tower and the stairs to the ground. "If you mean to do this, for the love of all the gods, don't look back."

29

14 Uktar, the Year of the Nether Mountain Scrolls (1486 DR)
Suzail, Cormyr

PHEONARD'S COLLAR MIGHT HAVE PROTECTED HIM FROM THE MAGICAL FEAR that raced out of Farideh, but the sight of the burning angel of Asmodeus alone sent him scrambling away. Wings of flame stretched from her back, the powers of the Hells pouring through her and through her and through her. The hateful rope held—for a moment she was suddenly panicked that it wouldn't burn the way her clothes wouldn't. But then she felt the flames eat into it, recognizing the hostility of the binding.

Farideh stood, straightened, a torch of unholy strength. She drew the rod from her sleeve, pointed it at the sellswords behind Constancia and Brin. A rain of brimstone pelted down on them, forcing the five men back. Brin stood frozen, shaking and horrified. Constancia opened her mouth as if she were going to scream—

A ball of fire struck Farideh, washing over her, feeding the halo of flames that surrounded her. She took a step back as it shifted her balance. Ilstan rose off the ground, more magic filling his hands. *Cast,* the powers seemed to hiss. *Stop him.*

Farideh seized the powers of the Hells and tore a hole through the fabric of the plane, diving through it, and stepping free behind a column off to the left, far from where the crackle of lightning leaped from the war wizard's hands. She searched for Dahl—found him staring at her from behind a pile of rubble, transfixed by the horror she'd become.

No, she thought. No, no, no.

There was no time to regret. Ilstan cast another blast of lightning at her, this time catching Farideh in its branches, burning the breath right out of her lungs. She gasped and cast toward him, a burst of bruised, angry energy that sizzled over him. Ilstan kept coming toward her.

"You cannot escape," he called, a promise and a plea. "I can't allow it. Please. You have the key."

Farideh scrambled backward. She spotted Brin, dodging the sellsword's renewed attack, his arms still tied. *"Assulam!"* she snarled, a bolt of ruinous magic bursting the ropes into a cloud of burning fibers. He ducked and grabbed one of the rocks from the ground. He turned toward Farideh.

Ilstan stalked toward her. As he passed the column, the floor beneath him gave a faint *click.* The smell of spirits gusted into the room and with a *whoosh* the trap ignited, catching Ilstan in its flames. Farideh cried out, her own flames extinguishing.

But Ilstan never stopped. His robes were on fire in places. His hair was burned away. The side of his face was a melted ruin from Devora's spell. He walked toward her, shivering with too much magic.

"I don't want to hurt you," he said. "But there's no other way. Don't you see?"

You don't want to hurt him, Farideh thought. But there's no other way. He might not be evil at heart, he might only have been driven to madness by the suffering of his god. But he was trying to kill her and the people she cared about.

"*Adaestuo,*" Farideh spat, sending another burst of energy crashing into the wounded war wizard, before she leaped through the plane again, this time landing beside Brin.

"Get them out of the way," she said. "Constancia and Dahl—get them back, as much away from the sellswords as you can. And Pheonard—you have to stop him."

"Right." Brin darted into the fray, toward Constancia and Dahl. Four of the sellswords were still on their feet. Constancia was freed and had claimed one of the dead men's swords. Dahl—her heart stuttered as a blade swung toward him. She cast another burst of Hellish energy at the attacker, narrowly missing Constancia.

Thwack, thwack, thwack—a trio of magical bursts struck Farideh in the back. Farideh twisted—rod outstretched. "*Laesurach.*" A vent of lava opened at Ilstan's feet, spewing fire as it roared to life. Farideh seized the pact once more, leaping to the far side of the fight where Pheonard had fled. The wounds in her back made her focus shatter, the powers of Asmodeus leaping up again, sending fire and fear racing over her skin. Pheonard darted out of her path, shouting at the sellswords, but the pain and the roar of the fire made it hard for Farideh to hear.

Ilstan lifted into the air as the lava fell away, drifting toward her once again.

Only one spell left, Farideh thought.

There were too many sellswords. Still Pheonard was on his feet. She heard Dahl cry out, a blade catching his arm, blood spattering. Brin grabbed hold of him, yanking him away from the attacker as Constancia bashed the sellsword with one armored forearm.

No more time to think. She turned the rod parallel to the ground and said a silent apology to the souls she was about to disturb. She yanked the rod upward as Ilstan's hand closed on her burning shoulder. "*Chaanaris!*"

The floor shivered like a skin, as spectral hands reached through the planes, climbing from the torments of the Nine Hells into the world of the living. They grabbed the sellswords' ankles, knees, pulled them to the ground as the souls tore at their essence, trying to regain what made them living.

As the trigger word left Farideh's lips, another pulse of power went through her—strange and cool as a spring breeze. Her nostrils were full of the scent of wintergreen and old books and candlewax. Her nerves were full of a humming that seemed to stretch across the whole of Toril, anchoring her from Waterdeep to Rashemen, from Harrowdale to Djerad Thymar. The air in her lungs turned electric. The powers of the Hells dried up, overwhelmed by this new magic. Her hands went wide, rigid, and the rod fell from her grasp.

What is this? her thoughts managed.

A gift, said a voice—said two voices intertwined. She glanced back at Ilstan, still grasping her by the shoulder, unmoving as magic poured out of him and into her. The flames had engulfed him as well, but they did not burn.

Then the power surged, the flames around her rising, the Hells hungrily scaling her bones, slipping past the strange magic. More spirits climbed through the floor, reaching toward Farideh as well as the screaming sellswords, but flinching away as they touched the flaming halo. Bullets of blue light streaked from her fingers, seeking out the sellswords trying to flee the hungry souls of the Nine Hells. Unerringly they struck.

Focus, Farideh told herself. She pushed the pact's magic away, as hard as she could, concentrating on the cool, binding magic. Let the souls go, that evil spell fade.

Missiles streaked from her hands, after the sellswords—she could no more direct them than stop them from peeling off her fingers. A handful streaked to Pheonard as he warded off Brin and Constancia and Dahl, failing against his shield. More scattered her allies.

And then one hit Dahl.

Farideh screamed, pushing back against the stunning magic as Dahl crumpled around the injury. She held tight to the powers of Asmodeus, the only thing keeping the hungry spirits from attacking her and Ilstan as well. One by one they sank back into the ground, and when the last one vanished, so did the surging blue magic. Behind her, Ilstan hit the stone floor like a corpse. Farideh's knees buckled and she fell to the ground, vomiting violently among the dead, until only sobs and bile came up.

Farideh forced herself up—there were still the sounds of fighting, there was still Dahl somewhere in the trap-riddled rubble. She saw Brin and Pheonard, swords clashing on the farther side. Someone caught her as her vision crumbled—Constancia, one hand on her holy symbol.

"Loyal Torm, aid this"—the smallest of sighs—"servant of your justice."

The ring of the sword on the whetstone screamed in Farideh's battered ears as the powers of the Loyal Fury washed over her, sealing her wounds with a feeling like being plunged into a forge fire. She gasped as the god's ungentle blessings passed, her burned lungs healed and whole.

"Dahl," she said.

Constancia released her. Pointed her toward Pheonard. Brin looked up at them, nodded once and feinted, forcing Pheonard to the right. "Hit the wall behind him. Now."

Farideh swept her hands up, a ball of energy collecting there. "*Adaestuo.*"

The blast streaked past Brin, past Pheonard and his collar, slamming into the wall. A faint *click*, the smell of oily spirits, and a very mundane gout of flames shot out of the wall, engulfing Pheonard. He screamed, clothes burning, and dropped his sword. He threw himself to the ground, rolling in the dust. Brin waved Farideh and Constancia to stay back as they skirted the rubble pile, heading for Dahl.

The nobleman managed to smother the fire after a few breaths, rolling to a stop near the central exit. He glared at Brin as he pressed up from the floor, his skin burned and his eyes wild—but in them the cold calculation of Helindra Crownsilver's repudiated blood.

"I won't fall easily," Pheonard said.

Brin crooked a finger at his uncle. "Come on. I still know a few more tricks."

But Pheonard only smiled—he wouldn't be baited. He moved instead toward the central exit, stepping backward—

Click.

The floor beneath Pheonard Crownsilver's feet fell open, swallowing him up with a cry of surprise that was cut off by a wet, horrible sound. Farideh rose up on her toes, trying to peer over the edge.

"Don't look," Brin advised. "They really do not like people going in the sewers unapproved."

Constancia's healing took care of the burns Dahl had suffered, as well as the bleeding wound on his arm. Farideh went to him, still shaking, as he stood. She reached for him.

Dahl took a step back. "Sorry," he said, catching himself. "That was . . . I wasn't expecting that. Any of that." His eyes searched her face, but he didn't come any closer. "Are you all right?"

"Mostly," she said. Her wounds would heal and so would his. Pheonard wouldn't succeed. But for Dahl and Farideh everything had changed, now that he'd seen what it meant to be the Chosen of Asmodeus.

"Ilstan?" Brin asked.

Farideh shook her head. "I . . . I don't think he survived." She looked back toward where the long-limbed wizard had fallen.

Only the dead sellswords remained. Ilstan had disappeared.

• • •

HAVILAR URGED THE hellhound north toward the wall, bounding through the Royal Gardens, past great manors all locked up tight. Raedra's arms around her waist were tight enough to keep her breath faint. They crossed the narrow lake that wriggled through the fine neighborhoods of Suzail, Zoonie leaping over the bridge without touching it.

"There's a tower ahead!" Raedra shouted, followed by the creak and crash of a catapult launching. Havilar searched the nearby buildings. She pointed Zoonie toward the low roofline of a stable and the hellhound sprang up onto the garden wall, across to the stables—roof to roof, until she could leap easily across to the wall, landing in an ungainly, puppyish heap among the archers.

"Stand down!" Raedra shouted. She leaped from the beast and ran to the edge, while Havilar checked Zoonie's legs.

"All good," she said, and the hellhound barked, scattering sparks.

"Oh ye Watching Gods," Raedra said. Havilar went to stand beside her.

At the edge of the Shadovar army, the dragon that had circled the city crouched, while the rest of the army moved steadily toward the city. Inky as a nightmare, big as the castle, the dark heart of Cormyr—it spread its great batlike wings and roared, sending a stream of greenish liquid across the ground. It made Havilar's stomach clench tight.

But that was not where Raedra stared.

Out of the gates a group of armored riders came, and at their lead, a snow-white horse.

"That's my father," Raedra said, her voice small. She shook her head. "What is he doing? That thing will kill him."

"He took armsmen," a voice said. A bashful-looking young man, wearing a Purple Dragon tabard over his mail had come to stand beside him. Baerovus, Havilar recalled, and wondered if she were going to be made to bow again. The prince didn't even look at her. "But not enough. He should have taken all the army. Or at least the ones you gave Erzoured. They are ready to ride."

Raedra's hand went to her mouth. "Oh no. Oh no." She looked at Havilar, her eyes wide and out of ideas. "He's *planning* to die. Because . . . Because . . ."

"Because you have dumb laws," Havilar said. She pursed her mouth, watching the dragon. It lashed its tail in an awkward fashion and crouched lower. Havilar frowned—it moved like one of the great, brutish wyverns that laired near Arush Vayem.

She blinked and suddenly she could see the beast within the dragon's skin. A wyvern—a big one to be sure, but not the ancient wyrm they were presenting. Completely beatable, she thought. Assuming they were skilled enough, and a little lucky.

"I can't let him do this," Raedra said. "I have to . . . I must . . ."

In that moment, on the outside, Raedra might have been as different from Havilar as the sun from the moon, but Havilar knew she had stood in her place.

It was the hopeless frustration of watching Brin twist under laws and expectations and promises he couldn't find his way out of and couldn't explain.

It was the useless sorrow of knowing she couldn't give Mehen back all those lost years.

It was the frozen, helpless horror of watching Farideh take the wizard's hand in the internment camp, before he whisked her away, a sacrifice to buy the rest of their lives.

Raedra could do nothing, as Havilar hadn't been able to do anything. But Raedra wasn't alone this time.

"Get back on Zoonie," Havilar said, climbing up herself. She said a little apology to Farideh and Mehen, for running right into danger. A moment later she said one for Brin too.

Keep calm, Havilar told herself. She leaned down beside Zoonie's ear and unfastened the muzzle.

"See the army in black?" she murmured to Zoonie. "If they get in our way, you can eat any of them you like."

The hellhound threw back her head and howled—a sound that made Havilar's bones ache—flames in her slavering jaws, before leaping off the side of the wall. They landed with a joint-rattling thud before the gate, and Zoonie took off, running after Irvel and his pure-white steed.

• • •

THE CLOSER IRVEL rode to the ghost of Thauglorimorgorus, the clearer the illusion became. The wyvern within tracked him, its serpentine neck swaying as he rode nearer, preparing to bite. Arrows sailed over Irvel, feathering the phantasm's wide wings and paining the creature as if they'd lodged in its natural appendages. There was no Thauglor, but not even the wyvern knew that.

Stocky, two-legged, far less intelligent than a true dragon, wyverns were still big, still ferocious, still dangerous with their poison-tipped tails. This one was black as a nightmare, it's neck stretched and it's eyes faintly glowing as though the Plane of Shadows had chilled its egg. The arcanist riding on the creature's back looked over his shoulder at the veserab swooping over the army as it approached, looking for orders. Atop the flying monster, Lady Marsheena waved a red scarf. At this distance, Irvel couldn't make out the Shadovar general's face, but he knew she was pleased. How could she not be—here was the King of Cormyr, playing into her trick.

She's been clever, though, Irvel thought. She has to know I've figured it out.

Behind him, the archers' horses screamed, unnerved by the beast. His own horse, trained to the intensities of battle, fared better, but he slowed, the closer they got, threatening to bolt. Stones sailed overhead, launched by the catapults on the walls, reaching for the encroaching siege engines. A blast of lightning struck the wyvern as Ganrahast lowered from the air beside Irvel's prancing horse.

"You have the kill," he said. "But no one will believe I let you race out here alone to face Thauglor." His wand crackled with a new spell. "Vainrence already thinks I'm mad for making him stay back with Baerovus and Oversword Greatgaunt."

Irvel set his lance, and urged the destrier into a charge. The horse might have wanted to flee, but it knew its duty and galloped toward the wyvern. A well-timed hail of arrows, a thoughtful blast of icy energy—the wyvern's attention was drawn away as Irvel's lance forced through the phantasm, and into the beast's true hide. The wyvern screamed, thrashed away, trying to bite the broken lance free. Irvel wheeled the horse away, checking the progress of the Shadovar army—closer, ever closer.

Irvel dismounted, pulled Orbyn free of its scabbard. Sunlight breaking through the cloud cover glinted on the faint tracery of runes along the blade. Arrows peppered the phantasmal Purple Dragon's wings as he faced the beast. An arcanist cast a bolt of crackling energy. Irvel batted it away with his shield and brought the Edge of Justice around to strike the fell wyvern. The blade cut through the scales along the beast's left leg, but not as deeply as he'd hoped. Orbyn might be keener and stronger than any other weapon Irvel had held, but the wyvern's hide was tough. Blood slicked the wound, a sheen of red over the inky scales. The beast screamed and snapped at him. Irvel pushed its teeth away with his shield, the force of its attack rattling his bones. Ganrahast's spells lit the air all around them, keeping the four arcanists dancing, keeping their attentions from Irvel.

The wyvern's tail dived over its injured wing, aiming for Irvel. He scrambled to the side, letting the spike plunge into the ground, sinking its poison into the dirt instead. The beast flapped into the air on its tattered wings, raking at Irvel with claws so large they filled out the phantasm's shape. One caught him, tore through his mail sleeve for the length of his upper arm, and ripped the shield from his arm. Orbyn sliced between the toes of the other, neatly bisecting the foot in a spray of bright red blood.

The wyvern roared again and spat a cloud of thick greenish steam. It burned Irvel's nostrils and throat, the iron tang of blood, the sour scent of disease. He held his breath as it rolled across the field, the archers scrambling back. That much, at least, was no illusion. The wyvern hung in the sky, its foot clutched to its chest. The arcanist on its back goaded it to land, to end Irvel. One good strike to the soft points around the skull—

The wyvern dived at him, teeth bared. As he jabbed Orbyn toward the soft under-jaw, the beast shied. Its tail whipped around, quick as a striking snake. The point hit Irvel in the chest, right below his heart. The force of it tossed him from his feet, onto his back. The impact was intense on its own—crushing his breastplate against his ribs. But then he felt the cascade of heat, spreading from the impact point, the fell wyvern's poison coursing through him. Right to the heart, he thought. I am slain.

Ganrahast tossed another burst of fire at the wyvern, forcing the beast back, away from the fallen king. "You have to get up!"

"I don't think I can," Irvel managed.

A howl that reverberated through his very bowels echoed over the battlefield. The wyvern jerked its head up, searching for the fearful source. The thunder of ten thousand soldiers shouting chased the strange screams.

Watching Gods, Irvel thought. Don't forsake us.

• • •

THE IMPACT OF the hellhound hitting the ground jolted all the remaining fear out of Raedra. Not Shade, not the dragon, not bloody Alusair, pressed upon her thoughts. She wasn't going to let Irvel fight the Purple Dragon alone.

"Aim for the eyes," Havilar shouted, as if she could hear Raedra's thoughts. "The eyes, the nostrils, the soft part under the jaw. Everything else has too much armor to it—you'll be batting for ages and it will get tiresome. And watch out for the tail."

Raedra fought to pull Rissar free as the hellhound's choppy gait threatened to toss her off. Arrows zipped past them, flying wide—those that didn't evaporate as the war wizard's magic protected her.

You are an Obarskyr, she told herself. There is fire in your blood and steel in your word. She wrapped one arm around Havilar's waist as Zoonie bounded over a fallen horse and drew Rissar with her other hand, holding the jeweled short sword high. She looked back over her shoulder, at the gates of Suzail, as they cracked wide. Trumpets sounded and the army poured out. At their head, Erzoured on a powerful bay.

Vainrence swooped down beside her, magic holding him in the air. "Princess, what in the Nine Hells do you think you're doing?"

Raedra turned back to her father and the dragon. He lay on the ground now, Ganrahast over him. The dragon tossed its head in the air, eyes suddenly on the hellhound. A sizzle of dark magic burned through the air, streaking right for the princess and Havilar. Vainrence waved a hand and the magic spattered against the wave he created, scattering wide. There were three more of them on the ground, their focus split now between Ganrahast and the hellhound.

"Princess!" Vainrence shouted.

"A moment!" Raedra managed. Her eyes stayed locked on her father, feebly trying to rise. The hellhound skidded to a stop before the King of Cormyr, before the terrible Purple Dragon, and Raedra leaped from her back, sword in hand.

• • •

THE WORLDS OF the living and the dead seemed to layer over each other, the wyvern becoming ghostly, the path to Kelemvor's kingdom opening up all around Irvel. Once more, he could swear Halance Crownsilver was standing beside him, looking benignly amused, as if he could only worry so much about the troubles of the material world. Atop the wyvern, the arcanist traded spellblasts with Ganrahast, keeping the Royal Magician moving. The wyvern pulled back, considering its prey.

Get up, Irvel thought, straining against the poison's tide. If the dragon didn't die first, then what good had he done? Cormyr would have been better off if he'd died in the Hullack or on the battlefields outside Saerloon, if he let Marsheena's pageant end the way she'd scripted it. He forced himself up on one elbow, putting all his energy into moving his legs. Ganrahast shouted. Something large skidded in the dirt behind Irvel.

He looked up at the wyvern's head looming over him, about to strike. Hal reached for him. *Come on, old chap. You're all done here.*

The wyvern, all shining teeth, plunged toward Irvel.

A flash of mail, a flash of jewels. Raedra leaped over her father, a jeweled short sword in her hand. Like an angel of battle, she lunged, soundless, as the beast reached to snap him up, and Rissar sank to the hilt in the great beast's golden eye, stinking black blood and the oozing jelly of the wyvern's eye slicking her arm to the elbow.

The dragon screamed, trembling as the blade punched through the fragile bones of its inner skull. It yanked away from Raedra and the blade, a last thrash of impulse. With every shred of strength that remained in Irvel, he grabbed hold of his daughter's ankle, pulling her toward the earth as the dragon sought to lift her away. Rissar broke loose of the creature's skull with an ugly pop, and Raedra hit the ground beside Irvel in a crouch. He saw the phantasm shatter, the wyvern fall away, dissolving from Irvel's sight.

Raedra leaned over him. "No, no, no!" she cried. She patted his cheek as if she could stir him from the edge of death. Irvel smiled at her, the poison racing through his veins, clouding over his mind. It wasn't the ending he'd hoped for, but it was an ending that Cormyr could make good use of.

• • •

Irvel's last breath rasped from his lungs, his pale eyes staring up at the clearing sky, and a part of Raedra felt as if it died too. She felt it slink from her, the wish to curl up, to weep, to try and shake her father back into breathing—it was there and then it simply wasn't. She would grieve him all her days, but she had to let him go. The *pop* of Rissar breaking through the dragon's skull seemed to still vibrate Raedra's skeleton, as if the weapon resonated with the burst of bone.

To the north, the army of Shade broke over the rise. But from the Horn Gate, a legion of new-made soldiers and Purple Dragons poured out, not even Erzoured willing to leave Raedra and Irvel to the dragon.

"Raedra!" Havilar shouted as another of the arcanists' spells dissolved in the war wizards' casting. She slashed her glaive at the arcanist who'd leaped off the dragon's back, interrupting his spell. As he attempted to draw something new together, something to cast at Havilar, the hellhound lunged, seizing him by the neck and shaking him like a ragdoll. Havilar jumped away from the beast, toward Raedra. "Help me put him on her back. Quickly!"

"I'm not riding back just yet," Raedra said as Ganrahast and Vainrence settled beside her. Raedra turned to the army of Shade, to the veserab that hung in the air, conveying General Marsheena high over her army. She pointed the bloody sword at Marsheena.

"Your turn," she murmured to herself, as the army of the Purple Dragon swept in behind her.

EPILOGUE

RISSAR
THE WEDDING BLADE

. . .

The only depiction of Rissar in the Hall of Gazes, they call the painting "The True Marriage of Queen Raedra." The young queen, moments from inheriting the crown, seems a weapon herself, the Blade of Cormyr as she sprints toward the Purple Dragon Reborn, her father dying at her feet. The beast is feral, unstoppable, the embodiment of the chaos that would rend Cormyr apart. But Raedra is as cool as a moonbeam, the faintest smile of anticipation painted on her face as the jeweled sword's tip touches the fearsome dragon's eye. Here is the moment where she speaks her vows with action: to honor and protect the Dragon Throne until her dying breath.

No one knows, the true events so long past, what the symbolism of the snarling black dog, fire in its jaws, is meant to be, nor the tiefling who stands at her back, warding off the shadows with a polearm.

. . .

445

30

Y THE SIEGE'S END, RAEDRA COULDN'T HAVE SAID IF IT HAD BEEN A HANDFUL of days or a handful of months. She stopped counting sunrises and moons, she slept when she couldn't stand any longer, regardless of where the stars were. The Shadovar army was neither as powerful and nightmarish as Marsheena would have had Cormyr believe, nor as easily beaten as many would have hoped. But the people of Suzail never wavered, never flagged. One day or sixteen days or seven hundred days, they remembered what their king had sacrificed. They remembered their princess riding out upon a beast tamed from nightmares, and killing the Purple Dragon once more. Cormyr would not fall to Shade. Not while the Obarskyrs still drew breath.

For sixteen days the battle raged, siege engines battering catapults, catapults knocking veserabs from the sky. Shade should have retreated, but it seemed as if Marsheena knew she would answer to High Prince Telamont if she fled too soon. Battles just as fierce raged in the tunnels and the sewers, the war wizards proving their value to the realm over and over—not to mention the stranger things that lurked below. Raedra found herself more than once, when confronted with reports of neatly dispatched Shadovar that no force below could claim, thinking of the scowling ghost in the Royal Court and what she might still do for her kingdom.

On the twenty-fourth day of Uktar, reinforcements came in the form of shadow-stepping warriors, and the walls were briefly breached by the shades. They were fierce and they were determined, bolstered by their goddess's blessings. Many died at their blades, but not a one of them opened the gates, and after, it was a badge of honor to have killed one of the warriors of the Hall of Shadows.

Raedra smiled to imagine Varauna in the company of veteran soldiers and powerful war wizards—no one able was exempt from duty, and the noblewoman had been there to bury an arrow in the eye of a shade battling into the gatehouse.

Auspicious, the overswords all said.

The arrow that launched a thousand "ready swords," Varauna crowed.

For sixteen days, no one sat upon the Dragon Throne. For once, Raedra didn't worry about what the nobles would do or wouldn't—there was too much at stake. For every ambitious upstart, there was an elder who shortened their leash. For every calculating old wyrm, there were a dozen young things with their patriotism on their sleeves to encircle them. If there were further traitors in their midst, they heeded the example of Pheonard Crownsilver and decided now was not the time to strike after all. Raedra's orders were followed as though she were regent again—many stemming from Baerovus's observations. Brother and sister might well have shared the throne for sixteen days.

To the north, in Arabel, war wizards sealed the portal in the Forgotten Keep, cutting Shade's path off. Without access to Netheril, the siege of Arabel was finally broken.

Then at dawn, on the Feast of the Moon, the celebration of the dead, the army of the Western Marches rode down from Arabel and crushed what remained of Shade against the walls of Suzail.

Not a single Shadovar soldier was spared.

"Between the Army of the Western Marches and the ones we've recruited," Oversword Greatgaunt said, "we should be well-positioned to liberate Marsember without too much trouble. More so if the Army of the Purple Dragon can return." But then there were the reports of Shade marching toward Myth Drannor—the war wasn't over yet, and Cormyr's aid might still be needed.

Erzoured had gained a measure of the public's respect, for everyone had expected the Baron Boldtree to use this moment of crisis and the army at his back to claim the crown. But Erzoured was too canny for that, Raedra thought, and instead claimed the prize she could not block him from: his army's admiration. He was a hero, for once, though still in his heart of hearts, she didn't doubt he was a blackguard.

"He can be tolerable," Maranth allowed. "If he's trying. If there are people to remind him."

Trying or not, Raedra had to admit she was a little relieved. In that moment, there were not Obarskyrs to spare, and she didn't need people worrying about the thinness of the royal line, about who would succeed whom, when they would leap so quickly to unclaimed bastards and Silver families. She would never trust Erzoured completely—no one could be that foolish and live—but the moment's respite she gained from him soaking up the adoration of the common folk was a boon.

And then there was Aubrin.

"I know about my father," she said, perched opposite him in her sitting area. They had buried Irvel that morning. Ganrahast stood behind her. Constancia Crownsilver stood behind Aubrin. He didn't blink. "About Havilar," she went on.

"What about her?" he asked in a conversational way.

Raedra frowned. "She raised him."

Constancia looked to her cousin, alarmed. Brin's eyes stayed locked with Raedra's. "Where did you hear that?"

"He told us what happened. And then she admitted to it." She saw the fear that lit his eyes. "She's put me in a very difficult position here."

Brin swallowed. "What are you going to do?"

"The law says she should be executed. You know that."

"You can't."

"I might have to."

Brin cursed and looked away. "You can't. Because I did it. She's lying for me. I brought him back."

"Aubrin," Constancia warned.

"The king was very clear about what happened to him," Ganrahast said. "You were not in the room when he returned."

"I stepped out," Brin said calmly. "Call a trial if you don't believe me. But who are your witnesses? A dead man, a tiefling, and a noble of the realm and purported Obarskyr. Whose testimony will ring truest?"

"Are you mad?" Raedra asked. "Are you trying to get your head lopped off?"

"Which is fairer?" Brin returned, a tremor in his voice. "To hold me responsible for all of this or to take it out on Havilar, who was only trying to make things right for me, when she couldn't possibly understand how to make that happen? The laws might make Cormyr what it is, but that's for good *or* ill, and I don't see how killing someone who was just trying to help the person she loved without the slightest malice intended helps the kingdom. I did it. It's my fault. Call your Dragons."

For a long moment, Raedra and Brin stared at each other, and Raedra wondered whether he was expecting her to call his bluff, or take up Orbyn in her own hands. Either, she thought, so long as you don't harm her. Oh, Aubrin, you are an odd one.

"I'm inclined to agree with all of that," she said. "And I think it evident that . . . *you* were unaware of the larger situation and my father's personal wishes. No one outside this room, apart from Havilar, knows what happened. I would be pleased to keep it that way. I'd be lying if I said I wasn't glad you brought him home again—for my own sake as much as Cormyr's. The gods only know what would have happened if he hadn't ridden against the Purple Dragon, as it were."

"You would have been all right," Brin said.

"We don't know that," Raedra said, "and we don't need to." She hesitated. "The marriage—"

"Raedra—"

"I don't care what's happening between you and her," she pressed on. "I am not marrying you. I am not marrying anyone who has so clearly muddled his past and his present. You have reasons for every step you've taken—and all of them are sensible on their own, even the nonsense with the silk—but together . . . they are a man who I don't want for a husband or a partner. Consider our engagement dissolved. You're free," she added.

"You needn't put it like that," Brin said.

"I shall put it however I wish. Much as I'd like to say that is all," Raedra went on, "if you are not marrying me, then we need to return to the matter of the legitimization. I intend to advocate it be ratified."

"Ye gods!" Brin cried. "How is that better?"

"It's better," Raedra said, "because at this moment there is entirely too much to worry about, without having to address the fact that there are only three living Obarskyrs."

"A fourth is not going to fix that."

"It improves it. I'll take what I can get. This isn't a point I intend to negotiate—"

"You will trap me here."

"If I need to."

"There's a problem, Your Royal Highness," Constancia interrupted. Raedra raised an eyebrow, and the knight straightened. "I wasn't going to say anything. But that was before . . . before this business about the late king and everything else. You see, in the battle in the tunnels, Aubrin was . . . struck by one of the traps. Mortally. He died. And I'm afraid I cannot keep it a secret any longer—I brought him back."

Raedra doubted she'd ever heard anyone lie so clumsily, but then she wondered if the Tormish paladin had ever lied in her life, Crownsilver or not. Brin gaped at Constancia as though she'd sprouted horns of her own.

"That seems a skill beyond you, lady knight," Ganrahast said.

"An artifact," she amended. "From the Crownsilver vaults. Aubrin is . . . my charge. I couldn't let anything happen to him. But the law is the law."

"And now his place in the succession is delayed," Raedra said. "How convenient."

"It is a bit," Brin pointed out. "I'm no barrier to you, this way."

"The throne hasn't been decided."

"Please," Brin said. "It's yours. And it will be a boon to everyone if there's no chance at all that some new Pheonard can rise up and try to use me to displace you. I'm not meant to be king." He smiled at her. "You, on the other hand . . ."

"You're still getting legitimized, whether you like it or not," Raedra said, standing. "I suppose you're going to leave now?"

Brin nodded, but he said, "I don't know. Everything's . . . it's all a mess right now."

"Try being forthright," she said. "Fight your breeding." She hesitated. "Good luck."

"If things had been different—" he began.

"Spare me," Raedra said. "If she hadn't come back, she would have still been in your heart. And I find I have to agree with my father. She's a charming young woman. She deserves someone who prizes her." Whether or not that was Aubrin remained to be seen, but since there was no chance at all that Havilar would remain in Raedra's sphere, it was hardly her business.

"Well done," Ganrahast said, as they walked to the Royal Court, trailed by a pair of highknights and preceded by a pair of Purple Dragons. "Almost a pity that couldn't have been worked out sooner."

"It wouldn't have worked before the siege," Raedra said. She could regret each action in turn, but to look at the whole, any piece resolved more quickly, more neatly, might have meant Suzail's defeat: if Brin had been on Calantar's Way, if they had married on time, if Irvel had returned safely and gone back to Saerloon, if Irvel had died in the Hullack . . . there would have been no one in Suzail to ride out like a madman against the Purple Dragon, to break Marsheena's spell of fear and release Suzail to fight as it must. And Irvel wouldn't have gotten to say good-bye to his family.

"Should he be needed," Ganrahast said, "we can always collect him."

"I'm counting on it," Raedra said. "But let's try not to need him."

In the chamber off to the side of the Royal Court, Baerovus was waiting for his sister. Baerovus and several nobles. Raedra's temper lit to see her brother cornered against the wall, avoiding the eyes of Lord Huntcrown and his cronies.

"My lord, the Dragon Throne has sat empty long enough," Lord Huntcrown cajoled. "Surely you see the need to step up."

"I suppose," Baerovus said, still looking at the carpet.

"You don't need a coronation, of course," Lord Ambershield said. "But it would soothe your subjects—a proper one this time. In the court."

"Must I?" Baerovus said. He looked around. "You are standing very close."

"It could be done by the end of the tenday," the High Chatelaine said, ignoring Baerovus's discomfort, and some old, almost discarded part of Raedra wanted to shove him out of the way and pull Baerovus into the tunnels where he could recover. She had been prepared to sit down with her brother and discuss what should come next. But watching him here, flinching away from these vultures, Raedra knew that the conversation wasn't needed. Her pulse hammered, but she held herself very straight and very still.

"Rover." Baerovus looked up at his sister, and all the nobles crowding him jumped at the sound of her voice. Good, she thought. "You abdicated," she said gently.

Realization lit the prince's face. "I did." He turned back to the lords. "I *abdicated*. That means, according to law, my claim to the throne loses primacy. I come *after* everyone else."

"You didn't abdicate, Your Majesty," Lord Huntcrown protested. "You deferred to your father's superior claim."

"But that's not what I *said*," Baerovus pointed out. "I said I abdicated. And rules are rules." He grinned at Raedra. "I'm not the king."

"Your Highness, don't strongarm him," Huntcrown said. "He doesn't know what he's giving up."

Raedra narrowed her eyes. "My brother is not a simpleton, Lord Huntcrown. In fact, he is very well versed in the law." She reached out a hand to Baerovus, and her brother moved to stand beside her. "He will make a fine advisor."

"So you mean to take the throne," Lord Huntcrown said.

Raedra smiled at the High Chatelaine. "By the end of the tenday, from the sound of things. I am the next in line after all. Unless," she said, her tone light, "you wish to start a civil war, Lord Huntcrown."

"Perish the thought," he said. Then, "Your Majesty."

"Good," Raedra said. "Then my lord, please excuse our brevity, there's quite a lot to do." The excess of nobles were ushered from the little room, the proper advisors sent for. There were other funerals—other brave souls who had not survived the siege and deserved a hero's rest. The pages returned with stewards and . . .

And the Dowager Queen Ospra still looked as weary as a person could be, but she stepped into the room, all grace and charm. Grief might have burned something vital from her, but Ospra Goldfeather had not become a jewel of the court by sitting idly by. She curtsied to her daughter, a true smile on her face, and Raedra was so grateful to have her mother on her side.

The hairs on Raedra's neck stood on end.

The ghost stood behind Ospra, her legs vanishing into a settee as if she didn't even notice it was there. Her scowl had softened, but not left.

Raedra inclined her head to the Steel Regent, the notice of one sovereign to another. Alusair's scowl quirked into a wry sort of smile. She nodded to her great-great-grandniece, and despite herself, Raedra felt as if that alone crowned her, as the ghost vanished from her sight.

• • •

IN THE GARDEN behind the tallhouse, Farideh wouldn't look at Dahl. "So are you ending it?"

"Gods' books—*no*," Dahl said. They sat together on the little stone bench beneath the arbor, the air around them grown cold with winter. "I'm just wondering if it would be better for you to wait for me. For me to go to Harrowdale alone. I'm asking what you think."

She gave a short laugh. "I think it sounds like you're ending it. How long is it to get to Harrowdale and back?"

Months, he thought, and dreaded it. "I'm not ending it, all right? I just . . . You were right. This is dangerous. Strange and dangerous. Maybe I was being a little flippant about it before. And then you turned into a burning angel and commanded the souls of the damned to tear apart some sellswords."

"That is the *second* time in my life I've used that spell," she said hotly. "I *hate* it. If I'd had another option—"

"Hey, hey. I'm not saying you shouldn't have." That was a lie. He couldn't get the memory, the echo of the fear that hit him right in the stomach as she changed, out of his thoughts. What should she have done instead? he thought. He still didn't have an answer.

He took her hand in his, as much to reassure himself as to reassure her. "I'm not saying you can't come. I'm only saying you were right. This is a lot to worry about—a lot I don't know if my family ought to be brought into. And I don't know how much control you have over that."

Farideh still wouldn't look at him. "So what would I do? Stay here?"

"I haven't thought through that part," Dahl admitted. He could hardly ask her to stay in Suzail, now that her family had no ties left to bind them there. "What do you want to do?"

Farideh pursed her mouth and shook her head. "I wanted . . ." She trailed off into a terrible silence. "I don't want to go where I'm not wanted."

"That's not what I'm saying."

"Then what *are* you saying?" She looked at him then, and it nearly tore his heart. "What do you want from me? You can't just bring up leaving me behind, as if it's the same if I stay or go. You said it didn't matter, and now . . . now it *matters*, now you're afraid I'm . . . what? That I'm going to set your mother on fire?"

"Don't be ridiculous," Dahl said. But she did hit you with that magical missile, he thought. An accident—whatever had happened with Ilstan was still a mystery, and with the war wizard's body still missing . . .

How can you even think of leaving her? Dahl asked himself. But then he thought of the burning angel, the ravenous souls of the damned—*how have you not run already?* There wasn't a doubt in his heart that if a soul said a word about Farideh being a tiefling, he would defend her to the last. But if they said anything about her being a Chosen of Asmodeus?

"You should go," Farideh said, even though her hands still knotted around his. "You have to pack and . . . what do I tell the others?"

He pulled her closer. "I want to make sure that you're ready for this. That's what I'm asking. That's what I want you to think about. I love you. I just want this to be easy." He bent to kiss her, and she turned her cheek to him.

"It's not going to be easy," she said. "You know that."

There's another answer, Dahl thought, even though he wasn't sure he ought to believe that. He kissed her and left the tallhouse, ostensibly to pack his things, to settle his plans with Vescaras and make certain the Harpers would not suffer at his absence. But instead he went to the Temple of Oghma and lay upon the floor before the idol.

The answer did not lie in the peace of Oghma. After uncountable hours of chasing the god's attention, trying not to beg for answers, Dahl sat up. He crossed his legs and rested his head in his hands.

He never gave you answers, Dahl reminded himself. You figured out the answers. You have to figure this one out too. That, alone, brought the faint warmth of the god's presence, and Dahl sighed.

She warned you, he thought looking up at the idol of Oghma. She told you she was a Chosen of Asmodeus and you didn't ask what that meant. You didn't want to know.

But you love her, and *that* is true. He loved her beyond all reason, and the very idea of never seeing Farideh again was so unbearable he rejected it out of hand. Everything that happened in the tunnels didn't change the fact he loved her.

It makes it harder, he amended. But it doesn't change it.

So there are two paths, he reasoned. Either you accept that she is bound like this, that she has a god's notice she wishes were gone. You stay and you stand by her and you accept what that means. Or you decide it's all too much and you let her go—you can't ask her to stay with you if you won't stay with her. It was that simple after all.

"Oghma's bloody papercuts," he muttered. He heard the acolyte's sharp intake of breath and winced. "Sorry."

He felt as though he were a novice again, relearning lessons. Think things through before you open your mouth, he told himself as he stood. He'd go back to the tallhouse. He'd smooth things over. They'd come up with some plan, what to do if the Hells intruded into Harrowdale. What to do if things got worse.

Everything would be all right.

"Well met, Dahl," a voice called from the alley as he passed. Dahl stopped in his tracks. There was Lorcan, wearing a human's skin, leaning against the wall of a bakery as though he were only out enjoying the chilly winter sunlight.

Dahl's pulse clattered. He can't do anything to you, he thought. Especially not here, in the streets. "What do you want?"

"A chat. Have you the time?" Lorcan asked, as though he couldn't bear to inconvenience Dahl. His cold black eyes promised only violence.

"You know, don't you?"

"I know lots of things," Lorcan said. "For instance—" He twisted his wrist and a glass globe appeared in his hand. Shining in the center was a little farmhouse. His mother came out the front door and rang a bell—highsunfeast was ready. "I know about this little farmstead," Lorcan went on, as Dahl's breath went still and cold in his lungs. Lorcan brushed his fingers over the orb, the image blurring away, changing to a company of Shadovar scouts, a shade among them, trooping across the fields of the Dalelands. "And I know about this lot, looking for farms to raid, heading right for that little farmstead.

"I also know," the cambion went on, "how to get you there. The travel takes an instant. You'll have at least three hours to get everyone out of harm's way. Or arm them all, if you're feeling reckless and heroic." He smiled, his eyes still cold and cruel. "Plenty of time, if you act now."

"What's the price?" Dahl asked, knowing that he'd pay it, knowing that he'd pay anything to be sure they were safe.

"Nothing much," Lorcan said. "Just this: I take you to Harrowdale, and you never, ever speak to Farideh again. You don't whisper in her ear, you don't yell across the room. Not with a spell, not with handsigns. Never."

Dahl kept his expression calm, though there was nothing Lorcan could have asked for that made him want to panic worse. "You don't think she'll have a problem with that?"

"I think she'll assume you did change your mind after all. That you don't want her cluttering up your life, frightening your blessed mother. And I don't think anyone will correct her. Because you also can't tell anyone about the deal. Those are the terms, and should you break either of them, I get your soul. Take it or leave it."

Dahl scrambled. "She said . . . She said you weren't allowed to harm me."

Lorcan laughed. "I promised that. You're very lucky, because frankly, there is not a soul on this plane I want to harm more. Your family, on the other hand, I made no such promises about. I can lead the Shadovar straight to them. I can make sure they can't hide. And when the army's passed, I can bring in my half sisters, and let them do the sort of unspeakable things the devils of the Sixth Layer are renowned for. And don't worry—I'll also be sure you have a chance to watch." He smiled. "Or you just never talk to my warlock again. Choose."

There would be a hole in the contract, an exception, Dahl thought. He was clever enough, he could find it. He had to find it—he couldn't say no. And Farideh . . .

"She isn't going to come back to you," Dahl said.

Lorcan laughed. "Oh, Dahl. You're not the hero of her story. You're an impediment. A sidetrack. Can you really stand there, considering this deal, and think you've won?"

"I don't think there was ever a contest," Dahl said.

"No," Lorcan said. "Because you aren't my rival. The sands are running, Dahl. What *are* you going to do?"

Dahl closed his eyes. "Take me to Harrowdale."

"A wise decision," Lorcan said, yanking him into the alley and opening the portal that carried Dahl the thousands of miles to his childhood home. "A pleasure doing business," Lorcan said, pushing Dahl out into the path that led back to the farmhouse, tucked against the edge of the forest there. The portal shut behind him, and Dahl started running, shoving aside the screaming panic that he'd made the wrong choice—*both* choices were wrong, and only this one meant no one would have to die. He pushed open the door without knocking. That's the cruelty of the Nine Hells, he thought. That's what you have to outsmart.

"Ma!" he shouted, running through the house. "Thost! Bodhar!" In the kitchen, they sat at the long table, a winter's spread laid upon the boards—his mother, brothers, their wives, their children, the farmhands, and Granny, perched beside the fire. His mother stared at him as though he were a ghost, and Dahl realized that he had no explanations to give them, no cover for how and why he was here.

There wasn't time. "Shadovar forces are heading this way," he said. "I haven't time to explain. We need to head into the hills. Now. All of us."

Whether his tone convinced them, or whether Dahl's family suspected he was more than just a secretary after all, mercifully they moved. As much as possible was packed into carts, the livestock driven up into the snowy hills.

"Leave a little," Dahl said. "They can't decide to follow." He made certain to leave the door standing open, to knock over the furniture and smash a window. Make it look as if someone else had already ransacked the place.

Up in the hills, as night fell, he crouched beside his older brothers, Thost and Bodhar, and watched the lights the Shadovar carried bob across the fields below, heading toward the farmhouse.

"How'd you know they were coming?" Bodhar asked.

"I'll tell you later," Dahl said. He took the little sending kit out of his cloak's pocket and with it, the bottle of scented ink he'd been carrying for months and months like a little talisman. The consequences of the deal hit him in the chest like a thrown stone.

"What is that?" Bodhar asked, scratching his graying beard.

"Ink," Dahl said, tucking it back into his pockets. He poured the lines of powder on the ground, relying on the light of the moon to find the right paths. He murmured the words of the scroll, thinking of Vescaras as he did. As the light of magic flared along the powders, he chose his words carefully, tapping them out on his fingers.

"An emergency's come up," he said in a hushed voice. "Gone to Harrowdale. No sendings left. I'll work on contact. Tell Farideh I love her. I will *fix* this—*exactly* that."

A pause, a crackle of magic. *Understood*, Vescaras's voice came back, faintly surprised. *I assume there's a reason you're not telling her? I'll bring your things back to Waterdeep.* Another pause. *Best of luck, Dahl. See you soon.* The magic faded, the light from the lines dimmed, and Dahl cursed Lorcan as many ways as he could.

"Who in the sodden Hells is Farideh?" Bodhar demanded.

"Never mind that," Thost said in his deep voice. "Who in the sodden Hells are *you*, little brother?"

• • •

ON THE FRONT steps of the tallhouse, Havilar shivered beside Farideh in the winter chill. "Do you think it's warmer in Djerad Thymar?" she asked. "I mean, I know Arush Vayem is colder, but it's up in the mountains, so . . ."

"I don't know," Farideh said. It wouldn't be warmer in Harrowdale, she thought, a knife against her heart. How long until she stopped thinking such things, just to test the pain of them?

Havilar leaned against Farideh and put an arm around her. "This will be good," she said, as though she were trying to convince herself as much as Farideh. "Just you and me. No dumb boys being *henishs*. We get to see Djerad Thymar."

"What happens if we see Arjhani?" Farideh asked. When Dahl hadn't returned that night or that morning, she'd taken it for her answer. She'd gone to Mehen and told him that they wouldn't be going to Harrowdale after all, and not an hour later he'd suggested they go to Djerad Thymar instead.

"I ought to," he said. "If for no other reason than to tell Anala not to bother me. And," he added reluctantly, "truth be told, it seems rough to send Dumuzi packing all alone."

"I wouldn't mind going with him," Farideh said cautiously. "Are you sure you want to go back?"

Mehen had sighed. "It's funny. I don't quite believe he's dead. Don't want to, I guess. He's still my father." He fixed Farideh with a grim, yellow stare. "I hope I don't leave you wanting to dance on my grave."

"Of course not!" Farideh said. "Don't be gruesome." He hugged her tight, rubbing the fringe of scales along his jaw against the top of her head.

"I'm sorry," he told her. "It's not easy. But he's hardly the only fellow in the world."

Farideh had pushed away from him then, smiled, and excused herself. "I'll be all right," she'd told Mehen, told herself.

"Arjhani," Havilar said loftily, hugging her sister closer, "has nothing on Kallan. If we see him, we'll just turn away. Because *karshoj* to him. Did you know Dumuzi is his son?"

"Did he tell you?"

"No, but it's completely *obvious*. I don't think Mehen knows. But who can tell?" She sighed. "I hope they're using their time wisely in there. Isn't it kind of hilarious that all of us sneak about, pretending that we don't have lovers, because someone might get upset?"

"Do you wish you'd told Mehen you were sneaking off with Brin?"

"Gods, no. But it's still funny."

"Not anymore," Farideh said. She didn't mean it to sound morose, but there was hardly another way for words to come out of her mouth just now. She found her heart scrambling every time a dark-haired man walked by, thinking surely, *surely*, this was Dahl with some explanation, some reason he hadn't come back. But every one of them kept walking by. He wasn't coming back.

Suppose something happened, she thought, not for the first time. Suppose he was attacked or kidnapped or worse.

But every time she thought that, she could only hear him saying, *Maybe it would be best if you didn't come to Harrowdale.* You loved him, she thought, but he didn't love you the same. She didn't want to believe it—she thought again and again of the stunned look he'd given her, that night after Teneth's, as if the whole illusion of the world had been stripped away, and he realized that he'd been fighting against it's very workings. *I'm in love with you*, he'd said, as if it were a revelation from the gods themselves. *I'm so in love with you.*

He was drunk, she told herself. He was reeling from reaching Oghma once more. You knew that. You know it.

"Do you think there's people who can block ghosts in Djerad Thymar?" Havilar asked. "Since they haven't exactly got swarms of clerics and things."

Havilar had told her of the ghost that possessed Brin and the dead sellswords. They'd compared it to the ghost from the internment camps, and Farideh's mangled dreams. Bryseis Kakistos, the Brimstone Angel—there was no one else it could be. Whatever she wanted, it couldn't be good.

Except . . .

Farideh couldn't shake the memory of the last dream of Asmodeus, the moment of darkness, the ghost suddenly kind-faced and warning her to hold tight to the amulet of Selûne. If she had to guess, what Asmodeus wanted and what Bryseis Kakistos wanted were opposed to each other. Which did not mean, she reminded herself, that either was the good option. Sometimes the choice is the least of the evils. Sometimes the only choice is a sacrifice.

"Do you think it's putting my soul in *peril* if I keep Zoonie?" Havilar asked. "Because I don't. But I don't know these things."

"Neither do I," Farideh said. "It seems odd that it would. You don't let her do evil things. Aside from the Shadovar she ate."

"*Never again!*" Havilar said. "She doesn't need to eat, and I don't want to clean up what comes out. Shades make for disgusting *aithyas*." She hugged Farideh again. "It's going to be all right. For both of us."

Farideh started to answer, but then a man entered the gate and for a moment her heart skipped again—but it wasn't Dahl, it was Brin. Clean-shaven and dressed in clothes for travel.

"Well met," he said. "And good morning."

"Well met," Farideh said. Beside her, Havilar went tense as a spring.

"You shaved," she said. He rubbed his chin, smiling nervously.

"I told you," he said. "As soon as I don't have to go to court anymore. And I don't. I've been . . . not *quite* disinherited, but nearly. And my cover has been compromised—there's no good reason for me to be in Suzail at all. So." He wet his mouth. "Do you think we could talk for a moment, Havi?"

"What is there to say?" she asked.

"A lot, I think. You don't have to change your mind, but hear me out? Please?"

Havilar clung to Farideh, as if she could anchor her to the front steps, as if she could stop Havilar from going. Farideh pushed her arm off. "It's all right. Go talk. I'll be there in a moment."

As the door clicked shut behind them, Farideh wrapped her arms around her knees, her breath a faint cloud on the air. You will be all right, she told herself. And some day you will believe that. But as much as she tried to insist that she'd known Dahl was going to leave her behind, the truth was, she didn't believe it. She'd believed in his promises and his smile and the sweet, rambling things he said as she drifted off to sleep.

You are going to be fine, she told herself. Because he isn't coming back. And that's better in the long run—he's safer this way.

When the man reached for the gate at the end of the pathway, Farideh startled, her pulse racing away from her. Once more it wasn't Dahl.

Instead it was Lorcan in his human disguise, strolling up the pathway, and the same image from her dream, the path to an unwanted happiness slipped through her thoughts, a ghost she couldn't quite exorcise.

"Well met, darling," he said. "It's been a while." He looked her over, and despite the fact that she had already tapped into the pact, ready with a blast of energy, that look sent a slow burn through her body.

Karshoj, she thought.

"You look well," he said. "Been keeping busy?"

"Plenty busy," she said. "What do you want?"

"To sort things out," Lorcan said. "I figure that we're even now. You got angry I left you when you needed me. Then you cut me out when I've only been helping. I forgive you. I see now how it feels. And I promise, no more contagions. Happy?"

Farideh shook her head. "Do you think this is about making me sick?"

"And," Lorcan added, "not listening. But I do listen. And you and I both know that this"—he gestured between them—"isn't meant to break on something so trivial."

"So trivial as poisoning me?" Farideh demanded. "No—it's not. It's all of it, Lorcan. You act as if everything's different, but it doesn't change. Do you think I can't tell the way you try to keep me alone? The way you bully me, even when—"

"Even when I give you everything you want?" Lorcan demanded. He climbed the steps toward her. "Could your paladin say that?"

Cold horror poured over Farideh. "What did you do? You said you wouldn't harm him."

"I did," Lorcan agreed. He tilted his head. "Don't you think it's more likely that he left of his own accord?"

It was—but that didn't mean it was so. "Did you do something to him? Are you the reason he left?"

"I can hardly answer that," Lorcan said. "I don't know his mind after all. And neither do you."

He was dancing, avoiding the question. Farideh stepped up to him, fire in her hands, shadows pouring off of her. "What did you do to him?" she cried.

But then Lorcan met her eyes. "Absolutely nothing," he said. He studied her face. "I suppose he's just not our kind."

The fire in her hands guttered out, and a moment later Farideh had to remind herself to breathe again. She'd been so certain—for a moment, she'd been so sure that Dahl had not left, that it was all Lorcan's doing. But Lorcan had never once lied to her. She felt fresh tears break down her cheeks, and she wiped them away.

"Darling," Lorcan said, taking her by the chin. He leaned close to whisper in her ear. "Don't cry for him. You were never his." He kissed her cheekbone, and even as she raised her hand to shove him away, her nerves all shivered. "I'll be waiting while you get your head on straight," he murmured. "Who else is going to protect you?"

"Don't touch me," she said.

He laughed. "Think about it for a while. You'll change your mind." He took the ring he wore around his neck and blew the whirlwind portal into being, drawing him back to Malbolge.

I won't, she told herself. She wiped her face again, and hoped beyond hope that that was true. That she wouldn't fall into that old, familiar path. That heartbreak wouldn't drive her back to Lorcan, shielded by the belief that she'd know better this time.

She shut her eyes and blew out a breath. This is what Asmodeus could promise you, she thought: a firmer heart. And maybe she should take it—there was hardly any way to escape so many wicked powers trying to snatch her soul. Why not sign on with the most powerful of them?

Farideh laughed once. Gods, you're gloomy. She took another deep breath, as if she could scrub it all from her thoughts, then turned to go back into the tallhouse, to find Havi and Brin, but as she did, once more, a man came to the gate.

"Well met," Vescaras called. "Farideh?"

Farideh's heart dropped like a stone. Every terrible thing she'd imagined to keep Dahl away rushed back at her—you idiot, you idiot. "Oh gods. What happened? What happened?"

"I don't know," Vescaras said. "I woke up last night to a sending from Dahl. He's in Harrowdale. There was some kind of emergency. He said to tell you that he loves you, and that he will fix this. And that he hasn't any more sendings."

She blinked. "He's all right?"

Vescaras shrugged. "To be honest, I have no idea what's going on. I don't know what emergency came up, or how he got there or why he told me instead of you. Should you find out—or should you know—kindly apprise us? There's no interest in losing agents, but Dahl particularly . . . well, we'd be worse off." Vescaras made a face. "Don't tell him that; he'll get a big head."

He's all right, Farideh thought. He's all right and he loves you.

And he went to Harrowdale in less than a day, she thought. And he couldn't tell you.

There was no doubt at all in Farideh's mind that some devil or other had gotten ahold of Dahl, and there wasn't a devil in the Hells as eager to harm him as Lorcan. But Lorcan never lied to her—and so it remained to be seen what new danger had intruded into her life and Dahl's.

Still she smiled. You are all right, she thought. And he loves you.

• • •

HAVILAR DIDN'T SIT when she and Brin came to the front room, and maybe that was why he didn't either. Her tail slashed against the floor, no matter how hard she tried to still it. You've decided, she told herself. And it doesn't matter what he says and it doesn't matter that you want him to say it.

"I'm not changing my mind just because you shaved," she blurted.

"I don't think you should," Brin said. "This hasn't been easy, and it hasn't been fair."

"I don't even really know you anymore," Havilar said—she reminded herself of that over and over. It's been eight years. He's someone else. He remembers someone who isn't you. That's where all the troubles start.

"Maybe," Brin allowed. Then, "But I want to know you."

Havilar moved around behind the sofa, so she could grab the back of it, hold it like a shield between them. "I don't know what that means."

"It means," Brin said, not moving, "I'd like it if we could start over."

Havilar shook her head. "That . . . No! We can't. Do you want to just pretend that none of this happened? That we're strangers and . . . What is that even supposed to do?"

You came back, and we just tried to pick up where things fell. It turned into a mess because you're right—you didn't know me, and I couldn't tell you so much. I hurt you, and I hate that. There's no one I've ever loved like you, Havi. No one else understands that, but . . . I love you best when you *are* yourself, when you don't tell me things because I want to hear them, when you remind me I'm being ridiculous or cruel. You're like my rudder." He pressed his mouth shut. "I messed up."

"*We* messed up," Havilar allowed. "I should have told you about Sairché. Whatever Lorcan said." She held tight to the sofa, as if it might be torn away from her. "So what are you suggesting?"

"I want to come with you," Brin asked. "We don't have to be lovers, or anything. Just . . . maybe we can figure out if we are suited, after all this time?"

Karshoj, Havilar thought. You are still in love with him, you pothac idiot. "I don't know."

"Can we try?" He shrugged. "Maybe you're right. We're too far apart. I hurt you too much—but then we'll just know you were right." He smiled at her. "Not a bad set of circumstances."

Havilar snorted. "You sound like Lorcan when you do that. But nicer," she added. He reached a hand across the sofa toward her.

"Well met," he said, grinning. "I'm Brin. Just Brin," he said. She took his hand in hers.

"It's nice to meet you," she said, giggling. It was silly, but it was sweet. Just like she remembered him.

• • •

THE CAMBION WAS clever, Bryseis Kakistos had to give her that much credit. The careful divisions of Sairché's mind meant the ghost could ride with her, could speak to her, but could not sift through her thoughts, nor could she wrest control of the body.

Yet, Bryseis Kakistos added, as she watched through Sairché's eyes as the cambion sought out a series of powerful warlocks and wizards. She had not shared the whole of her story with Sairché, the whole of her plan. Only enough to give her the impression that this would be the key to undoing Asmodeus—that this would be a prize his scheming daughter would forget all Sairché's failures to get. Let the cambion think Bryseis Kakistos was bound to her wishes. Let her think that Bryseis Kakistos was a tool to be used and disposed of. It failed them all in the end.

"Do you care," Sairché drawled, "if they survive?"

Not especially, Bryseis Kakistos said. *I will need a body, eventually. It will work best if it comes from a descendant.*

"And you're quite short of those," Sairché noted, waving the image to reflect a skeletal lich standing motionless beside a lectern with a large book on it. "We seem to have plenty of options for the spell in question. Any preferences on where to start?"

The portal opening washed Bryseis Kakistos in adrenaline, but Sairché merely waved the mirror back into quiescence, so that it only reflected herself, and the cambion man who was suddenly behind her. Handsome in the sort of way that made mortals make very foolish decisions indeed. He looked so like Caisys that Bryseis Kakistos laughed.

"My brother," Sairché murmured.

You never told me you were the children of the Vicelord.

Sairché's confusion couldn't be hidden. *Don't worry,* Bryseis Kakistos said. *You have quite a lot of company.*

A memory swept over her, pulling her attention away, into the past: the shameless wishes of the ghost, the ghost bound to her side. Alyona. *He's handsome,* Bryseis Kakistos allowed. *But when you are alive again, you'll see there's so much more for you now.*

It rushed her away, back into the past, and tossed her back out in the present just as swiftly. Bryseis Kakistos tried to cling to it—Alyona? Who was Alyona? But the memories were lost again, pulled away on the ever-circling edges of her damaged soul. She turned her attention to Sairché's, to the cambion man.

"Where is she?" Sairché asked.

"Which she?" he retorted.

Sairché gave him a withering look. "Farideh. The only she you give a damn about."

"Suzail, for now," he said, ignoring the barb. "Don't get any ideas—I plan to keep a very close eye on her in the near future."

Tell him Asmodeus does as well.

"So does Asmodeus, I hear."

Lorcan narrowed his eyes. "Sairché, don't pretend to be clever. Of course he does. Why would he ignore his Chosen?"

"He ignores them left and right," Sairché returned. "Three of them are already dead."

Ask him if he knows why she was made a Chosen.

Sairché stumbled at that—the kind of question the devils were loath to dig into, the kind of question that might draw the attention of Asmodeus. "Why do you suppose," her brave little cambion said, "that he made her one of his Chosen?"

"To make my life more miserable still?" Lorcan guessed. "Who knows? It's an odd choice, that much is plain. A nearly uncorrupted Chosen of Asmodeus? Shit and ashes, the Princes of the Abyss are probably rolling."

Sairché chuckled. "Aw, did your plans to corrupt her fall through?"

Bryseis Kakistos considered the cambion, the near image of his sire, and considered too, the dearth of descendants, the need for a solid form.

Ask him if he still takes her to bed, she told Sairché, plans for the next stage of her reincarnation neatly unfolding.

· · ·

ILSTAN NYARIL EMERGED from the sewers to the north of the city, still limping and wounded but sane. For the moment: The intermittent murmurs of the Lord of Spells were eating away at the clarity that last battle had bought him. The magic of the Weave was beginning to pull him in again. He would have to find others—other spellcasters—whose magic he could augment, whose spells he could improve with the blessings of Azuth.

. . . the seal is weakened . . . the key is found . . . the Lady of Black Magic is searching, searching . . . how is a devil like a wizard? . . . both bleed until they don't . . .

A healer, he thought. You have to find a healer. He sat down in the crust of snow and cast a cantrip. A needle and thread appeared and stitched the note into the sleeve of his robes in shimmery thread. If the madness overtook him again, here would be a reminder before it was too late. *Find a healer. Give the magic to another caster. Find Farideh. Rescue the Lord of Spells.*

You have to kill her, he told himself. Even if it made him squeamish—she might seem kind and safe and certain. But there was no escaping that she had been Chosen by the god who'd murdered Azuth, the god who no doubt kept him trapped. That she held the key to his release and return. That she had to die for Azuth to live, for Ilstan to be exonerated and cured of this building madness.

Find Farideh. Ilstan traced the roughly embroidered runes upon his robe's lap, and considered the setting sun. He began to walk toward Proskur—a healer first, then a way to track her. The right components, the right persons, and she would be easily pinned down, a sacrifice for the rebirth of Azuth.